Michael—Whose passionate idealism is complicated by his forbidden desires.

Frank—Michael's best friend from childhood, who shared his dreams, his doubts—and the woman they both loved.

Carolyn—The beautiful ex-nun whom neither man could ever fully possess.

Together they were caught in a triangular web of friendship and betrayal . . . three people out to save the world and plunged into the violent drama of an entire society ripped apart . . . and a love that threatened to become the deadliest snare of all. . . .

PRINCE OF PEACE

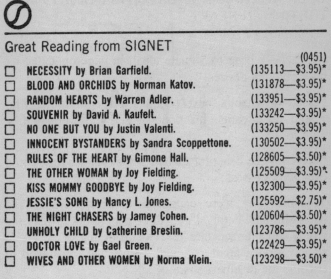

Great Reading from SIGNET

PRINCE
OF PEACE

JAMES CARROLL

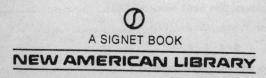

A SIGNET BOOK

NEW AMERICAN LIBRARY

For My Son Patrick

IN MEMORY OF
PATRICK HUGHES

ONE

Not many miles from the hill on which I stood they were prying great chunks of concrete off the mangled bodies of children. They were picking up corpses from ditches but leaving severed limbs to rot in the vicious August sun. And suddenly they were dropping from the sky again in their flashing Phantoms, blowing balconies off tall buildings, twisting minarets and smokestacks apart and stripping the trees of branches. They were pumping rounds of fire at targets picked off maps at random; their long-range guns were almost never silent.

But I didn't hear them. And usually I did not think about Beirut. I had not concerned myself with Lebanon, though everyone in Israel, even the brothers there at our remote priory, had thought of little else all summer.

I pulled the hood of my cowl forward for shelter against the sun. The desert wind snapped at the worn gray fabric of my habit.

Yes, to my ever-increasing surprise, what those words—priory, cowl, habit—indicate is true. I was a monk.

As in monk's bread? you ask.

As in jam. We were a small herd of bull-nuns, though the canonical constitution preferred to call us English Benedictines. We were a teaching order, centered at Downside Abbey in England. My priory, Holy Cross, was our contemplative outpost in the Holy Land. Our angels' island, as it were. The monks came there from sister monasteries in Britain and the United States. They came for three months, six, a year; for retreat or sabbatical; to renew their vows or—and alas, these fellows were always better company—to finalize their decisions to breach them.

I was one of the seven brothers who were there permanently. As the monastic argot had it, I was a lay brother, which phrase had always called to mind, forgive me, the interrogatory—"Lay, brother?"—of a hustling Eighth Avenue pimp. You, of course, are thinking, since you know your Benedictine history, Ah, poor lame-brained bastard! Lay brothers were the enlisted men of monasticism, the serfs, the Little Johns, who praised the Lord in meniality—Scoop that slop! Knead that dough! Stomp those grapes!—while the tonsured, the clerical officer class, aired their manicures, thumbed their breviaries and their noses. In the new Church, lay brothers were to be treated with all the dignity due the sons of God, a return to Benedict who brought democracy to the West. Monks were all equal in the Lord, *n'est-ce pas?* Still, some were more equal than others. The shit-work always fell to us.

Myself, I did not complain. But then I didn't harvest olives in the sun or scrape the cistern free of algae on my knees. I served as librarian and sacristan; no heavy lifting, inside work, a desk of my own.

The care of books remained, in my opinion, a noble function. Even those books. The bulk of my library consisted of outdated tomes, manuals of Scholastic philosophy mainly, and commentaries on canon law. You would not believe the dry-rot, the trivia, the efflorescent casuistry. Dust rose off every page. Papa John flung open his famous *aggiornamento* window, I'm convinced, less to let fresh air in than to throw such volumes out. The Church was entombed in their heartless formulations.

We Benedictines did not believe in destroying books, any books; we invented them, after all, in our *scriptoria*. Books were our sacred totems, our sacraments. And so Brother Librarians in England and America, on the theory that desert monks would read any old shit, sent us their mush-spined copies of the *Codex*, the *Devotio Moderna*, the *Imitatio*, the *Summa*, the *Oxoniense*, the *Moralia* and the *Etcetera*. Monk librarians on two continents knew of Brother Francis, bibliophile, fool and scholar *manqué*, who would receive each book gratefully, wipe it carefully and fondle it for a moment, even if for all the monk's bread in the world, he would never read it.

My duties as sacristan were less sacred. In fact they were mainly a matter of laundry. In the civilized world the sacristy, which is in effect the department of props and costumes, was always entrusted to Brother Swish, some monastic Edith Head. Not there. Me, I was an aesthetic minimalist. It was the desert after all, not Canterbury, and not Fire Island either. My simple responsibility was to see that Father Prior and each visiting priest had what they needed to concelebrate the daily liturgies. I spent much of my time therefore—this seems like an admission and would once have humiliated me to make it—ironing linens and vestments like a putzfrau. It would have humiliated me even more to confess, as I do now, that I had come rather to like it. There was a certain visceral satisfaction, one I could never have imagined in my previous life, in folding a Purificator precisely in thirds and creasing it with half one's weight on the old iron, transforming a balled, wrinkled cloth into a sacramental crisp and white enough to be worthy of the Sacred Species. As every housewife of the old school knew, and every confessor too, nothing pleases like making what was filthy clean.

"Ah, Durkin, you old fart!" I could hear my former colleagues bleating from the poker table in the faculty lounge, "And you hadn't even booze to blame it on!"

To which I'd have replied, better break your elbow than your knee. Better waste your liver than your soul. Ah, dear reader, what you'd never believe is that over those years at Holy Cross my gratitude at being there moved me more than once to tears. Of course it wasn't the *laborare* that did that, the menial work. I had not lost my mind. It had been an act of profound self-preservation when I took a lifelong vow of Stability to the Priory of the Holy Cross near the village of Tantur on the West Bank of the Jordan River. Once I'd had a thousand problems. But there I had only three: poverty, chastity and obedience.

You see, all I have to do is begin to sketch this story and I resort to self-sealing irreverence, the fake cynicism we came to expect of each other when the subject at hand was serious. But it can't be helped. My story begins in that monastery,

and my own impulse, now, to be chagrined by that, is
absolute. Still, I refuse it.

To put it as forthrightly as I can, I, together with my
brothers there, had accepted the call to build, day in and day
out, a living edifice of prayer.

"Come, come, Durkin!"

Let me say it, for my sake if not yours. My life's meaning
had become, despite itself—what else to call it?—holiness.
Shrinks say "wholeness" but miss by a mile what I'm talking
of: prayer, the desert life, spiritual existence, the Eucharist
and a strict observance of the monastic hours, from Matins to
Compline. How can I describe the life to you and not sound
addled, inane or, worse, sincere? Words fail me perhaps
because in that setting and throughout my years in it we didn't
use them much. Except for Sundays and feast days we continually maintained the Great Silence. In *lingua* that's *Magnum
Silentium*, which sounds like a weapon, and of course it is.
Silentium is the great enemy of *Sardonius*.

So there I was, in a monastery. And, offered with some
embarrassment but no apology, here is the meaning I began
to uncover there, but only on that day which would be,
though I didn't know it yet, my last.

It distracted enormously when events outside our enclosure
intruded. Like, if you will, the war between Israel and the
Palestinians. Not a week had passed that summer in which
one monk or another hadn't homilized about it at liturgy, and
every day someone prayed for peace with justice if he was for
the Palestinians, or for the survival of God's Chosen People if
he was for the Jews. I was known to pray for help in bearing
with special burdens, by which my quibbling brothers no
doubt knew I meant them.

A mere distraction? you say. That vicious, unending conflict?
That slaughter? Yes. For me, I admit it, until then. But then,
suddenly, for once it was not "distracting" me. It was obsess-
ing me. I had the eye all at once of a worried parent in time
of war, and I didn't miss a thing.

I saw, especially, Beirut. It was a city without windows. I
imagined all that glass in shards, a crop of blades, sprouting
underfoot. I imagined all those panicked sleepers running

from their tin bungalows without sandals, slicing flesh from bone, dancing on the streets, not in them. In the howl of wind that afternoon, for a change, I did hear them, wailers, gunners, dive bombers. I saw children. I saw girls. I saw one in particular pressing her entrails back into her stomach, but her wound was like the mouth of a shrieking Arab. And whom should she have hated? That wily devil Arafat, hiding in his sewer until the river of babies' blood overspilled a gutter on cue for television? Or should she have hated our own beloved Begin, more popular than ever, leader at last of the cossack charge of his dreams? Would he have known a pogrom if he was the one who ordered it?

I lived in Israel, but I was not a Jew; among Englishmen, but I was an American; as a monk, but I was not ordained. Once a scholar of some repute, I was the custodian of cast-off books and I did laundry. Therefore my opinions were so much sand in the brain. I tried to live without them, but on that day the war had begun to frighten me, and I knew why.

The sun was setting. The shadow of evening had already fallen across the distant desert valley. Beyond, on a butte just visible in the east, was the ruin of Herod's palace—Antipas, the Herod who beheaded John because his daughter asked him to. The ruin sat on a lonely pinnacle from which its privilege was to bathe in the golden light some moments longer.

I understood Herod better than the celibate exigetes did because, before I was a laundress-monk hidden in Judea I'd had my measure of prominence too, and more to the point I'd had a daughter of my own. I'd held her in my arms before her mother did. Those few moments after her birth—a tough cesarean; I'd thought they both were dying—remained for me the very definition of happiness, wholeness, peace. As she'd grown older and of necessity away from me, my devotion to her had only intensified. If she had asked for some crazed prophet's head on a plate and I could have given it to her, I might have once. Why then, you might well ask, had I abandoned her more than a decade before when she was seven years old and needed me more than ever? It will take all these pages to explain, and in a way they are addressed, first, to her, the long and complicated confession of a parent who lost his way. Let me say now only that she was the last of my loves whom I betrayed.

I faced the thing itself, the sun, and stared at it, which one never did in the desert, even at that moment when its lower edge was slicing into the earth like a saw blade into pulp. I turned slightly and faced Bethlehem two miles to the south. Behind me, eight miles north of a line of hills, lay Jerusalem. I was desolate but still pompous, and made much of that geography; a monastery between Bethlehem and Jerusalem, between birth and death, between the beginning and the end. As if it were the vision Jesus had from a hill like that—or from *that* hill—I had seen in that plain a literal army massing during the Yom Kippur War; hundreds of tanks, thousands of soldiers and in the darkness the blinking light of countless campfires spread across the valley like a reflection of the stars. It had become every army to me, a permanent vision, as the Arabs had become the Jews, permanent victims, and I had become inured to every plight but Herod's—who couldn't refuse his daughter. *His* Salome wasn't a seven-year-old; all my child wanted was her Daddy.

The wind picked up and I tugged at my robe absently, as if it were a blanket under which I had been sleeping badly. I shivered. I had been there, where to you the virtue of detachment would have looked very much like the vice of indifference, for a fifth of my entire life, and all at once I was afraid. How did Eliot put it? I had seen birth and death, but had thought they were different.

I slid one hand inside its opposite sleeve and my fingers touched the paper I had hidden there. The note was folded neatly as it was when handed to me by Brother Porter just before Vespers. Once in the chapel, in my stall, I had opened it inside the psalter and while my brothers had chanted, "Praise is rightfully yours, O God in Zion, Vows to you must be fulfilled," I had read my contraband message in a swirl of happiness and terror that nearly toppled me. "Jerusalem," it said.

Jerusalem! Not the ancient heartbreak, secret or memory. Not the city Jesus would have gathered to himself like a mother her child. Another Jerusalem than these, a mundane one in which traffic gets snarled, taxi drivers grunt at the size of tips, and tourists check into hotels.

I pulled the folded paper out of my sleeve and in the wind prepared to open it again. My fingers were trembling.

I remembered taking her into my arms, no, hands; she was too small for arms. The doctor had barely wiped her clean of blood, Carolyn's blood. Carolyn was my wife whom I worshipped, considering my worship a higher form of love when, really, much later, it was what drove her away. If I had left too it was only when I understood that she would never be mine again. I must have traveled in a trance. I had come to that monastery. I had presented myself to Father Prior who must have taken my derangement for devotion. I had been completely disoriented, but for one thing. I knew enough right from the beginning not to tell him the truth. If I had told Father Prior the truth, he'd never have let me stay.

"Truth? What is truth?" said jesting Pilate—Bacon's line—as he washed his hands. And I wonder now, sitting here, rubbing at the skin of my own truth, was it the question of a sophist or was he really tormented?

My anguish was permanent, but I had long deflected it. But that afternoon I couldn't. I opened the square of paper and in the day's last light, with my back to the monastery, read it for the second time. "I must see you tonight. I am at the King David Hotel in Jerusalem. Your Molly."

I flagged the rattling Arab bus that shuttled between Bethlehem and Jerusalem. The bus stopped for me as if it picked up vagrant monks at twilight all the time. With apologetic shrugs and my few words of Arabic I made the driver understand that I had no money for the fare. He waved me on. Mendicant Christians! What were our bizarre abnegations to him? I was grateful not to have the language. How could I have explained that a man of fifty, not perceptibly retarded, was violating a sacred vow by going into town without permission? Sometimes I saw my situation from the outside and it made me dizzy.

The bus was moving slowly. The road, winding up into the hills on top of which the city sat, was crowded with traffic. I had forgotten that, since sunset, it was Tishah-b'Ab, the late

summer feast which drew Jews to Jerusalem from all over,
including the controversial West Bank settlements. But this
bus was nearly empty because it was for Arabs. There were a
pair of old women in black shawls, three slouching youths in
Banlon shirts and jeans, and a thin, hawk-nosed man seated
by the door wearing, defiantly it seemed to me, the flowing
Arab headdress. West Bank Arabs tended not to show themselves on Jewish feast days, and for good reason. The fanat-
ics on both sides came out like goblins. They were the
sensitive ones who were like the rest of us, but with less
tolerance for life's cowshit. They'd rather be up to their asses
in blood.

And so Israeli security was even more rigorous than usual.
In Jerusalem, particularly in the Old City near the shrines,
body-searches would be aggressive. Even monks got their
flesh pressed on holy days, but I would not complain that
night.

From the bus window I watched as the bleak dark desert
landscape gave way to clusters of tall concrete apartment
buildings which monotonously but so effectively surrounded
Jerusalem. These apartment houses, hundreds of them filled
with immigrant Jews, were the ''facts'' which bolstered Israel's
resolve never to return East Jerusalem to Jordan. Since their
strategic purpose was clear and crucial—and justified, I'd
say—it didn't matter that the housing blocks, even at night,
were unbearably ugly. The gray half-light of television glowed
eerily in countless windows, and as we passed I wondered
why those Jews were not going up to the city for devotions
too. Was it Beirut? Were they watching the siege of the PLO
stronghold on their little Sonys? Or did each apartment have
its guard, its volunteer who stayed behind to resist when the
Arabs finally came? ''Remember,'' they would whisper to
each other on that holy night, ''the dogs attacked the last time
on the Day of Atonement.''

Tishah-b'Ab commemorates the two destructions of Solomon's Temple, the first in 586 B.C. over which Jeremiah
wept, and the second in A.D. 70 over which Jesus wept in
advance. These events, of course, have new meaning in our
century as emblems of that people's fear. On Tishah b'Ab
Jews remember all their destructions and their fear gives way,

rightly, to their rage. Israelis therefore by the thousand streamed into the city that night to approach the Western Wall, to place their prayers in its crevices and to stroke those ancient stones or, ritually, to strike them.

The bus driver let out a curse. The slouching boys sat bolt upright. The bus stopped and suddenly the glare of spotlights blinded us. Roadblock.

The door slapped open.

Uzi-toting soldiers clambered aboard, two, then three of them.

The first soldier barked at the driver a word I did not understand, but I heard it as "Goatfucker!" The driver cringed and appeared ready to throw himself at the soldier's feet.

Another soldier leveled his weapon at the man in the headdress. With great dignity the Arab turned his head slowly away to look out the window. The soldier forced him to stand and frisked him. As the Israeli jammed the snout of his gun into the Arab's neck, the man barely seemed to register his presence. I could see his grandfather turning that impassive face on a two-bit British overseer.

The third soldier was approaching me. I imagined him demanding to know by what authority I had left the monastery. Instead he shocked me by saying in a friendly voice and American-accented English, "Good evening, Father."

I couldn't bring myself to answer him at first. Was I afraid?

"You're from Holy Cross, I assume."

"I am indeed." I adopted a cocky tone that in no way corresponded to what I was feeling. "Very clever of you."

He smiled. He was proud of himself. "I grew up in Latrobe, Pennsylvania. There's a Benedictine monastery near my aunt's house. I recognized your habit. Of course, now I know the Franciscans', Trappists' and Dominicans' too."

"Someone as smart as you are should know better than to call me 'Father.' Don't assume all monks are priests. And don't assume all Arabs are terrorists."

"Believe me, we don't, Father. These searches are for everyone's protection. Especially tonight, we can't be too careful."

"But you've called me 'Father' again. You're not careful

enough to listen.'' I was aware that the other two soldiers had moved together on the three formerly slouching youths. Would the fools resist? Would there be shooting? I looked sharply up at the soldier above me. "We understand that you have to do this, but still it affronts what dignity remains to us."

Us? Was I throwing in with Arabs?

He nodded. He had been trained to be patient with the likes of me. We were the ones—the clergy, the Americans—who could cause them trouble. Clearly his job on this bus was to occupy the field of my attention so that his comrades could jam the rods of their guns into the collarbones and ribs of the Arab scumbags. As long as they were not too obvious about it they knew I would not protest. Of course he would attempt to ingratiate himself with me and of course—"Father" indeed! —his ingratiation would insult me. My resentment of his pseudo-deference, I saw too late, served his purpose.

One of the other soldiers called back to him. They were getting off.

"Good luck, Father," the Israeli said to me, and he saluted informally.

I stared at him. To my annoyance I saw that he was waiting for me to speak. "Shalom," I said.

The King David Hotel, touted spa of the Middle East, but famous first for having been blown up by young Menachem Begin in 1946. Nearly a hundred people died, many of them Jews. But its glory days returned. Nixon, Kissinger and Sadat stayed there. Also Rockefellers, Toscanini, successful salesmen from the Bronx and my daughter. Would I know her?

Once, in the alley behind our house on Brooklyn Heights, we were playing catch with an old tennis ball. In her exuberance—she was perhaps six at the time—she turned our game into a contest, "running bases" the boys called it, she said. I, not an athlete, was uneasy with her burst of energy as she tore up and down the narrow pavement, dodging my feeble efforts to tag her. She laughed continually. At a certain point I sensed that I would never catch her. She had me and she knew it. Her fuddy-duddy father. What child wouldn't squeal with delight to so defeat a parent? She zigzagged in, then out, daring to come close, but only to show how easy it was to scoot away. I remember how impatient she made me feel until I realized what was happening. My impatience changed in a sorcerer's flash to awe: my child was more alive than I was. She had a grace and fire all her own. I stood there slack-jawed, thinking, She is so fast! Happiness as brief as it was sweet overwhelmed me. Later I found Carolyn reading in the corner of our book-lined living room. Without explaining, I sat on the floor next to her chair and put my head in her lap and gazed up at her, silent until she asked and I said, "We have made a kind of masterpiece."

The King David Hotel had its name marked on its entrance in English, Hebrew and Arabic, an ecumenical gesture, but the doorman in his martial red jacket looked at me suspiciously. A monk on the loose? *Apostata et fugitivus?* You might think my Benedictine habit was what put him off, but the eccentric dress of religion was ubiquitous in Jerusalem. I nodded at him and pushed through the oversized revolving door.

I was uneasy because of the war and because of my daughter, but also because it was years since I had been in a city at night. It was all like a dream to me.

In the lobby, mammoth pillars of pink stone supported the massive beams of a blue ceiling which could have been the canopy of a Semite chieftain's throne room. King-sized chairs of cedar and leather spread across the lobby. Sitting in the chairs or strolling between them were impeccably tailored guests. The men were large but not portly. They were smoking. The women glittered. Everyone looked rich to me. At each pillar huge sunflowers, bunches of them in front of floor-to-ceiling swatches of damask, arched over us from antique pots. A group of American Jews clustered at the reception desk in front of me. Those men were wearing yarmulkes, those women sensible shoes. All seemed to clutch guidebooks and they nodded in unison while the concierge explained in accented English how the adjacent road snaked across the valley into the Old City. Even those tourists were going to the Wall to grieve.

Finally I caught the eye of the clerk behind the desk.

"You have a guest registered? A Miss Molly Durkin?"

He flipped through the file. He looked up blankly. "No, Father."

I resisted the urge to correct him. "Are you certain?"

"Quite, Father."

"Would you check again? I'm sure she's here."

The clerk made a show of fingering the registration cards. Suddenly, at a particular one, he stopped and looked up. "You said 'Molly . . .'?"

"Durkin."

He shook his head and continued through the cards.

"What was that one?"

He flipped back to it absently. "Maguire. Molly Maguire."

It must be that the color drained from my face because he was staring at me. Molly Maguire? I could not grasp it. Molly Maguire? As in the Irish equivalent to the Stern Gang? Her very name was an assault, a bomb.

Why had it never occurred to me that once Carolyn married him, Molly would have taken Michael's name? Michael Maguire. How long had it been since I'd thought of him? Did Molly call him "Daddy"? Had he legally adopted her? Involuntarily, my mind threw up a picture of his face, smiling with such fondness. Michael, you bastard! You fucking bastard! You always said you loved us *both!*

The clerk was looking at me wearily.

"That's her." I smiled. "Her married name. I knew her parents. I still think of her as Durkin."

"Room 722. You can call from the phone-bank there." He pointed to a shelf in a corner ten yards away.

I approached the phones slowly, knowing I would never use one. Because I could feel the clerk watching me, I went through the motions of calling her room, all the while depressing the engage button. If even clerks cast a disapproving eye upon me, how would my daughter look at me? She rejected my name?

As I crossed the broad sweep of marble floor toward the massive bronze elevator doors, it was like walking back in time. Memories tugged at me the way Arab boys did in the marketplace. I shook them off as I had ruthlessly now for ten years, but they clutched this time.

My daughter's four-year-old face was streaming with water. Her soaked hair framed her eyes. She had just climbed up to the float and now, arms spread, she was about to throw herself back into the lake where I waited to catch her. Her trust in me was absolute.

The elevator doors opened. The operator was short and obsequious. His bellhop's uniform looked wrong. Then I realized that his pitch-dark hair was cheaply dyed. His skin was not ruddy but flushed with age. He was too old to be dressed like that. I wanted suddenly to ask him, Were you here when Begin bombed the place? Were any young girls killed?

The elevator doors opened again, then closed behind me. I felt like a sleepwalker. How could my Molly have taken another name?

When I had last seen her she had pleaded with me not to go. Owing to the setting perhaps—she was sitting on the knee of the Hans Christian Andersen bronze in Central Park—she looked even younger than seven. Her hands fiddled in her lap with a twig. I was standing beside her. Her head was bent, but I could see that the stress of what had brought us to that moment had set its stamp on her face. With difficulty she said one last time, "Please don't go, Daddy."

"My darling Molly, I would give anything not to." I raised my eyes and saw Carolyn standing mutely, mournfully, a few dozen yards away, waiting for us to finish. I half expected Michael to be with her, but he couldn't have been.

Molly was sobbing then. I took both her hands in mine and I kissed her cheek. At once I turned and ran. Before I reached Fifth Avenue, I remember, it began to rain.

At Room 722 I stopped. I listened for sounds: music, water running, talking. There were no sounds. I looked down at myself. What would I say when she asked about my being a monk? What would I say when she asked me why I never contacted her?

I knocked at the door.

Immediately she opened it.

Her beauty was complete. She stood there in front of me, perfectly still, like an artifact, but with an expression of such human longing that it stunned me when I realized it was longing for me. In her face sadness showed, but as a resonance, a depth. Her loveliness was wonderfully familiar to me. I saw the fulfillment of the abundant promise that always set Molly apart as a child, but also I saw her mother as she was at nineteen. I wanted only to look at her, but my eyes were blinded suddenly by tears. While outside the hotel throngs mourned the destruction of the Temple, the fiercest grief I had ever felt took possession of me. I had spent twelve full years avoiding that emotion, though, and I simply, by an act of will, warded it off.

Neither of us spoke. She stepped aside for me. Finally when I was in the room and the door was shut and the moment had come when we might embrace, she said, "I am sorry for taking you from your monastery."

I searched her face for an indication of sarcasm, but found none. I couldn't think what to say to her.

She turned from me and walked efficiently to the window which opened onto a small balcony. She stood by a table with her back to me. In the distance, framing her dramatically, were the illuminated towers of the Jaffa Gate, and all too easily I imagined the red burst of an explosion, the chunks of stone over-ending through the air, the screams of wounded pilgrims. The enemy from Beirut had struck back at last. I could see that girl pressing her entrails back into the cavity of her stomach, only now I recognized her as my daughter.

"Molly, why are you here?"

"Mother sent me."

"Why?"

"She wants you to come home. She sent me to ask you."

What could I possibly say?

When I did not respond, she faced me. "Will you?"

The show of longing with which she greeted me was gone, replaced by a studied indifference, no, *detachment*, which seemed unbearably cruel to me. And, of course, familiar.

It was the perfect vengeance. I'd practiced it for years.

I approached her carefully. "Molly, you know, we've jumped into the middle of a conversation we're not prepared for. We haven't even said hello."

She averted her face. The water in her eyes glistened. "I wouldn't have come, but Mother asked me."

When I put my hands on her shoulders she did not resist.

In my *hands* I had held her, she was so small!

"What's wrong, darling? Tell me what's wrong?"

She nodded toward the adjacent table. A newspaper was open on it, the *International Herald-Tribune*. She touched it. "Did you see this today?"

"No."

I made no move to look at it. She picked it up and held the page for me to read.

"China Discards Maoist Vision."

My eyes fell several inches to a headline in the lower right-hand corner. The type was smaller, but I read it easily.

"Michael Maguire, Ex-Priest, War-Protester, Is Dead."

TWO

To recover the secrets of one's past and lay them bare in the inchoate hope that even disordered testimony reveals the wider meaning of those events that left us numb—one attempts it feeling a certain desperation. I have found it impossible to resist finally, this strange impulse to sit at my desk—lean to your ear—and speak. It is writing, I know, but it seems like speech to me. An unexpected faith enables me to think I am not talking to myself, for I believe despite the evidence of the blank wall above me that you exist, that you lean toward me, that these solitudes—the writer's in his study, the reader's in his chair—are one solitude. If I am telling you two stories, Michael's and mine, and how despite everything they became this one, can't I also hope I am telling yours?

Flaubert said the artist, the soldier and the priest face death every day. I say, bully for them! The rest of us face it once, maybe, and after that isn't everything just fucking awful? But also . . . aren't we aware only then that we're alive? How often can one glimpse that open secret? And how often is the structure of its story revealed? Pity the sacred trio—artist, soldier, priest—if they do this every day. They could not possibly sustain the grief, the awe or the understanding, so death, shorn of its intensity, must become like flossing, like brewing coffee, like mail falling through the slot. Death; the artist paints it. The soldier wears it with his ribbons. And the priest douses it with holy water.

But you and I watch death cross the land like a shadow once or twice in a lifetime, changing everything, and then we withdraw to our studies, our chairs, or to our lubricating wakes to tell the raucous and irreverent stories that alone make us know that we survived. You survived. I survived. Even if they don't know it anymore, the artists, soldiers and priests survived. And by God because *story* outweighs *history*—if I didn't believe that would I even begin?—so did the dead survive.

But dear old Henry James says, Don't state! Render! Don't describe what happens, let it happen!

So, my friend, I catch myself. No fustian pronouncements here, no lecture on the salvific effect of narrative impulse, no discursis on Coleridgean *biographia*. Don't explain, create! *Ex nihilo?* Not quite. The events and the people are real. And the time was that stretch of years in which we both came of age and went to the edge. This is the beginning, like all good ones, which contains the end. *Eschaton*, therefore. It was August of 1982. I was in Israel. And Michael Maguire was dead.

And with Molly, riding from Jerusalem, I could barely speak. I was filled with grief for Michael, but also for what I had not had with her. An infinity of tender moments seemed to have been squandered. I watched Molly's sparkling eyes and saw her mother's, that finely formed face, but every memory of Carolyn was a rebuke and I turned from it as I had ruthlessly for a dozen years.

Molly waited in the taxi down on the public road. She assumed I would accompany her back to America that night. She thought we'd returned to the monastery so that I could change from my habit into lay clothes. But what lay clothes? My overalls? How could I have explained to my daughter that her once distinguished father had returned to Holy Cross to ask the old goat prior for permission? The crunch of gravel under my feet was the only sound and it filled the night. It was only midnight, but not a light showed as I approached the monastery. Surely they had noted my absence at Compline. In more than a decade I had never missed an exercise.

With the hem of my habit in hand I leapt the stone wall and circled furtively behind the building toward the prior's room. Once beyond the chapel corner I saw that his light was on. I imagined him talking on the telephone to the Israeli police. But they would have been too busy on that feast night to

come out until the morning. A search of the wadis would
have been impossible in the dark in any case. If I had just
secretly gone off with Molly wouldn't they have assumed I'd
wandered into the desert in a mystical trance like Bishop
Pike? They would have revered my memory. Monks and
prelates *should* disappear without a trace, like Elijah.

This train of thought stopped me. I was standing in the
ludicrous arrangement of stone and cactus that the prior referred to as his Zen Garden. The door of his room stood open
to the night, and I could see him, a small, frail figure. His
bony shoulders protruded under his Benedictine robe. He was
bent at his table, like an old man over the wheel of a car. He
was not on the phone. A wedge of light fell toward me,
inviting my entrance, but I could not bring myself to approach him because suddenly I realized there was every
likelihood that this man for whom I had such disdain was
praying for me. And all at once my impulse was to throw
myself upon him and cry, "Michael is dead!"

Michael was on Nixon's enemy list. J. Edgar Hoover
denounced him before Congress. He was the most famous
priest in America for a time; the priest against Vietnam. You
remember him surely as one of the leading opponents of the
war. But there was a secret Michael whom many fewer knew.
Despite his reputation as an activist, he was sought out as a
Confessor by many Catholics throughout his years as a priest.
The elegance of his sensitivity drew people, and not only
from among the antiwar crowd. I never confessed to him
myself, but Carolyn did. Certainly their encounters in the
Sacrament sustained their intimacy and the irony in that, in
hindsight, seems particularly poignant to me.

Once I admitted to him that I no longer believed in God.
Such a statement seems entirely unmomentous now, but I
remember trembling as I said it then. Our certainties had all
flaked away like dried skin. Michael sat in silence for such a
long time that I began to wonder if he'd heard me. I was
unable to read his face. Finally he replied with a voice so sad
as to be completely unfamiliar. "None of us believes in God,
Durk, but we act as if we do because we love each other.
Otherwise . . ." He checked himself, as if he'd said too

much already. I never asked him, Otherwise what? But I must have known. We have to help each other cling to God while we can, because eventually we do each other in and then God is all there is.

What desolation I felt, standing there outside the prior's room, watching him. That old monk had been my spiritual father now for more than a decade. We had never overtly expressed affection for one another. I'd hidden from him in my wry irreverence; the trouble with religious superiors, I'd say to myself, is they think they are. He had shown me only his stern mask. His habitual expression had for years been a version of a desert shrub's. Yet, watching him at his psalter and imagining him praying for me, I felt a rush of, yes, love for the man and for the company of brothers who had received me as one not merely welcome but wanted. That I dared allow myself at last to feel such love for those men was how I knew that I was leaving them and their monastery forever. Leaving without a word. It would have been impossible for me to explain. What? That I had a daughter? That she was waiting in a taxi? That she'd come to take me to America? That I was going to my wife's side at her husband's grave? That he was my dearest friend, my enemy? How explain such riddles? What could I have said? Not so much to make the prior let me go—I was beyond permission—as to make him understand. But weren't we beyond understanding too? Hadn't we always been? When I'd arrived years before, a vagrant refugee in flight from dingy rented rooms where for months after Carolyn had left me I'd groped for a way to live and for the bottles of cheap booze that were always rolling under the bed. I'd told the prior nothing then. I could tell him nothing now. He would be shocked to find me gone, hurt perhaps, but not really surprised. What monk ever presumes to know in the dark shroud of his vocation what the old *Deus Absconditus* is up to now?

"On the river of tears," Picard says, "man travels into silence." That was what I had done, going there in the first place. And now, grief-struck, stunned at Molly's reappearance, at the summons she'd brought not from Carolyn, but from my own life, I was doing it again. I was leaving the silence in silence.

I stifled yet another urge to burst in on the prior to throw myself before him for his blessing. Instead I stepped back from his door into the shadows of the desert. Goodbye, dear father, I muttered. God keep you, I prayed, since I cannot. *Ad multos annos.*

I turned, faced Bethlehem for a moment. The stars were spread above me like a jovial throng, but like applause in church, affirmation from the night seemed wrong. This was loss, all loss. First Michael, my friend. Now Holy Cross, my only brothers. Gone, all gone. Already my years in the place were sliding away. I knew that I would someday account for myself to Father Prior and to my gracious confreres, but not then. In fact, of course, these pages are my accounting, and finally my mouth is at the grill of their cloister. Their ears are pressed against it and I am whispering, Oh my brothers, this is why I came to you and why I left.

I didn't need a blessing. I didn't need permission. What I needed were my passport—I was Frank Durkin now, not Brother Francis—and something to wear. I circled the monastery and entered it by the proper door. The halls were quiet. In a few hours, but long before daylight, the monks would rise and sing the nocturnal psalms and they would pray for an absent brother. I stopped in the chapel to pray for them.

And then, in the laundry room, I traded my habit for a denim shirt.

"Why did you stay there so long?" she asked.

I looked past Molly to the desert nightscape we were leaving behind. The taxi was halfway to Jerusalem, and the garish suburban settlements were coming into sight. "Because no one asked me things I had no answer for." I laughed modestly, just glad to be with her, and despite herself she laughed too. Such questions could only make fools of both of us, her for asking, me for never being able to respond. When I looked at her silhouetted against the window I wanted it to be that I'd just awakened and that she and I were two of a family which had survived the harshest winter without wood for a fire. We'd stayed together through awful times. Her mother was a spinner, and I was a miller and she was the girl the prince was wooing. We were going home now. My wife would be in the corner at her wheel, making clothes for me.

"I hate it," my daughter said, about the land we were passing through.

"Because it's barren?"

She looked at me. "Because it's had you all this time."

"It has and it hasn't, Molly. The best years of my life happened without me." I smiled again, trying to steer away from her mood and from my guilt. We weren't an inch from the fact of my having abandoned her. "Tell me about Mount Saint Vincent's. I'm surprised you wound up there."

"Why? Because bright young women don't go to Catholic colleges?"

"No, because it's where your mother went, and she wasn't . . . well . . . exactly happy there."

"She says she was. She says she loved it."

"Really?" I didn't disguise my amazement. So Carolyn had mellowed too. "Is she still working?"

"Better than ever. She has a major show on now, in fact, at a gallery in Princeton. A dozen new paintings. There was an article in *Time* magazine."

I was surprised again, but now I did disguise it because of the envy it implied. "Very colorful? Geometric forms?"

"Mostly whites. She works in whites and pastels."

"Color was her trademark. Great splashes of color."

"She's more subdued."

Weren't we all, I thought. I returned to the haven of silence. These exchanges with Molly exhausted me. There were a million things I wanted to know, but each of her answers was like the glass wall in the Marcel Marceau routine; I kept bumping into it until a kind of panic set it. When I stopped talking, so did she.

In a few minutes the taxi slowed down. There was less traffic on the road than earlier, but the roadblock was still there. The taxi driver stuck his head out the window. The three soldiers were standing mutely before a pair of black-suited, bearded Orthodox men who were wildly berating them. The driver joined in, adding his own sharp voice, a one man antichorus. He was a Jew and his curses, if that's what they were, were in Hebrew. The soldiers waved us through.

As we entered the outskirts of the city the taxi picked up speed.

"Everyone seems angry here," Molly said.

"They're at war. . . ." I almost called her "sweetie," but my tongue stumbled and the endearment remained unspoken. "It isn't anger. Everyone's afraid."

"But why can't they just live together? Why can't they just leave each other alone?"

She looked like a woman, but she wasn't quite. "They both want the same thing, Molly. That's the trouble. They can't both have it."

"What, land? There's plenty of land."

"Not 'land,' Molly. *Holy* land. Do we have time to take a detour? I'll show you something that will help you understand."

She looked at her watch. "We're supposed to be at the airport at two o'clock. They said the security check takes a long time."

I leaned forward toward the driver. "Can we get to Lod by two if we go through the Old City? I'd like to see the Wall."

"You have time, sir. But you'll have to walk. I can't get you closer than two blocks."

"Fine." I faced Molly. "I'd like to see it one last time myself."

"The Wailing Wall?"

"The Western Wall. You can't have come to Jerusalem and not have seen it."

"I came to see you." She poked me. "The Wailing Monk."

"If you only knew." I seized her finger and held it.

A few moments later we were walking hand in hand down the broad cobblestone ramp that led to the huge open plaza. We had been frisked by soldiers twice. The streets of the Old City and this route in particular were mobbed, even at that hour. Well before we saw them we could hear the throng at the Wall, the hum of prayers hung in the air like an electric effect, an otherworldly moan. When we came around a last bend the sight leapt at us, stunningly. Floodlights illuminated everything, the plaza, the mammoth Wall, the sea of black-hatted men. But, dominating it all, suspended above the Jews and their shrine, dwarfing them, dwarfing even that block-long construction of hewn boulders were the Dome of the

Rock and Al Aqsa, the great Mosque, which sat on the Temple Mount, occupied it, as if it was built at the beginning for Mohammed, not Moses.

Molly pressed my arm, her nails bit through my shirt. She had gasped and was not breathing yet. We stood where we were, straining to take in the spectacle. Thousands of bobbing Jews, beseeching not Yahweh but the stolid indifferent stone; the brilliant blue tile and the golden egg, the mammoth Fabergé, of the Arab shrine; and between them at intervals along the top edge of the Wall, like forged spikes, scores of Israeli soldiers at perfect attention with Uzis between their arms and breasts. Set in the blazing light against the pitch black of night, it was like a de Mille version of the apocalypse an instant before his ''Action!''

''There is a rock under that dome, an ancient boulder. Moslems believe Mohammed ascended into heaven from it, and that makes this shrine second only to Mecca. Jews believe that Abraham offered to sacrifice Isaac on the same rock, Molly. When God spared Isaac their religion was born. That's what they're fighting over.''

''What are all these people doing?''

''They are reciting the antiphon of Tishah-b'Ab. 'Every generation in which the Temple is not rebuilt is guilty of its destruction.' They'll be here all night, praying for the restoration of Solomon's Temple, which implies the destruction of the Dome and Al Aqsa. The Arabs are right to be afraid of piety like this.''

''Are you against the Jews?''

''No. I am afraid for them. And I am afraid of them. Many Jews feel the same way. What I wanted you to see was that *this* land is different. Step over here.'' She followed me up a set of stairs that led to a narrow alley winding back into the Jewish Quarter. From the top of the stairs was another view of another dome. This one was not illuminated, but even from several blocks away, its black unornamented form stood out sharply against the sky. ''That is the Holy Sepulchre. Christians revere it both as the site of Calvary and of the tomb from which Jesus was raised. This patch of earth is less than half a square mile in size; the three great religions of the world all believe it to have been touched directly by God.''

"And so they fight over it?"

"Yes. It's absurd, isn't it? What does God think, do you suppose?"

"I don't believe in God," Molly said. "I never understood why until now."

"You can't blame God for the madness of his people."

"He made them, didn't he?"

I poked her. "Not if he doesn't exist."

But she refused to treat this lightly. She turned from me. "I didn't say he doesn't exist. I said I don't believe in him."

"It is not easy here to believe in God. You're right about that." I was speaking softly. Molly gave no sign that she even heard me. "When I first came to Jerusalem I was put off by the shrines, even by the Holy Sepulchre. Bad art, contentious monks, superstitious tourists. The tomb of Jesus isn't even empty; a Greek priest with bad breath and no teeth waits in there to sell you candles. I hated the decadent religiosity of this place."

"But you stayed." She faced me. Her eyes were full.

I touched her cheek and I nodded. "There's an excavation cave I wish I could show you. It's being dug under a Russian convent not far from here. You go down, down, down, like into a mine, and you stoop through a tunnel to come out into a great, spacious cavern which is lit by naked bulbs. You stand before a large stone slab about nine feet long and three feet wide. It is unremarkable, an ordinary hewn piece of rock at your feet. You look down at it in silence for a long time, and finally you kneel and touch it and kiss it."

"Why?"

"Because it was the threshold stone of the city gate in the time of Herod. Only recently have archaeologists uncovered that section of the ancient city wall. They say it is certain that, only a few years before the threshold stone was covered by the rubble of the Roman destruction, Jesus of Nazareth stepped on it with his feet when he left the city to die."

Molly let her gaze drift across the city. "It's hard to picture Jesus here."

"Why?"

"Everyone's so mean," she answered sharply. She was

dangerously close to losing her poise. What was she afraid of?

"The world is mean, Molly. And it makes us mean. In his own way Jesus was mean too. The Incarnation wasn't puppy love, you know. Jesus was one of us, that's all. It could have been the Bronx, but it was here. God came *here*. That's the curse of this place."

Molly was silent. In her face the immobile nightscape showed. Her eyes seemed to look out from one of the city's tombs, and I saw how very sad she was. Not fear, but grief was what undid her. I saw for the first time that she was a young woman profoundly in mourning.

"Michael was a good friend to you, wasn't he?" I touched her.

She nodded shyly. Now the tears came. She stood erect, ignoring them. The breeze feathered her hair. "He was more than that. Forgive me for saying this, but he became like a father to me."

"I'm glad, sweetie. He was the best man I ever knew."

"You don't hate him?"

"I did. You've been asking me why I stayed here so long. It was to purge myself of that, to recover from it. No, Molly, I don't hate him. I haven't in a long time. That's why I'm coming back with you. I have to say goodbye to Michael. He was more than a friend to me too. And when I failed you as a father, I thank God he was there to take my place."

Molly lowered her head and whispered now, "You didn't fail me."

And I could think of nothing to say to her, or of any way to touch her, because we both knew that she was lying.

After a long time I said, "We should go." I took her arm and led her back along the cobblestone ramp toward the street where the taxi was waiting.

After the glare of the floodlit plaza the narrow arched-over passageway was too dark to negotiate hurriedly. As we passed them I could make out the corrugated shutters that covered the stalls and alcoves of merchants. In the cramped Jewish Quarter the stale air with its unfamiliar odor, whether of food or waste, pressed on us. Three Hasidic men on their way to vigil at the Wall brushed by us, and I sensed Molly stiffen, as if modern women knew instinctively of their contempt. At a corner a machine-gun-toting soldier looked up from a match with which he had just lit a cigarette. "Hi ya, Father," he said. It was the young American who'd stopped the Arab bus. There was a snicker in his greeting, and I realized that he thought he had caught me, a monk out of habit, with a beautiful girl in the middle of the night. I winked at him.

And at that very moment from behind us came the explosion, like the sustained clap of hailstones on a metal roof, and instantly it seemed to me that since I first laid eyes on the army in the Judean desert valley ten years before I had been waiting for that outbreak. Without thinking I pushed Molly to the ground. I had no way of knowing how close the bomb or shell or grenade was to us, though I felt a blast of heat and I was sure the ground under us had been jolted. The noise of the explosion hung in the air, and then, as it faded, other sounds grew to fill the night. First, of human screams, a great roar of screaming that was coming from the plaza by the Wall. And then, more immediate to us, the clomp-clomp of runners. When I opened my eyes to look, I saw squads of soldiers barreling past us. The American was gone.

Molly was pressed into the corner of a shuttered merchant's stall and I was on top of her. When I looked, I thought at first she was pushing her entrails back into the wound in her abdomen. But she was not. Neither of us was hurt. The explosion, it was only now certain, took place some distance away. At the Wall, or at the Dome of the Rock, or in the Holy Sepulchre. I pictured the night sky full of flaming debris. What had they blown to bits now, and whom?

Just as Molly and I were struggling to our feet the roar of the coming wave reached us. By the time we faced it, the wave of panicked, fleeing Jews was on us. Hundreds of the thousands from the Wall had squeezed into the narrow alley and were running blindly through it, screaming. Only the yard-square alcove we were pressed in saved Molly and me from being crushed in the stampede. We clung to each other as the throng's edge ripped at us. Molly had buried her face in my shoulder. Her eyes were tightly shut, but mine were open. I couldn't help but stare at the terror in the faces of those Jews. For that instant they were in flight from every pogrom, every massacre, every slaughter, every crucifixion men had ever inflicted on the creation of God. And I, in my corner, holding my grown child, watched with the eyes of a guilty bystander through which, unfortunately, I had seen everything.

THREE

M ICHAEL MAGUIRE was mobbed by a throng of panicked fugitives too, but he was not free to watch from the
edge of the road as I would be years later. The old men,
women and children coursing past him were as desperate to
escape as those I would see, but they pressed against each
other, always forward, forward, with greater restraint. They
were less an avalanche of terror than a glacier, and it was
about to become Maguire's job to stop it.

It was January 4, 1951, the first of his fighting days. He
was eighteen years old, had been in the army only since
August and in Korea less than a month. Almost from the day
of his arrival as a member of the 27th U.S. Infantry Regiment,
the American forces had been falling back, withdrawing
southward, collapsing around Seoul—not "retreating," the
officers insisted—in the face of the shocking onslaught of
Chinese troops. Maguire's company had been doing garrison
duty in the Korean capital, but now it too had begun its move
south. Maguire's platoon, consisting of seven GIs of whom
he was one, a corporal, a staff sergeant and commanded by a
second lieutenant, had been sent ahead the day before to
guard the railroad bridge over the Han River a few miles
below Seoul. But in twenty-four hours almost the entire U.N.
force of soldiers and equipment had been evacuated across
the Han, and now Maguire's platoon was one of only a few
U.N. units remaining on the north side of the river.

The platoon's problem was the mass of refugees. Whenever the radio crackled its warning that a train approached
they had to halt the flow of civilians long enough for the train

to cross. But there hadn't been a train now for nearly two hours, and it was difficult to imagine that the stunned, inexorable mob would obey them if they ordered a halt again.

The river at that point was half a mile wide, but it seemed narrower because ice, white shoulders of it stretching from each bank, had begun to close on the center channel where the current ran most swiftly. It was so cold that Lieutenant Barrett gave permission to keep the jeep running so that the GIs could take turns sitting on its radiator to keep warm. The bridge was a rigid, solid multispan suspension structure, a quilt of pig-iron girders on top of concrete pilings, that the Japanese had built during their wartime occupation. Ice floes had begun to jam up at the pilings. The retreating ROK Army had demolished the center span of the bridge the previous July when the North Koreans overran the south. American engineers had rebuilt it in October after the U.N. breakout and the recapture of Seoul. And now Seoul was about to fall once more, this time to the Chinese, and its population was once more fleeing south. Maguire and his buddies knew that the bridge would have to be dropped again, but if it wasn't done soon, the river was going to be frozen clear across anyway, and no one would need a bridge. "If the Chinks don't catch us," they complained to each other, slapping their sides, "the fucking cold will."

Later Maguire would grasp the chronology of the seesaw victories and defeats that characterized the first phase of the war, but that day he did not understand what was happening. MacArthur's autumn assurance that his army would be home by Christmas was repeated now as a bitter joke. In the previous summer the North Koreans had conquered most of the peninsula, but that was before the Americans came. After the great assault at Inchon, the GIs took the peninsula back almost easily. When Maguire got his orders for Korea as one of the tens of thousands of quickly drafted relief troops the war—the "police action" as the president called it—was supposed to be over. Draftees like him expected ninety-day turnarounds. Now he and his regiment and, as far as he knew, the whole U.S. Army were running for their lives, just like the expressionless, sullen refugees passing stoically by him.

To tell the truth Michael Maguire understood very little of what had happened to him in the six months since he'd graduated from Good Shepherd High School in Inwood. He was one of only three boys in our class to be drafted. The rest of us pretended to envy them and, though we worshipped our older brothers for having fought in World War Two, I can recall no one of our group who went downtown and enlisted. It was as if, instinctively, we knew that Korea was not the war we wanted. As to why Michael should have been drafted, no one knew. His fame as a schoolboy athlete had carried around the city, leading some to think the Selective Service only picked those most likely to make good soldiers. But Tubby McGaw was drafted too. More confusing still was the fact that Michael's long-deceased father had been a New York City cop. None of us remembered him but it was neighborhood legend how he'd been killed in the line of duty, thwarting a holdup in Pop Mahoney's Variety Store. It was as if the draftboard, instead of exempting the only sons of widows, went out of the way to call them. Maguire's father a dead hero? Then the army would give him the chance to be one too. By rules we were all familiar with, it was a chance Michael was compelled to take, for it was unthinkable that he should apply for a hardship exemption. He'd have been a shoe-in for it, but he felt bound by an honor code of which his father was the mythic exemplar. We were far from cynical about such things, but that honor code of Michael's seemed anachronistic to some of us even then. His willingness to be conscripted by events would set Michael apart, for good and for ill, for the rest of his life.

The war in Korea was not the war against Hitler, and aspects of it troubled right from the start, but it was morally compelling nonetheless. However difficult it is to imagine now, America seemed as invincible as upright then, and we were sure that our mission in Asia was thrust upon us by a pleading world. When Michael left Inwood, even those of us who thought he was a sap to go were proud of him. I was also grief-stricken. Already the bond between us was stronger than blood. He was my best friend and I was his. For a long time I felt his absence as a bodily pain, and I came to hate the war that took him from me, even if I believed in it.

Forgive me if I homilize about it for a moment, but Korea serves as the first bracket not only for this story—for Michael's life—but for the story of the tragic decline of America, which is of course our larger subject. It is only the failure of Communism to realize its own rhetoric that makes that first reflexive effort to oppose it seem naive. And it is only the recent collapse of belief in our own rhetoric about ourselves as free people defending freedom that makes our intervention in behalf of an invaded people seem militaristic. Contrary to present opinion, it is not that people were stupid in those days or prisoners of univocal thinking that draws all conflicts in black and white. They were neither morally nor politically shallower than we are. On the contrary they had a perception of one of the century's great facts, a perception since lost in the fog of our social, personal and political narcissism—that Communism is an inhuman system comparable to Nazism in every way but one: it works as a system of repression and conquest, but it cannot feed its people, and so eventually must fail whether opposed from without or not. The generation that fought Communism and contained it in Greece and Korea did not know that yet. I was an aware young man launched on a Greenwich Village phase of Camusian *engagement,* yet I did not know it. Communism, we believed, was capable of taking over the world. It is superficial therefore merely to fault Americans of that period for their paranoia, despite its dreadful domestic and international consequences. They moved—I should say "we" moved—in Eliot's phrase, "in the time between sleep and waking."

The point is that there were reasons, regarded as good ones then, and still so regarded by some of us, to perceive the Communists as monstrous. Every GI in Korea could have given them to you. Graphic stories of Red atrocities were a feature of basic training. What pimply-faced draftee could benignly contemplate the prospect of dying in a ditch with his balls in his mouth?

Later in life Michael Maguire would express the opinion that basic training was itself a kind of atrocity—a systematic numbing of individual conscience and will. His preoccupation by then would be not with how we were right about the Communists, but how we were wrong about ourselves. It would become his position that even a graced, generous society like America can be corrupted—will be corrupted—when its major effort is turned to the prolonged conduct of war. Basic training, his own experience of it, would therefore become a basic point of reference and a basic metaphor for the inhumanity into which America slipped. But that came later.

At the time, though, he knew something was dreadfully wrong with a system that celebrated and sought to nurture the sadistic in men. In a letter he wrote to me just before shipping out to Korea, he described with suppressed rage how his company's drill instructor had presented them on their arrival at Fort Dix with the gift of a pet rabbit, and how he had encouraged them to feed it and care for it and grow fond of it. Through the rigors of the training that rabbit—its childishly derived name was Thumper—sustained in Maguire and others the capacity for gentleness and warmth, feelings for which there were simply no other outlets. Maguire described how attached they became to Thumper. They fed the animal on scraps smuggled out of the mess hall. He described how on the day that basic finally ended and they were shipping out to various regiments bound for Korea, the DI gathered the company for his farewell talk. He took Thumper and, after fondling him and nuzzling him, he suddenly snapped the rabbit's neck with his bare hands and then threw it on the table and in quick order produced a gleaming bayonet with which he skinned and disemboweled it. Then he splashed on his men its blood, Thumper's blood, an unconscious mockery of the *Asperges Me.* And he swore that that was what the Commie bastards would do to any GI they caught alive, and so GIs just fucking well better do it to the Commie bastards first. Michael said in his letter that he was horrified by that drill instructor, but also by his own reaction to him, for in fact he accepted despite himself the slaughter of that rabbit as an image of Communists' skinning their prisoners alive, and it terrified him.

And now the ultimate Commie Bastards—Chicoms—had swept down on Seoul, whose citizens needed no Thumper lessons to be afraid.

Maguire watched as the Koreans funneled onto the bridge.

They hauled ladened carts or carried their possessions on their backs, boxes and even pieces of furniture strapped to the large Korean A-frames made of tree branches. Some women carried loads on their heads, like Africans, and they alone managed a stately pace in the otherwise jerking crowd. Progress was too sporadic and the press of bodies too close to ride bicycles, so those who owned bicycles pushed them. Babies rode in bicycle baskets or on smaller versions of the A-frame on their mothers' backs, wrapped like papooses. The faces of the men and women were so lacking in animation of any sort that it was possible, by virtue of that lack, to imagine the oppression under which they'd lived. If one had only their faces to go by, they'd have seemed sullen, not afraid. Their fear was communicated through the ferocious concentration of their energy on movement.

The faces of the children, though, seemed alive, despite their being wrapped against the cold so that only their eyes, noses and mouths were visible. They reminded Maguire of the Hummel figurines his mother collected, with little dashes of color for features and an air of porcelain fragility, as if just looking at them would make them break.

As they moved by, Michael waited for someone to look at him, but their eyes were fixed on the heels of those immediately ahead. Even when they were shoved into each other, as happened increasingly, no one protested. Maguire felt sorry for them. Only the eyes of the papoose children snagged on him. Well over six feet tall, thin, cigarette dangling from his lips, M-1 slung on his shoulder, he was the embodiment of the fantasy Asians had of good-looking, friendly but also somehow frightening Americans. When he waved or otherwise acknowledged that he saw them, the children looked away. Alone of everything he'd seen in weeks, their shy glances made Maguire feel that there was something in that frigging country to protect. What would Chicoms do to enemy children? Maguire didn't believe it, but the Koreans said they ate them.

"Maguire!" Sergeant Stone's harsh voice cut through the cold. "On the double!"

The ten men of the platoon circled the jeep, drawing as close as they could to its radiator. Their breath rose in white puffs, a winter flower that bloomed and faded above them magically. Lieutenant Barrett was standing with one foot on the jeep bumper. When the men were assembled he said, nodding at the radio on Tucci's back, "Okay, boys, we got the word. We get one more train through, then we move out."

"Across the river?" O'Hara asked.

"Hell, yes. You think they'd leave without us?"

"Fucking-A!" O'Hara slapped Bean's helmet with relief. Bean just looked at him.

Lieutenant Barrett went on. "It's time to be on our toes." Something in the lieutenant's voice frightened the men. Maguire had been afraid since arriving in Korea, not acutely and certainly not in any acknowledged way, but in a dull, constant mortification of all his senses, as depressing as it was secret. Now he felt his fear quicken. He shifted his glance to the others. They were all staring at Lieutenant Barrett, riveted, waiting. Despite the cold a thin line of perspiration could be seen on the young officer's lip.

"The next train only has one car, get it? It'll be a big tender, only instead of coal it has a load of dynamite in it."

"Oh fuck," Lennie Pace said. He was the big Italian kid who admitted that he was only sixteen years old, but he was so brawny he passed for eighteen easily. Everyone mispronounced his name—it was "pa-chay," not "pace"—but he'd grown accustomed to that in basic. He'd only been in Korea a week. His fright was palpable.

Sergeant Stone gave him a look. Its thinly veiled contempt seemed lost on Pace, but it unsettled Maguire. He remembered that the sergeant was a veteran of World War Two.

So was Lieutenant Barrett, who made no secret of his resentment at having been called up from the reserves. He seemed young but had been in combat in the Philippines, though not as an officer. That he was new to command accounted perhaps for his stifled uneasiness. "When the train passes, we hop aboard, get it?"

"Even though it's moving?" Sully asked.

Maguire saw that the other men were at least as afraid as he was.

"Falling off the train is the least of your worries, believe me." Lieutenant Barrett looked nervously across at the mobbed bridge and he wiped his lip. "So we're on the train, okay? The engineer's going to stop it right in the middle. Then we get off, okay? We cover the crew. They get a jump on us."

"You mean everybody gets off the train?"

"The train is stopped, Sully. After the crew, we hightail the rest of the way off the bridge on foot. On the other side we hook up with Captain Ray. Get it?"

"So what about the dynamite?" Pace asked.

"Pace, you're a stupid Wop, you know that?" Sergeant Stone belted the kid's helmet.

"No, it's a good question," the officer said. "Usually, they'd string the charges out all along the bridge. They'd put them on the pilings. But there's no time. They're going to just blow it right there in the middle. Right there in the train."

"What about the jeep?"

"Fuck the jeep," Sergeant Stone barked. "Shut up."

Maguire thought the sergeant was right. The men were only asking questions out of nervousness. Obviously Lieutenant Barrett knew barely more than they did.

"Our job," he said, "is to clear the bridge." He looked at his watch. "We have half an hour. The train just left the depot. The lucky people who are already on the bridge will have just enough time to get to the other side. Nobody else gets on, so let's stop these folks. We'll only use what force is necessary, but we'll use it. Any more questions?"

"Yeah." Sully raised his hand like a schoolboy. "What about the Chinese?"

"They're on the way, Sully. Listen."

The men listened to the dull roar of artillery from Seoul. For the first time they realized that it was closer.

"The engineers have already taken the other bridges down, fellows. This is the last one left across the Han. The Chinese want it. It's up to us to see they don't get it. If we don't clear it right now so that train can move out fast, we're going to have to stay here and fight them for it. About thirty thousand of them."

"Oh fuck," O'Hara said.

The men took up their positions. There were two roadblocks,

one at the entrance to the bridge itself and one about fifty
yards up the railroad bed. At each the makeshift gate was in
the raised position, letting people through. Sergeant Stone,
Sully, Bean and Jones manned the outer one while Maguire,
Brown, Pace and O'Hara manned the one at the bridge itself.
Lieutenant Barrett and Tucci remained at the jeep. When
everyone was in position Stone fired his weapon into the air
and barked repeatedly the Korean phrase which meant "Stay
back!" Both teams began to lower the gates.

Previously the effect of the gunshot and the order had been
immediate compliance. The refugees, once halted, waited
submissively for permission to resume. They'd thought nothing of waiting several hours. But now, as if they knew the
score, their reaction was the opposite one. They surged forward en masse. Women, old men, even children threw themselves against those in front. They ripped the logs of the
blockades from their leather hinges and tossed them aside like
matchsticks. The people crushed each other to get onto the
bridge. A-frames and carts were thrown into the river. Those
who stumbled were trampled. Refugees farther back on the
road pressed forward even harder. The knowledge of what
was happening rippled back; thousands perceived it at once.
Their escape was being cut off.

Cries went up: first of pain of those being crushed; then of
protest at the prospect of being left behind. Sergeant Stone
fired his weapon into the air again, and then the GIs did too.
But the barrage only increased the panic in the crowd. The
force of its surge doubled.

Maguire sensed that there was no stopping them, and he
could feel their panic seizing him and the others of his
platoon. What could they do? He for one was being swept
onto the bridge, like so much flotsam in a surf. Even if he'd
wanted to use his rifle he couldn't have raised it. He, Eddie
Brown, the colored kid, and Lennie Pace were each several
heads taller than the swarming Koreans, but they were
powerless.

Maguire could see that the four soldiers at the forward
roadblock had linked arms and were pushing against the tide
of people. But then Sullivan's helmet was knocked off when
someone clubbed him, and Bean simply disappeared as the
crowd overwhelmed him.

Later Maguire would realize that Lieutenant Barrett had seen Bean drop too, because it was at that moment that he hopped behind the wheel of the idling jeep, popped it into gear, and gunned it right at the mob. He was still picking up speed when he hit the line of people midway between the two roadblocks, midway between the positions his boys held. It was an instinctive act, but not an irrational one. Barrett never hit the brakes; the crunch of flesh and bone was what stopped the vehicle. Maguire would later swear he heard the thunk of steel against bodies and of bodies against each other, but the real sounds of impact were lost in the roar of the revving jeep engine.

Though he would not articulate it until much later, it was at this moment that Maguire understood for the first time that judgments about right or wrong can be completely irrelevant. War presents men with certain circumstances and they act. That's all.

Not quite all. Also they perceive; perhaps they perceive, despite their numbness, with special clarity. Maguire saw the heads of Koreans cracked open like melons, gray matter spurting out like vegetable pulp and seeds, as if a pumpkin truck spilled right in front of him. He saw bodies flung through the air jerkily, limbs flailing like swingles, faces crushed against chests or against backs; bodies sprawling on top of each other, then being hideously bulldozed as the momentum of the jeep carried it fully through the line. A score of people were mauled, a dozen horribly killed, but the shock of violence—the wave it made—was felt, could be seen to be felt, all through the dense crowd. The grotesque sight of those split skulls was fixed in Maguire's mind and would always dominate his memory of that day. The memory would make him sick. But he would also always remember that it worked. Lieutenant Barrett had stormed the glacier and stopped it.

Tucci was standing in the jeep firing the submachine gun above the heads of the people. The staccato of his weapon gave perfect expression to the violent fury that always follows the release from danger. The Koreans, hunched over, protecting their heads, had lost their impetus. The GIs were in charge again. Maguire and the others formed ranks in front of and alongside the jeep. They stood with their weapons cocked, a more formidable blockade than ever.

"Cease fire, Tucci!" Lieutenant Barrett called.

When Tucci released the trigger a shocking silence fell. The groans of the wounded Koreans could be heard and also the distant booming of artillery, but still there was silence.

"Sergeant! Is everyone accounted for?"

"Yes, sir!"

"What about Bean?"

"Here, sir!"

"Tell these people anyone who moves will be shot!"

Sergeant Stone rattled off a few words in the strange language. The Koreans gave no sign they knew they were being addressed.

"That's you, Tucci," Lieutenant Barrett ordered. "Shoot them if they move. Don't wait for me to tell you."

"Yes, sir." Tucci, poised above the scene like the statue of a hero, was not as cool as he looked. He had never fired the submachine gun in action before.

Barrett shut the jeep engine off and hopped down. "Maguire! Brown! Let's help these people!"

They laid their rifles aside and knelt, trying to pull the tangled bodies out from under the front bumper of the jeep. Bodies were piled there three and four deep, like, Maguire thought, in a concentration camp. At first none seemed alive, but as they pulled, some victims began to move. The cries grew louder. The vehicle had come to rest right on the railroad tracks. One poor bastard's head was crushed against the rail.

Maguire retched, but he only turned his head aside. He, Brown and the lieutenant worked steadily to free the people, to drag the corpses away and to try to comfort the ones who were alive.

One little girl, a shattered but howling figurine, was strapped to her dead mother's back. Her mother's neck was broken, and her expressionless face was perversely askew on her shoulders. Maguire freed the girl, who was barely more than an infant. When he stood up with her he found himself facing Lieutenant Barrett. The officer seemed suddenly horrified. "Jesus Christ," he whispered while staring at the bawling child in Maguire's arms. "What have I done?"

Maguire buried the baby's face against his chest. It was how he'd held that rabbit. He wanted to say, "We all did it, Lieutenant," but he couldn't.

The crowd was still at bay and the bridge was clear when the train arrived. It pulled into view behind the scolding sound of its own engine and Maguire wanted to feel relief, but he had maintained his nerve up to then only by blanking out his ability to feel anything. He had spent the time trying to comfort the injured civilians, applying first aid, wrapping them in GI blankets, clearing stones from under them, wiping their faces. He realized that he'd begun to imitate their stoicism.

He had to remind himself that now he was going to leave. The train had come, in a way, for him.

"Move that jeep!"

Maguire looked around to see who Lieutenant Barrett was addressing, but he was nearer to the jeep than anyone. It was still blocking the track, and the engine was steaming steadily closer. He hopped aboard the jeep, pushed the ignition button, and fiddled with the gear stick until he found reverse. He had to gas the engine to get the wheels over the iron rail. As he backed away from the track he continued to gun it instead of stopping; suddenly he knew that he wanted only to get away. He saw what he had in common with those Koreans, not stoicism, but heart only for escape. He careened backward in that jeep toward the riverbank, as if escape was waiting for him there.

Maguire would hear it said later that some men were made more acutely conscious by the bleak experiences of war, and it was true that his ability to see and smell and hear the minutiae of violence was heightened. But his ability to organize his perceptions into a coherent whole in which he was more than a detached observer abandoned him utterly. As far as he could recall he was barely aware throughout that episode of his own choices or even of his own reactions. It was a mad thing to do, for example, to send that jeep shooting off the edge of the cliff. It tumbled down the hundred feet of rocky incline and burst into flames just before it plunged through the ice. The gasoline fire was extinguished as quickly as it had ignited.

And Maguire, as if he'd practiced for a stunt show, had leapt free at the last instant, landed in a crouch facing the river, and watched until the jeep disappeared under a plume of steam. "Fucking thing," he said.

"Maguire! Maguire!"

The engine and tender were just crossing onto the bridge. The platoon was scrambling aboard. Sergeant Stone was waving Maguire's M-1 and calling his name, alarmed that he was being left behind.

Maguire had to run. The train was moving at a clip and he would not have made it if Brown and Pace hadn't pulled him aboard. He collapsed on the iron platform and then at last, leaving that nightmare behind, felt the first hint of relief.

But it was premature.

"Oh fuck!" O'Hara cried. "Oh Jesus! Fuck!"

The others saw what he saw. The wall of refugees had broken and they were rushing onto the bridge behind the train. Their grim stoicism was gone. The crowd of old men, women, boys and girls which had not moved for most of an hour was now a charging infantry, bellowing insanely as it stormed after them. Fatalistic Orientals? Shock victims? A defeated populace? Resigned to wait for its new masters? None of these. They were like the notorious primitive armies of Sun Tsu, which depended less on weapons than on dreadful masks and frightening noises. But a mob is not an army. It is moved not by discipline but by emotion. The Koreans were one creature now, an incarnation of feeling that went beyond fear or rage into something wholly other, something infinite. Even from a distance Maguire could sense that now their energy was going to overwhelm any obstacle they met, and to their horror the GIs realized that the refugees were catching up with them.

"Fix bayonets!" Lieutenant Barrett ordered.

It was difficult to do it on the jolting train, but no one hesitated. In a moment all seven riflemen had the long blades fixed to the barrels of their guns, and Tucci had the safety off the Browning. No one, not Maguire certainly, allowed qualms to surface. The Koreans were no longer old men and women, no longer children. They were an enemy whom the odds favored.

A boy of about twelve was the first to catch the train. He was reaching for the rail when Pace poised to harpoon him, but at that moment the train picked up speed and a gap opened between the boy and Pace's bayonet.

The crowd kept coming even though the train was leaving them behind.

But just as it seemed safe again, the train slowed. Maguire had forgotten that it was going to stop in the middle of the bridge.

The iron wheels began to screech, and steam hissed out from the undercarriage.

And the refugees began to close the distance. The train jolted to a stop.

"Get ready!" Lieutenant Barrett ordered.

Maguire couldn't believe what they were about to do. Tucci raised his submachine gun, and the other soldiers aimed their rifles. Maguire tried to find a middle-aged man to aim at, but all he saw were Pappa-sans and children. "Go back!" he screamed suddenly. "Go back!" Sergeant Stone started screaming at them in Korean, and the other GIs chorused, "Go back! Go back!"

Tucci fired into the crowd, and the front rank fell. Immediately there was a pileup as the onrush continued. The bodies of the Koreans, even the fallen ones, writhed as Tucci's bullets pumped into them.

Maguire couldn't tell whether the other soldiers were firing. He assumed later that he was himself firing, but he was never certain that he hadn't simply frozen while the merciless staccato went on around him. He wished desperately that the rabble-refugees had been a cavalry charging so that he could have aimed his gun at horses.

By the time Lieutenant Barrett gave the order to fall back, the engineers had already abandoned the train. Stringing detonating wire behind them, they were rapidly crossing toward the shore, and it was with infinite relief that the platoon took out after them.

It was impossible to run efficiently on the railroad ties, and the men stumbled constantly.

When Sully fell ahead of him, Maguire assumed he'd only tripped. He stopped to help him. Sully looked up with blood gushing out of a hole below his ear, then he collapsed, obviously dead.

Bullets pinged off the ironwork of the bridge.

Maguire was the first to see the flotilla of small boats in the river below. The channel between the iced margins was clotted with vessels. Scores of soldiers in mustard-colored uniforms were shooting at the Americans from the decks and superstructures of dozens of fishing boats and junks. "Chinese!" he screamed. "Chinese!" Some of the boats were already alongside the pilings of the bridge. The Chinese were grappling their way up.

The GIs ran even faster. The railroad ties were suddenly no obstacle.

Bean was shot. Lieutenant Barrett stopped for him, but then he fell too, clutching his chest.

Eddie Brown and Maguire scooped the officer up and, each taking an arm, carried him along. O'Hara and Pace started to pick up Bean, but he waved them off and they left him.

Tucci fired his submachine gun in a frenzy, and only then did Maguire realize that a pair of Chinese soldiers had just climbed over the railing right in front of them. The Chinese fell dead.

Tucci, Pace and O'Hara ran swifty ahead. Fifty yards from the riverbank Maguire and Brown with the lieutenant between them came upon the corpses of the two engineers who had been stringing the detonation wire. One of them had his arms around the black plunger-box. The other members of the platoon mustn't have realized what it was because they'd run right by.

"Get it!" Lieutenant Barrett ordered. "Leave me and get that plunger!"

"No, sir," Maguire said. "We're getting you out of here."

"Fuck you, Maguire!" The lieutenant wrenched himself out of their arms and fell violently to the track. His blood had soaked even through the heavy winter jacket, turning the olive-green to black. He looked desperately at Maguire. "You've got to get off the bridge and blow it!"

Maguire looked behind him expecting to see the Chinese soldiers, but the wave of Korean refugees, having swarmed over and around the halted train, was rushing at them again. The fucking refugees! They'd overrun the Chinese too!

Eddie Brown picked up the wire-wheel and began to string it out, moving backward toward the shore. Maguire picked up the plunger-box with one hand and with the other hoisted Barrett over his shoulder. He ran as well as he could. He and Brown reached the far end of the bridge at the same time. Tucci was there and once his buddies were clear he began firing back into the onrushing refugees again.

It took several moments for Brown to cut and attach the electrical wire to the terminal in the detonator. When it was ready he looked up at Maguire. "Okay!"

Maguire reached over and grabbed Tucci. "Stop firing! Stop firing!"

There was no need now. Let the poor bastards make it, a few of them anyway.

Tucci obeyed Maguire. He stared at him dumbly. Tears stained his face. He'd been weeping all the while. He'd also wet himself.

Maguire felt a shocking sense of control. It had all somehow come down to him. When the first set of refugees rushed past him off the bridge, a token quota of survivors, he pushed the plunger without hesitating.

For an instant, long enough to turn toward the bridge but not to see the faces, thank God, of the Koreans who hadn't quite made it, there was no explosion. Then it came as a simple loud clap, followed by a muffled dull roar. The earth of the riverbank registered the shock. It moved.

The iron girders of the bridge's three central spans were tossed into the air, along with mammoth fragments of the locomotive and millions of splinters of metal and wood. The dust of tons of enginecinder and the smoke from the huge combustion billowed. Yet through that chaos of debris and noise Maguire swore that he saw severed limbs arching through the air and heard the cries of babies.

"Hey, hey, LBJ! . . . At his side in demonstrations years later I was always aware of Michael's refusal to utter such taunts. ". . . how many kids did you kill today?"

FOUR

WHILE Michael went to Korea, I went to college. I
hastily set about putting away, in Saint Paul's phrase,
the things of a child, including, I'd have said with worldly
relish, the phrases of Saint Paul. The idea—and it is the
perennial idea of freshmen, one of the few they can be
counted on to grasp—was to reinvent one's personality. For
a punk from Inwood newly arrived at NYU in Greenwich
Village, the quickest way to do that was to claim the fiercely
romantic identity of the fallen-away Catholic. That meant
having to learn at once to disdain above all others the figure
of the Roman Catholic priest, that embodiment of smug
sterility and intellectual vacuity.

And then, of course, almost immediately, I fell under the
spell of Gerard Manley Hopkins. My attraction to him would
be permanent and his aesthetic would even be the subject
years later of my dissertation—"Instress and Inscape; the
Diction of G. M. Hopkins." In those days it embarrassed me,
as I was sure it did his Balliol friends, that he'd become a
Catholic and a priest. I agreed with critics who asserted that
his religious vocation had come at the expense of his literary
one. What a waste! we said as if we were horny schoolgirls
discussing the handsome curate. If Hopkins hadn't been a
priest, we agreed in every seminar, he'd have been a lesser
great poet instead of—how these distinctions mattered!—a
great lesser one. When he called himself "Time's eunuch" we
knew he was bewailing the mistake he'd made, the trick God
played on him.

Now I understand that of course his priesthood was precisely what drew me to him. For my kind the priest is the linchpin of belief. In all my religious phases—whether I was fallen away, newly found or only, in current argot, user-friendly—priests have been at the center of my consciousness, and that's part of what's made me Catholic.

And priests, as you know already, will be at the center of this narrative.

None more so, beginning in Korea, than Tim O'Shea.

Father Timothy O'Shea—he answered neither to "Padre" nor to "Major"—was born in Tipperary. His parents emigrated when he was a child and he grew up to become a priest of the Archdiocese of New York. He was trained in philosophy to be a seminary professor. Though overage he had entered the army with Cardinal Spellman's blessing when his brother Ned was killed at the Battle of the Bulge. It was an impulse born of grief and patriotism and also of guilt at his exemption, but he never served with a combat unit during World War Two. Perhaps that's why he felt obliged to stay in even when the war ended. After two tours at stateside VA hospitals he'd hated to admit it but he welcomed this new war, and he'd had Spellman pull strings for his assignment to the 27th Infantry in Korea.

Father O'Shea wanted to be with lads in their extremity, the way he hoped someone had been with Ned in his. He wasn't prepared to find that at the front most GIs ignored him and what the commanders expected of him was help with the USO tours. Still, he had not adopted that ingratiating and implicitly apologetic manner typical of military clergymen, as if they were by virtue of their calling not quite manly enough to keep company with soldiers. Father O'Shea knew what contribution he had to make, even if the men didn't. An army's effectiveness depends most on the ability of its members to believe in the justice of its cause. Since Augustine and Thomas, the Church had considered every implication of each question concerned with that very element of warfare. Once the morality of going to war (*jus ad bellum*) had been established, then participation in war (*jus in bello*) could be encouraged. Once the criteria of the Just War Principle had been met, in other words, it was important that the warriors knew it. Father O'Shea would hold your hand if you wanted, but mostly he wanted to help you think about what you were doing on a bleak spit of land between the Yellow Sea and the Sea of Japan. He wanted to help you do your grim work there as well as possible, and he wanted you to be proud of yourself for doing it. He resented the commanders who required him to arrange the USO events, but in fact he epitomized what they wanted from their chaplains. He was the best goddamn morale officer in Korea.

"God," he said, quoting Emerson's line as a motto, "will not have His work made manifest by cowards."

Most vocations to the priesthood are inspired ultimately by the example of another priest. The priests of Good Shepherd parish in Inwood had a reputation, as a group, for kindness, and the junior curate was widely considered to be terrific with kids, but the parish clergy had made no more overt impression on Michael than they had on me. Priests had certainly been a fixed part of his world—his mother was a volunteer at the rectory—but they were far less central to it than, for example, coaches had been. He was very young when his father was killed, or it might have been different. Until Korea he'd never needed a priest for more than encouragement from the bench at basketball games.

Father O'Shea found him sitting on a campstool outside the quartermaster's tent, futilely trying to warm himself by a small portable kerosine stove. It was late in the afternoon and the crisp blue of the sky was softening. The 3rd Battalion, Maguire's unit, was holding a perimeter position of the makeshift encampment. The regiment, about a thousand men, was dispersed on the four peaks of a hill mass that dominated the main road south. Its mission was to cover the 24th Division's flank while it dug in at Osan. The four hills overlooked the rugged valley that had been cut over eons by the Han, and the regimental patrols were on the alert for signs of enemy activity. Word, though, was that the Chinese had stopped at the river.

What remained of Maguire's platoon had been split up. He, Brown and Pace were assigned to Second Platoon in B-Company, and it was scheduled to go on patrol at dusk.

The other members were sleeping or playing cards in their tents. Maguire wanted the fresh air more than he wanted the rest or the warmth.

"Soldier, how are you doing?"

"Fine, Father." Maguire stood up and saluted, but it was clear from the priest's abbreviated return that he needn't have. Father O'Shea's bearing was lackadaisical. Not even his imposing uniform—the helmet with its white cross, the silver cross on his lapels, the major's gold leaves on his shoulders—overcame his air of informality. He pulled up another canvas stool and sat. He extended his gloved hand toward the stove.

Maguire stood awkwardly over him.

"Take your stool, soldier."

"Yes, sir." He sat.

"Cut the 'sir' crap with me, son. You're an Irish lad who ought to know better."

"Sorry, Father." Michael grinned. It came as a strange relief that this priest rejected martial despotism in favor of ecclesiastical.

"Where do you come from?"

"New York, New York, Father. Same as you."

"What parish?"

"Good Shepherd."

"Inwood? Is that right? Monsignor Riordan is an old friend of mine."

"Monsignor Riordan baptized me."

"No wonder you're good." The priest slugged Maguire's shoulder. "I hear you've been working on the railroad."

Maguire didn't react. At mess that noon some of the GIs sang the old folk song when he joined the tray-line, an indirect acknowledgment of what he'd done. It had made him uncomfortable.

When Maguire said nothing the priest was silent too for some moments. Then he said, "Lieutenant Barrett told me about it."

"How is he?"

"He needs to be evacuated. They're hoping for a chopper before we have to move."

"Is he . . . ?"

"He'll pull through. He's one tough soldier."

"I know. We'd still be over there if it wasn't for him. They mobbed us."

"I heard."

Maguire looked up sharply. "Did you hear what he did?" The chaplain nodded.

Maguire wanted suddenly for the priest to say that what the lieutenant had done, ramming that crowd with the jeep, was all right. But he veered away from that. "How's Jones?"

"He died this morning."

"Oh." Maguire exhaled slowly. It troubled him that he didn't feel more than a vague disappointment at that news. He'd liked Jones, though they'd never talked. He resolved to write his mother. "That's three," he said. "Plus the engineers; how many of them bought it?"

"Four. But Bean's okay. Just a flab-stab. Two other men have wounds that need more attention than they can get out here. Once the chopper comes . . ."

Maguire grunted and forced the mandatory irreverence of tone into his voice. "Tickets home."

"I guess those Chinese just showed up out of nowhere. Nobody thought they'd be in boats. You did damn well to get that bridge. Otherwise they'd be on us now. They could have eaten the whole division for lunch yesterday."

Maguire leaned forward to fiddle with the flame lever. He was grateful to have the chaplain's company, but he didn't feel like talking. That was why he'd left the tent.

Father O'Shea removed his gloves and offered him a cigarette. When they were both smoking he said, "I just wanted to be sure it wasn't bothering you."

Maguire stared at the cinder of his cigarette. "Shouldn't it?"

"It's got to bother a man some, a thing like that, but not so it gets in his way. I wanted to tell you about the principle of double-effect, in case you're interested." He waited for a reaction from Maguire. Emotional numbness was a sign of shock. The lad just worked his cigarette. "Lieutenant Barrett said it was pretty rough."

Maguire nodded.

"In many actions there's the intended good effect and the

unintended bad effect. If the intended good effect—say, the blowing up of a strategic bridge—is justifiable, then the unintended bad effect—say, the deaths of civilians—can be considered moral.''

Maguire looked directly at the chaplain for the first time. ''That's it in a nutshell, eh?''

''You don't seem convinced.''

''To tell you the truth, Father, I didn't think about it. Any of it. And I wasn't thinking about it now.''

''Just a fighting machine, eh? A burp-gun with legs?''

''Isn't that the point?''

''Hell no! We're Americans, soldier.'' Father O'Shea instinctively adopted a brisk authority as he spoke now. Nothing irked him more than the kill-and-masturbate mentality of drill instructors, as if that was all soldiering was. He was ''one of the guys'' until a moment like this, but now he was an oracle. His authority was what rescued men from their confusion. ''Americans, you hear me? We *think* about what we do. We know right from wrong and we stake our lives on the difference. Goddamnit, we bury men in the difference. That's what this war is all about. You want to be a burp-gun with legs, you join the other side. You want to be responsible for your actions, make humane decisions even in the heat of battle, always looking out for your buddies, then stay right where you are.''

''I see what you're saying, Father. But I don't think it matters much to the people who got blown up.''

''We pray for the dead, son. But we watch out for the living. It sure matters to Lieutenant Barrett. He's damn grateful to you for not leaving him out there.''

''I didn't think about that either.''

''No blame, no credit, eh?'' The chaplain surprised Maguire by grinning at him and putting his hand on his shoulder. ''What's your name?''

''Maguire.''

''I mean your first name, son.''

''Michael.''

''The Archangel. The leader of God's army against Lucifer.'' Maguire laughed.

''Monsignor Riordan christened you with that name? He'll

be damn proud when I tell him what you did. And when he tells your folks, imagine how they'll feel.''

Michael didn't say that his father was dead. The thought of that unknown ghost filled him, for a change, with calm. He'd scored every basket and lined every outside pitch and caught every buttonhook of his life with one eye on the man who wasn't there, and in our own small world where the legend of his hero father loomed we all knew it. ''Go, Michael! Go!'' we would cry from the stands as he led our teams to victory, but everyone knew that Michael drove so hard not because of our support but because of his father's absence. How could he earn that long-gone love? That was the void into which O'Shea stepped with his simple affirmation. For the first time in his life, Michael felt his father's presence.

When the priest stood up Maguire asked, ''Hey, did you just give me absolution or something?''

''Maybe I did, Michael.'' The priest muttered a quick blessing and waved his hand over him. And then he reached inside his field jacket and pulled out what Maguire assumed was a pack of cigarettes. Weren't chaplains always giving out cigarettes to people? But it was a book with blue covers, small enough to close inside one hand. The chaplain handed it to him. ''Here,'' he said. ''This was my brother's. He was killed at the Battle of the Bulge. I'd like you to have it.''

Instinctively Michael removed his gloves. It was the New Testament. He looked up at the priest. Years later, in describing this moment he would take refuge from its emotion in a Woody Allen line: I always carry a bullet in my shirt pocket in case someone throws a Bible at me. But at the time he was too moved to speak. The relief he felt came as a shock because he'd had no explicit idea how distressed he'd been. The priest had soothed the orphan-pain in him that was far older than a day. What had happened on the bridge had only uncovered it, and now, with this gift evoking so much—the New Testament, a dead brother, the Battle of the Bulge—he experienced a sense of embrace he'd never felt before. And at last he understood—how he needed this!—why we call them ''Father.''

*   *   *

That midnight an artillery bombardment began that veterans said was as bad as anything the Germans had ever thrown at the Allies in France. The Americans were pinned by the fire and even the patrols had to stay in their ditches. The frozen earth had resisted their efforts to dig out proper foxholes, but now the men wished they'd stayed with it. The ground on which they flattened themselves reverberated continually as it registered every shell that exploded on those hills. Some soldiers made fists of themselves in their shallow holes. Chunks of dirt and stone-chippings bounced off them endlessly. The noise of the heavy-caliber explosions coming after the piercing approach-whistles was so loud that their ears hurt, and they took to blocking them with the heels of their hands while their fingers pressed the cold metal rims of their helmets. Periodically, even through their gloves, they had to warm their hands, though, by stuffing them into their armpits. But quickly the noise of the bombardment was a worse pain again than frozen fingers. Now and then even that din was surpassed by the shrieking of a man who was hit. It was dangerous to look, for the popping of debris and shrapnel was constant.

It didn't take an Omar Bradley to deduce that the Chinese were advancing across the river valley during the barrage. Every man in the regiment knew that. But the bombardment went on so long—nonstop, all night—that they began to understand its purpose was not merely to cover that advance or even to neutralize their ability through shock, fear and disorientation to resist it when it reached them. The purpose of the aimed fire was to kill them.

The 27th Regiment was under orders to hold its ground, but only long enough to delay the onslaught. The American stand wasn't going to be made in the hills around Suwon, but at Osan. The regiment therefore was to withdraw before actually engaging the Chinese, and it was to link up with the main body of forces twenty miles to the south. But an orderly withdrawal was out of the question until the artillery fire stopped. Even panicked flight would have been impossible. And the artillery fire wasn't going to stop until the Chinese were ready to attack. By then what would anyone be able to do but run?

The terror of that night unhinged more than one man. Lennie Pace was crouched next to Maguire in the same ditch, and when a round landed close enough to singe their clothing, he tried to get out. Maguire and another GI grabbed him just as he was scrambling over the lip of the hole. "Let me go, you fuckers! Let me go!" Because of his size and toughness Pace threw the second soldier aside effortlessly. Maguire slugged him, but the punch seemed only to quicken his belligerence. Pace began to pummel Maguire, but Maguire clung to him. Pace tried to get away and he dragged Maguire with him. "You fucker!" he screamed. "I'll kill you!" Maguire held on until Pace fell into the fresh crater of a 175. It was still warm, but it was deeper and more secure than the ditches the men had dug, which were like shallow graves.

Even in the crater the hysterical soldier continued to slug away. Maguire covered his face and let Pace hit him. Most of the blows were lost in his heavy clothing or against his helmet. Eventually the Italian kid collapsed on top of Maguire. He was weeping. Maguire made no effort to get out from under him, but only closed his arms around Pace and held him. At first he envied him the catharsis, but then he realized that he'd shared it. They both felt purged. The terror of that night, Maguire saw, would be a bond forever.

In the release, the evaporation of tension that followed Pace's outburst, both men settled into a kind of sleep. One hears it said that such a drifting off is not uncommon during prolonged sieges. The psyche has its ways of escape even when the body doesn't. Some Londoners never slept well again after the Blitz ended, but during it, even in the rank discomfort of sewer tunnels, they slept like children. Neither the noise nor the cold, extreme as both were, penetrated the consciousness of either soldier for several hours.

Maguire woke first and he was amazed to realize he had slept. He actually felt a kind of refreshment. The artillery fire was still on, merciless as ever, but he wasn't cold. Pace was still on him, like a blanket. He was snoring lightly.

Maguire didn't move. Beyond Pace's collar, like a dream, he saw the morning star, Venus, hanging in the east above the notch in the hills where the sun would rise soon. Automatically Maguire's hand went to his breast pocket, to touch

Father O'Shea's New Testament, as if it was going to save him or already had.

On the roof of his apartment house on Cooper Street, Michael and I had slept out through countless summer nights, though not in each other's arms. Imagine the cries resounding through Inwood of "Fairies! You fucking fairies!" It would have been disgrace enough to have it known that we called the roof our "lone prairie" and pretended that the straining barrel-staved water tank was our Conestoga wagon. When Venus appeared—it was the last star to fade because of course it wasn't really a star but a planet which reflected the coming sun's light instead of getting washed out by it—he always woke up and nudged me. We New York City boys did not take our heavenly bodies for granted. In our pale night sky only the luminaries shone because the dispersed light of the city screened all the ordinary stars and planets out. New York was that way with people too, although we didn't know it yet. Shining in that firmament meant, fortunately, as we would learn much later and separately, either burning to extinction or reflecting the light of some other star.

Venus seemed closer than ever that morning in Korea, and even though the barrage was still on, it seemed to Michael he had already survived it. His lucky star. The night was almost over. And what better omen for the day than the worn little book in his pocket.

The good book. The Bible. The glad tidings of Jesus Christ. Michael was no more religious than any of us, but like us he'd gone to religion class, however automatically, every day of his school life for twelve years. He'd heard the Scriptures read every Sunday and most first Fridays for eighteen. Surely he could remember some proverb, some parable, some saying of Jesus that would help him now.

He squinted at the morning star and a line popped open in his mind like the "Bang" on the flag out of a fake pistol. "He was the light of men, a light that shines in the dark, a light that darkness could not overpower." He had read those words a million times while the priest recited them in Latin; they were from the Last Gospel with which every Mass ended. "A man came, sent by God."

Michael told me over Scotch whiskey many years later that

at that moment, half frozen, paralyzed under the weight of a shell-shocked soldier in a bomb crater on a desolate hilltop in Korea, he discovered for the first time that he did believe in God. He believed in the Resurrection. "What can I say? I saw His glory." He shrugged and drained his Scotch. "With Him on my side, who can be against me?" In other words, while fifteen thousand Chinese were steadily creeping toward him and his one thousand terrified frozen comrades, Michael Maguire accepted in advance whatever was going to happen to him, not only, as pious assholes were always doing, during the remainder of his life, but—much more difficult—during that very day. It was as if he knew how decisive it would be. I would wish many years later that he'd been killed.

The withdrawal began at dawn. Because artillery shells were still falling, though intermittently now, it was a retreat through a nightmare landscape, but the men of the 27th Infantry Regiment were so relieved to have their dreamless terror over that they pushed out energetically. Who wanted to wait for the Chinese charge?

It was impossible to assemble a proper convoy. The regiment's vehicles, marshaled along the main road, had been sitting ducks all night and the artillery had knocked most of them out. That meant forced march, which posed a heart-wrenching problem for the colonel in command: the wounded would have to be left behind. As of dawn, counting the casualties of the night shelling and those from the incident at the bridge two days before, there were fourteen of them. Two Medevac choppers had been promised the day before, but they couldn't come in during the heaviest bombardment. Though now it had eased, there was still no sign of them. It made no sense to leave behind a unit of healthy soldiers to defend the wounded until the helicopters arrived, because each aircraft could carry out only seven men. The fourteen, plus the medic, was stretching it already, and when the chaplain volunteered to stay behind, the colonel could not refuse. He said, "Take off your insignia, Father, and make sure Lieutenant Barrett isn't wearing his bars either."

Father O'Shea wasn't stupid. He wasn't going to fall into Chinese hands with gold leafs on his lapels. But he kept his crosses, on his helmet and his breast.

Word passed through the regiment quickly both that the wounded were being left behind and that the chaplain was staying with them. When Maguire heard it, he was just tying the flaps of the radio case that he and Pace had been assigned to carry. He looked up at the GI who'd told him, but he was gone already, scurrying down the side of the hill. He looked at Pace. "We can't just leave them here!"

"What the fuck, Maguire! What can we do?"

Maguire snatched up his M-1 and climbed quickly to the top of the hill. The wounded men were huddled on a level spot near the top of the next hill. Even without binoculars he could see Father O'Shea holding a man in his arms. They knew what was happening. Maguire searched the sky above the windswept hills, looking for the choppers. No sign of them. In the distance of the valley below, the figures of men jammed the roads, but these were not refugees. It was the massing army of the Chinese peasant riflemen. He scanned the spiny terrain of the nearby slopes, but there was no sign of the enemy there yet.

A round landed in the gully between the hill on which he stood and the one where the wounded lay. Maguire didn't flinch. After the night, the occasional shell now seemed benign. He squinted, trying to make out Lieutenant Barrett.

Pace was at his elbow. "Sarge says to move it, Mac!"

Maguire looked at Pace. "How can we just leave them?"

"Fast! That's how! Come on, Goddamnit!" Pace's agitation was intense. He'd survived the night, but it had left him manic and insecure. He'd clung to Maguire's side since they crawled out of the crater. He was terrified of being alone, but he was also terrified of being left behind. Their company had been detailed to take up the rear, but most of it had moved out already. He and Maguire were the last ones left except for the lieutenant, the sergeant and the radio operator. Their job was to get the radio gear down to the jeep waiting on the road. It was one of the few vehicles still running, and Pace hoped to get on it. "Come on, you shit!" His voice cracked with panic.

But Maguire said suddenly, "What's that moving? Do you see that? Is something moving there?" He pointed to the lower slope of the opposite hill.

The urgency in his voice cut through Pace's agitation and he too fixed his stare on the brush and boulders across the way. Bushes were moving and he saw it too. Both men stared, motionless, not breathing. Bushes were moving up the hill, toward the party of wounded.

"Fuck!" Pace said. "It's them!"

The Chinese had brush fixed to their helmets and their backs, and they were steadily creeping up the hillside.

Pace whispered, "I thought they charged, whistling, screaming, banging cymbals and throwing grenades."

"Maybe they're just the advance patrol. I don't think there are that many of them." Maguire threw the bolt on his rifle.

"Hey, man, come on! Let's go!" Pace started to back off. He was eyeing Maguire as if he'd lost his mind.

Maguire raised his arm and pointed to a spot in the sky above the farthest ridge. "Look, Whirlybird!" He felt a rush of happiness, as if the helicopter was coming for him. But the rescue wasn't going to succeed, he saw suddenly. The Chinese patrol was closing on the hilltop. They'd drive the chopper off or down it. Locks snapped open in Maguire's mind, and he saw what had to happen. There was no experience of decision, only of insight; his response seemed no more the product of choice than a sunrise is. The second helicopter appeared as a dot moving behind but in sync with the first. "Lennie!" Pace was already fifty yards down the hill, clambering backward. "Lennie!" Maguire went after him. He caught up to him easily and grabbed him. "Lennie, we've got to slow them down! We've got to give our guys some time!"

"No, Maguire! Let me go!"

"I can't do it without you, Lennie!"

"Fuck you, man. I'm gone. Get your hands off me or I'll tear your fucking eyes out!"

Maguire released Pace roughly. "You chickenshit!"

Pace whined abruptly. "Don't call me that." Suddenly he looked like the adolescent he was, at the mercy less of his fright now than of his buddy's contempt.

Maguire turned and started up the hill.

Pace called him and Maguire stopped.

"You think we can help?"

"We can get them five minutes maybe. It might be enough. But we have to make the Reds think there's a bunch of us at them. That's why I need you."

Pace caught up with Maguire. "Okay. Okay. But don't let the fuckers kill me, will you?"

Maguire smiled. "No, I won't." He said this soberly, as if he meant it, as if it was his to mean. "You got a grenade?"

"Yeh. A deuce."

"Me too. We have to get close enough to throw them. Then we pin them down with rifles, get it? You take the left flank through that crevice. I'll slip across here. Keep an eye on me. Don't do anything until I do."

"Not too close, okay?"

"Just watch the bushes, Lennie." Maguire slapped his friend's shoulder. "We can do it. Those wounded guys would do it for us." He felt responsible for the boy suddenly, Maguire's first experience of that sensation, and it seemed to him that his affection for Pace at that moment was strong enough to protect him.

As they set off Maguire had to stifle a whoop, as if they were boys at play. His flash of exhilaration did not cancel his anxiety but matched it. He was operating on instinct, like a natural driving for the basket. He didn't know from one instant to the next what the moves would be, but he was in such perfect control of himself that even Pace, sensing Maguire's innate competence, was able to come back from the edge of panic.

They were crouched low, descending the slope easily, each with his rifle and his pair of grenades slapping against his field jacket. The morning light was bright already, but the sun was not above the hills yet and a broad shadow stretched across the ravine that separated the two hilltops. Pace followed the contour line toward an outcropping of rock that would give him shelter, while Maguire plunged directly across the undulations of the rough terrain. When he reached a thatch of waist-high brush in the crease of the gully, he stopped and hid. He could count the Chinese, even in their crude camouflage—more than twenty—but he could no longer see the plateau where the wounded GIs lay. He couldn't see the helicopters either, but he could hear them approaching from beyond the hilltop. All at once he felt he'd made a terrible mistake. He'd surrendered his position on high ground and now was below the enemy. They had every advantage. But the high ground hadn't been in rifle range. He caught Pace's eye and waved him on. Pace's reluctance to leave his cover was obvious, but Maguire stared at him until he set out again. They angled up the hill behind the Chinese as the yapping sounds of the choppers grew louder. The Chinese heard the helicopters too, of course, and, obviously hoping to snare one or both of them, they began climbing toward the pinnacle with abandon, no longer creeping stealthily or taking care to crouch. Instead of slaughtering a few wounded, their glory could be the destruction of the dreaded American machines.

Maguire and Pace threw their grenades within seconds of each other. The explosions, coming out of nowhere and without the prelude of the artillery whine, stunned the rear-most Chinese, as if the earth itself had burst against them. The two Americans threw again, and by the time that second pair of grenades exploded, every Red on the hill had stopped. They never expected the enemy from behind.

The grenades killed or wounded a handful and the nearest Chinese took cover. Only those approaching the crest of the hill resumed running and, silhouetted against the sky, they were the ones Maguire and Pace chose as targets. The GIs were riflemen. This was what they'd trained to do, and they concentrated on lining up their sights and squeezing their triggers. They fired successive volleys, and the frontline Chinese began to fall.

A cloud of dust spilled over the ridge; the choppers were landing.

The Chinese patrol was under cover now, and some of its members had begun to fire back at Maguire and Pace, but against the shadow of the valley they presented obscure targets. Nevertheless Maguire fell prone behind a mound of dirt. He replaced the magazine of his carbine and pressed off several quick rounds. When he looked over at Pace it was like seeing a man about to walk off a cliff. Pace was still standing bolt upright and shooting his weapon efficiently, aiming carefully each time he pulled the trigger, as if he were on the firing range. Maguire wanted to yell "Get down!" but Pace wouldn't have heard him. Maguire resumed firing too; it was all he could do. Had Pace snapped? Or was it only his determination to show Maguire that he was not chickenshit? Maguire knew already that the big lunk was going to be hit, and that filled him with nausea and with guilt.

Like an apparition in a cloud the first chopper appeared above the lip of the ridge, lifting off unsteadily in a great roar, but instead of gaining altitude it jerked down along the curve of the hill toward Maguire. The second helicopter swooped up and immediately away.

Now the Chinese all over the hill began firing at the chopper instead of at Maguire and Pace, but the wash from the rotors kicked up a screen of dirt, and the peasant-riflemen were too agitated to fire accurately.

At first Maguire thought the helicopter, erratically dropping toward him from the hilltop, had been hit and was about to crash. But then he realized that its jerkiness was evasion, and that it was coming down to snatch Pace and him up.

Pace was still lost in another time. He had not been hit, though he continued to stand exposed, like a statue. But he was pressing off shot after shot. Maguire took his cue from him. All over the hill the Chinese too were upright, in the open, firing madly in the air, trying to bring down that helicopter. Pace and Maguire picked off one after the other of them. By now more than twenty Reds had been shot and still the brown hill was dotted with them. Maguire's estimate had been off by dozens.

The helicopter swerved and bounced in midair, as if it were being swung on a cable. A soldier was in the open door braced against the hatch frame, clinging with one hand to the lurching machine and, with the other, firing an automatic pistol down at the Chinese.

The chopper dropped dangerously and then hovered right above Pace. Pace reacted to it with shock, as if he'd just awakened. The noise and dust were infernal. Only an act of mind made it possible to see the thing as a rescuer, not monster. The skid-railing was just above his head and he could have grabbed it, but at that moment his back snapped in a sharp arc as he took a bullet. His body jerked again as it took another.

Maguire ran to him.

Unbelievably, gallantly, the helicopter waited.

Pace collapsed in Maguire's arms. That was it.

Maguire looked helplessly up at the man straddling the doorway. Wind tore at him. He was bareheaded and half-bald, naked without his helmet. Perhaps that was why Maguire had not recognized him. He was frantically gesturing with his pistol for Maguire to grab the skid. Only yards separated them.

Maguire's mind slowed down. Why didn't the man in the chopper jump down and help him save Pace? But that was impossible. Still he stared pleadingly up at him. Don't leave us here! He focused on the soldier's breast insignia off which light glanced. The silver cross. The man who'd been firing from the doorway was Father O'Shea.

The irony that his violation—his violence—should have so embodied his dedication stunned Michael. This priest would kill for me!

Michael shook his head and waved them off.

O'Shea was screaming at him, having dropped the gun and cupped his hands around his mouth, as the helicopter began to ascend. In the noise it was impossible to hear what he was saying, but then O'Shea, priest again, blessed him. Absolution. For an instant Maguire's eyes and the priest's met.

Michael told me years later that he felt in Father O'Shea's look an absolute affirmation, what he'd come to call, with Rogers, an unconditional positive regard. Michael might have called it by its other name—love—but his history with Father O'Shea was complicated by then. At that moment, though, he experienced the priest's gaze as if it were his dead father's or God's. The transcendence of that sensation, more than the violence around him, made him certain that he was about to die.

The helicopter swooped away, leaving behind in the relative silence only the popping of the Chinese guns.

Even that fell off to nothing as the last echo of the chopper engine faded.

Maguire listened and listened, but to Pace, not the enemy as it closed on him. He pressed the Italian kid against his own breast, the way he had that baby at the bridge, that rabbit in basic. He listened and listened.

He could have sworn he heard Pace speak: "You said you wouldn't let them kill me and I believed you."

But Pace was silence itself.

When his captors jerked Pace's body out of Maguire's arms, he saw a red mark on Pace's face, the impress of Maguire's own dog tag. He had crushed his buddy's face against it, stamping on the poor bastard's forehead for all eternity the negative of the ID number, rank, name, blood type and religious preference of the man who had led him to his death.

When the interrogators asked him their questions over the next thirty-three months, he answered as if he were reading from above the left eye of Lennie Pace: "Private First Class Michael Maguire, U.S. Army 73822094, O-positive, Catholic."

FIVE

THE Korean war could have saved us.
Forgive me that fustian pronouncement. The Korean war could have saved us? Saved us from precisely what, pray tell? What a wad of fibrous padding for cracks in the mind that statement is! Indeed. And I apologize. Unfortunately the statement is also true. If we'd learned from it, Korea could have saved us from the moral and political suicide we committed in Vietnam. Will future generations remotely understand what led America to squander her glory, wealth, moral position and the cream of her youth on distant conflicts of no true international significance, and to do so not once but twice? It is stunning to realize that a mere decade separated the ignominious end of the conflict in Korea and the launching of the doomed American effort in Vietnam. Were we asleep all that time?

In a way, yes. My friends and I, like the entire budding intelligentsia, were spellbound by the hocus-pocus of Cold War bombast. We believed that the transcendent political event of the era was the discovery that our leaders had "lost" China. Imagine. Congressmen, senators, diplomats, generals and presidents were regarded as having lost a nation of five hundred million people. As if it were a parking stub. Which of them, after that, would willingly be perceived as participating in the "losing" of anything else? Even Indochina, wherever that was? The nations of the world were like a hoard of marbles. For twenty-five years every president, military man and senior civilian to grace a table in Georgetown had his aggies to protect, his steelies, his walleyes, and his balls.

Now balls we understand about. We males are required, whether by nature or culture, to establish for ourselves and others that we have them. Rites of passage, journeys through the dark forest, Sacraments of Confirmation, Bar Mitzvahs, Eagle Scout ceremonies, fraternity hazing, panty raids, beerblasts—showcases all for two things. Balls. But it isn't enough to demonstrate potency, virility, once, at the beginning of one's manhood. Most of us have to do it again and again. Having established that we have balls, we have to regularly prove that we haven't "lost" them. Like we lost our parking stub or China or the war in Korea.

Unfortunately, by definition, the circumstances in which we must establish such a thing are rarely subject to our control. A bully shoves us in the corridor. A stranger asks our girl to dance. An army crosses a parallel of latitude. The process that ensues—ballbusting—is irrational and often degrading of others, humiliating for oneself and implicitly—here is the irony—emasculating. Like Korea was. Like Vietnam was. Like the behavior of boys on the prowl almost always is. But I am ahead of myself.

What I knew about balls in the autumn of 1953 was that Michael Maguire had them. Jesus, did he have them! He was a goddamn war hero, a repatriated POW, still tall, more erect than ever, as if he'd survived by holding himself rigidly at attention. His picture was in the papers and he was one of a group interviewed on television by Edward R. Murrow. Murrow had approved the Korean war and introduced his guests that night as "young men who had drawn a line not across a peninsula, but across the world."

Michael was thinner than he'd ever been, but not malnourished. He was gaunt, but like an ascetic poet. He had the lean visage everyone wanted in Greenwich Village. My friends there regarded the experience of the veterans as cavalierly as they regarded their own. I knew better. In the Village all experience was artifice, at the service of impressions to be made, whether on oneself—the Beats—or on others—the College Joes, of whom I was one. But men who'd been at war, men who'd seen violence and awful death at first hand, men who'd killed other men, nobly—these were creatures set apart, young gods to me. And none more so than Michael.

Having distinguished himself in combat he had then withstood pressures of what a phrase of the day tagged the "Red
Hell." Unlike others he had not compromised himself before
his captors. Only on his return did he learn that he had been,
while imprisoned, promoted to sergeant and awarded for
actions taken at the Han River bridge the Silver Star, and for
actions taken in the hills outside Suwon the Distinguished
Service Cross. For conduct while in prison he was awarded
the Legion of Merit and two Presidential Unit Citations. He
received this news as one chastened. I remember that on the
Murrow show, in contrast to his comrades, he displayed a
lively graciousness toward the Chinese and generosity toward
the Americans whom imprisonment broke. When Murrow
asked how he survived the brainwashing he replied that though
he was interrogated regularly he was never tortured, and that
his impression was that attempts to brainwash footsoldiers
like himself were rare. He said that airmen and officers who
resisted were the ones who deserved respect because they
were the ones the Chinese singled out. When Murrow pressed
him, he allowed that he did depend for solace on his Catholic
faith and, yes, he supposed that POWs with strongly held
beliefs might have had some advantage. Far from torturing
him, he said, his captors had permitted him to keep the one
possession that mattered to him, a small copy of the New
Testament. Murrow asked him to hold it up for the TV
audience, but Michael politely refused.

Michael Maguire was one of those celebrated in news
stories and sermons as proof that Americans, even in that
imbecile defeat, had conducted themselves with virtue and
manliness. If we hadn't beaten Communism, we'd stood up
to it. We'd contained it. Maguire and his kind enabled us to
believe that we were still good guys with balls.

I was more awed by his status than anyone, more admiring,
more moved to have him back. Yet weeks went by and I
didn't see him. I rarely visited Cooper Street anymore since
I'd moved to the Village and my parents had moved to
Queens. But it wasn't just a question of not having run into
him. How does one presume to kick the can with young
Hector? How does one bridge the gulf between the infinitely

mundane experience of a mere student—even one in the
throes of Village liberation—and that of a returned warrior, a
champion, a hero? We were both twenty-one years old, but he
was an archetype of manhood. I was an Honors senior in
Modern Literature and had the swagger for it. Literature,
after all, more than the life of license in Greenwich Village,
had rescued me from the cramped sullenness of Inwood. My
world had come to seem huge, bright and full of language,
language even the great Michael Maguire could not have
appreciated in its subtleties. But suddenly I wasn't sure. Who
had left whom behind? I ruthlessly compared myself to my
old chum and became to myself more a kid than ever. I "had
gone back and forth all night on the ferry" with my Millay,
but what was that? Michael had confronted the Waste Land
itself, and "had bred lilacs" out of it. I assumed really that I
would never see him again, except from a distance. The
war—my exemption from it as much as his achievement in
it—had changed, or so I thought, the very ontology of our
relationship, as if one of us had been ordained or canonized
or had undergone, as Christine Jorgensen soon would, a
sex-change operation. What would he say to me? What would
he think? His years in prison, his terrible time in combat—
what a rebuke each reference to his experience was to me.
When I'd heard that he was captured, I'd known at once that
he and I would never have the most important things in
common again.

During the long hiatus of the Panmunjom negotiations—
they lasted two years, even while operations named Wolfhound,
Thunderbolt, Round-up, Ratkiller, Ripper, Rugged and
Piledriver failed at places named Bloody Ridge and Heartbreak—I thought of him continually. But would he believe
that? When the prisoners came home, college boys felt more
guilt than joy. Wouldn't Michael think I did too? I'd been
gloriously freed from Inwood, that *parochia* we'd ruled together as boys, and had made a place for myself in the
downtown world toward which we'd looked with longing.
Michael had dreamed of college and digs in the Village too, a
life of ideas, literature, liquor and sex. I'd plunged far enough
into each to say I'd been there, and also enough to know the
dream of such things can never be surpassed. But would

Michael look at me now and see if not a hedonist and a coward, a frivolous aesthete? Would he see a weakling of the sort who went berserk in foxholes or who signed confessions in Chinese prisons? Later when I confided these insecurities of mine to Michael he laughed, though not cruelly. We were chums, he said, and would be always. Differences between us? Don't be a dope, Durkin! He didn't deny the differences but he dismissed them and therefore so did I. Now I see that perhaps we were wrong to. Michael Maguire was an anointed man. I would never be. We knew it then, but ducked. What we regarded later as the true beginning of our friendship was, after all, the beginning of the end of it.

Even before the sun was up that Sunday morning I was on the uptown A-train, headed for Good Shepherd and the 7:15 Mass. I hadn't been to church in a year, but this was a way to see Michael and perhaps, finally, talk to him. He was to be the main speaker at the annual Father and Son Communion Breakfast. Looking back on it, even given the insecurities I've described, it seems a curious choice of circumstances for our reunion, even if I'd wanted to make it seem a reunion of chance. Was I moved by an impulse I've forgotten? Did I in fact want to pray? The likelier explanation is that I wanted, first, to see him at remove, to see him before he saw me, to see him on the turf we'd had in common. We'd been altar boys together in that church and we'd roamed the parish hall as if we were proprietors of the place during bazaars and bingo and bake sales and talent shows and a dozen previous communion breakfasts. The first time either of us was made giddy by drink had been inside the huge sacristy closet where the deadly sweet altar wine was stored. The cheap but blessed sauterne was like cough medicine and we loved it.

The A-train clicked along like the Ellington tune, snaking under midtown, Central Park, Harlem, and Upper Broadway. There were few other passengers at that hour and so I found myself looking unselfconsciously into the black mirror of the windows. I worried that Michael would see what I saw. When the train periodically pulled into stations my eye was drawn to the bright posters and billboards on which were portrayed ruby-lipped women in calf-length skirts and pipe-smoking men in absurdly creased fedoras. It was a Sunday in December and there were scenes of couples under mistletoe and families at Christmas dinner which only heightened my sweet melancholy. A boy like me believed more firmly than he believed in God that he couldn't go home again.

At NYU I was regarded as something of a dazzler, I don't know why. I lived alone in a dark room below ground on Horatio Street, and in looking back it seems to me I spent an eternity at my table writing poems, whole afternoons walking the city alone or seeing Russian films in dingy movie houses. But I mustn't have been the recluse I fancied myself. In my junior year I was elected editor of the literary magazine and chairman of the Cellar Theater, a campus coffeehouse where we smoked and read our poems to one another. In public I was extroverted and humorous. I hit it off with the brightest of my classmates, and by my last year I found myself at the center of a lively intellectual crowd, mostly Jews, on whom the exotic airs of Bohemia seemed utterly natural. We gathered at night at the Cedar Tavern on University Place where we imagined ourselves hobnobbing with Jackson Pollock, Mark Rothko and their disciples. As would-be writers we fairly basked in the sporadic presence of Dwight MacDonald, Norman Mailer, Philip Rahv, Mary McCarthy, Delmore Schwartz and the old *Partisan Review* crowd. I had friends who insisted my poems were as good as anything that magazine was publishing and they were always threatening to go over to Rahv's table on my behalf. What a mortification it would have been. I could never bring myself to tell them how many times that magazine and a dozen others had already rejected my work. My fellow undergraduates thought of me as one of the two or three among them with *real* promise. I let them. I suspected the truth, however, that my flare for poesy would not outlast my adolescence. I would be a teacher like the rest of them.

My oh so worldly fellow students would not have recognized me by the feelings I was having on my way to Good Shepherd. The closer I came to the Irish neighborhood in which I'd been raised, the more inhibited I felt. By the time I got off at 207th Street and climbed out of the subway I had my overcoat tightly belted, my shoulders hunched against the

cold and my head lowered, eyes on the sidewalk, like some
bookish introvert come back to attend Mass with his mother.

The sun was up and Broadway, so domesticated there on
the far tip of Manhattan, was yawning and stretching like the
family collie. Terry Behan, the baker who claimed then to be
a cousin of Brendan's, but later when the writer was dissolute
would deny ever having heard of him, was winding down the
awning on his shop window. It was of pink canvas and
carried the legend "Baking on Premises." He didn't look at
me as I passed him and I did not greet him. I saw the church
at the end of the block. But for its size it was an unremarkable structure of gray stone set back from the street by a
stunted plaza and above the street by eighteen stairs. Many
people were going in for Mass, and most of them were
familiar to me. Automatically I took the stairs two at a time
as I had done since high school, which was when I discovered that the steps were too shallow for a grown man to take
in stride. The steps, I had decided one bold day in my six-
teenth year, were made for children and old ladies, like the
religion was.

I noticed in fact that the people approaching the church
with me seemed mostly to be women, which one would
expect at the early Mass. But this was Father-and-Son Sunday.
Where were the men and boys? I'd expected to see a dozen of
my schoolmates. Did I have the wrong weekend?

Even in my agnostic phase—never atheist; it was a distinction we made much of—I was a sucker for the silence of
churches. When I traveled in Europe during graduate school I
could never enter a cathedral without matching its hush with a
piquant inner one which was like a voice rebutting my
sophistication; God whispering, "Oh really?" The compelling atmosphere of the sacred depended in my case at least on
certain visceral feelings of guilt, and no place ever evoked
those more satisfactorily than Good Shepherd. The guilt I felt
that day was so pleasantly familiar it was easy to think of it as
an element of the holy. Even the obnoxious bustle of the old
women with their satchel-sized purses staking out their favorite pews could not dispel the old *mysterium*, and I welcomed
the sensation even as it welcomed me. The silence, the
unctuous odor of votive candles, the warped sheen of the

linoleum aisles and the hissing of the car-sized radiators touched off such warm feelings of belonging that I could have exclaimed, "Of course you can't go home again, but you can always go back to church!" I thought it was an original insight of mine when I understood that the church's main function is to be there to go back to.

This feeling of poignancy at Good Shepherd was as unexpected as sharp, and it filled me with a sudden sense of loss, not for belief or religion or Catholicism but for the neighborhood, the parish. I regretted not so much my own move away from it, but my parents', because as long as this was theirs it would have been mine. How could they have abandoned Good Shepherd? And for what? Queen of Queens? I resented my parents' move for the first time. So what that at last they had a little bungalow now and their own patch of grass. So what that they finally had a car. Wasn't it their job to keep my past intact so that I could wander through it now and then, nostalgically? It came as a surprise that my parents' choices, their lives really, could still impinge on mine. In the Village we thought parents counted for nothing. The best people, the ones we emulated, had never had them.

But at least the church of Good Shepherd was not like our apartment on Cooper Street. Those five rooms were someone else's now, with new wallpaper in the bathroom and pictures of different snow scenes on the walls. It was a relief that Good Shepherd, with its silence, odor, sheeny floors and hissing pipes was still mine. And if it was still mine after NYU, it always would be. Good Shepherd with its nuns, priests, old ladies, pamphlet racks, banks of red and blue votive lights, holy water fonts, pointed windows and mammoth electric lanterns under which I'd made a point since fourth grade never to sit was indelibly stamped on my soul, like grace. I did not realize until that moment how at sea I'd felt downtown, and how lonely. If I was at my desk too much or at the movies it was because no one I knew down there was an Inwood kid.

Like Michael. No wonder I'd come to see him here. In a park, a tavern or an Automat downtown I'd have been reduced to imitating Edward R. Murrow interviewing him. But here . . . I understood in a flash and for the first time that it

was this place that had made us friends. That alone would
have made it sacred.

I entered, dipping my hand, blessed myself, genuflected—
right knee to left heel—and slid automatically into the corner
by the confessionals.

"Msgr. Riordan," a lettered sign said over one, and I
shuddered. He'd caught me smoking in the schoolyard and
his mere stare had injected me with a terror I still felt five
years later. I took up a place by Father Walsh's booth. He
was a soft touch. The line of penitents waiting for him on
Saturdays could run for an hour after the monsignor had
returned to the rectory. You could confess to Father Walsh
having been sinfully aroused and he wouldn't ask you if it
was with yourself or with others.

I looked from worshipper to worshipper for Michael but
didn't see him. He was taller than I was from the age of
twelve and so all through high school had sat behind me, so I
might not have recognized the back of his head, but there
were almost no men or boys in the church anyway. Why
weren't they standing in the right rear corner where I was?
Even when the pews were three-fourths empty, my father and
his cronies always heard Mass from there because at sermon
time, but before the priest turned around to face the congregation, they could slip out the side door for a smoke. When my
generation stood there it was to arrive late and leave early.
But that morning in the last moments before Mass I was alone
in the men's corner and it took me a moment to remember
why. Holy Name Sunday was the one Sunday on which the
male hangers-back joined the congregation. They would be
wearing their funeral suits today and, having gathered in the
choir room behind the sacristy, they would any minute now
be entering the sanctuary in procession ahead of the priest.
They would file out onto the laity's side of the communion
rail and into the first dozen pews on both sides of the aisle.
Even from the back of the church I would know their bright
faces. The fathers would be red from the flush of weather,
age and drink, and the sons would be red from embarrassment,
unnecessarily since no one whose opinion they valued would
see them in their obeisance.

Except me, of course.

I was famous among my old friends for having lapsed. In my rare summer forays into Inwood taverns I had, in the drunken company of mates who now worked as apprentices to their fathers in the Irish trades and on the waterfront, sworn with Jefferson upon the altar of God eternal hostility against every form of tyranny over the mind of man. "Including if needs be," I loudly added, "the tyranny of God Himself."

Now what would they make of me, timidly hanging back in my dark corner among the purple draperies of the confessional booths? "Monsignor Riordan." The very name frightened me and I moved away from his confessional again, as if an arm was going to reach out from behind the curtain and grab me. It was the pastor's whisper I'd imagined, not God's; "Oh, really, Mr. Durkin? Eternal hostility?"

A stirring in the sanctuary rescued me.

I focused on the sacristy door. The bell tingled and the pair of acolytes entered. The congregation coughed once and rose. The silent procession of the Holy Name Society began and I held my breath, straining every faculty of perception, not for the monsignor or my father's cronies or my old school chums but one. It was he I wanted, he I was afraid to see.

Two hours later, after the Mass during which I'd wanted only to chat with my solemn neighbors, and the breakfast banquet during which I'd ignored their openings, I was nearly out of patience because I'd yet to make contact of any kind with him. In the shrilly lit cavernous parish hall below the church he was being introduced by Monsignor Riordan. We had eaten our scrambled eggs and toast and now were smoking and sipping coffee, carefully not clinking the cup and saucer. The pastor's legendary ability to unsettle his parishioners was related in part to the rude disproportion of size between his head, which was huge and topped off by a bush of gray hair, and his body, which was slope-shouldered, waistless and too small. Physically he was graceless and disjointed, but he was a cultivated man and an accomplished orator of the Bishop Sheen school. When he spoke, even in conversation, he commanded absolute attention. "And Father O'Shea told me that even at the last moment, Sergeant Maguire could still have saved himself. That helicopter was right above his head. All he had to do was reach up and seize it.

They were calling for him to do that. But did he? We know
he didn't and we know what he suffered as a result. But why?
Why didn't he latch on to that helicopter and hold on to it for
dear life, and let it bring him safely home? Well, I'll tell you
why. Because he wouldn't leave his brother to the mercy of
those atheistic Communists, that's why. Father O'Shea said
Sergeant Maguire was holding his mortally wounded comrade
the way our Blessed Lady held her dear Son down from the
cross. 'A Battlefield Pietà,' he called it. Sergeant Maguire
preferred the final comfort of his compatriot to the solace of
his own safety. Father O'Shea told me that there were tears in
his eyes as that helicopter pulled away—and Father O'Shea,
I'll tell you, men, is one tough Irishman—yet there were tears
in his eyes as he watched the Reds closing in on Sergeant
Maguire and his wounded *amicus*. And Father O'Shea said
running through his mind over and over was that great line
from Scripture, 'Greater love than this hath no man . . .'

  "And do you know what I said to Father O'Shea, men? I
said, 'You're damn right. Because he's his father's son and a
Good Shepherd boy, and that's how we grow them here.'
You know our motto: *Deus et Patria*. We teach our boys to
give their all to God and Country, because God and Country
have given all to us. Men, I want you all to stand up and
welcome home Sergeant Michael Maguire of the United States
Army."

  We stood and clapped for a long time, and more than one
of those men had tears in his eyes as Michael, resplendent in
his brown uniform with its simple row of colored bars pinned
to its breast, took his place at the podium. He was blushing
so fiercely and he was so thin and his hair was so short and
he stood so rigidly at attention that he seemed altogether
unlike himself. It was my first unobstructed view of him, and
I can't for the life of me tell you what I thought. I suspect I
was hoping rather desperately that he was not about to say
some version of "Aw, shucks, a man just does what he has to
do." But also I hoped he wouldn't second the monsignor's
saccharine canonization of him. I was not unmoved by the
facts of his heroism or by the monsignor's reference to his
long-dead father, but there were no tears in my eyes. I was
afraid for Michael, having seen for the first time the new peril

he had to deal with. Having survived the war as a hero, he had to survive the peace as one.

Finally the audience stopped clapping and sat again. When the last scraping of chairs had faded and quiet had settled over the men and their transfixed sons, Michael began to speak while staring at his hands, which were at rest on the podium. "I guess you're hoping to hear about the war, but I can't tell you much about it because I was only in combat a month."

He looked up and grinned and a few men laughed.

"It ended for me a long time ago." Michael let his eyes drift across the hall and I braced myself, thinking he would see me any minute.

"You probably want to hear about the Chinese prison camp I was in, but to tell you the truth there's not much to say about it. Two and a half years of nothing happening, nothing at all. What can you say about that?" He grinned again, but more awkwardly. He knew the audience expected some momentous statement and he was saying right off that he didn't have one to make.

"But Monsignor Riordan mentioned his good friend Father O'Shea, and I did want to say a word or two about him. Father O'Shea was in that helicopter because *he* had stayed behind with the wounded when it seemed certain the Chinese would take them. What struck me about that, and I think other GIs too, was that it seemed, well, not that surprising that the chaplain would do that. I mean he volunteered and all, and he didn't have to, and any other guy who volunteered to stay behind when the enemy is just down the hill, well we would have just thought he was nuts, you know?"

We laughed hard, all relieved at his lack of pompousness.

"But, well, Father O'Shea was a priest and I guess what I'm trying to say is that when the average Joe does something like that, he gets treated like a hero because the average Joe isn't supposed to stick his neck out. But well, if a guy happens to be a priest, then we change what we expect. A priest stays behind with the wounded and everybody says, Well, of course. He's a priest. That's what he's here for. And I guess that just makes me feel real proud to be a Catholic. I know I felt that way in Korea. See, in the army the Catholic guys feel sort of defensive about the priests, and when they're good ones, we're proud of them. Father O'Shea, well he was the best and everybody knew that. And it didn't matter if you were Jewish or even an atheist. He was with you no matter what you were. Of course if you were Catholic, he was *really* with you.''

He stopped while we laughed warmly. Monsignor Riordan was nodding dramatically at his place, feeding the laughter. It faded and Michael resumed, more solemnly. ''And I know that if Father O'Shea could have, he would have taken my place on that hill and later in the POW camp. He would have taken my place for any of it. And I'll tell you something, there were a lot of days when I'd have let him.''

We laughed again, but quietly. That audience of three hundred plumbers, cops, carpenters and telephone repairmen was beaming at Michael. Eyes glistened everywhere in the hall. Pride, admiration, gratitude filled the spaces above us, like angels. But the sons, teenaged boys mostly, had reason to squirm. Each of them at that moment, by virtue of not being Michael Maguire, was a disappointment to his father.

''People have told me I was pretty special because I was lucky enough to pull through the time in the camp in pretty good shape. It sort of embarrasses me because I know I shouldn't be getting any credit for it.'' Michael stopped and for an instant he looked right at me, but there wasn't a flicker of recognition in his eyes. Finally he said, ''I have to give credit where it's due and that's with God. This is the first talk I agreed to give since I got home. You can probably tell I don't do this much. I didn't do it at all in China.''

We liked him needling himself, and were edified by his testimony. This was an audience of devout men, but they had no patience for overt expressions of piety and would tolerate sermons only from the clergy, if that. But this kid had earned the right. They liked him for his reticence. He was still a blue-collar guy and knew it.

''When Monsignor Riordan asked me to talk to you I thought about it and I said I would because Good Shepherd gave me my faith. The monsignor knocked it into me.''

Laughs again and coughing, nods all around. Monsignor Riordan had been known to clip altar boys on the ear right in the sanctuary. Once, during Mass, when I gave him a finger towel that was wet he threw it in my face.

"And I figured this would be a good chance for me to thank God sort of publicly, which is something I promised myself I'd do. Or maybe I should say I promised Him. So anyway, that's what I'm doing up here. Not that God needs it particularly, but, well, I do."

And suddenly Michael stopped talking and bowed his head. We realized he was going to pray now, and we all automatically made some shift in posture, uncrossing our legs, scooting to the edge of our chairs, dropping our heads onto our hands so that we wouldn't have to watch. We snuffed out our cigarettes and as always we coughed.

Michael said so softly one had to strain to hear him, "Thank you, Almighty God, for getting me through and for bringing me home." He paused, then for a long moment was utterly still. I looked up at him. He resembled a statue, a GI at prayer. And I realized there was not an ounce of swagger in him, no artfulness or conceit. I don't know that I'd ever had the experience of seeing a person for exactly what he was. He was not a pretender of any sort, and he had come before us to claim nothing. Therefore we'd have given him anything. My anxieties in relation to our reunion dropped away. He was unlike anyone I knew. Straight as an arrow. Square as a die. A profoundly good man. I thought him beautiful.

"And . . . ," he continued softly, ". . . may the souls of the departed rest in peace, amen."

I made the sign of the cross too. Who was I kidding? Agnostic Fosdick! At that moment, because Michael Maguire believed in God I did. I was only the first of many people to react to him that way.

He looked up at us now, somewhat helplessly. We looked back at him.

Finally, Monsignor Riordan stood up and began to clap, and so did we. But I sensed a reluctance all around me. Applause was off the mark. Not even a standing ovation was what the moment wanted. The young sergeant had touched us all and had made every category we might have applied to him—hero, leader, saint—irrelevant. We just would like to have sat there for a moment longer and looked at him.

Before the applause stopped, Monsignor Riordan shook Michael's hand and smoothly drew him back to his place at the head table. He picked up his napkin and pulled his chair out. He nodded once at the audience, his first acknowledgment of the ovation, and then, only then, he looked directly at me and his eyes held mine, held me. His look made me feel caressed.

SIX

"HE is a tower unleaning," I said to myself, that opening line of John Crowe Ransom's, as I watched Michael greet the others. After the breakfast broke up a reception line had formed spontaneously. The men and their sons waited decorously to shake his hand, but I hung back. How could I possibly have greeted him that way, as if he were a politician I wanted favors from? On the other hand how could I presume to set myself apart? Maybe I was just one of the gang. From Olympus didn't all mortals look alike?

"Good morning, Frank," Monsignor Riordan said, startling me.

"Hello, Monsignor." I shook his hand manfully enough, but he'd set my insides to quivering, as always.

"What do you think of your old friend?"

We both looked across the hall at Michael, who was graciously, patiently saying hello to each man, not with poise exactly, but with an utterly engaging awkwardness that served both to underscore his virtuousness and to put the Society members at ease. "I think he looks good, Monsignor. Real good."

"So do you, all decked out . . ." With a judging glance he took in my double-breasted suit, my starched shirt and tie, my polished wing tips. I had my overcoat over my arm, and my wide-banded felt hat hung at the end of my fingers. Like all college boys of the day I dressed the part of a bank teller or an FBI agent.

". . . We don't see enough of you around here. You shouldn't forget your old friends, Frank."

"I don't get back much, Monsignor."

"I gather that. And you didn't go to Communion either."

I blushed despite myself. In the old days when we all went to Confession on Saturday, if you didn't go to Communion on Sunday, it meant you'd masturbated Saturday night or, if you'd had a date, you'd copped a feel. I remembered our all-purpose if unconvincing cover: "I broke my fast, Monsignor."

He grunted. "How are Mom and Dad? We miss them since they moved to Queens."

"They're fine."

"Your father talking to you yet?"

My father hadn't spoken to me for a year after I'd chosen NYU over Fordham. My objection to the latter wasn't the Jesuits or that it was Catholic, but that it was only across the river from Inwood. It meant I'd have had to live at home, and not even my father's wrath was enough to make me do that. My father eventually softened toward me, but my family would never recover from the wound of our breach. It mortified me that the pastor knew about it. His hostile pressing made me feel deprived of oxygen. "My dad and I get along fine, Monsignor."

"Good. Glad to hear it. I know your mother was broken-hearted."

I forced a smile. "She's fine too."

We laid off each other and let our gazes drift back to Michael. After a moment the monsignor said, "Father O'Shea told me he was simply the bravest soldier anyone had ever seen over there. He saved a lot of lives I guess, but you wouldn't know it from him."

It occurred to me that Michael's greatest achievement was to have forced this bitter old fart to suspend his mordant disdain. I'd never heard him speak admiringly of anyone.

"And Father O'Shea knows what he's talking about. He's the head army chaplain in Germany now." The monsignor looked at me. "A colonel."

"Is that right?"

He stared at the bridge of my nose—for every Michael Maguire there are a thousand bums like you.

The last thing I'd imagined for our reunion was that when

Michael and I finally met again our old priest-nemesis would be standing between us, but that is what happened. Michael was crossing toward us. When our eyes locked together I raised my hand to wave at him, but it seemed a wholly stilted gesture. Monsignor Riordan's presence? No, something else.

Now that I was facing my friend at last a new question had popped open in my mind. How would he take it that I'd created a personality around an imitation of him? Michael had always served me as a kind of compass of perception. With him what-was-what had always been obvious, and the things and styles that seemed good to him had by virtue of that seemed wonderful to me. He had been, and I gathered from his talk still was, both funny and solemn. They had seemed the perfect modes to me and I'd consciously tried to duplicate them in my own responses. I did not succeed, of course, but I became what I remain, ironic and pessimistic, the Greenwich Village versions of Michael's attitudes.

The closer Michael came the taller he seemed. He wore his nervousness quite loosely, as a given of the moment, as if awkwardness between us was the most natural thing in the world. He was the first to speak. "Welcome home," he said when he grasped my hand.

I had to smile; the son of a bitch welcoming *me* home! "Thanks," I said feebly.

"It must have been rough," he said. I realized what he was doing, turning all the shit they'd just been giving him on its ear by giving it to me. He was dodging the embarrassment of our reunion by making a joke on the leering Monsignor Riordan. Michael was proposing an improvisation. I caught it instantly, as if I was his drummer, as if this was Birdland.

"It wasn't that bad," I said. "You do what you have to do."

"I guess so. But I doubt if I could have."

"You never know . . ." I matched his grieving tone exactly. We were picking up where we'd left off. ". . . until you're in the situation how you'll react."

"Some men just have what it takes, I guess."

"Though really," I offered modestly, "I can't claim any credit."

"Well, you may not believe this, but . . ." Michael gave

me his most meaningful look. ". . . I wish I'd been there with you."

"Where?" Monsignor Riordan asked, bewildered.

It was time to turn the scat around. I answered him, "Korea. I just wish I'd been with Michael, that's all. He has what it takes, Monsignor. Don't you think?"

The old coot blinked at me.

"I appreciate it, Frank," Michael said.

Monsignor Riordan eyed us both, then muttered, "I misunderstood. . . ." He turned and took several steps, then stopped and said to Michael, as if he were a schoolboy after all, "Tell your mother I have some envelopes that need addressing."

"Yes, Monsignor."

We watched the priest leave the hall. He seemed stoop-shouldered and weary, and I felt a twinge of guilt, as if we'd been tossing lit matches at a derelict.

The hall was nearly empty. The Holy Name Society volunteers were noisily clearing the tables. Michael and I stood in awkward silence until I realized that he was waiting for me to speak. It would have been wrong to be sarcastic, but the prank with Monsignor Riordan had been such a relief that I wanted to prolong it. "As I was about to say before I was so rudely interrupted by Kim Il Sung . . ." I grinned cockily, proud to have remembered the North Korean's name. ". . . it's great to see you're back." I slapped his back to underscore the hackneyed pun.

"Did you miss me?" he asked somewhat mockingly, as if to deflect the banality of my welcome the way he had the others.

But I met him head on. "Hell yes, I missed you. What do you think?"

"I think you're a turd," he said.

"Who's a turd?" I punched his shoulder. It was rock hard, and he cocked his fist to punch me back.

He held the pose for a long minute, hooding his eyes like a boxer posing for a photo. Then he straightened up and laughed. "God, we were punks, weren't we?"

"Some of us still are, Mike."

"I thought when I saw you in church, That can't be

Durkin! You moved. Even your folks moved. I couldn't believe it when I heard they moved."

"Yes, they live in Queens. I never get up here anymore. I came up today to see you."

"Oh yeah? Not for the plenary indulgence?"

"Well, that too, naturally."

He looked away, as if our needling had run its course and he wasn't sure where that left us. After a moment he said, "How are they?"

"Who?"

"Your mom and dad. Mo."

"They're great. They love it out there. A yard, grass, their own tree, the whole bit. They flipping love it. Mo's in a nice Catholic high school. She calls herself Maureen now. My mother can still walk to Mass every morning and my old man has a clunker of his own. Everything's a dream but me. Me, I've lost my soul."

"Because you live in the Village?"

I shrugged. " 'N.Y.Jew' my father calls it. Famous for its urban campus, its liberal curriculum, its heterogeneous student body, but also for its atheists, Commies, dope fiends and transvestites. Professors stand in line to take whacks at Irish kids, to prove that there is no God but Sartre and Simone is his *savant*."

Michael said nothing. I realized that my blasé references would be lost on him, and I resolved not to show him up. The deprivation of his having not read a book in years only then struck me. The New Testament didn't count. "What about you?" I asked. "You get the GI Bill, right?"

"Rights."

Cracks, I thought. Everything is cracks. "I mean, are you going to use it, or what?"

"I don't know yet."

"When do you get out of the army?"

"I could be out now. My leave is up January first. I have to let them know by then."

"You wouldn't stay in?"

He looked at me sharply. "I wouldn't? Why not?"

I blushed. "Well, you know. Christ! It's the army!"

"And you civilians think the army is shit, right?"

His defensiveness stunned me. "I'm no civilian," I said inanely. I meant that the very notion requires a military point of reference.

"It's one of the things they say, you know. That civilians hate us. After the wars are over they just want soldiers to flush themselves down the toilet."

"You think the Holy Name Society hates you?"

He shrugged, pulled out a pack of Camels and lit one.

"If you did stay in, what would . . . ?"

"I'd apply for OCS. I guess they'd take me."

"You guess? Jesus Christ, of course they'd take you, after what you did."

He flicked the match, as if we were outside, and he said fiercely, "Let's cover that right now, Durk. I didn't do shit! Get it? Not shit! I don't want that what-I-did crap from you!"

"What crap?" I asked helplessly.

Michael's face was inflamed and his mouth had tightened in the way it always had when he was angry. His chin had a way of turning white, even while the skin from his neck up burned. I had a fresh ear now on the pitch of his emotions. He was puffing at his cigarette compulsively and his hand trembled. He was more tightly wired than I'd realized. I chided myself. What did I expect? It wasn't the Adirondacks he'd returned from that fall.

"I'm sorry," he said. "I think I'm on edge. I mean I know I'm on edge. I don't know what I'm going to do."

He stared at me. I remember how starkly I perceived his despair then. It was the despair of youth, the absolute conviction to which only the young are capable of clinging that the pattern of a lifetime is already set, and that never would zest, affection or spontaneity form part of his experience again. "Downward to darkness," is the feeling, "on extended wings." I was as young as he was, of course, and did not recognize the illusion for what it was, having not learned yet that despair overpowers us not once but repeatedly through life. Only in looking back on them are we capable of seeing how little true damage those fits have done us. At that moment, though, I felt only a bleak sweet kinship with Michael; I was as convinced as he was that the joy that had made us friends was irretrievably lost. But no real matter. Our despair would make us friends again.

"Maybe I'll do some coaching," he said after a moment. "Monsignor said I could lend a hand with the CYO league."

"Would they pay you?"

"I'm loaded. I've got two years' back pay piled up. Sergeant's pay."

"Wow. Well, maybe coaching's just the thing. You kept in shape, I guess, huh?"

"How many pushups do you want?"

"How high'd you get?"

"Five hundred."

"Jesus Christ, Mike! Every day?"

He smiled. "Morning, noon and night."

It was as if a bird had taken off from behind a bush by my feet, scaring me, but also giving me my first real inkling of what he'd been through. Fifteen hundred pushups a day? That was something I could understand. I'd never done fifty. All at once I realized that what seemed like strength to everyone else—the quality that pulled him through—was to Michael himself the most acute desperation. And I realized too that his ordeal had not ended. Now instead of Chicoms tormenting him he had us. We were punishing him with our distance from his experience, from the sickness of soul it left him with. The vicious routines required by mere survival had been suspended everywhere but inside him. A vacancy, willfully displayed, had come over him. A hero to the world, I saw at last, but a basket case to himself.

To my horror I found myself using the line he'd used on me in our shtick for the monsignor. "It must have been rough, Mike."

"Where the fuck have you been, Durk? I've been home on leave for weeks."

I had to look away, I was so ashamed. I'd been afraid to face him for fear of what he'd think of me. Yet I hadn't thought of him. It had never occurred to me that Sergeant Michael Maguire, D.S.C., Silver Star, could stand in need of me. "Mike, I'm sorry." I found his eyes. "I should have come up sooner. I was afraid to. You're a fucking war hero, you know. I'm a chump, a saphead."

He laughed. "That's true." He lowered his eyes bashfully. He regretted his outburst.

"But I'm here now. I came all the way up for you, and I want the credit. I even went to fucking Mass."

"Hey, come on."

"Sorry. But I mean I did, you know."

"Aren't you a Catholic anymore, or what?"

"I guess I'm not."

"Jesus!" he exhaled dramatically, as if he'd never met one of us.

I nudged him. "No atheists in foxholes, eh?"

"Do you know who said that?"

"No idea. Robert Service?"

"A priest said it. A priest said it on Bataan, a chaplain name of Father Cummings. You might like to know that he was killed later when the Jap ship carrying him and hundreds of other prisoners from the Philippines to Japan was sunk by an American submarine."

"God."

"Yeah, God. We had our own version in Korea: 'No atheists in foxholes, only assholes. The atheists are in college.' "

"Oh, fuck, Mike. Come on."

"Nothing personal, Durk. Hey, nothing personal."

"You said we civilians hate you, but that isn't it, is it? You hate us."

"Wouldn't you?"

"What, hate the people I was supposed to be defending? I wouldn't think so, no."

" 'A tidy foxhole,' we used to say . . ." He stared at his cigarette. ". . . 'and a tight asshole.' " He looked up at me. "I knew guys who shit their pants." He waited for me to react. When I didn't he said. "Hey, Durk, *I* shit my pants."

"Because you were afraid?"

"No. It was in the camp. I had the runs the whole time. Sometimes it just flowed out of me without my even knowing it, like I was a retard or something. Of course, there's nothing to clean yourself off with and you can't wash your pants. You know what happens? Do you?"

"No, I don't."

"You get used to it. You get used to the smell and to the crud in your pants and to the rash on your butt. And you don't have to be embarrassed because everybody else has shit in his pants too. At first I would pray for a solid bowel movement. I mean, can you believe it? Praying for that, Durk? But then I stopped praying about it because it stopped being important." Michael looked back at the Holy Name members who were stacking dishes onto a stainless-steel cart. "What do you think my fans would say if they knew their hero went around with shit in his pants for two years and nine months?"

"Hey, Mike, everybody shits, you know? Even the pope." As I said this I knew how off the point it was. Michael's caustic reminiscence seemed to fill a profound inner need of his, a declaration of the real, a rejection of the Hollywood fantasy people had of what he'd been through. Shit is real, no doubt about it. No wonder he was troubled: why should an experience of such prolonged and utter degradation have resulted in his glorification?

We were both, I think, aware of the irony that Michael's bitter remarks implicitly invited me into a new intimacy with him. Would I be the person to whom he could confide his experience? His true experience? Already I had some sense of how heroically he was fending off the reduction of his identity *into* heroism, and I saw how a willing friend—one to whom he could be everything but a hero—could help him. But for the life of me I could not think of a way to express my sympathy. Why couldn't I have said, simply, "You can tell me what it was like"? Perhaps because one cannot presume that such secrets as he had could be shared. Did I in fact want to be entrusted with them? If, as I have said, there was an invitation to intimacy in his show of bitterness, it was not enough. We were not ready for each other yet, that's what I felt. Suddenly I wanted to get away from him. I imagined myself saying, "Well, it's been cool. See you around." But that was equally impossible. I was paralyzed, neither here nor there with him.

"Anyway," he said. He dropped his cigarette on the floor. As he ground it out I wondered if it would do damage, but the floor was terrazzo.

He made no move to leave.

Since clearly we'd have each welcomed a way to prolong if not our conversation our time together, neither of us moved to end it. So we stood there stupidly in the corner of the parish hall. A long few moments of awkwardness passed before it was apparent that no one was going to rescue us.

"Want to walk me to the subway?"

"Sure thing," he said with counterfeit enthusiasm.

"You got a coat?"

He smiled. "No. Remember? I'm one tough s.o.b."

We left the hall and took the stairs in stride together. Outside I put my overcoat and hat on, but it didn't seem that cold and I felt citified. Michael didn't even turn his collar up. We walked with a studied casualness down Isham Street toward Broadway and the front entrance of the church. The sidewalk was deserted though the ten o'clock Mass was going on inside. It was that brief period when it was too late to arrive and too soon to leave.

Michael paused, and I thought he was reading the names of the clergy on the sham-Gothic sign nestled among measly shrubs off to the side of the main stairs. But he was staring at the weathered bronze plaque below the sign: a Celtic cross above the inscription "That Those Who Perished Shall Not Have Died in Vain," and then, "Catholic War Veterans, Shamrock Post 120, 1940."

Nineteen forty was the year the subway was completed from midtown Manhattan up to Inwood. The neighborhood celebrated that event, but it shouldn't have. That subway was what enabled my generation to escape.

I wasn't interested in Maguire's mordant preoccupation with the war or the dead. I turned and began to walk down Broadway toward the subway at 207th Street. Michael followed me, but I could sense his reluctance. I did not slow down for him. I passed the bakery, the shoe repair, the baby carriage store, the cavernous entrances to apartment buildings in which dozens of our schoolmates had lived. I passed the Green Acres Bar, the A&P, Connor's Funeral Home and two liquor stores. Not even the makeshift rack of Christmas trees in front of Manning's Fruit Stand stimulated my nostalgia. My earlier affection for the old neighborhood was gone without a trace, replaced by a much more familiar repugnance. I wanted out of Inwood, that cramped, small-minded enclave of dreary apartment houses and drearier people, the women forever pregnant, the men cheered not by home life or by work but only by the morose company of tavern-hounds and by the booze, the children eternally poked, pinched and chastised by mothers and nuns, and the whole throng of them cowed by priests to whom the great enemy was the world south of Dyckman Street where, notoriously, men and women read books and discussed ideas that had never been referred to in the seminary.

By the time Maguire and I reached the corner I knew that if I went down into that subway, leaving him behind, our friendship was over. I was furious at him. What the fuck was he doing back here? This was worse even than Queens! And what was this shit about the CYO, coaching Catholic kids for the monsignor? I faced him. "You know something, Mike, you ought to check out college. You ought to get a load of the Village."

"You love it, I guess, huh?"

"I'm the loneliest bastard you ever saw. If I died in my room tonight, nobody'd find me until the stench got to the landlord. But I'll tell you something, nobody steps on my hand down there." I was certain that he'd remember the time we were both altar boys, serving Monsignor Riordan's Mass. At Communion, the monsignor dropped a Host and it fell onto the floor at my feet, missing completely the gold paten I held beneath the chins of communicants just to catch the invisible crumbs. But this was the whole Host! the Body of Christ!—"Species" we called it, having our own words for such things—and on the cold, unconsecrated linoleum tile, and it was through my fault! Through my fault! Through my most grievous fault! Automatically, instantly, I bent to pick it up. I was going to put it on that golden plate, to save it, to rescue it, like Christopher did the Christ Child from the raging river. Alas, also I was going to touch it, and thereby compound the sacrilege, turn it into blasphemy. And so at the last moment, whump! Monsignor Riordan stomped on my profane hand with his hard black clerical boot.

Michael was staring at his feet.

"Mike, I have the feeling that if we just say goodbye now, then, well . . ." I couldn't finish the sentence. Direct expression on such a thing as the loss of one's oldest friendship was utterly beyond me. I felt an ominous wave of depression riding in.

"Then we've said goodbye," he offered with brutal matter-of-factness.

"Yes."

"And you don't want to do that."

"You do?"

" 'If such things as these are done when the wood is green what will it be like when it is dry?' "

I guessed his statement was biblical, or rather hoped it was, it seemed so weird. I didn't know what to make of it then, but now I see that epigram as the perfect comment on the situation. At twenty-one years of age were we going to behave like a pair of defeated old men whose choices had been worn down to nubs by a long streak of dead years? If we lacked boldness and vitality in our relationships then would we ever have had the qualities of youth? But in fact, then, Michael lacked both. He had been overwhelmed by the death of time itself, and now that he'd dropped the false front of his noble cheer it was obvious to both of us that time had yet to come to life again. The poor bastard had no capacity for the present tense. Later I would understand that, in that passivity and detachment from the here and now, he was like the survivors of many kinds of large trauma. He could have just returned from an icy peak in the Andes where he'd had to eat the flesh of his fellow plane-wreck victims. He could have just returned from a season on a raft at sea or from a year inside the embassy in Teheran. What he'd endured had ended, but it remained still more compelling than the "reality" he'd returned to. Not even familiar old Good Shepherd was real to Michael. Not even—I saw this suddenly—I was.

I punched his shoulder. "Hey, come on, keed. What say? Come downtown with me? We can ride the ferry. I'll read you Edna St. Vincent Millay."

He shook his head. When he looked up there were tears in his eyes. I'd never known him to cry. He said, "I'd like to do something with you, but not that."

"Okay, buddy. Anything you want."

He raised his eyes, as if to heaven. "I want to go up there."

I turned, facing down Broadway. Just beyond Dyckman Street, overshadowing Inwood, was the majestic wooded hill of Fort Tryon Park, and on top of it was the stone tower of the Cloisters, the museum that housed the Rockefeller collection of medieval art in stark monastic splendor.

"It's where I go," he said.

SEVEN

IN Europe Benedictines built their monasteries on mountaintops, and the hill in Fort Tryon Park overlooking the Hudson River was the perfect site for one. The Cloisters, of course, was not a true monastery or even an authentic imitation. It was a fantasy building, an ensemble of Gothic and Romanesque, constructed to display the pillars, doorways, arcades, stairways, frescoes, altars, holy water fonts, stained-glass windows, sculpted figures and tapestries that wealthy and cultivated American Protestants prized so highly in the early part of this century.

By and large the only Catholics who strolled the Cloisters' hallways in the forties and early fifties—the museum opened in 1938—tended to be the Irish who were employed to do so. Many Inwood men worked there as uniformed guards, including for a time, on Sundays, my father. Despite the fact that the museum was a stunning monument to the aesthetic achievement of Catholic culture, the Catholics of Inwood knew better than to consider it theirs. What were a bunch of moth-eaten old wall hangings or limestone statues with smashed faces anyway? Everyone knew that what counted in monasteries and convents were the monks and nuns and their spiritual works of mercy. And as for religious art, my people liked their statues painted and their crucifixes in good repair. The Cloisters seemed a peculiar, empty, haunted place to the parishioners of Good Shepherd, and they were content to ignore it.

Beginning in the mid-fifties the Cloisters would, however, enjoy a vogue among a new type of Catholic, that first sizable generation of intellectuals and aesthetes, mostly laymen, who considered themselves disciples of Thomas Merton.

Merton had haunted the Cloisters while a student at Columbia and credited it with prompting his conversion. He was the first of many young Catholics to embrace the spiritual aesthetic of French monks and the humanist theology of French intellectual laymen. The Cloisters' connection with Merton's conversion made it the object of pilgrimage—was all the consecration the museum needed—for Merton was the prophet of aesthetic Catholicism. Even I was aware of Merton, and if I held myself aloof in those days from the religious movement he represented, still I watched it, sensing perhaps that eventually it would claim me. I always understood what, at bottom, such Catholics were doing. I should count myself among them because finally, in the sixties, I did succumb. I played a small part in the New York version of aesthetic Catholicism as an editor with the liberal journal *Jubilee*, and as a *Commonweal* savant. I liked having a desk between me and my movements, but even that didn't keep me from coming dangerously close for a time to something like commitment. My knack for detached—some said smug— analysis rescued me, although not before I'd been dubbed the Bill Buckley of the left. I was devastated by that, of course, though Buckley, I heard, was flattered.

Catholics like me had tried and failed to liberate ourselves from the stifling parochialism of Irish American Catholicism by rejecting it outright. When we found we couldn't shake that complex of guilt, nostalgia, conviction and belief, we rejected our early experience of Catholicism by embracing a truer, higher form of the Church, an older one, a more rigorous one, which was at once beautiful and intelligent. How did we know? Eminent converts as different as Clare Boothe Luce, Heywood Broun, Hugh Kenner, Robert Lowell, Allen Tate and Tennessee Williams told us so. And, most importantly, the American Protestant elite, the Berensons and Eliots and Cramms and Mrs. Gardners and even Rockefellers (whom to our shame we secretly admired and envied) had told us so. It was they, after all, who'd given us our Cloisters. Only bigots accused the Protestant collectors of plundering the Middle Ages; they had rescued it from the crass Enlightenment and the profaning Revolution.

We could go up to the Cloisters, listen to the recorded Gregorian, stroll the ambulatories, gaze out on the wild Palisades from ancient arcades, thumb our laymen's breviaries and claim our place not only in religion or culture, but in the very cosmos. We indulged our highly sensitive souls and never feared for a moment that we were like our cousins in the Bronx whom we referred to contemptuously as "BICs," Bronx Irish Catholics. Certainly we were not like our parents, hustling up to Good Shepherd in the shadow of this very place. Good Shepherd was the only Catholic church on all of Broadway, they boasted, as if it was a glitzy show palace for the soul. It was the center of their impoverished lives, and they were always going to novena or to Benediction or to bingo, or, if it was morning, to a crudely gabbled Mass in which no one sang and in which the priest, vested in the laughable fiddleback chasuble, spouted from the kitsch-filled sanctuary his gibberish about the Building Fund. We preferred, in sum, our curators to our curates. We loved everything about the Church except its people.

But the Cloisters was still new to me when I went up there that day with Michael. How was I to know it would become a haunt of mine and a central symbol of my life, of what was right about it and—though it would take two decades for me to understand this—what was wrong? I think it fitting now that Michael who never embraced the pretensions of intellectual Catholicism should have introduced me to the place and that it should have been the scene of the rescue of our friendship.

We were sitting on an oak bench in the garden with our backs to the Hudson River. Naked quince bushes clutched the air grotesquely with fingerlike branches, and in the spaces between the sham buttresses of the Gothic chapel I saw my first espaliered pear and apple trees. It was nearly midday by now, but the gray winter light was still diffuse, as in the early morning, and if anything the day was colder. The arches of the portico and the terra-cotta tiles of the sharply sloping roofs so suggested balmier weather that the unreality of the

monastic setting was heightened. It was like being inside the
wallpaper in someone's bathroom.

A choir of monks was singing a Gregorian melody, which I
could identify now as *Gaudete in Domini Semper* but which
at the time seemed too mysterious to be enchanting. It was,
naturally, a record, but the loudspeakers were hidden and I
kept picturing stalls full of robed figures in the chapels through
which we had just walked. I was certain those rooms were
deserted, but still . . .

The walls of the large pseudo-refectory had been covered
with The Hunt of the Unicorn tapestries. For some moments
Michael had stood in front of "The Unicorn in Captivity,"
that exquisite and poignant portrait of the mystic animal in its
corral. Its white coat was stained with red liquid. Michael
said, "I thought at first it was blood. But it's not. Look, it's
juice dripping from the pomegranates in the tree." He smiled.
"See? Captivity's not so bad."

In another room were the faded, patched-together but still
stunning Heroes Tapestries, three of them; the pagan heroes,
the Hebrew heroes and the Christian heroes, all portrayed
alike on thrones with an abundance of crowns, shields, pikes
and drums. The faces of the men were unyieldingly fierce,
and it was possible to see them rallying throngs. Michael
pointed out to me that King Arthur and Charlemagne were
attended by cardinals and bishops; Joshua and David by
courtiers and warriors; but Alexander and Caesar were attended by entertainers and women. "I'll take pagan," he
cracked, surprising me.

He stopped in front of a small alabaster bas-relief that
might once have adorned the front panel of an altar. The
figures were worn and unlovely and the scene represented
was too cluttered with horses, riders and anonymous attendants to make much sense of. But Michael pointed to the
central figure, a helmeted man brandishing a sword, and he
said jokingly, "That's me." When I looked again I saw that
it was Saint Michael the Archangel. He was standing on a
dragon whose face was smashed, whether by the sculptor or
by time I could not tell.

The disembodied Gregorian music floating over the garden
unsettled me. My eye traced the cruciform brick walks to the

center of the garden, which was marked by a weathered white fountain, dry now. An adjacent plaque read "FROM THE REGION OF THE VOSGES, FRENCH (LORRAINE), LATE XV CENTURY. THE SHAFT AND PEDESTAL ARE MODERN."

"The shaft is modern," I said dryly.

Michael ignored me.

What shaft? I wondered. I couldn't see what the plaque referred to.

"So what do you think?" I asked vaguely. It was Michael and his mordant silence that was unsettling me, not the goddamn pseudo-monastery.

He shrugged. " 'To one man he gives the ability to speak with strange sounds; to another he gives the ability to explain what these sounds mean.' "

"What the hell does that mean, Mike? You're acting weird, honest to God you are."

He laughed abruptly and slapped my knee. "You know my problem?" He withdrew a small book from inside his army jacket. "I have this thing memorized, and phrases from it keep popping into my mind."

"What is it?" But I knew what it was from the Murrow show.

"A pocket New Testament. It's all I had with me."

"You mean in China?"

"Yes. That priest gave it to me. That chaplain." He handed me the small book.

I opened it at random, automatically. But the impulse frightened me, as if there would be messages, and I refused to read. Instead I fingered the worn pages. "I see what you mean, Mike. Damn, no wonder you went religious on me."

"I didn't 'go religious.' " He took it back and opened it as if he knew the exact page he wanted. When he read it was in a voice so full of animation, so much his own, that I heard the words as a personal statement. " 'Make room for us in your hearts. We have done wrong to no one, we have ruined no one, nor tried to take advantage of anyone. I do not say this to condemn you, for as I have said before, you are so dear to us that we are together always, whether we live or die. I am so sure of you, I take such pride in you! In all our troubles I am still full of courage. I am running over with joy.' ''

''Don't stop.''

''He just goes on about Macedonia. Who gives a shit about Macedonia?''

I wanted to touch his sleeve or something. ''Hey, I'm the one who takes pride in you,'' I said.

''Durk, let me be the one to say it for once, okay? I meant that about whether I lived or died. You were somebody I thought of.''

''I appreciate that, Mike. I really do. But mainly I'm just glad that . . . you lived.''

He nodded somberly. ''I keep slipping into moods. I can't forget some of it.''

''What?''

''Not everybody lived.'' He opened his book again, had his place in an instant and read, '' 'I saw another angel coming up from the east with the seal of the living God. He called out in a loud voice to the four angels to whom God had given the power to damage the earth and the sea. The angel said, ''Do not harm the earth or the sea or the trees until we mark the servants of our God with a seal on their foreheads.'' ' '' Michael stopped reading and looked at me as if he'd proved something. My blank return look seemed to confuse him. He resumed reading. '' 'And I was told the number of those who were marked with God's seal on their foreheads; it was a hundred and forty-four thousand, from every tribe of the people of Israel. There were twelve thousand from the tribe of Judah marked with the seal; twelve thousand from the tribe of Reuben; twelve thousand . . . ' ''

''Mike.''

'' ' . . . from the tribe of Gad . . .' ''

''Mike!''

He looked at me, then dropped his head into his hands. The New Testament fell to the ground. ''There was a guy named Pace in my platoon. Lennie Pace. He died in my arms. When I released him he had a mark on his forehead.'' Michael loosened his collar and pulled his dog-tag out of his shirt. ''This,'' he said, ''like a stamp, right on his forehead, only reversed. Michael Maguire. O-positive. Catholic. Do you know why?''

"Why what?''

"Why my name was on his head?''

"Because you pressed him so hard. You cared about him.''

"I got him killed. He would never have come with me, but I called him 'chickenshit.' He was a kid, he'd lied about his age. I mean he was like sixteen. I made him go someplace he didn't want to go, and then I let him down.''

"Jeez, Mike, you feel lousy about it, eh?''

"I mean, I didn't kill him, I know that. But it seems . . . I just feel very, very guilty, like I did something wrong.'' He looked up at me. "I survived.''

"That's not wrong.''

"It feels wrong though.''

"But it's not! It just isn't wrong, Mike.''

"I keep saying that to myself, Durk. I even think it was by God's grace. I say He spared me for a reason. 'But God in His grace chose me even before I was born, and called me to serve Him.' ''

"Maybe He didn't have a reason. Maybe He just likes you. And what's this 'serve Him' stuff? I mean, hell, if it was me I wouldn't have some condition on the thing, like you owed me your life or something.''

"I guess we owe it to Him anyway. I mean, at first I thought that the rest of my life was like a bonus. You wouldn't believe what Korea was like, Durk. I never thought I'd live through it. And then the camp . . . I never, never thought I'd live through it. But I did. And then I realized that my whole damn life was a bonus to begin with. You know? I mean we didn't have to be here at all. Or anywhere. The whole frigging thing is, like, extra. You know?''

"It's not how I usually think about it.''

"Me either.''

"But you sound kind of . . .''

"What?''

"I don't think you have to feel guilty because you survived something other guys didn't. And I don't think it leaves you with all this huge debt to God. You sound kind of beaten down by the whole thing, Mike. I think it's too bad the chaplain didn't give you a copy of *Catcher in the Rye* and let it go at that.''

"No, no. You're not getting it. This book saved my fucking life, Durk! It didn't beat me down! It's what let me beat them! 'Do not be afraid of anything you are about to suffer. Listen! The Devil will put you to the test by having some of you thrown into prison; your troubles will last ten days. Be faithful until death, and I will give you the crown of life.' ''

"Ten days, eh?'' I poked him.

"Give or take two and a half years.'' He laughed, and I realized it was his laugh that I had always loved most about him. His proud, dark-eyed, serious face became for a moment almost jaunty. Despite all of his anxiety, his edginess, it was apparent that his old self-acceptance undergirded him still. His laughter relieved me and made me feel bold.

"Tell me about the bridge,'' I said. "The papers always make it sound like a movie.''

He shook his head and his genial countenance became severe again. "I can hardly think about it.''

"Why? I thought it was the good stuff. Right out of *Gung Ho*.''

"The papers never mention the women and children.'' He stopped as if his statement explained itself. After a moment he added, half wistfully, "Whom I blew up.''

"Chinese soldiers, I thought.''

"You don't expect the army to give a medal to a man for killing refugees, do you? The bridge was jammed with refugees. We couldn't keep them back.'' He took out his cigarettes. "You think we can smoke out here?''

We both lit up. He stood and leaned on the wall facing the river. At first I thought he didn't want to be seen smoking by the monks. Or rather guards. Then I realized his gaze was fixed on the George Washington Bridge.

"It looked something like that,'' he said, "smaller, of course, and there were several spans instead of one big one. But from the hills it gave you the same feeling. A bridge, you know? There's nothing like a bridge.''

We stared at the George Washington Bridge and smoked in silence. From that vantage the bridge seemed nestled in trees. A second hill, the promontory of the park, the site, in fact, of the original fort, rose up between us and the rest of the island. One would never have known we were in one of the largest cities in the world or that the bridge below us carried more traffic, practically, than any other bridge ever built. I tried to imagine it blowing up, cars, trucks, buses, girders and people falling into the river. Women and children, he'd said. I could not picture it.

"The thing is," he said slowly, "I can't figure out how to get going with normal life."

"That's why you want to stay in the army?"

"Oh God, Durk, you think I want that? The army? The fucking army? I just don't know what else there is." He flicked his cigarette and watched it arc into the shrubbery below. "It's like Paul says. To some men He gives the ability to explain. But not to me."

"You were going to explain about the bridge."

"What really knocks me out is how it didn't matter that much about the refugees. I mean we tried to keep them back and everything. That was my platoon's job. But it was like trying to keep back the wind or something. They just kept coming at us. At one point the lieutenant drove his jeep right into a bunch of them. Fucking creamed them! Right in front of me! Must have killed a dozen right there." He fell silent for a time, then resumed. "After the bridge blew we watched from the hill. I could see the people in the water. It was a fast current. It was freezing. They didn't have a chance. There were a bunch of Chicoms in little boats, a force that had been trying to take the bridge by sneaking up from the river. We expected them to beat the people down or shoot them. I mean those people were their enemy, but you know what? The Chicoms helped them. They pulled people in until those boats nearly swamped. I remember thinking, Jesus! The Reds are rescuing people, and we're blowing them up! How do you figure that? I mean the Reds were so ruthless, ruthless! But we just blew those poor people up! We just drove our jeeps right through them. How do you figure it, Durk?"

"You know the answer as well as I do, Mike."

"Sure. War is hell; you got to break some eggs to make breakfast, right. You know something? In the camp where I was, Chung Kang Djin, just across the Yalu, seven guys confessed. They were pilots. They said they were dropping germ bombs, trying to get the plague going in Asia; we wanted to spread cholera, cholera! The Reds put them on a platform and they made the whole camp listen to them, about five hundred guys. It was shit, just pure shit! Insect bombs! Plague bombs! Christ! Who'd believe that? But you know what? If they'd picked me, it would have been a snap for them. They wouldn't have had to ream my ass out at all. I'd have confessed. I'd have said we blew up a bridge full of toothless old ladies. We drove our jeeps into them. And we didn't give a shit. I mean nobody gave it a fucking thought.''

"You did.''

"Not at the time I didn't. At the time I just went from one minute to the next. I mean I was scared, Durk! I thought I was going to die. I don't know half of what I did. You get into like a trance. I got home and they gave me these medals and there was stuff in the citations I never heard of. Like it wasn't even me. You'd think they were talking about a different fucking bridge. The citation doesn't even mention the refugees. I mean I remember what happened to them. I can't forget! We were kicking these pathetic old people off the train. Bayonets! We had our fucking bayonets fixed, Durk! God knows what I did forget! I know I had the bayonet on my rifle. I don't know what I did with it though."

"You didn't do anything with it, Mike. Come on.''

"I did enough. I just wish the Reds asked me to confess.''

"No, you don't.''

"I do too, Durk. I mean I really do.''

"That's what priests are for.''

Michael grunted cynically, and frankly I was relieved. The confessionals at Good Shepherd were made for whimpering admissions about masturbation and neglected night prayers. What Michael was doing right then with me was confession enough. But he said, "I wish Father O'Shea was around.''

I picked up the pocket New Testament from the ground. "For your penance he'd give you the Old Testament.''

Michael laughed and slipped the book into his tunic. " ' "Go back home to your family and tell them how much the Lord has done for you and how kind he has been to you!'' So the man left and went all through the ten towns telling what

Jesus had done for him; and all who heard it were filled with wonder.' "

"What had Jesus done?"

"He cast the man's demons out." The tale amused him and his eyes brightened as he told it. "He drove them into a herd of pigs and the pigs went crazy—two thousand in all, it says—and ran off a cliff into the lake and drowned. Of course everybody thought Jesus was great, but some poor bastard owned those pigs, and he was wiped out!" Michael laughed heartily. "Get it?"

"No matter what good thing you try to do, somebody gets the shaft."

"And you said the shaft is modern!"

We laughed hysterically then, in that delicious, unpredictable way of which only adolescents are capable. Some of our worst moments in Good Shepherd had been our best ones when we'd cracked up and completely lost control of ourselves, bringing on the wrath of nuns and priests, laughing until our bellies and our faces ached. There'd been a time when we hadn't been allowed to serve Mass together because all one of us had to do was clink the cruets to destroy the other. One time the priest farted and Michael laughed so hard he had to leave the church before Communion was even served. I managed to stay but I had an open wound inside my cheek for days.

So laughing in the Cloisters' garden like that rescued us. Only when we stopped did it seem awkward that we had thrown our arms around each other's shoulders. Michael withdrew his first. "Want to see something eerie?"

I surveyed the garden with dramatic eyes. "Eerier than this?"

He nodded and set off. I followed.

Inside the museum it was no warmer. A guard watched us coming in and I was careful to close the heavy oak door softly. If it had banged, Michael and I would have begun laughing again.

Despite our mutual inarticulateness, Michael had successfully indicated his plight to me, its range between fear and regret, but I was too young—the field of my concentration was cluttered with poses and insecurities—to understand that what he was in fact showing me was a crisis of conscience.

Catholics are schooled to make much of conscience from an early age, although even our notion of it as the one faculty that sets the individual apart from the community derives from Luther. We learn at first to treat conscience like a domesticated animal, a house pet always ready to bark a warning but also slightly underfoot and often damned inconvenient. But there comes a time when conscience turns on us, clawing, and we are perhaps more shocked when that happens than our neighbors who never regarded conscience as a friend. That shock, of course, serves the Church's purpose, for likely as not we seek refuge from the attack in the Sacraments, and for a time the ritual of Confession rescues us, renewing the very world and reestablishing our cozy place in it. But eventually even the Sacrament of Penance falls short of what we need, and that crisp joy at being part of a total system that works—an answer for every question, a word of absolution for every sin—begins to fade. Some of us begin our serious drinking then: "Booze ain't my problem, Father. It's my solution." And some seek new shoulders or bosoms on which to lay their heads: "No one's ever really understood me, darling, until you." And some rededicate themselves to the old ways. They continue to confess, but as an act no longer of renewal, but of nostalgia. Catholicism is the progression of conscience experienced first as childhood chum, then as irascible boss, then as the invincible enemy, then as the familiar adversary who loses to us now and again, and finally as the old acquaintance rarely brought to mind.

I knew already that Michael was not going to be like the rest of us, accommodators, arrangers, moral amnesiacs. His conscience was no leprechaun on his shoulder or prick at the base of his spine; no fog of guilt rolling in after drink or sex or a particularly snide crack about the Jews. Conscience defined his capacity for grappling directly with life itself, including but not limited to what was flawed about it. Saint Thomas says that we are drawn instinctively toward the Good, like plants to light, and it was that trait, more than a dark moralism, though he had streaks of that too, that set Michael apart. At a certain point, later in his life for a brief moment, he became the compass rose for America herself because he could make the right thing known as the only thing.

Even as a kid in Korea he made his moves like the natural he was. He had the moral equivalent to the acute physical coordination that made him an exceptional athlete. Grace; he was a man of grace. It was impossible not to follow him—"Go, Michael, go!"—whether on a fast break toward the basket or, despite all one's inhibitions, into an act of civil disobedience. But that came later.

Once in a heated argument I demanded to know how he could be so cocksure as to what was right and what was wrong. He said, "I'm sure because I breathe." Yes, his conscience was like his breath or the circulation of his blood. Despite what it cost him and others who were influenced by it, nothing could ever impede its steady rhythmic insistence. At various times he would be ignored—he was dismissed once by the exquisitely condescending *New York Times* as "a man of good conscience but bad judgment"—and even condemned. But for some of us the effect of his example was permanent. A compass rose? Perhaps he was more like Polaris itself. We understood what I sensed inchoately at the Cloisters that day. I glimpsed his determined struggle not to justify what he'd been part of or to excuse it or to condemn it even, but simply to shape it into the great point of reference—his own Polaris—by which he would steer for the rest of his life. Conscience? That cauldron into which he poured his considerable knowledge of killing and torture and despair and loneliness. Conscience? It overwhelmed every other faculty of his: intelligence, memory and feeling. It stripped him of his ability to moderate, as I learned both happily and not so happily, either his rage or his love. Conscience? We knew that Michael Maguire did not have a conscience. A conscience had him.

It was the book of course, the small volume of tissue pages, that rooted him. At first I took his feat of memorization as mere memorization, the mind's equivalent of his fifteen hundred pushups every day. But it was far more than that. Over the two and a half years, he had copied the Gospel line for line, in Paul's phrase, on the fleshy tablets of his heart. As meaning is present in the word, so that book

became present in him. It provided margins within which war
and death and deprivation and the destruction of his own
innocence could all be faced and, finally, used. It was an
instance of what had happened to Israel herself when all at
once, within a generation of Moses, its Book occupied, like
an army occupies terrain, the center of her awareness. From
then on every political, religious, aesthetic and personal judgment was submitted to what-was-written. Naturally writing
implies the writer whom Michael was as reluctant as Israel to
name.

It was a long time before he spoke to me of his crisis in
Korea as a religious conversion—who'd have thought a Catholic could be converted? I assumed at first the aura I sensed
that day in the Cloisters was an effect of the piped-in Gregorian
chant or the medieval art. But it wasn't. As I followed him
into the Gothic Chapel I realized the aura I was aware of
came from him. I sensed for the first time the presence in him
to which he rarely referred but to which, to my knowledge
save once, he habitually and absolutely deferred.

There was no sanctuary lamp in that chapel and instinctively I registered the absence of the Blessed Sacrament. So
despite the magnificent windows and the marble high altar
below the barrel-vaulted ceiling and the statues of the saints,
the chamber seemed sterile to me. Despite my sophistication
I'd have still preferred the BVM side altar at Good Shepherd,
holy card art and all.

I drew close to Michael, who was standing between the
laid-out tomb-effigies of a knight and a lady, the one encased
in armor and the other reposed with hands folded on a great
pair of breasts. But he was ignoring the breasts and the
effigies. "Something eerie," he'd said.

At that moment, profiled against a small arched window
with clear glass, *he* seemed eerie. A fucking saint? My old
buddy? It was bad enough he was a hero.

My mind fled the thought. My eyes went to the window
and out to the grassy slope of the promontory of Fort Tryon
Park. Maybe Michael would see it as a mountain in Korea
now, or as a hill in Galilee. But I didn't. From the south side
of that peak one could look out on the most seductive city in
the world. As teenagers Michael and I, like other rakes of

Inwood, had brought girls up there. Furtively, without swagger, we'd coaxed them into bushes, and we considered ourselves wild as pagans when we pushed our tongues against the gates of their teeth and pressed the heels of our hands against their wire-mesh bras. The truth was that our inborn inhibitions were near infinite, yet made worse by the looming Cloisters. We knew it was a museum, but it looked like a tower from which nuns were watching, if not God.

It seemed to me that Michael was still in the grip of those inhibitions, as it seemed to me that I was free of them. That freedom was what I'd gone to Greenwich Village to obtain. Three and a half years of the life at NYU had confirmed what I'd gleaned from the fierce denials of the priests and nuns at Good Shepherd—that sex is all. Though it would have mortified me to admit it, my sexual experience in the Village was episodic and unsatisfactory, but the illusion of my liberation was in place. I had an image of myself as one who knew what was what between the sheets. It was an image I would lose, of course; having discovered that sex is all, one discovers later that all is chaos. But at the time I considered myself an initiate, and that was enough to make me feel like a man.

I was more a man in that regard, I thought suddenly, than the famous Michael Maguire. Hell, he wasn't a hero or even a saint. He was just a virgin. What Michael needed was to get laid.

He was staring at a gray tomb-slab attached to the wall of the chapel just there. I could discern on it the scratched outline of a monk—the cowl, the tonsure, the steeple of his hands; the smug posture.

"Look at that," he said. "It's eerie."

I read the Latin inscription. *"Hic pacet venerand Pater Michel."*

"Here lies the venerable Father Michael."

EIGHT

"SOMEBODY I've never forgotten or forgiven myself for," Michael said to me many years later, "is Mary Ellen Divine. Do you remember her?"

I did vaguely, but I didn't answer him. He was in a confessing mood and I wanted to hear his story. I didn't want to short-circuit it with one of my cynical cracks. We'd been discussing an article of mine called "Sex and the Single God" in which I'd suggested that priestly celibacy was not only an aberration but a practical heresy since it implicitly denied the essentially sexual dynamic at work between the Persons of the Trinity. What claptrap! And I knew it at the time. I insist now that I was being at least partially ironic, although also, I admit, I'd allowed myself to think for a while that it mattered both whether priests got laid with permission or not and whether the Father, Son and Holy Ghost were real folks or just names we put on *Ipsum Esse*. I was happily married then, or thought so, and in the first throes of paternal bliss, and was inclined to reify both my family as the ultimate symbol of the tri-une God and fucking—"intercourse," we called it—as the great symbol of the divine interaction. "In His own image created He them; male and female He made them." It was a ludicrous twisting of traditional notions. In my scheme the Son became the feminine principle in the Trinity. But Michael took it seriously—he could be so fucking earnest—and it led to his impulse to tell me about his experience with Mary Ellen. My impulse to pile high the theological bullshit fell at once before an intense, slightly prurient curiosity. I'd have made an unworthy confessor be-

cause I wanted to hear the good stuff in detail and at the top.
What had he done to her? And when? I would not realize
until much later that what he really wanted to confess to me
that night but couldn't was his love for Carolyn.

In our time Mary Ellen Divine was considered the most
sophisticated girl in Inwood. She was a flat-chested, spidery
girl, and this was well before the type was fashionable. But
her dark eyes and bony face gave her a look of such intensity
that other, more conventionally attractive girls seemed uninter-
esting by comparison. After high school she got a job downtown in Macy's. Her looks were so striking that eventually
they put her behind the makeup and perfume counter. With
artfully arranged hair and applied eye shadow and rouge she
was like something out of a magazine. During high school
she and Michael had been friendly but they'd never dated. I
assumed that they didn't see each other again after he went in
the army. Not so. Michael didn't tell me at the time, but he
went down to Macy's not long after our encounter in the
Cloisters hoping to find her.

It was the week before Christmas, and he went into the
store on the pretense of buying a gift for his mother. He
approached the perfume counter obliquely, one of the throng,
as if he didn't know she would be there.

"Michael? Is that you?"

He feigned surprise. In truth he was not prepared for the
sight of the glamorous woman, not girl, she'd become. He
noticed her lips first, how red they were, opened in surprise
as she stared at him. She wore a formal black dress that
emphasized her slimness, and jewelry at her wrists and throat
that flashed like the seasonal lights against the department
store glare. At first Michael thought he'd made a terrible
mistake. He felt she'd left him far behind. He stood there,
surrounded by women, staring back at her, unable to remember what he was going to say. His speechlessness reinforced
the impression that he was completely startled.

"My God!" she said, moving toward him along her side of
the counter. "It *is* you!"

"Mary Ellen Divine!" he said, and he grinned.

They shook hands across the counter.

"What are you doing here?" she asked.

Suddenly it seemed juvenile to him to say he was shopping for his mother. It rankled that his mother expected him to go on living with her on Cooper Street after he got out of the army, which was one good reason for staying in. "I was just doing a little shopping."

She smiled at him. "For someone special?"

He nodded.

She gave him a look, as if she wanted to read his secrets, and then she asked casually, "Want suggestions?"

"Sure. Why not?"

She led him along the length of the counter. He had to weave between other shoppers to keep up with her. Finally she stopped. The display case featured small dark bottles of exotic fluids. Michael made a show of studying them.

"What's she like?"

"I don't know."

"You don't know what she's like?"

He looked up sharply, blushing. "Oh. No. I misunderstood. I don't know what she likes."

"If you tell me something about her perhaps I can make a suggestion.

"Well, she's . . . hard to describe." Michael lowered his eyes. He knew that he seemed smitten and he regretted the deception he'd stumbled into, but he was simply overcome by inarticulateness. Once he'd charmed girls with his talk, but that was before.

"Should I tell you what I like?"

"Sure."

"I like this." She reached down for a small bottle and brought it up to the counter top. She placed it carefully, as if it was fragile. "It's by Elizabeth Arden. It's called 'Garden of Delights.' It seems French, but it doesn't cost so much. It's cologne."

"That's nice."

"You haven't smelled it yet." She opened the bottle and briskly upended it on the inside of her wrist, then held her wrist for him to sniff.

He bent toward her. The sensuality of her pose, more even than the scent, was what struck him. He had never had the offer before of the inside of a woman's wrist. Her flesh there was whiter, and the veins were visible. It made him think of the inside of her thighs.

"It's what I'm wearing already, actually."

" 'Garden of Delights'?"

"Yes. Silly name, isn't it? But it's rather nice for seven dollars, don't you think?"

"Yes, indeed." In fact the last thing he felt prepared to comment on were the olfactory mysteries of women. His mother smelled of talcum powder, that was all he knew about it. He would never buy her cologne.

"Do you think she'd like it?"

"Is it . . . ? Gee, Mary Ellen, you've got me." He took the cologne from her. Its shape and feel resembled a Vitalis bottle, but the liquid was green. "I was thinking of something a little more . . . But if you like it . . ."

"I do like it, but there are other more special things." She smiled. "Things I can't afford."

"Like what?"

"Imported perfumes. From France."

"Could you show me some?"

"She *is* special."

He could only bring himself to nod. This deceit seemed ludicrous to him, and it was mortifying. He'd only wanted to conceal how foolish he felt, and how at sea. He was sick of the worship of his mother's circle of Good Shepherd biddies. He was sick of the goggle-eyed deference of the nuns and the chipper camaraderie of the priests who hailed him as if he was one of them. Upon his release from the Chinese prison he'd felt a great exhilaration, but that had faded and the confines of Inwood had been pressing in on him. Was the army his only way out? No wonder he was depressed. If anything, his rediscovery of our friendship only heightened this feeling because, after all, I was gone. Other people our age, even including the few old friends who were still around the parish, were uniformly stiff and uneasy in his presence. When he dared go into the neighborhood tavern, men bought him drinks and waited for his war stories. He'd bought his mother a television set when he'd first come home so that she could watch him on Edward R. Murrow, but in the weeks since his leave began, he'd watched it continually from the time it went on the air in the afternoon. He'd gone to Macy's looking for Mary Ellen partly out of his desperate but unadmitted loneliness, but more because he couldn't stay at home another day watching the antics of Kukla, Fran and Ollie.

"Here's one." Mary Ellen placed a tiny green vial in front of him. "It's called *Je Reviens*. That means 'I remember.' "

"It's French?"

"Parisian."

"Not a whole lot of it, is there?"

"She would just use a wee bit. It's the most wonderful perfume we sell. You'd know what I mean if you could smell it, but we don't open these. The assumption is, anyone who can afford it knows what it smells like."

"How much?"

"Forty dollars."

"For that little bottle?"

She nodded and laughed, and then started to put it away.

"I'll take it."

Mary Ellen looked up at him. "You're kidding."

"No, I'll take it. You convinced me."

"I wasn't trying to."

"You're a good salesgirl." Michael reached for his wallet. "Very good."

"You'll take her breath away, I promise you. My goodness."

He saw that he'd taken hers away. He handed her a fifty-dollar bill. "Can I get it gift-wrapped someplace?"

"Downstairs, beside the credit desk, just bring your receipt."

Mary Ellen turned away to write up the sale. She put the boxed perfume in a bag and brought it back to Michael. By then he'd had a chance to think of what to say. "Listen, Mary Ellen, I see how busy you are and everything, but I think it would be nice to shoot the breeze a bit, don't you? I mean, what a coincidence, running into each other like this."

"You look good, Michael. I'm glad. I'm glad things worked out for you." She handed him his bag, then lowered her eyes. "I prayed for you." She looked up quickly. "We all did."

"I know. I think that's why I made it."

They stared at each other and for a moment the bustle

around them faded and they were aware only of each other. Michael felt both that they'd been very close friends once, which was not the case, and that he'd never seen her before. Her beauty seemed unreal to him, as if she were one of the store's perfect mannequins. But for that instant her feeling, that worry, tinged perhaps with grief and also with the awe he'd grown accustomed to by then, communicated powerfully. She too saw him as a hero, and he sensed that she was drawn to him.

"Anyway, I was wondering how I could see you? Or when?"

Her eyes fell to the bag she'd just given him; what about his girlfriend?

He lowered the bag and deflected the problem it implied. "Or do you work around the clock?"

She laughed. "Not today. I work till six."

"Do you live in Inwood still?"

She nodded. He knew that she still lived with her parents on Isham Street.

"Well, I could ride the train home with you. I'm staying with my mother for a few weeks."

"I'd heard that."

"I have some other shopping to do. I could wait until you got off."

"That would be lovely, Michael."

"Maybe I could buy you dinner."

She stared at him, trying to read his expression, and she said nothing.

He spent the rest of the afternoon sipping coffee in an Automat. He watched the food-windows as if they were television sets.

At a few minutes before six he was back, but Mary Ellen was no longer behind the counter. For a moment he panicked, thinking she'd changed her mind and had slipped away. But then someone touched his elbow.

When he turned he was surprised to find not the glamorous woman with ruby lips, rouged cheeks and shaded eyes, and high-fashion dress, but the Inwood girl, in sweater and skirt, he'd known since they were children. She wore no makeup and her hair was in a ponytail. This second transformation stunned him even more than the first, and now he saw for the first time how truly beautiful she was. And also how familiar. Anxiety drained out of him. "My goodness," he said.

"You didn't think I go around like that, did you?"

"You didn't dress down for me?" He asked this ingenuously. He thought that if she had any appetite for him at all, it would be due to his uniform. It was why he'd worn it.

She shook her head. "Do you mind?"

"Heavens no!" He took her coat out of her arms and helped her into it. "Now I don't have to take you to the Rainbow Room."

It was dark and cold outside, but the sidewalks of Herald Square were crowded with shoppers. Men and women were holding each other and children were craning to see the scenes of Santa's Village in Macy's windows. A Salvation Army lady was ringing her bell, and from loudspeakers hidden above the elf-ridden window displays Bing Crosby was singing, "I'll be home for Christmas."

Michael had an impulse to take Mary Ellen's arm, but he checked it. He was nearly overwhelmed with the feeling that this was a moment he'd have dreamed of if he'd dared. A deep need of which he'd been inchoately aware was for that instant filled, and he felt suddenly free of his morose listlessness. It was possible for him to be inside such a scene, however contingently, a man with a woman on the streets of New York at Christmas. And not a mere man, but a soldier. For our generation the epitome of romance was the GI with his girl, and in our fantasies they were always either at the docks saying farewell or on those streets with snow falling and Christmas coming.

He bent toward her. "I meant what I said about dinner."

"I think that would be nice. I've already called my mother."

He laughed. What a pair they were! Sophisticated Manhattanites? Inwood Irish Catholics checking in with Ma. He was relieved, though, because she wasn't checking in with a man.

"Where would you like to go?" he asked.

"I'd like to walk first, wouldn't you? Have you walked up Fifth Avenue? Have you seen the decorations?"

"No."

"Michael, really! And you call yourself a New Yorker!"

"And I've never been to the Statue of Liberty either."

They kept their distance from each other as they cut across Broadway toward Fifth Avenue. They knew they were enacting a classic scene. The Christmas carols that wafted magically above them might have been the film score. They passed Santa Clauses and more bellringers. The laden shoppers were good-humored for a change and the mounted policemen at each intersection seemed a very emblem of the benign and joyous season. At Saks Mary Ellen pressed against the windows which displayed animated scenes of life in an Alpine village. "I think ours are better, don't you?"

Michael had barely noticed the Macy's windows, but it was his impression that they had nothing to compare with these lifelike mechanical figures that chopped wood and drove sleighs and toted baskets. Still he agreed with her vigorously.

At Fifty-second Street they crossed into Rockefeller Center to see the tree. They stood on the parapet above the skating rink, aware of the gliding couples and the smooth music, but their gazes were fixed upon the huge spruce decked so abundantly in gaudy lights that the tree itself, its limbs and needles and cones, had no substance. They had been raised to think of this scene, the tree and the rink, as enshrining Christmas every bit as much as the parish nativity, and it would fall short to say that they gave themselves over utterly to the prescribed sentimental enchantment.

"You know something?" Michael said.

She looked up at him. Lo and behold the first snowflakes began to fall at that moment. The film score swelled. Not even in his imagination would he have dared conjure an effect like that.

"I'll never look at this tree again," he said, his voice lowered, "without thinking of you."

Michael could read her. She was a young woman who had left other girls her age in the dust. She was smarter and more ambitious and not prepared for a moment to settle for the hemmed-in life of the old neighborhood. But she hadn't left it yet. She was like the princess of Inwood, but that had brought with it a grave problem: where were the princes? If they had energy or ambition of their own, they were gone. Michael knew that the boys who remained and with whom she might have been expected to make a life were nice enough. They were her friends and the sons of her parents' friends. But they had already settled for a world she found too small. She didn't know what she wanted, but she knew what she didn't want. And now here was Michael Maguire whom she'd always liked and who had always been so accessible. But he had become a legend, having shown such largeness of soul, such nobility, that it shamed her for having all those years taken his friendship for granted. He was like an apparition, a reincarnation, like one resurrected. And he had just said the most wonderful thing that anyone had ever said to her. The feeling was so unexpected, so poignant and sharp that she could hardly breathe, and this is what it was: here is my prince. She didn't forget for a moment that he had a girlfriend already, but that only sharpened her reaction to him.

At dinner in the Rockefeller Center Café just off the ice-skating rink, intermittently watching the pairs coast by in their languid ovals beyond the glass wall, they found their tongues. Each discovered in the other the all-too-familiar sense of hesitation, poised as both were on the very threshold of life. "I feel," she said passionately, "as if the world is about to open up for me and give me everything I've ever wanted. Only the secret word needs to be said, and I know what it is!"

"But you haven't said it."

She shook her head and sipped her beer. "Not yet."

"What are you waiting for?" He was ingenuous. She answered him with her stare. Michael knew, and he was taken aback by the knowledge. He said, "You are a bold girl."

"So I'm told. It's regarded as my failing."

"Not by me."

"But what if I was truly bold?"

"And did what?"

"Asked you to tell me about your time away."

"In prison?"

"Yes."

After a moment he said, "A Chinese government official came to our camp once and told us that World War Three had begun, and that the Russians had blown up New York with an atom bomb.''

Mary Ellen was aghast. ''Why did they do that?''

Michael shrugged. ''Just to knock us down some more. He said the U.S. had surrendered.''

''Did you believe it?''

''Do you believe things that happen to you in nightmares? After a while, when we didn't any more about it, I guess I decided it was just another turn of the screw. But by then I knew that it *could* happen and that was pretty awful too. The Reds do have the bomb. And they believe the ends justify the means. I think they're capable of anything.'' Michael checked himself. He had no interest in sounding like Senator McCarthy. He picked up the bowl of sugar cubes. ''There was a period when they kept me alone, although mostly I was with other guys. But the time they kept me alone nearly did me in. I had to think of things to keep my mind occupied, like keeping track of the days. My cell had a dirt floor, and so every morning under a corner of my mat I'd scratch the date. I kept it up for seven months and eleven days when they put me back in the camp. And you know what? I had the date right!'' He laughed, and his elation came back to him. What a triumph that had been. ''And another thing I did was to try to memorize the squares and cubes of the numbers up to a hundred.''

''Did you do it?''

He laughed again and nodded. ''The square of your age is 441, and the cube is 9,261. What I wanted to do was figure out a system, like a table or a formula that would simplify the multiplication. But I never could.''

''But you just did that all in your head?''

''Yep.'' He dropped the sugar cube into his coffee, then tapped his forehead. ''You wouldn't believe the gobbledy-gook I've got up there.''

''Monsignor Riordan told my mother you read the Bible a lot.''

He shrugged and said, defending himself from the implicit charge of piety, ''It was all I had. The New Testament, actually.'' He smiled. ''That's not what I mean by gobbledy-gook.''

"I'm surprised they let you keep it."

"They took it away during my time in solitary. You never knew what was coming with those guys. When they gave it back, I was afraid they would take it again, so I memorized a lot of it."

"But they let you keep it."

"Naturally. I think once you've protected yourself from something, it doesn't happen."

She thought about that. "You had to protect yourself against so many things . . ."

"Yes," he said easily enough, but she had spoken straight to his heart. Her simple statement seemed full of connotation, as if at last someone understood what he'd been through. It wasn't that they'd tortured him but that on the merest whim and at any moment they could have. "The question always was, How can this or that serve their purposes? An extra ration of rice or an unexpected move to another camp or a doctor showing up with malaria pills; no matter what they did, even if it was an improvement, you knew it wasn't for you. It was for them. Even when it came time for my release I found myself wondering, How will they use my freedom against me? Even now sometimes I wake up in the middle of the night and I can't believe there isn't a guard outside my door."

"That's just your mother," Mary Ellen said.

They both laughed hard. Inwood mothers *are* like guards. Mary Ellen's crack punctured his melancholy and he was grateful to her. He felt more and more exposed to her and more and more relaxed.

"You know what I learned?" he asked intensely. He felt as though he was shaking off the lethargy of three years. "I learned how tough we can be, how defiant."

She responded with a slight movement of her brow. What did he mean?

"I thought that we were raised by the nuns and priests, by our parents, to be good little boys and girls, obedient and unquestioning. I mean, wasn't that the point of all the stuff at Good Shepherd, the demerits and the stars, the rewards and punishments, the indulgences and the years in purgatory? I thought the whole system was to keep us in line. But you know what? We've been raised to a standard, and they held us to it so that when the time came we could hold ourselves to it. We weren't raised to be deferential and obsequious at all. We were raised to make judgments and live by them. 'Don't you know that God's people will judge the world? Do you not know that we shall judge the angels?' We're Catholics, Mary Ellen. We stand for something. And it makes us stronger than other people. It really does. I saw it with my own eyes. And the Communists know it too. That's why they hate us. But they also respect us. Catholics have to lead the fight against Communism.''

''Like Senator McCarthy.''

This was six months before Joseph Welch said, ''Have you no sense of decency, sir, at long last? Have you no sense of decency?'' And Michael was not equipped to evaluate the performance of the senator, but he wasn't enthralled by him. Unlike Mary Ellen and Inwood Catholics generally, he did not take his virtue for granted. No, the senator from Wisconsin wasn't what he meant at all. But he had a point. It was important to keep your eye on the ball, Michael would have said, and the ball was Communism, and how to lick it. He said as much to Mary Ellen.

Then they both fell silent, having lost the poignant, personal note of their talk in what must always seem by comparison the banality of politics.

After the waiter cleared their dishes and they were smoki their second cigarettes, Michael said, ''So they think yo bold.''

She nodded and looked at him through the smoke, touchin her cigarette to her lips artfully. She *was* sophisticated, anc he guessed that she'd had experiences with men that her mother didn't know of.

''Why exactly?''

''Because I don't believe that all the dreams have already come true. I don't believe that all the fabulous new worlds have already been discovered or that all the great ideas have already been thought up.''

''I don't believe any of that either.''

''I know you don't. It's obvious. You've got your hat set on something special.''

"It shows?"

"I'll say."

"I wish you could tell me on what. I'm kind of at sea."

"You should go to college."

"I'm going to, one way or the other."

"And become what?"

Michael had not declared himself even to this extent before, and suddenly it seemed to him the conversation had taken a dangerous turn. "A lawyer maybe," he said. "I'd become a cop like my old man was, but to tell you the truth I've had my fill of guns. I'd like to do something that makes the world better, you know? You don't think that sounds hokey, do you?"

"I like hokey."

He trailed the cinder of his cigarette through the ashes in the ashtray. "Lawyer's work can be kind of dull though. Searching through the fat law books for legal precedents and all that. In the law I think they *do* believe that all the great ideas have already been thought up. I'm not sure."

"What does your friend think?"

Michael looked up sharply. He confessed to me that his first thought was, "Who, Durkin?" Then he realized what she meant. A coy thrust. He said, "She leaves it up to me."

"Smart girl."

"Yeah."

They could see through the windows that the snow was falling heavily now and they agreed it was time to head uptown.

On Fifth Avenue in front of Saint Patrick's Cathedral they paused. A service of some kind—carols perhaps or an Advent Mission—was in progress inside the Gothic church, and the snow was luminous against the brilliant blue windows. Michael and Mary Ellen stood there staring at the cathedral as if, magically, it would reveal its secrets to them. Was this the shrine of an Alpine village? Was it the insides of a spherical glass paperweight? In what way, exactly, was this real? To them at that moment Saint Patrick's was the most beautiful structure in the world and, sophisticates though they were, they shared a swell of pride that Fifth Avenue's masterpiece was their cathedral. Could Michael have imagined that only seven years after that moment he would prostrate himself on the floor of that very sanctuary to be ordained to the holy priesthood, and only seven years after that he would in its offices scandalously refuse to obey the explicit command of Cardinal Spellman? As if he had imagined not only these things but a whole life of heroic loneliness, he abruptly turned his back on Saint Patrick's and took Mary Ellen's shoulders in his hands. He intended to tell her the truth, that there was no other girl, that these hours with her had been his first truly happy ones since coming home, and that for the first time it seemed possible to him that he could do something with his life. Something worthy of his father's memory, worthy of his own having been spared in battle and in prison, worthy even of her!

"Mary Ellen," he began. But words failed him once more. Instinctively he veered into phrases he knew by heart. He spoke them passionately, loudly, his voice rising above the noises of the avenue. " 'Then a great sign appeared in heaven . . . a woman clothed in the sun . . . and . . . the moon under her feet and a crown of twelve stars on her head.' But the dragon was angry with the woman and went off to make war on her offspring. 'Then war broke out in heaven! Michael and his angels fought against the dragon who fought back with his angels, but the dragon was defeated . . . Then I heard a loud voice in heaven saying, ". . . Now God has shown his power as king! Now his Messiah has shown his authority!" ' "

"Michael, you're making me nervous."

He checked himself and released her shoulders. The intensity of his emotion had him shaking. "I'm sorry," he said. "It was the woman, the idea of the woman. I saw you."

She shook her head. "You said everything they did served their purposes. Maybe the Communists let you keep that Bible to . . . "

"Make me nutty?"

She dropped her eyes. She had a Catholic's distrust of a Bible quoter.

But he crooked his finger under her chin and lifted her face. "I'm not nutty, Mary Ellen. I know I'm not the archangel and I know I'm not the Messiah. But I do feel like I was

spared to do God's work. I think they let me keep that New
Testament because He wanted them to. It was His way of
introducing Himself to me. I know how strange it seems. It's
strange to me. But also very real. I mean, I'm here. That's
the basic thing. And why should I be when fifty thousand
other fellows didn't make it? Well the answer is obvious to
me. Something very important won't get done unless I do it. I
know it sounds conceited or pompous, but I have the feeling
that the world needs me."

"Maybe not the world, Michael. Maybe just a little part of
it."

It was as if he didn't hear her. He said, "It's such an
awesome feeling that, well, it's kind of paralyzed me. I
haven't known how to get going. But now after talking with
you I see that the way to start is just to start. For me it was a
start just to walk into Macy's this afternoon."

"What do you mean?"

He reached inside his coat and took out the small gift-
wrapped box. "This is for you. I bought it for you. *Je
Reviens;* is that how you say it?"

"You mean . . . ?" She stared at the gift, not daring to
touch it.

"I don't have a girl, Mary Ellen. Only the dream of one."
Michael would say to me later that that was the first moment
in his life when he'd stood on the near edge of love. He
would stand there again, even more painfully, more happily.
He saw her eyes fill. He said, "And she is a woman clothed
in snow."

"This city," E. B. White said, "which not to look upon
would be like death."

Michael and Mary Ellen looked upon it from the second
hill in Fort Tryon Park. They looked upon it regularly. As the
days lengthened they would meet at Dyckman Street and
follow the pathway up the wooded slope and around the peak
on which the Cloisters sat. Michael never took her into the
museum, never showed its treasures to her as he had to me,
and that fact alone would have tipped me off to what was
coming.

He and Mary Ellen went up the hill to watch the sun set

behind the George Washington Bridge. They held hands but
only once they were inside the park, as if the streets of
Inwood would whistle at them. Often, once the golden mist
of evening had faded to black, they would sit on a favorite
bench and kiss. As the weather grew warmer and the color
returned to the tips of the trees and the smell of forsythia
hung above the hillside and the earth underfoot grew dry
again, they sat on patches of grass to be alone. They stared
out at New York, talking, held in place by the sight of the
city that embodied their longing.

One balmy evening in May he took her hand and led her,
unopposed, to a remote grove. He took her into his arms and
they held each other. Her strong, narrow body matched his,
pressed against him. Her hair was against his face and through
strands of it, as through the wispy young leaves, he looked
out upon the city. It was time for them to be lovers.

They had begun this before and stopped. Michael had
discovered her breasts and explored her waist, the curve of
flesh at her hip and the patch of rough hair between her legs.
Mary Ellen had rubbed herself against him purposefully, to
the point of his ejaculation, mortifying and stunning, inside
his trousers. They courted, in other words, like what they
were, children of another age, taking for granted their inhibition as well as their acute sense of sin, and paradoxically
taking extreme delight, one lost to the present generation, in
both. They were in no hurry, as if they knew that in sex
anticipation is sweeter by far than what follows. They would
take possession of each other as lovers, in other words, only
when the rites of passion, longing and trespass had been
fulfilled.

Tonight.

He undressed her even as they remained standing. She
shivered when he drew her sweater back and off her shoulders.
She let him find the clip of her bra. That his hands shook
pleased her. She would never have permitted a man of experience to do this to her. When her skirt fell and she bent to
remove her pants, then straightened, naked, he stepped back
to look at her. This body, he felt, which not to look upon
would be like death.

And she closed the distance between them. She fixed her

eyes on the buttons of his shirt as she undid them. And she spoke. Her voice seemed distant, disembodied. "Michael, you have to tell me one thing." He waited. When she had his shirt unbuttoned she stopped and looked in his eyes. "My mother told me you're going to be a priest."

He nearly fell. "Oh, Mary Ellen, that's not true. That's not true at all."

"Monsignor Riordan told her. He told her I should leave you alone."

Mary Ellen laughed awkwardly, as if she'd brought the subject up against her will. She was only trying to dispel the ghosts of Inwood, ghosts she was sure could never claim Michael Maguire.

He took her into his arms and pressed her. Her breasts flattened against his chest. But suddenly she was wooden. She sensed that he'd drawn her into his embrace so that he would not have to look at her. "Oh, darling, you know how I feel about you. I love you. Everything else is far away and unimportant."

It stunned her that he hadn't denied what they were saying. His deflection seemed like an admission, and it panicked her. "He said you've applied for the seminary, that they've accepted you, that you begin in the fall. He said he's been tutoring you in Latin. Is it true?" Her voice was a whisper. Her weight was on him and her mouth was by his ear.

He did not answer. He could have said, "I haven't quite made up my mind to do it." Or he could have said, "What else can I do with my life?" Or he could have attacked the monsignor and her mother; why can't Catholics leave their bright young men alone? Why do they fold us in, corral us, ruin all our options but one? Of course he knew why; it was the genius of the system. His generation would be the last of which it was true, but the best, smartest and bravest boys were tracked inexorably toward one thing. The Great Vocation. Even angels bent their knees to priests. No one ever asked, Since when do angels have knees?

"Help me," he could have said, "to tell them no." But say no to God? He said nothing. He could not answer her.

She dressed herself. He watched her. It was as if a door

closed slowly on a room. He would always think of it as the best room in the house.

Before she turned away she said, "I'm the one who helped you make your mind up, aren't I?"

He nodded. She had given him not the courage, but the will.

Tears overflowed her eyes. She was so hurt.

She said, "And you wanted to make love to me so that you'd have done it once. Right?"

He didn't answer.

"Right?" she insisted. Her voice rose sharply, and all at once her anger swept her hurt aside.

He stepped toward her.

"Don't touch me! Just answer me! You wanted to make love to me so that you'd have done it once! Right? Right?"

"Mary Ellen . . ." Of course, what she said was true, but he only saw it now. He'd never meant to hurt her.

"You goddamn saint!" she screamed. "You goddamn saint!" And then she turned, broke through the virgin branches that enclosed them and was gone.

Michael's hands trembled as he buttoned his shirt.

When he left the grove he walked to the peak of the hill and looked down on the city. The Cloisters loomed, a shadowy fortress, behind him. He told me that he wanted to concentrate on Mary Ellen, to memorize what they had had and what she'd looked like and what the touch of her flesh did to him. But he couldn't because, despite himself, his mind reeled off what he'd memorized before. "After this I saw an angel coming down from heaven. He had great authority and his splendor brightened the whole earth. He cried out in a loud voice . . . 'Whoever is meant to be captured will surely be captured. This calls for endurance and faith on the part of God's people.' "

NINE

E V E N if I had been able to imagine being a priest myself—
they lived well, after all, did good things, had in their
spheres great power and a leg up in getting their poetry
published—I couldn't have stomached the thought of burying
myself alive for six or seven years in a seminary. A seed bed,
literally, from the same root as semen; often referred to
accidentally by Catholics as the cemetery.

Most American seminaries, like Dunwoodie in Westchester
County where Michael did part of his training, would have
reminded you of the eccentric lavish country estates of extremely wealthy Protestants of the sort whose art collections
wound up at the Cloisters. In fact many began as the estates
of such people and came into the Church's possession only
when the great fortunes began to fade under the burden of
taxation in the period after World War One. It is an irony of
American Church history that the leaders of the immigrant
Church were financially in the position to ape the fabulous
style of the WASP elite just at the moment when the WASP
elite could no longer afford it. Of course, bishops were
exempt from the other great tragedy, besides taxes, that befell
the aristocracy about that time too—the shortage of good
servants. And so Carnegies and Mellons and Lawrences and
Biddles and Fricks retrenched somewhat, while Catholic orders and dioceses converted their splashy mansions into novi-
tiates and seminaries. Now in the Berkshires of Massachusetts
and on the Main Line of Philadelphia and on the fashionable
North Shore of Lake Michigan and in the hills overlooking
the Hudson Valley the great prince archbishops—Spellman of

New York, O'Connell of Boston, Mundelein of Chicago and Dougherty of Philadelphia—realized their poor boy dreams for country places of their own.

These seminaries had their acres of rolling lawn and their formal gardens with trellised rosebushes and clipped boxwoods, their lakes and ponds stocked with bass and their nine-hole golf courses complete with practice ranges and winter greens, all meticulously tended by legions of immigrant—though not Irish, who were above such work now—or colored gardeners. Now part of the grounds, however, were given over to football fields and baseball diamonds. To the tennis courts were added bunkerlike handball courts, but the swimming pools, with their threatening air of sensuality, were covered over for basketball. Amid cultivated groves of spruce and cedar loomed artificial grottoes, evoking Fatima and Lourdes, but also the cement-over-mesh "mountainside" in the zoo. To these shrines the boys were expected to come daily, pacing along the winding tidy pathways from one Bavarian-style "station" to another to tell their beads. Tell them what, you ask? No doubt how grateful they were, as the sons of the low and foreign born, to have been admitted to the world—for this was the delusion of that generation of ecclesiastics—of the American aristocracy.

Those places are mostly empty now. Despite their tax exemptions they cost too much to run. Even as conference centers or Job Corps training sites or retreat houses or old folks homes they turned out to be simply too drafty, too impersonal, too much the depressing relics not of one age, but of two. That the Catholics are stuck now with those lumbering white elephants in the Berkshires and the hills above the Hudson is the last revenge of the WASP elite who built them in the first place.

And of course the main reason they are empty is that today there are only a tenth the number of boys presenting themselves as candidates for the priesthood. In Michael's day the seminaries were jammed. Thousands of young men, beginning at the end of World War Two and continuing through the Catholic heyday of the fifties, entered every year. A huge expansion of facilities was required and the edifice-complex bishops built thousands of schools, churches and hospitals everywhere in America. It is both an achievement and a revelation that they did so without constructing a single architecturally distinguished building, adding sham-Gothic wings to the gracious old mansions or replacing them altogether with the sterile brick and poured-concrete of fifties "modern." One order sent off its plans for a new seminary building to the Vatican for review. The Vatican office wouldn't think of faulting the architect for his mundane design, but it did note that he had failed to include toilets and baths for the seminarians. It responded with the question, *Suntne angeli?* Are they angels?

They weren't angels. The seminarians were robust young men, talented, smart, well groomed, aggressively American. lovers of ball games. Their talk was full of slang and they were jazz buffs and devotees of Broadway musicals. But the life they led in the seminary derived from a fierce European regimen that hadn't changed in its essentials since the Reformation. Every Catholic seminarian in the world had his daily schedule, his course of studies, his style of dress, the length of his siesta and even his right to toilet facilities supervised by one curial office in Rome. The most minor detail of daily life (the Latin words, for example, with which seminarians awakened each other in the morning: *Benedicamus Domino! Deo Gratias!)* was considered as sacrosanct as the most major—that, say, the seminarian had slept alone that night. Every such detail, minor and major, was codified and had been for centuries.

The young men had such vitality, such abundant goodwill. and the Church herself enjoyed such a cheerful burst of energy in the period of her "arrival" in America that no one seemed to notice that the ideology underpinning all this building was fossilized. The classroom method of seminary education was intended to be a confrontation with the mind of Saint Thomas. But, first, it was conducted in Latin, a language which few professors, much less students, truly mastered. And, second, the structure of Thomas's thought was misunderstood. His masterpiece, the *Summa Theologiae*, has its origin as a record of a vital dialectic, a Socratic conversation that was supple and dynamic. Instead of teaching his method, most professors simply recited the record of it, so that Thomism was taken to be a kind of catechism for clerics. The monotony of the rote review of *Quaestio, Sed Contra* and *Responsio* was relieved only on those rare occasions when the class penetrated, as if by accident, to the genius of Thomas, glimpsing his still revolutionary insight, for example, that faith is not opposed to reason, but dependent on it, and vice versa. More often, the monotony was relieved not by understanding but by youthful snickers when the bland meaninglessness of the endless text-bound consideration was interrupted by a line made wonderfully ludicrous by loss of context, as in "Man in sexual intercourse is an animal," or "No part of a foot is a foot," or "The whiteness of a man's teeth primarily belongs not to him but to his teeth."

As undergraduates in philosophy, seminarians were expected to divine what Thomas, citing Aristotle, meant by potency and act. As graduate students in theology they were flogged with his distinction, also derived from "the Philosopher," between the *esse* and the essence of God. They were told that their vocations hinged on their successfully grasping such material, but no priest they knew, often including the professors themselves, showed the slightest sign outside the classroom that any of it mattered. Even the Five Proofs of God's Existence, which few remembered beyond the exam, would be of little use in the parish where priests weren't famous for arguing with atheists.

What counted for success in the seminary was mastering that peculiar mode of high-toned mediocrity—to be devout but not pious, savvy but not intellectual, athletic but not physical, self-confident but not arrogant, deferential but not insecure, jocular but not sarcastic, friendly but not intimate with anyone—that developed as the dominant personality type of the American Catholic priest.

Thomism was not taught in seminaries as a way of opening the minds of students to great ideas at all, and it did not matter for the life of the Church that the long, arduous academic program of the priestly formation system was a complete sham. The *Summa Theologiae* was one of history's few works of true genius but by the twentieth century its function as the base document of Catholic thought was merely metaphorical, and in fact the dry, static, constricted framework of the professors served that symbolic purpose better than a vital appreciation of the original theology would have. The *Summa* fit perfectly with the culture of immigrant Catholicism because, as presented in the seminaries, it embodied that sense Catholics had that there are only so many questions and in the symmetry of God's creation there are just that many answers. Perfect happiness—what we called "beatitude"—was possible to Catholics because we participated in a divinely ordained system in which the one set, *quaestio*, could be matched with the other, *responsio*. Even if a particular professor or priest didn't know the answer, someone did. The rector maybe, or the bishop. Certainly Saint Thomas did, or God. The rigid authority of Catholicism derived not, as Protestant critics particularly in America held, from the archaic monarchism of the papacy or a perverse vestigial love of feudal aristocracy, but from a deliberately sustained and unabashedly premodern philosophy that put hierarchy at the dead center of existence. And of course this *philosophia perennis* was not regarded as a system of thought, but as an expression of the Truth Itself. As long as they subscribed to it, what others experienced as the absurd, alienating pressures of life in the twentieth century had no discernible effect on those young men. The seminary discipline that we outsiders would wince to hear described kept seminarians, as an expression of the day had it, on the beam. Or as their motto had it, in all things, they kept the Rule and the Rule kept them. It was an ordered life on the way to Orders.

No wonder they loved America. It had given them their castle-seminaries where they could, on feast days at least, listen to Ella Fitzgerald and Duke Ellington in their music rooms, but where, also, they could pretend to enjoy not as remote historical figures but as present masters Aristotle, Augustine, Anselm, Abelard and Aquinas. They could be in the world but not of it, or was it of but not in? We never knew. The totalitarian quality of seminary life and its cultivated anachrony alerted them to the dangers of materialism and license that so infected their age. Or, as they might have put it about their *horae* if they'd known Robert Penn Warren to quote, "It is not dead. It is simply weighty with wisdom." All they knew finally was that how they lived made them feel

so much a part of the most important project they could
imagine that their responses, despite all the Jansenist gloom
of centuries of Catholic moral teaching, were instinctively
optimistic. During their golden age, seminaries of the Catholic Church in this country, in sum, took a huge crop of gifted
boys, nurtured an irresistible camaraderie that made their
common rooms and refectories puerile, discouraged true distinction among them, yet enabled them to lay a near
permanent—though as it turned out years later, a merely
apparent—hold on a rare American happiness.

One of the ways to prevent the emergence of an intellectual
or personal spirit of true excellence in seminaries was to
segregate the smartest and generally most promising young
men from the rest. Among the diocesan clergy, as opposed to
the religious orders like the Jesuits or Paulists, this actually
occurred when top prospects from all over the country were
sent for their theological education either to the North American College in Rome or to the Theological College at Catholic University in Washington, D.C. These two theologates
produced the ecclesiastical elite from which future American
theologians, canon lawyers and bishops were invariably taken,
and that fact alone is enough to make one wonder about those
places, but that's my prejudice, isn't it? Of course it is.
Prejudice is my starting point on the subject of the American
Catholic hierarchy. In fairness I should rein it, but, hell,
fairness was excommunicated from the Church some time
ago, and not by me. Let me make my simple point about
these seminaries. Training of the leadership was the stated
intention of the system, but perhaps its more telling effect on
the Church at large was to remove from diocesan institutions
the very element, the "leaven" in the metaphor of Scripture,
that might have raised the standard of the whole American
parish clergy through the period of its greatest prestige when,
ironically, it was about to be put to its greatest test. But
maybe not. I'm an opinionated cynic on the subject, but it
seems evident nevertheless that even the flower of American
Catholic manhood lost its bloom in those places too. Not to
say its virginity.

But let me tell you about Michael's school because it's

important for our story to understand what happened to him there. It happened to everyone who went through the place.

The Catholic University was founded with papal approbation in the late nineteenth century by bishops who were moved by the booming American embrace of higher education, and they encouraged their fellow bishops to send students and faculty, and religious orders to locate houses of study there. These bishops were enlightened enough to foresee the importance of professionally trained clergy and an educated laity, even though the immigrant poor who made up the bulk of the Church's members at the time did not seem to require intellectual sophistication either of themselves or of their leaders. But those bishops who look like giants, in Newton's image, only because they were succeeded by dwarfs, were not enlightened enough to imagine, nor were the structures of American society yet fluid enough to permit, that large numbers of Catholics could be educated in the great American secular institutions of higher learning. The impulse to establish the Catholic University of America was thus part of a larger pattern of duplicating the prevailing social structures, which led to the founding of such venerable institutions as the Catholic Boy Scouts, a Catholic Forestry Association, a Catholic Lawyers Guild, a Catholic War Veterans and a Catholic Philatelist's Club. By the time a fellow name of Francis Spellman was archbishop of New York it seemed the most natural thing in the world for him to preside over a Catholic debutante ball at the Waldorf Astoria. Spellman himself aspired to be the Catholic Frances Parkinson Keyes. He wrote a little-known novel called *The Foundling* which fell short, frankly, of her *Came a Cavalier*.

In short, the Catholic University of America became the centerpiece of a great Catholic subculture. It was an authentic monument to the aspirations of the simple people who built it. It was endowed not by a few bequests of wealthy people but by annual collections proudly taken up in every Catholic parish in America, as if this university was an extension—and of course it was—of the parish school. But it was supposed to be more. The dream was that it would embody in the New World the great tradition of Saint Thomas's Paris. Weren't universities invented by clerics, after all, under the sponsorship of popes? But CUA failed to distinguish itself and never made it to the first rank even of Catholic universities like Georgetown and Notre Dame and dear old Fordham where, having been launched on the seas of academe with my doctorate for a sail and my bluster for ballast, I pulled quickly in. Not much of a journey, you say, from Washington Square to Fordham Road, but the idea was to stay in New York. I dropped my heavy-duty anchor on a lightweight teaching job. The Jesuits loved my work on Hopkins for its anticlerical tone and thought of themselves as open-minded for hiring an Irish agnostic from NYU. I was better than a Jew. I didn't tell them about Inwood or that my best friend was a seminarian or that finally ending up at Fordham felt like coming home.

It was the perfect time to come to Fordham. In the next decade even an out-of-fashion ideo-Socratic like me—I hated the seminar method and only asked questions of my beloved imbeciles to wake them up—became a campus fixture, one might almost say a campus light. It helped that as we moved to a shiny new campus in mid-Manhattan, my Jesuit competition on the faculty—those bright would-be sons of my own Hopkins—began dropping like flies in the priest-exodus of the sixties. And lo! To keep me from an assistant's slot at Columbia, they would make me the youngest full professor in the place! They even would give me my whack at running the department just as Marshall McLuhan came on board with his barrels of bullshit about Swedish massage. He made me look unoriginal and unopinionated. I didn't mind the former—it is not a teacher's job to be original. But I couldn't forgive him for the latter. What does a teacher have but his opinions? Nor could I forgive him for earning so much more money than I. He couldn't touch me in the classroom, but his books on the end of books sold wonderfully. I used to wink at him in the corridor to let him know that I knew, but wouldn't tell. I seriously intended to challenge him to debate, but before I could the war hit us, made all the talk about McLuhan seem absurd—which was its one good effect—and made, eventually, the ground open up beneath my feet and swallow me.

But my failure is another subject. I was talking about Catholic University's. Even the Methodists, whose equivalent nineteenth-century movement resulted in Boston University,

Northwestern, SMU, Emory, Southern Cal and my own NYU, outshone the Catholic bishops. Still, CU became and remains the center of the effort to educate American priests and nuns. Perhaps it was handicapped impossibly by its clerical orientation, though some of its priest-faculty, Fulton Sheen for example, or John Tracy Ellis, had left enduring marks. Of course CU has had its achieving laymen too. Among the alumni of its famous drama department are Jon Voight, the midnight cowboy, and Ed McMahon, the midnight card.

The site chosen for the university in the 1880s was on a hill just northeast of Washington, and over the next seventy-five years, around a first modest hall of lecture rooms and a primitive observatory where presumably the priest-astronomers asked forgiveness of Galileo, there clustered the monasteries, convents, postulates, juniorates, theologates and colleges of Paulists, Benedictines, Redemptorists, Oblates of Mary Immaculate, Claretians, Capuchins, Christian Brothers, Xaverians, Salesians, Oblates of Francis de Sales, Carmelites, Carthusians and half a dozen competing factions of Franciscans. Each of these places housed students who attended the university or faculty who taught at it. By Michael Maguire's time there, Catholic University and its religious satellites so dominated the growing new section of Washington known as Brookland that it was referred to as "Little Rome." It was the perfect setting, that genteel but modest neighborhood with its quiet tidy streets and small tract houses on quarter-acres of grass, each with its garage; the little tudor shopping centers with ample parking; the sprawling parks where Little League and Pop Warner flourished. Brookland was an early suburb and as such a type of world into which the entire postwar generation of American Catholics was moving. The fifties boom was for the Church too a suburban phenomenon. Newly ordained clergy weren't going to serve in the gloomy parishes—"Saint Paul's," "Saint Mary's"—of the decaying cities, but in the bright new all-purpose parishes—"Our Lady of Hope," "Holy Innocents"—of the sparkling child-dominated suburbs. The knotty-pine cheer of such places already paneled their lives.

Thousands of young religious were at large in Brookland. On its streets monks, friars and cassocked seminarians could stroll in their medieval robes without the least self-consciousness. The officials deferred to them and the merchants gave them discounts. On the class-free mornings of Holy Days they could attend en masse in a local moviehouse special gratis screenings of features in which Bing Crosby was forever paying off the mortgage of the new church and Ingrid Bergman was perpetually taking her final vows. Brookland was an enclave like Vatican City itself, complete and entire, and across its boundaries the junior clergy were forbidden to go, except in the afternoons of those same Holy Days when they might hike across the city to Arlington for the Tomb of the Unknown Soldier or down to the Smithsonian, wondrously cluttered with the wax figures of Indian chiefs and the original Spirit of St. Louis. Not that larger Washington was regarded as wilderness or that the institutions of government weren't prized by those highly patriotic Catholics, but that, for all their success, the last vestige of that old alien feeling had yet to be removed. In truth it wasn't the *world* they were in but not quite of, but their beloved America.

In the fall of 1958 Michael Maguire began his second year at Catholic University's Theological College. Washington was continually abuzz with news; events that would shape the future followed each other in quick sequence that year. The president, acting on his own authority and with no particular regard for the precedent set, sent the U.S. Marines into Lebanon to restore order and bolster a friendly government. The Supreme Court, applying its own four-year-old principle, affirmed the right of embattled black children to attend a segregated school in Little Rock, Arkansas. "Here come the niggers!" the rednecks cried, and they were right. The first American satellite was successfully shot into space. Nikita Khrushchev became the premier of the USSR. A grand jury found that quiz-show winner Charles Van Doren, the son of my own literary idol, was a fake. The U.S. Food and Drug Administration was sponsoring tests on an oral contraceptive that would free women from the fear of pregnancy. Ché Guevara and Fidel Castro routed the last of Batista's troops to complete the liberation of Cuba. Stereophonic recording was developed and among young people outside the seminary the hits of the year were Buddy Holly's "Maybe Baby" and the

Kingston Trio's "Tom Dooley." 1958 finished Elvis as a musical innovator—he went into the army—but it launched a trio of Liverpool teenagers who called themselves "The Silver Beatles." Any one of these events would have justified Eldridge Cleaver's comment made about Rosa Park's refusal to relinquish her seat to a white man on a Montgomery bus: "Somewhere in the universe a gear in the machinery had shifted." Taken together they support the view that the era of tumultuous change we call "the Sixties" actually began in 1958.

But no event of that year was more fraught with significance for the young men studying for the Roman Catholic priesthood than the death of the man who had come to embody everything triumphant, timeless and secure about their Church, but also everything static, rigid, morose and moralistic. He was an Italian, born Eugenio Pacelli, but revered by two generations as Pope Pius XII. When he died that fall many Catholics reacted as if some law of nature had been transgressed. His Holiness dead? That was no gear shifting, but the machinery shutting down. A kind of tensing—that glandular "Achtung!"—swept the Church, and with it the unexpected visceral knowledge that the last of the ancient command societies, dating back one and a half millennia, was, like an old Roman, about to fall on its sword. Catholics sensed implicitly that the ecclesial structure that had enabled their achievement in postwar America could continue serene and unshaken, immutable as well as infallible, only if Pius, as some thought he might, lived forever.

Seminarians were ordinarily restricted in their ability to follow the news. It wouldn't do to have them distracted by the man-chasing sensations of Jayne Mansfield or Marilyn Monroe. Let me say, aside, that the wholesome movie stars like Doris Day and Grace Kelly were vastly more seductive as fantasy figures to such repressed young males. After all they, like the "innocent" actresses, were being taught the manipulative values of chastity. The most insightful actress of the day, by the way, was Jane Wyman, being the first American to see through Ronald Reagan. But actresses are not my subject, alas. If they were I'd pay homage to Brigitte Bardot, who rescued cinematic eros from the weirdos on

Forty-second Street. It was a great day for us Puritans when
we learned that sex was art. But seminarians, I was speaking
of seminarians.

Reports of goings-on in "the world," whether sex-related
or not, could only make it more difficult for the boys to keep
their eyes on the ball, in Michael's phrase, which was not
God but the thirteenth century. And so by and large newspapers,
magazines, radio and television were forbidden unless there
was a Catholic angle to the event reported, Edward R. Murrow interviewing Senator and Mrs. Kennedy, for example, or
any Notre Dame football game. This restriction, of course,
played its part in the larger strategy of seminary discipline,
which was to reduce those young men, even those best ones,
to the status of dependent children. Seminarians were being
trained in subservience, and no one had embodied the totalitarian system in which obedience was synonymous with humiliation better than Pius XII. He had run the entire Church
the way every rector ran his seminary. When the cardinals of
the Church sequestered themselves in the Sistine Chapel to
elect a new pope, their Consistory became the top news story
of the day and seminarians across America were not only
permitted to follow it but expected to.

The places of honor in the students' common room at
Theological College belonged to two pool tables and a Ping-
Pong table. The television was a small-screen floor model
with a battered wood cabinet, the hand-me-down gift of some
faculty member, and it was impossible, even after the head
student and two others lifted it onto one of the pool tables, for
more than a couple of dozen fellows to watch it at one time.
There were a hundred and twenty-two soutaned theologians in
the room, the entire student body not counting the eight who
were in the kitchen washing dishes, a chore everyone took
turns doing except the deacons. Deacons could smoke too,
though not in front of the others. Theirs were the petty
privileges of a petty elite; the last lesson in how to be a priest.

It was the free period after the evening meal. Ordinarily,
during those thirty or forty minutes, they all donned sweaters
over their cassocks and went out in raucous groups of three,
always three because more was impossible on the neighborhood sidewalks and fewer was forbidden. For a seminarian to

stroll alone was antisocial, and for a pair to go could indicate an incipient "particular friendship." For obvious reasons homophobia thrived in the seminary culture, and not only among the faculty. Seminarians were alert for any sign of intense feeling in themselves or others. Affection reaching to any depth at all set off alarms, and you can imagine what that did to their capacity for friendship. And so as trios they strolled along Michigan Avenue or down Fourth Street or onto the CU campus to check the progress of "the shrine," the National Shrine of the Immaculate Conception, the massive Romanesque basilica that after intermittent construction over thirty years was nearly finished. With its pencil-sharp K. of C. bell tower and its brilliant blue mosaic beach ball of a dome, it already dominated the northeast hill of Washington as completely—and wasn't this the point?—as the Episcopal National Cathedral dominated the northwest hill. Unfortunately the Protestant Church was a classic Gothic masterpiece while the National Shrine seemed garish even to the unaesthetic Catholic donors whose names were being chiseled on pillars in the vast crypt. There was a story, in fact, that on the morning of the day that the great dome was dedicated at last the Blessed Virgin Mary herself appeared on the massive shrine plaza and said to two humble seminarians, "Tell the bishops that I want them to honor me by building on this very spot a beautiful church."

But that evening, despite the mild late October weather, they weren't outside. They were attending as well as they could to the tiny television. A hush fell over the room when Walter Cronkite reported the amazing news that the Consistory had still not chosen the new pope. The smoke had risen black twice that day, indicating two more futile ballots. Speculation now, he said, was that the cardinals, divided between progressive and traditionalist factions, were deadlocked. Cronkite went on to other news, but the seminarians ignored him, bursting into heated conversation of their own. Many took offense at the newsman's implication that liberal versus conservative politics, not the guidance of the Holy Ghost, would determine the outcome of the papal election. Others, the more worldly ones, thought it naive in the extreme to expect a secular commentator not to impose some human analysis on the sacred process.

Gene O'Mally didn't care, frankly. He was worried about the game. The next day Theological College was playing the Paulists, and on the Paulists' court. O'Mally was the captain. He was a type and I know all about him. They came through Fordham by the gross. Even as I remember what Michael told me of him I can read his mind. He'd played basketball for Notre Dame, and he knew better than anyone that his team didn't have it. Hell, it was embarrassing. They'd lost six in a row now. Even the Capuchins in their fruity beards beat them, and the Paulists had won the league the year before.

Some people thought the seminary basketball league was frivolous, the litniks and the eggheads, but O'Mally's opinion was that God was as glorified by a nice lay-up as He was by the *Tantum Ergo*. But he also thought it was a disgrace to have all these effete religious orders trouncing the diocesan guys of TC, and he was going to do something about it. If he didn't, the Paulists, who could be vicious bastards, were going to run off a hundred points against them.

As the seminarians began to drift out of the common room—they had to be in their rooms in ten minutes for the night study period—he slid into line behind Mike Maguire. Oh, if he could just get the son of a bitch to play tomorrow, that would do it! Not that they'd win, but O'Mally just wanted to keep it from being a rout. Maguire, at six-three, was taller than anybody on the team, and the guys from Dunwoodie said he was good. In fact O'Mally had seen him shooting baskets by himself the previous spring, and he had the touch. The ball just floated off his fingers, like it had helium in it. He'd knocked off ten in a row from all over the court. But Maguire wouldn't play, and he didn't even shoot baskets by himself this fall. For sports all he did was swim laps in the CU pool. When O'Mally'd approached him in September he'd declined pleasantly enough, but firmly. He'd said he wanted to concentrate on studies and that b-ball wasn't his sport anyway. Maguire'd made a joke about being older and said his jock days were over. But O'Mally's theory was that Maguire was used to being the big shot. He never referred to the war-hero stuff himself, but everybody else was always aware of it. Hell, a lot of guys looked at him with a kind of awe. Maguire seemed oblivious to that, but probably he secretly lapped it up. He probably wouldn't play ball unless he was the captain. Well, O'Mally had decided during that miserable game against the Capuchins that if that was what it would take to get Maguire on the team, it was okay with him. He'd resign the damn captaincy and offer it to Mister Wonderful.

"Hey, Mike, how goes it?"

"Hi, Gene-o, how you doing?" Maguire was a year behind O'Mally, but at twenty-six, he was two years older. He'd gained weight since entering the seminary in New York four years before, and had lost the ascetic leanness and gray pallor he'd brought home from China. He was stoop-shouldered now, but no more than many tall men, and when he tired, his face took on a bony, haggard look. Still he was an imposing, robust man, devoid of boyishness, a handsome black Irishman in his prime. In the opinion of his superiors and most of his colleagues his physical stature was more than matched by other less tangible qualities of character. Once, on a bet, he skated out onto the freshly frozen lake at Dunwoodie. When the ice, which was too thin, began to crack he went faster and soon he was furiously skating across the lake, ahead of the crack. A gully of black water opened up behind him, but he never hesitated. He made it all the way across the lake, and the seminarians who saw what he'd done said to themselves, though not to each other, "Here is a man I want to be with."

Some of the fellows, however, could never master their ambivalent feelings about him. It was less a problem at TC than it had been at Dunwoodie, but even among the theology students in Washington there were men for whom Michael's background was an insufferable rebuke, as if he'd risked his life in combat and endured years as a POW precisely to make them feel inferior. What his fellows were not aware of, for Michael kept his feelings to himself, was the fact that he felt deprived of the very sense of manhood, of power, his years in Korea and China had given him. This man who'd survived war and withstood brainwashing had been cut down to size

too by the chickenshit of seminary life. It had been like a
return to the suffocating, child-pinching world of Inwood.

Once, the previous winter, he'd asked permission, as he
was required to, of Father Farley, the gruff rector, to go ice
skating on the Reflecting Pool at the Washington Monument.
Father Farley said no, which so surprised Michael he
involuntarily, for it was practically insubordinate to do so,
asked why. The rector replied that it was dangerous. Dangerous!
The water in that landscaped artificial pool was only three
feet deep! At Dunwoodie Michael had skated across that
cracking ice above twenty feet of water. "Go, Michael, go!"
Michael Maguire had been a war hero! Had killed people!
Had saved many lives! Stop, Michael, stop!

"Dangerous, Father?" he asked, his face reddening.

Father Farley stared at him.

After a long time, a critical time in Michael's life, he
turned and left the rector's room, but not before saying, as he
was required to even though he'd been refused, "Thank you,
Father."

Michael worried, in other words, as much as any of them
did about appeasing the great authority figures of rector and
faculty, and he spent all of his energy, like the others, trying
to dazzle not two parents but two dozen of them. If there was
a difference between Michael and most of the others it was
this: he was man enough to suspect what was happening to
him. He was becoming what Saint Paul called a "eunuch for
the Kingdom of God." And there's the key. He would never
have tolerated it, but he had inherited a belief and had yet to
question it that the emasculating shit of life in the Church was
the absolute will of God.

Seminarians are inveterate nicknamers—they call each other
"Fuzz" and "Spade" and "Champ" and "Wolfjaw" and
"Bishop" and "Sleepy," always with a needle—and in
Dunwoodie Michael had been tagged as "Mister Wonderful."
Few had the nerve to call him that to his face, and it had
evolved, as such handles do, first into "Won-ton," as if he
was being ribbed for an interest in China, and then simply
into "Won," pronounced "Juan." Michael knew better than
to show how it insulted him, and he'd grown used to the
complicated feelings his fellows had about him. But their

bitterness, when it surfaced in a cold look or a snide crack, could depress him, and Michael had learned in Dunwoodie that nothing was served by outshining the others unnecessarily. That was, in point of fact, why he'd stopped playing basketball, a game at which since Good Shepherd no one he'd played with could touch him.

"What do you think, Won?" O'Mally asked. "Who's going to get it?"

There were Vatican-watchers among the seminarians who had all the leading candidates—the *papabili*—doped out. That crowd lived for Church gossip and it was them Michael kidded when he said, "Walter Cronkite, Gene-o. I think Walter Cronkite."

One of the wags would have come back with a Cronkitish, *"Et vos ibi!"*—"And you are there!"—but O'Mally wasn't famous for his wit and his Latin was far too workmanlike for cracks. He said, as they rounded a corner into one of the long dark corridors off which each man had his room, "But it's got to be an Italian."

At first Maguire thought that O'Mally was responding to his remark about Cronkite, but in fact he'd ignored it. Michael couldn't imagine that Gene-o really wanted to go on about this. There was nothing new to be said on the subject. In recreation and in every class for days now the Consistory had been the only topic. If they all talked about it compulsively it was surely because the interregnum was implicitly threatening. Where was Holy Mother the Church without her Father figure? "I hope it's Triozzi," Maguire said. "At least he knows the U.S. I think a lot of those Italians think we're all Baptists over here."

"He doesn't have a chance. Too young."

"That's true. Only sixty-three."

They both laughed.

"When we're sixty-three," Maguire said, "it'll be nineteen ninety-five."

"Speak for yourself, old man."

"That's right, I keep forgetting. I'm a delayed vocation."

They stopped at Maguire's door. The pause there should have been the briefest possible, like one of them getting off a moving sidewalk. They were discouraged from talking at each other's doors, and absolutely forbidden, for the usual reason, to cross the threshold of another seminarian's room.

"Actually, Won," O'Mally said awkwardly, "I wanted to ask you something."

"What's that, Gene-o?" Michael waited. It could have been anything from switching a dishwashing assignment to help with his Canon Law notes.

"You probably know the team isn't doing that hot."

"Hey, the season's early, Gene-o. It'll pick up."

"It's a third over, Mike, and we haven't won a game. And we haven't played the toughest teams yet. Even the Capuchins beat us. Talk about mortification! Lord!" O'Mally fingered the row of cassock buttons that bisected him as neatly as a shrimp's vein.

Michael liked O'Mally. When he'd first come to TC, O'Mally had called on him somewhat formally to say welcome. It was a studied act of kindness—he repeated it for all the first-year men—but Michael appreciated it nonetheless. Later he understood about O'Mally's preoccupation with the basketball team and realized he was in fact scouting the new class, but that didn't seem to take from the gesture's sincerity. O'Mally was the kind who could talk with feeling and a pseudo-Freudian erudition about the importance of athletic competition as a sublimation of the sexual drive. Not that he would credit Freud, of course, who was still regarded as an enemy of religion, or for that matter, not that he would even know that the theory he was parroting originated with the notorious psychoanalyst.

"Losing is one thing," Michael sympathized, "but getting murdered is another. It's enough to make you want to quit, I'll bet."

"That's why I wanted to talk to you. We can't quit, of course. I mean, jeez, what a disgrace that would be. And imagine how that would look in my file. Farley would love it."

If seminarians were obsessed with Farley's opinion of them it was because no one got ordained without his recommendation. Students at TC were rarely fired, but the culture of seminary life required a constant insecurity. The rector and faculty nurtured it and students—remember, these were all men in their twenties—played into it. It was another of the ways in which the slave-master mentality of priests was inculcated. By the time a man makes bishop he has spent a lifetime cooperating in his own humiliation, and he can't understand, now that he's in a position to humiliate others, why they don't cooperate too.

"Anyway, quitting isn't what I wanted to talk to you about. I was hoping you might reconsider and come out." O'Mally leaned against the doorjamb.

Maguire snapped on his desklamp, then sat on the edge of his perfectly made bed. "I know it's not easy for you to ask me, Gene-o."

O'Mally smiled. "It's not so bad."

"I'm not the easiest guy in the world to approach."

"That's true."

"I'd really like to help you out, but . . ."

"Hey, it's not me I'm asking for, Mike. It's the other guys. Jeez, talk about demoralized. You know what I'm saying to you? Your brothers need you. I mean it's that simple. Your brothers need you. Not because you're so terrific yourself." He smiled winningly. "But God happens to have given you certain gifts. You're taller than any of us. You can shoot. And you're tough. And why did God give you those gifts? Not so you could hang out with the litniks in the sacristy. God's favorite people are the jocks, everybody knows that. And you're a ten-talent guy if there ever was one. But you're just burying your talents like the fellow in the gospel."

" 'Well done, good and faithful servant,' " Maguire laughed. " 'You have been faithful over a little. I will put you over much.' "

"Just put me over tomorrow when we play the Paulists." O'Mally's face darkened. "You're probably better than I am, Mike. I think you probably ought to be captain."

"Don't be ridiculous. The guys elected you captain. What's my being captain have to do with it?"

"I thought maybe you'd come out if you were captain."

Michael stared at O'Mally. " 'You wicked and slothful servant'!" he said good-naturedly, disguising the insult he felt. Why didn't this son of a bitch take a hint? Michael simply didn't want to play. Think of it as an act of independence, one of the few he allowed himself in that world where conformity and dependence were the great virtues. It wasn't only the faculty you had to please, finally, but all your peers too. Everyone's opinion counted but your own. Here was O'Mally saying that in *his* opinion Maguire was a vain, arrogant showboat who could be bought off with the measly honor of being team captain.

"It would look good on your record if you were captain," O'Mally pressed.

"My record looks okay, Gene-o."

"Not if they think you're a loner, Mike. This is your chance to do something for the community."

How had such a small thing become so big? How could Michael's *not* playing basketball reflect badly on him? But O'Mally's thrust had struck home and Michael felt a moment's panic. Did they think him a loner? If his fellow seminarians so regarded him, wouldn't the faculty learn of it? Wouldn't Farley?

"Look, Gene-o, I'd appreciate it if you didn't press me on this." What Michael meant was, "Please don't tell on me." He knew that his act of autonomy was an offense, but there was little enough autonomy left to him and he had instinctively to protect it. How ironic that a last pathetic defense of his balls should have required the rejection of sport.

O'Mally shrugged and opened his hands. He was about to say a final word.

"Mister O'Mally!" a voice boomed down the corridor. It was Father Farley. "Get to your room!"

O'Mally flashed a stricken look, then disappeared.

The next morning Michael woke feeling a fresh insecurity about his status, and so he resolved that during theology class, at his first opportunity, he would dispel any possible impression that he considered himself apart from the others or, God forbid, better, by joining in the discussion with unusual energy. Class participation was one of the things you were judged on.

De Ecclesia, Ecclesiology; the subject of the class was the Church itself, and the ongoing Consistory had led the profes-

sor to focus for some weeks on the concept of Apostolic
Succession. On that notion—that the bishops and popes of the
Church are linked in an unbroken line to Peter and the
Apostles themselves—rested both the legitimacy of Catholic
Orders and the Catholic claim to spiritual and juridical superiority to the Protestant denominations. For days the professor
had been displaying the charts of the historical record, the
conclusive if mechanical evidence that Catholic claims were
true. It was like an endless relay race with each bishop a
runner taking the baton—God's Grace—and handing it on to
the next. No matter that, far from sleek, ascetic athletes, most
of them were like the characters Orson Welles portrays,
pampered, self-indulgent, dictatorial and vain. The idea of
Apostolic Succession was as central to the Church as the idea
of the Balance of Powers was to the U.S. Constitution. From
it derived the basic Catholic doctrine that the authority of
bishops and pope came not from the people, but through the
Apostles from Christ Himself.

"Any questions?" The professor blinked above his notes.
He was an old man named Father James Ford, but because
he'd always abbreviated his first name, "Jas.," and also, of
course, because there was nothing modern about him, he'd
been discreetly dubbed "Jazz" by seminarians years before.

Michael raised his hand and Father Ford nodded. "While
there is no pope, Father, who can be said to hold the power
of the Keys?"

"Why, the power rests with the whole Church."

"But then it reverts to the pope once he's elected?"

"Precisely."

"Thank you, Father."

Jazz blinked out at him.

Michael had hoped to get something going, but even he
knew what a dustball his question had been.

"Anything else?" Jazz recognized another seminarian.

"In order to be in contact with the Apostles somebody has
to be a member of the Church?"

"That's correct, although, as you know, the Holy Office
distinguishes between *in re* membership and *in voto*. Who
can tell me what this distinction means?"

No one moved.

Father Ford grimaced, as if their ignorance was a physical pain of his.

Michael raised his hand. "In *re* means 'in fact' and *in voto* means 'in desire.' "

Jazz nodded. "One can be incorporated as a member of the Church *in fact*, as we are, or one can belong to it *in desire*, as in the case of a man who wishes to act in accord with the will of God. Why is this distinction important, Mister Maguire?"

"Because it's how we get around the doctrine that there's no salvation outside the Church."

The class gasped at Michael's phrase "get around," and braced itself. Michael realized it was a slip. He'd answered, stupidly, with what he really thought. He tried to bury it by going on. "Father Feeney was condemned for concluding that those outside the Church are *ipso facto* damned. That has never been the Catholic position. The Catholic position is only that there is no salvation outside the Church. And we can affirm that because *in voto* everyone is, in potency at least, even atheists whose 'desire' may be implicit, a member of the Church."

"Even Luther?"

"Yes, I would say so."

"Well, you're wrong. Membership *in voto* is available only to those who have had no opportunity to know the truth. Luther was a heretic and apostate." Father Ford was angry. To him Luther wasn't an obscure figure from centuries before but an enemy who still threatened, the embodiment of rebellion. If he had been squashed the first time he'd used a cocky tone with his professor the Reformation would never have happened.

Michael said nothing.

"Do you understand now?"

"Yes, Father," Michael answered.

"And is understanding Church doctrine our purpose, Mister Maguire, or is our purpose 'getting around it'?"

"Understanding, Father."

"I expect you to remember that, young man."

"I will, Father." Michael felt sick. He continued to stare back at the professor, but not defiantly. He was afraid to lower his eyes for fear it would seem coy.

Father Ford snapped his notebook shut and stood. The

class stood. They recited the Latin prayer and, then, once the priest left, burst into muted conversation, a release of tension.

Michael walked from the room without talking to anyone, but when he saw O'Mally ahead of him in the corridor he grabbed his arm. "Hey, Gene-o!"

O'Mally faced Michael. "Boy, Maguire, you got the hot-foot that time, didn't you?"

Michael made a face, a quick intake of breath through gritted teeth. "And I was just trying to play the damn game. Speaking of games . . ." He paused. He knew what he was doing. One way out from under the awful feeling of having been slapped down would be to do what this kid had asked. Michael wanted to belong. He had felt a new blast of the old *voto*—the desire to appease. Finally it came to that, and the walls around the last small part of himself that he had not surrendered just collapsed. He felt like a child asking a harsh playmate, ". . . Do you still want me for this afternoon?"

"Pick!" the Paulist guard cried and moved toward the top of the key, driving O'Mally into the other Paulist who'd set himself.

"Switch!" Michael called, sliding away from his own man, the pick, to cover the guard. The guard went up for a jump-shot and Michael went with him. When the guard released the ball, it was still arching slowly upward when Michael slapped it away.

"Shit!" the Paulist said, but the play moved quickly away from him as O'Mally led yet another TC fast break. Approaching the key he drew one of the two defenders and dropped a short pass to Maguire who was coming in right behind him. Maguire drove into the left slot, drawing the other defender, then fired a pass across to Tommy Coogan, the second TC guard, who was open for an easy lay-up.

"Beautiful! Way to go, Coogs!"

Coogan crossed to Maguire on their way upcourt. "Mister Wonderful," he sang, "that's you."

Michael grinned. With less than ten minutes to go they were leading 74–70. TC hadn't beaten the Paulists in four years. Michael had already scored twenty-four points, but his real value to the team seemed to be the way in which his concentration and his hustle—his discipline—communicated to his teammates. He had a rare *esprit* and they caught it. On the basketball court his natural grace, his instinctive willingness to take risks, asserted themselves. It was the opposite of the inhibitions he felt throughout the rest of his life. He was a man of action again. Why had he denied himself this pleasure? So as not to show the others up? To protect a little autonomy for himself? Or had he refused to play because he *was* a loner? No, not that. Suddenly he knew. He had denied himself this pleasure—driving, shooting, passing, scoring—because it *was* pleasure.

O'Mally had scored nineteen points, a personal high. Even if they couldn't quite hang on to win, although at last he believed they were going to, this was already the happiest day of his life. During his two years at Notre Dame, the truth was he'd been a substitute and he'd never really experienced until now the true ecstasy of the game. All he'd wanted was a ringer to keep the score respectable. It never occurred to him that what he'd get was everybody at his best together.

The Paulist forward took a bad shot. None of his teammates was in position for the rebound and Michael snagged it easily. He passed off to O'Mally for the run upcourt.

O'Mally's heart was in his throat. This would make it six, a lead of six!

But something happened.

The carillon in the Knights of Columbus bell tower at the shrine exploded with a loud peal of bells, and in quick succession bells began to ring loudly from the crenellated tower of the adjacent Paulist house and then from the Redemptorists' beyond the playing field and from TC across the wooded ravine behind the basketball court. The bells in the tower at the CU faculty residence began ringing too.

The players drifted. O'Mally started to throw a pass at Coogan, but Coogan wasn't paying attention. He was looking goofily up at the sky as if for a show of angels. Bells were coming from Trinity College across Fourth Street.

The referee blew his whistle; time out.

They all stood there listening as the bells from religious houses all over Brookland began to sound. It was the most extraordinary thing.

"Habemus Papam!" one of the Paulists cried. "We have a pope!"

And with that, the Paulists and the TC guys filed off the

basketball court, some without picking up their sweatshirts. They were all dressed alike in tan workpants or old black cotton trousers and T-shirts. They didn't wear shorts. They crossed the driveway en masse and funneled quickly into the common room of the Paulist House. As a religious order, the Paulists took the vow of poverty, which meant that they had a new, expensive, large-screen television mounted nicely where everyone could see it. On the screen was a photograph of Saint Peter's Basilica and a correspondent on radio hookup was describing through static the white smoke that even then was pouring from the chimney above the Sistine Chapel. He said the cardinals burned their ballots without wet straw and that's why the smoke was white.

A few moments later the correspondent said that the first unconfirmed report was that the new pope was named Roncalli. Walter Cronkite came on then and awkwardly explained that Roncalli had not been mentioned as a possible pope. For the moment they knew nothing about him, not his first name, the see of which he was Ordinary, his age or the stripe of his politics. Nor did they have a photograph. The newsman flashed that twinkle of his, though, and said it was safe to assume that Roncalli was Italian.

The seminarians didn't laugh. A somber crowd, they pressed forward, listening, waiting to glimpse their future.

Michael looked out the window. O'Mally was still standing on the basketball court with the ball between his forearm and his hip, as if he expected the game to resume. "That guy," he thought, "doesn't have his priorities straight."

Later, by the time he told me this story, by the time he'd finally thrown off the pall of priestly subservience, long after the famous fresh air that blew into the Church with the election of John XXIII had grown stale, and after Eisenhower's Lebanon had become Johnson's Vietnam and Civil Rights had become Benign Neglect and birth control had become abortion and Lennon had become Lenin and the world had learned that at Auschwitz the smoke from the ovens was white because the victims' bones lacked fat enough to blacken it, Maguire had decided that O'Mally was the only guy of all who got it right that day.

TEN

THE breakfast dishes hopped when the monsignor slammed his hand down on the table. "The son of a bitch!" he said.

"Who?" Father Rice asked mildly without looking up from the *Times*.

"Moses! The son of a bitch!"

Father Rice raised his head and shook it once at Michael. "He doesn't mean the prophet."

Michael checked himself; Moses wasn't a prophet, but it wasn't a deacon's place to correct a priest, not even a vain, pompous one like Henry Rice.

The monsignor muttered under his breath while he read the article to its conclusion. Then he looked up at the table. Father Rice and Michael were the only ones left. Father Keegan was in the church already for the eight o'clock Mass, and Father Mahon was in the common room where he could have his morning drink in peace. Since Father Rice remained buried in his newspaper, Monsignor Ellis addressed himself to the new deacon. "He is one son of a bitch."

"Robert Moses?"

"He says this neighborhood is blighted. Blighted!"

Michael watched the pastor as he began to read the news story again. The Triborough Bridge and Tunnel Authority planned to demolish certain buildings on the West Side—"warehouses and dilapidated dock facilities"—to expand the access ramps for Lincoln Tunnel, an expansion made necessary by the in-town congestion resulting from the completion two years before of the third Lincoln Tunnel tube. The accompanying diagram indicated that one ramp would empty onto Forty-third Street, right in front of the parish school. Michael had only arrived at Holy Cross from Washington two days before, having been freshly ordained to the deaconate, which was, in effect, a kind of internship, the last phase of training before ordination to the priesthood. Michael would be working in the parish all summer and looked forward to his first experiences of pastoral ministry. But so far the talk had been of nothing but Moses's plan and the threat it posed to the safety of the schoolchildren. The old priest trembled visibly as he read. Michael looked in vain for signs of the bright, good-humored man he must have been in his prime. The first thing anyone ever said about Monsignor Ellis was that he had won the United States Amateur Golf Tournament in 1911, the year he entered the seminary. This was 1960; he was seventy years old, and his arthritis had kept him off the golf course for years.

He looked up again at last, fixing his stare in Michael's direction, but his eyes remained unfocused. "He won't get away with it, the goddamn child-hating Jew."

Neither Father Rice nor Michael commented.

Monsignor Ellis pushed his chair back from the table and stood up. His body creaked. "I'm going downtown."

In the argot of the New York clergy "downtown" meant the Chancery Office at Fiftieth Street right behind Saint Patrick's, and even priests for whom the trek was uptown referred to it that way. Holy Cross Church as on Forty-second Street at Ninth Avenue. The school was on Forty-third.

"The cardinal won't let this happen."

At the dining room door the pastor stopped and looked at Michael again. Now he did see him. "What'd you say your name was?"

"Maguire, Monsignor. Michael Maguire."

"What do I have you doing?"

"The hospital, Monsignor. I'm taking Communion to the hospital."

Monsignor Ellis nodded.

"And Father Mahon's going to take me over to the school this morning. He thought I could help the sisters get the children ready for the May Devotions."

"He would!" Monsignor Ellis said bitterly, and he left.

After a moment Michael said to Father Rice, "What did he mean by that?"

The priest turned the page of his newspaper, foppishly shooting a French cuff free of the black sleeve of his sharkskin clerical suit. He eyed the day's stock listings while he said, "The kiddies are the only ones left who can stomach Father Mahon's breath. They think he's funny. The nuns probably tell each other the poor dear's had a stroke. The school is the one parish duty, aside from the early Mass, that Monsignor hasn't had to take away from him. Of course, Father Mahon considers himself more overworked than ever. Hence his interest in you."

Rose came in from the kitchen and began to clear the dishes. She was even older than Monsignor Ellis; she limped just the way he did, as if her knee was arthritic too, though it wasn't. She'd been the housekeeper at Holy Cross almost as long as he'd been the pastor. Whenever he left the table she cleared it immediately, whether the curates were finished eating or not.

"Morning, Rose," Michael said.

She nodded at him and took his coffee cup.

Father Rice snapped his newspaper shut, stood noisily and left the room. As a rule he and Rose did not address each other unless the monsignor was present, in which case they were ingratiatingly courteous to one another.

Rose, mightily balancing a tray of dishes, left the room. From inside the kitchen she threw the switch that doused the dining room lights. Because the heavy curtains remained closed, it was as dark in there as it would be at night, though Michael knew that an April morning was shimmering outside. He sat at his place for a few moments longer thinking, What in God's name have I done to myself by coming here?

But he reminded himself it was only for the summer, and he knew he could bear anything until September when he'd return to Washington for his last year of theology. These two days at Holy Cross had given him his first taste of the ferocious chill inside which most American priests must make their lives, and it stunned him. But he refused to take it as more than an isolated instance. The priesthood was a lonely life, he knew that. But there was a consolation in the manly fellowship priests shared, and he was sure that in most rectories there was cheerful conversation at table and good-humored wisecracking around the television. Here, however, each priest had his own set in his room and apparently they were never together except to eat. A rectory full of loners, he thought. The seminary was right to discourage that tendency in the men. The evening meal the night before had taken a mere fifteen minutes from start to finish. Father Mahon might be a drunk, but he was the only one who'd showed even a mild interest in Michael. He decided to join him in the common room.

"What's on?" he asked, entering, surprised to find the television on.

"The *Today* show, my boy. Have a seat." Father Mahon slapped the leather hassock with his free hand. In the other he held a highball. He sat placidly in an easy chair, his legs slowly opening and closing. He grinned at Michael, then turned his attention back to the television show, sweeping a long strand of reddish-gray hair across his mostly bald pate.

"Monsignor went downtown to see Cardinal Spellman about the school," Michael began. "He said the archdiocese would never let the Triborough Authority get away with it."

Father Mahon grunted and sipped his drink. A large burly Irishman, it was easy to picture him behind an Inwood bar, serving drinks, or at an intersection waving traffic through, or, for that matter, in his undershirt operating a jackhammer.

"What do you think, Father?"

"It's not what I think. It's what I know."

When Michael realized the priest wasn't going to tell him, he pressed. "What would that be?"

Father Mahon looked at him. "Old man Moses and Spelly have a deal. No doubt about it. That ramp is going onto Forty-third Street and that's it. You watch."

"But the archdiocese would have a case. Imagine rush hour. How many cars use Lincoln Tunnel? Good Lord, the hazard would be enormous. I agree with the monsignor. It seems quite callous."

"Robert Moses? Callous?" Father Mahon laughed. He continued to laugh; inappropriately, Michael thought.

"They could route the ramp some other way," Michael offered.

"No need." The priest chuckled again, then stopped. He faced Michael. "Can't be any hazard to the children. can there, if there's no school?"

The two men stared at each other.

"What do you mean, Father?"

Dave Garroway was talking with Burt Lancaster about his new movie, *Elmer Gantry*.

"What do you mean, Father?" he repeated.

"Hey, Mike, call me Ed. You make me feel like an old fart. That what they call you? Mike?"

"Yes. Or Michael, either one."

"You're the war hero, right?"

"I was in Korea. Forgive me, Ed, but I don't follow what you said there, about there being no school."

Father Mahon lifted his shoulders dramatically, grimacing. "I've said too much already."

Michael stared at him.

"Let me put it to you this way, Deacon. Old man Moses and Spelly are like this." He held up a pair of crossed fingers. "Have been since the Saw Mill Parkway deal. Moses bought a corner of the property at Dunwoodie for two million dollars when he brought the Cross County into the Saw Mill. Same corner the real estate guys said was worth about fifty grand. He bought Spelly off, but good. And *for* good."

"How do you know about that?"

"I was procurator at Dunwoodie at the time. Nineteen forty-seven. They've been scratching each other's backs ever since. You think Moses would defy Spelly on something like this? You think Spelly would defy Moses?" He snorted. "Poor old Arthur. He's just the last to catch on."

"But you said . . . "

Father Mahon snapped his fingers at Michael. "It's gone! I said it's gone!" Father Mahon leveled his voice, and for a moment he seemed a different person, alert and sober, an Irish DA. "You go look at that diagram again, Mike. Notice two things. To bring that ramp out on Forty-fourth Street they'd have to reverse the direction of traffic going all the way across town, but that would screw up their fancy new

alternating system completely. Second, to bring the ramp out
on Forty-third, they've got to have twice as much street on
both sides. They've got to take the school for that. You can
bet Spelly got a pretty penny for it, not that we'll see a dull
nickel.''

"Well, they'd build a new school then, right?''

Father Mahon laughed.

"What about the children, Father?''

The priest tapped his head. "They will have thought of
that. So happens old man Moses has just finished tearing
down most of Clinton for that nice new Lincoln Center of his.
Cut the heart right out of Saint Paul the Apostle two parishes
up. You know the church on Fifty-ninth Street? Looks like an
armory?''

Michael nodded.

"A thousand families evicted! Shipped out to Jersey or
Bay Ridge or Flushing, like that!'' He snapped his fingers.
"So Saint Paul's has a school but no kids. Down here we got
kids but no school. Just sixteen blocks away. A couple of
used buses get donated and bingo! Problem solved! So what
if it cuts the heart out of this parish. We're just 'blight'
anyway. Relax, Deacon. All things come to him who takes it
easy.''

"Is this all . . . a surmise . . . of yours?''

Father Mahon seemed to think the question bordered on the
insolent, but he decided, what the hell, not to take offense.
"You mean has anyone taken me into his confidence? Or
sought my advice?'' He laughed. "I can figure it out, my
boy, because I don't expect to be consulted. Poor old Arthur,
on the other hand. His problem is he thinks he's the pastor of
this parish, can't imagine he wouldn't be in on the planning.
Ought to know better by now. There's only one pastor in
New York, a roly-poly red-cheeked bowl of Jell-O, the
Cardinal-Leprechaun. Only this Jell-O's got arsenic in it.
This leprechaun has a rapier hidden in his shillelagh. I know
it. Bob Moses knows it. And now even our wet-behind-the-
ears war-hero deacon knows it. Want a drink?''

"No thanks. I'm on my way to the hospital.''

"I used to have the hospital.''

"Did you?''

Father Mahon stared at Michael, his eyes full of self-pity. "Yeah."

Here was a man, Michael sensed, who had tilted with Spellman and lost. He shuddered, as if he was seeing into the future, the shell of another man, the husk. He looked away. "I'll check in with you when I get back. We're going over to the school, right?"

"Sure. Got to show you around while it's still there." Father Mahon started. "Hey, don't say anything to the nuns, okay? Don't say anything about that to anybody. I'm just an old asshole breaking wind."

"I won't say anything."

The pastoral duties of the deacon include preaching, baptizing and bringing Holy Communion to the sick. As Michael went that morning from room to room in Saint Clare's Hospital, dressed in black suit and Roman collar, carrying the small ciborium and placing on the outstretched tongues of patients, young ones as well as old, men as well as women, the thin white wafer, the Blessed Sacrament, the Lord Himself, he realized that for a long time he'd carried a picture of a man doing exactly this. A picture of the priest who'd bent over his father at the end, a picture of Father O'Shea distributing Communion on a hillside in Korea the night of the barrage, a picture, he saw now, of the man he longed to be. It was to a hunger of his own that he brought the sacred food.

In one room there was a barely conscious man whose head was completely bandaged. Only two holes remained in the swaddling, one for breathing and one for an eye, which moved toward Michael when he touched the man's hand. Michael saw the eye register his collar, then settle on his face. Disembodied in that way, the man's eye flashed eerily, like an animal's in a cave. But then Michael sensed how it was pleading and he guessed the man was dying. He stood by him silently for a long time, holding his hand, returning his gaze. Then he said, "God bless you and keep you." All at once the man squeezed Michael's hand fiercely. Michael had never felt such an expression of gratitude before. He returned the pressure on the man's hand, not in mere sympathy, but with gratitude of his own. "I'll come back every day," he promised. For you, he thought, but also for me. This patient, like the others, was making possible for the first time in Michael's life—himself. That was what he felt. Until those first "priestly" moments—the patients all regarded him as a full-fledged priest; why wouldn't they?—it was as if he had always been someone else, and now at last, touching the bandaged man's hand, the pale cheek of an old lady, the arm of a teenager in traction, the bed of a burn victim, he touched himself with just that tenderness, just that acceptance. Ironically he knew that when they looked at him it was someone else they were seeing. He was an image of Christ now, a sign of His love; he was himself a sacrament. He'd become Michael Maguire by being more than the man of that name, and less. That was the point of the Roman collar, the point of the priesthood, and in fact it was the point of the rigorous abnegation one underwent in seminary. It was all worth it. He felt awed and humbled, profoundly unworthy. Yet, also, prouder and stronger than he'd ever been in his life. Thus, despite the glimpse he'd had that morning of the lifelong stalemate of rectory living and its effect on men who had begun every bit as hopefully as he did, and despite the premonitory chill Father Mahon gave him, Michael felt a surge of happiness to be in the ministry at last. Had he ever been happy before?

Father Mahon and Michael had lunch that day with the nuns in the teachers' dining room off the school cafeteria. The difference from the scene in the rectory was extraordinary. Father Mahon himself, free suddenly of bitterness and sarcasm, glowed pleasantly, and not only because of liquor. The women had an enlivening effect on him, and he conducted himself with an old-fashioned courtly flair that charmed the sisters. A dozen nuns and half a dozen lay women came and went, each with her tray, in a pleasant bustle. The talk was friendly and animated as they exchanged anecdotes about the morning. Three nuns had led a second-grade field trip by subway to the Central Park Zoo, and they recounted in hilarious detail each phase of it. One child had climbed into the Pulitzer Fountain at the Plaza Hotel, a younger Scott Fitzgerald.

Michael had trouble squaring these women with the image he carried of the grim crones of his childhood in Good

Shepherd. In the seminary the only nuns he had encountered
were the self-effacing Mexican sisters who prepared the meals
and did the laundry. These women were Sisters of Charity
and though their traditional black habits and stern Mother
Seton bonnets, not veils, were grim enough, the nuns themselves were not. For one thing they seemed young, though in
those days it was impossible to tell with precision. Sister
Rita, the principal, reminded Michael of a Muriel Spark
heroine, that witty liveliness and bright intellect not flaunted
but definitely on display. She wasn't fifty, he was sure.

He'd expected them to defer to him and even to address
him as "Father," but they didn't. Father Mahon introduced
him as Michael and that was what they called him. Each
woman he met found some way to make him feel welcome.
After lunch Father Mahon excused himself to go back to the
rectory—to say his breviary, he explained. No one winked,
though Michael sensed that they all knew he was going back
to drink himself to sleep.

Sister Rita showed Michael around the school. Holy Cross
was a weary brick building dating back to the late nineteenth
century. Only its arching, story-high paned windows distinguished it as a structure, but its corridors and classrooms
were brightly plastered with drawings, cut-outs and the win-
ners of poster contests. The floors were spotless and the
windows were too. It was attended at that point by seven
hundred and fifty boys and girls, a third of whom were Puerto
Rican, a third Irish and a third Italian. "We should be called
'Unholy Trinity,' " Sister Rita said. The division was an
accident of fluid demographics; a decade later the neighborhood would be almost entirely Puerto Rican and no one
would call it "Hell's Kitchen" anymore. A decade after that
the neighborhood would be full of affluent young professionals who thought their handsome brownstones, restored to
perfection, were all the more wonderful for having stoically
survived three generations of screaming filthy children. There
would be few children by then, of course, anywhere in
mid-Manhattan.

It didn't take years of pastoral experience to see right away
that the school was the liveliest thing in the parish. The
people came faithfully to church, but it was in the school,

Michael realized, that the Church came faithfully to them. Take the matter of Spanish, for example. None of the parish clergy spoke a word of it. Sister Rita, her assistant and two other sisters were fluent. And the other nuns were all studying it in a special course at night run by the parents of children.

"Do you speak Spanish, Michael?"

"No, I don't," he admitted. In his embarrassment he offered the usual excuse. "Isn't it important to help the immigrants learn English?"

Sister Rita bristled somewhat. "Puerto Ricans aren't immigrants, are they? I mean of course they're American citizens, as you know. And many of them feel they have the right to maintain their Spanish heritage. And that enriches us as well, don't you think?"

"Yes, it does." He felt chastened but also chastised, and he had to stifle an old resentment.

"Some people feel that Puerto Ricans aren't quite as worthy of their attention as the Irish are."

" 'Some people' wouldn't by any chance be Irish, would they?"

Sister Rita laughed. "Father Mahon says you might be available to work with us."

"I'm looking forward to it."

The nun looked at him directly and said in a frank, unapologetic way, "We could use a man around here."

"I'm only here for the summer, Sister, and I assume the school year ends soon."

"Now is when we can really use you. This summer we're trying something new. We're going to have programs in the school that we hope will involve not just the students but their families as well. We'd like the school to be a real center of the community here. This neighborhood is full of life. We want to celebrate it. We want to bring it out into the open. The school gives us our entrée. The people cherish it. We want to help them cherish themselves. We could use your help if you're not busy elsewhere in the parish." She smiled; where else was there?

Michael felt like he'd walked out of a gloomy, unfriendly woods into a clearing that was splashed with sunlight, littered with flowers. "I'd very much like to be part of that, Sister, in any way I can. I'm at the hospital two mornings a week, but that's all."

"Good. I'll talk to the monsignor about it. Come into my office. I'll call him."

And just like that she did. Michael sat in a straight-backed chair opposite her desk. It was the chair, he realized, for mulish pupils. A saccharine portrait of the Sacred Heart hung on the wall behind her. Her approach to Monsignor Ellis was direct; she asked to have the deacon assigned to the school's Summer Outreach program, and she winked at Michael while listening to the pastor's response.

"Yes, Monsignor, we'll keep him busy, I promise you."

Her face changed and she listened again. Obviously the pastor had something else on his mind. Michael guessed that he was telling her about his meeting at the chancery. After a moment she said, "All right. I'm sorry. I'll talk to Sister Laurice about it. Thank you, Monsignor." When she hung up she looked at Michael and shook her head sadly. "He says the altar boys don't fold the finger towel properly. 'They just flop it in the dish,' he says."

"He didn't mention the Lincoln Tunnel ramp?"

Sister Rita reacted carefully, with a hint of the devious that suggested how the nuns and priests distrusted each other. "No, he didn't. Why should he have?"

"Well, it was in the paper this morning."

"I know."

"I would expect you two to be talking about it."

Sister Rita nodded. "Anyone would."

"But you don't?"

"The Lincoln Tunnel ramps have been in the works for months. Monsignor Ellis has insisted it would come to nothing. He refused to consider the possibility that they would actually run that traffic by our school. We decided we had to proceed without him."

"To?"

"To protect the children. We're going to take it to the parents. To the neighborhood."

Michael smiled. "The Summer Outreach program."

"That's right. It's called 'building community.' "

"It's called 'community organizing.' "

Sister Rita shrugged. "Public opinion; Robert Moses always needs to have public opinion on his side. That's how he operates. But he won't have it this time. Not when 'the good sisters' get through with him. We're going to get the ramp moved. It's our summer project, and you've just been assigned to it."

"Great!" Michael said, and he let his pleasure show.

"You haven't met my assistant principal."

"No."

Sister Rita looked at her watch. "She'll be back in twenty minutes. You should meet her. It's her show. Can you wait?"

"Sure," he said. "You're the boss."

Michael waited in the reception area outside the principal's office. Half an hour later a tall, slim nun breezed down the hallway. When she saw Michael she smiled at him but kept going. He stood and said awkwardly, "Hi."

She stopped. "Are you the new deacon?"

"Right. Michael Maguire." He put his hand out.

"I'm Sister Anne Edward." She had a striking aquiline nose and lively blue eyes, one of those nuns whose gift of presence was enhanced by the habit and whose face was made to seem radiant by the dark frame of the abstracting religious headgear. Michael guessed that she was younger than he was. When she took his hand he was struck by the force of her grip—it seemed unfeminine to him—and in some way he did not approve of in himself, he was put off by the forthright manner in which she returned his curious stare.

"I was just going in to see Sister Rita. I think she's waiting for me." She took a half-step toward the door, but paused like a girl on a porch who wasn't ready to say goodnight.

"I know. She wanted me to meet you."

"Oh." She smiled and blushed; you were waiting for me?

Michael gestured. "So lead on. I think she's waiting for both of us."

They went into Sister Rita's office. Even before the principal greeted her, Anne Edward said, "They wouldn't give them to me. They said the specific plans are not public documents. They were utterly condescending to me."

"What plans?" Michael asked. He hadn't noticed how agitated she was.

But now Sister Anne waited for the principal to nod before replying, "The tunnel ramp blueprints. We wanted to see exactly where on Forty-third Street the access will go."

Sister Rita said, "We can't start making an issue of it until we can show exactly what our problem is. We have to convict the planners with their own testimony. We need the documents. They've been very clever in keeping all the public talk vague and the diagrams sketchy, but we know they have detailed plans, and there have to be alternative plans too."

"Have you considered what the alternatives might be?" Michael asked.

"Forty-first Street," Sister Anne said. "They have to have considered it. They have to have drawn it up. It's what we'll be pushing for. That's why we need that plan too."

Michael realized it had never occurred to her that the school could go altogether; it hadn't occurred to either of them. He nearly blurted it—"The school is gone!" Father Mahon had said—but he checked himself instinctively. Already an incipient clerical loyalty inhibited him, despite his instinct that the initiative for the real welfare of the parish had fallen to these women. "Who has access to the blueprints?" he asked.

"Just officials," Sister Anne replied. "The Pharisees and the Scribes. Aside from Triborough, only the City Construction Coordinator, who also happens to be a fellow named Moses, the Planning Commission, chaired by a fellow named Moses, and the Traffic Bureau."

"The Police Traffic Bureau?"

"Yes."

"Well, that's not run by Moses."

Sister Anne studied him. Her hand came lightly up to her lips and remained so for several moments. Her expression was both frankly interested and perfectly natural. Another woman, looking at a man like that, would have been thought perhaps somewhat overly personal. But Sister Anne Edward was clearly more interested in the subject under discussion than she was in this new young clergyman.

Michael felt himself begin to blush. He couldn't explain to her what he was thinking, and she would conclude that he was stupid. A mulish pupil after all. But he had just decided to find out before this went any farther just exactly what the threat to Holy Cross School was.

At police headquarters everyone nodded at Michael, and some officers even touched their hats. The shows of deference made him all the more self-conscious. He never for a moment was unaware of his Roman collar, and he felt vaguely guilty, as if despite his deaconate he was not truly eligible yet to wear it. The laity did not know about the distinctions of orders, major and minor, porter, acolyte, exorcist, subdeacon, deacon, priest, bishop. Were there stages of virginity? To the people you were a priest or you weren't. If you were, you wore a Roman collar, heard confessions, said the breviary, had Sunday dinner with your mother and never paid for tickets—concert, baseball or traffic.

On the sixth floor was the office of the Deputy Commissioner for Operations. Michael presented himself to the receptionist.

"Hello, Father," she said, a middle-aged woman with her dull hair in a bun. "What can I do for you?"

"I'd like to see Deputy Commissioner Kerr, if he's in."

She consulted the diary. "Do you have an appointment?"

"No, I'm sorry."

She stood up. "Whom shall I say . . . ?"

"Just say Joe Maguire's son Mike is here."

She studied him. "Father Maguire?"

He shook his head. "No, please. Just say Joe Maguire's son."

"Mike?" She pursed her lips disapprovingly, then disappeared into the adjoining office.

Michael focused on the oversized seal of the New York City Police Department that hung on the wall behind her desk. Its design—a pair of warriors flanking a shield below an eagle—was familiar to Michael because it dominated the Medal of Honor certificate displayed since his childhood in the living room of Cooper Street. Whenever Michael thought of his father, it wasn't the face of a man he conjured, but a

place—the treeless hill in the Queens cemetery, bare except
for the crowded rows of tombstones, from which one looked
across the East River at the crowded rows of skyscrapers. As
a boy, during those sad, pensive visits, it had been easy for
him to think of the Chrysler and Empire State buildings as
giant tombstones. What had been hard was having any specific sense at all of who his hero-father had been.

"Mike?" the voice called from the office, and then Ray
Kerr, the deputy commissioner, who as a young cop was Joe
Maguire's partner, came through the door. "My God, Mike!"
Deputy Commissioner Kerr was so fixed on Michael as he
approached him, hand extended, that the Roman collar didn't
register. "Good to see you, Mike!" After shaking hands
heartily, the two men stood back and looked at each other.
The policeman's white shirt was resplendent at the shoulders
with gold braid. They laughed at their costumes, but then
Kerr said with alarm, "Hey, you're not ordained already?"

"I'm just a deacon, don't worry. Would I get ordained
without you there? It's next year."

The commissioner flicked Michael's collar. "Well, you
look wonderful. Christ, you must break the heart of every
dame in New York City."

Michael smiled. "I would if they had hearts."

The receptionist had resumed her place at her desk.

"Right, Marie?" Kerr said. "Don't the best-looking guys
always go in the priesthood?"

"Yes, sir."

"Come on in, Mike." They went into the deputy commissioner's office and sat in studded leather chairs. Marie brought
coffee. Ray Kerr asked about Michael's mother and took
obvious pleasure in hearing Michael describe her. She couldn't
have been better, particularly now that Michael was in the
city again. The commissioner told Michael about his own
children; his daughter was in law school, but his son had quit
high school to work in a garage. He shook his head, a bare
hint of the disappointment he felt, then fell silent.

After a moment, Michael said, "Ray, I have a favor to
ask."

"You name it, Mike. I'd paint the stripe on Fifth Avenue
green for you."

* * *

Michael did not open the tube that held the blueprints until he was alone in his room at Holy Cross. The sun had begun its decline over New Jersey and the priests had already gathered in the rectory dining room for the evening meal, but he spread out on his bed the plans entitled "Manhattan Entrance Plaza, Expansion." It took him some moments to orient himself, and the first several sheets, while indicating other buildings on Forty-third Street, did not refer to the school. The width of the ramp entering Forty-third, however, was indicated as ninety feet, while the width of the street itself was indicated elsewhere as sixty. Thirty feet were going to have to come from somewhere. He found a sheet marked "Demolition," on which a wedge-shaped blue shadow angling intown from Forty-third Street and Tenth Avenue was superimposed on the plots of existing buildings. Holy Cross School clearly fell within it.

It was not as if he went down to dinner intending to keep it secret, but the mood at the dining room table derailed him. Monsignor Ellis had just rebuked either Father Rice or Father Keegan. Both men were flushed, bent over their food. Father Keegan, a frail priest of about fifty, had seemed timid before, but he was cowed now. Father Mahon smiled at Michael obliviously, his face still creased from sleep. Michael's entrance altered the silence, without ending it. The priests ate their soup daintily, but the sounds of spoons against dishes dominated. When Michael had taken his place and spread his napkin in his lap, the monsignor said coldly, "Nice of you to join us."

"I'm sorry," Michael said, automatically. Once he would have hated himself for his subservience, but by now it was ingrained. No one spoke. Rose served grossly overcooked lamb, and they went to work on that. It was going to be another fifteen-minute meal. Michael knew that it wasn't his place to speak, but he simply could not tolerate either the silence or the suspense.

"Monsignor Ellis," he began, "how'd it go this morning?"

It seemed to Michael that the three curates froze for an instant.

Monsignor Ellis, however, did not miss a beat. "Darn well!" he said. "Darn well!"

"How so?"

The pastor leaned toward Michael and gestured with his fork. "The cardinal gave me his personal assurance that there was no cause for concern. He's not going to let anything befall the children of Holy Cross." He resumed eating.

Michael looked quickly across at Father Mahon, but he was intent upon the bread he was spreading with oleo. After a moment, Michael asked, "So the ramp will be rerouted?"

Monsignor Ellis looked sharply at him. "Isn't that what I just said?"

Michael held the pastor's eyes for an instant longer than he should have, and that "insolence"—its implicit "No, that is not what you said, nor obviously what the cardinal said" —released the old man's fury. "Goddamnit! I will not have this at my own table! I will not have it! Do you understand?"

Michael thought it wasn't necessary to answer, but he was wrong.

"Well, do you?!" the priest shouted.

"Yes, Monsignor."

Nothing more was said.

Within five minutes the dreary meal was over and each of them had retired to his room.

Michael was shaken by the pastor's anger. He considered rolling the blueprints up and stashing the tube of them in the trash in the alley, but only for a moment.

"In for a penny," he said to himself, feeling something he hadn't allowed himself to feel in years. He picked up the phone and called the convent.

To his own surprise, when the phone was answered, he did not ask for Sister Rita, but for her assistant, Sister Anne Edward.

ELEVEN

THE next morning he found her in the schoolyard, a drab paved quadrangle that could have served as the exterior set for a prison film. She was supervising the ten o'clock recess, and the children were swarming like bees. Unlike the other nuns who had taken up their positions in the schoolyard and stood watching like sentries, Sister Anne Edward had joined in the games.

The game was kickball, and it was her turn to kick just as Michael arrived. She didn't see him. Otherwise she'd have been self-conscious when she hiked her skirts and charged the rolling ball, inadvertently displaying her old-fashioned ankle shoes, granny shoes, and a black-stockinged calf. She made contact with the ball—*thunk!*—and it sailed over the heads of the nearest children. But an eighth-grader in left field caught it in the air just as the nun rounded first base, and there was a resounding groan from her side.

Michael recognized her, of course, as the *Life* magazine cliché of the high-spirited young nun—"Good kick, Sister!" But her liveliness charmed him nonetheless and he was still applauding when she saw him. She laughed as she approached. "Were you watching?"

"Yes. You're good. The kid was lucky. That should have been a double."

"A double! That was a home run! I was robbed!" She grinned.

"Well . . ." Michael made a swatting gesture with the cardboard tube he was holding. "Try taking a crack with this."

"Are those the plans?" she asked, sobering.

"Yes."

"May I see them?"

"Out here?"

"I suppose not, but . . ." She looked around. "Wait a
minute. I'll just tell Sister Laurice to cover for me." She ran
across the schoolyard to another nun. She had to clutch the
rosary beads hanging from her cincture. Returning to Michael
she slowed to a walk because he was watching her, he
realized, and so he looked away. Clothed in that particular
habit—a black bonnet instead of a veil and wimple, a modestly waisted gown with flowing skirts instead of a scapular
and multifolded robes—she looked more like a nineteenth-
century New York Society widow than a medieval abbess,
more like the Victorian Mrs. Seton, whose dress the habit
memorialized, in fact, than like Eloise. Still, the effect of her
clothing was the same. It made her another creature entirely,
a mysterious otherworldly person who was unlike lay people
or even priests. It made her a nun.

"We can go to the teachers' lunchroom off the cafeteria.
Nobody will be there now. We can get some coffee."

"That would be great," he said, and they walked to the
school side by side. Children waved and called her name, and
some ran after her to clutch her hand for a moment before
running back to their games. Each child she greeted or touched
seemed special to her, and Michael sensed that each was.

She stood at the hot plate while the water heated, fussing
with napkins and spooning Nescafé into cups. He listened to
the faint swishing of her clothing, the rattling beads. Those
subtle sounds were familiar to him from his boyhood, but at
Good Shepherd School he had never watched nuns in the way
he was watching her. Her body was lost in her habit and from
behind not an inch of her skin was visible, not a wisp of hair.
The vague outline of her slim figure, her efficient posture and
carriage, suggested an unsensuous womanliness, but even
that abstractly. Why then should her image have been the one
to gnaw at the strange but necessary detachment he had
cultivated over six years? But he knew why. She had given
herself to God. She was a Bride of Christ. She was safe. He
would never have allowed himself so blatantly to watch a real

woman or think in this way about her. Sister Anne Edward was vivacious and pretty and smart, but what drew him to her finally—with a shock he realized that this was the first time he was in a room alone with a woman his own age since entering the seminary—was that she, like him, was, in one of the all-time fabulous phrases, a dedicated virgin. That meant not only that she too was trying to build a life around an inexplicable but compelling attraction to God, but also—and more importantly—that she was no threat. She was not automatically suspicious of him or condescending. He didn't have to prove to her that this choice was a worthy one. Outsiders would regard them as life's losers—who else became nuns and priests?—but they knew differently. Their vocation was a courageous rejection of the superficial and the sordid, a generous embrace of a life of service, the most ennobling calling there was. With anyone else of their own generation they'd have felt foolish and defensive. With each other, already, they felt better about themselves.

"Cream?"

"No, thanks. Nothing."

"No sugar?"

"No, thanks, Sister."

She served the coffee, then took a chair across the table from him. "You should call me Anne. I call you Michael."

"Okay." He smiled. "I never called a nun by her first name before."

"You still haven't."

"Anne."

"That wasn't so bad, was it?" She laughed and sipped her coffee. The sleeves of her habit fell back each time she raised the cup to her mouth, and he saw her forearms. She wore a man's watch. Her wrists were pale and he could see the faint blue lines of her veins. Other girls her age put perfume there.

"Like I said on the phone, it's bad news." Michael pushed his coffee aside and unrolled the Triborough plans. Anne Edward leaned forward. "Right there. See?" Michael planted his forefinger firmly. "The whole school is marked for demolition."

For a moment she said nothing. Then, exhaling dramatically,

she leaned back in her chair. "And the monsignor says, 'Don't worry!'"

"Monsignor Ellis has his head in the trench, but that's because Moses is shooting live ammo. Obviously these plans are going through."

"No, they're not."

Michael shook his head. "Anne, if the cardinal has given the green light, and I'd say there's reason to think he has—"

"The cardinal doesn't understand the needs of this parish. If he did, he'd never permit the destruction of the school. The school is all there is at Holy Cross."

He said nothing.

"Don't you agree?"

Loyalty to his fellow clerics, whom she was criticizing—what did it require? He could say, No, there's also the hospital ministry, there are the daily Masses, there's the bingo. But those were rote exercises, and he already knew it. Only the school had life. He nodded, a small concession, but for him important. A break with clericalism. "Why else would I be here with you? I haven't shown these plans to the priests."

"They would say what you said, that it's all over. But do you know why they'd say that? Because the priests don't care about the school. They don't care about the children. Why should they fight for them? But if Robert Moses was coming through here taking away their liquor cabinet or their three days off a week or their free passes to fancy restaurants, *then* you'd hear a howl! *Then* they'd be on the cardinal's doorstep! And *then* Moses would think twice. But the priest are fatalistic now because all Moses wants to take away from the parish are its children."

When she sipped her coffee now her hands were trembling, and Michael saw that she herself wasn't nearly as bold as her speech was. When she looked at him across the rim of her cup, he saw that her eyes were full.

"I don't blame you for being angry," he said. She was right. It was an outrage. These nuns were right and the priests were not supporting them. Well, by God, he thought, I'll support them. Even if they're bound to lose. Now clerical loyalty *required* that Michael throw in with Anne Edward.

Should he have let these nuns defend the parish alone? Should he have ignored what he saw in her eyes, what her speech revealed, what she was telling him? They needed the priests! They needed him! He said, "You love the children, that's obvious."

She put her cup down. "Of course we do. What sense does our life make if we don't love the children?"

Michael nodded. What a simple statement of the nun's vocation. Priests fall back on clerical privilege or on the transcendent function of administering sacraments or on the exercise of ecclesiastical power or on the superior social status they occupy in an immigrant community. Nuns fall back only on the people they serve, or on God. Michael was surprised by a wave of admiration he felt for her, and he wanted to express it. "Holy Cross is lucky it has you."

"Our order has been in this school for seventy years."

"And you?" Michael smiled.

"This is my second." She laughed and touched the corner of her eye. To purge a tear? "But I care about it as if I've always been here."

"Where were you before?"

"In the juniorate. In training. I came here right after I took vows. I felt so lucky to be assigned here. It's considered a privilege in our order because the people of this parish are so good."

"How'd you wind up in the convent, Anne?"

With a quick look she conveyed both that she did not take his right to ask such a question for granted, but also that she welcomed his interest. "The sisters in my high school; I thought, what fantastic women! They were so happy, their lives were full of meaning. I fell in love with them." She blushed but did not drop her eyes. "I fell in love with Christ." She laughed and added, self-mockingly, "Isn't that what girls in high school are supposed to do? Fall in love?" Despite her irony, however, Michael sensed the strength of her vocation. There was no equivalent for priests to the religious woman's fiercely romantic attraction to the mystical life. It was at root, of course, an attraction to the great dream figure of all time. Jesus was the ultimate Mister Goodbar.

"It's a great system, isn't it?" he said. "Now you're in a

school impressing young girls with *your* happiness, with the meaning in *your* life.''

''Yes,'' she said, but there was a hint of darkness in her that made him wonder, How happy?

She went on, ''Maybe that's why the school is important to me. Schools are where we sisters do our work. Schools are where we sisters come from. We take care of our schools because they take care of us.''

Michael nodded. He looked around at the corners of the room and suddenly realized that teaching nuns had been eating lunches in there for decades. Robert Moses was assaulting the ghosts of all those nuns too. A long line of fantastic women! Yes, Michael looked at her and thought that.

Perhaps she sensed these feelings in him because she continued to blush. When she didn't speak, the silence loomed between them. She picked her cup and saucer up and stood, but because her hand shook the cup rattled and she had to quiet it with her other hand. This was not like her, he sensed. She was ordinarily more self-possessed. Was he the cause of this tension? he wondered. Or was it only Robert Moses? She came to his side of the table and took his cup. She smelled of soap.

''Thanks,'' he said.

While she rinsed the cups and left them to drain, he rolled up the blueprints and put them into the tube.

She dried her hands while crossing to him, then dropped the towel on the table and reached for the cardboard tube just as he did. They picked it up together, each with a hand. The tube joined them. Their eyes met.

''I was going to take it,'' she said. ''I have to show Rita.''

''I have to get it back to the commissioner's office.'' Surely she understood that. ''We can't keep it.''

''But we need these plans, Michael. They prove our point. If we're going to rally the parish, they have to know what we're up against. They think it's just a widened street.''

Michael felt sick suddenly. What was she asking him to do? What would the commissioner say if he didn't return the plans? What would the monsignor say if he found out? Or, good God, the cardinal!

He felt the pressure from her hand on the tube. She was

pulling it toward herself. It was as if she was pulling him.
They were physically close and no doubt since they were
young and ripe, there was an erotic aspect to the charged field
between them—they held each other's gaze after all for a
long time—but it was not only that or even primarily. They
were making a compact with each other, an alliance. And
Michael didn't realize that that was what they'd done until,
despite his inhibition, he let go of the tube, to let her take it.

Monsignor Ellis had assumed it would be the usual May
procession from the schoolyard to the church front where the
pale statue of Mary in its small grotto would be garlanded
with roses as it had been every year since he put it there in
memory of his mother. He hadn't presided himself in some
years, but that hadn't mattered. Now it made him seem like a
fool that he wasn't there, as if he didn't know what was what
in his own parish. The first phone call was from a *New York
Times* reporter, and the second was from the chancery.

An hour and a half after the end of the regular school day
and well after such devotions were usually held, all seven
hundred and fifty Holy Cross children filed down Forty-third
Street, nuns herding them like collies. That block was little
traveled for Manhattan, and as they always did when the
pastor or the principal requested it, the police had closed the
street. The girls were wearing their Communion and Confirmation dresses, and certain of them were carrying bouquets.
The boys were wearing white shirts and blue ties, and their
shoes were polished. As they marched along they sang, ''O
Mary, we crown thee with flowers today, Queen of the
Angels, Queen of the May.''

Neighborhood women leaned from their windows up and
down the street to watch. One wiped a tear from her eye with
the corner of her apron: such innocence! And what the world
would do to it! It was a lovely spring afternoon befitting the
ceremony, and the sky itself was blue as Our Lady's cloak.
Father Mahon, looking stately and benign in his alb and
gold-encrusted cope and attended by acolytes, each with his
candle struggling in the breeze, stood on the top stair of the
church entrance like a potentate reviewing his parade. He
seemed indifferent to the implication when the nuns steered

the cross-bearing eighth-grade boy and the garland-bearing eighth-grade girl at the head of the procession past the church, around the police barricade that closed the street and out onto the Ninth Avenue sidewalk, going downtown.

It was the height of rush hour, the sidewalks were crowded with the usual peddlers, but also with secretaries, shopgirls and clerks on their way home from work. The avenue was already jammed with automobiles heading for Lincoln Tunnel and buses for the Port Authority. Before the May procession intruded, the commuters had achieved, despite their numbers, the efficient, steady progress of their daily exodus. The alteration in the rhythm of that progress caused by the Holy Cross children was slight at first, but it was enough. Dozens of pedestrians slowed, then made room for the procession by spilling out into the street. Drivers cursed them, but they too slowed. At the intersections where the streets cut into the avenue, nuns raised their arms at the auto traffic as if it was Red Sea water. The commuters were amused at first, and they waited even if they had the light while the sisters waved the children through. ". . . Queen of the Angels . . ."

Policemen who saw it knew damn well what the effect of the disruption would be, but they had all been in such processions themselves, though not in midtown at rush hour. They weren't going to tell the nuns to beat it. They stopped traffic altogether and nodded at the sisters as they passed. One truck driver leaned out of his rig and joined in the chorus: " . . . Queen of the May . . ."

The decorum of the children was perfect. Those boys and girls, ordinarily the after-school bane of the fruit merchants and of the cops and of the newsstand hawkers, now went by with their eyes cast down and their hands in steeples.

But it was apparent on second glance, third at most, that this May procession was different. In every tenth rank of children was a pair of seventh- or eighth-graders carrying between them a large sign blazoned with the letters *S.O.S.* And trailing the procession were the ten tallest children carrying a large blue banner with white letters that read, "Save Our School From Robert Moses."

Michael had been walking behind Sister Anne Edward. He caught up with her. "You were right, Anne! You were right!'' His exuberance overflowed. ''You are *fantastic* women! Fantastic!''

She laughed. She was delighted with how it was going too. ''You're not so bad yourself, Deacon!''

He fell into step with her. Taking the procession out onto Ninth Avenue had been her idea, but Sister Rita wasn't convinced until Michael had joined Anne in arguing for it. Without permits, which the police would never have granted, it was illegal to disregard traffic signals as they were doing, and the tie-up was building. ''I think we have their attention,'' he said.

She gestured over the heads of the children at the line of automobiles. ''They drive through here every day without a thought for the neighborhood and what they do to it. Maybe now they'll get the idea that people live here.''

Michael waved at a glaring motorist, and through his grin he said, ''They get it, Anne. They get it.''

Under her breath she said, ''They look mad, don't they? God, I hope nothing happens.''

''Relax. Nothing will happen. It's a May procession! The folks who use Lincoln Tunnel will just get home late for dinner, that's all!''

Anne touched his arm. ''I hope so, Michael. I wouldn't admit this to anyone else, but the whole thing makes me nervous. I can't believe we're doing this. Do you think it will really make a difference?''

''Hey, the parents and children of Holy Cross School have to be reckoned with, right? Now Moses will know it.''

''And so will the cardinal.''

Michael grimaced. ''Let's leave him out of this.'' He clutched her arm, and they laughed like adolescents who had just defied a parent, although the parent didn't know it yet.

Her eyes flashed with delight. ''Thanks, Michael.'' In that setting, despite her habit, she was the opposite of the churchly women enshrined by piety. The meek Bride of Christ? The Mother of Sorrows? The Woman Bathed in Tears? Her heart pierced seven times? Passive? Forbearing? Long-suffering? O Mary, we crown thee with flowers today? Not this woman. She was neither tough nor hard-boiled. On the contrary, she was caring and vulnerable. But threaten what she cared about and she became strength itself. She seemed more alive and more full of energy than any woman Michael had ever known. (What? All three of them?) It pleased him to think that his support had helped her to muster the nerve for this. She had helped him to muster his.

A stymied driver honked his horn angrily, and Michael waved at him. "Bless you, brother!" he called.

"Michael!" she said, half-teasing, but only half. "We shouldn't take pleasure in their discomfort."

"Yes, we should! It's them or us, Anne. And my money is on our side!" (What? All three dollars?)

She grinned at him happily. "We're doing it, aren't we?"

"Damn right. I'm going to run ahead. Try to keep the line up to pace here, Anne. I'll slow them a bit in the lead. And I want to make sure nobody bothers the kids when they make the turn at Thirty-ninth Street. Hell, I want to walk in front with them! This is great, Anne!" He clapped his hands and threw his fist in the air. Michael Maguire was a man of action again at last. Spontaneously he blew her a kiss as he turned and then, with an athlete's stride, ran out into the street and along the line of the procession. There were singing children on one side of him and irate motorists on the other. One could almost hear that young, smitten nun saying to herself, "Go, Michael! Go!"

By four-fifteen traffic all over midtown had slowed to a virtual halt, and the first radio reports were going out about what the WINS reporter dubbed "The SOS Parade." What was this anyway? Parochial school kids taking on Commissioner Robert Moses? What did he want with their school anyway? His Mid-Manhattan Expressway had been shelved, hadn't it? But you never knew. It was one thing for Moses to be blasted by Sutton Place matrons over his destruction of a playground above the East River or by the left-wing crowd who wanted Joe Papp to put on Shakespeare in what Moses called "my park," but Catholics? Nuns? The archdiocese? Was the commissioner taking on the cardinal? That would be the battle of Titans! *Find out what the hell is happening over there!*

By the time the procession had wound its way past the new

Port Authority building at Forty-second Street, down to Thirty-ninth, across to Tenth Avenue and back up to Forty-third Street, bollixing traffic for an hour, the news organizations represented at Holy Cross included the *Herald-Tribune,* the *Post,* the *Daily News,* WMCA, WINS, WOR and a camera crew from WPIX-TV. The *New York Times* reporter who'd called the monsignor told his editor nothing newsworthy was occurring, and he would, after the storm broke that evening and the next day, be roundly rebuked.

After the last hymn was sung, Mary's head fittingly crowned and the throng of children dismissed with a blessing by Father Mahon, Monsignor Ellis appeared from inside the church vestibule. He had obviously been waiting for Father Mahon to finish. The pastor looked at the rheumy priest with contempt as the altar boys led him past, into the church. Then he faced the crowd. The children had begun to disperse, but many of their parents were there now, filling the street. They, together with the reporters, waited for Monsignor Ellis to speak. He fingered the row of red buttons on his cassock, but not nervously. These people didn't threaten him. Only phone calls from the chancery did that, and by God he was going to see that he got no more of those on this matter!

"I have a statement to make," he declared in his preaching voice. He waited, skillfully collecting their attention. Cameras ran. He said, or rather, proclaimed, "The May devotions of this parish have the sole purpose of honoring Our Blessed Lady. They have significance for the Church, but not for the world. Therefore some of you have wasted your time in coming here, unless of course you have been edified by the innocence of our children, which would be to the good. As for those of you who are parishioners: my dear people, I appreciate your concern. Rumors abound. Next we'll hear that our beloved church itself is marked for demolition! Nonsense!" He paused, then repeated that word, slamming his fist into his palm for emphasis. "I am authorized by the cardinal himself to say that nothing anyone does with Lincoln Tunnel is going to bother Holy Cross School one bit! You can rest assured, my dear people, that the cardinal would not permit it, and . . ." His finger shot up; this is the last word. " . . . neither would I!"

He turned away abruptly and disappeared into the church. The reporters murmured in protest, but no one went after him. This was another era. The press had yet to stumble upon the fact of its omnipotence, and newsmen hadn't begun to claim the right to ask anyone anything. They began to drift away, wondering what the hell had happened to the story.

When a camera crew from a TV station goes out, though, it's different. They *have* to get something whether it's used on air or not. The footage of the procession, of angry motorists shaking fists at altar boys, of the sweet girl on the ladder placing a little rosebud crown on the head of the statue, was all too good to waste. But there had to be some one-on-one with somebody in authority. The longshot of the monsignor on the steps wasn't enough. But he was gone. At first the TV crew foundered. Then, instinctively, they drifted toward Tenth Avenue instead of Ninth and found themselves in front of the convent. A tall young nun was standing there, as if waiting for them, in her stark, black, oh-so-photographable costume. She was holding oversized rolled papers—perfect visuals— and she said so sweetly, "May I help you?"

Michael watched the broadcast on the late news that night alone in the rectory common room. Father Mahon was already asleep and the other priests were still out. At first his solitude depressed him, but as the news segment came on he was profoundly relieved that he didn't have to watch it with the others. WPIX broadcast a first that night: a nun, without a hint of overt defiance but with a steely undertone all Catholic viewers recognized, apparently contradicted the pastor of her parish. The heart of the report was a dramatic juxtaposition of Monsignor Ellis's brisk denial that the school was threatened and Sister Anne's statement, buttressed by the set of blueprints she displayed, that the Triborough Bridge and Tunnel Authority intended to condemn the school the week after the term ended and to complete its demolition by the middle of July. When the reporter asked her why the archdiocese had not addressed the issue, she replied that the archdiocese had expected the matter to be resolved quietly, at the parish level. Unfortunately that didn't seem possible now. She and the principal and the parents of Holy Cross were confident that the archdiocese would now intervene and Monsignor Ellis would be shown to be right after all. There would be no problem about the destruction of the school because, the Sister of Charity said, the cardinal would not permit it. The news report concluded with the revelation that Robert Moses had been confronted by a reporter only moments before, coming out of a reception in his own honor at the Tavern-on-the-Green. He claimed never to have heard of Holy Cross School and said that, anyway, he was in the business of building things, not tearing them down. When the reporter told him the nun had Triborough blueprints that assumed the demolition of the school, he said, "If she has our blueprints, then the nun's a thief."

After the news, Michael changed his mind and decided that even the biting sarcasm of Father Rice or the cloistered murmurs of Father Keegan would have been preferable to what he had—the company only of an ominous dread so palpable that it might have been another person opposite him in the gloomy room. What the fuck had they done? What would happen now? He felt like that rebellious teenager again, but now his parents had been sent for by the headmaster. He snapped the television off, poured himself an inch of whiskey and sat again. The chair creaked, then the room filled with silence.

Within minutes restlessness overwhelmed him. He went to his room, donned his rabat, collar and suitcoat and went out. On the street he turned automatically toward the convent. He stopped in front of it and stared up at the one room from which light shone. Hers? Had she seen the news? Did they even have television in there? With a shock he realized he didn't know. He'd known nuns all his life, but at what distance! Tonight he wanted to know how she was feeling. Was she afraid? But why should he know her innermost thoughts if he didn't know what color her hair was? He had watched her walking in that procession, watched the swish of her skirts, waiting for a glimpse of her flesh, a flash of white at the ankle or the nape of her neck, as if such meager sights would have opened to him her secrets. The arms and ankles and hair of certain premodern nuns were more alluring, vastly more erogenous, than the displayed pubes of vacuous movie stars are today. Michael was disgusted with himself. It's sexual, he thought. Only sexual! But he shook himself. Of course that wasn't so. It wasn't *only* anything.

He suddenly had the image of himself as a moonstruck courtier looking up at the window of the infinitely unattainable princess in her tower, and he laughed. Where was his mandolin? He laughed. Instead of long golden tresses up which he could climb, she had a shaved head. His life was a fairy tale on its ear. He was jealous of the charming prince for whom she was saving herself, but, alas, that was Jesus.

He realized for the first time that he had become in some way ridiculous. He was worried about her? But she was not the one who had, apparently, handed herself over to a piety of deference and submissiveness. Why wonder if she was afraid when, so much more to the point, he was. Afraid of Cardinal Spellman? Monsignor Ellis? Robert Moses? But Michael Maguire had medals to prove his courage. What were such old coots to him? What had happened to him over these years? But he knew. He had known all along.

It humiliated Michael to admit it, but what he was afraid of was the world outside the seminary, outside Orders, outside the Church. He was afraid of the world's dreary rootlessness, its shallowness, its paucity of transcendent meanings, what seemed to him a vast milieu of self-squandering. He equated it both with the shrill terror of the battlefield and with the devouring angst of his years in prison. The Church had saved him and had become his refuge, the rock on which he'd built a life for the sake of others. But somehow this fine, one might even say noble, choice had been trivialized, demeaned. He was no longer an honorable man whose strength of will was legendary; he'd been reduced by the process of ''priestly formation'' to a passive, dependent subject. Now that he had, almost despite himself, dared to defy the Great Parents—and hadn't he done even that out of the arrogant illusion that he was supposed to be in charge, at the head of parades?—he was terrified of getting slapped down. And for now at least he depended totally on the will of his superiors for his place in the snug, safe haven of the Church. So of course he was afraid of the cardinal and the monsignor. They were the ones who could force him out, exclaustrate him.

But wait! With startling clarity he saw that Sister Anne

Edward was the one to be wary of, the one to fear. He saw that she was going to be the one to take the weight now, and that if he stood with her, he was gone. He would be kicked into the world, alone and with nothing. He would have kept faith with her, but he would have failed his vocation, his commitment and God. He would be cursed forever.

But how could he not stand with her? He had encouraged her, supported her, cheered her on. It was Lennie Pace all over again, but now his immunity from consequences, his own safety, wasn't up to luck or the bad marksmanship of the enemy. It was up to him.

Years later he told me that he walked to Greenwich Village that night, thinking to visit me. I was by then shackled by Freshman Composition to my junior post at Fordham. He realized at the last moment, rightly, I think, that I would have understood his anxiety less well even than one of the crusty priests he lived with. He was suffering a particular kind of panic, the discovery that beneath the illusion of clerical strength and altruism, he was utterly without direction, will or potency. Priests, he thought, could understand this, and that made him all the more afraid of not being one. He continued to walk all the way to the Battery, and then back. "In the dark night of the soul," Fitzgerald said, "it is always three o'clock in the morning." Michael did not know it, but it was a measure of his courage that he simply allowed himself to feel that desolation, even though he was years from understanding it. He was wrong to think it was just seminarians who panic when they finally see what they've become. Hell, every man has a night like that soon after the trajectory of his life suggests itself. That's when most of us get serious about drinking or sex or work or prayer. Michael walked, he told me later, just walked.

He followed Broadway up through Times Square. A derelict, sprawled against a building, spied his Roman collar and called out, "Hey, look at that! A fucking priest!"

Michael waved. "How'd you know?" And they both laughed.

At the newsstand on Forty-second he bought the morning papers. There was nothing on the *Times*'s front page or the *Trib*'s, but the *Daily News* blared, "Moses: 'The Nun's a

Thief!' '' and featured a photo of Sister Anne Edward above the caption, "Sister Mary Felony."

Michael studied the picture. Her eyes were large and, framed by the black headgear, emphatic, looking directly at the camera, directly at him. Her face seemed extraordinarily expressive, caught in a moment of intensity, and he could almost hear her describing what Holy Cross School meant to the children, to the families, to the nuns who'd given their lives to it and to the thousands of New Yorkers who'd learned to think and believe there. She was the defender of them all, and their rights had become the center of her life. Michael knew he was not like her in that.

He folded the papers under his arm and walked slowly through the last of night, aware of the sour air of the city in his nostrils and on his tongue. It seemed to him that the recognitions he had wearily come to finally, even those, were things he could find a way to live with. But here was another one, and it was impossible; he was not concerned with the school or the parish or even his own vocation as much as he was concerned with her.

From his room he telephoned as early as he dared. When the phone was answered Michael had a moment of panic in which he couldn't remember her name, and he felt very foolish. A nun answered brusquely, "Holy Cross Convent."

"May I speak to Sister Anne Edward, please?" He had an adolescent's dread of identifying himself. He didn't recognize the awkward boy his feelings had reduced him to. It was a mode he'd bypassed altogether.

"One moment," the nun said, and he was relieved.

When Sister Anne came on there was no animation in her voice.

"Sister Anne, it's me, Michael. Forgive me if I'm calling too early." He tried to picture her. Was she dressed? Was the phone pressed against her black bonnet? When they went down the hall for the telephone did they cover their heads?

"I've been up forever, Michael."

"Me too," he said. "I never went to bed." Walking away the night after years of monastic discipline had been, even in his mood, an adventure and his exhaustion pleased him.

Indicating it was like bragging. "I couldn't sleep after the news show. I wanted to say you were magnificent. I almost called you right then. I was really proud of you."

Sister Anne was taken aback by what he said and for a moment couldn't speak. He would learn soon enough that his simple statement of support thrilled her, relieved her, enabled her once more to believe in what she'd done. She'd been expecting him to back away. "If you had called," she said, "you'd have found the line busy. Mother Superior called from Tarrytown."

"What did she say?"

"I'm transferred."

"What?"

"I'm leaving shortly, Michael. I'm glad you called. It's a chance to say goodbye."

"But why? Everything you said was perfect. You even gave the chancery its way out." He knew it wasn't true even as he said it, and in a part of himself he didn't approve of, he hoped they would get her out, that they'd make her disappear.

"I didn't have permission."

"For what?"

"For anything. The procession, which she called 'a profane use of the sacred'; the television interview, which she called 'the height of impudence.' "

"You weren't impudent."

"I *felt* impudent, Michael. I really did. It communicated. Mother said I was contemptuous. And do you know what?" Michael realized that she had begun to weep. "I am."

They were both silent for a moment, then Michael said, "But Sister Rita backed you up, didn't she? She's the local superior. She was in on everything."

"Mother gave it to her too. She 'deceived the pastor!' We're both . . . Oh, Michael, Mother said they're pressing charges. They're claiming the blueprints are stolen property."

"That's ridiculous, though. It's a red herring."

"Rita's frightened. It's not her fault. She's the one who said I didn't have permission."

"Oh, God."

"It's not her fault. You can't imagine what it feels like over here, like we've done something awful. Apparently the cardinal's very upset. He called Mother himself. He's furious. He says I put him on the spot."

Michael laughed. "I guess you did."

Sister Anne Edward laughed too. "I did, didn't I?"

"Wonderfully. I admire you enormously." He paused, to choose his next words carefully. This was thin ice but he wasn't flashing across it this time. "And I'd be proud to take my share of the blame with you."

"Michael, you can't! You're just a deacon. The cardinal would fire you in a minute. I'm telling you, he's furious."

"But, God, Anne, I led the parade! We all did it. You. Me. Sister Rita. Even Father Mahon."

"Well, I'm the one on record."

"But you shouldn't be alone."

"Michael, I can take it!" she said, suddenly impatient. "I knew what I was doing. Let me see it through."

His lungs clutched in his throat. He couldn't think what to say.

She said quietly, "I loved going down Ninth Avenue with you. It felt wonderful to me. I felt free and strong and was doing something I believed in. I still believe in it. And I'm grateful to you for that." He sensed her gratitude and her affection; once he'd have soared with happiness for either.

She was letting him off the hook. If he was going to stay on the hook with her, now was the time to say so. But he simply couldn't. It was a moment that he'd remember for the rest of his life.

"Where are they sending you?" That's it; a cool question, a little distance.

"The Mother House for now."

"In Tarrytown?"

"Yes."

"I'll call you."

The nun laughed, but not bitterly, as far as he could tell. "Not there you won't."

"I'll come and see you. I'll pass as your confessor."

"What I'll need is a lawyer. Michael?"

"Yes?"

"Be careful." And she hung up.

He stared at the phone, thinking, What is this? The Iron Curtain?

Michael found Father Mahon in the common room, drink in hand, though it wasn't nine yet. He was hunched over the *Herald-Tribune* spread on the hassock. When he looked up at Michael he was smiling. "He's dead," he said.

"Who?"

"Moses. Did you see what he said?"

"I did."

Father Mahon laughed and slapped the paper and leaned back, spilling his drink. "He's slipping. The old Bob Moses would have kept his mouth shut and won. He'd have said he was too busy planning the World's Fair, and then they'd have asked him about that. Now the son of a bitch thinks he can say whatever the hell pops into his head."

"I think they might be serious," Michael said. "I just talked to Sister Anne Edward and she said they're threatening to press charges."

The priest stared at him for a moment. "But the plans aren't stolen."

"It says 'Property of Triborough' all over them."

"But you got them from the cops."

"I did, that's right. But I don't—"

The phone rang. Father Mahon was the priest on duty and he immediately got up, composed himself and crossed to the wall phone outside the common room. "Guess what?" he said a moment later. "It's your cop friend."

Michael took the call. Then, obviously shaken, he went back in to sit by Father Mahon, and he indicated the priest's drink. "Maybe I should have a belt of that."

"I wouldn't recommend it. What did he say?"

"He had no idea the blueprints were controversial. He assumed I'd returned them two weeks ago."

"And he doesn't want his name associated . . ."

"That's right. I promised to keep him out of it."

Father Mahon sipped his drink and raked what hair he had nervously. He eyed Michael. The booze wasn't calming him the way it usually did. The first drink worked wonders most of the time. He said, "Damn. Now maybe she is a thief."

Michael lit a cigarette, but his hands shook.

Father Mahon was thinking out loud, not quite addressing himself to Michael. "These bastards would spike their mothers for the extra base. And, Jesus, maybe Moses didn't make such a dumb move after all. Suddenly the damn issue isn't the school anymore. It's the blueprints." He fell silent for a moment. When he looked up, his gaze had sharpened. "They can't press charges. Spelly can't let them rough up a nun. He and Moses will have talked already. Moses will agree to lay off. Spelly will agree to get the troublemakers out of here."

"She's gone already."

Father Mahon nodded. "No more processions, no more S.O.S. School year ends. Go ahead with plans. Moses gets his ramp. Spelly gets his cool million, or whatever. Holy Cross gets it in the eye. One, two, three." He drained his glass. "And you, my boy, will have learned a lesson."

"What if I called up the reporter and said I was the thief."

The priest grunted. "I knew you were a war hero. They didn't tell me you were a kamikaze pilot. You ask an easy question. The answer? One, you call up your reporter. Two, Spelly boots your ass out, making you just another schmuck layman for whom he has no responsibility. Three, they *do* press charges and, four, you go to jail." Father Mahon got up and crossed to the bar. "You'd just like to make it a little more difficult for them, wouldn't you?"

"Yes," Michael said. He wanted to find a way to stand by Anne. He wanted to find a way to live with himself.

As the priest poured his drink, he said, "Only one son of a bitch around here can do that."

Michael waited.

Father Mahon took a swallow, then faced him. "Me."

"You?"

He nodded, and he said gravely, without bravado, "I could stop the bastards in their tracks."

Michael waited.

"I was the presiding priest yesterday. I had the vestments on. I had the holy water. That was *my* procession, not some nun's!" His eyes flashed and suddenly there was a veteran preacher's energy in his voice, conviction, solemnity. A throng was before him now, a throng, Michael realized, of reporters.

"I am the priest in charge of Holy Cross School. It is the duty and privilege assigned to me by the pastor of my parish. I am responsible for the welfare of that school, and the idea to save it from the expansion of Lincoln Tunnel was mine! *I* stole those blueprints! *I* told the nuns to make those signs. *I* told the kiddies to march down Ninth Avenue! And I regret none of it. And I come before you now to say that God won't let Robert Moses make a laughingstock out of one of my nuns! A thief indeed! The only thing that girl has ever stolen are the hearts of the countless children to whom she has dedicated her life. Robert Moses, for all his power—and yes, for all the good he has done—must not be allowed to demean the sacred vocation, the infinite sacrifice of every nun in this city! A thief? This Bride of Christ? This woman clothed in mystery? We do not expect those of other faiths to adopt our beliefs, but we insist that they respect them! Robert Moses has insulted every Catholic in New York. The man already controls every park, every bridge, every tunnel, every highway, every public works project! Does he also want to steal, like a *thief,* the archdiocese of New York? Is it his to decide which Catholic child shall have access to a parochial school? Is it his to decide which woman is worthy of the veil? Is it his to decide which Catholic parish lives or dies? I tell you it is not. And if you doubt my word, then I bid you, go downtown to that beautiful old cathedral, named for the patron of the humble Irish immigrants who have broken their backs and spilled their blood to build the great *public* monuments of this city for which Robert Moses, like a *thief,* steals all the credit. Ask the leaders of the great Irish building trades about that! And ask the Irish contractors if *they* think nuns are thieves! And at Saint Patrick's Cathedral, you ask His Eminence Francis Cardinal Spellman who *still* controls the archdiocese of New York and who alone has authority over its parishes and schools and who alone has the cherished responsibility to protect its children from the anti-Catholic assaults of the secular world and its women religious from the gratuitous insults of outsiders! You ask Cardinal Spellman who the thief is! I promise you he will neither repeat nor countenance the vile slander of Robert Moses!"

Father Mahon stopped. He put his drink down. His hand was steady. And then he looked at Michael.

Michael wanted to stand and throw his arms around the priest. Here was a spar to grab hold of! It could keep him from sinking! He said, "Do you think you could repeat that for the record?"

"You're damn right I could."

"You'd take a lot of heat."

Father Mahon laughed. "That's the difference between me and you. I'm 'a priest forever.' " He laughed again, as at his favorite joke. "Spelly would have fired me years ago if he could. He can't fire me now. Anyway, I'm going to make him a hero. The minute Moses thinks Spelly's on the way in, he'll back down."

"I think we should have it in the school cafeteria."

"Will you be with me?"

"Of course," Michael said, but once again he began to calculate the risk. And then, instantly, guilt overwhelmed him. First he'd hidden behind a nun, and now behind a whiskey-priest.

"Just nearby, son. I'd appreciate having you nearby." Father Mahon's eyes filled and he turned toward the bar where his drink was. Then he checked himself. "I better leave this alone for a while."

Michael stood and crossed to him, took his arm and pressed it. "You're a good man, Ed."

"I used to be." For a moment they were suspended in the silence of the room.

"I'll call the reporters," Michael said.

Father Mahon nodded. "I think I'll make a visit to the Blessed Sacrament; collect myself, you know?" He tugged at his collar, straightening it. A wily smile crossed his face. "Let old man Moses dump his shit now on a priest of the Roman Catholic Goddamn Church!"

TWELVE

"**H**E built all these roads, didn't he?"

Sister Anne Edward nodded, but remained silent.

Michael kept his eyes on his driving. He'd borrowed my car, an old Ford famous for not starting on rainy days, but that day was bright and hot. It was mid-July, and Michael had driven out to the Mother House in Tarrytown to pick the nun up. There was a block party at Holy Cross celebrating the victory and Sister Anne Edward, unknown to her, was going to be the guest of honor.

"Saw Mill River, Deegan, Taconic, Cross Bronx, Cross County, Henry Hudson. Incredible," Michael said. "And we beat him."

Sister Anne Edward harrumphed and repeated what Moses had said at his press conference the week before. " 'I planned to build the ramp on Eleventh Avenue at Forty-first Street all along. This confusion is what happens when the public intrudes itself on the planning process prematurely.' "

They both laughed.

And then they fell silent again and watched the gracefully cultivated knolls of the parkway passing by. Moses did build a hell of a lovely highway.

After a few moments Sister Anne Edward said, "My parents live here." She pointed to an exit sign. "Dobbs Ferry."

Michael glanced at her with surprise. Her family had money? He almost asked her; how rude. Instead he said, "They must like having you so close."

She gave him a look. "We don't go home, you know. I

couldn't even attend my sister's wedding last year. My father was wild. He wishes I'd quit."

"Really? How about your mother?"

She shrugged. "She'd rather have the grandchildren, I think, than the Grace. She'd never say that, of course."

He looked at her again. Her parents' ambivalence about her vocation was a sure sign that they'd begun to make it in America. "What does your father do?"

"He's an importer."

"Successful?"

She nodded and smiled. "Diamonds."

Michael whistled dramatically, but perhaps he shouldn't have been surprised. Even if she was typical in her nun's romantic and self-denying attachment to the Lord and to the cloistered sorority, she was unusual in her capacity to muster self-assurance and will when the chips were down. She had not been your typical nun on TV, but that was Dobbs Ferry ego she had fallen back on. Marx was right: everything was a matter of class.

"Industrial diamonds," she said, "not ornamental. He's not Harry Winston." She paused.

Michael thought, Who is Harry Winston?

"He was going to sue the *Daily News* for calling me 'Sister Felony.' He was wild. They both were."

"But not at you?"

"Oh, no. They're not like that. They're on my side." She faced away. "Unlike some people I can think of."

"Has Mother Superior eased off?"

"She doesn't even talk to me."

"I was hoping she'd send you back to Holy Cross now that the dust is settling."

"I'm afraid not. I've been assigned to the library at Mount Saint Vincent's College in the Bronx. I'm going to be dusting books."

"Oh, God! How long will that last?"

"The sister whose place I'm taking was there seventeen years. She'd still be dusting but she died."

"Oh, Anne."

"I'll have all the time in the world, but she said I'm not to paint.'' She let him see how devastated she'd been made to feel.

"You paint?"

"Yes. It's the most important thing about me.''

It seemed to Michael she was rebuking him for his ignorance, and he felt suddenly ill at ease. Why should he have known anything at all about her? They'd hardly ever talked about themselves. He'd visited her three times in June, but they had talked stiffly in the Mother House parlor, and only about the uproar at Holy Cross after Father Mahon's press conference. That he knew so little about her was an affront, perhaps, when compared to the charged air between them, the unexpressed but potent intimacy that he'd felt from her side since that first meeting in the teachers' lunchroom. She had communicated a certain affection, but he was sure she also felt disappointed in him. He had let her take the heat alone, after all, and now she was telling him in detail what that was like. Had she bristled because, really, she was angry at him? No. Not that. She had bristled, he sensed, because she had shared his intensity of feeling, and now his ignorance about her made it seem misplaced. Well, ignorance can be dispelled. "You grew up in Dobbs Ferry?"

"No, Bronxville. We moved when I was in high school. They have a fabulous swimming pool." Was she bragging? No. She was showing him that her parents' affluence had become as strange to her as it would be to him.

"A pool would be great on a day like this, wouldn't it?" He looked over at her, eyed her habit. "You guys must get hot in those things."

She smiled winningly. "They tell us to offer it up for the poor souls in Purgatory. But do you know what I think? In July we *are* the poor souls in Purgatory. I think I'm being punished for sins I committed in an earlier life.''

"Maybe you were a thief.''

"No, no, to deserve this?" She lifted a fold of her habit in her lap. "I must have been an ax-murderer.''

"That explains everything. You're deadly.''

Michael knew that she was desolate. He admired her for covering her grief but it wasn't working. If he'd been she it wouldn't have been the prospect of dusting shelves forever that would have depressed him, but the massive disapproval. The parish school's victory had been her defeat. If her superiors disliked her now, didn't that mean, finally, that Jesus did? Wasn't *that* what she'd be feeling? Michael wanted to touch her, to reassure her. Jesus had said, "Let the children come to me." Jesus would love Anne Edward more than ever. "Tell me about the painting you do. Have you been painting long?"

"I studied a year at the Art Students League after high school. They liked my stuff. I wanted to be an artist and a nun both."

"Why do you say 'wanted'?" The word made him nervous. Even if I hadn't pressed him into a study of Gerard Manley Hopkins, Michael knew how difficult it was to square artistic impulses with life in the Church. "Birds build," the poet groused, "but not I."

She did not answer him at first, but only stared out at the snaking road, the passing trees. She leaned into the wind at her window for the air, then faced him. She explained, pensively, "Until now the Order encouraged my work. My novice mistress was a sculptor who'd studied in Europe as a young woman, and she thinks I have real talent. She was the first one who enabled me to take myself seriously. She said I could glorify God with my gift. But now Mother tells me painting was a privilege, and it became the source of my vanity."

"Your vanity?"

"That's what she called it. Anyway, there was a problem even before this. Once I was assigned to Holy Cross my own work came last, just because there was always so much to do in the school. I love the children. I could never say no to them." She stopped talking. Michael thought she was finished. He looked at her. She was staring at him. She said, "I think to be an artist in the religious life, one would have to be in the cloister or in the novitiate or someplace. The only nuns I know of who are serious about art are Benedictines."

"It's hard to think of you as a contemplative. You're too good with people. It would be a waste."

"And dusting library books won't be?" She laughed, but at last her bitterness showed. She looked across at Michael and said, "If I was a contemplative I would have to talk to you through a grille."

"I'd hate that," Michael said quickly.

"Me too." She blushed and began to fuss with the rosary beads in her lap. "It's bad enough this way," she said, her voice barely above a whisper.

Michael knew what she meant. There *was* a grille between them. It thrilled him to think she hated it too.

She looked up brightly and said in a change-the-subject voice, "You know something about the contemplative life, I think."

He shook his head. "Not me."

"I mean the POW camp. I gather your vocation came from that."

"That's *my* previous life. It's like it happened to someone else. Whatever you've read about prison camps, remember this: writers always make life better and worse than it really is."

"But you came out of it wanting to be a priest."

"I did, yes."

"Why?"

This was the first time anyone had ever asked directly for an explanation, and Michael felt his face redden. He deflected her. "You tell me first. Why are you a nun? A rich girl, an artist, a rebel. How'd it happen?"

She shrugged. "I told you. High school. I fell in love." She looked right at him. "Jesus ravished me," she said blatantly. "He carried me away."

"And now?"

"I still love him. And of course, now I have my vow. But I haven't heard much from him lately. I think he's away on business." She grinned, then added, "I'm not a swooning teenager anymore, but I still believe. Now it's your turn."

Michael was in trouble. How could he possibly match her honesty? Or her feeling? Jesus was a compelling biblical figure to him, not a lover. "I want to serve the Church," he said automatically. It was a weak statement, and he knew it. He took refuge in lines from Maritain. "I want 'to celebrate the Eucharist, to assist the sick and dying, to console the afflicted, to instruct the Catholic people, to intercede for all and to bear witness to the truth.' ''

"All that and golf on Wednesdays."

"Those are in fact the things I want to do. I didn't mean to sound pompous."

"Seminarians and young nuns have to sound pompous when they bare their souls."

"Are you baring your soul?"

"I would if I knew how. To you."

Michael was aware that the steering wheel was slick with perspiration. My hippo of a car lumbered along the serpentine parkway, and he found that he had let the speed drop to twenty-five. He gunned it back up to forty-five. Anne's simple statement unhinged him. What would happen if they put *those* feelings into words?

His reticence didn't stop her. "I'm having my problems, as you can tell. I have no one to talk to."

"You can talk to me, Anne," he said, not glibly. "I'd like to be your friend." It was a dangerous statement but still within bounds, he thought. Wasn't the ideal of such friendship held out to priests and nuns by hagiography that so emphasized the bonds between Saint Therese and John of the Cross, Saint Francis of Assisi and Saint Clare and, for that matter, Abelard and Eloise? Even Pius XII was known to have had for over forty years a special friendship with the nun who served as his secretary. But Michael was hip enough to know how easily such impulses between celibate men and women, who were poised on the brink of permanent adolescence, slipped over into puppy love, spiritual fingerfucking. He was right to be uptight.

Anne for her part veered away from the issue. She brought her hands together in front of her mouth, impishly.

"Can I tell you who I remind myself of? You won't laugh? Or think me 'vain'?"

"Of course I won't."

"Joan of Arc," she blurted; then added with mock solemnity, "she was condemned by the Church too."

"The judges of Rouen weren't the Church, Anne. Cardinal Spellman's not the Church and neither is your mother superior. They're wrong and they're unfair, but you mustn't think of them as the Church. The Church is the people of Holy Cross and they love you."

"They'll barely remember me, Michael."

"You saved their school and they know it." Michael almost told her of the plan to honor her at the block party, but checked himself. The secret—what joy it portended—was more precious than before. "They appreciate what you're putting up with."

"Will they appreciate it seventeen years from now?"

What could he say?

After a moment, she touched his arm. "I'm sorry. I'm having an authority problem."

"I don't blame you. You've been blasted by the very ones who should have supported you."

"You know something, Deacon? You're the only one who has. . . ." She stopped and leaned toward the window for a moment. ". . . You and my parents. I've been feeling somewhat bereft." She closed her eyes. Wisps of her hair tore free in the wind; blond, he thought. "The judges of Rouen may not have been the whole Church, but they sure were a part of it."

"They made Joan a saint, right?"

"I suspect she'd have settled for a few more years as an ordinary mortal." She faced him again. "Look, that's the point. I love Holy Cross. I love the Church. I love my Order. But I'm not going to give up my painting for any of them. I'm not going to be a martyr. If that's what the religious life requires, then I want no part of it."

"I wouldn't want part of it either, if I thought that's what it required."

"But you don't."

"No, not at all. You're right that authority is the problem here. We agree about that and we agree on what to do when authority is in the wrong. Hell, you take it on the best way you can. You rant against it." Was he really saying this? It was an act of his and he knew it. And she would know it. How had he ranted on her behalf? He felt nowhere near this brave, which of course was why he pretended to. "You try to change it. But you accept in principle its fundamental structure."

"Even if that means martyrdom?"

"Martyrdom is your metaphor, not mine. That's not how I feel about my life."

"Metaphor?!"

"I—"

"You don't feel this way because you're not the one who's on the spot!"

"I know that," he said quickly, guiltily. How he wished she wouldn't say it. "I've kept my head in the trench, and I don't feel right about it at all. You've really been out there by yourself." He glanced over at her and saw tears on her cheek. It happened that just ahead there was one of those rest area/picnic groves off the parkway and he swung into it and stopped the car. He leaned toward her and touched her shoulder while she wept as quietly as she could. She seemed so vulnerable. How he wanted to protect her, but he knew how he had failed her.

As if she read that in him she raised her hand to his and pressed it against her shoulder, and her body, until then a remote abstraction, took over the field of his perception. He felt suddenly through her habit the sharply defined bone of her left clavicle. He became aware of the clean odor of her skin, that nun's soap smell he'd noticed in the teachers' room. But now it seemed intensely erotic to him. She was more woman than nun and for a moment it was possible to forget all that kept them apart. He touched a tear at her cheek with the back of his free hand, then let his finger fall to her lips. She opened them and took his finger between her teeth and bit him just sharply enough to cause him pain.

He trembled. She was waiting. Ravished? Had she said ravished?

He pulled away.

She leaned against the door and turned her face from him. All he could see was the black of her habit.

When he resumed driving, he used his old trick, reciting Scripture, but to himself. "No one hates his own flesh," Paul said. What the fuck did Paul know? "He nourishes and takes care of it as Christ cares for the church." Right. Sure he does. Oh yeah.

Later, in a disembodied voice, he asked if it would be

possible to see her paintings sometime, and she said yes, that very day, for there were several at the Holy Cross convent. She was polite about it. She'd love for him to see them. By the time they arrived at the parish they had their controls in place again. But it was different. Their shared embarrassment— they had a secret now—was what made them friends.

The block party was an ethnic bash: refried beans on soda bread; Italian ice in waffle cones. Children had their faces painted. The fire hydrant at the far end of the block was open, and boys in underpants wildly dashed in and out of the geyser. On the church steps an accordionist and a fiddler rendered Irish jigs while a couple of dozen elderly men and women with bright Irish faces and slightly glassy eyes kept each other company, nodding to the music. The gents kept threatening to ask the wizened colleens to dance, but never did. In the street, in the center of the block, several nuns had organized a game of Red Rover. Ten or fifteen children were arranged on a side, and every time the line held there were great cheers.

Michael felt that after years of pacing a room alone—for compared to this the seminary seemed that isolated, that pointless—he'd been released to the world. The festivity and the sun and the city itself all seemed to applaud not only him and not only Sister Anne at his side, but the two of them together. Now that they had their distance again, and in the context of the parish celebration, he dared to think that somehow they might yet find a way to ransom one another. He didn't leave her side. Not this time.

In the schoolyard the older kids had yet another game of kickball going. A man in a white shirt with bunched sleeves was rolling the big balloonlike ball at the kicker; it was Father Mahon. Michael and Sister Anne made their way toward him. When he saw them he pulled out of the game and came over to embrace Anne warmly. He tugged her back down the block toward the church. Parishioners greeted her, though the nuns kept their distance. Michael was looking for Sister Rita because he knew that Anne would be looking for her too.

A few moments later all the activity was suspended as the throng gathered at the foot of the church stairs. When Father Mahon had their attention he thanked the ladies who had prepared the food and the men who'd hung the decorations, and he said he hoped everyone would play games and dance in the street until dark. After that he hoped they wouldn't keep the fathers awake since everyone knew that priests in their rectories went to bed early and often. They all laughed, the more so because he was poking fun at himself. Then he introduced Mrs. Heaney, the president of the Mothers' Club. She could hardly be heard, but that didn't matter because everyone knew what she was saying. It was her job to present Sister Anne Edward with the felt banner the mothers had made. The young nun was quite moved, but she managed to unfold the gift and hold it up so that everyone could see it. "Sister Anne Edward," it read, "you S'd our S. Thank you. With Love from the Parents and Children of H.C." The people applauded loudly and Sister, for the barest moment, buried her face in the banner.

I was there. I stood on the edge of the crowd, utterly ignorant of the meaning of what had just happened, but nevertheless affected by it. That was the first time I'd laid eyes on Sister Anne Edward and I remember straining to see her because of the notoriety she'd received, and also because Michael had described the impression she'd made on him. As was arranged, I'd come uptown to pick up my car. Sister Anne was to return to Tarrytown with one of her fellow nuns that evening.

While I made my way through the crowd toward Michael, I was thinking what happy people those parishioners seemed to be, so unlike the sullen freshmen for whom I was endlessly diagraming compound, complex and simple sentences on blackboards in those days. I hadn't expected to find myself envying Michael, but as I saw the open fondness with which the people of that neighborhood engulfed him, I did.

I hooked up with him and his nun friend just as another nun did, the principal, Sister Rita. And so it was that I witnessed the awkward encounter between those two women, once so dear to each other. I could, of course, have had no idea how decisive that meeting would be not only for Sister Anne Edward, but for each of us.

"Oh Anne, it's so good to see you," Sister Rita said, but she made no move to embrace her or to shake her hand.

"Mother was kind to let me come," Anne Edward said stiffly, but even I sensed the power of her emotion. Was she afraid? Angry? Hurt? Was she going to cry?

"We managed to get Monsignor Ellis to call her." The principal smiled awkwardly. "What old nun can refuse the pastor?" She paused, then added, "I wanted to write you."

"I wish you had."

Rita lowered her eyes. "I was advised against it," she said miserably.

Then Michael noticed me, and he made the introductions. I knew I'd interrupted something, but it was clear even to me that the women needed more privacy than was available there for the talk they wanted to have. Michael described me as his oldest friend, and he draped his arm around my shoulder, but the tension between the nuns continued to dominate. They moved, as if to go off together. Sister Anne Edward said to Michael, "Thank you for coming for me. I enjoyed our talk."

God, they're formal with each other, I thought. Like Mennonites. What did I know?

Michael said, "Don't forget, before you go back, you're going to let me see your paintings."

"That's right," Anne said, with a relief that first displayed to me her desire to be with him, and that flash of warmth unaccountably filled me with relief too.

But the other nun interrupted. "I'm sorry, Sister, that's one of the things we have to talk about."

"What do you mean?"

"Your paintings are gone."

"Gone?"

"I had to send them to the Mother House. I sent all your things over a month ago."

"But they never gave them to me. Not my paintings! What did they do with them?"

"I don't know." Sister Rita lowered her eyes in exactly the way she had before. I realized it was a form of hers, an act of piety. There was even a name for it, I would learn: "custody of the eyes."

Not even I believed that she didn't know.

"You *do* know!" Sister Anne said, furious.

"I'll tell you later."

"Tell me now please, Sister."

"All right." The nun spoke as I imagined nuns spoke to their confessors, with more whine than penitence. "Mother told me at first to destroy your paintings. She said she should never have allowed you to pursue it. I pleaded with her. She relented and told me to send them to her instead."

"So that *she* could destroy them! Why didn't you call me? Oh Rita!"

Sister Rita looked up sharply. "You know why I didn't call you!"

"No I don't. I truly don't."

The women were suddenly at a standoff. Each had unfurled what she thought of as the truth. I glanced at Michael who hinted at his own frustration with a quick upturn of his eyes. I mistook his attitude at that point for clerical or at least masculine condescension.

Sister Rita abruptly turned away and cut through the crowd. Sister Anne Edward faced Michael. "Do you still want to see my work?" Her voice trembled with emotion. I recognized her defiance even without understanding it. And I sensed how large this moment was for her, without knowing why.

"Yes, of course."

"Can you drive me?"

Michael looked at me. I'd been counting on my car, but I said, "No problem, go ahead, I'll see you later."

Michael shook his head. "Come with us." He looked at her. "That would be okay, wouldn't it?"

I sensed her disappointment; how could Michael want me along? But she said, "Sure. The more the merrier."

And that is how it happened that I drove them that afternoon to her parents' house in Dobbs Ferry.

That town struck me as a place brimming with happiness, or is that how those of us raised and still living in the grim corners of the crowded city always felt in our rare forays out to the posh suburbs? Her family's house was large, set on a carefully landscaped knoll and surrounded by elm trees, which made it seem more private than it probably was. It certainly seemed less hot than Manhattan had, though we arrived in the middle of the afternoon and the temperature must have been near a hundred. The trees cast a benign pattern of moving shadow over the house, but that was no relief. I could not imagine how Michael managed in that collar and suit of his, much less his nun friend in her habit. The relevant heat had seemed, of course, to be in her, that plugged volcano, and I sensed her fury and her hurt despite the inconsequential chatter my presence imposed on them. Our ride up the Saw Mill River would have been less awkward if they had sat together in the back seat of my car. That arrangement at least would have reflected the reality of our relationships and allowed them perhaps a snatch or two of real talk about the inflamed decisions they were coming to. As it was, Michael had insisted on her riding in the front with me. I didn't understand yet how desperate he was to get his distance from her. I only knew that I felt entangled between them at once and I didn't like it.

The house, when we entered it, was cool. Sister Anne Edward ran ahead, calling for her parents. We followed as far as the entrance hallway which was dominated by an elaborately curving staircase with a gleaming mahogany banister. Michael grimaced at me and shrugged. We mirrored each other, slouching with our hands in our pockets, trying to seem casual, though obviously we felt like interlopers.

"I'm sorry to drag you out here," he whispered.

"No sweat." I pointedly ran a finger through the slick of perspiration on my forehead.

"Look at this." He crossed behind me to a large painting of a barn wall in winter. In it snow was falling in a keen wind; icicles hung from a wrecked gutter and the gleam of frost defined the grain of the unpainted wood. The painting captured perfectly the sparkle of winter. "Just looking at it cools me off."

"Is it signed?"

The name *C.P. Campbell* was carefully printed in the corner, and the year, 1956.

I stood back and said, "It's stunning."

"Thank you," Sister Anne said, from behind me.

We faced her. "It's yours?"

She nodded and looked at it wistfully, as if remembering

flakes of snow whirling around her canvas. She grinned. "That's the north wall of our barn at our farm in Vermont. I painted it in each of the seasons. My father says he keeps this one out here because he can't afford to heat it." She approached the painting, resting her fingers on its frame for a moment, as if to reassure herself that it, at least, existed. Then she brightened. "I'll show you others, but first come meet my parents. They're outside."

We followed her through the narrow corridor that ran behind the staircase. The walls there were hung with several dozen family photographs, and I saw, displayed like treasures, the faces of children, a girl in a hammock, two boys clutching a dog, a man at the helm of a boat, a beautiful woman posed in a satin gown on the very staircase we had just left behind. They seemed creatures from a brighter world, and the flash of their smiles filled me with envy.

The corridor led to a solarium, and its french doors opened on a broad stone terrace. A lawn sloped gradually down over a distance of about fifty yards to a blue and white island in the green, a swimming pool. A man and woman were reclining on chaises longues and they remained oblivious to our approach until Sister Anne clutched her rosary and her hem and broke for them, crying out, "Mommy! Dad!"

"My God, it's Syr!" her father cried. "It's Syr!" He was up and running to meet her, a grinning, vigorous man in his fifties, tanned and muscular. When they embraced, I felt something of a jolt, as if the shock of their bodies colliding registered in me, but I think it was more the sight of that large, quite physical man clad only in his bathing suit taking that sternly garbed nun in his arms and whirling her around and around so that her black habit flew.

Her mother, knotting a terry robe, quickly joined them. When they hugged the two women burst into tears.

Michael and I stood oafishly by until her father noticed us. He approached Michael with his hand extended. "Hello, Father! Welcome! I'm Ed Campbell."

"I'm Michael Maguire, Ed. And this is Frank Durkin."

As Campbell shook hands with us he eyed his daughter. It was obvious something was wrong. She was sobbing against her mother's shoulder. When she realized we were watching she pulled herself together and brought her mother over to meet us.

Mrs. Campbell was a slim, tanned woman whose hair was partly blond and partly gray. She had the posture of a tower and her face, though lined, seemed young. When I took her hand I felt drawn in by her, and my unease left me. Her name was Anne.

Anne and Edward, I realized. Anne Edward. My first lesson in the naming of nuns.

Ed Campbell offered us beers, but then a better idea hit him. "How about a swim, fellows?" Before we could respond he led the way back to the house, saying that between him and his two sons they had suits galore. As we followed, Michael looked back at Anne who watched us smiling, as if the pleasure for her in seeing her strong-willed generous father override us was enough. I glanced back at her once more as we went in the house and was struck by—I could say *moved* by—the mammoth sacrifice nuns make. She had forsaken herself, and even there in the embrace of her home the stigma of her clothing, of her choice, set her apart. No swimming for Sister.

But I saw too, amazingly, why she'd done it. Only in that setting, heightening as it did the extremity of her situation, could I grasp its meaning. In her vowed life, in her hyperchaste body, in her loss of free will, she contradicted the world itself, its bondage to time and its steady quest for comfort. On that day in her merciless garments she contradicted the weather itself, and that act alone seemed transcendent. She was Crane's "wink of eternity," a spot of black in the glare on which it was possible for an instant to rest an eye. The great oppression is that things are what they seem and no more. Nuns deny it. How simple once one understands. And what fools they are unless the rest of us are wrong. Nuns teach us, if we let them, that we want to be wrong. If we don't let them, they're no bother unless your best friend gets involved with one.

In her presence so far that day I had been uncomfortable, and I hadn't fathomed Michael's apparent attraction to her, but now I saw her as an image less of rejection than invitation. In her radical straining against the flow of things was there some meaning for me? For my sense-ridden but senseless life as an aging boy-wonder whose zeal for literature had been swamped in the backwash of classroom drudge-work, and whose once cherished, oh-so-modern belief in "the dearest freshness deep down things," in the "shining shook foil" of "experience" had grown stale, like bread left out on the table overnight? What began in the Village as a permanent "liberty" in the sailor's sense had become for my generation, or my crowd at least, even as we drifted from the great promise of school into rather ordinary jobs, the lockstep, nose-to-tail of canine heat. Even as I gave my stirring early lectures on "The Wreck of the Deutschland" (which Hopkins dedicated by the way to five Franciscan nuns), I was always half thinking of the weekend and of getting laid. This nun made me uncomfortable, I realized, because her chastity-on-display seemed addressed to the likes of me, and I could admit it only when I'd met her parents whose lively bond with each other seemed not Manichean, as one like me would expect in the progenitors of the celibate, but downright voluptuous.

So Sister Anne Edward was straining against the flow of herself, as if her point wasn't at all that the world is evil, but that, even though it is good, it is far from enough. Life even in a loving family, even in a beautiful house, even as a promising artist, is not enough. How much less is it enough if life is among lonely Village girls who dream of Edna St. Vincent Millay and so believe us when we tell them that we part with our despair by parting our legs and whispering to each other like literary whores—give me "Baby, oh baby!" any day—"Death devours all lovely things," or "Love is not all; it is not meat or drink." After we have cheapened not only talk but good writing, no wonder the woman of silence reminds us that there is more, far more, not only than the worst, but than the best. That was why the radical denial implicit in Anne Edward's vocation had taken the form of a radical embrace. Had she been raised by lovers? Then she had to have for herself the Greatest Lover of them all. To my own surprise, I understood. In my last glimpse of her across the lawn I marked how she bent her head toward her mother and they laughed, and a rare affection fluttered above them.

When, suited, we went back out and across the lawn to the pool, they were gone.

Michael and I plunged into the water while Ed went back into the house for the beers. We rejoiced in the sheer release from the heat and I, for myself, felt momentarily freed of my Young Werther melancholy. The thrill of the wet cold enlivened me and I had, as it were, a brief foretaste of what was soon to come. Michael and I swam independently at first, then splashed one another boyishly, like a couple of Cooper Street kids away at camp for the first time.

Michael noticed before I did. He stood up in the pool abruptly, the water at his waist, his strong chest dripping, and his jaw suddenly slack. I turned to see what caused this shock in him.

She had just stepped off the terrace onto the lawn and was coming toward us in an unornamented, unskirted dark bathing suit of the sort competitors wore, but it registered as nudity, the simplified lines of her limbs, her long, elegant legs, her bare arms undulating sexually, as if to walk was an erotic act. Her cropped blond hair was short as a boy's, which made her long neck seem flaunted. Watching a lewd stranger coyly raise her nightgown at a window would not have been more electrifying than watching this virgin place one bare foot after the other in the grass. Her naked ankles! Her undraped thighs! She came not self-consciously but solemnly, as if taking possession of territory or enacting a rite of primitive religion. Drops of water clung to her. Had she just showered? To shave herself perhaps? Her skin was white as porcelain, cool, the Victorian ideal, but she seemed otherwise like a figment of the avant-garde, something out of Existentialist Paris, lacking only a cigarette and a hurt expression.

A faint smile and the barest color in her cheeks were the only hint of the bashfulness she surely felt. How long had it been since she'd so exposed herself? I pictured her before her childhood mirror, removing her anachronous garments, the black yardage, the linen at her throat, the constricting starched bodice, the layered underwear. And when she saw her parts whole, her breasts with nipples rising and her hips, her broad pelvis, the delta between her legs, her body in its prime come back to her, did her juice flow? Certainly she knew what an apparition of desire she would be to us.

In fact, I heard from Michael's lips a quick short cry, an "Oh!" that made me look at him.

His face was the face of a man who'd taken a severe blow. Without the water to float in I think he'd have been reeling. His disorientation was apparent, and his questions flashed in his eyes. Who was she? And what did anything he'd learned or vowed or prayed over have to do with the agony of this wanting? What were all those memorized verses of Writ to him now? He wanted her and his wanting trapped him. By then the choice was not between her and God or between her and the Church or between her and the priesthood, but between her and himself.

Because I cared for him as a friend my thought for an instant was how to help him. I knew right then of course that his pain would not be soothed until he took possession of her, and I think I knew also that eventually, no matter what promises to whom were broken, he would.

When I looked back at her I forgot him. As she approached the tile apron of the pool her step quickened, and she raised her arms together over her head, flaring her breasts, and then springing into the air, feet together, carving an arc through the heat with her flawless dive.

She swam underwater half the length of the pool, right at Michael, like a predator, and she surfaced two feet in front of him. "Hello," she said. But her meaning was, Here I am. What are you going to do?

"Venus Rising," Michael answered, but the rakish greeting had nothing to do with what he felt. I read his agony, though I didn't understand it yet. He was naked to himself for the first time. What was he going to do? Precisely nothing. Why? Because he *was* nothing. He would never know humiliation like that again.

She began to blush. Clearly she had planned her moves to this point, but no farther. She folded her arms across her breasts and let her face fall. Neither Michael nor I looked away from her. It would have been the merciful thing to do, for her counterfeit boldness had failed her utterly and she felt terribly exposed. But it was impossible to take one's eyes away. She was simply the most beautiful woman either of us had ever seen.

To my astonishment I was the one to steer us past that moment by saying simply, "Your father calls you 'Syr.' "

She nodded and laughed. "For 'Syrup.' Karo syrup." She laughed again. "My name is Carolyn."

Michael said sadly, quietly, "It's a lovely name, Carolyn."

And she raised her face to him exactly as she might have had he hooked a finger under her chin. I saw the worship in her eyes. For years I would try to forget that moment and its meaning. They beheld each other so steadily, so exclusively and for so long that I became embarrassed and dove under the water.

When I surfaced she had swum away. Her parents were approaching with refreshments. Michael called me, drew close and whispered, "As soon as we can you have to get me out of here."

Carolyn never returned to the convent. As Michael and I left that day, he took her aside for a moment. I saw them kiss, like a pair of figurines. Tears ran freely down her face when she followed him to the car, then stood waving as we drove away.

Michael didn't speak.

Finally, as we crossed into Manhattan, I had to ask him. "What did you say to her?"

"I said 'Goodbye.' I can't see her again."

"Why not?" I asked, though I knew the answer. I asked it calmly, though my heart soared with happiness. I cared not a whit for his agony then, and though I was in its debt, I did not for once admire his ruthless will.

"Because I love her," he said simply.

I nodded, as if my only meaning was that I understood.

THIRTEEN

OUR TWA flight from Tel Aviv arrived at Kennedy at 1:45 in the afternoon. My daughter and I took an hour to clear customs. Molly was carrying only a shoulder bag and I had nothing, save my toothbrush and passport, but that heightened the official's suspicion. When he asked me my occupation I wanted to say smuggler.

Then we were in a taxi sailing up the ramp of the Triborough Bridge. Ah, Moses! The cabbie cut dangerously in front of a truck. Molly and I exchanged a glance, then smiled; this was more dangerous than the terrorist-ridden road from Jerusalem.

New York was golden in the afternoon sun and my eyes feasted on the skyline, the most familiar sight there was. Only then, beholding the jagged frieze, did I realize how I had hungered for this city. I was nearly overwhelmed by a longing for the life I had denied myself.

The taxi took us directly to the cathedral.

Not Saint Patrick's; the funeral was to be held that night at the Anglican Cathedral of Saint John the Divine on Amsterdam Avenue near Columbia University, and that had loosed a flood of feelings that surprised me and disturbed me. At first I thought Carolyn had preferred the Episcopal Church and I was shocked. Had they converted? I asked Molly, and she said no. They had quietly continued to worship as Catholics all those years, mainly at the Jesuit parish not far from their apartment on West Seventieth Street. Since it was a church staffed by Order priests who had never known him personally—though perhaps some of them had played basketball against him—Michael had been able to go there with a certain, essential feeling of anonymity. Molly said that he and her mother had come to love the place.

But it hadn't mattered.

When, after Michael's death, Carolyn had called the Jesuit pastor, he had regretfully referred her to the chancery of the archdiocese. The chancellor had told her that Michael would not be allowed to be buried from a Catholic church. As an unlaicized but married priest he was an excommunicant, the archbishop had said. Canon law forbade him both a Church funeral and burial in sacred ground. The archbishop regretted it too, and he was sorry it came as a surprise. But, he'd said, he was sure Michael Maguire himself had understood the consequences of the decisions he'd made.

I was too stunned, when Molly told me, to realize how furious I was and how hurt, for myself as well as for Michael. What an obscenity such a last rejection was, even if, by Church standards, it was somehow defensible. I was confused by the fact that Molly seemed to have no particular reaction to the profound insult her mother had suffered. Was that because she expected no better from the Church? She didn't believe in God, she'd said. Wasn't it to her advantage to be free of those petty distinctions, as if, on any rational scale, it mattered, now that Michael was dead, which church he was buried from? Hell, from Molly's point of view Saint John the Divine *would* have been preferable. It at least was an authentic Gothic masterpiece, far more beautiful and, even unfinished, more imposing than the Fifth Avenue bauble, Saint Patrick's. And no mere museum like the Cloisters, Saint John the Divine had at least been the scene of vital human events of broad significance: huge ecumenical gatherings on the crisis of the city, on the meaning of the Holocaust, on ending racial conflict. Duke Ellington conducted his concerts of sacred music in that cathedral and was buried from it. Great festivals with jugglers and aerialists and minstrels, and countless productions of plays and chorales and symphonies reaffirmed the ancient connection of religion to art. And once, while FBI agents waited nervously to arrest him, Michael preached against the war from the cathedral's great pulpit.

Aside from Cardinal Spellman's famous sermon condemning—and therefore launching—the movie *Baby Doll*, and the funeral of Bobby Kennedy, what had ever happened of more than parochial interest at Saint Patrick's? Ironically, of course, Michael was ordained in its sanctuary, but that would be cited by the chancellor as the very reason his funeral could not happen there.

As the grotesque meaning of the archbishop's statement became fully apparent I involuntarily but graphically conjured an image of him, at once ingratiating and hostile: "The archdiocese regrets, the cardinal might wish otherwise, but the new pope, you see, has reinstated the traditional emphasis on the absolute and permanent character of priestly vows. After a regrettable period of laxity in the wake of the Vatican Council, the Church no longer contradicts herself in these matters." He smiled sadly, in my fantasy, shrugged, turned his hands out. What could one do?

And I was thinking, yes, the new pope. Not the Hamlet Paul VI was, but Shakespeare's Brutus, slayer of brothers. The new pope ran the Church the way the Party wanted to run Poland. Michael Maguire was for a time the Lech Walesa of American Catholicism, and he was not forgiven. It was my mistake, of course, to think he might have been.

So the taxi took us to Saint John the Divine. As we paid the cabbie and got out, the heat blasted us. It was as hot as the desert.

I stood looking up at the mammoth dark structure with its rose window, the tracery dominating the glass in daylight, its portal gargoyles leering down at me, its tympanum saints indifferent, and the carved stonework ribs of the entrance arches soaring to their crowns. The cathedral was too large, as if a mere human person was unworthy to enter alone. We should have gone in as members of a throng. But I reminded myself: *This* cathedral has welcomed outcasts. *This* cathedral has bent itself to Michael.

But I was immobile there before it.

It will be cooler inside, I told myself. The Gothic windows will be brilliantly illuminated by the fierce summer light. Saint John's was a perfect rendition of man's most magnificent expression, and, compared to it, all the box-forms of Manhattan's architecture, from the looming Behemoths downtown to the sterile dwellings across the avenue behind me seemed as impoverished as the thatched-roofed mud cottages in medieval villages, as if contemporary people too invested all their greatest treasure, skill and art, despite themselves, in the house of God.

Still, I did not want to go in there. Michael was laid out in some crypt chapel under the vaulting, tracery, clerestory, triforium, arcade; under buttresses, capitals, mullions, voussoirs, keystones and acres of leaded glass. A cruciform jewel.

But I knew Michael and knew then with a certainty infallible as the pope's that where he belonged that night was at the head of the aisle of even the most undistinguished Catholic church in New York. Good Shepherd, say, in Inwood, which I was sure he never ceased to love. "Durk!" I could hear him screaming at me. "Durk! Don't let them do this to me! Get me back where I belong!" And even in my imagination the panic in his voice was absolute.

In primitive religion the worst fate was to be a lost soul, a spirit improperly dispatched from the world and condemned therefore to an eternity of aimless wandering. And whose religion, when it comes to death, is not primitive? The new pope was right. My fury at him showed it. *These things do matter.* Scratch us and we are all primitives, desperate for the ancient rites done in the ancient way. The pope was only doing what he had to do to protect those rites. Michael Maguire was a priest forever, bound by vows he had renounced. Were we now to say his ordination in Saint Patrick's didn't matter? If that most solemn act of the Church did not matter, what did?

And who was I to judge the chancellor for pronouncing his anathemas? I had cut Michael off before the Church did. I had turned on him even more heartlessly. He had been bound by the implicit vow of our friendship and he had disregarded it. More than anyone he had known what Carolyn meant to me and he had been the only one who could have taken her and he had. Was I now to say his betrayal didn't matter? Hadn't Michael understood, as the chancellor put it, the consequences of his decisions?

What, that he should wander aimlessly forever? Could we mean it? Without the only blessing, the only forgiveness that he'd have wanted? Of course the Protestants could welcome him now, and the dean of the cathedral no doubt would asperge the coffin himself. But why not? Michael had not offended the Protestants. He had not betrayed them. To an entire generation he'd been a hero, the Prince of Peace. Only to the few of us who loved him most had he been the vilest enemy. I saw suddenly what I had in common with the cardinal. And also, since the Church had so resolutely condemned Michael, why Carolyn had needed me to come home. I was there, I understood finally, to pronounce the absolution that saves a soul from hell, and I knew, to my horror, that I could not do it.

Molly and I mounted the stairs and at the huge center portal—the lower of the pair of wrought-iron hinges was above the level of my eye—I found the ring handle that indicated which panel served as the quotidian door. But it didn't budge. I went to the side portal and tried its door, but it too was bolted. Only then did I recall that in the cities of America, God's house, even in the middle of the day, is locked from the inside.

Our path around the side of the cathedral took us through the garden which was elegantly laid out around a stunted steeple, a relic from some English town perhaps, which looked, when seen whimsically, like the topmost part of a church that was otherwise completely buried in the earth. An underground church, as it were. In fact the structure was an outdoor pulpit that hadn't been used in years, and I remembered being struck by its archaic beauty once before. I had been standing by it years ago when the agent of my destruction ambushed me.

"Molly!"

A boy of about eight, dressed nattily in a little blue blazer, had called her from a bench and was now running toward her. He was sobbing.

Molly dropped her bag and took a few steps toward him, and they embraced violently. He left the ground and for a long time she held him. I marveled at her strength, at the strength of her affection for the child, and I was filled with awe at that epiphany of her goodness. She was my daughter!

And it ripped me anew that the degradation of my love for her mother had degraded in turn my fatherly love for her. Else would I have left? Else wouldn't I have fought Michael for at least my daughter's love? If I had been there she would never have taken his name. I was filled with regret, but also stern acknowledgment that opaque hardening is the only law that heartbreak knows.

When finally Molly turned to me with her arm around the boy's shoulder, I was in no way prepared for it when she said, "This is Eddie, my brother."

But I must have suspected it. Surely otherwise I'd have consciously entertained the possibility. Staring at the boy whose face, even wrecked with emotion, had the dark Irish charm peculiar to his father, I knew that I was looking at an extension—no, the consummation—of the adoration I'd seen in his parents' eyes that first day at the house in Dobbs Ferry. No wonder I hadn't wanted to contemplate this possibility. For the first time in many years I felt the full force of Carolyn and Michael's love for each other. It was glib of me to claim earlier that I had put my resentment behind me. Perhaps I could even have felt bitterness toward this child, but the intensity of his grief overcame me. Michael was his *father!* I knew what it was to feel bereft as he felt. And I knew what it was—though I had broken faith with this knowledge—to comfort a child who yearned for a father's touch. "The fathers of families . . ." Suddenly, I longed for Michael anew, to clap his back for what we had in common now, and quote Peguy: ". . . those great adventurers of the modern world."

"Eddie," I said, while he shyly avoided my gaze, "are you named for your grandfather?"

The boy nodded and collapsed against Molly again, and I sensed that Carolyn's father had died at some point too. I looked at Molly with my question, and she flicked her eyes, yes.

When the boy pulled himself together I wanted to tell him I was sorry, but the words seemed cruelly glib, and I suddenly felt exhausted. Was I up to this? How many time zones had I crossed? I rolled down the sleeves of my shirt; that child was dressed the way I should have been. What was I doing there?

"Mommy's in the church." He indicated the doorway at the south transept. "I can't go in there because Daddy . . ."

Molly took him again. Without speaking we agreed that she would wait with him in the garden. He clung to her gratefully, and I crossed slowly to the stairs. At the threshold of the church I stopped. Inside the darkness beckoned, soothing and cool. I thought of the threshold stone of the ancient gate of Jerusalem, the one Jesus crossed. Then I entered the everlasting moment the cathedrals preserve for us.

It took some moments for my eyes to adjust to the dark, and at first all I could see were the brilliant blues and reds of the towering windows. There was not a sound in the vast church. As I moved to the center of the cruciform, my sight sharpened. Stairs to my right led into the sanctuary. The elaborately carved wooden stalls of the choir framed the space in which the high altar stood. Beams of sunlight filtered down upon it magically.

I did not presume to enter the sanctuary—lay brother, still—but crossed to the far aisle and followed it into the apse of the cathedral because I knew that in the classic plan the chapels are behind the choir in the alcoves formed by the easternmost buttresses. As I wound past the sanctuary and the altar and the bishop's throne, it wasn't Chartres I thought of but Saint Patrick's. For all their differences, those places inside were very much alike.

As I approached the chapels I instinctively slowed my pace, all at once conscious of the click of my sandals on the stone floor. I was aware of Carolyn's presence even before, as I passed a last column, she came into view. She was kneeling with her back to me before a subtly illuminated statue of the Virgin, and I froze. The sight of her, bent like that in prayer before the icon of Mary, that great sufferer, confounded me. An avalanche of emotion—love for her and infinite sympathy, grief for my friend, infinite loss—crashed down on me. I had no choice but to turn away and retrace my steps, back around the aisle to the choir. I could not breathe, and for an instant the dread phrase "Heart attack!" flashed before me. I slipped into a choir stall, a monk's stall, and collapsed, burying my head in my arms, weeping.

When I raised my eyes and beheld the sanctuary, it wasn't that moments had passed, but that years had fallen away.

Carolyn and I took places toward the rear of Saint Patrick's just as the great anthem of pipes and horns unleashed waves back and forth across the vault of the cathedral. The congregation rose to its feet and the flourish was followed by the grand processional antiphon, the ancient Gregorian *Ecce Sacerdos Magnus,* Behold the Great Priest! And the bobbing procession-cross flanked by candles led the long train of paired-up *ordinandi* vested in white albs with stoles slashing across their chests as deacons wear them, golden chasubles folded like large waiter's towels over their arms, into the body of the cathedral. The procession came nowhere near us but we were easily able to pick Michael out because he was the tallest deacon. He carried himself with a natural grace.

They wound through the nave and up the stairs into the sanctuary. Trailing them, between his chaplains, poking the floor with his crozier, was the diminutive figure of Francis Cardinal Spellman. It was the first time I'd ever laid eyes on him, and from where we stood, he seemed slightly ludicrous, that roly-poly cherub in miter and velvet slippers, like a newspaper cartoon of the time called "The Little King." It was the spring of 1961 and in fact Spellman's power was in decline. His worldwide influence had depended on his intimate relationship with the aristocratic Pius XII. He and the Peasant Pope, John XXIII, had not hit it off. John had raised Spellman's old rival, Cushing of Boston, to the College of Cardinals. As if that wasn't enough, the Kennedys had embraced Cushing too, and now after that winter's inaugural, the nation thought of the old coot from Boston as the preeminent American Catholic prelate. But here in New York, Spellman was still in command, and if New York was all that was left him, he would be more in command there than ever. Anyone who dismissed him, in other words, as a roly-poly cherub, made a big mistake. Spellman was the *Sacerdos Magnus,* and anyone who doubted it had only to watch this line of handsome, robust young men in their prime—men who'd have been the prizes of recruiters at firms all over Manhattan—kneel before him at his *cathedra* one by one to have their hands bound in linen cloth. In that consecration each made his obeisance in a ceremony derived from the feudal rite of fealty; obeisance not to God or to Jesus or to the Church, but to this man, to this—as the argot puts it with rare irony—Ordinary.

Spellman addressed his question in the Latin: "Do you solemnly promise to respect and obey me and my successors?" Michael like the others did not hesitate with his "I do." Years later he would openly break that vow and I would applaud him for it, thinking stupidly that he would keep his others. I would only wonder, not understanding yet how thoroughly that seminary meat grinder had chewed his ego up, what took him so long.

I remember the jolt with which he slammed his drink down on the table late one night. "Goddamnit, Durk, I *want* someone to obey! I *want* someone to respect! Authority is the basic principle of my life, and look what I've done to undermine it!" He had his finger on the irony of what he'd become. I said, cruelly perhaps, "You just want your daddy, Michael." He looked at me with shock in his face, as if he hadn't seen that elemental orphan's wish as a motivating force behind his vocation.

After making the vow of obedience, the *ordinandi*, in the metaphoric and dramatic climax of the ritual, prostrated themselves on the sanctuary floor, assuming the posture of the dead. Twenty or thirty corpses in white, utterly immobile for the transfiguring duration of the litany of the saints. Its strains, sung antiphonally between the schola, its precious falsetto, and the entire congregation, its ragged base, rose like incense to the vaulted reaches where the faded red hats of Spellman's predecessors hung rotting from the crown joint of the intersecting arches.

> *Kyrie Eleison!*
> *Christi Eleison!*
> *Kyrie Eleison!*
> *Sancta Maria, Mater Dei . . .*
> *Ora pro nobis.*
> *Sancta Michaeli Archangeli . . .*
> *Ora pro nobis.*

And so on through dozens of arcane names—Athanasius, Sebastian and Basil, Perpetua, Agatha and Felicity—men whose bodies were pierced like pin-cushions with Roman arrows and women whose breasts were crushed with Appian Way paving stones.

> All holy men and women, saints of God . . .
> Pray for us.
> Lord, be merciful . . .
> Lord, deliver us.
> Bless these chosen men . . .
> Lord, hear our prayer.

My true feeling surfaced even as I sang. Those poor sons of bitches! Chosen men? One can always tell God's chosen ones—Jesus, the Jews—when they get nailed or gassed. I rose up on the kneeler, straining to see Michael lying there, like a dead man, one of a massacred crowd. I could not tell which was him. Spellman knelt smugly above them, like Moses having laid low a band of Pharaoh's thugs.

Moses! I remembered Spellman's part in the humiliation of Carolyn less than a year before, and I was angry suddenly that Michael would bind himself to that petty tyrant. But my anger fell before my pity. Poor Michael! What was he doing to himself? At that moment surely he was in the grip of a vicious despair. Perhaps he was undergoing, victim of that liturgical enactment, a true foretaste of death. Or was he facing the facts about himself? That his touted bravery had driven him headlong from the world; he was dead to the world now! No human feelings in him from now on, no weakness, no vulnerability, and no autonomy. One of God's true heroes forever. Surely he saw the sham of it! Surely he knew that his priesthood was a blessed sleeve, a maniple, in which to hide the stump of his cowardice! Why else would an American male of my generation cooperate in the denigration of such a ceremony? I was utterly scandalized by it, and I think even now that I understood its radical character, therefore, far better than that edified throng awash in its ocean of sentiment. The ordination of a priest is an awesome, artful and affirming act only to those who buy the whole package, and I didn't.

Michael in fact was not seeing it my way at all. He told me later that he lay there on that cold stone floor in the grip not of despair but of euphoria. The Church to which he was giving himself, its theology, its liturgy, its discipline, was as seamless as the round of chanted music echoing above him, and he felt that the eyes of heaven—all those Felicities and Basils—*were* upon him. His clinging reservations, his shame at what he knew he'd become when he'd failed to stand with Carolyn, and the huge self-doubt I imagined as his burden had fallen away or had been lifted with the airy litany and incense to the shadowy cavern above. When he stood at last, it was no act of abnegation to kneel once more before the cardinal for the imposition of hands and the investiture. "Receive the yoke of the Lord, for his yoke is sweet and its burden light." As the cardinal crossed the stole on Michael's breast, he felt his heart lighten, for he believed fully for the first time that he was indeed called by God, no, seized by God, captured by him—he would almost have said "ravished"—to be held forever. The relief he felt came from the obliteration of his conflicts. There was no issue any longer of which choice to make, for with a clear-headed self-awareness, arrived at over seven arduous years, he had made his choice. That other human beings have to make their choices repeatedly, even their life-shaping ones—especially their life-shaping ones— was a fact without relevance for him.

The contradictions implicit in the Catholic priesthood—slav- ishly obedient men are expected to use mature judgment exercised with flair in their pastoral positions; men uncon- sciously in revolt against intimacy and domesticity are ex- pected to nurture the family lives of others—simply did not exist for Michael Maguire at the moment of his ordination. He willingly suspended his disbelief so that Cardinal Spell- man could seem a dignified figure of magnanimous authority, the congregation in Saint Patrick's a veritable choir of the moving spheres, and his own life stretching out before him an adventure of transcendent significance. The illusions were in place. Michael accepted with great joy the chasuble of charity upon his shoulders and the oil of kings upon his hands. He touched the chalice of gold and the paten with the sacred Host upon it. "Receive the power to offer sacrifice to God and to celebrate Mass for the living and the dead."

A priest undergoes, in the phrase of Saint Thomas, an ontological change, a change so fundamental that it reaches to the very core of his being, making him, according to this theology, a completely different creature. But Michael's happiness that day, he would tell me, derived from his experience that he became the man he always thought he was.

It was the previous September, only weeks after that day at Dobbs Ferry and after Michael had returned to Washington for his final year of seminary, that I had first called Carolyn at her parents' home. I talked to her on the telephone two or three times before I quashed the feeling that I was a thief and finally asked her out. We began in a tentative way "to see each other," a phrase then light years away from its present status as a euphemism for fucking. We first came together, in other words, the way porcupines, in the old joke, make love—very carefully.

Carolyn had suffered not one but two traumas, for she'd lost Michael and, even more shocking, the Church. If she'd been the Bride of Christ, now she was—and this was the feeling Catholics had about ex-nuns and the feeling Catholics expected ex-nuns to have about themselves—His unfaithful former wife. For a girl who'd been raised to expect affirmation and acceptance, it was a stunning blow to find herself in a situation of failure and rejection. Her parents stood by her, and no one openly derided her, but the shame hung over her nonetheless. It made her feel that she would never recover, would never know happiness, would never again bask in the easy love either of God or the Church, not to mention of a man. The greatest agony, of course, was in having had for a moment, then lost, the love of such a man as Michael. Hadn't it seemed in its intensity, its purity, the perfect gift from God?

Initially my company was a solace to her because I was Michael's friend. I could tell her stories about our boyhood, and she could describe the enthralling first discovery of her feelings and the pain she experienced at his rejection. She could describe her confusion; how could God's gift have become her sin? How could her urgent desire to serve the children have caused her disgrace? How could Michael have left her alone with such trouble? If she'd done nothing wrong, as I kept telling her, why was she consumed with sorrow? "Help me understand, Durk!" she'd cry. "Help me live with this!" And I did. She was no failure to me, no reject, no pariah, and eventually she knew it.

After a while she began to enjoy my company for its own sake, and she began to regard me in relationship to herself, not Michael. Only then, and most carefully, did I reveal my feelings to her, but still the effect of my admission was to make things more confused than ever. Now when I invited her to my somewhat shabby Village apartment, was it to make love to her? When she came to my apartment and I didn't make love to her, was she disappointed? I wanted her sexually more than I'd ever wanted any girl, but I had no intention of pressing her in any way. But, as a virgin, was she waiting for me to overcome her hesitancy? In order to have her, did I have to pretend that I was Michael? Looking back on it now, it seems a miracle that our relationship at last became clear, became *ours*.

We'd had dinner at the New Port Alba, a homey Italian restaurant just below Washington Square, and we headed out into the cold—it was February. We were going to Grand Central so that Carolyn could catch her train to Dobbs Ferry, but crossing the square we came upon an old lady who was trying without success to wrap herself in newspapers. She was blue with cold, wearing only a pair of sweaters and a wool knit hat. Without thinking, I took off my coat and draped her with it. It was a navy pea coat, easily replaced, and so it was not an act of great generosity. Still it was utterly unlike me. I crossed that square every day and hardly ever registered the derelicts. My impulse came from Carolyn, not that I was, grossly, out to impress her, but that, in her presence, such expansiveness came naturally to me. I not only loved Carolyn but loved myself as I was when I was with her.

The old lady cried, "God bless you!"

And as we walked away, Carolyn put her arm around me, to warm me. "You're good," she said.

She was looking at me with such affection that I replied, "Gee, maybe I'll go back and give her my shirt."

But now we had to stop at my apartment so that I could get my other coat, which meant we had to hurry to make her train. It *was* cold. We walked on as quickly as we could toward my place, Carolyn leaning on me, rubbing my arms, me reciting loudly Millay's "Recuerdo."

> We were very tired, we were very merry,
> We had gone back and forth all night
>   on the ferry.
> We hailed "Good morrow, mother!"
>   to a shawl-covered head
> And bought a morning paper, which
>   neither of us read;
> And she wept, "God bless you!"
>   for the apples and pears,
> And we gave her all our money
>   but our subway fares.

"Oh, Frank," she said excitedly, "could we do that?"

"What, give her all our money?"

"No. Ride all night on the ferry."

"Sure we can, kid. Stick with me."

"I mean it. I've never been on the ferry."

"Could we wait till August?"

"I didn't mean tonight." She pushed me, and I started to run. She followed, playfully. The truth was I didn't want to take her on the Staten Island Ferry. It was a cliché. It was where I'd gone with other girls, which was why I happened to know "Recuerdo." Reciting poetry into the wind worked wonders. I hadn't tried tricks like that on Carolyn. But, hell, the ferry didn't have to be a trick. It cost a nickel. It offered a great view of New York. It ran all night. And no one bothered kissing couples if they kept their clothes on.

"Hey, why not?" I said suddenly, stopping her. "Want to?"

"The ferry?"

"Sure! What the hell? It's a perfect night."

"It's freezing!" she laughed.

"You're telling me! What do you say?"

"Let's get your coat, then we'll flip a coin."

"Okay. That's a deal."

We ran the few blocks back to my apartment, holding hands, and my mind was filled with her image, how beautiful she was, how untamed, how untouched. It was the most I frankly hoped for, running, joined to her, like that, hands only, and such was my happiness that I thought it could be enough. By the time we got there we were both winded. Carolyn collapsed across my tattered overstuffed reading chair, while I caught my breath against the wall. We were grinning at each other like exhilarated kids. I took my topcoat from its hanger and put it on. She stood up. I produced a quarter and held it toward her on my thumb. "Still game?"

I saw a hint of insecurity in her eyes, but she nodded.

"Heads if by land, tails if by sea."

I flipped and it was tails. We both stared at the coin, stunned, as if that etched George Washington had just cried, "All aboard for Staten Island!"

"Oh," she said. When we looked at each other, I saw how vulnerable she felt. What was this anyway? And I resolved to leave my sure-fire poetry at home with all my hard-learned wiles and moves and savvy calculations. I was not on the make anymore. That, perhaps, was what she sensed, and what, as Frost said, made all the difference.

She said, "I'll have to call my folks."

"What will you say?"

"I'll say, 'We're very tired. We're very merry.' And not to wait up for me in Dobbs Ferry."

"You're good," I said and grinned. I was aware that those were the very words she'd said to me in the park. She'd made me feel not noble precisely, but, well, worthy. Worthy, I realized suddenly, of her.

She went to my phone. As she dialed, her hand shook slightly, but it wasn't her parents who made her nervous. When she told her mother that we were going to ride the ferry, it seemed ludicrous to me, but apparently her mother encouraged her, said it was just the thing for young people to do. It would mean missing the last train, Carolyn said; she'd stay in a hotel. It underscored the difference between our backgrounds when her mother did not object. In Inwood even that bright, self-assured young woman would have been scolded home by midnight.

When Carolyn hung up the phone she turned toward me. When our eyes met we realized together that we were in a completely new situation.

It was the first time an evening had passed in which Michael had not been mentioned. That told us.

It was unthinkable that we should have withdrawn from one another. That told us.

And now, by the same instinct, we knew that the Staten Island Ferry was nothing to us. We weren't going anywhere. And none of this was spoken or needed to be.

I let my coat fall from my shoulders. She started to unbutton hers but her hands could not manage it. She plunged them into her pockets and let her eyes fall instead. She couldn't look at me. She couldn't move. It was my place to cross to her, to take her hand, to show her what to do. But it was as if we both were virgins. I crossed without speaking. My arms went around her; I kissed her. But she was afraid, and I couldn't help but sense it.

"Shall we just go?" I asked.

"No. Durk, you're so good to me." When she looked up there were tears in her eyes. I must have been a blur to her. "I need you, Durk. Without you I'm nothing."

"Oh, that isn't so, Caro." I took her in my arms again, wanting to press into her what I thought. How wonderful you are! How beautiful! How good! But I saw too the other truth about her. She was bereft of any purpose in life, and of course she would be. She had been beloved of the Lord, and now she was His outcast. When her sisters, then Michael, had turned their faces from her, who was to say God had not? I knew her despair as if it was my own. She was nothing, nothing, nothing.

And therefore, ironically, at last, she was mine. To spare her the pain of her loss I'd have returned her at once to God or Michael. Having begun by wanting her, now I wanted only her happiness. My happiness was that neither God nor Michael seemed interested.

She wept quietly against my shoulder.

"I love you, Caro."

She shook her head. Yes? I know? Or could it have been, I love you too?

All at once her arms were around my neck and she was pressing her mouth against mine. I was opening her coat; she shrugged it off, barely pulling away; then I was undressing her while she kept coming at me with her mouth, as if finally the only pain she'd ever felt was hunger. I told myself it was hunger for me. Me, I said, she wants me! I nearly believed it. She was weeping all the while. Ungodly, frightening noises came from her. She pressed her fingernails into my neck, hurting me, and I had her by the hair, by the ears, by the bones in her face. I kept saying, "I love you, Caro," but she was the one who had us locked together. She was the one whose longing peaked first, who would not be denied. By the time we'd moved to my bed, naked, and had crashed down onto it, it was impossible to say who was taking whom. I knew that everything she had for a man who was not Michael was there for me. He was in my brain, whether in hers or not, but that didn't stop me from devouring her. Figments were nothing to me. Not even her body was a dream; it was the ultimate physical expression, those clasping legs, those curving breasts, the smell of perspiration, of crotch. And my body had never been so responsive, so alive to every sensation. We were weightless with each other.

I received what she could give gratefully. Her gift changed my life. Please don't think it pathetic of me, but because Carolyn found it possible to settle for who I was, I also could. If she had rejected me then I would never have accepted myself. So there's the great irony: because I knew she loved Michael more, that she loved me at all seemed miraculous. It was like *redemption* to me. I was the Earth after Copernicus, not wounded that I wasn't the center of the universe, but so awed by what that genius had revealed that I was glad to have a corner of the universe for my own. But metaphors fail me utterly. Copernicus indeed! I am simply saying that what peace with myself and what pride in myself I have ever known came from Carolyn that merry night.

I was for her the other thing, the lover absolute. It is a rare thing to act without reservation, without pretense; that was my virginity. Ineptitude, yes. Our timing was off, but who was clocking? There was awkwardness, but no mirror in the mind, no detachment, no dream of someone else. It was a simple, heartfelt cleaving. I felt the special weight it was to be initiating her, and sensed hovering beyond the ghost of Michael that other, holy ghost, her first chosen spouse, the Lord. But even His shadow seemed benign.

She embraced me—was this *my* suspension of disbelief?—as if I was quite enough for her.

Naturally, for a range of reasons, we felt somewhat awkward at Michael's ordination a few months later. As it happened, his ordination took place not long after we had become engaged. Carolyn, who had had no communication whatsoever with him and hadn't been invited, did not want to go. I insisted. I knew that I could not compete with a memory or a dream, whether hers of Michael or Michael's of her. My friendship and my love depended on their adjustment to what was real, and that would never be more apparent than at his ordination. But at the last minute Carolyn said she simply could not face it. She wasn't coming. We quarreled. It was a flashpoint, and she understood that if she did not come with me, then our relationship was at an end as well. It was the moment of her choice. The misery in her face made me think of Father Zossima's line—you understand by now that I take refuge in profane quotations the very way Michael did in sacred ones, and Dostoevsky remains a favorite—"Love in practice is a harsh and dreadful thing compared to love in dreams." Carolyn was looking up at me from the edge of my bed and as she said finally, "You're right," I was aware of her handing herself over to me in a way she hadn't yet. It was as if she had curled herself into a small wad and held it up between her fingers. I bent to her and put my hand under her head with a tentativeness that made my hand tremble, and I kissed her. She pulled me down onto the bed, on top of her, and with an abandon she had yet to demonstrate and I had scarcely suspected she was capable of, as if her acquiescence released all sexual restraint at last, she made love to me.

And made us late. I was acutely aware, not smugly so, that even while Michael, hands folded inside Spellman's, made his vow, my sperm was moistening the fold between Carolyn's legs.

At the end of the ceremony each of the newly ordained priests went to a section of the main communion rail or to a side altar to bestow on his family and friends his first priestly blessing. Carolyn and I approached with awe for what had just happened to our friend, but also with a more mundane fear that our appearance together at this moment would undermine each of us. As the line moved slowly forward I watched Michael raise his arms and eyes to heaven, smoothly and solemnly as if he'd always done it, and then cut the air in a cross and press his now consecrated hands onto the bent head of his mother. It moved me nearly to tears to see her. Michael took her by the elbow then and helped her up, and when he embraced her she almost disappeared in the wrap of his golden chasuble.

By the time Carolyn and I presented ourselves at the altar rail and knelt before him, he had blessed several dozen people. I couldn't help but grin up at him, and as he bent toward me with impressive solemnity I was afraid he would think me irreverent. But at the last moment he winked and my anxiety disappeared. Hell, after all that tossing and turning, it was Michael! My oldest friend, my friend for life! Ontological change or not this was still the man I'd grown up with. The distance between us and even the awkwardness I felt about Carolyn evaporated. No woman, no Church, no God, no meaningless observances or penances or humiliations were going to wreck our friendship.

Even my argument with his piety disappeared for the moment. In the case of Carolyn I had been the beneficiary of his self-denial, but otherwise I'd been depressed to watch the transformation of my strong-willed, active friend into a dependent, necessarily passive cleric. I thought the alleluiahs with which the Church propagated such abnegation—''I am a worm'' was how the great Thomas à Kempis put it, ''and no man''—was so much shit. But all at once I saw the thing differently. Now that he was a priest, perhaps I saw the other side of that self-surrender. Maybe it wasn't cowardice. Perhaps it wasn't mere masochism. Maybe that ancient impulse of religious men and women—"abandonment"—did express some kind of wisdom. Maybe even a sophist punk like me could understand it.

As I tell you this story now, looking back on that moment from a vantage two decades later, it is obvious to both of us that my suspicion of "holy obedience"—the ecclesial version of "wholly owned"—is intact. Still, even now, remembering how moved I was in that first encounter with him as a priest, I admit that something else was at work. Something else was in him. Hadn't it been superficial of me to dismiss Michael's experience, his choice? Wasn't it possible to see his self-surrender not as an act of feminine piety, but as a bold image of what we all do every day—this blind handing over of ourselves to the blank future? What if the cardinal *was* an authentic sign of God's presence, a proclamation exactly that God draws near to us in what is ordinary? What if Michael's belief in the Church, in other words, was true?

"Why do priests carry chocolate pudding in their wallets?" we Village anticlericals used to ask. "For identification. Har. Har. Har."

Why then was I weeping?

Michael loomed over me like an angel. He seemed a man of tremendous virtue and strength, and if I could have, I'd have put my hands in his and sworn fealty, not to God, to him. But with great sweep and priestly panache, he deflected my mind back to God, away from him. It was what he would always do to me. *"Benedicat Deus omnipotenti . . ."* And with his large athlete's hands he pressed down on the crown of my head, pressed so hard I imagined him praying like some fundy, "Believe, Durk! Believe!"

It had been six years since I'd discarded the faith and now, to put it simply, I took it back. Hell, even Wallace Stevens, the most eloquent agnostic of all—he wanted poetry to take the place of the God he couldn't believe in—became a Catholic on his deathbed. So did I have to wait until I was dying?

Oh, sure, you say, how they soften after college, once they have a job, when they fall in love and start thinking family.

Can't send the kids to Sunday school if you don't believe in Sunday.

Maybe that's all I was doing, ending my adolescent apostate phase on schedule. But at that moment, with Michael pressing on my head, it seemed to me that God Himself—the Heavenly Condor—had swooped down, talons flashing, to seize me by the hair. I "had trod, had trod . . . bleared, smeared with toil." Not only that, "I had fled Him down the nights and down the days." But in Michael He had followed me. He was my "ransom, my rescue, my first, fast, last friend." Christ. Jesus Christ. He came back to me.

You see, what Michael did for me that day, pressing down, was to bring me back to myself. I was born like this. I am Catholic like I am freckled, like I am smart, like I am, under all this flippancy, afraid. Michael revealed to me how much I wanted to believe, and he reminded me that wanting belief is having it. That is the chief way in which belief differs from sex.

I felt defenseless. I wanted to tell Michael that I loved him. But my affection was swamped by tidal waves of guilt and remorse. How unworthy I was of this man, of his friendship, of his blessing. How unworthy I was of God. Those were the feelings I had. I wouldn't know how true they were until years later. I seized Michael's arm and like a self-loathing peasant—this gesture of subservience had always disgusted me, but it was the perfect primordial act—I pressed my mouth to his hand and kissed it.

If Carolyn's presence next to me upset him I did not see it. I was too ambushed by my own emotion—by my experience, for this is what it was, of conversion—to notice anything of their encounter, but when I looked at her as we both stood to leave the rail, I saw the black streaks of mascara beneath her eyes. She looked like she'd been beaten.

The reception for the *ordinandi* in the Cathedral Hall was jammed. Long tables were spread with sweet rolls and finger sandwiches. Hatted ladies were dispensing coffee from huge aluminum urns. The families of the new priests were crowding them. Flashbulbs, forbidden in the cathedral itself, were popping everywhere.

Priests' mothers were already laying claim to the linen bands in which their sons' hands had been wrapped during the anointing. It was the privilege of the mothers of priests to be buried with their own hands wrapped in the strip of white cloth that would still, years later, be stained with the sacred oil.

On smaller tables were displayed the priests' new chalices and patens which the laity could ogle but not touch. Also on those tables were tidy stacks of holy cards commemorating each man's elevation to the sacred state. I took one of Michael's. On one side was a Daliesque picture of Saint Paul, kneeling with a sword, looking up to heaven. For a holy card it was a manly pose, a dismounted warrior after all, exactly what I'd have expected from Michael. On the reverse side was a line of Paul's, a selection that frankly surprised me. "In my own flesh I fill up what is lacking in the sufferings of Christ for the sake of His Body, the Church." And beneath that verse were the words, "Reverend Michael Maguire, Ordained a Priest, May 22, 1961. Please Pray For Me."

I handed it to Carolyn and despite myself said, "I hadn't realized anything was lacking in Christ's suffering." Carolyn read the card and gave it back to me, apparently uninterested in what Reverend Michael did in his own flesh. Even in the flush of my "conversion" I thought the quotation smacked somewhat of smugness and self-pity, but I saved the card. Years later I would come across it in my Bible and see that it expressed perfectly what he'd done.

As we moved through the crowd, Carolyn clung to my arm as if the scene in the becolumned hall was foreign to her. She was afraid she would see someone she knew, someone from the Sisters of Charity. She was afraid those mothers of priests would point at her and snarl, "She used to be a nun." She didn't look it. She wore a trim tan linen suit with a bright blue silk blouse open at her throat. Her blond hair with which she'd lashed me that morning—she would never wear it short again—was in a perfect pageboy, and she wore a pillbox hat as becomingly as Mrs. Kennedy did. She had repaired her makeup and now held herself, despite the nervousness I could sense, with the poise of a movie star. Beautiful women have a right to feel ill at ease in the basements of cathedrals.

When Michael finally entered, his mother was on his arm. Her arthritis made it impossible for her to walk without help. He saw us, left his mother with his aunts and hurried across the large room. If space and decorum had permitted it, he'd have run. He arrived with his arms open and an expression of happiness I'd never seen in him before. He embraced us both, singly and with great feeling.

"Hello, Father!" I said, grinning again and abandoning for once everything but the pride and affection I felt for him.

" 'Call no man father,' you son of a bitch!" He laughed hilariously and clapped my shoulder. "Do it again and I'll break your arm." He was joking, but also making a point. Some priests are addressed as "Father" by everyone. If they were allowed to marry they'd be called "Father" by their wives.

To Carolyn he said more soberly, but with that broad smile, "I'm so glad you came." Obviously, he meant it. He took her hand.

"Congratulations, Michael," she said, then broke into a grin of her own. "Now they can't fire you."

"But I can't fire them either."

"What is all this about firing people?" I put in happily. His bondage was my freedom.

He turned her hand over in his own, fingering the modest diamond I'd given her.

He looked quickly at me and at last I saw a brief show of hurt in him. "My God!" he said, too stunned for the moment to veil his reaction.

All at once it seemed to me that every word Carolyn and I had said to each other and every tentative gesture of the flesh we'd shared were available to him as if now, ontologically indeed, he had mystic powers to penetrate our secrets. Could he know that not two hours before she'd ravished me?

I blushed and started to explain. "We'd have told you before . . ."

But he stopped me. He put an arm around each of us. His reaction was a denial of the visceral, an act of will and of generosity. But everything—particularly the solemn commitment he'd just made—required it. "I'm so pleased! I think it's wonderful! It makes me very happy.'' He crushed us together. ''You can be my family.''

For a moment we three held each other tightly. It was what I'd hoped for.

When we separated Carolyn brushed her pancake makeup from his cassock. She said to my utter amazement—we'd never discussed asking him—''Michael, we were hoping that you'd marry us.''

''Of course I will,'' he said instantly. ''I'd never forgive you if you didn't let me.''

They stared at each other and for a moment they forgot that I was there. Carolyn had said in effect, ''I came to your ordination; I want you at my wedding.'' I could sense the flow between them, the understanding, the effort to accept what was real, as well as the effort to transform their feelings into something new. But also I saw how they drew each other out of the world in which the rest of us lived, and I knew that I was forever banned from the deepest place in each of them. Of course I was wounded and jealous, but frankly I didn't know of whom. I wanted both of them the way they had each other.

''When are you planning it for?'' he asked.

''August,'' Carolyn said.

Michael slapped his forehead. ''August!''

''Why?''

''I haven't had a chance to tell you yet about my assignment.''

What was to tell? Weren't priests always put in parishes? Our Lady of the Vouchsafe, Saints Maureen and Doreen, Saint Joseph by the Way. And weren't the new ones always put in charge of bingo and the altar boys and the annual picnic? But Michael's enthusiasm surprised me. Clearly the news of my engagement to Carolyn had not derailed him.

''What is it?'' I asked.

''Do you remember Father O'Shea? That chaplain in Korea?''

The one whose life he'd saved, the one Michael had longed to talk to. Sure I did and said so.

''He's retired from the army. He's a monsignor now, and he's with the Catholic Relief Service here in New York; he runs the Far East Refugee Rescue operation. He's asked for me as his assistant. I'll be in a parish but only part-time. He and the cardinal are going over there this summer after the Eucharistic Congress in Manila. And I'm going with them.''

''And you won't be back in August?'' Carolyn asked.

''Not until September.''

After a moment of rather awkward silence—Carolyn's mother had already begun making reservations, and Carolyn herself was prepared to take his unavailability as another rejection—I said, ''We'll just do it in September then.''

''Great!'' Michael seemed to mean it, and it relieved me to see Carolyn's face soften toward him again.

At that moment people in the crowd behind Michael moved aside, opening an aisle. They fell silent, and craned to see the approaching figure. He was invisible to me because he was so short, but I knew it was Cardinal Spellman. It had to be. I exchanged a look with Carolyn. Who needed this? She was blushing, and I put my arm around her. I knew how vulnerable she felt. She'd been valiant, in my opinion, up to then.

Michael wore a stricken look too. It was for fear of this moment that he had not invited Carolyn to the ordination. He knew better than anyone what Spellman had done to her. And now he was sworn as Spellman's vassal. Or was it serf?

''Father Michael,'' Cardinal Spellman said, beaming up at him.

Michael bowed smoothly from his waist to kiss the prelate's ring, then said, stiffly, ''Your Eminence, let me introduce you to some friends.''

Carolyn and I each managed to kiss his ring. It was a gesture that couldn't have come less naturally to me, but Carolyn accomplished it smoothly, with a graceful half-curtsey. Still, she blushed furiously, and when Spellman, still holding her hand, said, ''We've met before, dear, haven't we?'' I thought she was gong to faint.

What would have happened to Michael's new career if she'd said right then, ''I'm Sister Mary Felony, Your Eminence. You saw my picture in the paper.''

But she stammered, ''You administered my Sacrament of Confirmation, Your Eminence.'' She forced a smile. ''That was fourteen years ago.''

Spellman put his hand on her forearm and asked, as if it was important to him, "What parish was that, dear?"

"Saint Peter's in Bronxville, Your Eminence."

He nodded. "And did I meet your parents?"

"Yes, you did, Your Eminence."

"And your mother is as beautiful as you are, if I recall." He smiled at her endearingly. He was like an old pol working the crowd, shuffling through what we all knew was his routine, but still we were affected, charmed even. His touch was light, and he held onto Carolyn's arm as if it was the most natural thing in the world for him to do so. He seemed benign, fatherly even, and I found myself softening toward him. I was nearly won over when he said to Carolyn with real feeling, "It is the great privilege of my position to administer sacraments to handsome young people like you. And then . . ." He grasped Michael's arm, while holding onto Carolyn's, an ironic if unintended linking. ". . . to think it is my honor to ordain God's new priests. Every night I get down on my knees to thank Him." He grinned suddenly. "Oh, but goodness, you don't want to hear an old priest boasting about being on his knees!" He looked at me. "And aren't you proud of Father Michael today!"

"Yes, I am," I said.

Spellman dropped Carolyn's arm to press Michael's with both hands. "We're proud of him too. It's not often the Church receives a man like Michael Maguire into her service." He was looking at me as he said that, but I sensed that Spellman was addressing Michael. He'd have been aware of Michael's war record, of course, and it would have carried great weight with a soldier-worshipper like Spellman. Now he was manifesting his attachment to Michael, though, of course, like all priests, he could only do so indirectly. "We expect great things from this young man."

Spellman still did not look at Michael, or else he might have witnessed the look Michael exchanged with Carolyn. There was apology in it, as well as misery, embarrassment. Michael's standing was considerable, obviously. But it had begun with his refusal to stand by her. With his standing, he felt, *on* her.

"And has he told you what we've planned for him?" the cardinal asked.

I nodded. "About relief work?" I couldn't remember the name of the agency.

"The most important work in the Church," Cardinal Spellman said. "Father Maguire is going to pick up where Doctor Tom Dooley left off, aren't you, Father?"

"It would be an honor to think so, Your Eminence."

I knew that the heroic doctor had died only months before. Spellman had been at his bedside. Spellman had pronounced him a saint.

The cardinal said, with a sudden fierceness, "Tom Dooley's people are suffering more than ever, aren't they, Father?"

Michael nodded.

"And Father Maguire is coming with me to see what can be done to help them."

"Where?" Carolyn asked, despite herself. Tom Dooley had worked in Laos or someplace. Hadn't Michael just said the Far East? But what was that to her?

Cardinal Spellman looked blankly at her. "Vietnam," he said.

FOURTEEN

IT was one of those steaming mornings of the monsoon when the air over the lush terrain grew hot faster than the air over the bordering South China Sea. When the resulting massive thermal draft began to rise it sucked at the wet sea winds which then moved steadily inland, across the low coastal hills to the rugged mountains that formed the spine of the country and separated it from the Kingdom of Laos. And everywhere the rain fell.

The convoy of seven black Citroëns sped along the glistening paved road that would come to be called Route One when the Americans came, the only proper name for a north-south coastal highway. Affixed to the bumper of each automobile, although not to the escorting military vehicles, were two flags; the red-striped saffron flag of the Republic of Viet Nam, and the yellow-and-white flag, displaying the triple tiara and the keys of Saint Peter, of His Holiness the Pope. The tires of the automobiles hummed a steady sibilant, but the passengers for the most part remained silent.

They stared out the half-open windows and let the rain-soaked breeze refresh them, and they eyed the green blur of jungle, watching steadily. For wild animals? The spirits of ancestors? For friendly farmers? Every hundred or two hundred yards, even in the desolation of that countryside, a government soldier stood at present-arms, but with his back to the cars as they passed. No mere honor guard, those soldiers were outfitted for combat and charged with preventing an attack on that convoy. They had swept the highway for mines and booby traps. Now they were watching for signs of

the guerrilla force that totally controlled the scummy swamp
world in the delta region far to the south, around Saigon,
making travel outside that city a nightmare. The guerrillas
lived, as one of their slogans said, like owls in the night and
foxes in the daylight, and they were known for striking,
almost mystically, just when a traveler thought himself most
safe. In addition to ambush those on foot had constantly to
beware their punji traps, concealed pits with dung-encrusted
bamboo spikes. Vehicles regularly tripped mines and hidden
grenades, and once-innocent obstacles like fallen trees or
collapsed culverts now certainly meant attack. In less than a
year as an organized force the Communists had already assas-
sinated more than four thousand village heads and district
chiefs. But their random assaults were even more fearsome.
On the road it didn't seem to matter whether their victims
were women or children or even supporters of the Great
Struggle, and that capriciousness only made the terror they
inflicted more stunning. In Saigon in those days Americans
were famous for refusing to leave the city. Government officials did so only with escorts, and the rich landlords who had
to visit their holdings disguised themselves as peasants.

But here in the northernmost region between Hué and the
border with North Vietnam, the population was loyal to the
government and the guerrillas had yet to make an impact. But
the three brothers who ruled South Vietnam, President Ngo
Dinh Diem, his counselor, Ngo Dinh Nhu, and Ngo Dinh
Can, the viceroy of Central Vietnam, were prudent men. The
sentries they had posted all along the road from Hué to Quang
Tri were members of their crack personal guard. The Ngos
were taking no chances this morning, not on such a great
occasion and not with such guests.

In the first car, but behind the military escort, Cardinal
Spellman rode with his old friend, the fourth Ngo brother,
Archbishop Thuc. Riding on the jump seat, facing them, was
Monsignor Timothy O'Shea, and in the front seat, beside the
driver, was Father Michael Maguire. The three Americans
had arrived from Manila only the night before, and now they
were speeding to Quang Tri, the northernmost city in South
Vietnam, where Spellman and Thuc would preside at a cere-

mony attended by the elite of the country, marking the dedication of the huge new basilica of Our Lady of La Vang.

Archbishop Thuc, between puffs of his cigarette, said, "It will be like Lourdes, *Eminenza*." He spoke with a pronounced French accent, though the title he used to address Spellman was the Italian. "La Vang will be the spiritual bastion of the country."

"All you'll need are the miracles," Cardinal Spellman replied. Michael caught a glimpse of him in the rearview mirror, and looked for signs that he was being facetious. There were none. Thuc nodded smugly. The miracles would come.

"We have built this shrine," Thuc said, leaning toward Spellman, "with the donations of all the people, even peasants. They gave their *sous* to thank Our Lady for the deliverance of her Catholic children."

Michael wondered, Would these "peasants" be at the dedication? Not likely. He had an American's distaste for the word, and it told him what he didn't like about the Vietnamese prelate. He carried himself like an Oriental Richelieu, and in his thin, ascetic visage, his dark, brooding eyes it seemed to Michael there was something merciless.

Thuc touched Spellman's hand familiarly. "Who would have been thinking fifteen years ago we would be together today, with my brothers serving the people? We owe our success to you, *Eminenza*."

Michael strained to hear what Spellman said. In Manila, just days before, he had heard an Australian priest refer to Ngo Dinh Diem as "Spellman's seminarian." The priest explained that Diem had been forced into exile in the late forties. Ho Chi Minh had murdered one of his brothers, so Diem was fiercely anti-Communist, but he wouldn't support the French either. He'd had nowhere to go until his brother Thuc intervened with Cardinal Spellman. Spellman liked Diem's personal style—he was a pious, ascetic Catholic who attended Mass daily and who'd taken a private vow of chastity—and he took him under his wing. The Australian priest claimed that Diem had lived in one of Spellman's seminaries from 1950 until 1954. Michael was skeptical and said so. Hadn't he begun his own seminary course in 1954? And in Spellman's diocese? But the Australian insisted it was true, and in fact it was. Though Diem spent most of 1954 in a Belgian monastery, before that he had lived at Maryknoll, just a few miles from Dunwoodie. It amazed Michael that he hadn't heard of Spellman's connection with Diem before. The Australian had seemed to think there was something sinister in it, but, if it was true, Michael thought well of it. What should the Church use its influence for if not to bring to power worthy politicians who were inured to corruption and dedicated to Christian moral principles? Michael had said as much to the priest.

Spellman shook his head. "We are mere instruments, *n'est-ce pas?* We owe our success to Providence."

Thuc nodded, patting Spellman's hand. "And to Our Lady."

"With a little help from the U.S. Navy," Monsignor O'Shea put in gruffly. Spellman withdrew his hand from Thuc's and laughed, as O'Shea knew he would. As a cigar-chomping, tough-talking Irish ex-chaplain, O'Shea took more latitude with the cardinal than most priests, but that was why Spellman liked him. Frankly, Archbishop Thuc's deference bordered on the overweening and that never went far with Spellman. What O'Shea and Spellman knew was that if the Catholics of Vietnam had been delivered by Our Lady, she had made damn good use of the navy ships that brought a million of them from North to South after Dien Bien Phu. Tom Dooley, whose books had made that exodus famous, and had made the support of Catholics in Vietnam good politics in America, had begun as a navy doctor.

Spellman pointed to O'Shea. "And, I might add, a little help from Monsignor's Catholic Relief Service. How much do you calculate CRS put up for the early refugees, Monsignor?"

"Thirty-five million dollars, Your Eminence."

Spellman looked at Thuc. "And now the U.S. government has asked CRS to oversee the increased aid the president promised."

"Food, clothing and supplies," O'Shea said. "But also money. Some people aren't wild about the idea."

Thuc leaned toward O'Shea. "But we need those things. Our people *need* them."

"I know that, Your Excellency. But some people are a

little nervous about our serving as a government channel. We've been raising our own funds up to now, as you know. In America we have this little thing called separation of Church and State.''

Spellman grunted. "Forgive Monsignor O'Shea, Archbishop. He has an immigrant's zeal for American institutions.'' Spellman chuckled. "We natives understand there's a certain flexibility.''

Thuc shrugged. "It is only sensible to use the Church for aid. In my country only the Church is everywhere.''

"That's the point,'' O'Shea said. "That's why we've agreed.''

"And I'm going to depend on you, Peter Martin . . .'' The archbishop's Western name jarred Michael, but he realized at once it shouldn't have. It was his version of an Oriental's plastic surgery on his eyes. ''. . . to see that all goes well. President Kennedy does not want any confusion, any scandal. He wants to make an impact on the problem, and fast. That's why they're not waiting until the aid distribution structures are established between the governments.''

"You can depend on me, *Eminenza*. And on my family. You know that.''

Spellman nodded. "I told our secretary of state that Vietnam would be the only country in the world where the ruling class didn't get rich off Uncle Sam. He said to me, 'How can you be so sure of that, Cardinal Spellman?' And I said, 'Because Diem and his supporters are my people.' I told him, 'The Ngos are a great and ancient Catholic family. They're not lackey converts who submitted to baptism to win favor from the French.' I said, 'The Ngos are real Catholics, Mister Secretary. They're incorruptible men of their word, absolutely trustworthy.' And do you know what he said to me? He said, 'Your Eminence, your endorsement carries a lot of weight in this office.' ''

Monsignor O'Shea gestured with his unlit cigar. He was dying to smoke it, but Spellman wouldn't have it in the car. "Your Excellency,'' he said, "what the cardinal intends to emphasize, if I may speak . . .'' O'Shea looked quickly at Spellman, who nodded. ''. . . is the delicate position we are in. The new administration—a Catholic administration—has asked for assurance that the emergency aid program can efficiently and securely be administered through the structures of the Catholic Church. The last thing Jack Kennedy needs is a Church-related snafu, if you receive my meaning. And no black market. We want *your* personal assurance, Excellency. You should understand Cardinal Spellman's position with his own government. We are talking tens of millions of dollars here. Cardinal Spellman is depending on your government and on your family, Excellency. But first he is depending on you. Does that state the case fairly, Your Eminence?'' O'Shea plugged his mouth with his cigar.

Spellman nodded briskly. ''I go from here to Rome for Vatican approval. Caritas International will be the umbrella agency you'll relate to. It will be a Vatican-sponsored operation, but we'll all know where the relief is coming from. No one will mind the Church involvement if the hungry are fed and the naked clothed. Monsignor O'Shea will coordinate from our end. I have a meeting with Secretary Rusk as soon as I return. He wants my answer.''

''By all means, *Eminenza*. I give you all assurance you ask. My brothers and I already discussed this. We had indications you might be speaking of such subjects. We are agreed. Aid will continue to be distributed through the Church, under my supervision.''

Spellman stared at Thuc.

Until Thuc added, ''Not through the party.''

Spellman nodded. It was then Michael realized that this was the assurance the cardinal wanted. Michael didn't know it yet, but the party, the Revolutionary Personalist Labor Party of Vietnam, was the personal fiefdom of Diem's neurotic brother Nhu and already there were fears in Washington that he could not be controlled. The idea was to keep power tilted as much as possible away from him, even then. Thuc was seen to have a certain independence and they wanted to reinforce it.

Michael had assumed that at some point during that car ride he'd be introduced to Thuc, but he wasn't. He was just the junior ADC in the front seat, the guy with the chauffeur. He wasn't supposed to contribute to the conversation, and he wasn't expected to listen. But he had listened, carefully. This was the beginning of his education in new realities.

He felt somewhat awed when he realized what subtle brokering had been going on, and it excited him to see men like himself—*Church*men—in the thick of international power politics. Vietnam may have been a remote, backwater country, but it was a hell of a long way from Inwood. The more he saw of Spellman the more impressed he was. There was more to the man than the Saint Patrick's Day parades he presided over. If Diem had begun as his protégé, wasn't it admirable that Spellman was still working to get him what he needed to succeed? This maneuvering had been going on for a decade or more. While Americans, including Michael, had regarded Spellman as an affable but essentially parochial builder of schools and hospitals, he had been building a nation. And Spellman now was like an architect returning for a supervisory check on the structure he'd designed and which was nearly complete. A new nation, and its symbol, a basilica, in fact. Yes, the architect, Michael saw. Tom Dooley was the patron saint. And because of the support generated by the cardinal and the doctor together, the guarantor of that Vietnamese triumph-in-the-making was now John Kennedy.

The worldwide defeat of Communism would follow quickly upon the heels of the eradication of poverty and hunger, and this generation of Americans and Churchmen had made that their priority. *That* was why Kennedy excited men like Michael; he represented a country and a Church reinvigorated and on the move. He was the world's equivalent of Pope John. Pope John's hope and John Kennedy's urbane optimism infected the age, and the two strains they represented came together no more elegantly than in one movement, Tom Dooley's movement, and in one man, Ngo Dinh Diem of South Vietnam. Michael remembered how, at his inauguration, just two days after Dooley's death, President Kennedy gave perfect expression to the ideals of the CRS and Medico and activist priests, he suddenly saw, like Spellman, O'Shea and even himself. They would go anywhere, to fight any foe, to pass on the torch of freedom, that God's work on earth might truly be their own.

*   *   *

The convoy slowed as it approached the outskirts of Quang Tri.

"Good Lord," Monsignor O'Shea said. The car had just rounded a curve leaving the thick green tangle of jungle behind. The land on either side of the road had been cleared for planting, but the fields were jammed with Vietnamese, thousands of them. The rain poured steadily off their conical hats, veiling their faces with sheets of water. The people waved and cheered, holding aloft rosaries and crucifixes, medals of the Virgin and rain-streaked pictures of the Sacred Heart. The closer the convoy drew to the city, the more solidly packed the crowd was and the louder their cheers became. Umbrellas began to appear as city-dwellers began to outnumber the peasants.

Monsignor O'Shea twisted in his jump seat to touch Michael's shoulder. He said, as if an emotion had taken him by surprise, as if the others were not there, as if he had the right to speak so intimately, "When those moments come, Michael, and come they will, when you wonder whether the life you've chosen is worth it . . ." Monsignor O'Shea paused to make the full weight of his feeling felt. His eyes were fixed on the grateful faces of the Vietnamese. ". . . remember this. Carry this scene, son, in your heart."

Michael nodded, though in fact he was embarrassed. He'd wanted to be included in the worldly talk before. He wasn't up for O'Shea's pieties. He said feebly, "It must have been like this going into Paris with Ike."

The monsignor snorted and turned to Spellman. "Don't you love him for that comparison, Your Eminence? He's comparing you to Ike."

"If I'm Ike, Tim, that makes you George Patton, and you remember what happened to him."

O'Shea winked and pointed his unlit cigar at Thuc. "And that makes your brother Charles de Gaulle."

Thuc grinned and shook his head. "No, thank you, Monsignor. One Charles de Gaulle is quite enough."

By the time the convoy pulled into the city proper, all four of the clergymen had fallen silent and were simply watching the mass display. Hundreds of thousands of people, more than the entire population of Quang Tri, were standing in the

rain, cheering or clapping mahogany sticks together or waving their yellow-and-white papal—not American—flags. The
din of the rain on the automobile roofs and the incessant roar
of the crowd made conversation impossible, and in any case
the members of the president's party were too moved for talk
by the time they arrived at the basilica of Our Lady of La
Vang, a huge structure made of cinder block or brick and
faced with bright yellow stucco. However much the people
loved their leaders, though, they weren't allowed anywhere
near them. Rows of soldiers banked the entrance plaza, even
though the only people admitted to the basilica grounds as
such were appointed lay representatives of each of the country's
two archdioceses, eleven dioceses, and eight hundred parishes.

Inside the church all was cool, dry and silent, though it too
was packed. The elite of the nation were there, perhaps two
thousand of them, sitting in their pews, facing forward, absolutely still. From behind they were a sea of heads. The
women's were covered uniformly with black mantillas, as if
the pope himself were coming. The men's heads were all
uncovered, but the uniformity of their black gleaming hair,
sharply parted, was striking too. Though Diem, Nhu, the
archbishop, the cardinal and their attendants arrived amid
considerable commotion, no one in the church turned to look
at them. They would be signaled when to stand and when to
look. Aside from that commotion the only sounds were the
occasional rattle of rosary beads or the crackle of pages
turning in prayer books. This congregation, in its recollection,
its "custody" of the senses, was the fulfillment of a nun's
dream.

Cardinal Spellman would preside over the dedication ceremony, though the celebrant of the accompanying Solemn
Eucharist was to be Archbishop Thuc. Serving him as deacon
and subdeacon were a pair of Vietnamese prelates. Michael
and Monsignor O'Shea vested in surplices to serve as chaplains to the cardinal. Michael's job was to be sure that the
missal was open to the proper page every time Spellman
needed it, and Monsignor O'Shea was responsible for the
relic.

"What's that?" Michael had asked, eyeing the black chalice case that O'Shea had brought on board the airplane in New York. They hadn't left the runway yet.

"You wouldn't believe it."

"What is it? Your chalice?"

The monsignor shook his head. "It's Saint Joan's toenail."

"What?"

"Joan of Arc, you've heard of her?" O'Shea began to laugh despite himself, and so did Michael.

"Her what?" The two priests were still laughing when the stewardess asked them to buckle up.

"It's Spelly's gift to the people of Vietnam."

"Jeanne d'Arc's toenail?"

"We shouldn't mock it, Michael. Stop laughing."

"I always wondered, did she paint them?"

"Come on, Michael."

"Where the hell did he get her toenail?"

"Saint Joan's in the Bronx. They had two."

"Oh, Jesus."

"Come on, Michael. Cut it out."

"But, Monsignor, she *had* to paint them! It's Joan of Arc, right? She had to paint them with asbestos nail polish!"

She'd been burned at the stake, cuticles and all. O'Shea had blushed and said defensively, "Don't you believe in miracles?"

And now at the basilica Michael watched as Monsignor O'Shea solemnly handed the gold reliquary the size of a cigarette pack to Cardinal Spellman. With like solemnity Spellman placed the relic in the aperture in the stone slab of the high altar. Then the clergy stepped back while the stonemason—an unlikely-looking Vietnamese worker in white gloves and tails—closed the aperture with a fitted stone, then troweled cement over it.

"The bodies of the saints lie buried in peace," Spellman intoned in Latin, "but their names will live on forever." And the choir sang the verses of a Psalm while he incensed the altar.

Michael and O'Shea exchanged a glance, and for a moment Michael felt like an impish altar boy controlling his giggles. How could they believe in this crap? he thought. The toenail of Saint Joan, Christ! It was to purge the Church of such mumbo-jumbo that Pope John had recently called the Council.

Everyone around Michael, though, was profoundly moved. Archbishop Thuc was weeping openly while the other Vietnamese clergy lined up to kiss the stone. Saint Joan was their patroness, the warrior-woman, the heroine of all that was good in France. And Vietnamese Catholics, Michael saw suddenly, were as French as Roman, and that came as a shock. How Vietnamese were they? he wondered suddenly. It was a reservation, a first, small one, he wasn't ready to deal with. He veered from it.

But his mind tricked him. Joan of Arc! He veered toward the image of that saint. He pictured her, saw her exactly, that warrior-woman. But Joan of Arc was someone else to Michael. Wouldn't he have pictured her walking toward him across a lawn? Wouldn't he have remembered her asking, "Can I tell you who I remind myself of?"

Anne. No, Carolyn. In her simple bathing suit, the simple perfect body of a saint. With her short blond hair, like Joan's, with her long, elegant limbs, her flaring breasts, walking toward him. Then, in the trick of his mind, she was raising his fingers to her mouth and biting him just sharply enough to cause him pain.

"The bodies of the saints," he'd have repeated to himself, "lie buried in peace, but their names—Oh, Carolyn!" He'd have considered himself free of this. He wouldn't have been able to think of her without feeling again the intense pain of his humiliation. ". . . live on forever."

By the time the Solemn Mass of Dedication was over the rain had stopped and the noon sun shimmered gloriously. The reception for dignitaries was held at the Governor's Palace, and it spilled out into the minutely designed Japanese garden. Steam rose from the broad green leaves and from the glassy surfaces of ponds. The white pebbles of the pathways glistened. The guests hovered in the shade of trees and gazebos.

Michael watched the Vietnamese with a certain detachment. By and large he was ignored, and that was fine with him. He was trying to decipher his feelings. He wanted to understand what he was seeing. The men were like mandarins, though dressed in dark Western suits and ties. They carried themselves with that combination of swagger and subservience characteristic of those who know their exact place in the structure of power. In Vietnam that place was determined, even for Christians, by the fates of heaven. But, like his equivalents everywhere, the mandarin lives to hold sway over many more people than hold it over him. They ignored Michael and even O'Shea because only Spellman of the Americans had a defined place in the structure of their world. He was its patron. Every male present owed his position and probably his life to the ruddy, bald, jovial prelate, and each one knew it. And now Michael knew it. The man who made princes of the Church made princes of the world as well! Michael felt like an initiate in secrets, and even to be a junior associate of the cardinal gave him a sense of power. His Roman collar had never seemed more magical.

Spellman was the one Westerner toward whom the Vietnamese elite felt none of their habitual ambivalence. They waited patiently in line to kiss his ring, a gesture that came more naturally to them, with their sweeping bow, than to Americans. It occurred to Michael that perhaps another reason they took so warmly to the archbishop of New York was that, unlike most Caucasians, he was as short and doll-like as they were.

Monsignor O'Shea caught Michael's eye. He raised a finger toward him, and Michael crossed the room promptly. O'Shea had just lit his cigar at last, and was standing by the doors to the garden, to blow the smoke outside so Spellman wouldn't whiff it. "So what do you think?" O'Shea asked.

"Of what?"

"Of our president."

Diem's toast had been a rambling monologue that made no sense, but Michael said, "Seems like a good man."

"We're damn lucky to have him. If it wasn't for him Ho Chi Minh would have this whole country by now and where would these lovelies be?" He jerked his thumb at the elegant Vietnamese.

"At reeducation meetings."

"Well, you of all people should know what that means."

Michael lit a cigarette. Chain-smoking was something he

had in common with Diem. He and the short man in the white suit both reeked of tobacco, but Diem's olive-skinned fingers didn't show the nicotine stain like Michael's did. Michael sensed that the president made O'Shea uneasy and he wondered why. What did O'Shea know? Obviously he knew a lot. Michael looked around the room at the prosperous Vietnamese. "Well, you have to give him credit. He feeds the sheep." Michael smiled at O'Shea. " 'If you love me, feed my sheep.' I guess that's what we help with, eh?"

"We'll have our work cut out for us when we get home."

"I gather. Thuc has his cut out for him too."

O'Shea nodded. "Now that he knows Spelly will be watching he'll perform. The man runs a very tight ship."

"But obviously he's dedicated to his brother."

"But these guys are old-fashioned Catholics, Michael. He's the bishop. In his area, they leave him alone. They want the people fed more than anyone. Nothing improves here until the people eat. Diem and Nhu know that. So does Kennedy. That's the point."

O'Shea stopped talking when he saw approaching a tall, thin American with angular features. He was wearing a white suit as were most of the Vietnamese. "Monsignor O'Shea?" he said. He seemed worried. He ignored Michael.

"Yes?"

"I'm John Howe."

"Mister Howe! Nice to meet you." They shook hands. O'Shea turned to Michael. "Mister Howe and I have had correspondence. Mister Howe is an AID officer at the embassy in Saigon. What, the 'Commercial Import Program,' is that what you call it?" O'Shea smiled, and then said to Michael, "He's been a big help." He said to the embassy man, "This is Father Michael Maguire, Mister Howe. Father Maguire is my new assistant in New York."

Michael and the man shook hands. There was something about him that Michael experienced as utterly new. He didn't know what it was but it drew him in. He watched carefully as Howe turned back to O'Shea. "Monsignor, I'm glad to have a chance to chat with you," he said smoothly. "When I heard the cardinal was coming I hoped you'd be with him."

O'Shea smiled. "It's nice to see you too."

Howe was holding a tall drink and he sipped it then, as he looked out across the crowd. For a moment Michael thought that was it—two men who'd exchanged letters but never met, greeting each other. Howe glanced at Michael and they nodded awkwardly. "How do you like Vietnam, Father?"

"I've only been here a day." Why did Michael feel wary? What was it about the man that unsettled him? He was almost as tall as Michael. He was fair, but he was no newcomer to the tropics and his skin was a tawny red. He was Michael's age, not quite thirty, but little lines, like spokes, creased his face, as if he worried a lot or grimaced.

Howe said to O'Shea, "When you're in Saigon, I'd love to show you around."

"Thanks, Mister Howe. I'm afraid our schedule is full up though."

Howe stared at him. "I was hoping you might have time to stop by the embassy."

Despite the suppliant statement, there was a hint of the imperial in it and Michael caught it whether O'Shea did or not.

O'Shea simply shook his head and smiled. "Sorry."

Howe glanced at some nearby Vietnamese, then let his eyes drift across the crowd again. Suddenly Michael recognized him as a figure out of a magazine, an advertisement. He should have been wearing a dinner jacket, and this should have been a country club dance. His handsomeness, his poise, his grace were part of a package and Michael realized it was one he himself, despite his kind of handsomeness and poise, did not possess. John Howe was a man from a different world. It was a world Michael's people only read about, or, if they gained access to it, it was as servants.

Howe said brusquely, "But you got the letter I sent you two weeks ago?"

"No," O'Shea answered. "We've been in Manila."

"Well, that's all the more reason I'd appreciate some time, Monsignor." Something in Howe's voice was familiar too.

"What's your problem, Mister Howe?" Good old Tim, right to the point, if gruffly.

But Michael noted that Howe didn't flinch. "I've been led to believe that once the new Vietnam assistance appropriation

passes the Congress, Cardinal Spellman expects the major
share of funds, food and supplies to be distributed through
your agency."

O'Shea shrugged. "We've helped out here and there in the
past."

"Indeed so. You've done wonderful work. CRS is the best
private agency in Vietnam. But it's *private*. U.S. government
relief should come under U.S. government auspices."

"Through *your* office."

"In point of fact, yes."

The two men stared at each other. Michael waited for one
or the other to yield, but neither did. Michael sensed but did
not understand the depth of their antagonism. This Irish
priest. This highborn American diplomat. Unlike each other
in every way, but at that moment they were twins in their
disdain.

Michael sensed also, though, that Howe, unlike O'Shea,
would never make his resentment explicit. Howe veered
smoothly and said, "We share the same objective, Monsignor."

"That's right. But we don't share the same structure.
There are nearly a thousand Catholic parishes in this country,
all *over* this country, not just in cities. Those parishes are
what the experts call 'indigenous institutions,' Mister Howe,
and local people *already* look to them for assistance. What
could your office possibly hope to set up to match that?"

"But Monsignor . . ." Howe reined something. Michael
couldn't decide whether it was his impatience, his anger or
his condescension. "The point of U.S. government relief is
to help *all* the people of this country, not just the Catholics."

"Wait a minute, Mister Howe! Wait a damn minute! If
you're saying the Catholic Relief Service and Caritas International benefit only Catholics, then I take strong exception, do
you hear? Strong exception!"

Howe put his hand up. "I'm not saying that, Monsignor.
I'm not talking about your agency. I'm talking about Vietnam."
He smiled suddenly and said quite warmly, "You and I are
on the same side. The last thing I want to do is offend you."

Michael believed him, and, despite himself, he was drawn
to him. For one thing, he'd recognized what was familiar in
his voice. Howe had a subtler version of the New England–

Harvard accent that made Jack Kennedy's speech so appealing. Michael wanted to hear him out. "What's your point, Mister Howe?"

Howe turned to Michael. "What percentage of people in this country are Catholic, do you think?"

"Quite a large percentage," O'Shea put in, but Howe ignored him.

Michael calculated. The population of South Vietnam was seventeen million. More than a million Catholics had fled the North. They must have joined at least three or four million others. The French were there a long time. He said, "A third. Thirty to forty percent."

Howe nodded dismissively. "Less than ten percent, Father. Including the refugees. Yet every governor of every province is a Catholic. Every senior officer in the army is a Catholic. The farmers who receive favored treatment in the land reform are Catholic. The students in the schools . . . the diplomats abroad, all Catholic. No offense, but where are the Buddhists? Where are the Confucians?"

"And where is the Church of England?" O'Shea asked bitterly. "Right, Mister Howe?"

"Hey, Tim." Michael took his elbow. O'Shea's tribal sensitivity embarrassed Michael.

But O'Shea didn't give a shit about embarrassment. He leaned toward Howe. "If your nice liberal American sensibilities are offended by the primitive practices of the natives here, perhaps you're in the wrong country. Why don't you put in for Italy? I'd be glad to ask the cardinal to say a word for you when he meets with Mister Rusk next week." O'Shea pulled on his cigar, satisfied with himself.

Howe smiled thinly. This immigrant shaman had no power over him, whatever his illusions. "Monsignor, you've taken what I said personally. That's not how I meant it."

"You've slurred the Catholic Church, Mister Howe. That may not be a 'personal' matter in your religion but it is in ours."

Howe nodded. His resignation was evident. He would withdraw now. His dignity, his self-esteem, would be intact. O'Shea, of course, and his assistant, would feel shabby. Howe said, "I look forward to cooperating with the relief effort however it is set up. Who will your representative in this country be?"

"Archbishop Thuc."

"I mean day to day, Monsignor. Who's going to handle logistics?"

"One of the archbishop's priests, Mister Howe. I'm sure you can find out from him."

"I assumed you'd have an American here."

"We don't work that way in the Catholic Church. We're a transnational institution." Unlike some I could name, was implied. "As I said, the structure is in place. And it's reliable."

"I'm sure it is." Howe shook hands with O'Shea. When he turned to Michael, wasn't there a hint of pleading in his eye? Can you help me with this character? Michael shook his hand noncommittally. Howe said, "Good luck, Father." Then he raised his drink in a mock toast and left.

O'Shea snorted and said to Michael under his breath, "Goddamn Prod! Typical! Trying to make religion the issue when it's just a run-of-the-mill turf fight. Shops all around him in that embassy are gearing up, military and agricultural development, health and sanitation. But he's just trickling along at the same old rate, surplus rice and CARE packages. He sees the boom coming and is afraid he'll be left out. He wants his hand on the spigot instead of mine. That's all."

O'Shea was ranting, it seemed to Michael. He'd rarely seemed so agitated. Michael said, mainly out of loyalty, "You stopped him cold when you said Spelly would be meeting with Rusk."

O'Shea nodded. "These guys are all alike. An eye forever cocked on that next promotion. I'll tell you something funny— he'd *love* to get shipped to Italy. Those Episcopalians just swoon for Italy." O'Shea slapped Michael's shoulder as if celebrating a victory over the old enemy, but Michael knew that Howe held them both in contempt. Michael was perplexed by his own inability to simply sweep the man aside, as O'Shea had. Was that because Howe was right? Or was it something else? Why did Howe appeal to him?

O'Shea was still jabbering. "It's people like him who worry that Kennedy's going to put holy water in White House commodes. If you ask him what a commode is, he looks down his Brahmin nose and says, 'I don't know. I'm not a Catholic.' ''

"But he had a point, Tim."

O'Shea stiffened. "Is that so?"

"Only about wanting an American. It might make sense to have an American on the spot. You said yourself, Thuc has to know Spelly's watching. An American priest might keep him honest."

"Goddamnit, Michael. He's an archbishop of the Church. He *is* honest."

"He'll have pressures from his brothers, and you know it."

"Forget it. Spelly leaves Thuc alone. Once the stuff leaves New York it's their show. That's the way it's always been."

"Not with Dooley, it wasn't."

"Tom Dooley was special, Father. The people over here worshipped him. He saved this nation's hide. Anyway, the CRS has guidelines. We use local clergy where possible. You know that."

Michael nodded. He'd said enough. He looked across the room, blithely, hoping that O'Shea did not sense his surge of feeling. My God, he thought, an American! What an arena this would be. Not a desk in New York, not a parish in Queens. Not altar boys and Legion of Mary meetings. But a major role in what Kennedy called a "massive joint effort" to help democracy grow out of the ashes of conflict between colonialism and Communism. Here was a cause that mattered! How he wanted to alleviate suffering. Yes. But how, also, he wanted to leave behind the demeaning, petty restraints of the junior New York clergy! There was more, far more, to being a priest than the submissiveness of rectories, the banalities of parish life, and Michael Maguire, for one, was going to have it.

He told O'Shea he was going for a fresh drink, but instead went after John Howe. He found him in the spacious palace foyer, by the entrance. A servant had just handed him his hat.

"Mister Howe, just leaving? I was too." Michael fell into step with him. "Perhaps we could walk a bit." Howe eyed him for an instant, then nodded. The two men left the Governor's Palace together. Outside its gates the city was teeming. The press of the crowd made conversation difficult, so they moved through it in silence.

The dedication was the occasion of a great festival in Quang Tri. Farmers and their families from the surrounding countryside had come to town, and so had fishermen from the coastal villages. The narrow streets were crowded with food stalls at which the pilgrims vied for their midday meal. The foodstuffs were exotic—bird's eyes, fish heads, little heaps of slimy grubs harvested from inside palm trees, and piles of vermicelli, "little worms" indeed, which Michael mistook for pasta. The two Americans slowly moved through the crowd, towering over them. Those Vietnamese who acknowledged them addressed Michael in singsong French, *"Bonjour, mon père!"* Michael nodded, but Howe, as if addressed himself, returned their greeting in Vietnamese.

Soon the crowd began to thin as townspeople drifted inside for siesta. A few blocks from the basilica the neat white-washed buildings of the central district gave way to rows of corrugated-roofed shanties. Tens of thousands of refugees had yet to be settled, and these were some of them. Children surrounded Maguire, tugging at his soutane. Their dark eyes implored, and Michael realized with a shock that the children were hoping for rice. He was a priest, wasn't he? He looked helplessly at Howe, whom the children had pushed aside and ignored. "You see," Michael wanted to say, "this is the difference between us. This is why I became a priest."

Michael pushed through the children, and he and Howe left them behind.

"Good Lord," Michael said.

"Shocking, isn't it, when you see it close."

"Yes. They're so desperate. It's why we should find a way to work together, don't you think? They're the ones we're working for."

"I couldn't agree more," Howe said. He looked at Michael with surprise. He hadn't expected conciliation.

Michael let his curiosity about Howe show itself. "Where were you before Vietnam?"

"The Congo two years. Before that Brazil."

"Always in relief work?"

Howe nodded.

"You speak Vietnamese, I noticed."

"Just a few words. I'm still learning."

"I admire that. I'm lousy at languages. Except Latin."
Michael grinned self-mockingly. He saw that this was the
assignment Howe wanted. O'Shea had been unfair.

At a hut farther along a family of six or seven hovered at
the doorway. Two of the children, perhaps ten and twelve,
each had a scar on one side of his head where there should
have been an ear. Michael saw their parents in the shadows;
their ears had been mutilated too. They watched from within
their hovel with the peculiar, angled stance of the partially
deaf. Michael had to look away. "Did you see that?"

"Yes," Howe said. "They're from Bao Lak, a province in
the North next to China. The Viet Minh there were notorious.
It's said they had a special penalty for anyone caught listening to 'evil words.' They ripped your ear off with pliers even
if you were a baby in your mother's arms. Do you know what
the 'evil words' were? The Catholic Mass."

"God."

"I'm not indifferent to what Catholics suffered in the
North, Father."

"I know that," Michael said. "I saw the point you were
trying to make to Monsignor O'Shea."

"I couldn't believe his reaction, frankly."

"I think he was trying to tell you that religion and politics
don't mix."

Howe stopped and faced Michael. "Forgive me, Father,
but that's quite fatuous, and I think you know it. Religion *is*
politics here. Why do you think this basilica was built in
Quang Tri? To anchor the Catholic population by the border
with the North, to discourage Ho Chi Minh from crossing,
that's why! The archbishop claimed in his sermon that the
basilica was built by the donations of all the people. I couldn't
believe no one laughed. The basilica was paid for by lottery
tickets that Diem's police made the whole population buy.
Everyone knows that here but Spellman. Hell, Spellman doesn't
even know this is a Buddhist country."

"Yes, he does, Mister Howe." Michael reined his clerical
defensiveness, which seemed banal compared to Howe's
emotion.

"Well, Diem and his people don't know it. The U.S. government shouldn't be playing to their weakness. And their weakness, Father, frankly, is a shocking level of intolerance toward the majority of Vietnamese, and that has a religious aspect. That's all I'm saying." As abruptly as he'd stopped, Howe began walking again, leaving Michael to catch up with him.

Which accounted perhaps for the irritation he felt suddenly. Who the hell was Howe to lecture him? To club Spellman and O'Shea with his high-toned moral sensitivity? Wasn't his concern a bit overdelicate?

But Michael realized something about Howe then, trailing him by a pace, watching him move intently through the streets without seeing them. Howe was used to moving in a world of ideals and principles. Wasn't that the point of a Harvard education? Didn't men like Howe always know how other people, other nations, fell short of standards? Wasn't that—the moral shortfall of the other—their expertise? How angry it could make them, how impatient. "Hey, wait a minute!"

But Howe kept up his stride, ignoring Michael.

Maybe it was Howe's standards that appealed to Michael. Certainly his obvious dedication did. Michael admitted that the novelty of Howe's passionate idealism was stunning. So what that his own instincts, by nature and training, ran another way. Michael, like his kind, was pragmatic. The human condition was not a scandal to him, but a given. As far as Vietnam was concerned, in his opinion, religious pluralism could wait awhile. Democracy was the end, not the means. What mattered now was getting people fed. But Michael wasn't interested in debating his differences with the AID officer. What he was interested in, he admitted finally, was getting over here and playing on this team. Michael Maguire wanted off the bench.

He grabbed Howe's arm. They faced each other.

"You were also saying you could use an American priest."

"What?"

"As liaison between Archbishop Thuc and your office."

The two men stared at each other. Michael was aware of a current between them that had nothing to do with their positions.

This could have been happening on a football field or in a school corridor or in a barracks. Michael recognized Howe as a man he wanted to be with. But Howe, perhaps sensing it, looked away. And Michael felt foolish.

"Yes," Howe said calmly. When he looked at Michael now it was with masterful detachment. "That would enable us to help with the relief effort."

"And to monitor it." Michael could be cool too. "You'd like to make sure the distribution is equitable, that *everyone* gets what they need. That's fair enough. I agree with you. And I agree that an American priest could help open up some lines of communication. I'd like to be that priest. . . ." Michael almost said "John" but he sensed that Howe would continue to call him "Father," and so he didn't use any address at all. "And you could help me get appointed."

Howe shook his head. "I don't understand."

"Cardinal Spellman and Monsignor O'Shea don't see the need as of yet. But I think if the suggestion originated at the upper levels of the State Department . . ."

"You've gathered, I think, that my influence there is limited. If I had my way His Eminence wouldn't be involved in Vietnamese affairs at all."

"Cardinal Spellman was involved in Vietnam when you and I were still in high school. It might help for both of us to keep that in mind. The point is, can't you make some recommendation? What if you compromised? What if you offered to support the distribution of relief through CRS, but with one condition. Wouldn't that carry weight?"

"The condition being . . . ?"

"Me."

"By name?"

Michael shrugged. "Why not? You could tell them you discussed it with me, at your initiative, of course. I'd report as much to Monsignor O'Shea. You could say my background would be a particular asset."

"What background?"

"I was a POW in China for nearly three years." Michael smiled. "I know the Oriental mind."

Howe stared at Michael, who read him. Hadn't he dismissed this priest only moments before? Now he was looking again, and for the first time he saw more than a Church functionary. There was a man here, with a history. Howe said with a certain deference, "That's the kind of thing they love at State."

Michael nodded. "Spellman loves it too. It proves his priests are real men, you know?" Michael grinned. He often mocked himself, but it wasn't like him to mock the cardinal. That he also mocked Howe for *his* nod to the mystique of war prisoners was inadvertent. "The point is, if you make an issue of it, there's a good chance they'll do it. His Eminence wants this operation to go smoothly, and he also wants his people in the middle of it."

Howe nodded. "All right. It could help, your being here." Howe hesitated, then added, "I think I could work with you."

Michael smiled. Was that supposed to be a compliment? For a Catholic priest, he was okay.

"May I ask you, Father, why you're interested?"

What could Michael say? To feed the hungry, clothe the naked, preach the good news to the poor? He too had *oblige,* if not *noblesse.* He checked his resentment and said what men in ward rooms and officers' clubs always say. "This is the action, isn't it?"

Howe's face broke into its first grin. For all their high-toned social concern, however differently expressed, this was the truth between them, what they had in common, and each saw it. "It sure is, Father. It sure is."

FIFTEEN

A MONTH later, Carolyn and I got married. I'd expected it to be awkward, having Michael as the priest, and so had Carolyn, I think, although we didn't talk about it.

But it wasn't at all, mainly because, lo and behold, Michael carried the ceremony off like an old smoothie. You wouldn't have believed how cool he was, how relaxed, witty, outgoing, affectionate. The ceremony was in the tailored yard of the house in Dobbs Ferry, so there was none of the anxiety that comes so naturally to wedding parties in churches, and Michael led us through our vows with such grace, such patent joy for us that even Carolyn, I thought, conquered her reservation. Oh that fucking reservation! For myself, holding her hand and pronouncing my promise, while feeling the weight of her gaze upon me, I never expected to be happier. Hell, I guess, as it turned out, I never was.

And what a relief it was to find Michael so excited about his own life. And with reason. As he described what he'd experienced—or rather discovered—in Vietnam, a great drama unfolding and a prospect that he would play an important role in it, I found myself thinking, God, Michael's world is going to be huge, so vastly larger than mine.

"So what do you think?" he asked.

"Sounds good," I said noncommittally. Was I just too much the cynic to respond to his enthusiasm? Was I jealous? Or was I simply unable to grasp what he was saying? What the hell did I know? Vietnam to me, as to almost everyone in 1961, was someplace near where Yul Brynner waltzed around with Deborah Kerr. Michael was whistling a happy tune, all right. And that was fine with me, though I suspect my eyes glazed over as he went on.

The weary nations of Europe, with their empires collapsed and their Enlightenment secularity bankrupt, could look now to a rejuvenated Catholicism and an America on the move. The pope and the president, the two Johns, all that shit; he was convinced of it. And he told me—how he would blush when I threw this back at him later—that Diem was an Asian Thomas More. So who was Cardinal Wolsey? I wanted to ask. That was Thuc, of course, though no one knew that yet. In Michael's view the Ngos' promise was enormous, and *that* was why it was crucial to go to their support. Ngo Dinh Diem, having been nurtured by American Catholicism and sponsored by it, now embodied its triumph.

Michael's triumph.

It is almost impossible now, given how badly that project turned out—which puts it rather mildly, doesn't it?—to imagine that Vietnam could ever have embodied such a dream. But it did. Still, even then I sensed that Michael's conviction was also a matter of something else. I didn't understand what he was really telling me until I looked across at Carolyn; she winked at me, and I realized that, of course, he had to go out now and save the world. Only the world itself, redeemed at last, could fill the hole that the loss of that woman had cut in him.

It was some months before Michael's assignment to Vietnam came through. Archbishop Thuc, of course, opposed having an American watchdog in his front yard, and he tried every way he could to get Spellman to change his mind. O'Shea had his reservations too. Was Michael seasoned enough? Would he walk with the roll of the place? But Spellman liked the idea and he liked having a priest who impressed the people at State. Michael arrived in Vietnam in January of 1962. He took up residence in the cathedral rectory in Saigon, but he had almost no contact with Archbishop Thuc from the very beginning. The first surprise was that the archbishop lived not at the cathedral but at Freedom Palace on Tu Do Street with his brothers. The second surprise was that his fellow priests had apparently been ordered to cooperate with Michael to the minimum, and beyond that to have nothing to do with him. He made the round of orphanages, refugee centers and hospitals that were being supported by the CRS. The European and American volunteers welcomed him, but Vietnamese relief workers, including nuns and priests, reacted as if he'd come to spy on them. In a way, he admitted to himself with a certain shame, it was true.

In Saigon he depended more than he'd have wanted on the Americans at the embassy for orientation. But, hell, the Vietnamese would hardly talk to him. And for some reason, John Howe didn't seem that anxious to school Michael in the local realities either. When they finally did get together, perhaps a month after Michael's arrival, it wasn't for a tour of AID projects or for briefings even. It was for tennis. Howe suggested it. Michael demurred. He didn't have a racket. It wasn't his game, really, he said. Howe insisted; he had two rackets. Michael knew the type. He liked to take on inferior partners now and then just to demonstrate the difference between pretty good and first rate, but what he said was, "If you're going to be in Saigon, you'll have to take it up. Everything important happens at the Cercle Sportif."

The Cercle Sportif was the high-walled colonial-era tennis and swimming club that the French planters had built for themselves. Its glory days were past, but it was still the nearest thing to an elegant spa in Saigon, and the remaining French elite now shared it with select Vietnamese, European and American diplomats and, lately, to everyone's chagrin, the news photographers and reporters who were coming to Saigon in ever greater numbers.

Michael met Howe at the front gate and was immediately embarrassed. Howe was decked out, scrupulously, in tennis whites. Michael was wearing black canvas basketball shoes, plaid Bermuda shorts and a blue sport shirt. He'd been afraid of this. Howe didn't flinch as they shook hands. Howe handed Michael his extra racket, and, as he followed him into the compound, Michael felt like Goofy the Dog.

To the right were the tennis courts, half a dozen of them, all clay, brilliant orange, and all in use. Other players sat at tables on the terraced lawn, watching. Everyone was dressed in white. To the left was a large swimming pool. Michael's eye went immediately to a pair of bikini-clad *colonistes* who sat on the near edge talking loudly in French. There were Vietnamese women, also in bikinis, less voluptuously endowed, but with long gleaming black hair that they displayed by tossing their heads. Beyond the pool was the awning-covered café leading into the *maison*. Men in white linen suits sat at tables with tall drinks in front of them, watching the *jeunes filles en fleur*.

Howe led the way toward the courts. "We're up," he said, as a doubles match ended. Michael felt a rush of anxiety as he unbolted the racket brace. Tennis was one of the games seminarians mastered, but he'd never played anyone in white before. Suddenly he realized he had no standards. How good had the guys in the sem been? How good was he? Michael had an athlete's pride. He did not want to be humiliated. It was bad enough that when he passed the players who were leaving the court they cast disapproving glances at his shoes. When he looked down he saw that the tread of his soles, a pattern of circles and triangles, was clearly imprinted in the clay. Oh, Christ!

During the warm-up hitting, when the spectators sized up newcomers, Michael's timing, naturally, was completely off. He missed shot after shot or sent them looping into adjoining courts. Howe had the smooth, steady stroke of someone who'd had his lessons early; by comparison Michael was a flailer. He knew he was already the perfect image of a fool. The perfect image, in *this* world, he thought, of a Catholic priest.

It took him most of the first set, which went all too quickly, to realize what was wrong. He'd played his tennis on all-purpose seminary courts, asphalt, never clay. On asphalt the ball sizzled, skipping across the surface, and Michael had developed a style that depended on speed and power. But the ball positively died on clay, and slow, careful moves, accurate placement and finesse were what counted. Michael consciously adjusted, and began to play better. He lost the second set, but not as badly. And by the third he realized that the spectators who'd dismissed their match earlier were watching intently. Michael matched Howe point for point and in the eighth game broke his serve. He won 6–4. When they shook hands at the net, Michael realized that Howe was shocked. Howe was embarrassed.

When they left the court, attendants had to come to repair the damage Michael's shoes had done.

They crossed the terraced lawn, went by the pool and took a table in the café under the awning. They complimented each other on the game. Howe said they were well matched and should play regularly. Michael promised to get the right shoes and they both laughed. They ordered drinks. Howe asked the waiter to bring them towels.

"So how has it been going, Father?"

Michael shrugged. "Pretty good. I've been learning my way around. We have a new center in Bien Hoa. I've been trying to help with that."

"Good." Howe smiled formally, then he wiped perspiration from his face and glanced around. Where were the damn towels?

Michael said, "I'm sorry I haven't been able to arrange your meeting with the archbishop. He hasn't even deigned to see me yet. I wouldn't say he's overjoyed at my being here."

Howe nodded. "He's no dummy. He knows you're one guy who could cause him trouble."

The waiter delivered the towels before Michael answered. He wanted to say, I didn't come here to cause anybody trouble. He didn't like the way Howe took it for granted that he shared his disdain for the archbishop.

They wiped their faces and their necks.

Michael said, "I visited an orphanage in Can Lo where the nuns and priests sleep on stone floors so that the children can have the beds."

Howe looked up at him sharply. "Why do you tell me that?"

Michael shrugged. "I was moved by it. There are dedicated priests and nuns in this country."

"I know that." Howe stared at Michael, making it obvious that he did not want his criticism of Thuc and Diem and Nhu reduced to primitive anti-Catholicism. "Hey, look," he said, "we can go around in circles, me saying the Catholics are bad, you saying they're good. So what? You know what my problem is. It's a Buddhist country."

The waiter interrupted again, this time with their drinks. Howe thanked him easily. Unlike Michael, he took the man's servility for granted.

When the waiter left, Michael leaned toward Howe. "Look, Catholics may be the minority here but they're in power not because of some conspiracy but because they're educated, they have Western values, and they appreciate what Communism can do to a country. I don't think it matters a damn how many province chiefs are Catholics. The question is, are they doing their job? The way I read recent history, I think they are."

Howe pushed the sugar bowl aside. "Can I give you a slightly different version of that history?"

Michael stared at him, sipped his lemonade, waited. He wanted Howe to quit beating around the bush with him. He knew they would never be friends until they could speak with each other frankly. And Michael admitted, he wanted to be friends with this man.

Howe nodded. "First, about this crap that Diem rescued the Catholics in the North from the Red Devil murders. Pure bull, Father."

"Wait a minute, Howe. What about that day in August, we saw those people with missing ears? You were the one who told me what their crime was, hearing Mass."

Howe waved his hand dismissively. "I was telling you what the people said, what they believed had happened. But it probably wasn't true."

"How do you know that?"

Howe worked at breaking up the sugar cubes in his tea. The ice was melted and he snapped his fingers at the Vietnamese waiter and barked several Vietnamese phrases at him. He waited for the boy to return with the ice. The interruption had the effect of defusing the challenge that had been implicit in Michael's question. While dropping a few cubes in Michael's drink as well, he said, "Because I know a guy who brags that he made that story up himself. An American. An Agency man who ran a string of 'black propaganda' agents whose job was to spread rumors like that among the Catholic population, to feed their panic. The Viet Minh were perfectly capable of mutilating people, but their

targets were collaborators, not Catholics. There was no poetry to it—an ear because of the Mass you'd heard. That
came from the CIA. I've heard that some of those agents
carried out atrocities themselves, to frighten the people into
running.''

"But why? Who cared if the Catholics stayed or moved?''

"Think about it. Who was better known in the rectories of
New York than in the villages of South Vietnam? Diem, the
George Washington of Southeast Asia. But who the hell in
this country ever heard of George Washington? When his
people needed him most, fighting the French, he was living
the high life in Spellman's seminary, giving tennis lessons to
you guys." Howe grinned, but only for a moment. "Diem's
power base was in Washington, not Saigon. And only one
group could change that for him. The Catholics in the North.
They could become his base. So he had to attract them south,
or drive them there, like cattle. Hence the U.S. Navy. Hence
Doctor Dooley. Hence Cardinal Spellman, all portraying the
Ngos as the rescuers of the refugees, when the case was just
the opposite. That migration of a million people was the great
CIA success of the decade, better even than the coups in Iran
and Guatemala.''

Michael sipped his drink. "I'm a little slow, John, aren't
I? You're with the Agency, of course.''

Howe shook his head. "Not on your life, Father. Their
manipulation of your Church and your Churchmen is not only
cynical but stupid, doomed to fail. Catholicism will never be
anything here but a vestige of colonialism, and colonialism is
dead. I don't think the CIA knows that yet.''

Michael smiled awkwardly. The sweeping, and compelling,
indictment of his Church embarrassed him, but he was not
prepared to acknowledge this. "So remind me. Why was it
you wanted yet another Catholic priest over here?''

Howe did not answer him.

Michael pressed. "You said, if I recall, that you wanted
communication, but you haven't asked me anything about the
local church. You said you wanted a meeting with Thuc, but
obviously you regard him as one of the Borgias. What the
hell do you want, John? Why am I here?''

Howe only stared back. Suddenly the man's inaccessibility

infuriated Michael. Then he saw it. "Good God, you think I'll come around, don't you? I'll see it like you do, and I'll make my report to Spellman, whom you hold in contempt in every way but one. He's still the key to controlling Diem."

Howe laughed. " 'Controlling Diem!' Everybody is controlling Diem—Spellman, Kennedy, Nhu, Madame Nhu." He stopped abruptly and pointed to the far tennis court. "See that guy over there, playing doubles? That's our esteemed ambassador. His partner is the CIA chief of mission. They're playing against two guys out from Washington who are supposed 'to appraise the current situation.' Everything depends on what those men say. Oh, sure, Nhu makes them nervous, but he's paid to. He makes Diem look good by comparison. They never talk to anyone—forgive me, Father, for the theme! —but Catholics. And you know what else? They never leave Saigon. So Diem controls them. He controls Kennedy. He controls us."

"I leave Saigon, John," Michael said with bravado, "and no one controls me."

"Good for you." Howe stood up. Had he said that snidely? Michael thought so until he added somberly, "It is important that you see what's happening. That's all I wanted. That's why I hoped you'd come."

Howe gathered his rackets and turned to lead the way out.

At that moment a good-looking American woman approached him. She was wearing whites and carrying a racket of her own. "Jack," she called.

He opened his arms as she came to him, and without a thought they embraced and kissed blatantly. She might have been his lover, but, if so, Michael sensed, not his only one. Nor was he hers. She said, "Play with me. My partner didn't show."

Howe said, "Who was your partner?"

"Annie."

Howe winked at Michael. "Well, in that case . . ." As long as it wasn't a rival. He turned to Michael. "This is Sally Doubleday, Father. Sally writes for *Newsweek*. This is Father Maguire, Sally. He's with Church Relief."

Michael and the woman shook hands. She eyed him boldly, but he expected that. Now he was glad he wasn't wearing whites. He wasn't just another dashing correspondent or Foreign Service dandy. He never liked being different except when he saw how it piqued a pretty woman's interest. What really piqued that, of course, was her realization that he wasn't on the make.

She looked back at him once as Howe went off with her. Michael watched them both, but it was the change in Howe he was aware of. He was so much more relaxed suddenly, jovial, even, and high-spirited. Obviously Michael had an inhibiting effect on the man, and he regretted it. They would remain strangers. When Michael realized that Howe hadn't followed through on his suggestion that they play tennis again, he felt put down. Should he have let the bastard win? Was this a country club? Was Michael Maguire a ball boy?

He left the Cercle Sportif, knowing he wouldn't return, and angry because of it. But then he chastised himself. He wasn't in Vietnam to improve his social standing.

The month that Carolyn and I got married, September of 1961, the Communists took over a provincial capital just outside Saigon. They held it long enough to flaunt their impunity and underscored it by decapitating the Catholic province chief. Though we heard nothing about it in America, the raid was the beginning of a new level of terror. It frightened the people of Saigon, and the method of mutilation terrorized even the sophisticates and the Catholics. As Vietnamese they still believed that a decapitated person is condemned to an eternity of headless exile, the worst of all possible fates.

The Communists proceeded with their hit-and-run terror among the rural population and with their brutal assassinations of local officials. And it worked. The illusion of Diem's control collapsed. By the time Michael had arrived in Vietnam that winter it was obvious at once that the CRS estimates of the numbers of refugees, displaced persons and orphaned children were already outdated. The relief program he'd come to help administer, once seen as mammoth, would barely touch the surface of the problem. Michael assumed at first that that was the result of the new Communist-sponsored violence. Indirectly, it was. But the immediate cause of the

people's misery was a tactic that had been adopted by the
Diem government, the elaborate fortification of central villages, "agrovilles" or "strategic hamlets." It was a tactic
that had worked against Communists in Malaya; in Vietnam
the French had tried to hold every village and had failed. So
now most villages were evacuated; it was a second mass-
movement of Vietnamese under Diem. But these people were
not Catholics and they were not willing, so their resettlement
had to be forced. The Americans called it "Operation Sunrise,"
and Maxwell Taylor referred to the program as "a great
national movement." But in practice it was violent and brutal,
and the supposedly idyllic "agrovilles" were in fact concentration camps. By the end of 1962 ten million peasants had
been confined to these heavily guarded centers, working their
fields and paddies in the daytime and returning to the "hamlets"
at night. Thousands of peasants who resisted this resettlement
were thereby branded Communist and killed. Hundreds of
thousands of others, terrified by the awful, alien crossfire
they found themselves in, crowded into the cities, burdening
them impossibly. Almost overnight Diem, as if ignorant of
the sacrosanct character of the tie between the Vietnamese
and his home village, the village of his ancestors, had created
a grave crisis of personal and spiritual identity for his own
people. He had made them into exiles in their own country.
In the beginning his problem had been that they didn't know
him. Now it was that they hated him. And exactly as he
expected the American government to provide his army with
weapons to enforce his policies, he expected the Church to
provide his displaced and demoralized population with food,
clothing and medical care.

It was an impossible job and Michael Maguire was one of
the people who had it. The longer he was in Vietnam the
more his focus narrowed. No longer did rhetoric about a new
polity, a *via media* between right and left, appeal to him. His
days were taken up with endless rounds of meetings with the
various volunteer agencies and Church officials who were
responsible for getting the supplies out to the countryside. In
fact, Michael, whose duties had been only vaguely defined
when he'd arrived, became a kind of troubleshooting dispatcher.
He was the guy who ran from one logjam to the next, kicking

them loose, from bureaucracy to ministry, from dockside to truck depot, from the American embassy to the offices of the archdiocese.

And most of the time, like all Americans, he was in Saigon. And from Saigon, as refugees poured in by the thousands with their horrible stories, it was impossible not to believe that the Communists had gone from their ruthless assassinations to a policy of mass murder. Ironically, when reasons began to appear for hedging his support of Diem, Michael, like the leaders in Washington, stiffened it. The more of the victims' suffering he saw, the more he accepted the arguments of the anti-Communists. And he accepted the government's position that until order was restored, even if that meant extreme defensive measures, like the "agrovilles," nothing else could happen. Given the urgency of the situation, concerns about Catholic predominance seemed irrelevant. It was just as well he wasn't seeing Howe. If the AID officer came at him about the Ngos' religious intolerance, Michael would have reacted as O'Shea had, spouting the old chestnut that anti-Catholicism is the anti-Semitism of liberal Episcopalians.

But then one day Howe showed up. He burst into Michael's office without knocking. Michael was on the phone with a French warehouse owner who'd been looking the other way while his workers pilfered rice to sell on the black market. Obviously they'd done so at his behest.

Howe said, "Can you come with us, Father? I think you should."

Michael held his finger up and repeated his threat to the Frenchman, and promised a visit, then hung up. He looked at Howe. "What?"

Howe calmed himself by wiping the perspiration from his hands on his khaki trousers. He wore an open-necked short-sleeve white shirt and no coat. On his head was a baseball cap with a B on it, Boston. "Come with us. Right now," Howe said. He let his agitation show, an amplification of his abrupt demand.

"All right." Michael stood and buttoned the black soutane he wore most of the time, as the Vietnamese clerics did. He picked up the stiff linen collar from his desk and fitted it around his neck as he followed Howe out into the brutal midday heat.

Howe had an embassy car, a Ford or something, and Michael sat beside him in front. In the back was the striking figure of a saffron-robed Buddhist monk, an elderly man. His bronze skin was tight on his shaved skull and his eyes were fixed on a point beyond. Michael glanced back at him but the monk did not speak and Howe did not offer to introduce them. Throughout the time it took them to clear the city and drive well into the countryside, the three maintained their silence, and by then it had come to seem natural.

My Tho was a river settlement in the delta region south of Saigon, formerly a fishing center but now one of those towns that had been swamped by refugees. It took two hours of fast driving through unsafe country to reach its outskirts where they were impossibly slowed by the thick traffic of carts and staggering families. One never saw Americans in the smaller towns in those days; the American command was only about twelve thousand strong.

Michael said, "It reminds me of Korea," though for the first time he noticed that the Vietnamese had no equivalent of the Korean A-frames for carrying their loads. The people carried their bundles or their children in their arms, and seemed doubly burdened.

"I hate to do this, but . . ." Howe leaned on the horn and gunned the engine threateningly. The refugees made way.

Howe addressed the monk in Vietnamese. The monk responded and made a pointing gesture. The monk, Michael understood, was the one giving directions. After winding through several blocks' worth of crowded streets, they pulled into a broad, open square, and the scene they came upon disturbed Michael because of the suffering it implied, but it also filled him with pride.

An outdoor food line was in progress. Old men and women, children, the parents of families, refugees of all kinds were waiting patiently for their turn at the huge vats of rice from which Vietnamese Catholic nuns were scooping ample bowls full. Beyond the vats, small sacks of rice, enough to sustain a family for a week, were being distributed. The refugees had the blank look of the displaced, but that was normal. A nurse was moving among them, checking their sores and wounds.

Michael looked at Howe for his explanation.

Howe said, "Don't you notice something?"

Michael looked at the scene again. It was all as it should have been. There were government soldiers behind the rice vats with their weapons ready, but that was standard too. No one was being bullied. And food was being given indiscriminately to everyone.

"What am I missing?" Michael asked.

"Look at the line."

Michael traced the line as it snaked back and forth across the square. Hundreds of people were waiting. Then he saw it. The line of refugees, each with his personal bowl, was issuing from the open portal, like tape from a roll, of the church on the far side of the square. The Catholic church. Michael crossed toward it, with Howe and the monk behind him. And as he did he suddenly felt an ominous dread. What could he possibly find in there? He began pushing through the crowded square more roughly, though ordinarily he was most gentle with people in that situation. The closer he came to the church the faster he went. At the entrance he pushed a man aside. At first, because of the dark, he couldn't see. He felt the cool air rushing over him. Then his eyes adjusted. He saw that the line of refugees wound into the church through a door opposite and down the far side aisle to the sanctuary, then up the center aisle to where he was standing. In one way, out the other. Apart from a pair of crying children, the people were silent.

He walked into the church and crossed to the third aisle, which was not being used. As he walked forward he stared as hard as he could toward the sanctuary. What was happening up there? He saw a priest, no, two priests, one vested in cope and alb, the other in alb and stole. Acolytes stood by with candles, and candles flickered on the high altar. The priest was speaking to each refugee in turn, and the refugees were bowing. And then . . .

No! Michael stopped where he was. The refugees were not bowing. Each was in turn putting his head over a basin. A basin to catch the water which the priest was pouring over each one's head. The priest was baptizing them.

"No!" This time he said it aloud.

I simply must put in here what every kid in Good Shepherd grew up knowing, that the crime of the British against the Irish was embodied in the fact that the thin soup the government offered to the starving victims of the Great Hunger came at a price: only those who renounced their Catholicism were fed. As here only Buddhists who submitted to it were.

"No!" he cried. He was running down the aisle, then across the transept, pushing the Buddhist refugees aside to get at the priests. The acolytes scattered, splashing candle wax on themselves. Michael upended the table on which the basin sat, splashing water about, and he snatched the Sacramentary, the book from which the celebrant read the ritual words, out of the hands of the assistant priest. Then he took folds of the main priest's golden cope in his hands, and he shook the man, a frail, pathetic Vietnamese who tried to hide his face behind the stylized silver scallop shell he'd been using to scoop the water. The shell fell to the floor. When he released the priest, Michael had to clasp his hands together to keep from striking him.

Archbishop Thuc refused to give him an appointment. But Michael expected that. A few days later it was Ash Wednesday. Michael went into the cathedral well before dawn to pray, but not only to pray. He wanted to be kneeling, cassocked, in the front pew before the president's bodyguard arrived from the palace to secure the cathedral. The Ngos would be attending the early-morning Mass; they would wear their ashes on their foreheads, like flags, all day. And the archbishop would preside.

When the security people arrived, they ignored Michael, a priest at his breviary, an American. He was conscious of the movement behind him as the churchgoers who had to identify themselves with special passes began to arrive and fill up the pews. There was a stir about twenty minutes before the Mass was scheduled to begin. Michael turned and saw Madame Nhu striding down the center aisle, dressed in black, her head suitably veiled with the traditional mantilla. She clasped a white prayer book at her breast. Her long red fingernails shone like blood against the white book cover. Her eyes were downcast, as if she was approaching for Communion. Behind her were a pair of bodyguards. She'd have ridden over from the palace with Thuc. Diem and Nhu would come together at the last minute.

Michael closed his breviary, rose, genuflected, opened the communion rail and went into the sanctuary. He genuflected again, then crossed to the far left corner, to the sacristy door. He used his key on it, and went in.

Thuc was standing at the vestment case with the amice in his hands, a small white kerchief, the first of several pieces of ceremonial clothing the priest dons. Next to him was an assistant priest, holding the alb ready. In the corner beyond stood a mean-looking Vietnamese in a tan suit, the archbishop's bodyguard.

Before anyone could react, Michael crossed to Thuc and said, "Your Excellency, Cardinal Spellman has asked me to give you a message."

Thuc stared at him, frozen. Then abruptly he turned and addressed his assistant in Vietnamese. Michael thought at first that his ploy hadn't worked, but the assistant hung up the alb, turned and left the sacristy by the hallway door, followed by the bodyguard. Then Thuc looked Michael in the eye.

Michael said, "I was in My Tho three days ago. I was at the church of Sainte Hélène."

Thuc's expression was blank, though Michael was certain he'd been briefed.

"Refugees were being offered food and medical care on the condition that they accept baptism in the Catholic faith. By the time I arrived, hundreds had already been put through the form of the sacrament."

Thuc's eyes widened. "But that is a violation of canon law."

"Indeed so, Your Excellency. That's why I stopped it. And why I am talking to you about it today."

Thuc shook his head sadly. "The curé of Sainte Hélène is a man of no judgment. I shall, of course, remove him."

"Your Excellency, I am informed that churches at Long

Xuyen, Can Tho, Dalat and Nha Trang are conducting similar mass baptisms in conjunction with the distribution of food.''

Thuc looked shocked. ''Impossible.'' He waited, perhaps to see if Michael could produce evidence, then reiterated. ''No, impossible! Père Theiu at Sainte Hélène could perhaps behave in this way, thinking in his confused situation that we want this, but no one else. I'm sorry, Father. It is impossible.''

''If you issued a statement guaranteeing the religious rights of the Buddhist population, your priests would be less likely to make such mistakes.''

Thuc made a dismissive gesture. ''The religion of the pagans is a *pot au feu*. Confucians one day, Taoists the next.''

''They are Buddhists,'' Michael insisted. The archbishop's evident contempt made him angry, but it also stunned him to realize how ignorant he himself was. What were these distinctions? What was Buddhism based on?

''They are Confucians in good times and Buddhists in time of trouble. It is not serious religion.''

''Leave that aside for a moment, Your Excellency. Clearly the ability of the government to control the country requires the loyalty of the Buddhist population but the Buddhist leaders feel—''

''Ah, the leaders, Father! They are Communists. The followers can be won over. But the leaders are Communists. That is well known.'' Thuc glared at Michael, satisfied with his statement of the decisive fact.

Michael saw there was no point in arguing about the rights of Buddhists. Error has no rights, *n'est-ce pas?* The point was to let him know that the baptism shit had to stop. It was sacrilege and it was bad politics.

''Cardinal Spellman's expectation, Your Excellency, is that the relief program will be kept apart from politics and also from religion. He wants me to emphasize that with you.'' Michael wanted Thuc to think he'd already heard back from Spellman. It didn't matter that he hadn't. He knew that Spellman would agree with him. Spellman would be furious at Thuc when he got Michael's report. ''We are responding to simple human needs; we are not proselytizing.''

Thuc nodded. "Of course not."

"Cardinal Spellman has asked me to be watching, Your Excellency. Just so you know."

Thuc did not respond. Michael knew that, in addition to the influence he could bring to bear on American policy, Spellman held the key to the realization of Thuc's great personal ambition, being elevated to the status of cardinal. Even as Spellman's mere agent, Michael felt the thrill of his power over the man and frankly relished it. Thuc tied the ends of his amice, and began reciting the prayers for vesting. Michael took the alb from its hook and handed it to him.

During the Mass, Michael knelt at the overstuffed prie-dieu in the sanctuary. He received his ashes from the archbishop—"Remember, man, you are dust, and unto dust you shall return"—then watched while the Ngos knelt at the communion rail: Diem, Nhu, Madame Nhu, and Ngo Dinh Can, the other brother, the shrewd governor of Hué. The archbishop smudged each of them, then each devoutly crossed himself. All at once their piety disgusted Michael. Whatever their political ambitions had been at the beginning, now they considered themselves the anointed of God with a sacred mission. Their arrogance was obscene.

After the Mass Michael hired a pedicab to take him to the Vinh Hoa Dao pagoda. Already the heat, the dirt and the noise of the overcrowded city made it unpleasant to be outside, and the jostling pedicab, with its crude wheels rattling over the cracked pavement, not to mention its association with class oppression, increased Michael's discomfort.

At the pagoda, one of the great temples of Vietnam, famous for its own beauty and for the exquisite ancient carvings and statues it was furnished with, Michael had to step gingerly up the broad sweeping staircase that led up from the avenue because refugees were all over it. Hundreds had made the steps of the pagoda home.

Michael entered the temple, and the tranquillity, the sweet incense, the soft light instantly soothed him, and the transcendent beauty of the large carved Buddha, which sat where in a church the altar would have been, made him want to kneel.

A young monk approached him and bowed. His head was shaven and his left shoulder was exposed. His feet were bare.

Michael spoke the name of the monk who'd taken Howe and him to My Tho, Thic Nhat Than. The young monk bowed again and indicated that Michael should follow him.

They crossed the large, shadowy space and went through a series of smaller darker rooms until finally they came out into a garden, an exquisite, otherworldly enclosure with pools, plants of many kinds, glorious flowers and a maze of paths, brilliantly paved with round, smooth pebbles of white and black like stones of the Japanese *go*. It was impossible to think that the teeming desperate city was all around them. Even the sky above seemed bluer, less indifferent.

The young monk led Michael to the veranda at the far end of the garden and there he found Nhat Than, on his mat, robed in saffron, a calligraphy pen in hand.

Michael bowed. The monk looked at him stoically. He was at least seventy years old. Every pain, loss, every happiness, of each of his years had been transformed into that great, silent dignity.

Michael spoke to him in his halting French. "It will not happen again. If you hear any reports of it, tell me at once. I will stop it." He vowed to himself, this, if nothing else, would be his work here, however long he remained.

Still the old monk made no reply.

Michael said, "And if I may be so bold, Honored Teacher, I would like to ask your help. I would like to learn about your people. I would like to learn about your faith."

Thic Nhat Than eyed Michael carefully. Then, even while sitting, he bowed.

SIXTEEN

SOMEWHAT more than a year later, two men died a week apart from each other, one in a Renaissance palace in Italy and one at a crowded intersection in the center of Saigon. And after their deaths, everything was different.

Pope John XXIII died on June 3, 1963. No one knew it at the time, but his magnificent vision for the renewal of the Church, the humanizing of it, would be thwarted, not maliciously but nevertheless effectively, by his successors, the Self-doubting Pope who was obsessed by his own suffering, and the Commissar-Pope who is obsessed by his own power. John's instinctive embrace of the world and his belief in its goodness were replaced by the traditional suspicion. Though his Vatican Council continued without him—many Churchmen, like Spellman, had expected it would last weeks; it lasted years—and though certain superficial aspects of Catholicism did change, the Church's essential post-Reformation note—world-wariness—reasserted itself. Suddenly the Ecumenical Movement stalled, pluralism as a manifestation of vitality was rejected in favor of the former rigid orthodoxy; the introduction of democratic procedure into the structure of the Church was undone and the ancient disdain for women and for non-Christians and even for Protestants was quickened. Some Catholics remember John fondly, as a kind of miracle, but if you push them they will say he was the Pope of False Promises, and it would have been better if he hadn't started what he wouldn't be around to finish. You detect a hint of disillusionment in my tone, *n'est-ce pas?* And you think to yourself, How unlike him.

And then, the second death. On June 11, 1963, an old man climbed from an automobile and squatted on the pavement at a main Saigon streetcorner. He was a Buddhist monk named Quang Duc. He was surrounded by a thousand monks and nuns, and then by thousands of other people, including journalists, because everyone had heard what he intended to do. Quang Duc waited patiently, running an acorn rosary through his fingers, while two disciples doused his saffron robe with gasoline. The eerie sounds of chanting, but of nothing else, filled the square as the monks and nuns offered their prayer for him. Then Quang Duc said, "I return to the eternal Buddha." He struck the match himself. Instantly he was aflame. The plume of smoke, unlike the smoke over Auschwitz, was black with the lard of human flesh. And quickly the stench of the burning bonze, even more than the heat, drove the inner ring of monks back, though the farthest away pressed forward. Police tried to break through, but the holies prevented them. Witnesses shrieked in horror and by-standers wept. Quang Duc's devoted followers continued to chant, and all the while photographers and film cameramen took their pictures. After ten minutes the charred body of the old monk fell over. Nothing he had done in his long life had the effect his death would have. Within twenty-four hours the photograph of his body in flames would appall the world, stun the leaders of America and give the American public its first, though by no means last, shock of pure horror from Vietnam. Within weeks the leading Vietnamese poet and novelist Nguyen Tuong Tam would kill himself, perhaps a dozen other monks and nuns would publicly burn themselves to death, one nun would ritually hack her hand off before an altar, hundreds of Buddhists would begin a hunger strike, and tens of thousands would take to the streets, all to protest against the vicious despotism of Ngo Dinh Diem. Quang Duc had exposed it to the world for what it was.

Pope John had dreamed of eliminating from the Church once and for all the implicit intolerance, self-righteousness and triumphalism that periodically in its history had become explicit in tragically violent forms. But in the very season of John's death, a fanatical Catholic army whose generals mourned his passing was unleashed against a populace because of its

religion, and it happened in Cardinal Spellman's protégé's
Vietnam.

"They've lost their fucking minds, obviously." Howe threw
the dispatch on his desk and looked across at Michael. "The
esteemed governor of Hué, brother of our esteemed president,
brother of our esteemed archbishop, brother of our esteemed
chief of torture, brother-in-law of the Dragon Lady, has now
issued a decree forbidding anyone from wearing Buddhist
robes in a public place."

"Oh, God," Michael said. The police and Buddhist mobs
had been skirmishing for days. "What will happen?"

"First reports are that now everyone in Hué, from taxi
drivers to Catholic students, have declared themselves Buddhists and donned the robes."

"Good for them."

"Yeah." Howe turned in his chair to look out his window.
His office occupied a corner in the rear of the embassy and its
single window opened on the parking lot where the marines
kept their jeeps. Beyond the lot was an iron picket fence and
a side street, along which pedestrian and auto traffic moved
as usual. The chaos in Hué had yet to break out in Saigon.
"And all that shit is hitting the fan because of flags."

Howe didn't need to make his reference explicit. Archbishop Thuc had banned the display of the Buddhist flag, and
the Buddhists had gone crazy.

"So what about the bombing? I heard there was a bombing
up there." Michael had come to the embassy not to fence
with Howe about the absurd denouement of Catholic-Buddhist
conflict, but to learn if the rumors he'd been hearing about
the violence were true. He had workers in Hué, and two
American Maryknoll priests whom he'd befriended were there.

"A car blew up inside the old city," Howe said. "There
were many casualties. We don't yet know how many dead,
how many wounded. Governor Can issued a statement already saying it was the Viet Cong. He says the Viet Cong
have taken over the Buddhist movement." Howe smirked.
"As if they needed to. I think the V.C. are probably on
vacation. Let the Buddhists and the Ngos finish each other
off."

"When can I get a casualty list, John? I have friends up there."

Howe jotted something on a notepad. "I'll keep an eye on the wire for you. I'll call you."

"Thanks."

"So, can I ask you something?" He paused. Michael didn't bat an eye. He and Howe had had frequent if somewhat formal contact in the last year. They respected each other and kept each other posted but they had not become friends. Michael no longer felt that as a disappointment, and he no longer allowed himself to take Howe's aloofness as a personal or social rejection. Michael didn't know it, but he had drawn on his innate Irish knack for turning aside the snub. "What is Spellman saying now? What's he going to do?"

Michael had to look away. If they had become friends he might have admitted that Spellman never responded to his communiqués. At a certain point he'd begun describing in detail the mad behavior of Thuc and the other Ngos. At about that point the replies had begun to come, not even from O'Shea, but from O'Shea's assistant. The replies had a theme: keep the relief going. Separate it however you can from politics. And that's what he had done. Michael forced himself to smile at Howe. "You think the cardinal and I are on the phone each week? Come on, John. What do I know? Anyway, what does it matter at this point, what Spellman thinks?"

"When we've got the Asian version of the Inquisition going on here? We've got Frankenstein's monster; but you know who Doctor Frankenstein is, as well as I do."

Michael nodded. "But he's irrelevant to it now, John. These people wouldn't listen to the *pope*. I mean, Madame Nhu, Christ! She calls the monks who burn themselves the 'barbecued bonzes.' Nhu is hooked on opium. The archbishop thinks he's Torquemada. And Diem considers himself an Oriental El Cid taking on the Moors. The whole family thinks of itself as sent from God. This is their moment to come down from Olympus with thunderbolts. So who's going to listen to Spellman?"

"Kennedy," Howe said abruptly. "Kennedy has people telling him that when Diem wins this battle, everything else will fall into place. They're saying swallow your misgivings, look the other way while the monks burn themselves, and while the soldiers shoot the people in the streets. They're telling him that those are Communists in the streets and that the Buddhists are Russian agents. If Spellman broke with Diem, it would help Kennedy to.''

Now Michael saw for the first time why Howe had cultivated him, even to the extent that he had. All along Michael had thought Howe wanted to influence events in Vietnam—to see that the aid was distributed equitably—but now he saw that Howe wanted to influence Washington. He said nothing.

Howe leaned forward across his desk. ''The question, Father, has become, At what point does the Church proclaim its opposition to the regime it created? When every Buddhist in Vietnam is dead?''

''Wait a minute, John. Don't talk to me about the Church. This is the American embassy, where Diem's money comes from. You talk to me about distributing aid. Ninety-five percent of the aid coming into this country goes to Diem's army. That's *your* people doing that, not mine. Tell *them* about Hué, John. Not me. And not Spellman either. Just because the president's a Catholic doesn't mean he's waiting to be told by the hierarchy what to think. He's waiting to be told by you people, Goddamnit! Hawkins and Nolting are the ones he depends on. So get to them, John!''

''I can't,'' Howe said evenly, coldly. ''People with my point of view have been shut out, and you know it.''

''Maybe you shut yourself out, John. You look down your damn nose at everybody. You slug us with your offended sensibility. You're surrounded by moral pygmies, aren't you? Who isn't your inferior, John?''

Howe flinched, but that was all, and Michael regretted at once having cast the issue in terms of inferiority, or rather, having admitted that those were the terms that mattered. He regretted especially having so exposed his feelings, and therefore having underscored once more how they were different.

Howe sat at his desk, immobile, staring back at Michael. He wasn't going to speak.

Michael said, more to cover his embarrassment than to press the point, ''If this was Africa and the Ngos were a clan of Ashanti chieftains at war with another tribe, you'd be much more tolerant. You'd still be horrified by the killing, but you wouldn't take it personally."

Howe said in a steely, cold voice, "How much more has to happen in the streets and villages of this country, Father, before you take *that* personally instead of the petty slights you imagine having suffered from me?"

The answer would come soon enough. First, President Diem declared the nation's pagodas closed and he sent troops to surround them, though not just any troops. The raids on the pagodas in which dozens of monks were murdered and scores more wounded were carried out by the elite Catholic units modeled on the American Green Berets. Diem claimed that the pagodas had been taken over by Communists.

By the next morning, word spread through Saigon that thirty monks in the Xa Loi pagoda near Freedom Palace where the Ngos lived had been shot by government troops. When Michael heard of it he tried to call Howe, but he couldn't get through. Later he would learn that Nhu's agents had cut the embassy telephone lines. The Americans would know less than ordinary citizens, and they would not be able to protest until it was too late.

Michael went at once to the Vinh Hoa Dao pagoda across Saigon. It was easy to get there that day because for a change the streets of the city were empty. The Saigonese knew when to stay at home. The broad, sweeping staircase leading up to the temple, usually so crowded with refugees and knots of students, monks and nuns, was utterly deserted. As he ascended the stairs in the eerie quiet, he slowed his pace and resolved to take in every detail of what he was about to see. He knew before he saw it.

The magnificent pagoda had been ransacked and half-burned. The great gilded-wood figure of Buddha in the sanctuary had been toppled, and its face had crashed into the floor. Benches were splintered, shrines demolished. The charred heavy curtain along the far wall still smoldered, and the roof above that quarter of the pagoda had been consumed by the fire. Apparently a rainfall had doused the flames once the flames had opened the roof to the sky.

Michael walked through the far doorway, through the series of small rooms, into the familiar courtyard, as he had done dozens of times coming to see Thic Nhat Than. The garden had been wrecked too; plants were uprooted and strewn about, large palm trees had been felled and lay now like great timbers across the ruins. Statues had been smashed to bits. As he walked he expected to come across corpses, but he didn't, and that made the chaotic scene all the more bizarre, all the more ominous.

As he approached the veranda where he'd met Nhat Than, where they'd talked, each in his broken French, and where he'd allowed himself not only to share the Buddhist elder's dream for Vietnam, but also to feel the spell of his holiness, Michael was slowed by an awful stench. It was an odor unlike any he'd smelled before, and it made him feel sick. He thought of stopping, turning around and running away. I'd have gotten the hell out of there myself. But he didn't.

He mounted the three stairs and pushed a tottering rice-paper screen aside.

Thic Nhat Than, the Venerable, the Beloved, the Spiritual Master, was lying in two pieces before Michael. Only a foot-long deep purple river of coagulated blood joined his head to his body. On his severed face was frozen a look of pure horror.

"So he had John beheaded in prison . . ." Michael slammed his eyes shut against it. ". . . and the head was brought in on a plate."

Michael knelt. Instead of praying for the monk or uttering the Catholic words—he was instinctively respectful and would have observed only the Buddhist rubric if he'd known it—he stifled his infinite repugnance and picked up the old man's head and placed it against the trunk of his body. Instead of praying for him then, he began reciting the Act of Contrition for himself and for us, his people, for we had done this. But even that reciting he did automatically, a reaction in shock. In his mind other words replayed themselves, words he had not thought of in years, Tim O'Shea's words, in that faintly accented Irish voice saying, over and over, "God will not have his work made manifest by cowards."

When at last Michael stood, a man behind him said, "Amen."

It was Howe.

They stared at each other blankly. Michael just shook his head.

Howe said nothing, not "I told you so." Not, "Are you satisfied?" Not, "Now do you understand me?" Not, "This is why I wanted you here."

Michael said, "I'm going to New York. I'm going to tell them."

"Good."

"But first . . ." He looked down at the remains of Thic Nhat Than again, then around the garden. His voice cracked as he said, "Do you think we should bury him?" There were no shovels but Michael realized that, given his emotion at that moment, he could have dug forever with his bare hands, through gravel, through stone. He wanted to rip out the hearts of Thuc and Nhu and Diem. He wanted to twist their heads off with his hands.

"No. His people will be back. They're the ones to look after him."

"Why did they leave?"

Howe shrugged. "They were afraid." He looked down at the corpse. "Not many men would have defied them by staying like this." He looked up sharply. "Would you have?"

Michael shook his head, no.

"Me either," Howe said. When he looked at Michael it was with an admission: I'm a man like you, just like you. All he said, though, or needed to say was, "Let's go."

They started across the ruined garden. Michael stopped and picked up a large fallen palm frond. He retraced his way to the veranda and placed it gently on Nhat Than's body, to cover him.

Michael had the airport cab drop him off at the Empire State Building, where the CRS offices were. But Monsignor O'Shea was not there.

Michael was exhausted. He'd been traveling, space available, on MATS flights for two and a half days. It would have made sense to sleep, but in his mind by then the situation in

Vietnam had become even more anarchic, more violent, and his mission, therefore—for that is what it was to him—was urgent. He shaved in the office washroom, borrowed a fresh collar from one of the CRS priests, left his bag there and set out for the cardinal's house on Madison Avenue.

The walk took Michael up the best stretch of Fifth Avenue, and after a year and a half, it was a foreign world to him, one to which, in his state, he had no particular reaction. He passed mannequins and travel posters, windows full of books. He cut between secretaries and shoppers with painted toenails and high-heeled sandals, the girls in their summer dresses, as the early Irwin Shaw so exactly put it. Taxicabs gunned at him as he crossed the streets and pretzel-sellers hawked. But he was indifferent to it all. Even as he cut down Fiftieth Street, which runs between St. Patrick's and Saks, that cathedral for consumers, he remained mentally and emotionally clutched, as if a lump of dough had congealed in his lungs.

The cardinal's residence was a gray, neo-Gothic mansion, one of the city's great houses, but the fact that it abutted the cathedral on one side and on the other faced the Villard Mansions, one of the great houses in the world—though in those days a major publisher and the chancery of the archdiocese occupied its separate wings—made the cardinal's own four-story abode seem modest, though not particularly friendly. Michael tried to shake himself from his strange, almost panicky mood by taking its half-dozen stairs jauntily, and swinging the door open as if he did it every day. In fact, like the vast majority of New York priests, he had never been in the cardinal's house, and he had never expected to be. Even the cardinal's own staff lived down the block in another building, with the cathedral staff. For other prelates, dignitaries, grand marshals of parades, the cardinal's residence was the setting for receptions catered by the Waldorf Astoria; for would-be mayors, governors and even presidents, it was the source of an invaluable benediction. But for common clergy, the cardinal's house was trouble.

It was unheard of that a priest should go there unsummoned, and Michael hadn't even called ahead. After the bright morning sunshine, the dark, paneled entrance foyer closed on him

like night, and it was only a voice from a room to his left
that gave him a clue to protocol.

"Yes? May I help you?"

Michael pushed the door open. An elderly woman sat at a
typewriter. The room was cluttered in a Victorian way, overcur-
tained, overfurnished, ill-lit. The woman herself, with pinned
hair and a doily-lace collar, seemed musty, left behind by
another time.

"I'm here to see the cardinal. I'm Father Maguire from the
CRS."

"CRS?" She was not impressed by his collar.

"Catholic Relief Service."

"Oh." She picked up the phone and dialed. "Monsignor,
there's a young priest here. He says he has an appointment,
but not that I know of." She listened, then squinted at
Michael. "What did you say your name was?"

"Father Maguire."

"Father Maguire, he says. From the CFM."

"CRS," Michael corrected, but she ignored him.

She hung up the phone. "Monsignor Dugan's office is on
the second floor. You should take the elevator there. His
office is right next to it."

"I'll just walk up. The stairs . . . ?"

"Take the elevator, if you please, Father. Monsignor said
you should take the elevator."

They didn't want outsiders wandering around the building.
The elevator would enable them to track him. He thanked the
old lady, who only stared at him glumly.

The elevator was closet-sized, and the clunking of the
manually operated doors reverberated through the walls of
that part of the building. The engine thunked into gear when
he pressed the number, and then whirred piercingly as the
cubicle rose. A time machine, he thought, out of H. G.
Wells. When it stopped, the doors opened. Monsignor Dugan,
the cardinal's secretary, a man as short as Spellman but thin
and sharp-featured, was standing opposite Michael with an
open show of quizzical irritation. For a moment Michael
thought he wasn't going to let him out. Michael recognized
him as the priest who'd served as master of ceremonies at his
ordination, where he'd proved himself a virtuoso of the pro-

found bow and the obeisance. Michael felt suddenly like an altar boy who was about to be rebuked for his slothful genuflections.

"Father Maguire?"

"Hello, Monsignor." Michael put his hand out.

Monsignor Dugan shook it, not limply but not firmly either. His quizzical look made it clear he was trying to recall if anyone had told him that Father Maguire was returning from Vietnam. He cocked an eyebrow, waiting for an explanation.

Michael could not assess at first what he was up against, though Dugan had the reputation of being impossible to get by. Priests often said it would be easier to get in to see Mayor Wagner or Senator Javits or even Governor Rockefeller than the cardinal, not that any of them wanted to.

"Miss Leonard says you have an appointment?"

"Her mistake, Monsignor. I told her that I'd come to see the cardinal. She assumed I had an appointment. But I don't."

"Well, Father, surely you understand that it's impossible. I'd have had Miss Leonard say as much to you, but it would have embarrassed her to do so. We don't have priests coming in off the street and expecting His Eminence to drop everything to see them."

"I understand that, Monsignor. I would not think of doing such a thing myself, but I arrived within the hour from Vietnam. It is urgent that I see His Eminence at once."

"About what?" Dugan asked carefully.

"About Ngo Dinh Diem."

Dugan stared at Michael. What he knew about were parishes, the ones in hock, and priests, the ones who drank too much. He knew about the schools, the efforts of the lay teachers to unionize, and the seminaries, that certain professors were spouting the ultraliberalism of that Swiss heretic, Kung. He knew about the downtown bankers who could get broker's fees cut and city hall hacks who could get the building code waived and the Aqueduct regulars who tracked the big bettors. He didn't know about Vietnam. Suddenly he realized that this young priest occupied a square on which Spelly, against advice, had placed a stack of chips. He knew the stack was teetering. "Come with me," he said, leading the way into his office, "and I'll check the cardinal's calendar."

"I have to see him right now, Monsignor."

"That's impossible." Dugan faced Michael. He stood with his back to his desk.

"Would you ask him?"

Monsignor Dugan had been vaguely aware of the furor over recent events in Vietnam, but if there were implications for the archdiocese in that madness, he had missed them. "Are you here to discuss your work with the CRS? Is that the point?"

"Yes."

"Well, then . . ." He sat back on the edge of his desk. Only now that he saw how to deal with this did he allow himself a hint of kindliness. "Then the appropriate thing for you to do is to take it up with Monsignor O'Shea or Bishop Swanstrom. If need be, they will approach the cardinal."

Michael shook his head and said firmly, "I'm the one who's here, Monsignor. I'm the one who wants to talk to him. I've traveled for two and a half days to talk to him. If he won't see me, all right. But I'd like you to ask him."

Neither man would look away. Finally the secretary softened. "Shall I put it that a brother priest seeks a word of counsel?"

"If you like," Michael said, though inwardly he recoiled. These bastards always had to have the upper hand. You came to them as a subject or a suppliant, nothing else. Only the wackos caught Spelly's eye. But hell, maybe it was true; maybe Michael was like the alkies and the Casanovas, just another Father Fuck-up, a little younger than usual, and with his problem clothed in Asian intrigue. "Tell him I've just this moment arrived."

Monsignor Dugan nodded and left the room.

A few minutes later he reappeared, crooked a finger at Michael, then turned and led the way through a shadowy corridor to the cardinal's office.

The room was dominated by a large crystal chandelier which filled it with light, and after the gloom elsewhere that surprised Michael. Centered under the fixture was a long Catalonian refectory table with six ornately carved wooden chairs, and on the table were dozens of neatly stacked books and reports. On one wall was a portrait of the late pope, not John, but Pius. On another was the carved wooden crest of

Spellman's cartouche, his coat of arms, which featured in elaborate serpentine the tassels of his red hat. On a third wall was a portrait of Spellman's predecessor, Cardinal Hayes; he was a stern-looking man who seemed to be glaring out at his successor's office disapprovingly. Below that painting was a leather wing chair arranged to face the cardinal's desk, which occupied the alcove of the bay window that overlooked Madison Avenue. The curtains were open and additional light poured in from the street, enveloping the cardinal himself who sat at his desk, back to the window, staring at Michael.

He was the sixth archbishop of New York, had occupied the chair since 1939 and had become for Catholics and most other Americans so much the epitome of a Roman Catholic archbishop that it was easy to forget that there had never been one like him before. His round smiling features were so familiar to New Yorkers because he loved to appear in public, at dedications and benefits, neighborhood festivals and civic celebrations. His commitments seemed wide-ranging and his presence to the life of the city seemed freewheeling, but in fact everything he did was calculated for effect. His purpose from the beginning had been to make an impact far beyond the confines of the Church and he did. His great accomplishment as archbishop was a subtle one: he had secured for himself a place of real influence among the power brokers and aristocrats of the nation in a way that no other Catholic prelate ever had, and he, more than any single figure, represented the arrival of the Catholic Church as a political and social force equal to any in America. He could be genial and friendly, but he never forgot his function for the Church, and that was to collect power, as much power as he could, not to aggrandize himself, but to reinforce the position of a community which even as recently as his own youth had been an oppressed, fragile collection of immigrant groups with little in common but their feelings of inferiority and their faith in the Church of Rome. His job had been to slam the door forever on the era when Catholic sensibilities could be ignored or violated or made mock of in this country. And so he had, from his position as archbishop of the greatest city in America, intruded himself into every area of the nation's life, from Cold War strategies as the Military Vicar to standards of popular entertainment as head of the Legion of Decency. Even if his patron, Pius XII, was gone, and even if his simple theology was being called into question by the Vatican Council, and even if, at seventy-five, he had lost a measure of vigor and had, for example, to lean on his chaplains to ascend the stairs of the high altar, he was still a man who knew what he was. He was authority itself. He was the cardinal.

"You know Father Maguire, Your Eminence," Dugan said.

Michael approached the desk as Spellman stood. He was wearing a red-trimmed black cassock with a broad silk sash. His short-cropped white hair framed his zucchetto, the red skull cap which, with its little center tab, Spellman adjusted, an absentminded gesture. When he offered Michael his hand, it was palm down, indicating that he expected, even across the expanse of desk, that the junior priest would kiss his ring. Michael did so gracefully, and he said, "Thank you for seeing me, Your Eminence."

"Father Maguire, are you all right?" Spellman looked at him intently, and Michael was surprised to sense his concern. "You weren't expected home, were you?"

Michael shook his head, but before he could speak Spellman turned to Dugan. "Did you offer him coffee?" He looked at Michael. "Have you eaten?"

"Yes, thank you," Michael said, though he didn't remember his last meal.

"Tell me what's been happening," Spellman said intently. "It must be chaos there."

Michael exhaled and felt his body relax into the chair. At last he was here, about to tell his story to the one man who could make it better, make everything better. He felt not only that he'd come home, but that he was with—though there was no personal justification for this feeling—his father. "Your Eminence, it's worse than chaos. For weeks there has been a well-organized, quite deliberate effort to destroy the Buddhists. All of the Buddhists. By now hundreds of monks and priests have been murdered. Thousands are in jail for no offense beyond their religion. And pagodas all over the country, small ones and great ones, have been ransacked and burned."

Spellman was shaking his head sadly. Light glinted off his

rimless spectacles, making it seem for an instant that there were tears in his eyes, but not so. He said, "It must have been awful, seeing it up close, as you did."

Michael stared at him, perplexed for a moment until he realized that Spellman thought the trouble here was with his priest; poor Father Maguire, what terrible things he's been through. Michael sat forward. "Your Eminence, it is a religious vendetta. President Diem and his brothers have broken confidence with you. They are abusing the Catholic Faith terribly by conducting such operations in its name. A monk I knew personally was murdered in his sanctuary. His head was cut off."

Spellman continued to shake his head. "Inexcusable," he muttered.

Michael waited for him to say more, but he wasn't going to. "But, Your Eminence, my point is about Diem." *Your* Diem! he almost added.

"The *New York Times* thinks Diem is mad. They get all worked up because our nice pat American distinction between Church and State is not observed in Vietnam. But what about Israel?"

Israel? Michael couldn't comprehend this at all.

Spellman leaned forward. "There are religious groups in violent conflict in Israel too! What does Mr. Sulzberger say about that?"

"But in Vietnam, Your Eminence, we're talking about government violence against its own citizens."

Spellman's eyebrows went up. "Well, the main violence, of course, is against the Communists. It's a war, isn't it? You know what a war is like, Father. You know that better than I. Sometimes there are abuses. Obviously, those soldiers were on a rampage. But what did the Buddhists do to provoke them? A country at war can't have thousands of citizens in the streets trying to bring down the government, can it? We wouldn't have allowed that here during World War Two, I'll tell you."

Michael was stunned. Was Spellman offering a defense of the assault?

Monsignor Dugan appeared at Michael's elbow, surprising him, with a cup of coffee. Michael took it, though he thought the strong, black brew would make him sick. He thanked the monsignor, who withdrew.

After a moment the cardinal sat back, bridged his hands under his chin and asked, "What do you believe about Buddhism anyway, Father?"

"Theologically?"

The cardinal nodded.

Michael was instinctively wary. Was this the question of an Inquisitor? "I believe, as Pope John put it, that they are men of goodwill whose hearts have been imprinted with God's Law."

"But they are, whether culpably or not, prisoners of error."

Michael tried to sip the coffee. His hands shook and it spilled.

"Don't you agree?"

"I think that in Vietnam this week they're being treated as worse than that."

"Perhaps with reason, Father. Perhaps reasons you and I are not privy to. What if the Buddhist movement has been infiltrated? What if their leaders are Red sympathizers? What if their pagodas and temples were the sites of cell group meetings? What if they abused their sanctuaries by using them to stir up subversion? What if they are actively trying to bring Diem down so that the Communists can take over?"

Michael suddenly couldn't think of what to say. The gap between their points of view seemed infinite.

"Furthermore, Father, you have jumped to a conclusion that is completely unwarranted and, I might say, unjust."

"I have?"

"By holding Diem and Nhu responsible for this latest crisis. It is not their doing, whatever the justification or lack of it. Neither Diem nor Nhu ordered those troops against the pagodas."

"Your Eminence . . ." Michael felt as if he was humoring an hallucinator. ". . . Nhu's personal army did these things. I was there."

Spellman nodded and said calmly, "You've been traveling, Father. There have been developments. Certain of Diem's most trusted generals ordered the raids without authorization, conspirators who hoped to cause an uprising and the overthrow of democracy. Nhu revealed their names yesterday, after they were arrested. The Ngos are as upset about the excesses against civilians as you are."

Michael stared in disbelief. Was Spellman convinced of this fantasy?

"I have been in communication throughout the crisis with the Vietnamese ambassador in Washington."

"That's Madame Nhu's father! You can't believe him!"

Spellman looked sharply at Michael: Don't use the imperative with me, young man. He said, "I have his word that his government deplores the killings in the sanctuaries and I accept it. So, I gather, do President Kennedy and Secretaries Rusk and McNamara."

Michael saw suddenly what the Ngos were trying for—in one move to eliminate their Buddhist opposition *and* the dissident generals who threatened from within—and he realized that if they pulled it off they would be unstoppable. The *Times* was characterizing the entire family as mad, but this ploy was ingenious. Even at the moment of greatest outrage, they had given their sponsors in America an irresistible reason to stick by them—this "madness" was going to work! It would give them total control of their country. Weather this storm with us, they promised in effect, and *then* we'll unleash our evil genius on the Communists. You will have an invincible bastion—like Israel—in Southeast Asia.

"Your Eminence," Michael said slowly, "I bow to your more intimate knowledge, but, as you know, I have been there for a year and a half, and I feel it is my responsibility to report to you exactly what I have witnessed. Archbishop Thuc has delivered public diatribes on many occasions against the Buddhists. He has said again and again they have no rights. He has encouraged their slaughter. The crisis is a direct result of his fanatical speeches."

"But Archbishop Thuc is talking about the Communists, Father."

Michael nearly came out of his chair. He spilled coffee on the rug. "No, no, he's talking about the Buddhists! About *holy* men and women. About ninety percent of the population. The Ngos are bringing disaster to Vietnam and they must be stopped. *You* must stop them."

Spellman shook his head. "Your experience is valuable to me, Father. And I appreciate getting it firsthand from you. But you don't have the big picture. You're *too* close. *Too* involved. What you don't see is that the Communists are within an inch of taking over Vietnam. It would be their greatest victory since China. And the slaughter, of Catholics certainly, but also of Buddhists, would make what's going on now seem tame. In other words, the big picture suggests that now, more than ever, it is time to support President Diem and I do." He spoke with a finality that was intended to end this conversation, and it did.

Michael sank back into his chair, staring at his coffee.

"You've done a good job in Vietnam, Father. I've had nothing but positive reports. Even though it's been difficult, you can look back on your service there with pride."

Michael looked up sharply. What? Look back?

"And I think your experience will serve us in good stead. We're about to launch a new fund-raising drive called 'The Children's Relief Fund.' It's geared to assist the overburdened orphanages in Vietnam. You know about it." Michael nodded.

"I want you to head it up."

"But that would mean . . ."

"Coming back here."

"Your Eminence, I'm not ready to come back." Michael had to stifle the alarm he felt. "I can't leave Vietnam now."

"But your purpose is to help the victims of that war, isn't it? This is a chance to do something big for them. For the children, Father. For the orphans. I can sense your conviction, your passion, your concern, and so will the other bishops—so will the Catholic people. Your job will be to quicken the conscience of the entire American Church."

Spellman was right and knew it. Michael Maguire would be irresistible on the subject of what he'd seen in Vietnam. The money would pour in and new orphanages would go up all over that beleaguered country.

And, more to the point, Michael Maguire would be back in the States, in the bosom of the Church, where he belonged. Spellman wouldn't have considered for a second allowing such an angry, righteous young priest back into a situation of such moral and political complexity. But he would forbid and command only as a last resort. He liked his priests to feel honored by their assignments. He preferred their enthusiasm to their resentment. Spellman was nothing if not an inspired manipulator of his own men. "What do you say, Father?"

Michael only stared at him. There was a chamber in his brain in which the cardinal's words had not registered at all. There, images of what he'd seen in Vietnam continued to flash, but like a stark film with no soundtrack. A feeling of utter exhaustion came over him, and he wanted suddenly, irrationally, to lie down on the thick carpet of the cardinal's office. Perhaps then the tranquillity of that place would soothe him. He could close his eyes against everything he'd seen. When had he had such a feeling before? Such longing for peace, for escape, for quiet? He could have his rest if only he did what they wanted.

"You're one of my best men, Father," the cardinal said quietly. "I need you to do this for me. I'd consider it a personal favor."

It was in China, in the camp commandant's office. They'd refused to let him sleep for days. They'd wanted him to identify those of his fellow prisoners who were officers. He never did. It had seemed to him he'd learned to sleep even while standing up, even while they kept questioning him.

Michael snapped himself alert. This was not China. And he was not being asked to betray anyone. He was being asked to save the children of Vietnam. Yes. He was being asked to tell Americans what was happening there. Yes. He felt that peace coming over him. The peace of assent. Yes, he would do it. For the children. For the cardinal. For God whose Will it was, he thought, which then embraced him.

SEVENTEEN

Two months later Michael was in charge of arrangements for the press conference at which Cardinal Spellman was to announce the beginning drive of the Children's Relief Fund. The press conference was to be held at Idlewild Airport because the cardinal was leaving for Rome for the third session of the Vatican Council. His departure would give reporters a news angle that what they would surely take as just another Catholic appeal for money lacked.

Public interest in the council was growing, and not only among Catholics. Americans were beginning to sense what forces it was even then unleashing. Cardinal Spellman himself, however, did not yet understand its meaning. He was leaving for Rome as the senior prelate of the most fabulously successful national Church in the world. In the previous ten years the Catholic population in America had grown by 44 percent, and the number of children in Catholic schools by 65 percent. There were twelve thousand more priests in America than there had been in 1950, and in the same period the number of seminarians had doubled. And the prodigiously generous Catholic people of America contributed millions of dollars not only to their own parishes and schools, but to the offices of the Vatican and to the Church's worldwide works of mercy. To Spellman, those were the things that counted. He had expected in the first session the year before that the Council Fathers in Rome would want to know how American Catholics were doing it. But he was surprised. The Council Fathers, inspired by Pope John, if not the Holy Ghost, had so far shown no interest in wealth, in buildings, in numbers, or

even in the kind of power represented by a Catholic in the
White House. Their concern was simpler: had the Church
become so obsessed with its own survival that it had forgotten
its true mission—to proclaim the Gospel, to serve the poor, to
work for peace and justice in the world?

But frankly that wasn't the question on anyone's mind at
Idlewild that day. In the popular press the council was still
treated as a kind of ecclesiastical Super Bowl, and the religious press was preoccupied with Church gossip. Several
dozen reporters had shown up, including camera crews from
two New York stations. When they had assembled in the
makeshift auditorium, a rarely used waiting area off the main
concourse, Michael went to the VIP lounge where the cardinal was waiting.

The room was lit like a cocktail lounge, and its walls were
covered with a cheap version of the dark paneling salesmen
might associate with rich men's clubs. The clergy dominated
the place. Two auxiliary bishops, several monsignors and half
a dozen priests were accompanying the cardinal to Rome.
They and their clerical chums who'd come to see them off
were standing in groups of three or four, talking softly. The
cardinal was sitting in a corner. As he approached, Michael
realized that one of the priests with His Eminence was Monsignor Ellis, the former golf champion and the pastor of Holy
Cross. Michael had not seen him since his deacon summer.

Monsignor Ellis turned slightly in his upholstered swivel
chair and fixed Michael with a stare. Spellman continued to
talk to the priest on his other side. The monsignor sat rigidly
upright, as if he wore a corset or a backbrace. Though he had
to crane up at Michael, who towered over him, his expression
achieved the familiar condescension. He looked more distinguished in his black suit with the tab of red at his throat than
he had that summer in his cassock. A black fedora dangled
from one hand, and he held a freshly lit cigar in the other.
"Well, well, Mister Maguire. How are you?"

"Hello, Monsignor. Quite well, thanks. And you?" Michael put his hand out.

Monsignor Ellis transferred his cigar, and without rising,
shook Michael's hand. "I guess it's 'Father' now, isn't it?"

Michael smiled. "For a couple of years, Monsignor."

When Spellman saw him, he stood up. Monsignor Ellis stood then too and took the cardinal's elbow. "I guess I was wrong about this one, eh?"

"You've been wrong about a lot of things, Arthur," Spellman said good-naturedly. Then to Michael, "Are you ready for me, Father?"

Michael said he was and led the cardinal back to the waiting reporters. But Ellis's comment preoccupied him. It was the first indication he'd had that the pastor had recommended against his ordination, and the realization stunned him. It wasn't simply that someone in authority had considered him unfit—though for a man who'd long been accustomed to the approval, even admiration, of his superiors that would have been blow enough. The shock he felt was more acute than that. Throughout the Holy Cross School controversy he had kept his head in the trench, and it still shamed him that Carolyn had taken the heat alone. Robert Moses and Cardinal Spellman may finally have yielded on the school, but they had blown Carolyn to Shanghai. The Church had made itself her enemy. And Michael had chosen the Church.

To discover now that Monsignor Ellis had disapproved of him anyway added to Michael's shame, multiplied it. He could imagine the old fart banging his table and saying, "Hell, if you'd had any guts you'd have stood up with that girl when she needed you! Then I'd have voted for you!" But of course he knew that Ellis's negative vote had been a simple effort to obliterate everything associated with what surely was the great embarrassment of his priesthood. He'd have voted against Jesus if he'd been the deacon that summer.

"Gentlemen, thank you for coming." Michael stood behind the microphones, but ignored them. They had been set at the cardinal's height, not his, and he'd have had to kneel to use them. "The cardinal will make a short announcement, then will entertain your questions for about fifteen minutes." Michael paused, looking over the audience. The Catholic press—the diocesan newspapers from New York, Rockville Centre, Brooklyn, Newark, Bridgeport and Hartford, the stringer from the Catholic News Service and writers from the Catholic magazines—was fully represented. Religion reporters from secular newspapers and wire services were there,

and the TV crews from the pair of local stations. Michael
didn't know them personally, but it was easy to imagine who
they were. Uniformly middle-aged, gregarious men, smokers,
drinkers, somewhat shabby in their old suits and frayed shirts.
They'd begun their careers in journalism with the usual enthusiasm and perhaps more than the usual promise. They tended to
be literate, liberally educated and, for journalists, reflective.
But for one reason or another they'd slid from paper to
paper—big-city daily to suburban weekly to diocesan—or
from desk to desk—Metro to Obit to Religion. They were
men who'd been shunted aside, and the news they covered
was unimportant not only to their editors but to them. If the
rare major story did break in their area—like the Vatican
Council—these poor bastards were bumped by the first-stringers
or the foreign guys. Except for a couple of them, they had not
even been to Rome and weren't going now. Michael resolutely refused to make anything of it, but he knew full well
that only failed reporters regularly covered the events that
formed the core of his life.

But it wasn't the sight of the regulars that gave Michael
pause. A young man in the third row had caught his eye. He
wore heavy black-rimmed glasses, and his thick red hair was
disheveled enough to suggest he rarely combed it. He looked
nothing like the others. He was staring intently at Michael,
and his air of expectation alone would have set him apart
from his blasé colleagues. But there was something else.
Suddenly Michael realized what had snagged his attention.
The young man was not wearing a suitcoat; he sported an
ill-knotted, gray knit tie on a faded brown workshirt. But it
wasn't a workshirt. It was an old woolen army blouse like he
had worn himself once.

Michael cleared his throat. "It is my honor to present the
archbishop of New York, the Military Vicar for the United
States Armed Forces, His Eminence, Francis Cardinal Spellman."

Spellman, so short and stout, so bald, so ruddy-faced, was
in no way a figure of imposing physical presence. When
garbed in the elaborate episcopal vestments he seemed slightly
ludicrous. But when he wanted to, he could transcend his
cherubic manner utterly, conveying more than a hint of his

immense authority. He took his power for granted and so had
no need to flaunt it. But when it was time to make a serious
point, he knew how to do it. And nothing in his entire
ministry was more serious than this. Oh, he wanted the funds
to be raised and the orphans to be cared for, of course. The
Children's Relief Fund was a fine idea, but not only for its
own sake. He wanted Americans to remember that in the war
against Communism their commitment had long since been
made. Nothing reminded them so well, he knew from years
of doing this, as the forlorn face of an orphaned child. He had
that face in mind as he finished reading what Father Maguire
had written for him. "In the last year alone more than a
hundred thousand Vietnamese civilians have been killed and
perhaps three times that many wounded. It is impossible to
say with precision how many children have been left homeless and parentless by this violence, but surely the figure is
many tens of thousands. The country and the cities are full of
boys and girls, hungry, ill clothed and terribly afraid. In the
chaos of the fighting no one will care for them if we do not.
That is why the Catholic Relief Service of which I am
episcopal director has launched this emergency effort, and
why I call upon all Catholics and all Americans of goodwill
to join us in it."

Spellman raised his eyes from the statement. "It should be
emphasized in addition . . ." he began.

Michael studied his hands. He had been hoping the cardinal wouldn't ad-lib. It was impossible to predict what he
would say.

". . . that these children are on the frontline of our war
against Communism. It isn't a flood or an earthquake that
rendered them homeless, motherless, fatherless. The Reds did
that. They are doing it to the Vietnamese, but who they'd
really like to do it to is us. Which is why we must stop them
there. Otherwise, tomorrow it will be Australia and day after
tomorrow it will be Hawaii. It is impossible to exaggerate
what an evil force we are dealing with." Spellman stopped.
Like an expert preacher he let the silence gather and build
before going on. "Many of the children we want to help were
forced to witness the beheading of their own parents." He
paused again to let the men see how this moved him. "And

we know for a certainty that the Reds would have murdered the children too, but they let them live because, alive, they are a drain on the resources of the struggling democratic government. But we are determined that not even such heinous tactics as these shall succeed! That is why we call upon Americans to do their part to see that democracy and freedom and Christian values survive in Vietnam. Only in that way will they survive here.''

Spellman nodded at the reporters to indicate that he was finished.

Their hands went up. He pointed at an overweight gray-haired writer in the front row and said, "Hal?"

"Your Eminence . . ." The reporter struggled to his feet and had reference to his pad as he asked his question. "What do you think the chances are that the Vatican Council will allow some use of the vernacular in the Mass?"

Spellman flashed his famous twinkle. "If I have anything to do with it, none."

The reporters laughed.

"How much longer," another asked, "do you think the council will last?"

"I'd say we should wind it up this month. The bishops of the Church are busy men and have to get back to their dioceses." He smiled again. "I know I do."

"Will you be making your usual tour of army bases this Christmas?"

"Of course I will. This will be my twentieth year. I have to go; Bob Hope needs me. Besides, what would I do with all those Camels?"

The men laughed again. Spellman had been distributing packs of cigarettes to the GIs since the war. The tobacco company not only gave them to him to do so, but embossed each pack with his name and seal.

The cardinal swatted out answers to half a dozen like questions as if he was a coach drilling grounders to his infield. He was amusing and engaging, especially for an archbishop.

Then Spellman recognized the young man in the brown shirt. "Your Eminence," he began. His nervousness, apparent as he stood, set him apart from the regulars. "I'd like to ask about Vietnam." He paused. Cardinal Spellman stared at him, and the room grew utterly quiet, but for the whir of the TV cameras. The young man glanced over at one of the cameras, then went on. "We're supposed to be defending democracy there, right?"

"Yes," the prelate said carefully. "That's right."

"Why are you against elections then?"

One of the cameras stopped filming.

"I'm not against elections, son. Who said I was against elections?"

"You did, Your Eminence." He fumbled with a sheaf of papers. A notepad fell to the floor, but he found what he was looking for. "You said that the elections called for by the Geneva Convention would be, and I quote, 'taps for the buried hopes of freedom in Southeast Asia.' "

"Oh, you're talking about Geneva. That wasn't binding on anybody." Spellman glanced over at Michael, his irritation flared.

Michael raised his finger at the newsman from the second TV station, and in turn he whispered in the cameraman's ear. The cameraman straightened and snapped his camera off too.

"I respectfully disagree, Your Eminence," the young man continued. "The Geneva Convention called for elections in nineteen fifty-six. The government of South Vietnam has flagrantly violated—"

"The government of South Vietnam never signed that convention!" Spellman's face had turned crimson. Unconsciously he lifted himself on his toes. He gripped the podium, as if that pressure would spill off his tension. "And neither did the United States! Everybody knows you can't have fair elections with the Reds."

"So you are against elections."

"Rigged elections, yes."

"But when Ngo Dinh Diem held his own plebiscite in the South in nineteen fifty-six against the Head of State Bao Dai who had appointed him, he won by ninety-eight percent. Wouldn't you call that 'rigged'?"

Spellman answered with his fiercest stare. "Who are you, young man?" he asked finally. "I don't believe we've met."

"My name is Nicholas Wiley, Your Eminence. I'm with the *Catholic Worker*."

Spellman smiled. There was a stir in the room as the reporters nudged each other. The strained atmosphere eased. "Oh, the *Catholic Worker*." Spellman nodded sagely, then said, aside, "Some of my best friends are Catholic Workers."

The reporters laughed loudly. Several clapped. They were glad for the release of tension. They knew, of course, that the cardinal was referring to the controversy that ensued the year before when the *Catholic Worker* crowd publicly challenged him during the Archdiocesan Cemetery Workers' strike. But Spellman had crushed the gravediggers' union, and the *Catholic Worker*'s picket-line hadn't impressed anyone but kooks.

"I'm glad you people are taking an interest in Indochina. You tell Dorothy Day for me, will you, that she should preach her pacifism to the Reds."

The reporters chuckled, enjoying themselves now. This could have been embarrassing, but the cardinal was chewing the punk up.

"I go way back with Dorothy," Spellman said. And, again aside, with a showman's timing, "I'm the one who gave her permission to use the word 'Catholic' for her newspaper. I guess for 'Worker' she went to Joe Stalin."

Now the reporters were slapping their knees.

Nicholas Wiley took his glasses off and looked around. He was blushing and seemed disoriented. What could he do now but slink off? But suddenly he pointed his glasses at the cardinal. "You were talking about the children! You said the Communists were the assassins! But the International Control Commission reports that the South Vietnamese Secret Police are systematically murdering Buddhists even as we—"

Cardinal Spellman threw a glance at Maguire, who stood abruptly. "That's it," he said firmly. "Thanks very much, gentlemen."

Michael's crisp statement belied what he was feeling. Buddhists? Had the kid said Buddhists? But instead of welcoming Wiley's challenge as a version of the one he himself had tried to mount against Spellman, Michael resented it. The kid reeked of self-righteousness and was obviously a nut. His raising the issue like that would only confirm Spellman in his

certainty that no one but kooks had questions about policy in
Vietnam. It would have been pointless to admit the anger he
felt toward the cardinal for his refusal to defend the Buddhists,
and it would have been humiliating to acknowledge his pee-
vish irritation at the punk who'd spoiled his press conference,
so Michael channeled both feelings into the pretend authority
with which he adjourned the session.

Before Wiley could protest, all the other reporters rose at
once. He tried to say something, but his words were lost in
the bustle.

The VIP lounge had been transformed by the clerics with
their dominating black suits and flashing gold Chi-Rho-
embossed cuff links, with their boisterous laughter and waving cigars, into a rectory common room. Even though it
wasn't noon, there were drinks all around—the flow of booze
was the great advantage of traveling.

It was a scene Michael had been relieved to return to after
the loneliness of Vietnam. The camaraderie of priests, their
great, if often biting, wit, their addiction to stories well told,
their minds finely tuned to political nuance, their knack for
deflating pomposity—these things made Michael glad to join
their company. There'd been several rectory parties—*gaude-
ami*—in his honor since his return, and when the fathers
sang, in reference to his old seminary nickname, the show
tune "Mr. Wonderful," he was surprisingly moved.

When Michael walked in then, some moments after
Spellman, the chancellor gestured at him and pointed toward
the cardinal. Michael crossed to where he was sitting.

"I don't appreciate that one bit, Father. Not one bit."

"I'm sorry, Your Eminence. I should have checked him
out. I have no idea how he heard about the press conference."

"There were television cameras present. Those people only
want to embarrass me."

"It won't happen again, Your Eminence."

"And I didn't appreciate that statement I had to read
either. Not one mention of what it's all about over there. I
had to bring it in myself."

"My thought was to emphasize the children, Your Eminence.

My thought was to leave politics aside, especially now that the situation there is so . . .''

"Well, you flatter yourself to call that thinking. It's not politics to speak out against Communism in season and out. It's faith and morals. And, Father, don't you forget it.''

Michael had to look away. Everyone in the room was listening. He'd have felt abused and humiliated, perhaps, but his stronger feeling was one of embarrassment for the cardinal who, in Michael's opinion, was quite plainly making a fool of himself. But wasn't that Michael's way of deflecting his true reaction? He was deflection itself now.

The cardinal was finished with him. Michael took his leave, saying, "Good luck in Rome, Your Eminence.'' But Spellman ignored him.

When Michael had crossed the room, Don Duff, a priest who lived down the hall at Saint Gregory's, the Manhattan rectory he'd moved into, handed him a Bloody Mary. "That was rough, buddy,'' he said.

Michael nodded. "He's a little touchy, isn't he?''

"You'll get used to it.'' Duff smiled wanly. "And if he really takes to dumping on you, he'll make you a monsignor.''

The two priests raised their glasses to each other.

Then Duff said, "You know what Adam said to Eve, don't you?''

"No. What?''

" 'Stand back! There's no telling how big this thing is going to get!' '' Duff grinned.

If only all things were as simple as weather, Michael thought as he crossed the airport parking lot toward his car. In October, New York weather is either hateful or glorious and on that day it was quite the latter. The air, even over Long Island, had been scrubbed clean by the austere night, and now the late morning sunshine bathed everything it fell upon in warmth. The sky into which the airplanes climbed was cloudless, a perfect pale blue like the inside of a porcelain bowl.

One of the new passenger jets roared and Michael looked up at it. We marveled at aircraft in those days, the way we now do at microchips. Planes were still the great emblems of

modern genius, and of course under Kennedy we had just
launched the contest of all time—to build a better plane than
the Russians and fly it to the moon. But Michael was neither
an engineer nor an outer-space patriot. He automatically saw
the silver fuselage and wings as a cross, then chided himself
for piety. It was an old habit. In the prison camp a decade
earlier he'd disciplined himself to look for crosses everywhere—
in the plaster cracks, in the weave of his palm-leaf mat, in the
shadows cast by the stockade grilles. Three trees on the low
sky. Now he'd have said there were crosses enough in life
without looking for them.

He was relieved that the press conference was over and that
Spelly was gone, and he promised himself that he would not
soon be in a position again to take such shit from anyone.
After the autonomy of life in Vietnam it was a shock to be
back in a position of such overt subservience. He hoped he
could get used to it again.

As he pulled his car, a late-model black Chevrolet, out of
the parking lot and onto the road that gave access to the
expressway, he saw a hitchhiker. It would not have occurred
to him to stop, but he recognized the young man's disheveled
red hair, black-rimmed glasses and, obscured by a tattered
lumberman's jacket, his army shirt.

Only after he'd begun to apply the brakes—after it was too
late—did Michael realize that the sight of the kid pissed him
off again. The last thing he wanted to do was ride into
Manhattan with him. But he stifled his feeling with charity,
the reflex-kindness priests were schooled in. Anger, resentment,
bitterness they could show only to each other.

"Want a lift?"

"Oh, Father. Hi." Wiley was embarrassed and he hesitated.

"I'm headed for midtown," Michael offered.

"Oh. Well, I'm going to the *Worker*."

"Chrystie Street, right? Hop in. I'll drop you off."

"Oh, no," Wiley said, but he was getting in. "I'll just go
to midtown with you. That would be great."

He carried an olive canvas satchel slung from his shoulder.
It was stuffed with papers and books, but Michael recognized
it as an army gas-mask bag. So the kid did his shopping in a
surplus store. The shirt meant nothing.

Once he'd joined the flow of traffic Michael asked offhandedly, "Are you actually writing something about the cardinal's press conference?"

"I didn't mean to upset him."

"I don't think you did," Michael said automatically. If he instinctively denied the cardinal's anger, how much more readily would he disguise his own. "I doubt he's given you a further thought."

"He should give the point some thought, though."

"What, the Geneva Accords? Believe me, Cardinal Spellman has thought more about those than the diplomats who wrote them."

"You agree with him?"

Michael swallowed. "Sure I do." Who was Wiley after all? "The Geneva Accords were a French sell-out, my friend. They really were."

"De Gaulle says Vietnam should be neutral."

"Tell that to Comrade Ho."

"Did you ever read the Vietnamese Declaration of Independence? The one Ho wrote?"

"No."

The young man fumbled in his bag and pulled out a leaflet. "This is how it begins. 'All men are created equal; they are endowed by their Creator with certain inalienable rights; among these are Life, Liberty and the Pursuit of Happiness.' " He looked up from the page in triumph. Refute that, Your Holiness!

Michael remembered what Adam said to Eve: Stand back! Why should he rise to this kid's bait? "You said your name is Nicholas Wiley. I'm Father Michael Maguire, Nicholas. Good to meet you."

"Nice to meet you, Father." Nicholas leaned back against the seat. He put the pamphlet back in his bag, then took out a small cloth bundle. He put the canvas bag on the seat between them, and fell silent. Maybe he didn't want to talk about Vietnam either.

Wiley unwrapped the bundle in his lap. He spread the cloth, like a napkin, on his knees. There was a small block of wood the size of a cigarette pack, and a penknife. He opened the knife, then began to whittle. He looked across at Michael. "Do you mind? I'll watch the shavings."

Michael smiled. "No. Go right ahead. I like to watch an artist work."

Wiley sliced away at the wood. Michael drove in silence.

After a time, Michael, casting a glance at the canvas bag between them, said, "I like your bookbag."

Wiley looked at it, then went back to his carving. "Thanks."

"You know what they used it for?"

"It was for my gas mask."

"Yours?" Michael took his eyes from the road long enough to look at Wiley's face.

"I was in the army."

Michael tried to conceal his surprise. "So was I."

"What, as a chaplain?"

He shook his head. "GI."

Wiley seemed uncertain whether to believe it or not. "I don't think of priests as having been in the army."

Michael laughed. "My thought exactly about Catholic Workers."

"Well, I didn't last. I was only in for seven months. I'm a C.O."

"They let you out?" It was nearly impossible for Catholics to claim C.O. status because they could not base their pacifism on their religion. Everyone knew that Catholics were allowed to kill.

"I was discharged on medical grounds."

"Oh."

"I mean psychiatric. They decided I was loony."

"Are you?" Michael looked at him again.

"Depends on how you define it. Maybe. I know something snapped in me during basic. Maybe it was my mind."

"Or maybe your conscience?" Michael felt an inexplicable rush of sympathy for the kid, almost an attraction.

Wiley grimaced. "It's good of you to admit the possibility."

Michael thought of his own experience of basic, of that day when the DI took their pet rabbit and snapped its neck and disemboweled it with a bayonet. "I remember basic," he said, and for the first time he felt ashamed that he had not protested in Thumper's behalf. "They try to numb you, don't they?"

An expression of gratitude crossed Wiley's face. "Yes,

that's right. That's exactly right. They want to turn you into a robot."

Michael nodded. Of course they did. How else could they get you to attack pagodas without hesitation? But that was someone else's army, not ours.

"If you think that," Wiley asked suddenly, "how come you're working for Cardinal Spellman?"

Michael shrugged. "I'm working for the Church, Nicholas. I'm working for the children of Vietnam."

"But the children of Vietnam are victims of their own government. Why isn't the cardinal opposing Diem by now? Why aren't you?"

But he was, wasn't he? Michael veered from the boy's question. "Perhaps because it's a little more complicated than you'd like to think. Ho Chi Minh may have plagiarized Thomas Jefferson, but he also heads an army of men who cut testicles off village chiefs and stuff them in their mouths until they choke to death."

Where had that come from? Michael realized at once and with horror that it was an image he had not from something he'd heard in Vietnam, but from one of the sadistic harangues of his basic training drill instructor, years before.

Nicholas stared at Michael, then energetically resumed his carving. After a few moments he asked, almost absently, "Were you drafted?"

"Yes. I was just out of high school."

Wiley calculated. "Were you in Korea?"

"Yes. I wasn't a C.O."

"I gathered that. Cardinal Spellman refuses to support C.O.s. As Military Vicar, he orders his chaplains not to write letters for them. Did you know that? He thinks we're cowards. Is that what you think?"

"That you're a coward? No. You seem to have the courage of your convictions. I know what guts it takes to buck the army. Cowards are people who go along with the crowd."

"You really think that?"

"Yes."

"Then why weren't you an objector?"

"Hey, look, Nicholas, I'll grant you your point of view. You grant me mine. Okay?"

Traffic slowed for a stoplight, which turned red just as they approached. Neither of them spoke until it turned green again and they were going. Michael knew that he had to be wary of his anger at the kid. The self-righteousness of purists always got to him. "I'll tell you, Nicholas, Korea was a bitch. We did stuff no human being should ever have to do, but there was no choice. Even in a Just War, you do what you have to do, number one, to survive and help your buddies to survive, and, number two, to get it over with quickly so the killing stops."

"What stuff?"

"What?"

"That human beings should never have to do?"

"Blow up bridges with people on them."

"You did that?"

"Yes."

"Is that why you became a priest? To atone?"

The question infuriated Michael, but he channeled his surge of feeling into his grip on the wheel. "Christ atones, Nicholas. We don't."

"But you're running the Children's Relief Fund. Was it children you blew up? Is there a connection?"

Michael drove mutely, but he knew the set of his mouth would give him away. No one had ever asked him questions like this before. What upset him was not the young man's effrontery, but the knowledge that these were questions he'd wanted to ask himself. Even to ask if there were connections between his past and his present was to see them. The orphans in Vietnam were, of course, the children of the Koreans he'd killed. It was a link he'd never allowed to come to consciousness while he'd been in Vietnam, but now, perhaps because that conflict had become somewhat remote and therefore manageable, it seemed obvious. But the orphans for whom he worked were something else too. They were the *anawim*, the least of God's children; they were the sheep whom Jesus said to feed.

"I guess I'm off base, asking that."

Michael shrugged. "Sure, there's a connection. Everything is connected to everything else." He looked at Wiley as he stopped the car for another light. "How old are you?"

"Twenty-two."

"I was twenty-two when I entered the seminary."

"Delayed vocation, eh?" Wiley grinned.

It struck Michael how young he'd been—as young as this kid—but he remembered feeling so old. Already the army and the war and the time in China and even Mary Ellen Divine had been behind him. Now it was ten years later and he felt much younger, as if that grim distant past belonged to someone else. When he looked at Wiley part of what seemed familiar was his premature weariness. Barely an adult, yet he solemnly carried, as Michael had, the weight of the world's great sins. Well, wasn't it that a certain kind of Catholic boy imagines at twenty-two that he is the Messiah come again? Whose shoulders wouldn't stoop under that burden? "So I went in the seminary, and you joined the *Catholic Worker*." Michael put his car in gear. "Two sides of the same coin. 'Be ye perfect.' "

"I don't think so. I'm not trying to be perfect."

"You're trying to be pure."

"The difference between us . . ." Wiley had adopted the lecturing tone he'd used with Spellman. ". . . is that you're satisfied to pick up the victims of the violence. I'm trying to stop it. The Church has always served the State as a kind of ambulance service. It's like at an intersection where people keep getting run over. The Church will nurse their wounds. It will even build a hospital on the spot. But what it *should* do is go downtown and speak the truth to power until they put up a stoplight at that intersection so that people will stop getting run over. But that would be politics. And the Church doesn't involve itself in politics."

"It seems to me that Dorothy Day has picked up a few victims over the years. I didn't know she was opposed to that."

"She isn't. But Peter Maurin says that serving the poor has to lead to political action in behalf of the poor. The mission of the *Worker* is twofold. The soup kitchen is only half of it."

"And you're the other half?"

"You know, you're just like the cardinal. You people think the *Catholic Worker* is this weird bunch of zealots. You

pat us on the head for the soup line, but you go 'tsk, tsk,' just
like Wall Street when we push against the systems that keep
our soup line crowded. You think our ideas are naive and you
hold Dorothy Day in contempt."

"That's not true. I don't know a single priest in the
archdiocese who holds her in contempt." Michael looked at
the blade in Wiley's hand. He'd been cutting at the wood
furiously, and now he was gesturing with it. Threateningly?

"Oh, yeah? Well, why hasn't a single priest in this archdiocese joined her on the picket line?"

"Because priests have other things to do, Nicholas. If you
don't know what, ask Dorothy. She'd be the first to tell you
that the members of the mystical body have different gifts and
different responsibilities. Do you really think she would welcome priests on the picket line? I don't."

"Peter Maurin says priests belong in the world."

"Peter Maurin is a Frenchman, isn't he? He's a Personalist,
right? The masses are saved by leaders who embrace renuncia-
tion and serve through the purity of their intentions. Et cetera."

"Personalism is the philosophy underlying the *Worker*.
That's right. Peter Maurin is a disciple of Emmanuel
Mounier's."

"Well, I'll tell you something funny, Nicholas. Ngo Dinh
Diem is a Personalist too. Personalism underlies his regime.
Ngo Dinh Nhu was a friend of Mounier's in Paris. The Ngos
consider themselves moral exemplars, and that's their problem.
Personalism is the root cause of the evil in Saigon."

"Evil? You think Saigon's evil?"

"How can I not think that after what they've done to the
Buddhists and the students?"

Wiley stared at Michael. "I don't understand you, Father.
I mean, you keep coming at me from different places."

"I just think it's ironic that Dorothy Day and Ngo Dinh
Diem have something in common."

Wiley nearly gasped. "Diem's a dictator!"

But when Michael looked at him, Wiley burst into laughter.
Dorothy Day in her sphere was a dictator too, and no one
knew it better than the people who worked with her. The
difference between her and Diem was that she imposed the
Divine Truth she possessed on a small group of disciples and

by force of her personality, while Diem imposed it by force of an ever-increasing American arsenal on an unconverted nation. Michael said, "I just think people should be a little less inclined to take their own virtue for granted. You know why I like Kennedy? Because he's not that great a Catholic. Good Catholics make me nervous." Who was he now, John Howe?

"But Kennedy backs Diem."

"Not for long. You watch. Diem's days are numbered."

"I hope so."

"Yeah, but you also hope for Ho Chi Minh, and I'll tell you something, that bastard is doing his best to see that that society collapses completely. And then he'll walk in and set up his utopian state in the rubble. Terrific. Maybe so. A humane socialist society out of what's left. Fabulous. But what about the kids whose parents have been killed? What about the kids who have to live like animals now, fighting over rat meat in back alleys, or selling their sisters to the highest bidder? I know of fifty thousand kids over there right now who are going to starve to death by the end of the year if I don't come through with something for them. Malnutrition, disease, famine, not to mention what the actual warfare is doing to them. You know what we're seeing now? Adolescent suicides! Unheard of in Asia! Children killing themselves because their lives are so horrible, or maybe because they figure their younger sisters and brothers will have a little more rice with one less mouth to feed. See, I think those kids matter, Nicholas. I doubt that your friend Ho does. To him, they're just more casualties of history on the bloody road to Revolution in the sky. Not me, though. I don't even care about Democracy, Nicholas. Or Land Reform, or elections, or the goddamn Geneva Accords. I care about the kids, that's all. And I'll tell you something. Their two best friends, maybe in the world, are fellows name of Spellman and Kennedy, who refuse just to brush off their clothes and walk away."

Wiley said nothing, and Michael's emotion receded behind the abrupt cloud of his embarrassment. He had not so exposed those feelings before, not to a layman and not to his fellow priests. In front of priests it was permitted, even expected, that he would display his surliness or his frustration, but not his exuberance, not his extravagant commitment. In front of lay people he was to display his moderation, his reserve. But about the children in Vietnam he had none.

They crossed Brooklyn in silence. When the towers of the bridge came into view, Michael's eye lifted. Being back in the city still exhilarated him, and his love of New York ambushed him regularly, the way it had when he'd come back from Korea. The sun glistened off the steel web of suspending girders, cables, stays, shrouds and wires. For a moment Manhattan was mere backdrop to this marvel, and the airy skyline only served to emphasize the gothic solidity of the stone towers. The achievement of engineering and imagination represented in the span took his breath away. It made him think of Saint Patrick's Cathedral, and indeed it had been built by the same Irish artisans, masons, stone-cutters, steelworkers and hod-carriers. Many of them died at their work.

Bridges! Michael and I grew up under their spell. Perhaps all island-folk do. From Inwood we'd climbed on dares up the parapets of the George Washington, and we'd dropped water-balloons on boat traffic from the New York Central Railroad Bridge and we'd smoked our first cigarettes in the dank riverbank shadow of the soaring arches of the Henry Hudson. New Yorkers never outgrow their enchantment with bridges. Carolyn and I, after our Village phase and when we'd had Molly, would buy a house we couldn't afford on Brooklyn Heights just because from its living room we could see the bridge, this one, Thomas Wolfe's bridge, Hart Crane's, Maxwell Anderson's and Arthur Miller's. Michael used to sit with me and watch the sun set behind it while I'd recite from Wolfe: "The Bridge made music and a kind of magic in me, it bound the earth together like a cry; and all of the earth seemed young and tender."

"Wonderful, isn't it?" I'd ask at last.

And he would tilt his glass like an old vaudevillian. "Hell of a lot of trouble to go to just to get to Brooklyn."

Crossing with Wiley that day, Michael went back in memory to that other bridge. With its pig-iron girders and stumpy pilings and its jury-rigged center span, it was nothing compared to this American masterpiece, not material for metaphors, poems or songs, no music, no magic.

His memory of that Korean bridge had come to him over the years with a certain regularity, and unconsciously he had ritualized it, had transformed it into the slow-motion climax of an arty war film. At the center of his memory was the explosion, the simple loud clap, the iron girders somersaulting through the air amid the millions of splinters and the dust of railroad cinders and the billowing smoke. He knew that there had been people on that bridge, and he had seen some of them in their particularity at the time—the Pappa-san, the shrieking old lady—but he never pictured them when he remembered the explosion.

But now as the car crossed with a bump the first metal-expansion joint—the threshold of the span itself—he remembered for the first time in years that other scene at the threshold of the Korean bridge. Lieutenant Barrett had just rammed his jeep into the throng. Michael had stooped to free a howling child from the straps tying it to the mangled body of its dead mother. He had taken that child in his arms, and he remembered that it refused to stop crying no matter how he jiggled it or cuddled it. Tears gushed out of its tiny almond eyes and oh what piercing shrieks that baby made. And suddenly the face he was seeing was an old man's face, its frozen look of horror, Thic Nhat Than's face, his severed head. Involuntarily he said out loud, "Oh, Christ!" And then he heard Barrett ask, "Oh, Christ, what have I done?"

"What?" Wiley asked.

"Nothing." The car rattled onto the iron grate, and the loss of solid roadway registered as a dangerous swaying, a drifting of the wheel in his hands, a loss of confidence in the car. He leaned forward over the wheel to concentrate on driving. Now it was the Manhattan skyline that dominated the field of his sight, Wall Street to the left, the Empire State Building and the Chrysler Building to the right. From Brooklyn the jagged magnificent row of skyscrapers always reminded Michael of the rows of gravestones in his father's cemetery, but that was an association he veered from, and he felt his control slip further.

Control; John Howe had said the question was how to control Diem.

But now Michael's question was how to control himself.

He tightened his grip and focused on the infinite detail of the great bridge as they went not over but through it. Finally his eye settled on the bright sky at the end of the tunnel the weave of girders made.

"Have you ever visited Chrystie Street?"

"In fact, I have."

"When you were a seminarian, right?" Wiley was folding his block, knife and the chips of wood back into their cloth. As he'd promised, he hadn't left so much as dust on the seat or floor.

Michael wanted to ask what he was carving, but it seemed, ironically, given their conversation, an overly personal question. He said, simply, "That's right."

"Funny thing, Father. You guys come like pilgrims to the *Worker* when you're in the seminary, but you never come back after ordination. Why don't you reverse the trend? Come on in and have lunch with us."

Michael looked at his watch. The car engine was still running and they were sitting outside the *Worker*. Derelicts had already begun to line up along the sidewalk. "I'm sorry, Nicholas, but I can't."

"Come tomorrow then. Come as our guest. You wouldn't have to work the line. I think Dorothy'd like to meet you."

"And I'd like to meet her, but . . ."

They stared at each other. Each was aware of the charged field between them. To his amazement Michael felt powerfully drawn to the kid. The strange energy that army psychiatrists had found pathological registered on Michael as vitality and eagerness. Nicholas Wiley was more alive, it seemed to him suddenly, than anyone in that crowd of urbane clergy he'd left behind. Wasn't that why in the kid's presence he had faced, if only briefly, the ragged feelings his time in Vietnam had left him with? No priest had yet asked him what it was really like there or how he felt about having left. If he'd gone into the *Worker*, it wouldn't have been to see Dorothy Day. There were domineering saints and mothers enough in every priest's life, and that was why they stayed away. It was Nicholas Wiley Michael wanted to be with. He had an impulse to confide in him right there. Confide what? He was aware that he hadn't even told Wiley explicitly that he'd been in Vietnam. Korea was easier to speak of, and that alone suggested how deep his feelings ran. Too deep, he thought, for a kid like this. But hell, even to himself he was boxes inside boxes, secrets inside secrets. All he knew was that when something shook him, he rattled.

"You're busy."

"I am. Yes."

"Okay." Wiley opened the door and got out. He leaned back into the car and flashed a winning grin. "But if you're ever down in the Bowery again, you know where to come, right? There's always room for one more when you're feeding two hundred and fifty."

"Thanks. I'll remember."

As Michael drove away an acute loneliness overwhelmed him and he thought, But if you're feeding thousands there's never room. He slammed the wheel with the palm of his hand. He was furious, but not with the *Catholic Worker* or the cardinal or the friendly but shallow priests he would now join for lunch. He was furious with himself.

EIGHTEEN

ON All Souls' Day, the day of the damned, Jean-Baptiste Ngo Dinh Diem and his brother Nhu, both disguised—fittingly, though pathetically—in the cassocks of priests and cowering in the sanctuary alcove of a modest Catholic church in a Saigon suburb, were seized by rebel officers of their own army. The president and his first counselor were then shot and stabbed repeatedly, like victims of mad killers.

The people of Saigon knew that the Ngos were dead when radio stations played Chubby Checker's "Come on, Let's Twist!", a song that had been outlawed as lewd under the Law for the Protection of Morality. They poured into the streets and danced.

Archbishop Pierre Martin Ngo Dinh Thuc, the primate of all Vietnam, was in Rome for the fall session of the Vatican Council. He would not return to his native country. We would all forget him, and assume that he was dead until one stunning day we would read in a tiny paragraph on a back page of the *New York Times*, as I did not long ago, that he was at last formally excommunicated by John Paul II. But here's the hitch. He was drummed out of the Church not for having incited the slaughter of Buddhists, but for consecrating as bishop a mad Spaniard who claimed, comic-strip fashion, to be the pope. So much for the New Morality.

Madame Nhu would certainly have been killed alongside her husband and brother-in-law, but, as you may recall, she was in America on a lecture tour, angrily denouncing John Kennedy for having withdrawn support from Diem the month before. In October I had been present to hear her Dragon

Lady diatribe at Fordham and to see our right-wing student body, to my intense shame, give her a standing ovation. When, a few days later, she was awakened in a fancy Beverly Hills hotel with the news of the coup and the murders, she ranted maniacally that God would swiftly punish those responsible.

Three weeks later, as she no doubt saw it, using the instrument of Lee Harvey Oswald, He did.

Now, looking back on it, one is tempted to see in President Kennedy's death meanings which at the time were irrelevant to it: if Kennedy's ascendance epitomized the triumph of American Catholicism, his assassination on the heels of Pope John's death and that of Spellman's protégé, Diem, revealed the hollowness of that triumph, nay, the utter vanity of it. If Kennedy's appeal to youthful idealism mobilized a generation to work for civil rights at home and the Peace Corps abroad, his absurd death made their disillusionment—their "days of rage"—inevitable. If Kennedy had in fact been the young god we considered him in our first grief, then he had been taken from us because we were mere mortals not worthy of him; worse, in the downward spiral of our self-doubt, we wondered, Weren't we all somehow guilty of his murder? And wasn't it therefore meet and just that after it, as after Diem's slaying in Vietnam, all the devils were loosed upon both lands? When the anointed king is killed, the law of nature is rent, the heavens open, the earth splits and the plagues come. Vietnam got "Big" Minh and the curse of a renewed American "friendship." We got Big Lyndon, whose own death would take place a decade later on the very day that the American phase of the Vietnam war—the fruit of that "friendship"—would end.

It was impossible at the time of Kennedy's assassination to arrange that avalanche of events and feelings in any intelligent pattern. All we could do was behold and ache, and marvel at the shock, the largest shock our generation would experience. We hadn't even known he was in Texas.

What were you doing when you heard the news? Even now, twenty years later, we ask that question and thereby reestablish for each other, for a moment, that bond. The loss

we felt made us friends. A vast illusion of intimacy—we
were a 190-million-member family—was what we got that day
instead of meaning. We ask each other what we were doing
when we heard the news, but we don't have to ask what we
did then, because we know. For three days we all did the
same thing—sat groggily before our televisions and watched.

Me? When I heard, I was pacing ritually in the fathers'
waiting room at Saint Vincent's Hospital in the Village.
Carolyn and I had been married for two years. We'd moved
to a small apartment on Cherry Lane, across from the theater.
We considered ourselves very *avant*, me with my poetry, she
with her painting. Sometimes I would pose for her in the
nude, but only on two conditions, that she not paint my face
and that she take off all *her* clothes too while standing at her
easel. She never would, of course, being a "serious" artist,
but sometimes we ended the session by making love. It was
my reward. But however Bohemian we considered ourselves,
Carolyn and I reacted to the discovery that she was pregnant
like a pair of Micks from Inwood. What happiness! What a
relief to think we could begin now to live the way we'd
always really wanted to, the way, in truth, our parents had.
Didn't we set about turning our ascetic, ill-furnished flat into
a cozy nest, doilies, rockers, throw rugs and all! A nest to
which we could bring our baby home.

I had intended to be with Carolyn throughout the birth, but
her labor ended abruptly in an emergency cesarean, and I
had been expelled from the operating room. I still find it
nearly impossible to relate the two events, but our daughter
was born less than an hour after the president was shot.

By the time the doctor came into the waiting room to tell
me all was well, it was crowded with nurses, staffers and
other doctors, all gathered around an old chocolate-colored
Philco. It was still assumed that an elaborate plot had un-
folded in Dallas, and there were reports that Lyndon Johnson
had been shot too. No one seemed to know where he was.

"You have a beautiful daughter, Mister Durkin," he said.
"And your wife is fine. I think they'd like to see you." He
shook my hand, then moved toward the radio.

How can both of these things be true? I thought. But that
was the extent of my reflection. I was tempted neither then

nor later to see them as elements of one mystery, as a metaphor of the ambiguous, life out of death, that sort of thing. The events were completely separate, of totally other orders, yet each one left me numb.

The corridor was deserted. From inside the patients' rooms sounds of the morose narration wafted from radios and televisions, but the recovery room where Carolyn lay was unfurnished, empty except for her bed and medical paraphernalia.

Her eyes were closed. I approached and touched her arm and only then did a flood of relief and gratitude course through me.

But I had another, more powerful experience. It is like admitting to the foulest blasphemy to say now that I, alone of all Americans perhaps, thanked God that afternoon that He'd taken Kennedy. It could have been Carolyn, I thought, as if in the Divine economy—this was the irrefutable given of that moment—it had to be one or the other.

She opened her eyes and smiled at me. Then I wept.

"Have you seen her?" she asked finally.

I shook my head, trying to grasp both that there was this baby now, and that Carolyn knew nothing of Dallas.

"Go see her. She's beautiful."

We think of joy as the opposite of sadness, but it isn't. The sadness of that afternoon was monumental and, in a way already sensed, permanent. It did not yield to happiness, but neither did it make happiness impossible. The joy I discovered beholding my daughter was unexpected and unprecedented, but it seemed so natural that I gave myself over to it as if I'd always planned to.

Molly fit in the crook of my arm, a perfect loaf, and I loved her without limit from that first moment. I have referred already to the "ontological change" that traditional theology claims as an effect of ordination, a notion I had dismissed as meaningless. But to my amazement that arcane phrase described what had happened to me. The birth of that child made me a new person, a different sort of being altogether. She taught me in that first encounter that the most radical separation of all is between people who have brought children into the world and those who haven't; is between the way I was before that moment and the way I was after it. You

probably think of me as an opinionated snob, but believe me I
am humility itself compared to what I was before my daughter's
birth. She called forth from me primordial hope such that
even the president's death could not shake.

I returned to Carolyn's room. She was sleeping and so I
stood above her and watched. She stirred and smiled and
slept on. Her bliss, partly of the drugs, was total. When she
awoke she squeezed my fingers and mouthed, "I love you."

I kissed her.

She said, "I dreamt that the president was killed."

"You didn't dream it, darling. He was."

"Is that why you were crying?" she asked. Disappointment dulled her eyes. She'd thought I was crying just for her.
I knew I couldn't explain that, in fact, since I had thought she
was going to die, I was.

Soon they moved her to the room she shared with another
woman. The television, of course, was on. And we, like
everyone, stared at it, as at shadows in the cave.

Carolyn drifted in and out of sleep. Periodically nurses
brought Molly in, and Carolyn held her. Then, since sedation
prevented Carolyn's breast-feeding her, I fed our baby until
she slept. I took her back to the nursery because it was my
wife, I thought, who needed my attention. Even when she
was awake we hardly talked. I sensed that as the grim reality
registered on her, Carolyn began to hate Oswald for what
he'd done not just to Kennedy or to America, but to us. He
had destroyed the purity of her joy. Was this a world into
which a child should come? To her, the juxtaposition of the
two events made them equally absurd, and by that night she
was in the grip of a depression I could not penetrate.

When I returned the next day, that gloomy Saturday during
which the rain fell everywhere in the East, she was withdrawn still. There were of course physiological reasons for
her state. The ferocious labor alone would have sapped her
strength, but the traumatic cesarean on top of it left her
nothing with which to fend off the tidal wave of feeling. The
spinal had caused an immobilizing headache and that, as well
as her abdominal wound, required further sedation.

I knew what she'd been through and what she was on, but
again and again I thought she was having such intense reac-

tions to the assassination and to the birth that she simply couldn't share them with me. She seemed such a distant, passive stranger that I feared at first our baby would be affected by her detachment. But not so.

All day long we craned up at the television set while dignitaries filed past the flag-draped catafalque in the East Room. When Jackie appeared, Carolyn touched my hand and said, "She lost her baby in August." When I looked at my wife, she was biting her lip so fiercely I asked her to stop.

She brightened once, when Michael Maguire called to ask if he could visit. His call was a stunning surprise. We'd had no idea that he was back from Vietnam.

It was Sunday, early enough that no visitors were allowed, except fathers and, naturally, clergymen. After rapping softly on the door, he pushed it fully open and stood there. He had lost weight and his black suit hung on him. His Roman collar no longer fit and his eyes were like grottoes. I found the sight of him shocking. He looked unwell to me, haggard and nervous the way he had when he first came back from China.

Carolyn raised her arm toward him. He went to her, took her hand, then visibly checked his impulse to lean down to her. *Oh, kiss her!* I thought. *Kiss the poor woman!*

The blur had gone from her eyes. "We have the most beautiful baby," she said. In the vibrant timbre of her voice happiness at last displayed itself, and I was profoundly grateful to Michael for having come.

She looked at me. "Oh, Frank, take Michael to the nursery. Show him Molly."

"No," he said, still holding her hand. "First, let me look at you."

I turned to the window. It seemed unfair to watch them and, frankly, I did not want to see. The sun was shining that day, and I fixed upon a bright pigeon smoothing its tail-feathers on the ledge of the building opposite. The pigeon leapt into the air without warning, dipped, then rose, disappearing above the roof lines. Behind me David Brinkley was describing the riderless horse. I hugged myself and turned.

Michael and Carolyn were both watching the television. They had dropped each other's hands. Michael had lit a cigarette. The woman in the next bed, though her curtain was drawn, could be heard saying into the telephone, "They're bringing him now. Do you see it?"

To muffled drums, the cortege wound into view. The ceremony for which we had all been longing had begun, though this was only the transfer of his body from the White House to the Capitol. I remember the formation of soldiers ahead of the horse-drawn caisson. I remember that stallion, "Black Jack," with the empty saddle and the boots reversed in its stirrups. The military trappings were unfamiliar, but altogether the impression was one of a traditional, well-known ritual and it soothed us. The army band struck up the Death March as the formation turned onto Pennsylvania Avenue by the Treasury Building. Behind the caisson were the limousines. What could his wife possibly be thinking? What could she be saying to her children?

Michael said, "So many people went to Confession at Saint Patrick's yesterday that they set up confessional screens in the sanctuary. There were even more penitents than during the Cuban missile crisis."

"Why do people feel so guilty?" I asked, somewhat bitterly. I could have spouted my own theory. They're Catholics, aren't they? And isn't it easier to condemn yourself and endure any punishment than to believe that perhaps God cares nothing for the world? But that would have been my oh-so-worldly self speaking, the one who wasn't surprised when cruel things happened. My other self, the one into whom Michael had pressed belief at his ordination and to whom both Carolyn and now Molly were miracles of affirmation, knew that people feel guilty because they are not worthy of the gifts God gives.

"I don't think it's guilt, Durk. I think people are afraid to die. If it can happen to him . . ."

"That's how I feel," Carolyn said abruptly, surprising us both.

I expected Michael to respond with something perfectly consoling, but he didn't. He was as inarticulate as I was, which relieved me. I crossed to her side and took her hand. She looked up at me gratefully.

For some moments we simply watched, one man on either

side of Carolyn, as the funeral cortege made its way down
Pennsylvania Avenue, which was lined with throngs of silent,
wounded people. It was like a dark parody of an Inaugural
parade.

I resented it when the network switched us back to Dallas,
the announcer explaining that Lee Harvey Oswald was being
taken to another jail and promising us a glimpse of the man
who had done this to us.

A crowded corridor; "There he is," the newsman said. I
craned, despite myself, to see the piece of shit.

And then that moment of alarm, chaos, shouts and a wildly
tilting camera. The reporter kept screaming, "They've shot
him! They've shot him!" and all I could think was that by
some mistake technicians had rerun, yet again, the awful
sound from Friday.

A woman screamed in the corridor outside Carolyn's room,
and then loud footsteps. Michael immediately went out, as if
he knew someone needed the last rites. I remained with
Carolyn and with that first-ever televised act of murder. I sat
on the bed with her and she clung to me, and I thought, This
is what it's like when we all go crazy.

"Is Molly all right?" she asked suddenly.

I'd forgotten her completely, and now the commotion in
the corridor—an assassin loose in Saint Vincent's!—was a
threat. I went out. Two orderlies were arranging a woman on
a stretcher by the nurse's station. Michael was holding her
hand.

Through the broad nursery window I saw that Molly was
sleeping contentedly.

"She's perfect," I told Carolyn. "Sound asleep." I resumed my place on the edge of her bed, and she held on to
me again, so fiercely it made me happy. The news reporter
was more coherent, but he was still near hysteria and he kept
repeating, "Oswald was just shot! Lee Harvey Oswald is
lying on the floor! He's been shot! There are policemen
everywhere here. I did not see who did it!"

I realized that only seconds had passed. I had apparently
run to the nursery and back, and I was out of breath.

The confusion on the television screen continued. It was
impossible to think of any image that crossed it as real, as it

would have been impossible to anticipate that all the most devastating of those images would become clichés, these clichés. David Brinkley came on and stammered at us. And then we were watching the spirited riderless horse prancing its stately way up Capitol Hill.

When Michael came back into the room he said, "Did you hear her scream?"

"Yes. What happened?"

"She had a seizure of some kind, epileptic, I think. Did you hear what she said?"

"No."

"When she regained her senses she looked up and saw me kneeling over her and she screamed, 'A priest! Oh, God! Am I dying?' "

Michael's weary face broke into that familiar grin of his. "I'm the harbinger of death," he joked.

I felt a pang for him and opened an arm. He came into our embrace, more mine than Carolyn's. Once more the feeling we had for each other, that essence of friendship that would sustain us through nearly, but not quite, everything, asserted itself. While Lee Harvey Oswald breathed his last and while President Kennedy's remains approached the place from which he had said, "Let the word go forth . . . ," the three of us laughed quietly and shared thoughts, as Mrs. Kennedy would describe them, "that lie too deep for tears."

"She's beautiful," he said, though Molly was sleeping on her stomach and wrapped in the tight sleeve of blanket so that only the dark crown of her head was showing. We each leaned on the glass as if to draw as close to her as possible. "What a weekend to be born in. Durk, you should save the papers for her."

My impulse was the opposite, to shield her from those events, even to deny them. I changed the subject. "How long have you been back from Vietnam?"

"A few months."

"And you didn't call us?" I stared at him.

"I've been busy," he said, but he was blushing, looking at his feet.

"What have you been doing? You seem exhausted."

"I was in Los Angeles Friday. I took the Red Eye Special home. I could have stayed out there, but I wanted to be in New York. It was dawn when I got back. There was a message at the rectory from Mom about your baby. That news redeemed the other news. It made me very happy for you both. In fact it made me happy for the world. The Talmud says that when a funeral procession intersects with a wedding march, the mourners must give way."

"You've become ecumenical, Michael. I remember when you only quoted the New Testament."

He laughed. " 'Now war arose in Heaven, Michael and his angels fighting against the dragon.' " Facing me, he said soberly, "I was so glad they were both all right."

"It scared hell out of me, what Carolyn went through. Still does. Seems like that dragon has drawn close this week, waiting to snatch people we love."

"I felt that way. My first impulse yesterday was to go see my mother." He rolled his eyes self-mockingly, as if he of all people was a momma's boy. He was in fact a dutiful son. "Then I walked downtown from Good Shepherd."

"In the rain?"

"Yeah." He smiled. "The rain was good, purifying, cleansing, you know?"

"Yeah, like a carwash."

"I wound up at Saint Patrick's and went in to pray. That's when I saw all the folks at Confession. I went to Confession myself."

"I assumed you'd been hearing them."

"It's the first time I actually just went, you know? Like one of the people."

"I hope the priest gave you the same kind of shit he gives us."

"I chickened out." He smiled again and, leaning on the glass, cupped his hand to light his cigarette. "I figured I could either tell him I masturbate or tell him I'm a priest, but I couldn't tell him both."

"Let me guess."

"I said I'm a priest and confessed that four times I prayed the breviary without paying attention, and I genuflected twice without actually touching my knee to the floor. Oh, and that

I've said Mass without wearing the maniple four hundred and seven times.''

We laughed softly for a moment, but when he put his hand on my arm it was sadness we shared.

''So then you left the cathedral and found a phone booth and called us because it was the loneliness you felt that seemed sinful.''

He met my eyes. ''That's right.''

''We've missed you, Michael. *Why* didn't you call us? And you never wrote. We were going to be your family.''

''I don't know how to answer that, Durk.''

''Just don't tell me how busy you are. I'll have one of those cigarettes. Thanks.''

We stood in silence, smoking, looking at the baby. Finally he said, ''You just never know what's going to happen, do you? I mean we all thought we had everything laid out. Kennedy was just hitting his stride. He was just getting control of things.''

''Are you talking about Congress, or what?''

''I'm talking about Vietnam.''

I stared at him, I'm sure blankly. I wanted to ask him what it was like there. Had he seen those monks burn themselves? I wanted to tell him that I'd been worried about him. But I didn't know how, thinking, still, in those days, that you didn't just say so.

''I don't know what his death will mean,'' he said. ''Something terrible, I'm afraid.''

I watched him smoke. He was already considering the consequences of Kennedy's assassination for the nation, for the world, for his own work. I saw how we were different. I was still in the grip of that present. Implications and consequences were nothing to me. Our brush with death—for what is childbirth but that, and what was Dallas?—had made the future an enemy to whom I was going, eventually, to lose my wife and daughter. Therefore I refused to think about it. I preferred to bask in the baby's presence—she was the present tense itself. Otherwise, like most Americans, I preferred the suspension of time in television that weekend; we knew instinctively that if we prolonged that awful moment, before it ended it would soothe us.

"What do they have you doing now?"

"Fund-raising." He smiled. "I'm a bingo-priest at last." He smoked his cigarette for a moment, then said, "I run something called the Children's Relief Fund. The idea was to build orphanages over there, but we can't keep up with the numbers. Since Diem's death, thousands of homeless Buddhist children are showing up. They were afraid before to show themselves to Catholic priests. Imagine."

I sensed the fury that filled him, but I barely understood it. Vietnam was more than I could think about.

We smoked and looked through the glass at the room full of babies. I remember thinking they looked like potatoes wrapped in foil.

"Molly. Carolyn said you're naming her Molly."

"Yes. Molly Saint Vincent Durkin." I laughed, but Michael missed my joke. "Edna Saint Vincent Millay was born here. Her parents named her for the hospital."

"You're kidding."

"No, really. Well, I'm kidding about naming Molly that. Carolyn and I laughed at the thought because Saint Vincent was a patron of Mother Seton; Mount Saint Vincent's was to be her exile. Just being here as a new mother is joke enough for her. Molly's middle name is Anne, for Carolyn's mother."

"And 'Molly'?"

"Snagged from the mists of our Irish past. We're lucky she was a girl. We hadn't agreed on a boy's name. I wanted 'Cornelius.' "

Michael laughed. "No wonder you didn't agree."

"Caro wanted 'Michael.' "

He froze with his cigarette halfway to his mouth.

"I'm kidding. She wanted 'Earl.' " I grinned at him.

He dropped his cigarette on the floor and stepped on it. I wanted him to admit that the reason we hadn't heard from him or seen him till now was that he still loved Carolyn. Now, of course, I understand that I wanted him to admit that as a way of punishing him. I wanted to see the pain he felt. I wanted to see the extreme of his loneliness. I'd have said at the time, though, thinking myself sincere, that I just wanted an honest conversation; I wanted the source of our awkwardness out in the open so we could deal with it. I'd convinced

myself that since I loved him too, it was no big problem that
he and Carolyn loved each other. I was custodian of Carolyn's
love, not its proprietor, and I always knew it. But I'd have
said that was more than enough for me. I was there day after
day, and I was certain that over time familiarity alone would
soften her heart to me.

Carolyn and I had not talked about Michael, and his absence since our marriage had made it impossible for any of us
to normalize our feelings, to grow accustomed to them, to
tame them. His being away kept the issue alive for both of
us, kept him a figment, a dream, a threat, which now I see
was why, whether innocently or not, he did it.

"It's the worst thing about celibacy," he said. The direct,
abrupt reference to his condition surprised me. He lit another
cigarette, and I realized he wasn't going to finish the thought,
as if he'd begun it aloud inadvertently.

"What is?"

"Not having children."

Because of Molly, I saw that he was right, but I rushed to
reassure him. "You have all those children whom you help."

He laughed. "Do you know who I spend my time with,
almost all of it? Monsignors. Church bureaucrats. The heads
of Catholic Charities or Offices for the Propagation of the
Faith. In Sioux City one day and Mobile the next, and L.A.
the day after that. Always in chanceries. You know what a
chancery is in wrestling? Any hold that imprisons the head."
His bitterness surprised me.

"But you're building orphanages," I said. "You're taking
care of children whose fathers are gone. You're a father,
Michael, to thousands of them."

"But I never get to hold them." He looked at me. "Could
I hold her, Durk?"

"Sure you can." Even if I'd known that one day Molly
would have his name instead of mine, I'd have let him do it.
He was my friend, and, having seen his pain, I wanted to take
it away.

Saint Gregory's is a neo-Gothic church on East Seventy-
ninth Street, and the rectory is a large stone building adjoining it. When Michael returned there late that afternoon, the

steady rain and the shadows from the nearby buildings made
the place even gloomier than usual, and it was with a shudder
of reluctance that he mounted the stone stairs from the street
and went in. He didn't go to his room, even to hang up his
soaking coat, because he dreaded being alone, but also because he had no television. He went to the common room,
and heard the reassuring hum of Walter Cronkite's commen-
tary even as he pushed the door open. But his heart sank
when he saw that, even though the television was on, none of
the priests was there. Walter Cronkite had been describing the
line of mourners passing the catafalque in the Capitol Ro-
tunda to an empty room and that seemed to Michael, suddenly, the saddest moment of the weekend.

He poured himself two inches of Scotch and sat in the big
armchair in the center of the room that the pastor reserved for
himself. He hoped the whiskey would dull his sense of
isolation, but if anything it only sharpened it. An hour passed.

A bell was ringing somewhere in the building. At first
Michael ignored it. But it kept ringing. The doorbell, he
realized. Why wasn't someone answering it? Weren't there
staff people? Wasn't there a duty-priest? But then he realized
that he not only felt alone in that building. He was alone.

The bell rang again.

He put his cigarette down and went to answer it.

When he opened the front door, there to his surprise was
the kid from the airport press conference. What was his
name? Wiley. Nicholas Wiley. It was dark by then but still
raining. Wiley's coat was soaked and his hair matted, and
Michael's first thought was, Where's your hat?

"Hi, Father."

"Nicholas . . ."

"I hope you don't mind my coming by. I've been thinking
a lot about things. I mean, when something like this happens,
you realize you better just go ahead and act on the impulses
you have."

"Come on in."

"No, I can't." He looked up at the rectory. How un-
welcoming it must have seemed to him.

"In out of the rain, anyway."

Wiley stepped past Michael, then Michael closed the door. They faced each other in the ill-lit foyer.

"This will just take a minute," Wiley said. He fumbled in his coat pocket, then pulled out a small packet wrapped in brown paper and handed it to Michael. "This is for you."

Michael took the package, but he was looking into Wiley's eyes. The boy seemed intense and alert, utterly in control of himself, but also brimming with feeling.

Wiley said, "You were nice to me, Father, and I liked you a lot. And I was hoping you'd visit us at the *Worker*. And then when the president . . ." He lowered his eyes, but only for a moment. "You were one of the people I felt close to. And I guess I thought, well, he'll never know unless I . . ." He shrugged and smiled shyly.

Michael felt ambushed, completely unprepared both for Wiley's expression and his own sudden, nearly overwhelming sense of need. Wiley had pierced it like the truest arrow. Michael channeled his feeling, his surprise, into the act of unwrapping the package.

It was a hand-carved wooden cross, two inches high, on a leather thong. It was stark and delicate. It was strong. Michael felt a rush of emotion. When he looked up at Wiley, their eyes met. When had he ever felt such a blast, like furnace heat, of another's affection? "Nicholas, it's beautiful."

"I made it."

Michael looked at it again. He remembered the kid whittling in the car that day. "It's just beautiful," he said. "I'm very touched."

"You were nice to me, Father," he repeated.

Michael looked into his eyes again. He wanted to say, I refused your invitation. I put you out of mind. I was afraid of what you wanted from me. He said nothing. Instead he put the cross around his neck. It hung at his breastbone. He fingered it. "I'll always wear it, Nicholas."

"You don't have to say that."

"No, I will. I really will. I want to."

"Well . . ." Nicholas smiled, he was so pleased. "I guess I better go."

"You won't stay? Have some coffee?"

"No." Of course not, and they both knew it.

They shook hands then, warmly.

At the door, watching Nicholas plunge out into the rain, the dark, Michael called, "Thank you. I really mean it. Thank you."

Nicholas waved. And Michael thought, This is what it's like when an angel comes and rescues us. No, not angel, he realized then. But son.

The cavernous Saint John the Divine seemed brighter then, but it was only that the pupils of my eyes had dilated. Our eyes, the "windows of our souls," in the nuns' phrase, can become accustomed to the most impenetrable dark.

I was kneeling still in the choir stall on the margin of the sanctuary, but the time had come for me to stand and go to her. Oh, Carolyn! How memory revived my worship! How magnificent you were! How bottomless your courage! It had been the great privilege of my life to be the awed man at your side on the day of our daughter's birth. Those were the things I wanted to say to you.

The sound of my sandals clicking on the floor seemed eerily distant, unrelated to the steps I was taking as I wound back toward the rearmost chapels. At the Lady Chapel I saw the Virgin Mary, hovering, suspended gravity, but Carolyn was gone, and I was filled with panic. Had I lost her again?

I turned and retraced my steps along the ambulatory. Just as I passed the arched entrance to a small room behind the choir, a sound stopped me, a faint groan. After a moment's hesitation I crossed into a jewel-like baptistry. Windows high up in its tower admitted light, but transformed it, and the air itself seemed sacred there. The font was a carved marble masterpiece the size of a pulpit. Beyond it, against the far wall, was the casket, Michael's casket. I could hardly look at it. My eye gratefully came to Carolyn who was kneeling there with her back to me. She had a hand on the coffin, and that detail recalled a pose of Jacqueline Kennedy's. Grief choked me. There was no Walter Cronkite whispering here, and for once the comparison with the death of the president, which was the loss against which my generation measured all other losses, was inappropriate. This could have been the first death ever; that could have been Eve there, mourning Adam. But who would that have made me?

I approached slowly, as quietly as I could. Even from behind she was familiar enough to arouse a familiar ache. Had it really been a decade, a dozen years? Her blond hair, now riddled with gray, was pulled back and piled upon her head, exposing her neck. She was wearing a simple blue dress, belted at the waist. She was forty-four years old, but there was no thickness in her body yet. The sight of her curving flesh reminded me, though really I had never forgotten, of the dream it was to be inside her. Sunday afternoons, sex, the newspapers, Bloody Marys, cigarettes, Billie Holiday and complacencies without the peignoir. While pretending to idle through the *Times* I could watch her as she left our bed without covering herself to cross our bright bedroom—bleached floorboards, white walls and a ficus in the corner—to answer the telephone. Her nakedness from a distance was thrilling too, more exotically perhaps than up close, the thrill of the voyeur. I could study her body, her pert buttocks, her taut thighs, her ruddy breasts. When she had been aroused her breasts kept that lively piquant color for a long time. If the phone call was from someone she liked, she would whirl on the toes of both feet, a pirouette, and lift her hair from the nape of her neck and throw her head back with pleasure. She might signal me with a snap of her fingers, then put them to her mouth, meaning, "Cigarette, sweetie!" I would toss and she would catch. Her toned nudity was free of the extraneous and her movements were completely natural, musically natural, having neither flats nor sharps. She was as easy with herself in front of me as a model before her artist and perhaps, come to think of it, all the hours she had spent in studios with an eye on the nude was why. But there was nothing impersonal in my gaze, and I could study her for hours. I liked it when those phone calls lasted. When she finished and she came back to the bed I would spring out from behind the paper and take her. She would laugh and I would know that she had sensed my watching, that she had displayed herself coyly, foreplaying me.

Oh, Carolyn, I thought, without you I have been a man with no use for arms!

She was aware of me. I sensed the tension in her even before her head came up and her shoulders straightened. Once more my grief and longing took second and third place to panic; the panic of having found her. What would she say to me? And I to her? It was wrong, I felt all at once, my being there. I was no helper. I was no friend. I had not forgiven Michael. I had not forgiven her. I had tried to flee my hurt, but I had nursed it.

Slowly she stood and turned.

Her face was like wreckage, but her eyes did not falter. She looked at me directly, with that old resolve. Which then disappeared, and her will collapsed, and she shrieked, "Durk!"

She came at me with abandon, the way once she came at both of us, to hurl herself into that swimming pool.

Now she hurled herself into my arms. "Durk!" She had pronounced my name only once, but in that vaulted space, the sound hung over us like a canopy. And when her weight hit me, I absorbed it and held her. I was immovable at that moment, as a tree. "Durk!" She landed against my chest. My despair by hers was nothing. I had never taken such a blow before.

Her hair was at my mouth, but before I could look at her my eyes were caught by the sight of someone else, a figure in the shadows, standing just yards away, her mouth agape. Carolyn's shriek had frightened her, even as her appearance out of nowhere had frightened me. She was, I saw at once, a Vietnamese girl, about eight years old, and she was crying.

Light from a bank of candles flickered behind her. She was an apparition.

My mind leapt to what it recognized—that naked Vietnamese girl running down the road, fleeing blindly, running at her photographer with fresh American napalm bubbling her skin the way the sun bubbles tar, running at him as if his photograph would heal her. It did not, of course. Instead it scorched me and you, a branding iron, the fiery tool that told us and everyone who we had become.

And now I understood that this girl was Carolyn's other child and that in her Michael had found an orphan of his own for whom to make a home.

NINETEEN

I<small>T</small> was the night of February 12, 1965. The Tonkin Gulf Resolution had passed Congress almost unanimously the previous August. Only the month before, on January 20, Lyndon Johnson began his own term as president, having won the office as the peace candidate. Less than three weeks after the inauguration, only five days ago that night, in retaliation for a bold Viet Cong attack against a U.S. Army barracks—a single barracks—Johnson ordered the first air bombardment of North Vietnam and decided to send two hundred thousand troops to the South.

But Michael was not thinking about those doomed efforts. That night his focus was narrower than the fate of Vietnam or the soul of America. As he watched the sky from the observation deck at the main terminal at JFK, he was thinking about the twenty-six children, all burn victims of napalm or white phosphorus bombs, whose plane was due in soon. This was the first attempt to bring Vietnamese victims of the war to America. It was sponsored by a Swiss humanitarian organization called Terre des Hommes which had already arranged for hospital beds and doctors' services in leading medical centers in Europe. In Vietnam doctors could do hardly more than wave flies away from the oozing skin of people unlucky enough to have been caught in a "hit" of napalm, and there were more and more "hits" every day. The gelatinous gasoline adheres to flesh absolutely and smolders indefinitely, leaving burns too deep to be treated in field hospitals and deformities too acute to be remedied without drastic and sophisticated medicine. Broken bones, ripped flesh, fractured skulls were one thing, but the little monsters with melted chins and no eyelids and charred blue skin and fused fingers were another. As the numbers of burned children increased and as more and more of them died agonizingly on the stone floors of the orphanages—cots, mats and sheets, which stuck to the wounds, only made their condition worse—even Catholic doctors took to administering merciful overdoses.

Now the Swiss had organized an effort to make that unnecessary. They hoped the initial evacuations would grow into a massive airlift of napalm victims, first of children, then of adults, to get them the treatment they needed. So, with no help from the U.S. government, Terre des Hommes was bringing its first flight of wounded children to the States on a chartered, specially fitted airplane. The Swiss organizers had gone through their Vatican contacts at Caritas International to find a coordinator of the effort in America. As you recall, Caritas was the parent organization of the Catholic Relief Service, and that was how Michael Maguire came to be standing on the deck at JFK that night.

Everything was ready. Seven ambulances were on the tarmac, nurses were standing by and units were prepared at Columbia-Presbyterian, Roosevelt and New York hospitals. Teams of some of the best surgeons in New York were scheduled to begin treatment of the children in the morning. At Michael's side were the Terre des Hommes representative in New York, a young plastic surgeon from Columbia-Presbyterian, and the former monsignor, now bishop-designate Timothy O'Shea, whom Cardinal Spellman had recently named as his auxiliary for the Military Ordinariate.

"Cold," O'Shea said. The four men stood with their shoulders bunched and their hands plunged in their coat pockets.

"What will the chill do to the kids, Doctor?"

"Same as it does to us. Nothing more."

"I'd think it would disorient them, their coming from the tropics."

"It disorients me," the doctor said, "and I'm from Jersey City." He shivered dramatically.

"They're late," the Terre des Hommes representative said. He was a Swiss diplomat, a middle-level administrator at

UNICEF. "They would not be late if it was a government plane."

Michael leaned toward O'Shea. "Did you hear what Monsieur Hurot said, why the army wouldn't make a hospital plane available? The spokesman said it was inhumane to take an Asian child out of its native environment."

"Well, that spokesman should be fired," O'Shea said.

"No, just burned," the doctor said brashly, "and then taken to Vietnam so he could see what a humane environment it is."

"Worse were the airlines," the Swiss diplomat said. "If they transported burn victims, even the mildest cases, they said their other passengers would experience discomfort."

"Their *paying* passengers."

"Well," the doctor said, "I can see why the government wouldn't do it."

"Oh really? Why?" Monsieur Hurot asked.

"Simple. They can hardly ask the American people to support Johnson's new buildup if it's targeting children with napalm. This is their dirty little secret. They sure don't want it opened up in New York."

"Neither do we," Michael said. "If the press gets onto these children, Saigon will never let us bring out more."

"They certainly aren't targets anyway," O'Shea said.

The doctor gave O'Shea a quizzical look.

"It is not American policy to bomb civilians."

"Oh really? You think we're waiting here for military personnel, average age eleven?"

"Let's not turn these children into debating points, Doctor. They are tragic victims of war." O'Shea's voice was firm.

"I don't call it 'tragic,' Reverend. I call it criminal."

"Despite my collar," O'Shea said sharply, "I'm not quite so facile with moral judgments."

"I prefer to think of it as a medical judgment, Reverend. Napalm is medically contraindicated for human beings."

Michael interrupted them, placing an arm on each man. It was an argument he'd had his fill of. "Gentlemen, this is not the Fulbright Committee. Take it easy."

"The plane should be here," Monsieur Hurot said.

"Maybe it landed," Michael said. "Maybe it's making its way to the gate."

Monsieur Hurot turned and led the way into the terminal. The doctor followed him. As Michael started, O'Shea took his sleeve. "Why the hell is he here?"

"He pulled together the team of doctors, Tim. He's more important to this than any of us."

"He sounds like an SDS kid."

"In the operating room, his rhetoric won't offend."

"You just better hope he doesn't get quoted."

"He won't. He understands. He's in this for the long haul, Tim. He wants this flight to be repeated as much as we do."

"I'm sick and tired of our military people being maligned. Hell, you know as well as I do that Americans don't kill civilians."

Michael stopped abruptly. "No, I don't know that." He stared at O'Shea long enough for the older man to realize he was thinking of the bridge across the Han River. But Michael wasn't interested in talking about that either. He said, "What I do know is that Americans don't provide hospital planes."

"There's a war going on, Father!" O'Shea blew up. His face was the color of the monsignor's tab at his collar. "And American boys are dying in it. I would expect you to appreciate what that means." He swung away from Michael and stalked toward the long spiral of terrazzo stairs.

And Michael watched him, as sadness clutched his chest.

"Hello, Father."

Michael had been standing a little apart from the others. They were out on the tarmac now, near the ambulances. The plane had landed, but had yet to taxi into view. A light, cold drizzle had begun to fall. He turned toward the voice that had greeted him. It was Nicholas Wiley. "What are you doing here?" he blurted. They'd seen each other irregularly in the past year and a half, meeting for coffee, going for long walks in the park, and Michael had always been glad to see Wiley, but not then, even though it had been months since their last encounter.

Wiley sensed Michael's displeasure, but he grinned. "Waiting for the A-train?" Wiley's hair was long now, hiding his ears. He wore a floppy leather hat and an army field jacket on which was prominently displayed the chicken-foot peace symbol. A camera case was slung over one shoulder, and over the other the familiar canvas bag.

"I'm sorry, but you can't stay."

"Why not?"

"No press."

"What does that mean, Father? Where do you think we are? Russia?"

Michael looked nervously out at the airfield. The green-and-red wing-tip lights of half a dozen taxiing planes crossed in eerie patterns, and the sharp blue runway lights glistened in the rain like lapis beads. No plane seemed to be approaching yet. He faced the young man. "Are you still with the *Worker*?"

"Yes. I'm the managing editor now. Dorothy likes the way I stack bundles."

"I saw your name in the *Reporter* also, just a few weeks ago, wasn't it?"

"Yeah, I string for *NCR* sometimes."

Michael nodded. "Good for you," he said, but that decided him. The obtuse and obscure *Catholic Worker* was one thing, but the *National Catholic Reporter* was an ambitious and irreverent liberal weekly that would splash this story all over the country. The project would be finished before it started. He took Wiley by the arm and led him away from the ambulances, toward a nearby hangar building. Once they were under its eaves, out of the rain, he stopped. "Look, Nicholas, you can't stay here. You simply can't. I'm telling you to leave."

Michael's tone jarred Wiley. "Hey, Father, you can't talk to me like that."

"The hell I can't! You're unauthorized out here. This is off-limits to the public."

" 'Off-limits'!" A fierce expression crossed Wiley's face. "What is this, the army?"

"Yeah, it's the army, Nicholas." Michael pushed him once, firmly, toward the hangar door. "And I'm your son-of-a-bitch sergeant! Now move!" He pushed him again. In the back of his mind a voice said, This isn't the way to handle the kid; sweet-talk him, take him in. But Michael was angry, at the mercy of anger. He pushed him again.

But now Wiley pushed back. "Hey! Cut it out!"

The two men were squared off, and the next move had to be blows. They stared at each other, puffs of breath steaming from their mouths and nostrils.

This was a mistake, Michael saw. He hadn't anticipated Wiley's resistance, but he should have. The kid had taken on the army, after all. Michael raised his hands, palms out. "I'm sorry. I'm out of line."

Wiley eyed him carefully.

Michael backed off. "You do have a right to be here."

Michael's surrender disarmed Wiley. "Why don't you want me?"

"Because we can't have publicity. You know what we're waiting for?"

"Vietnamese children, burn cases. I have a friend at Columbia, in the medical school. He told me. I didn't know it was your project, though."

"Nicholas, if these kids become the focus of antiwar shit, then that's it. We won't get any more out. It's that simple."

Wiley did not react.

"Do you see my point?"

"But doesn't that play into the army's hands? Doesn't it serve their purpose to keep the outrage hidden?"

"Obviously, we can't debate this here." Michael looked past Wiley toward where the others were waiting. Still no sign of the airplane. He made a show of resignation, but in fact he'd had a new idea. "How about this? You can stay and watch the arrival, but you don't ask any questions of anybody, and you don't take any pictures. Then, tomorrow, come up to my office. I'll give you a full interview, an exclusive interview, and I'll get you into the hospitals."

Wiley agreed immediately.

But Michael intended to get in touch first with Dorothy Day. She believed in the primacy of meeting simple human needs. She was a master of publicity when she wanted it, but she would understand that sometimes it was deadly. He was sure he could convince her to call Wiley off.

"There is one thing I'd like to ask you, though, Father."

"Shoot."

"What's Monsignor O'Shea doing here? Didn't the cardinal just appoint him Military Vicar?"

"Yes, he did. Why should that disqualify him from being here?"

"These children are napalm victims, right? That's the U.S. Army, Father! The V.C. don't use napalm."

"The army wasn't aiming for these kids, Nicholas. You know that. Not even the fucking marines *try* to burn children." Michael realized that, like a coin that had been flipped, he had just changed sides. Discussions of the war were futile and infuriating for him because he could argue—he could feel—both positions.

Wiley smiled suddenly. "I never heard a priest say 'fuck.' "

"Did I say 'fuck'?"

Wiley nodded sagely and Michael laughed.

Wiley said, "At Berkeley someone hung a banner out that said, 'Fuck Communism,' and the John Birchers didn't know whether to rip it down or make one of their own."

Michael remembered what he liked about the kid, how his earnestness was tempered by humor. His guileless vulnerability was a relief after the habitual self-protecting calculation of Michael's own kind. "How've you been, Nicholas?" he asked suddenly.

"I'm in therapy now, Father." He looked away shyly and touched his hair. He could have been a hippie; Michael realized he *was* a hippie. "The army shrink told me I should get some help, but it took me a long time to see it. My doctor's a good man. He says I have a problem trusting people, but that maybe I can learn to trust him." He looked sharply at Michael, and a wave of insecurity crossed his face. "You think it's okay, don't you?"

"What, therapy? Sure I do."

"Some priests think it's a cop-out. I guess Freud had his problems with the Church, eh? Dorothy thinks we should just have Spiritual Directors, and let it go at that."

"I don't agree with her, Nicholas. I've known a Spiritual Director or two who could have used a shrink." Michael slapped Wiley's shoulder in a friendly way. He was aware that the ground had shifted under them. The young man's defiance had been replaced by the old deference of a Catholic seeking the approval of his priest. "I'm glad you're taking care of yourself."

"I guess I have some stuff to deal with."

"We all do."

"Could we talk about it sometime, Father? I mean, it's been a while since we got together."

"Sure, Nicholas," Michael said quickly, the pastoral reflex. But inwardly he was backpedaling. The kid seemed needy and unstable, prone like most radicals to politicizing his own insecurities. If they'd found it impossible to become friends the previous year it was because Michael could never quite relax with Wiley. Much as he wanted to he couldn't be himself. The kid was a little strange. "Though, you should check it out with your counselor. We wouldn't want to work at cross-purposes with your therapy, would we?"

"There are some religious angles, though, that my doctor can't help me with. Like, he doesn't agree with pacifism, but I think that's because he doesn't understand about the Crucifixion. Nonviolence always leads to the Cross. I know that. But the Cross leads to the Resurrection."

Michael looked toward the airfield. It seemed to him that one plane in particular had begun to make its way toward them, a four-engine Constellation. If so, that was it.

Wiley talked on as if he'd forgotten what they were doing there. "My therapist calls it 'passivism,' and he thinks Martin Luther King is a passive-aggressive. But, hell, so was Jesus! But what are we supposed to be, aggressive-aggressive? I mean, what's so bad about being passive-aggressive if it builds up the Kingdom of God? Or liberates God's people? Or ends the war? Gandhi says we have to be prepared to die for nonviolence, and that's what I think too."

"Nicholas . . ."

"But my therapist says Gandhi has nothing to do with me. That's what I mean, how can I—"

"Nicholas, I think the plane's here. We have a deal, right?"

Wiley's eyes went out of focus for a moment, strangely. Then, as if he'd snapped his own lapels, he seemed to remember where he was. He followed Michael's gaze out to the airfield, then assumed his earlier manner. "Right," he said. "No pictures."

"And don't talk to anybody."

"And I can see you tomorrow?"

"Yes, but only about the children." He resolved to call Dorothy Day, but had the feeling he should be calling the kid's doctor.

They walked out to the ambulances and joined the others. The rain was falling harder, and as the airplane closed in, the wash from its propellers swirled the ground puddles and whipped the air. The men had to hold their hats.

As Michael watched the plane porpoising slightly as it slowed and cut an exact arc behind the "Follow Me" truck, he knew very well what the moment meant. It had been more than a year and a half since his time in Vietnam, and since then the beleaguered country had become a mystical kingdom to him, a bewitched realm of the unreal with mad rulers and spiraling violence and a fairy-tale curse of reversals that turned every "improvement" into yet another unsolvable problem. He had been charged with relieving the suffering of Vietnamese children, and he had preached their cause with eloquence and feeling in pulpits and chanceries all over America. But in fact, however acutely he made others feel it, the suffering of those children had become a remote abstraction to him. Even the horror of napalm had until now generated a visceral reaction, but at the moral level more than the personal. It was the *idea* of its use that offended him, the *idea* of its effects that outraged him, the *idea* of burned children that made him afraid his country had lost its way. He could not tell you the name of any of its victims. He could not imagine what it was to hold one or love one or lose one. He was like the pilots who pressed their buttons in rarefied cockpits high above the earth. Whom the pilots injured Michael sought to heal, but from the same distance and with a like detachment. When he realized this about himself he shrank from the knowledge. Tonight, thank God, it was going to change. He wanted to take the first child he came upon into his arms, but even that image was wrong, a product of his quite American insensitivity, his sentimental abstraction, for burned flesh cannot be embraced without increasing the victim's agony infinitely. All one can do, really, for such children is to gaze upon them, find their eyes and not let them see you flinching. What they do for you, on the other hand, is obliterate your aloofness. Michael was ready for that, and he was smart enough to be afraid.

The Constellation stopped. Groundcrewmen ran under it with blocks for the wheels, while others pushed an aluminum staircase against the fuselage. A caterer's truck coasted forward to nestle inside the wing. Its hydraulic lift, holding wheeled stretchers instead of food containers, rose slowly. Finally the airplane's doors opened.

The Terre des Hommes representative was the first to mount the stairs, followed by the doctor, Monsignor O'Shea and Michael.

An air force steward saluted each of them inside the aircraft entrance, and that was the first sign—that he was military—that something was wrong.

Monsieur Hurot was speaking animatedly in French to a woman dressed in nurse's whites. The doctor squeezed by them toward the after-cabin where the children were. Michael followed him while O'Shea, who was fluent in French, remained with Hurot and the nurse.

It was Michael's first time in an airplane outfitted with pallets instead of chairs. It reminded him of those submarine movies, the walls lined with double-bunks, naked bulbs casting garish light, but only over the aisle. In the bunks all was shadow, and the children stirring under sheets were like creatures hiding in alcoves. No, it wasn't a submarine, he thought suddenly. It was a cave, a catacomb, and the bunks were the niches into which the martyrs were rolled. The Catholic tradition of embedding saints' relics in the altar began in that first generation when all Masses were said in secret and, because there was no other space in the tunnels under Rome, upon the tombs of the slain. In places, he thought, like this.

The doctor was leaning into a bunk, examining a child. He turned away abruptly and leaned into another to examine the child there.

Michael saw the face of a girl, her eyes hard upon him. To his relief, her face had not been burned, and though he sensed her fear and her discomfort he found it possible to smile at her. She was covered to her throat with a heavy woolen blanket, and belts strapped her in. The second sign that something was wrong.

The doctor went quickly down the aisle, bobbing from cot to cot. A pair of nurses stood aside for him, and a Vietnamese civilian, a man in a white shirt open at the throat, waited at the far end of the cabin. It was to him that the doctor finally blurted, "But they are not burn victims!"

Michael was right behind him. "What?"

"These children have not been burned. There isn't a burn case in here."

"What do you mean?" Michael's eyes fell to another child, a little boy perhaps eight years old whose ravaged face was so thin it seemed his cheek bones were devoid of flesh altogether. His eyes were lost in their sockets.

"They're sick, obviously. But they're not burned." He faced the Vietnamese. "What is this?"

The man seemed shocked. "Why, these are the children for Terre des Hommes. They are cardiac patients and victims of polio and leukemia. They are to receive treatment here."

Monsieur Hurot burst into the cabin behind them. "They have switched the children! There are no wounded children on board here at all!" He pushed past the nurses and past Michael and confronted the Vietnamese. "Are you Doctor Nguyen?"

"No. Doctor Nguyen was not able to come. I am Doctor Cao."

"I've never heard of you! You haven't been working with our people."

"Nevertheless—"

"But this is incredible! Where are the war-wounded? Our agreement with Doctor Ba Kha was quite explicit. We were not airlifting the chronically ill. This was not to be mere pediatrics! We were airlifting war-wounded children!"

"Doctor Ba Kha has been replaced."

"What?"

"Doctor Ba Kha is no longer minister of health." The Vietnamese doctor leaned toward Hurot and began to talk in French.

"Speak English!" Michael ordered. He understood already what had happened, and though his shock was total, he was not surprised. Neither Johnson nor Khanh, that month's ruler of Vietnam, could allow children mutilated by U.S. fire-bombs to come to New York. It had been naive to think they might. Still he had never felt so angry. His fists and jaw were clenched, his body rigid, as he held himself utterly in check. What? He should have hurled himself against those stricken children, as if it was wrong of them to have polio and not third-degree burns? Or against the nurses and the doctor who had cared for them? He was just learning what was truly maddening about the Vietnam war, both for those who fought it and those who fought against it: the real "enemy" was never there when you were ready to attack.

"My government approved this project," the Vietnamese said gravely, "because certain cases require treatment we cannot provide as well as hospitals in America." He gestured down the line of bunks. "These cases. Other illnesses and other conditions we handle adequately. Your organization wants to help our children. If you think these children do not need your help, examine them."

"But the napalm victims!" the young American doctor said. "Where are the napalm victims?"

"Napalm?" The reference seemed to mystify the Vietnamese doctor. "Napalm is used against the Communist soldiers."

Michael looked down at the boy beside him. From inside the caverns of his eyes he pleaded, as if he were a healthy child like any other, but only asking to be released from the tomb of his body. Michael touched him. "Lazarus," he thought. "Come out."

TWENTY

"**Y**O U were there, Tim, damnit! You know what they pulled!"

O'Shea turned his chair slowly toward the window behind him. The view from his office on the sixty-fifth floor of the Empire State Building was hypnotizing, but the rain from the night before had continued and intensified. Sheets of it blurred New York. Queens was gone in the mist. He wondered if airplanes were flying at all. "We're lucky this isn't snow," he said in what remained of his smooth Tipperary accent.

"Tim!" Michael leaned across his desk. "Will you not talk to me about the weather!"

"Oh, Michael," O'Shea said mournfully. "I hate it when you go all earnest on me. It's how I know how young you are." He continued to look out the window, and his silence was absolute.

But this was a pretense of detachment on his part, one Michael saw through. He had a reaction of his own to what had happened the night before, but it certainly was not anger at the South Vietnamese government. He'd let Michael draw him into something he had no business with. He wouldn't have gone near that evacuation airplane if he had thought it was controversial. Whether knowingly or not, Michael had tossed him a hot potato, and O'Shea hadn't gotten to where he was—or, rather, where he'd be in a few weeks when he was consecrated bishop—by juggling those. But he wrapped his uneasiness in his tough-Irish-priest demeanor, as if the only issue that morning was his young assistant's emotionalism.

351

He said, disarmingly, "Did you hear about the hippie liturgy they had at the Paulist church? They sang Negro spirituals and the priest gave a flower to everyone, along with rye bread Communion. God knows what they did at the kiss of peace. Probably passed around a—what do they call it?—fag."

Michael knew he was not expected to respond and he didn't.

"If they consecrate rye bread, what does transubstantiation do to the caraway seeds, do you suppose? You were good in theology." He continued to stare off vacantly.

Michael sat down in the chair facing the desk; all right, Monsignor, I'll wait until you're ready to talk to me.

Finally O'Shea faced him. "Your friends got their facts wrong. Something was lost in the translation."

"That's not it, Tim. The Vietnamese welshed. They fired the man who'd made the deal. Somebody got to them."

"And who would that be?"

"I'd like to know, Tim. Wouldn't you?"

O'Shea shook his head. "No. To what end? Michael, if the evacuation of children is a political problem, then we can't help with it, can we?"

"That wasn't my thought."

"Well, you'd better make it your thought."

"Why is it 'a political problem' to want to take care of wounded children?"

"It shouldn't be."

"It is, because their presence here would pose an obvious question, and there isn't a good answer for it."

"It is not your job to ask that question, Michael." O'Shea leaned toward him. "We talk about love and tolerance all the time around here, don't we? Maybe we've had it easy. I mean, love and tolerance toward refugees and children, that's a snap. But what about love and tolerance toward the men who are trying to keep Vietnam from sliding into the Communist pit?"

"These are the thoughts of a man who's preparing for a new job," Michael said.

"Don't insult me, Michael. It's how I feel regardless of my appointment."

"But as auxiliary bishop for the Ordinariate, you'll be paid not just to love and tolerate the military, but to bless it."

"That's right. And I'll do that with enthusiasm because I believe in the American military, and I accept the essential justice of our cause in Southeast Asia." After waiting for a comment from Michael, he leaned back in his chair and folded his hands at his chin. "Don't you?"

To Michael's surprise, it was not the interrogatory of a moral philosophy professor, nor even of an ecclesiastical superior, but the concerned question of a friend. No one had put it directly to Michael before, and he knew that his inability to answer with a simple yes was, in the arc of his life, literally momentous. He said carefully, "It's dawning on people that maybe the V.C. can win this thing. And if that's what they're thinking, well, you know what happens then. 'Justice' goes out the window, and what comes in are all the air strikes and artillery headquarters will give you."

"That's war, Michael. We've been through it."

"Not against guerrillas, we haven't. You're kidding yourself if you think the just-war categories still apply."

"But I think exactly that."

"And if what you call 'unintended side effects' have become the means?"

"Look, Michael, get off your high horse. Vietnamese civilians are getting mauled. I know that. But what can we do when the V.C. disguise themselves as peasants?"

Michael stood up. The older man's cool rationality seemed suddenly obscene to him. "We can admit that the rules of war simply don't apply. Obviously that has become policy. Why don't they say it instead of denying that it's happening?"

"You know why."

"Yes, because Americans don't want to be told they've become barbarians!"

O'Shea made a point of not responding to that.

Michael felt stupid suddenly. In 1965, even among the opponents of escalation, it was still unthinkable that we should simply abandon to the Communists the country we'd helped to create. (Of course, years later we did.) Michael sat again and tried to deflect the feeling that he'd made a fool of himself. It was a common experience of ours in those early convoluted conversations about the war, that what began as a clear instinctive revulsion at the endless escalation ended in a suspicion that one simply was not tough enough or pragmatic enough to see the thing through. We dreaded above everything the accusation that we suffered from, as the Bundys were always describing it, a failure of nerve. We were always eyeball to eyeball—not with the Russians; what did they care for the punji trap of Vietnam before we fell into it?—but with ourselves.

Michael forced a grin. "Maybe you were right. Let's talk about the weather."

But now O'Shea was serious. "You don't think I should take my new job, do you?

"No, that isn't what I think." Michael was confused. What made this impossible was the way in which talk about right and wrong seemed increasingly out of place. Was that so in the thick of every war? Maybe the just-war theories were for the homefront folks, to spice their conversations. "I think it's a minor miracle that Spelly appointed you. I think you can make a difference, Tim. The chaplains will take their cues from you. They are the guys on the spot. You can help them remember what they're for besides saying Mass on jeeps."

"Maybe you can help me remember."

Michael leaned forward. "Everything I think about it, I learned from you."

The two men held each other's eyes, both aware of the strong, manly feeling that bound them. "So remind me," O'Shea said.

Michael nodded and responded as if elaborating the point of a dissertation. "Chaplains are for helping GIs and officers to do what's right. Right action, Tim. That's the main thing. Chaplains are for preaching a clear morality even in the middle of an ambiguous war." Michael smiled and raised a finger. "They should say, 'Don't fuck over innocent people. If you do, God fucks over you.' "

"So to speak."

"Keep the boys nervous about their immortal souls."

"You learned that from me?"

"Tim, I'll tell you, in Korea we were never nervous

enough about that. You no doubt remember a lieutenant who drove his jeep right into a crowd of refugees. He had his reason. At the time I thought it was a good one. But we didn't think twice about it, and we should have, because the next time you don't think even once."

"The DI would say that thinking twice interferes with the soldier's job, and maybe makes it riskier for him."

"And he'd be right. In a firefight it might slow the soldier down just enough to make him lose. But that risk is worth it if other times it slows him down enough to prevent murder. It's a risk I'd take."

"Would you have fifteen years ago?"

"You tell me."

O'Shea nodded. "You were sensitive to this stuff. But frankly that's what set you apart."

"It's what you call 'going all earnest.' "

"It is, and I admit it. And it's why I keep you around, despite your fucking foul mouth." O'Shea grinned. "You're my barometer, Michael. You've always been. How will I know the weather without you? Maybe I should bring you along. Want to work in the Ordinariate?"

Michael shook his head.

"Of course not; silly thought."

"Actually, my next job is what I wanted to talk to you about, Tim."

"Good. Because it's on my mind too."

"I'm resigning from the Children's Relief Fund."

"What?" O'Shea was genuinely surprised.

"It's the right time, Tim. The Relief Fund's in good shape. Anybody can run it now. I want out." Something in O'Shea's expression startled Michael, a glimmer of hurt perhaps, a wound. Michael thought about the difference in their ages, more than twenty years. Once it had seemed an infinite stretch, but now Tim O'Shea seemed not all that much older. That meant both that Michael was getting up there—he was thirty-three—and that Tim, having begun as a surrogate father, had become a friend. This was going to be difficult. "And the man who takes your desk will want his own people."

"What if the man who takes my desk is you?"

"What?"

"You, Father." O'Shea smiled. "Bishop Swanstrom and Cardinal Spellman both agree. You're the man for the job, Head of the CRS Refugee Project. Spelly was going to tell you himself."

Michael was flabbergasted. After director, it was the most important job in the agency. He was far too junior. "God, Tim, you're not serious."

"Sure am. I expected an argument, but everybody agrees. You've done a hell of a job with the Fund. And the bishops you've dealt with are at Spellman all the time, how good you are. And I told Swanstrom frankly that if he didn't give you the Refugee desk I was going to ask Spelly to transfer you to the Ordinariate."

"And when was I going to be asked?"

"What?"

"Am I the pawn in your chess game, or what? You expect me to be grateful, don't you? I'm not surprised when the cardinal plays God with his priests' lives. I don't expect that from you. Why wasn't I the first person you talked to about this?"

"Well, because, of course, I knew you'd want it."

"But I don't, Tim."

"Oh, God!" O'Shea slapped his desk and pushed away from it, slamming back in his chair. His eyes went to the immaculate ceiling, and he muttered, "Give me patience." Then he bent forward and pulled a drawer open for a cigar. He calmed himself by trimming, licking and lighting it. "All right," he said through the smoke, "what's up?"

"I want you to send me back to Vietnam. While you still have the clout here, resurrect my old position or create a new one. On-site relief administrator, liaison with the local Church, liaison with AID, an appointment through Caritas, I don't care. But I want to go back to Vietnam, and I want a Church position."

"Good Lord, Michael! You know I can't do that. You've done your bit over there. And the last thing they need now is another American."

"But the buildup would justify it. If there are two hundred thousand military, there will be thousands of AID and State people. Nobody would think twice if you sent me back over."

"What for, Michael? What the hell for?"

"To find those children. The ones who were supposed to be on that airplane last night, and to get them out. And to get the others out."

"Don't be ridiculous. That's the most foolish thing I ever heard."

"You said I'm your barometer. I'm telling you the pressure is falling fast. Johnson has decided to wind it up, and it's going to be vicious. I'm not talking moral theology, Tim. I'm not talking right and wrong. That's for your chaplains to do. I just want to get those kids out. I want to get them to hospitals that can treat them. It's a goddamned outrage, what was pulled last night, and they're not getting away with it. Terre des Hommes says there have been a million child casualties since nineteen sixty-one, in just four years, and that was before LBJ decided to make the goddamned war . . . "

"You're a priest, Michael! Watch your language!"

"Oh, it's language that seems obscene, is it?"

"Your overreaction is what disturbs me. A million casualties? Where does that figure come from? What do a bunch of Swiss do-gooders know? Take it easy."

"So maybe it's *half* a million! Maybe it's only a hundred thousand! Okay? But why the hell are they sending us polio victims? Don't tell me to take it easy!"

"I *will* tell you to take it easy, Father. And I will tell you to remember who you're talking to."

"I'm talking to you, Tim." Michael checked himself. "You were there last night. You heard what the Vietnamese doctor said. They're going to hide what's happening now. They're going to deny it. Imagine what that will mean to the children. They'll have to bury them alive. They won't even get to field hospitals. They won't get first aid. Tim, somebody has to get over there. Somebody has to find those children and get them out."

"Monsieur Hurot is way ahead of you. Isn't that what Terre des Hommes is doing?"

"But to what effect? You said it yourself, a bunch of Swiss do-gooders. But I'm an American. I'm a decorated veteran;

I'm a war hero, and I'm a Roman Catholic priest. I work for Francis Cardinal Spellman. Let the army try to flick me aside!''

O'Shea snorted and waved his cigar. "And let Francis Cardinal Spellman find out what you're up to."

"How can he be against saving children?"

"If they become a dove cause célèbre?"

"They won't. You know me better than that. I'm no dove."

"I was beginning to wonder."

"And my purpose is to help Vietnamese kids, not the SDS and not the Fulbright Committee."

"Don't be ingenuous, Michael. Suppose the army fights you. Suppose they make the not unreasonable case that the sovereignty of the Vietnamese government in caring for its own people has to be respected. Or suppose your worst suspicion is true and there's a conspiracy to keep the condition of wounded children secret and therefore out of treatment. You're telling me that at that point you wouldn't go to Fulbright about it? Or the press?"

"If that was the case, of course I would, and you'd help me, right? But you believe like I do that our military people are decent, and that all any of us need is a little moral clarity. Well, this is a way to get some."

"Don't be racist about it. Maybe Saigon cares about its own citizens too. Maybe the ARVN are decent too."

"I'd like to think that what happened last night was just a foul-up, some timid bureaucrat's decision. There's no set policy on evacuating victims yet, and I want to get there before there is one. If I can find out the facts—how many war-wounded children, where they are, what they get for treatment—and if I can take the facts to the right people, then we won't need a patched-together Swiss airlift. The army itself will get those kids out, on military aircraft and to military hospitals. Hell, Tim, I'm talking about something bigger and better than the Berlin Airlift!"

"But you're not the U.S. Air Force, Michael."

"That's right. I'm the Catholic Relief Service, and I know that people working in this office helped generate this war.

By God, people working here now can at least get the wounded taken care of.''

"You've just made the case for why you must stay here and take my job. CRS needs you at the top.''

"I can't.''

"Why?''

"Because half a dozen guys can do this job, and no one but me was on that plane last night. I made a promise to those children, Tim.''

"You've made a prior promise, Michael. A solemn one, a vow.''

" 'Obedience and respect.' ''

"That's right.''

"Tim, I'm asking you to help me keep that vow. You can do it. You know you can.''

"You want to be the new Tom Dooley.''

"Why not?''

"Actually, it's not a bad idea. There's only one problem with it. The brass won't let you in, not if they know what you're up to.''

"That's why it has to be a Church job. We don't ask the brass, remember?''

"Spelly would. He wouldn't send you over there without checking it out with Washington.''

Michael stared at O'Shea. "When the cardinal refused to let me go back before, he made it seem like the issue was how much more good I would do from here.''

"And he was right.''

Michael shook his head. "He slid one by me, Tim. He just didn't want me over there. He was afraid of what I'd see and what I'd do.''

O'Shea thought for a moment, then nodded. "He still would be, Michael.''

"That's why I need you, Tim. I'd like to slide one by him.''

"What, I'm supposed to lie to him?''

Michael said nothing.

O'Shea turned away, swiveling toward the window. "Michael, God . . . I don't believe you're asking me to do this.''

"Tim, I'm only asking you to let me go."

He swung back abruptly. "Rubbish! You're asking me to sponsor the next Don Quixote! You think you're Tom Dooley? Do you know who you'll be? Father Coughlin! It's always a disaster when priests involve themselves in politics, and that's what you'll be doing. You know it too, otherwise you wouldn't be asking me to cover for you with the cardinal. Good God, Michael! I'm about to be made a bishop!"

"I know that."

"Well, why are you putting me in this position then?"

Again Michael remained silent. He had to look away from his old friend.

O'Shea smoked his cigar. Finally he said quietly, "It's my first stack of real chips, and you want me to bet it all on you." He looked at Michael. "I owe you, don't I?"

"You owe me nothing, Tim."

"Except my life. You don't think I've forgotten that, do you? You've never asked me for anything before."

"I want you to let me go because you think it's the right thing to do."

"It's the most foolish damn thing I ever heard of. You have no business over there. And if you step on toes, it will reflect on CRS and embarrass me, and bring the cardinal down on both of us. Hell, I've just begun allowing myself to look forward to a nice career in the hierarchy. You could finish it before it gets off the ground."

"Tim, you're not responsible for what I do."

"The hell I'm not. At least give me credit for the risk I'm taking."

Michael smiled.

O'Shea said, "There's an opening on the Indochina Council of Volunteer Agencies. You'd represent Caritas. We could justify it by saying you're the only one with experience in the field. Actually, it's been a problem, trying to think of whom to send."

"Do you think I'm nuts?"

O'Shea answered carefully. "No, I think you're right, Michael. I think you're courageous and right and your feeling about it moves me. And I'm glad you pushed me. I can handle Spellman. But I'd appreciate it if he didn't read about you in the *Times*."

"He never reads the *Times*."

"I'm serious."

"I don't have an ax to grind, Tim."

As Michael stood up to go, O'Shea got off one last shot. "Are you sure you don't want to take twenty-four hours and think it over? Whoever takes this desk . . ." His cigar hand idled along the edge of it. ". . . gets made monsignor. You'd be the first in your class, Michael. A leg up."

"For my career in the hierarchy?" He grinned.

"It's priests in power who can do the most good. Don't forget that."

By the time they get there, though, Michael thought, after a lifetime of toeing the line for the sake of their next promotion, they've forgotten what "good" is. From many years before he heard O'Shea's lilting, Irish voice saying on that battlefield, "God will not have his work made manifest by cowards." But O'Shea was no coward. He'd just proved that once again. Michael said, "The sooner you come to power, the better, Tim."

"Monsignor Michael Maguire. I like the alliteration."

"Hell, Tim, a monsignor's a 'Domestic Prelate,' right? A former one yourself, you know what that is. He's the guy that makes the pope's bed."

"No, Father, that's the 'Papal Chamberlain.' The 'Domestic Prelate' makes the cardinal's bed."

TWENTY-ONE

NICHOLAS WILEY was waiting for Michael at his office.

Goddamnit! Michael thought, when he saw him. He hadn't called Dorothy Day yet. It was more important than ever to get Wiley off the story.

"How you doing, Nicholas?" They shook hands. The kid seemed nervous and ill at ease. "I'll be right with you."

Michael went into his office and closed the door. Now what? Damn!

He crossed to his desk, sat and picked up the phone. He got the *Worker* number from information, dialed it, asked for Dorothy Day and waited. When she came on the line he said, "Miss Day, this is Father Michael Maguire at the Catholic Relief Service."

"Yes, Father?"

"I'm a friend of Eileen Egan's, Miss Day."

"I know that, Father. She has spoken of you."

"She and I have often talked about the admiration we share for your work."

"Thank you, Father."

"Miss Day, I have a problem, and I need your help."

"Yes?" In her firm, quiet voice, the appropriate deference—no more—was implicit.

"I have Nicholas Wiley here. He wants an interview about a certain CRS project having to do with Vietnamese refugees."

"I know about it, Father. Nicholas told me. He didn't indicate there was any problem."

"I can't have him writing about it, Miss Day. Publicity

will bring the government down on this. You understand about finessing authority."

"I understand about speaking the truth to power, not finessing it."

Michael told himself to be careful. With her "Yes, Father, no Father," it was easy to think of the woman as a Legion of Mary type. She was a Catholic Emma Goldman. "I can't give him the interview, Miss Day."

"But he said you promised it to him."

"I did, yes."

"Well then." She said nothing else. A silence fraught with sanctimony.

"I was hoping you'd take my word for it, my word as a priest, that right now publicity would destroy our ability to help these desperate people. I was hoping you would take him off the story."

"I can't do that, Father."

Oh, Christ, he thought, the principles! Which would it be, freedom of the press or the rights of laymen in the Church? "May I ask why, Miss Day?"

"I have no authority over Nicholas Wiley."

"If I can respectfully disagree, your authority over him is absolute."

"Nicholas Wiley doesn't work for me anymore, Father. He's no longer with the *Catholic Worker*."

"He told me you'd made him managing editor." Was the kid a liar? "He said that only last night."

"He was my managing editor, but he's not now."

"Well, when . . . ?"

"This morning, Father. As of this morning."

"Why?"

"I don't feel free to say. You'll have to ask Nicholas."

Michael was too surprised to respond, and Dorothy Day didn't help him. "Well then," he said finally, "I guess that answers my question."

"Was that all, Father?"

"Yes, Miss Day. Thank you very much."

"You're welcome, Father. And Father . . . ?"

"Yes, Miss Day?"

"Would you pray for us, please? Particularly today we could use your prayers."

"Certainly, Miss Day. I'll put you on the paten at noon." He looked at his watch. The archdiocesan seminarians were touring the U.N. that day, and he was scheduled to say Mass for them at the U.N. chapel. She'd think it an awfully establishment place for worship.

"Why, thank you, Father."

After he hung up, Michael had to stifle his dislike for her. Saints are great in heaven, as Cushing loved to say, but they're hell on earth.

How had Wiley crossed her? Sex? A girl in his bunk? That would get him kicked out on the spot, but he didn't seem the type.

Michael buzzed his secretary and asked her to send Wiley in.

"I guess I'm early, Father," he said, entering. He was holding his brimmed leather hat and still wearing his field jacket. His canvas bag hung from his shoulder.

Michael was aware now of what he'd missed before, the haggard, spent look, the red splotches on his skin, the disheveled clothing. Nicholas hadn't shaved and his long hair was matted at the ends. He'd been caught in the rain. Michael guessed he hadn't been to bed. "Take your jacket off, Nicholas. Have a seat." Michael felt sorry for him suddenly. Whatever he'd done, he hadn't deserved to be turned out in weather like this. The *Worker* had been his home since the army. "Do you want some coffee?"

Wiley shook his head. "I try to leave caffeine alone." He removed his jacket and let Michael take it. He remained standing.

"I used to have a field jacket like this. I should have kept it, eh? I'd be the counterculture priest." Michael smiled. While he hung up the jacket he asked, "Why do flower children love army clothes?"

"Because they're the color of the earth." Wiley answered as if he'd thought of it before. "When you take the militarist insignia off, the clothes are beautiful." Suddenly he grinned. "Just like soldiers. When you take our weapons away, we're just peaceniks and priests.'' He flashed a V-sign. "Peace, Brother. I mean, 'Father.' ''

"You can call me brother if you want.''

"I'd rather call you Mike.''

"That's okay too, although Michael is what I go by.''

"I've never called a priest by his first name before. I doubt if I could do it.''

"My mother manages, and she's a lot more old-fashioned than you are. Why don't you sit down?'' Michael pointed to the large vinyl couch, the room's only piece of furniture aside from the desk and chair. They both sat on it, in opposite corners. Michael hiked his leg up, taking his ankle in his hand and facing the young man. He was aware that his own clothing, his trim black suit and clerical collar, was the sartorial opposite of Wiley's jeans, workboots and blue shirt colorfully embroidered with, in point of fact, flowers.

"Nice office,'' Wiley said.

The office was smaller than O'Shea's, the linoleum floor was bare and the walls were unadorned except for a Mexican straw crucifix above the couch. But the window looked out on midtown, facing north. Even in the haze the great green patch of Central Park stretched before them like a carpet. There was definition to the clouds now, as if the storm was breaking. "I like it,'' Michael said.

"Great view.''

They looked at the city in silence.

"You were wrong before, Father, about me being a flower child. Flower children have no politics.''

"How would you describe your politics, Nicholas. As *Catholic Worker*?''

"I'm against the war. That's the main thing.''

"That's not 'politics.' Everyone's against the war, especially the people who have to fight it.''

"Our GIs throw prisoners out of helicopters when they refuse to talk. I'm against that.''

"We don't have to argue about the war, Nicholas. Why don't you tell me about the *Worker*? What happened?''

For a moment Michael thought Wiley was going to cry, such a forlorn look crossed his face. But he said, "The *Worker*'s nowhere, Father. People dying in Vietnam, and on

Chrystie Street nobody even talks about it." He reached into his canvas bag and pulled out a pair of tattered photographs that had been clipped from newspapers. He held them out to Michael who took them.

One showed a boy the trunk of whose body was mutilated by burns; the skin was gone and the bloody tissue was exposed. The other showed an old woman staring at the camera without affect, and holding in her arms a charred log. After a second look Michael recognized the log as an infant. "I've seen photographs like this, Nicholas."

"I can't get their pictures out of my head, Father. I go to sleep at night, their faces are in my head." His helplessness was unconcealed now. "I wake up and I wonder if I didn't dream up the war, my private nightmare. But then those pictures are still in my bag and the morning paper always says we're escalating. Sometimes I think it's making me nuts."

Michael hesitated. The kid was clearly asking for help, but he was already in therapy. Michael knew he should steer him back to the doctor. But it struck Michael that Wiley, in his emotion, was to him what he himself had been only minutes before to O'Shea. He remembered how touched he'd been when Wiley gave him the wooden cross he was wearing even then inside his shirt. "What's been going on with you?" he asked.

"A lot."

"I gather."

"It shows?" Wiley smiled thinly.

Michael nodded. "Mildly. But I just talked to Dorothy Day. She told me there'd been a problem, but she didn't say what it was."

Alarm crossed Wiley's face. "Why were you talking to her?"

"I'll tell you that in a minute, but why don't you tell me what happened first. I get the feeling you'd like to talk about it."

Wiley stared at his hands. They were large hands, and the flesh around both thumbnails had been gnawed. He did not speak.

Michael waited.

After a long time, Wiley whispered, "She kicked me out."
When he raised his head to look at Michael, water spilled out
of his eyes.

"Why?"

"Because . . ." His mouth twisted with a misery that
throttled his capacity to speak. He continued to look at Michael as the tears came and then he began slowly at first,
soon violently, to sob.

Michael slid next to him, to put his hand on his shoulder.

At last when he could speak he told his story. "Last night
you wouldn't talk to me, but Doctor Levine did. He explained how those poor kids had been substituted for the
wounded ones. I couldn't believe it. And I watched you and
Monsignor O'Shea going around being polite to everybody
and helping that Vietnamese doctor, I just couldn't believe
it."

"We were trying to help those children, Nicholas. Even if
they weren't the ones we expected, we couldn't just send
them back."

"I know. But last night it just seemed to me like you were
letting them get away with it. I kept thinking, what did they
do to the kids who were *supposed* to be here?"

"I kept thinking that too."

"But it, like, made me crazy, Father." Wiley dropped his
eyes to his hands.

Michael had to prod him. "How do you mean, Nicholas?"

"I walked into the city."

In the rain? Michael thought. From the airport?

"I guess I was in kind of a trance. What hit me last night
was that when I became a C.O. I sort of washed my hands of
the war, like Pontius Pilate. After I got out of the army, I
thought I was home free, that all I had to do was, you know,
keep my own nose clean. So I went to the *Worker* where, I
mean, down there everybody's a saint, you know? Voluntary
poverty, feeding the hungry, the brotherhood of man, all that
stuff. And as for war, well, we're just against it period, you
know? But so fucking what? We can feed the hungry until
there's no food left, and that's just fine with the army. They
don't even know the *Catholic Worker* exists. It just hit me
last night that the *Worker* is completely irrelevant, because

nobody down there is doing anything to *stop* it. God knows what the army is doing to those kids! But what are *we* doing to stop it?"

"Did you say these things to Dorothy Day?"

"I did, yes."

"And she didn't like it?"

"I walked all night. Finally I got back to the *Worker* this morning. It was later than I thought. I had no idea what time it was. I mean, that's stupid . . .." He laughed. "The sun was up, but I didn't even notice. When I showed up, the morning soup line was almost over. At seven we serve oatmeal and cornbread. I'd forgotten that it was my turn to work the line. Dorothy was there and she sort of criticized me. She said—right there in front of all these old derelicts—that I was thinking too much of myself lately and not enough of others."

"What did you say?"

"I asked her if I could talk to her in private. And she said no, that I should just get into the kitchen and do my job. But I didn't move. I think I just stood there looking at her. Everybody in the room got real quiet. And then I just said what I had to say about the *Worker*."

"That it was irrelevant?"

"Yes, and that everybody who didn't work to stop the war was just as guilty of it as McNamara and Johnson." Suddenly Wiley started laughing bitterly. "What an asshole! Can you picture it? There I am surrounded by these poor old farts who only want to eat their cornbread so they'll have something in their bellies to soak up the shit-wine they drink, and I'm preaching a sermon to Dorothy Day about resistance! What an asshole!"

Michael didn't laugh. All this time his hand had rested on the kid's shoulder. Now he withdrew it. "But you had a point to make."

"Oh, and I made it. Do you know what Dorothy said when I finished? She said, 'Now go in the kitchen and do your job.' "

"And did you?"

"No." He stopped laughing. "There's the rub. I said I was going up to my room to write the story of the wounded children who couldn't get out of Vietnam. I told her that I was coming to see you about it. And I told her that from now on everything I did was going to have one aim—stopping the war. And she said that was fine, but it wasn't how things went at the *Catholic Worker*. And I said, 'You mean I'm out?' And she just nodded her head, her fucking head, like she was the queen of England. And I saw that as far as she was concerned I was just gone. I didn't even exist anymore. And you know what's funny? I thought she loved me."

Michael was stunned. "You know what, Nicholas? I felt after last night very much like you did. You called it 'crazy.' I don't think it's crazy at all."

Wiley raised his head sharply. "But you didn't take it out on some poor old bum."

"What do you mean?"

"There was a guy sitting there, just one of the street people, an alkie. I knew him. His name was Slate. He started yelling at me not to talk about America like that. I ignored him. Those old guys are all right-wing lunatics if they're anything. But he picked up his bowl and threw it at me. It hit me on the side of the head. It didn't hurt that much, but, well it made me snap, I guess. I don't even remember thinking. I just went across the table at the guy. I mean, an old wreck who can hardly climb stairs, and there I was pounding the shit out of him, as if he was McNamara. There I am, the great C.O., the pacifist, the would-be war resister, beating the shit out of the poor bastard. They couldn't pull me off him, and the next thing you know . . ." He lost control of himself for a moment, crying, then regained it. ". . . there's blood all over his face, and he looks like one of those people in my dream or in the pictures I carry, like a bomb has hit him. But it wasn't a bomb. It wasn't the army. It was me."

"You know what, Nicholas? I didn't pound somebody, but I might have. We both have strong reactions. You know who we remind me of? Peter. Saint Peter." Of all the characters in the New Testament, Michael was drawn to Peter. And in that way—for his contradictions, flaws, extremities, for his *brio*—he was drawn to this boy too.

Wiley snorted. "Speak for yourself, Father. I feel like Judas."

Michael shrugged. "Same difference. Judas and Peter both

did the same thing. They both betrayed the Lord. The difference between them was in what happened next. Judas refused to let go of what he had done. Peter allowed Jesus to forgive him.''

"Peter didn't beat the shit out of anybody."

"Oh, really? He cut the high priest's servant's ear off with a sword. Who are you, Nicholas? The worst son of a bitch to ever come down the pike? Come off it. So you lost your temper. So you beat somebody up. Hell, he asked for it. Obviously, who you wanted to pound was Dorothy. Maybe you did a pretty good job of redirecting your anger. I mean, I'd say she really let you down. I'd have been damn pissed if I was you. So you're capable of anger. Big deal. You're capable of violence. Welcome to the human race.''

"I think maybe I broke Slate's nose. It was bleeding bad.''

"He'll survive.''

"I'll find him. I'll make it up to him.''

"Good idea. And while you're at it, why not make it up to yourself?''

"What do you mean?''

"People like you and me, Nicholas, we tend to take the weight of the world on our shoulders. Like the wounded children; we have the same reaction. You carry your pictures around. In my own way so do I. As if we're the ones dropping napalm on them. Don't get me wrong. I think we have to feel it, and I think we have to do something about it. But we shouldn't beat ourselves for it. We're not burning those children. Look, I have a certain history, and so do you, and maybe we both feel some guilt about it—you for getting out of the army, me for not getting out. Bonhoeffer says guilt is an idol. We cling to our bad feelings and beat ourselves with the past when what we should do is let go of it, like Peter did. Once you let go of guilt, then you go out and change the world.''

"But how?''

"By daring to live as a forgiven man.''

"I don't know how to do that, Father.''

"You start by listening to me when I forgive you. Would you like to call this 'confession'? Would you like absolution?''

"Yes. I'm really sorry for what I did.''

"I know you are. Bow your head, Nicholas." Michael put his hand on the kid's head and pronounced the Latin words. He was thinking, It's the people who don't care about the war who are the sinners. The moderates, the balanced ones—they're the crazies. This kid, he thought, is decent and brave. I should be more like him.

After making the sign of the cross, the priest was silent and his usually churning mind became calm and then, as it were, empty.

Neither acknowledged it, but they were praying.

"What's my penance, Father?"

"Some breakfast, now, with me. Let's blow this place." They went down sixty-five floors to the coffee shop in the mezzanine. They took a booth. Michael insisted on Nicholas's eating, and to encourage him he ordered bacon and eggs himself, despite his obligation to fast before Mass. Nothing provoked the Lord's wrath more quickly than the heartless observance of ritual law. The people who'd left the wounded man in the ditch were on their way to church.

Nicholas touched a napkin to his mouth. "You were going to tell me why you called Dorothy."

"I wanted her to pull you off the story. I guess I didn't need to bother, huh?"

"I'm still on it, Father. I want to find out what happened to those other kids."

"You won't find out from me, Nicholas."

"I have an appointment with Monsieur Hurot this afternoon. He said last night he'd tell me everything he knew. I'm also meeting with Doctor Levine."

"They won't talk to you. They were stunned last night like I was. But they're still committed to the project. Publicity now will wreck it."

"Well, I'm committed too. I think America should know what's being done in its name. We have to get people's attention, and I think this will do it."

"But who would you write it for?"

"Don Thorman." The publisher of the *National Catholic Reporter*.

Michael calculated. He had met Thorman in Kansas City.

In fact, Thorman was on the Midwest committee for the Children's Relief Fund. He was a gruff, amiable man, jealous of his prerogatives as a layman and a publisher, but also a responsible journalist and, beneath the irreverent mode, a traditional Catholic. Michael would talk to him. He smiled at Wiley. "You know you guys have been causing trouble since New Testament days."

Wiley looked at him quizzically.

" 'Jesus was speaking to the multitudes when his mother and his brothers appeared. They were anxious to have a word with him, but they could not draw near in that crowd, because of the press.' "

Wiley laughed, but only briefly.

They sipped their coffee in silence.

Nicholas said eventually, "I have to admit I'm disappointed. I thought we had a deal." He eyed Michael steadily, demonstrating, given what he'd been through, a remarkable resilience. Michael had not expected to be called to account for his broken promise.

"All deals were off after what happened."

"You mean because the army reneged on you, you could renege on me?"

"It wasn't the army, first of all. We were dealing with the government of South Vietnam."

"You're not responding to me, Father."

"Frankly, Nicholas, I'm not interested in a relationship with you that's defined in terms of an issue, even *this* issue. I'm aware that something personal has happened between us."

"I am too. And I'm grateful for it. You have me back on my feet. But now that I'm there, you've got to deal with me."

"Do you know what Jesus said to Peter after he forgave him?" Michael lit a cigarette, then gestured at the dishes on the table between them. "They'd just finished breakfast on the shore of the Sea of Galilee. Jesus said, 'If you love me, feed my sheep.' He said it three times, once for each time Peter'd denied him. 'Feed my sheep. Feed my sheep.' " Michael stared hard at Wiley. He wanted very much to win him over. "He didn't talk about issues or about saving the world or about converting Rome or about ending wars. He talked about a concrete, immediate, simple need. Someone's hungry, feed them. See, Nicholas, you and I can go on until we're blue in the face about the war. But meanwhile there are these kids with an immediate need for medical care, and I'm going to get it for them. And you know what? I've got three problems: I've got the government in Saigon, and I've got the U.S. Army, and I've got you. All three of you do the same thing. You put issues—whether it's stopping Communism or stopping the war—before people. Take those pictures out of your bag again. Look at those kids. Don't stop me from getting them to a doctor, Nicholas. Don't use them to make a name for yourself as an antiwar reporter.''

"That's not it, Father."

"Are you sure?" Michael realized that now he was doing to the kid what Dorothy Day had done, accusing him of thinking only of himself. Michael knew, like Dorothy did, how vulnerable Wiley was. Before Michael had been urging him to let go of his guilt, but now Michael was using it against him. But he had to. At bottom, for all his Karl Rogers, he was just another Catholic priest controlling the behavior of a boy by undermining his belief in himself.

Wiley looked away. "Well, who does that make you, anyway? This isn't exactly the shore of the Sea of Galilee. And you're not Jesus."

"I know that."

"Am I the sheep you're feeding, is that it?"

"No."

"Well, you want me to act like one. You want me to just close my eyes and forget about the war."

"No, I don't. I want you to go after them, Nicholas, aggressively, responsibly. I think you're right to raise questions and to try to make people think about it. But find another way into it, that's all I'm saying."

"A way to make people pay attention, because it has to stop."

"You can do it. Write about your experience as a C.O. People need to hear that story."

"What are you going to do?"

Michael hesitated. He had to overcome an instinctive reluctance to tell him. "I'm going to Vietnam. I'm going to organize the rescue operation myself."

"Let me come with you," Wiley said instantly.

"No," Michael said. "You wouldn't help, Nicholas. I'm going to be dealing with the army. You'd have to get your hair cut."

"Why the army? I mean, Christ, they're the ones who are dropping the shit on them."

"Nicholas, I'm not coming back until it's army policy to care for the civilian casualties they cause."

"No way, Father."

Michael shrugged. "It's the only way we can fight a war like this and not lose our souls."

"Father, I don't believe you! A war like this can't be fought, period. What, first the U.S. spends a fortune dropping napalm on people, then it spends a fortune flying them back to the States for good old Blue Cross–Blue Shield? You're wacky! I thought I was wacky! The thing is to just stop it!"

"They won't just 'stop it,' Nicholas. Like it or not, that's the fact. Given that, what do we do? We have to conduct ourselves as humanely as we can."

"You'll be their window dressing. They might just latch on to your idea. It would be the perfect way to whitewash what they're doing. Jesus! At first I thought you were naive, but now I get it. You're right. They just might do it! A humanitarian airlift of wounded women and children. It would be brilliant!"

"That's right."

"But they'd be using you, Father."

"I'd be using them, Nicholas. I don't give a damn about anything but those wounded people."

"You're pretty sure of yourself, aren't you."

"I'm going at their jugulars, at their weak point. The commanders in Vietnam learned to think of themselves as soldiers in the war against Hitler. They're the original boys in white hats. They'll kill you, but only if they can think of it as an act of virtue. Honor, Nicholas. That's the deal with these guys. Honor, duty, country. And that's where you go after them. Honor, not guilt. Think of them as soldiers, not Catholics."

"You love soldiers."

"When I read about the V.C. assault at Bien Hoa, it was easy for me to imagine it: the shouts, the chaos, the absolute terror you feel at a burst of explosions right by your head, and guys you ate breakfast with falling over in front of you with their guts spilling out in the mud. At a moment like that the orders officers give don't mean shit. Soldiers just react, and you know what? They react for each other as much as for themselves. In a battle, soldiers have an instinctive generosity. Each man's own survival includes as the same thing the survival of his friend. The whole world should live that way. We should all be like soldiers in the heat of battle."

"But you're talking about killing."

Michael studied him. "Which makes it bullshit, doesn't it?"

"I guess. Except . . . ." Wiley pushed crumbs with his little finger.

"Except what?"

"I wish I had friends to look out for, friends to look out for me."

Michael nodded. The kid wanted to go with him to Vietnam. But it was impossible. Nicholas Wiley belonged in Vietnam less than anyone. He had just been kicked out of his womb, the *Worker*, and now he was wandering around with his umbilical cord in his hand, looking for another to plug into. If not a womb, a cause.

Why then was Michael ambushed by the urge to take him along? Come with me, kid. Write the story. Be my partner. Let's take them on together.

But Michael knew. Through his shirt he fingered the cross that Wiley had made for him, that had so soothed him once. Michael was going into combat of his own, and he could have used a buddy too, someone whose survival was intertwined with his. A Lennie Pace.

Lennie Pace. Michael hadn't thought of him in years. But Lennie, despite Michael's explicit promise—"I'll take care of you! Depend on me!"—had not survived. Was that when Michael had begun going his way alone?

He nearly asked Nicholas to come. What adventures they'd have shared! How different things would have been for both of them!

"Look," he said. "I'll tell you what. We can watch out for each other in another way." Michael grasped Nicholas's forearm across the table. "We can pray for each other. Let's pray for each other every day. You know that line of E. E. Cummings? I'll carry your heart, Nicholas. I'll carry it in my heart."

TWENTY-TWO

On the Vietnamese calendar, 1965 was the Year of the Snake.

That year saw the first outbreak of racial violence in American cities and the beginning of the massive rejection by American young people of their parents' values and prejudices. It was one shock after another. In the spring the American embassy in Saigon was blown up and we saw in that flash the fate of the entire enterprise. In the summer James Meredith was shot on his walk through Mississippi; how familiar such fire from ambush would become. In the fall David Miller burned his draftcard at a demonstration in New York, and with it our traditional assumption that the Law was the friend of Justice. In the winter was held the first large, celebrity-studded antiwar rally in Washington; those pioneer marchers would not have believed—so momentous did the occasion seem to them—how little they and their millions of successors would affect the course of the war.

Nineteen sixty-five was the year in which Pope Paul VI visited the U.N., crying, "No more war! War never again!" But that year also, as if to remind us what else he stood for, he formally absolved the Jews of blame for the death of Jesus.

By the end of the year American troop strength in Vietnam would be approaching two hundred thousand, the air war—"Rolling Thunder"—against North Vietnam would have succeeded only in solidifying the resolve of Ho Chi Minh and his people, the underpinnings of the American economy would be destroyed, and it would be apparent to many that the

Vietnamese Communists' willingness to die ran far deeper, even, than the obvious American willingness to kill. Tragically, it would take eight years and the deaths of many hundreds of thousands, the destruction of the Indochinese environment and the obliteration of ancient Vietnamese and Cambodian culture before the American government saw that too. Nineteen sixty-five was the Year of the Snake all right; we didn't know it yet, but the snake was us.

"Ah, dear man," you say, "you sound like what you are, a fugitive monk in the throes of memory."

It is true. Once, at an earlier point in history, men like me came into their own, bewailing the disintegration of standards and blaming it ultimately on the unfettered human appetite for war. *They* were fugitive monks in the throes of memory exactly, Benedictines like myself in point of fact. And for a thousand years they made slaves of themselves to an idea, an ideal, a hope, that human beings can live with each other charitably, at the service of learning, art, a just society and God. They preserved the greatest of human thoughts—Aristotle's, Plato's, David's, and Saint Paul's; invented the most humane of social organizations—the jury, the monastery, the university and the modern city; sang the most exquisite music—chant; and created the most beautiful artifact of all—the Gothic cathedral. And when their era was over, their Enlightenment successors, the direct antecedents of the pragmatic humanists who brought us Vietnam, looked back upon it with disgust and called it—that time of fugitive monks in the throes of memory—the Dark Ages.

What Vietnam in 1965 reduced to for Michael Maguire was the noise of helicopters.

At first he found it frightening and disorienting, and if there'd been another way of getting around the country he'd have taken it. But he was a hitchhiker. He had to take what he could get. Having clambered aboard a command copter or an empty Medevac or one of the giant troop-carrying Chinooks, he could close his eyes and think he was in Korea. But in Korea helicopter use had been sporadic, limited to evacuation functions. In Vietnam, helicopters, massed in formations of dozens of aircraft, were at the heart of American strategy.

The Air Mobile technique of swooping in from the sky while Cobra gunships covered and great clouds of dust rose above GIs leaping from their Chinooks like young gods reinforced their sense of being lost in a surreal world that had nothing to do with them. Michael didn't ride on *those* helicopters, of course, but still the machines disoriented him and came to embody everything sinister about the war, just as they did for GIs.

And oh, the fucking noise! Michael compared it to being inside a commercial clothes dryer, an analogy you'll find unhelpful unless you too have climbed into one of those giant tumblers, as he and I did in the basements of Inwood apartment houses. Once you braced yourself against the ribbed tank, you hollered, "Yo!" and your partner dropped in the penny and pushed the button. The trick was to hold yourself rigid at all points so that, as the tank revolved, you didn't bump. The game was to see if you could make it through the entire seven-minute cycle. Michael and I were a team because neither of us trusted anyone else to shut the machine off when through dizziness or fatigue we let go and began to bump. We called it "Niagara Falls."

"This is like going over Niagara Falls," he called to the machine gunner next to him, a perspiring black sergeant who was braced between his weapon and the steel frame of the lurching chopper, but half-leaning out of the open hatch. He nodded, but in the noise he hadn't heard what Michael'd said. He rode as if he'd been in helicopters all his life; he knew better than to try to make small talk.

Michael leaned into the wind a bit, to cool himself. He wore a short-sleeve white shirt, open at the neck, and black cotton pants. His face and arms were a deep red from four months of the fierce tropical sun. He'd arrived in Vietnam in March, at the beginning of the hottest season of the year. On his feet he wore the ubiquitous tire-rubber sandals of the Vietnamese. Soldiers, like the gunner, rarely saw mufti-clad Americans outside Saigon—even reporters were required to wear khaki in the field—and they assumed he was a CIA man. Despite his black pants, which Michael made a point of wearing as a vestige of the clerical, no one guessed he was a priest. Occasionally, in fact, he was chided for wearing the uniform trousers of the Viet Cong.

Despite the rigors of his itinerant, unsettled life and the wearing frustration of endless blind alleys and the numbing effect of what he saw when the alleys led somewhere, he looked and felt far healthier than he had when he arrived, a sallow-faced do-gooder, a citified stranger to physical exertion. Four months in Vietnam was long enough to make him feel that he hadn't left in the first place, but also long enough to dull the shock he'd felt at first at how different the country was now that an American army occupied it.

In four months he'd discovered only handfuls—hundreds, not thousands—of war-wounded children. He had encountered the maddening intransigence of GVN officials, the glib optimism of the American mission, the condescending detachment of journalists and the refusal of Vietnamese pacifists, the Buddhists and the students, to trust him. All the while he had watched as hoards of GIs poured into the country, and everywhere he went he saw bases and barracks under construction. And everywhere he heard rock'n'roll—"I can't get no . . . no, no, no . . . satis*fac*tion!"—blaring from AFN Radio.

One scene in particular stood out in his memory. After his first weeks of searching the countryside for the burned children, going from hospital to orphanage to refugee center and finding none, he'd become convinced that hundreds if not thousands of mutilated children were being kept hidden by the government. He'd returned to Saigon in a frenzy of anger and concern, as if the burn cases were prizes he was being cheated of. He could think of only one man who could help him find those children, John Howe, who by then was the deputy chief of AID at the American embassy. Without even stopping at the rectory where he was staying, Michael went to Howe's office, but Howe wasn't in. He was playing tennis at the Cercle Sportif. Michael went there.

He found Howe sitting at a table on the veranda with three other men in tennis whites. They'd obviously finished their match some time before, but their necks were still draped with towels. They were smoking and sipping drinks. As Michael approached, he saw that Howe looked thin and sickly. His gaunt, bony body contrasted with the healthy suburban look the others had. It was a shock to see Howe's decline. The country had worn him down.

When Howe saw Michael crossing toward them he stood up. "Father Maguire! My God! I'd heard you were back!" The warmth of Howe's greeting surprised Michael. What he'd remembered about the man was his aloofness.

"I'm sorry to come on you like this, Jack, but I have to talk to you."

"Sure. Sure." Howe looked at his partners, then said, "Fellows, this is Father Mike Maguire. He's, uh . . ." He looked at Michael. "Are you still with CRS?"

"Actually, I'm here for Caritas now. The Council of Volunteer Agencies."

"I thought you'd have come to see me before this."

"I've been in the countryside, Jack. That's why I want to talk to you."

"Are you the padre," one of the others asked, "who's been looking for the burned babies?" He was a lanky Southerner whose voice was implicitly disdainful.

Michael bristled, but controlled himself. "Burned babies?"

"Well, isn't that what you folks call them?"

"Father, this is Colonel Tom Vintner," Howe put in. "He's the chief public affairs officer for the air force here."

The colonel sipped his drink. Michael noticed now that it was straight whiskey and it was probably not his first. "That's right, padre. I'm the guy who reporters come to for their burned babies. Reporters just love burned babies."

"And what do you tell them, Colonel?"

"Why, the truth, padre." Vintner leered at Michael contemptuously.

Howe took Michael's arm. "Let's go, Father."

"Hold on, Jack," the colonel said. "You want the truth, padre, right? Even if it's unpleasant?"

Michael was aware that people near by, including the first Caucasian women he'd seen in many days, were watching them.

"Does the good padre have the stomach for the truth? That's the question."

Michael leaned down to him, placing his hands on the

table, bringing his face close to the colonel's. "So what do
you tell them about the napalmed children?"

"Why, that the only napalmed children in this country are
the little thieves who burn themselves with pilfered gasoline
when they try to cook with it, and those fuckers deserve
anything that they get."

Michael reacted without thinking. He smashed the man in
the face, knocking him backwards off his chair.

The bathing beauty on the diving board froze, the play of
the doubles match at a nearby court stopped, the people at the
surrounding tables fell silent. Everyone stared at Michael
Maguire. Michael was more stunned than any of them.

Colonel Vintner struggled to his feet, dazed, and only the
sight of his own blood flowing from his mouth, staining his
shirt, seemed to make him realize what had happened. He
lunged toward Michael, but Jack Howe stopped him.

"You were off base, Colonel," Howe said.

Vintner shook his fist at Michael across Howe. "You stay
the hell away from me. I'll tear you apart."

Michael didn't move.

Finally the colonel's other friends coaxed him back to the
table. Howe took Michael's elbow. "Come on. Let's go."

Outside the compound Michael faced the AID officer.
"Christ, Jack, I didn't mean to put you on the spot."

"He had it coming. I've wanted to do that myself a dozen
times." Howe grinned. "I don't have your flair or your right
jab."

"Or my short fuse. It's the one thing I can't stomach
cracks about. Jack, you've got to help me. I've been all over
the damn country. I can't find those children. There have to
be thousands of them. The government is hiding them, and I
have to find them."

Howe shook his head. "Father, that's cockeyed. You're
completely wrong."

"What, you think the only kids getting burned by napalm
have stolen it to cook with?"

"Of course not." Howe looked away, and a pained expression unlike any Michael had seen from him before crossed his
face. "I guess you don't know how bad it is here now." He
looked fiercely back at Michael. "When the air force dumps

its shit on a village, Father, nobody lives, get it? It's so fucking lethal that if it touches you, you're wasted. Women and children? Hey, *pas de problème!* Because we got a body-count going now, and it's how we know we're winning. That means every dead Asian, even a child, is tagged—literally on his toe—as a Communist. Get it? That's why there are no civilian casualties. Colonel Vintner will tell you all about it. I wish you'd killed that fucker.''

Michael took a step back from Howe. Once he'd longed for an expression of feeling from this man, but now Howe's emotion frightened him. His eyes were distended and perspiration poured down his face. The buttoned-down, ever-cool aristocrat that Michael had known before was gone; in his place was this hothead. Such anger seemed, in Howe, like madness. And it revealed as much as anything what the war was doing.

Howe took a handful of Michael's shirt. ''Vintner will tell you! Because of our incredibly accurate targeting and our humane warn-and-clear techniques! No civilian casualties whatsoever! Because every dead Slope is *ipso facto* a dead Cong!'' Howe was shaking Michael now, and Michael saw that it wasn't perspiration only on his face, but also tears. ''And *that's* why there are no wounded children for you to rescue. Because they are all dead!''

The chopper dropped. Michael turned to look out the small window. The dramatic green mountain peaks past which they swooped seemed like the props of a boy's model railroad. Nestled at the base of one of them was a brilliant blue lake—an oval sheet of mirror—and on its shore Michael glimpsed the flat white roofs, each emblazoned with a red cross, of the hospital compound. The adjacent town, a collection of bamboo huts clustered around a large, twin-spired Spanish-looking church, was An Hoa, the Vale of Peace, an ironic name now since the fighting had recently come here too. An Hoa was only fifteen minutes by helicopter from the huge new air base at Da Nang, and the Americans had selected it as the site of a supply depot and light aircraft landing field, both of which were even then under construction on the shore of the lake opposite the hospital. It was toward the construction site that the chopper angled. Acres of jungle had been cleared and already a runway was being poured. Heavy green machinery—bulldozers, graders, dump trucks—crawled around on the rich dark earth like beetles. Still the region hadn't been cleared of Viet Cong, and Michael had been warned that the An Hoa Hospital—run by a group of German volunteers, not the government—was known to treat Communists.

"Here we are!" he shouted to the gunnery sergeant, and he jerked his thumb at the hatch.

The sergeant did not bother to watch as the helicopter landed.

Maguire was the only passenger. He hopped out. The rotor wash of air tore at his clothing. There was no reason to run, but he did, from habit. Everyone ran away from helicopters, in that familiar hunchback's crouch, as if they couldn't stand the noise or thought it was going to blow up or draw Charley's fire.

A dozen plastic bags, each with its yellow tag, were arranged neatly in three rows of four on the apron of the square of pavement. Marines began hauling them to the helicopter; American corpses were what it came for.

Michael watched from a distance until the chopper, still brisk despite its sad load, was airborne again. The gunnery sergeant stared at Michael from behind his weapon. Michael checked an impulse to wave at him. An eerie silence—though not really silence, since bulldozers worked near by—filled the air once the helicopter was gone.

A person whom he did not recognize as a woman until she spoke—she wore tan slacks and a loose tan shirt, dark glasses and a floppy white hat that obscured her face—approached and said, "Father Maguire?"

"Yes."

"Inge Holz. I am the nurse from Malta."

Malta was shorthand for the group that ran the hospital, the Aid Service of Malta, a Cologne-based organization of Catholics who did volunteer work in reparation for the crimes Germans inflicted on the Jews. "I come for you with our jeep." She smiled and put her hand out. Her brisk, one-pump

German handshake surprised him. A pretty European woman was the last thing he had expected to see in An Hoa.

From the ground, looking up, the surrounding mountains were a rich blue, not green, and the lake along which they drove reflected the peaks against the cloudless pale sky. The near hills had been terraced by farmers, and the neatly hedged walls of piled stones, each defining plots of soil, which grew progressively larger according to the contour, lent the scene the tranquil, tidy air of a travel poster. At the foot of the hills drawing water from canals fed by the lake were rice paddies and at one point the road itself formed the dam between the body of water and the squared-off paddies. The nurse pointed to them and said, "The rice crop has fallen. Do you know why?" She looked at Michael. When he did not reply, she said, "Because it is here in the rice fields that the Buddhists have their dead buried. So many dead, so many killed, the seedlings choke."

Michael no longer reacted to such epiphanies with shock, and he knew why. The corpses were piled inside him too by now, choking feeling. He was afraid of his own numbness. "Around here?" he asked. He wanted to confront directly what she was telling him. He wanted to learn how the local horror was unique. "It's been that bad?"

"Since the marines, yes."

"They're trying to secure the area for their base, I guess."

"Always before the Viet Cong had left us alone. Now there is reason to come. They have something to attack. The marines have made the area less secure, not more. That is very bad, you understand."

"And your hospital treats mainly victims of the fighting?"

"Now, yes."

"And before?"

"Always leprosy."

Michael shuddered despite himself and fell silent.

He found himself thinking that the nurse's accent was wrong. The Europeans in Vietnam were French, not German. Germans were from that other war, that just one. He reminded himself that despite what the Ministry of Health official in Da Nang had said about her hospital, she was not the enemy. Sidelong, he looked at her. She had sharp features, and her face, what he could see of it for the hat and he glasses, was weathered brown. Premature lines at her mouth and eyes indicated the disregarded weariness that was habit ual among volunteers. He watched her hands playing upon the wheel and gearshift. She drove with an *esprit* that bor dered on the reckless, but which stimulated him almost erot ically, even as he held on. The only flesh that he could see besides her face was that of her hand and forearm. He traced its outline until her skin was lost in the rolled sleeve. A perspiration stain emphasized the seam of her shirt. Now he saw the form of her breast. She raised her hand to tuck an elusive wisp of blond hair—how had he not noticed it?—up into her hat.

"How big is your hospital?" he asked, to rein his mind.

She shrugged, downshifted efficiently to take a curve, then speeded up again. "One hundred twenty beds, five nurses, one permanent doctor and two doctors from Da Nang. We have six clinics in surrounding villages, but since the marine it is impossible getting to three. Those clinics are, so to speak, closed."

"Have the Communists taken them over?"

She nodded. "That can be possible."

"I heard the NLF is strong everywhere out here."

She laughed. "Not in the daytime."

It was difficult to talk in the open jeep. His questions tripped over one another in his brain, but he waited. He wanted to see her face more clearly when she answered him. He sat back against the worn seat and enjoyed the wash of air. The scenery was stunning. The lake amid the mountains, like water in a cup, reminded him of the lake at Bear Moun tain up the Hudson where the priests of Good Shepherd took altar boys on camping trips.

Soon they approached the hospital compound. *"Voilà,"* she said, turning in.

Michael saw four whitewashed stucco buildings, only one of which was two stories high. Huge overarching palms cast delicate shadows and a breeze off the lake cooled the air. Between the buildings were makeshift shelters, palm branches stretched across bamboo frames, and under them were the inert forms of dozens of Vietnamese men and women. At first Michael gasped, thinking they were corpses.

Fräulein Holz noticed his reaction. "They are the families of our patients."

"But they look dead, like a massacre."

She shook her head. "It is siesta, Father. Even during war the people need siesta." When she'd brought the jeep to a halt and shut the engine off, she said, "I told you one hundred twenty beds. What I have not said is in each bed two patients, and in children's ward, three."

"Do you see burns in your hospital?"

"Not often."

"When I came over I was very conscious of napalm."

She shrugged, callously. "If all weapons were like napalm, Father, people like us would not be needed."

"Forgive me, but there is a question I must ask you. I was told your hospital and dispensaries supply the Viet Cong with medicine."

She seemed amazed. She said, "They steal our medicine. We can do nothing."

"Do you lock it?"

"Of course we lock. Our medicine is precious. We have to ship it in from Germany."

"The government doesn't supply you because you are considered partisans."

She reached across from the driver's seat and took the cigarette he offered. While she lit it from his match she shook her head. "The government does not supply us because we will not black market with the district chief. He asks always a quarter of our drugs."

"You don't treat the Viet Cong?"

"We treat diseases and wounds."

"V.C. wounds?"

Inge Holz smiled at him through her smoke. "Is this *Beichte*, Father? Confession?"

"I think you ought to know what I've been told. Your hospital would be closed if you weren't German nationals."

"We treat all people who come to us."

Michael stared at her, then nodded. "Good. Then I'll stick up for you. The Council of Volunteer Agencies was asked to withdraw its certification from you."

But she wasn't grateful. "You collect evidence? Why should I believe you are a priest?"

Michael smiled. "I am, really."

"But perhaps a priest with the CIA. Priests in this country work for the government. What will you do with me, some head-shaving, no?" Now she smiled, but cynically.

He shook his head. "Nothing so exciting. Just what I said in my letter. Just a survey of hospital facilities for the Council." He paused. "When I first came, it was to lay the groundwork for an evacuation of wounded children to the States, but I've had no luck with that."

"Luck!" She laughed, then looked at him bitterly. "Why should you have luck here?"

She got out of the jeep, flicking the cigarette away. He followed her, for his tour of her hospital.

Children ranging in age from perhaps eight to twelve years old were gathered on their haunches around Michael in the shadow of a palm tree in the hospital yard. It was late afternoon of the next day, and the children, having overcome their bashfulness, were helping the tall American practice his Vietnamese.

In his time Michael had mastered not many more than a dozen rudimentary phrases. He had no gift for language. But he'd won the children over with his animation, his flamboyant gestures, his great-hearted but finally laughable rendition of words they took for granted.

"*Chào ong,*" he said earnestly.

The children laughed and clapped their hands at him because the phrase meant "good morning," and here it was afternoon. None of them dared correct him.

"*Tôi la, Père Michel.*" My name is Father Michael. "*Tên ông là gi?*" What is your name? He repeated the question until one of the children answered him, a boy who said his name was Tran. Michael bowed to him. The other children grew silent. Everyone waited for Tran to speak, as politeness required.

"*Ông sẽ ô lai bao lâu?*"

Michael made him repeat it very slowly until he understood; how long will you stay?

"*Thú-nam,*" he answered. Until Thursday.

Tran bowed, making it clear that the exchange satisfied

what need he had to expose himself to the stranger. After that Michael found it impossible to draw out the children further. It was then, to prolong the encounter, that he began reciting all the phrases he could remember. He came to one that a boy in Pleiku had taught him. *"Doàn thanh niên ta Vung lòng tâm tri."* We, the youth of the nation, must remain firm and determined.

Abruptly the children rose and scampered away, to rejoin their relatives under the bamboo shelters.

Inge Holz had been watching from the veranda of one of the buildings. Michael stood and crossed to her. "What happened?"

"They are afraid of that."

"Of that saying?"

"It is not a saying, Father. It is a line from the national anthem. The ARVN soldiers must sing it while marching, but in the villages singing this is dangerous crime. The NLF will cut out your tongue."

"I thought it was just a slogan."

"What is 'slogan'?"

"It's, well, just a saying."

"So. But here, nothing is just slogan."

Michael looked across the compound. The children had dispersed. He couldn't see them. He wanted to run after them and say he wasn't testing them. He wasn't trapping them. He wanted to apologize. He felt disgusted with himself.

He remembered the paper he was holding, a leaflet one of the children had given him. He held it up. "Is your Vietnamese good enough to translate this?"

She took it and read in a dead voice, but without stumbling, "The wicked Viet Cong have stored weapons and supplies in your village. Soon air force gunfire is going to be conducted on your village to destroy these Viet Cong supplies. We ask that you leave your village, as we do not wish to kill innocent people. And when you return to your village repel the Viet Cong so that the government will not have to fire on your village again."

Inge Holz handed the leaflet back to Michael and turned and walked away from him.

TWENTY-THREE

CROSS from the hospital compound was the lake Michael had seen from the helicopter. Along its edge ran a sliver of a beach, and he was walking it, barefoot. It had been four days since he'd arrived. He'd visited the dispensaries that were still active there and he'd interviewed the Malta staff. It was time to move on, but Michael was in the grip of an unusual lethargy. He didn't understand anymore what he was doing there. His round of visitations seemed pointless.

The water lapped gently against the cuticle of sand, and Michael let it bathe his feet as he walked absently along. Perhaps half a mile from the compound he was startled to come upon a bather's towel stretched on the beach, and near it a tattered straw basket. A pair of pilot's sunglasses lay on the towel next to a propped-open book. He looked out at the water. In the glare it took a moment to spot the swimmer, a moving speck far out in the lake. Who was it?

He looked at the book. The title was in German and at first he assumed he wouldn't know it, but then he saw the author's name, Ignace Lepp, and recognized the title, in translation *The Christian Failure*. It was a book Michael had read in the seminary, an indictment of the German Catholic clergy for its willingness to cooperate with Hitler. He picked the book up. Inside the cover was written the name, in tight, European script, *Inge Holz*.

Why is she reading this? he wondered. He stared out at the lake. She was so far away. As he watched the speck growing even smaller, he found himself imagining her body moving through the water, arms and legs working, head turning up for air, hair trailing. It was a surprise to him how easily he could call up her image—her body was lithe, not voluptuous, but lovely—and only then did he realize how her subtle womanliness had affected him.

Crazily he thought of the notorious Viet Cong ploy: maidens swimming naked in a lake, waving at passing GIs, beckoning them. The GIs drop their rifles, dash across the sand, undoing their web-belts, then fall suddenly through a punji trap, taking dung-coated razor spikes the length of their bodies. Seduce and destroy.

Michael shuddered and dismissed the image. What was happening to him?

He took off his shirt and his black chinos, stripping to his brown, army-issue boxer-shorts. Absently he touched Wiley's wooden cross at his chest as he walked into the water. When it was waist-deep he dove in and went after her. He was a strong swimmer, and before long he'd caught up with her, and simply fell into pace. They matched each other, stroke for stroke, until she turned over on her back. He did likewise and they began the return lap. They never looked at each other or spoke. Michael fixed his concentration on the fierce blue of the sky. By the time they reached the beach again they'd been swimming in sync with each other for twenty minutes. What a relief to have left behind the jarring edginess that had made their encounters so awkward. The fluidity of swimming, the instinctive common rhythm of their timing, made Michael feel as though they'd been intimate with each other.

She went ahead of him to her towel. He felt self-conscious about being in his underwear but stifled the impulse to pull on his chinos quickly, lest she think him prudish. The brown shorts in fact were perfectly modest. He sat on the sand a little apart and watched her drying herself. She wore an ordinary blue bathing suit. As she toweled her hair he saw the magical impress of her nipples through her suit; the sight stirred him, but also underscored his inexperience; nipples grew erect either through arousal, wasn't it, or cold?

Her hair was long, to her shoulders, half-brown, half-blond. It brushed at her shoulders, at her breasts. His eye fell to her deeply tanned legs, their subtle curves. He saw the

flash of white between her thighs where she had not shown
herself to the sun. She seemed oblivious to the effect on him
of her drying herself. He stared at her as if he'd rarely seen
the feminine form so displayed, which was true, of course.
Inadvertently, naturally, she was outflanking his careful,
measured, clerical reserve.

She offered him her towel. He declined.

She spread it again and sat.

To his regret she put on her sunglasses. He reached for his
shirt, for his cigarettes. He offered her one and she accepted.
He crossed to her, lit their cigarettes from one match, and
then sat an arm's length and a little more away.

He couldn't think what to say. I admire your work? Why
aren't you modeling fancy dresses in Berlin? Where'd you
learn to swim so well?

He said finally, "I noticed your book."

She glanced at it and nodded.

"Not what I would call beach reading."

She pulled her knees close to her chest and linked her arms
around them. "Difficult reading," she said, "for a German
Catholic."

"Is that why you joined Malta? Is that why you are here?"
How had Nicholas Wiley put it? To atone?

She shrugged, moved the book aside absently with her
foot. "In Mainz, my own archbishop. He gave sermons at the
cathedral. He said the Jews were termites."

"Termites?"

She thought she'd mispronounced it. "An insect that destroys a house by eating the wood. *Die Termite.* I remember
the word distinctly. That week houses in Jewish Quarter of
Mainz were for the first time burned."

"You remember that?"

"Yes."

They fell silent, smoking.

After a long time, Michael said, "So you're from Mainz.
I'm from New York."

"Ah!" She buried the tip of her cigarette in the sand.
"Cardinal Spellman."

"That's right."

"He came at Christmas to the air base at Da Nang. They

wanted us to go there for his Mass. All the volunteers, to receive his blessing. To kiss his ring. I would not.''

Michael stared at her. He sensed the depth of her feeling. Her strength. She reminded him of someone. Carolyn, of course.

She said, ''To hear him preach against the termites.''

''Cardinal Spellman doesn't speak for me on the subject of Vietnam, Fräulein.''

''Oh? Who does?''

Michael had to think about it. ''No one.''

She nodded. ''So it was with us.''

He shook his head. ''I understand your point of view. You think of me as just another marine, but I'm not.''

''You think because you visit hospitals that makes you different. But you ride in their helicopters. You are friendly with the men who do these things.'' She looked at him sharply. The sun glinted off her dark glasses. ''Forgive me, Father, but you are like the girls who wait outside their camps. When you are there they are happy about what they do. All the better if they can . . .'' She shrugged instead of finishing.

''. . . screw me.''

She laughed. ''Yes.''

''Am I so different from you? Anybody here who tries to soften the blows becomes part of the situation that makes them possible.''

''I do not like your war, Father. I do not want that you Americans do these things here, and I think you should make a stop.'' In her anger her English grew more confused.

''Me?''

''Yes.''

''You think I should just go home and lead the rosary in a parish in the suburbs?''

''You said you wanted to help the children. So you go home and tell your people what their soldiers and pilots do to the children.'' She looked away. When she put her hand to her mouth, Michael saw that it was trembling.

''Fräulein . . .''

''I was four years old, but also sing 'Deutschland über Alles' in church. I see priests making the Nazi salute from the altar.''

He reached his hand across to touch her shoulder. "I'm not one of those priests, Fräulein."

"You are Spellman's priest, yes?"

"And should I wear a yellow star?"

She slapped his face, hard. He ignored the blow. "Are you Germans all alike?"

"My God, I think, yes! So now some of us are here. You will also leave it to your children to denounce twenty years from now what your country is doing?"

"Fräulein, you are wrong."

"If I was wrong, you would not listen. But always you listen, though you know now what I am saying. Why is that?"

He couldn't answer her.

"You have seen it with your own eyes. You know I am right."

It was as if she'd hit him again; this time he felt it. She was forcing him to see what these months had taught him, cost him. Spellman's priest? Yes. He was back to that, at last. A man with no conscience of his own. No capacity to act. This war had the blessing of the one to whom he'd handed over his soul. Therefore he couldn't oppose the war, he could only hate it. Now it was Michael who trembled. He tried to control himself by fumbling for a cigarette, but when he struck a match he could not keep it lit.

He felt naked suddenly. This woman was staring at him. He *was* naked. He turned away, pretending to turn from the wind, to light his match.

When he had his cigarette lit he rubbed his hair, then pressed the heels of his hands against his eyes. "I ride on helicopters, yes. Once I rode with twenty American kids, GIs, just like fellows I grew up with, fellows like me. Except for one thing. They were all dead. I was the only one in the helicopter alive, the only one not in a bag." He stopped for a moment to breathe, then said, "And the Vietnamese, the *loyal* ones, the *Catholics* at your hospital, won't even recite a phrase from the national anthem! Christ! And we call it 'Winning Hearts and Minds'!" He slammed his fist into the sand. "Also known as WHAM!"

After a moment Inge Holz said softly, "They are not Catholics."

"They have pictures of the Sacred Heart and the pope hanging in their hooches."

She laughed. She reached across to squeeze his arm, the first sign of warmth she had yet shown him. Her eyes twinkled at him, to her he seemed so naive. She saw how devastated he was. "They have pictures of Ho Chi Minh too, but hidden. They know we are a Catholic hospital. They think we want those pictures everywhere."

Michael laughed and slapped his forehead. Her touch had soothed something in him. "They were so nice to me. I thought it was because I am a priest."

"They are nice to you when you are so nice to them. I have watched you with patients. You are a kind man. You are not a marine. I did not mean to say that."

Now she took off her glasses and let him see her eyes. "Father," she said, "I talk to you directly because I see you with my people. I see you are good."

He did not look away from her. Suddenly she made him feel all right. As if she knew how much he wanted her to, she touched him again, resting her hand on his arm.

He was acutely conscious of the feel of her fingers, how they had no weight, but caused sensation right to the bone. He wanted to take her into his arms and bury his face in her hair. Are you in love with someone? he would ask. And when she said no, he could ask her to be his friend. That was how he'd put it; perhaps we can be friends. He imagined her agreeing. She would stop being aloof and accusing. She would be like him; vulnerable, unsure of what such feelings meant, afraid of expressing them, yet desperate to.

Ah, poor Michael. The man's loneliness, just thinking of it, undoes me. It was of course the loneliness of a man at sea with himself, a man approaching yet another impossible choice. That loneliness we all know. But his was the further loneliness of the avowed celibate. Figments of women were as much at the center of his inner life as any man's but his figments were of a type. The love of his life, remember, had been a nun. He was immune to the charms of Saigon whores and of the pampered, bikini-clad *colonistes* of the Cercle Sportif. The tough-talking American women correspondents struck him, with their swagger, their blatant if rough-hewn sensuality, their lust for gruesome copy, as crude parodies of the male safari-jacket type. The nurses he'd encountered were noble and strong, like this German, but they lacked her attachment to the full truth. Her willingness to see beyond the victims she treated to their victimizers, and the rare ability to sustain compassion for the first while honing her fury at the second were what moved him. Michael wanted to be like her. And, yes, he wanted to possess her. He was like many priests; only purity could seduce him. When he looked down at her then, the lines of her body, the tracery of her womanliness, breasts and hips, thighs, dominated his perception. The vise-grip in which he held his desire—priest's vice—loosened for a moment. If he imagined lying with her, naked; if he imagined making love to her, it was because she, unlike the whores and *colonistes* and adventurer-correspondents, seemed the opposite of everything he'd encountered in Vietnam. But wait. Wasn't it his fear exactly that once he disavowed his place in the middle of the road—it is necessary to pursue the war, but we should do so humanely—his grip on moderation itself would slip? If he could call into question his patriotism, the bedrock virtue, what would happen to his other commitments? To his celibacy? In other words, didn't both his priestly vocation and the integrity of his fresh rejection of the American war depend on his carefully sustained detachment? Detachment from her? If he was going to place himself above the moral standard of his own people, he could do so only as a man of virtue. With this woman he could perhaps have softened the pain he felt because of the war, but wasn't it his duty now to keep that pain sharp and find a way to act on it? The thing was to stop the war, not his hurting. Thus, he steered not only their talk, but his train of thought away from his attraction to her. Ah Michael, you poor fuckless bastard!

He withdrew his arm and lit cigarettes for both of them. How do couples manage such moments now that no one smokes?

They were silent, staring off at the lake.

Michael hadn't a clue what to say, what to do.

He thought of Nicholas Wiley who seemed wise now, in his moralism, his simplicity. Michael fingered his cross, and it filled him with affection for the kid, a rare longing to see him. He said, "A friend of mine gave me this. He says about the war, 'Just stop it! That's all. Stop it.' "

"When enough people say that to them, they perhaps will."

"Maybe whether they would or not, people should say it."

Inge picked up *The Christian Failure*, looked at it for a moment, then opened to a dog-eared page. "In nineteen thirty-nine our bishops made a joint statement," she read. "Catholics must 'do their duty in obedience to the Führer, ready for sacrifice and with commitment of the whole being.' " She snapped the book shut. "I wish someone had said 'Stop it!' " She dropped the book into her bag. With her cigarette dangling from her lips, she stood and folded her towel. She dropped it in her straw bag, then withdrew a worn white lab-coat, which she donned as a robe. "I must get back."

Michael pulled on his trousers and shirt and walked with her. Neither spoke. At the entrance to the compound, she stopped. He sensed something stiffen in her, a decision made, a resolution. She held his eyes and said quite deliberately, quite carefully, "I want you to come into An Hoa with me tonight."

That was all she said, all she asked of him, but suddenly his throat was dry and he could hear the blood pulsing in his ears.

They walked in silence. The dark forms of palm trees were silhouetted against the night. The mountains beyond the lake were visible only as the black nothing above which the sky, by comparison, seemed a shade of coal blue. Ahead of them, at a distance of half a mile, were the spires of the church. No lights shone from the village. The country lived permanently in blackout.

"The cool air feels good," Michael said at last. He had to deflect the tension he felt into talk.

Inge said, "You know what happens in Vietnam at sunset, don't you?"

He heard something whimsical in her voice, something girlish, and he was drawn in by it. He was aware for the first time of her cologne. Had she worn that for its effect on him? "What?" he asked.

"The gates of the underworld are said to be opened and the souls fly out, naked and starving. They fly back to their home villages and are eating the food left for them on their family altars."

"Sounds like the Viet Cong."

"Vietnamese feed not only their children, but their ancestors."

"You love them, don't you?"

"Yes. It breaks my heart, what happens. You say that—'breaks my heart'?"

"Yes."

The sound of helicopters in the distance stopped them. They listened as the noise grew louder. They stared up at the dark sky, but saw nothing. The aircraft flew without running lights. Soon the sound of their engines began to fade. It was impossible to say how many there were.

Michael said, "In Saigon, when there is rumbling in the distance, people in the cafés hope it isn't thunder because they don't want it to rain, they'll have to go inside. They listen and then say to one another, 'Oh good, artillery fire. Oh good, bombs.' "

Inge nodded. "Europeans and Americans."

"No. Vietnamese. I've heard Vietnamese say it."

She shook her head. "Someday soon they will bomb An Hoa."

"Why do you say that?"

"Because of the marines across the lake. They cannot have a village here. If there is a big village, always there will be NLF, what their leaflets call 'wicked Viet Cong.' "

"Are you worried for the hospital?" Michael asked, but he was thinking he was worried for her.

"Of course worried. We're in the middle, no?"

They walked on in silence then.

Once in the village they went directly to the church. Inge rapped the heel of her hand on the large mahogany door. In a matter of seconds it opened and a shadowy figure stepped aside for them. Michael recognized the form, even in the pitch-black of the church, of a cassocked priest. Once they'd entered he closed the door softly behind them, then led the way into the darkness. It took Michael a moment to realize why that darkness was wrong; not even the sanctuary lamp, indicating the Presence in the tabernacle, burned.

At an altar the priest lit a candle, then faced them. He was Vietnamese, taller than most of his countrymen but considerably shorter than Michael and extremely thin. His Roman collar hung loosely at his throat. His black hair fell across his forehead. It was impossible to say how old he was—perhaps thirty, perhaps fifty—but a certain fierce vigor showed in his face. His black eyes fixed on Inge Holz, and he greeted her softly in Vietnamese.

She responded with a whisper, and Michael sensed at once the current of their relationship.

The priest faced him. *"Mon, Père,"* he said gently, *"bienvenu à l'église de Vinh Son."*

Michael looked blank.

The priest read his small embarrassment, and said, "Welcome, Father, to the church of Vinh Son." They shook hands.

"Thank you." Now that his eyes were adjusted, Michael looked around. It was a typical Catholic church, the dominating high altar, its gaudy crucifix with painted corpus—Jesus a pale Caucasian—and two side altars, one for Joseph, one for Mary. They were standing in front of Mary's altar, and the candle the priest had lit was a small votive candle in a blue cup. "Vinh Son?" Michael asked.

"Vinh Son," the priest repeated. "Vinh Son Da Sal."

Vincent de Sales, Michael realized, as the French pronounce it. He nearly laughed. Saint Vincent. Good old Saint Vincent, patron of the order to which Carolyn had belonged, patron of the hospital in which Molly was born. *Vinh Son!* When he told me this story, he smiled. By then the Church was like a haunted house to us, and certain saints like ghosts.

The Vietnamese priest was staring at him intently, taking his measure. Finally he said, "You know of the Struggle?"

It took Michael a moment to realize what he was referring to. He said cautiously, "The Struggle; I know the word. It is used to mean 'resistance.'"

"Not 'resistance,'" the priest said softly. "In Vietnamese 'Struggle' is to rebel with all one's life-force."

"It refers to the Buddhist Struggle, no?" That movement

had brought Diem down in '63 and lately it had shown signs of quickening once more.

"It is not only Buddhists who seek a third way between the Communists and the generals. Some of us do also." The priest studied Michael.

Michael showed him nothing.

"Inge told me perhaps you would like to learn. I thought to approach you as a brother priest."

Michael suddenly thought, This might be a trap! He said warily, "Every Vietnamese priest I've met is loyal to the Saigon government."

"But of course they would appear so to you. We are loyal first to God, second to the Church and third to our people. The government does not command a priest's loyalty." He smiled. The strength of his conviction communicated, but he was speaking gently. "It is the same for priests everywhere, no? Even in America?"

"It should be."

"It is so with you?"

Michael said carefully, "My government commands my loyalty as a citizen, not as a priest." He looked at Inge quickly. She was staring at him, waiting for him to declare himself. But still he felt wary. He said, "The Buddhists are tools of the Viet Cong." It was a provocative statement, one he didn't really believe, but he felt instinctively that he had to stiff-arm this priest. Why had he brought him here? What did he want? "Communists do not command my loyalty either."

"Nor mine, but the NLF is not run by Catholics. My government is. That puts me in a special position, you agree?"

Michael did not answer.

The Vietnamese priest continued to smile, inappropriately, Michael thought. Then he realized that his smile was his disguise. The priest said, "I attended seminary in Paris. My thesis was on Tocqueville. You know what he said about the Ancien Régime? 'Our government resembles the Mass for the Dead: there is no Gloria, since there is nothing to sing about; no Credo since there is nothing we believe in common; a long offertory where much money is collected, and in the end, no Benediction.' " The priest's smile was gone.

*   *   *

"What do you mean, 'run by Catholics'?" Michael asked. "The time of Diem is passed."

The priest made a gesture with his hand: Maybe yes, maybe no. "You remember the Ngos' Can Lao?"

"The secret organization?"

"Yes. Police, spies, provincial leaders, generals, a shadow government, all Catholics. It was the source of their power. Those men did not disappear when Diem and Nhu were killed. They simply withdrew somewhat, to wait. And now it seems the time of waiting is over."

"Why?"

"Nguyen Van Thieu," the priest said simply.

Thieu was the new chief of state. With Air Vice-Marshal Nguyen Cao Ky he had been running the government for less than a month.

"Thieu is a convert to Catholicism, a devoted, pious man, and many of the former Can Lao members see in him a new Diem. They have secretly begun a new organization, the Nhan Xa, called in English 'The Revolutionary Social Humanist Party.' Many of the old alliances have simply been struck again. Their purpose is the old one, to save Vietnam not just from Communism but from Buddhists. *They* are the ones who have convinced Lodge and Westmoreland that the Struggle for a Third Way is Viet Cong. Your government would love to have Catholics in power again. They will welcome Nhan Xa."

"What about Ky?"

"Ky is a comedian. Only Americans think of him."

"But Thieu only came to power this month. None of the others have lasted."

"He will last, I promise you, until the war is lost, or until he is dead."

"Or until the war is won."

"It won't be won."

"If Nhan Xa is secret, how do you know about it?"

"The leader is my own bishop, Nguyen Van Thuan. In our country a bishop has no secrets from his priests. Do you know him?"

"No."

The priest nodded. He was accustomed to such ignorance. "He replaced Thuc."

"Diem's brother."

"That is correct. You believe Diem's family was removed from power in nineteen sixty-three."

"It wasn't?"

"You know the myth of Hydra, the monster slain by Hercules? It had nine heads, and when one was cut off, it was replaced by two others. My bishop, Thuan, is the son of Diem's sister. The Ngos are the hydra family of Vietnam. They still control the Church. With Nhan Xa, they will control Thieu. They will control America."

And it all began, Michael thought, in the Maryknoll seminary where Ngo Dinh Diem had spent his years in exile as Cardinal Spellman's ward. Jesus Christ! he thought. Am I the only one who knows this? Michael looked at Inge again. This must sound to her like the resurgence of the Nazi party. Well, wasn't it like that? Michael remembered that, once, his horror at what the Ngos were doing had taken him, furiously and so imprudently, to Spellman's residence. And Spellman had coopted him completely.

Michael faced the Vietnamese priest. "Why have you brought me here?"

"Because I want to tell you what I and some brother priests are going to do."

"You trust me?"

"Of course. We are eleven Catholic priests. Who can we trust if not a fellow priest? On July twentieth in all of Vietnam, in Hanoi as well as Saigon, in Haiphong and Hué, we Vietnamese will mark the Day of National Shame. On that day it is ten years since the Geneva Agreement divided our country in two. And on that day we priests from parishes all over South Vietnam will go to Saigon in behalf of our people. There will be many Buddhists in the streets, many demonstrations. The government will say the demonstrators are Viet Cong. But no one can say that about Catholic priests. We will make a simple prayer, a procession, a Way of the Cross. We will go from the president's palace to the American embassy, and we will be saying what the Buddhists say. The National Shame is what we have allowed to happen in our country. We can relieve our shame only by protesting the source of it: 'No More America in Vietnam!' No more American soldiers in our cities. No more American bombs on our villages! No more American murder of our people!''

Michael was not breathing. The priest's indictment filled *him* with shame. ''And you are telling me this because . . .''

''We want you to join us.''

''Making twelve.''

The priest smiled. ''Unintentional.''

But Michael's thought was, One of the twelve was Judas. He remembered Nicholas Wiley. Judas and Peter; what made them different was how they handled their shame.

Inge Holz spoke finally, saying to Michael, ''I told Pham that you are ready. If this offends you, then is my fault.''

What Michael noticed was her use of the priest's name. She did not call him ''Father.'' He looked from one to the other. ''But I am an American. That seems wrong, given what you're saying.''

The priest nodded. ''In a way, that's true. But there are good reasons. You are a priest like us, and that emphasizes that we are speaking as Catholics. As priests we all object to government, you to yours, we to ours. And as priests we all proclaim the Gospel's independence from narrow, political causes of whatever kind.'' He paused. ''And there are other reasons too. If you are with us, then the police will hesitate to move against us. We do not want our procession to be interrupted before the people see us.''

Inge Holz said, ''If you are not with them, the police will put them off the street at once and we may never see them again.''

The Vietnamese priest ignored her, as if that was not his concern. ''And your participation will attract the attention of news reporters from Europe and America. We do not burn ourselves, like the bonzes. They might therefore ignore us.''

Tim O'Shea's one request to Michael: ''Don't let Spelly read about you in the *Times*.''

Michael could think of a dozen reasons to say no, good ones. But his impulse—and it was to say no, to be sure—sprang from none of them. He was afraid.

''We are asking you to join us on the Day of National

Shame, and on each day after that when we will repeat the procession until the war ends or until they stop us.''

Michael stared at him. The gaunt, shadow-ridden priest seemed all at once an upright cadaver. Shall these bones live? But it wasn't Suu Van Pham who'd been reduced to bones. Michael saw that his own belief in his own mission, his own identity, his own position was completely collapsed. He looked out on an infinite stretch of ruins, a vast plain littered with dried, lifeless bones, the remains of all he'd once sworn by and lived for. The futility of his effort to alleviate suffering by working, timidly, within the structures of Church and government was undeniable now. The absurdity of his own life slammed him, and he felt for the first time ever disgust at what he'd become. A clerical camp follower, yes. The army's holy whore. The cardinal's. His self-loathing was surpassed only by his despair.

Dear reader, such a moment would have undone you and me, would have finished us. We'd have gone off, regarding the Vietnamese priests as foolhardy, self-aggrandizing martyrs. We'd have claimed to prefer organizing quietly among Catholic clergy and developing what we would call ''authentic'' opposition, ''practical'' dissent. We'd have refused, citing if not our vow of obedience to America's Sunshine Prelate or our obligation to the poor refugees served by the CRS, our debt of loyalty to Tim O'Shea. They couldn't undo his consecration because of us—he was a bishop forever—but they could keep him an auxiliary forever too.

And we'd have been nearly right; there were honorable reasons for men like us to say no to Suu Van Pham. Honorable reasons to pretend that nothing had changed, to insist that the invitation from this ghost of a priest was not, at last, an annunciation, a conscription, an act of God. You and I, dear reader, would have slipped away, wishing the Vietnamese dissenters well, promising to pray for them. And only we'd have known what cowards we were and how we'd just destroyed ourselves.

But Michael Maguire was not like the rest of us, any more then than he had been in Korea or would be later. His capacity for fear, and for retreat, matched ours, but when forced by events to face the truth, at last, he did so willingly.

I would have deflected the truth. Perhaps you would have. Michael embraced it. Confronted with that vast plain of dry bones, the bones of the slain, the bones of his own savaged dreams, he stood with upraised arms and cried, "Live!" In him despair became hope, collapse became conversion, and fear was changed into the source of action. Such transforming will is the hero's gift, and he had it. And we remember him through these pages because, oh, we need it.

Michael nodded at Suu Van Pham. "I am honored that you should ask me to join you. *Adsum, Pater,*" he said firmly. It was the ancient declaration that each of them had made at ordination. "Send me," it means. "I am ready."

Father Suu Van Pham led Michael and Inge Holz to the rectory. In the kitchen he drew the blinds, then lit a fat, short candle on the table. He took a crucifix from around his neck and placed it next to the candle. He poured a glass of wine and set out a third of a thin loaf of bread. Then they each took seats and joined hands. For a few moments they prayed in silence. Then Father Pham raised his eyes to Michael. "You have a favorite passage of Scripture, Father?"

In Michael's mind, the pages fell open of the small New Testament Tim O'Shea had given him in Korea, and he recited from Paul's letter to the Ephesians. " 'But now in Christ Jesus you who were once far off have been brought near in the blood of Christ. For He is our peace, who has made us both one, and has broken down the dividing wall of hostility, by abolishing in his flesh the law of commandments and ordinances, that he might create in himself one new man in place of the two, so making peace; and might reconcile us both to God in one body through the Cross, thereby bringing hostility to an end. And he came and preached peace to you who were far off, and peace to those who were near; for through him we both have access in one Spirit to the Father.' "

When Michael fell silent, Pham opened his eyes and looked at him. He completed the passage. " 'So then you are no longer a stranger or a foreign visitor. We are fellow citizens with the saints and members of the household of God.' "

The two men leaned toward one another and embraced. *"Pax tecum,"* they said.

Then each one kissed Inge Holz, whose eyes were bright. When Pham touched his cheek to hers she whispered something. Michael knew what—"I love you"—and he understood.

"Shall we say the Canon in Latin, Father? Or English?" Pham had the wine and bread arranged in front of him on the plain unfinished table.

Michael had never done the Mass so informally before. Though the mode would become trivialized in the post-Council era as "home liturgy"—that impoverished rite shorn of vestments, stripped of gesture and rubric, devoid of eloquence— one's first experience of the transcendent event so simplified, so freed from the sterile medieval accretions, called up its own special awe. The unadorned Mass could evoke magnificently that Last Meal in the Upper Room, but for Michael that night the breaking of the bread at the deal table in the blacked-out rectory was like something done in the catacombs, an act of the underground Church exactly. Wasn't the world outside raging? Wasn't it full of enemies? Weren't soldiers raising crosses on every hill? And in this shocking dispensation weren't the old loyalties replaced by a new one, modest and absolute at once? Underground, freed from trappings, the Eucharist becomes itself again, a simple meal, an act of life against death, a sacrifice. And likewise the Church. Michael felt that he was at Mass for the first time, that finally he had come home.

Latin was the vernacular of martyrs.

English was the argot of men who dropped canisters full of napalm on children.

But this was an act of communion—First Communion— with a people whose forgiveness Michael Maguire longed for.

"In your language, Father, please," he said. "In Vietnamese, let us pray."

TWENTY-FOUR

MICHAEL MAGUIRE was the tallest of the twelve, and he walked in front.

His first problem had been where to get a cassock. The Vietnamese priests were too short. Even Pham's soutane would have barely reached Michael's ankles and he'd have looked like an oafish altar boy. Ludicrous as it seems, the project of finding a cassock that would fit him preoccupied him in the days before the demonstration. If Michael Maguire was going to do this, appear in a public protest against his own government in a foreign capital, then he was going to look like what he was—a responsible, some would say important, American priest. He finally found an air force chaplain his height at Tan Son Nhut Air Base, a friendly Chicagoan who greeted Michael as if they'd been classmates. Michael told him he needed the cassock for a prayer service at the embassy.

The day itself was humid, and even in the early morning, rain threatened. July is the heart of the wet season in Saigon, and it was certain that the skies would open at some point.

Nevertheless by midmorning the streets and boulevards of the city were jammed with citizens. Few of them were demonstrators, and almost none of them had come in from the countryside. The government had coopted the move to turn the anniversary of the Geneva Accords into a protest and had declared it a national holiday. Also, soldiers were posted outside the city to prevent residents of refugee camps, displaced villagers and Buddhists from the countryside from

407

coming into Saigon. Traditional Vietnamese had disdained
Saigon when it was the French capital. Now that it had
become the center of the American occupation with the degradation and corruption that brought, they hated it. And so on
that day the government simply kept them out.

The Saigonese, on the other hand, were cynical and
indifferent. As long as the generals kept the war in the
country, and as long as the Americans stayed in the Cowboy
Bars on Tu Do Street and the MPs kept the drunken soldiers
away from their daughters, they ignored the government.
They did business, that was all. On this day they closed their
shops, though, and strolled the city as if it were Paris.

The Buddhist Struggle Movement, which had turned out
hundreds of thousands of protesters against Diem, and which
in a year, in 1966, would bring Saigon to the brink of chaos,
was quiescent now. Thousands of its leaders were still in jail,
and the Catholic opposition was wielding its power more
subtly. Only students could be rallied in numbers that summer,
and to them the condition of a divided Vietnam was less a
National Shame than a fact of political life they had grown up
with. A day of protest against the government that protected
their draft-exempt status and against the Americans who brought
them their beloved Everly Brothers and blue jeans was more a
lark than an act of conscience.

In sum, if you weren't looking that day, you might not
have noticed the earnest demonstrators, though two small
groups of them were easily identifiable. A single file of
saffron-robed monks snaked through throngs of white-suited
men and ladies in flowing *ao-dai* dresses on Lam Son Square
before the Continental Palace Hotel. Some of the monks
struck shoulder-drums and others carried signs saying,
"Vietnam for the Vietnamese" and "Down with U.S. Intervention in Vietnamese Internal Affairs," and "One Vietnam" and "All Life Is Suffering." The Buddhists and the
students, perhaps one thousand all together, were going to
spend the day chanting and praying in front of the American
embassy.

The Catholic priests did not want to be taken as an adjunct
to the Buddhist demonstration, as, being so few, they would
have. So they changed their plan. They would avoid the

embassy. It was Michael who suggested that instead they take their procession to the MACV Headquarters which that summer were still in a three-story French villa in a residential neighborhood. In fact it was a better place to make their point since their objection was not to America or Americans, but to the American military buildup. They did not know it, but no demonstrations had been conducted at the headquarters before, and because of what they started that day, it would be moved soon to a secure concrete building in the middle of Tan Son Nhut.

At the Presidential Palace they prayed the rosary in Latin before the huge elaborate gates on the other side of which deferential guards watched nervously. The guards were obviously relieved when the priests set off, in single file like the Buddhists, but behind the tall American. Michael carried the procession cross. Pham carried their only sign, which said in English and Vietnamese, "We Pray For Peace. Stop Killing Our People." Each of the other priests carried a candle and his breviary. As they walked they recited the Psalms.

The procession took them down Thong Nhut Street, a broad boulevard that had until recently been lined with graceful elms. But it was a bald street now and had a ravaged look. It had not been bombed, but the elms had been cut down early in the summer to accommodate the huge American trucks that were bringing soldiers and supplies in from Tan Son Nhut, which by July was, and would remain for years, the busiest airport in the world. "Thong Nhut" meant unification, and at the opposite end of the boulevard from the palace was the National Zoo, which gave rise to a Saigon joke; what Unification Street unified were not the halves of the country but the monkey houses at its either end.

The crowds who were long accustomed to demonstrations of Buddhist monks could not ignore these Catholic priests, not even a mere dozen of them. The people eased aside for them and craned to read their sign. The priests walked solemnly past stymied pedicabs and boys who were forced by the crush to push their Lambrettas along the sidewalks. It may have been the National Day of Shame, but in Saigon—wasn't this typical?—it had the look of a festival. The shops were closed, but at improvised stands along the curb, sellers hawked flowers, decorations and black-market goods—transistor radios, Zippo lighters and Timex watches. Even these cagey merchants gawked when the priests went by. The street urchins—the Vietnamese called them *bui doi*, the dust of life—who pestered browsers for coins or, when they dared, picked their pockets, stood back. Catholic priests rarely left their churches or appeared in public in groups, and they never criticized the war. Old men pointed to the sign Father Pham carried and then fell to arguing about what they'd seen. Was it the funeral procession of a Spiritist sect? Were they Palm Tree Prophets? Was the man in front Caucasian? As word spread ahead of them that they were coming, people both came to the street to see and moved away from it out of certainty that such a demonstration would soon draw government riot police.

For his part Michael felt that he was enacting a dream he'd had years before. He remembered walking in single file with other POWs from one camp to the next, through Korean and Chinese villages, until finally they were brought to the prison camp at Chung Kang Djin across the Yalu. Asian faces had stared at him all along the way. In some towns they had jeered and hated. Now they were staring again, and again it was their hatred he was aware of, though no one cursed him or raised a fist. But they would have if they'd known! They'd have screamed at him and torn at his clothing. They'd have spit. "What are you doing in Asia again? Why can't you leave us alone?"

He remembered the mob of refugees rushing at him. He'd been ready with his bayonet, but had been spared using it. Once all the Americans—the Occidentals—were safe, he'd blown the Asians to smithereens. And now, fifteen years later, more powerfully than before, sorrow flowed from him. This procession was an act of penitence. This should have been Good Friday. "O my people, what have I done to thee?"

When he'd first come home from Korea, Michael had struck me as Ransom's "Tower unleaning." He was so erect, so spare, so stripped of the superfluous, so radical, so rooted! But wasn't he still? The impression those twelve priests made as they moved slowly through Saigon's streets was in large part an impression *he* made, towering above everyone in sight, setting the pace for the others with his steady cadence and holding at the level of his brow the ornate brass crucifix, the racked body of Jesus facing away from him and toward the city, toward the people and toward the army offices to which they marched.

Now they were reciting, in Latin, the Second Psalm. "Why do the nations rage and the peoples utter folly? The kings of the earth rise up, and the princes conspire together against the Lord and against His Anointed: 'Let us break their fetters and cast their bonds from us!' He who is throned in heaven laughs; the Lord derides them."

It was a new idea. To Michael Maguire the kings of the earth against whom the Scriptures railed incessantly had never included the leaders of his own country. But now that he had heard the words of the prophets as addressed to *him* and to *his* people—as opposed merely to, say, the Sodomites—revelation occurred as for the first time. America was not exempt from the judgment of God. Nor, for that matter, was the Church! The kings of the earth and the princes conspire! Nguyen Van Thieu and Nguyen Van Thuan! Lyndon Baines Johnson and Francis Cardinal Spellman!

"Serve the Lord with fear and rejoice before Him; with trembling pay homage to Him, lest He be angry and you perish from the way when His anger blazes suddenly. Happy are all who take refuge in Him!"

Michael Maguire embodied in himself, without knowing it, the end of the great American Catholic Success Story. He was, first, its crowning achievement—a Silver Star Priest. His Catholic Faith had never seemed more glorious than when it enabled him to withstand the pressures of a Chinese prison. His Catholic Faith had made him a patriot and a hero, and the Church celebrated him as if the purpose of the Incarnation was to make us better American citizens. Michael Maguire was what all those seminary estates up the Hudson and along Lake Michigan and in the hills of California were trying to, in their word, "form." He was the man with twin loyalties, *Deus et Patria*, and they were equal, matched, one at the service of the other.

But the seminaries, not understanding the risks in such

exposure, had confronted him with the Word of God. It was a domesticated Word, to be sure, one that had left unmoved and unchanged generations of seminarians before. But Michael Maguire, thanks to the chance gift of Timothy O'Shea, had begun his confrontation with the Word of God in the Chinese prison, and a seed was planted well before he entered the "seed bed." It would take years to bear fruit, but when it did, it would set him apart from almost all his brothers.

He understood inchoately that the Word of God was what kept him free in prison, and that taught him that the Word of God is freedom itself. "You cannot imprison the Word of the Lord." Paul's antiphon came back to him. You cannot imprison the Word of the Lord in a phrase like *Deus et Patria*, for the Word has nothing to do with America. Michael's anger blazed suddenly at all he'd been taught, at all he'd believed, at all he'd built his life around. His anger blazed, purifying, cauterizing.

You cannot imprison the Word of God in a national purpose, in a Cause, in a culture, in narrowly defined—nationally defined—religion. By walking in that procession with those Vietnamese priests, speaking not for Communism or Buddhism or the reunification of Vietnam or the defeat of the Dominoes—speaking only for the sacred right of innocent people not to have fire poured on their heads, Michael, having been captured by the Word, had become its instrument.

"The Word of God," Paul says, "is something alive and active. It cuts like any double-edged sword, but more finely. It can slip through the place where the soul is divided from the spirit, or joints from marrow."

It can even slip between the words "America" and "Catholic," and can declare that from now on they should be presumed to have nothing to do with each other. What had seemed our moment of glory—this is what Michael saw—had been the beginning of our disgrace. John Kennedy embodied both when he said in his great Inaugural—how we cheered him for it; these words more than any prepared us for Vietnam—"On earth God's work must truly be our own."

The eyes of every Asian that fell on Michael Maguire, who hid his own behind the blurring crucifix, flared with hatred. He seemed to hear their voices sputtering.

What has "God's work" to do with firestorms above our cities? What has "God's work" to do with throwing our sons out of helicopters? What has "God's work" to do with cutting off our ears? With herbicides, defoliants, white phosphorus or napalm? What has "God's work" to do with body-counts or "Cong catchers"? With forcing live flare rods into the orifices—mouths, anuses and vaginas—of men and women, the sons and daughters—even if you despise us as Slopes, Slant-Eyes and Gooks—of the Almighty, Everlasting, Vengeance-seeking, Justice-loving Lord God! You dare call what you do "God's work"! You dare invoke that Name! That Word! You scum! You worm! Leave! Begone! Get out! Let my people go! Yes, *my* people! It is Yahweh who speaks! The Lord of History, Creator of the Universe, Absolute Future toward Whom all time pulses, God!

The Military Assistance Command–Vietnam Headquarters was easily distinguished from the other turn-of-the-century villas in which the French colonial elite had lived, because from its roof sprouted a forest of antennae. White and silver communications disks tilted toward the dull sky, which seemed lower. Rain was closer.

In front of the villa a sandbag barrier four feet high blocked half the street, keeping traffic in the far lane. There were no crowds on the sidewalk here, though curious, perhaps foolhardy, Saigonese were trailing along behind the procession now.

The two MPs at the villa gate saw them coming and called for reinforcements.

The priests now recited the *Te Deum*, the hymn of praise that every Catholic priest of that generation and before knew by heart because he recited it as a prayer of thanksgiving as he left the altar after Mass. "You overcame the sting of death and opened the kingdom of heaven to all believers. You are seated at God's right hand in glory. We believe that you will come and be our judge. Come, then, Lord, sustain Your people, bought with the price of your own blood, and bring us with your saints to everlasting glory."

Death, *mors*. Blood, *sanguis*. Judge, *judex*. Your people, *tuus populus*.

The words reverberated in that space between their souls

and spirits, between their bones and marrow, as they closed the last distance to the American building.

By the time they reached the sandbag barrier, two squads of combat-ready American soldiers were filing out of the villa, rifles at exact angles across their breasts, obscuring their faces so that they need not look the demonstrators in the eyes.

What Michael fixed upon were the gleaming bayonets; he remembered his own and what he'd have done with it, all too willingly. A fresh wave of feeling flowed in him, but now for the first time that morning, his sorrow and anger having kept it at bay, it was fear. It flowed as cleanly as blood would once a rifle's blade had pierced him.

He began to pray, reciting numbly, "Come Holy Spirit, fill the hearts of your people. Enkindle in them the fire of your love." Then in his own voice, he whispered, "Oh Christ, help me do this."

The soldiers marched out of the compound, into the street, and as the priests stopped in a single line in front of the barrier, the soldiers split into two files and surrounded them. They were uniformly tall and burly, physically intimidating. The first blow was their appearance. There were perhaps fifty, and more than half were black men.

The sergeant barked an order, and the soldiers froze, ready.

Then a Vietnamese officer addressed a command to the priests. Disperse at once. Michael fixed his eyes upon the brass cross. It hadn't occurred to him that they wouldn't be allowed to stand peacefully in the street, for a time at least. The Buddhists conducted their demonstrations with impunity. But of course the government had learned to live with Buddhists, and the news media had long since ignored them. But Catholics! And priests! And an American!

With a high-pitched whine, a large army truck, the familiar olive canvas, backed up the street toward them. More soldiers?

Michael looked around quickly, hoping to see reporters, cameramen, American or European witnesses. None. The citizens who had been following had been stopped by a line of police a block away.

Suu Van Pham began reciting, in Latin, the Sixtieth Psalm. "Hear, O Lord, my cry. . ." The others joined in. At least if they had to be arrested, Michael thought, it would be by Americans.

"From the earth's end I call to you as my heart grows faint. You will set me high upon a rock; you will give me rest, for you are my refuge, a tower of strength against the enemy."

Even before the truck stopped, the flap was thrown back and Vietnamese Rangers began jumping out. They were carrying heavy wooden riot sticks. Immediately, though no priest resisted, they began to club them. Within seconds each priest had been bloodied, then roughly picked up and hurled into the truck.

All but Michael. A pair of American MPs had snatched the crucifix from him. Taking him by each arm, they dragged him into the headquarters building.

Within ten minutes the demonstration was over. The truck was gone. The dropped breviaries and candles, the crucifix and Pham's sign had been swept away. The bystanders, including reporters, half a block away had seen nothing, owing to the wall of burly American soldiers. The entire demonstration might have been a fantasy, a mirage. And the bystanders were dispersed then anyway when the skies opened finally, with a great clap of thunder, for the rain.

Michael was kept in a bare room, alone, for more than two hours. It was furnished with a plain wooden table and two chairs. He tried to pray but couldn't. The sound of the lock turning in his door startled him. He straightened in the chair and put his hands palm downward on the table and he watched as the door opened.

"Jack!" Michael stood. Relief surged through him, an absurd happiness. It was Jack Howe, in his white suit, his slick black hair carefully parted above his haggard face. Howe looked gaunt as ever, and stern, but the tension in which Michael had held himself so rigidly went at once. When Howe offered him his hand Michael took it in both of his and shook it gratefully.

"Are you all right, Father?"

"Yes, but you've got to get me out of here. They've arrested my fellow priests. I've got to get to them."

"Sit down, Father." Howe withdrew his hand.

"But, Jack—"

"Sit down," he ordered.

Michael stiffened. He watched in silence while Howe took a pipe from his pocket and lit it. Had he ever seen Howe smoke a pipe before? As he puffed it alive he said, "That was a stupid thing to do, Father."

"Where are my fellow priests, Jack?"

"The Viets have been taken to the Center for Political Reindoctrination at Bien Hoa."

"That's a prison! That's where V.C. terrorists are taken."

"You people didn't expect rooms at the Caravelle Hotel, did you?"

"What law did we break?" Michael stared at him; had he ever seen this Howe before?

"I thought you had more savvy than this, Father. They used you." Howe looked at Michael mournfully.

"Everybody uses me, Jack, even you." Michael was trying to stretch his mind around what, at last, it knew. "You told me once you hated the CIA. Now that I recall, perhaps you didn't explicitly deny working for it, however."

"I wish I could have told you, Father," Howe said simply.

"And now they've sent you in here because you're famous for getting me to eat out of your hand."

"Father, I asked to be the one to see you."

"Why?"

He shook his head and shrugged. "Because I know why you did it."

"I did it, Jack, because of things you taught me."

Howe stared at his pipe.

"You stayed with it too long, Jack."

Howe's eyes widened. "Maybe so. But now it's moving too fast to jump off."

"I'm off." Michael stood up. He recognized Howe's situation, that familiar despair, but it came as a surprise to find he had no sympathy for him. "Take me to Bien Hoa."

Howe stared at him.

"I mean it. If the Vietnamese priests are there, then I want to be with them."

Howe relit his pipe. It was a gesture into which he could

channel his insecurity, and when the pipe was lit all traces of it were gone. He said officiously, "Father Maguire, you are being taken to Tan Son Nhut, being put on an airplane and sent home. Your visa has been revoked."

"I'm not going, Jack. Not even for you, buddy. You'll have to go back and tell your bosses that you couldn't work your magic with me this time."

"Oh, really? What are you going to do?"

Michael answered with a resolve he did not know he had. "I'm going to return to the Presidential Palace and I am going to retrace the steps that we took today, and I am going to stand outside this building until curfew. I will observe curfew because I have no intention of breaking the law. But I will repeat the procession tomorrow and the next day and the day after that and every day until my fellow priests have been freed."

"That won't be necessary, Father. Your fellow priests will be freed as soon as your plane leaves the ground. The government has no interest in making heroes of them."

"I don't believe you, Jack. I don't believe the government here. You're all fucking liars. You free the priests. Then talk to me about leaving."

Howe studied the bowl of his pipe for a moment, then turned abruptly and left the room.

More than an hour later another man came, this one in khaki. On his collar were the silver eagles of a full colonel.

He offered Michael his hand. "Father Maguire, I'm Father Paul Fitzmaurice."

Only then did Michael see the silver cross on his breast pocket. This was the Theater Chief of Chaplains.

"I have a message for you." He put a piece of paper on the table and sat.

"Already?" Michael smiled. He understood suddenly that they'd have been on the wire to New York. As he picked up the teletype sheet, he said, "Good old Tim O'Shea."

The chaplain shook his head. "Not Bishop O'Shea, Father. It's from the cardinal."

Michael's stomach constricted. Why hadn't he expected this? Had he been living in never-never land? He sat, stunned.

When he saw that the communication was in Latin, he did

not breathe. The first thing his eyes fixed on were the paren-
thetical citations by number of canon law. He was being
formally ordered back to New York under solemn obedience.

Michael looked across the table at Fitzmaurice. "It must be
the middle of the night in New York! They woke Spellman
for this?"

The chaplain nodded. "They want you out. Every American in Vietnam is furious at you." Especially including me,
his attitude suggested.

Michael looked at the paper in his hands. "I don't think
the cardinal is too pleased either."

"They're threatening to force CRS out of Asia altogether
because of you."

"Good Lord."

"What did you expect?"

Michael looked sharply at the chaplain. "To be able to
stand peacefully in front of an American building, to express
an opinion."

"This isn't the States, Father. You're damn lucky they're
not charging you with treason."

"What?"

" 'Aid and comfort to the enemy,' Father. You've heard of
it?"

"Don't accuse me of treason, Colonel." Michael's anger
swelled.

Fitzmaurice shrugged, backing off. "Look, you give every
priest over here a bad name. You're the first American citizen
to join these kooks. How do you think that looks? An American priest demonstrating against his own superiors!"

"Westmoreland and Taylor are not my superiors."

"Over here they are. This is war, Father. I don't think you
understand that."

"That's one thing I do understand, Colonel. I know war
when I see it, and I know when the rules of war are being
violated. I've been in the countryside; have you? I've seen
this war from the villages; have you? You should get your
chaplains out of the officers' clubs and into the free fire
zones, then tell me this is war. This isn't war, Colonel. It is
mass murder. It is genocide."

The chaplain said mournfully, like a hurt mother—a common form among certain clergy—"I take your refusal to call me 'Father' as an insult, as you no doubt intend it."

"Not so. I simply find it impossible to think of you as a priest."

"You've got a nerve."

"A nerve is right! A raw nerve, involving some brother priests of ours who had the shit kicked out of them with American GIs looking on, and who are now in Bien Hoa, a torture-prison. And you know it. I'm not leaving here until they're free."

"The Viets can take care of themselves, Father. They knew well enough what they were getting into, even if you didn't." The chaplain nodded at the teletype sheet. "You don't have any choice in that matter now. That's God's Will you're holding in your hands."

Michael dropped the paper on the table. "I want you to tell whoever sent you in here I'm not leaving Vietnam until those priests are free."

"That's a solemn command you have there, Father, from your Ordinary himself. You recognize the canonical formula surely."

"Yes, I do."

"And you recall the consequences if you disobey."

"I believe the progression runs from suspension to interdiction to excommunication, doesn't it? But it's a little more complicated than my saying yes or no to a solemn order. Since they've chosen to play this canonically, Colonel, instead of, say, pastorally or even fraternally, they'll have to follow the form to its conclusion. That means they have to issue the order three times before the penalty is incurred, which gives me a little time, doesn't it?"

"And they told me you young priests didn't know your canon law."

"Some of us know it well enough to hide in it."

"But what about CRS? It won't have the benefit of canonical due process. The army can just shut it down. Do you want that on your conscience?"

Michael shook his head. "They can't do it. The Catholic Relief Service! It's the largest private foreign aid agency in America. It operates in seventy countries. It gets clothes and food to ten million people. There are three hundred CRS workers in Southeast Asia. And the board of directors has some of the most powerful men in America on it. What MACV has if they shut down CRS is bad publicity. Everybody from Uncle Walter to the *New York Times* to, maybe, the head of Caritas International comes to me to find out what happened. And do you know what? I'll tell them. And that, Colonel, is what they'll obviously do anything to avoid."

"You're pretty cocky, aren't you?"

"Not at all. I'd vastly prefer that none of this was happening. I wish I was the third curate in an upstate parish."

"You may get that wish before you're finished."

Father Fitzmaurice stood.

"And you tell them I demand to know by what authority I'm being prevented from leaving this building."

Fitzmaurice shook his head, genuinely bewildered. "This isn't the States, Father. Do you want them to turn you over to the Vietnamese?"

"That's exactly what I want."

"They can't and you know it."

"Then get our brother priests out of Bien Hoa."

Minutes after the chaplain left, Jack Howe returned. "All right, here's the deal. You're free to go. But you get the woman away from this building."

"What woman?"

"The German nurse. She's been standing outside all afternoon. Tomorrow the priests will be released. They'll be brought to the rectory of the cathedral where you can greet them. Then an army driver will take you to Tan Son Nhut, and you'll board a plane for the States. And you will never come back to Vietnam."

"You make it sound like I'm a criminal, Jack. Is that what you think after all these years? After all you've seen here? That I'm the criminal?"

Howe did not drop his eyes. Clearly he had decided that this priest wasn't going to make him feel guilty. He had his battens in place now.

"All right, Jack," Michael said, "I agree."

Howe nodded briskly and left the room.

Inge Holz was waiting beyond the sandbag barrier. The ain had stopped and the late afternoon sky was clear and bright. When Michael came out, she rushed forward and mbraced him. She began to question him in a rush, but he ut his finger to his lips and led her away from the headquarers building. In the middle of the next block he unbuttoned his cassock and took it off. He laughed. "I should have left his there. I borrowed it from the air force." He draped it over one arm, and put the other arm around her shoulder. "I hink they let me out because they sensed you wouldn't go way."

"I wasn't certain you are still there, but where else can I go?" Her calm had never broken, but he saw how alarmed she'd been.

He told her that Pham and the others would be released the next day, and that he'd agreed to leave Vietnam.

"And you believe them?" she asked.

"I'm not going until I see them."

"But when you go they can do anything."

"They can do anything now, Inge. My being around guaranees nothing."

"But how can you leave? Without you they are there forever. Pham won't stop now. He'll need you again."

"No. He needs his own people. That's all. If I have work o do, it's with mine. Pham doesn't need me. Maybe he doesn't need you either." Michael hadn't planned to say that. What business was it of his?

"What do you say?" She held herself against what he'd said, as if it was the first blow of many.

"He's a priest, Inge. You know what I mean."

She slipped out of his arm and ran ahead. She dodged hrough traffic to cross the street away from him.

By the time he caught up with her, she was sobbing.

"I'm sorry," he said, as he took her arm.

She continued to walk at a clip, but she didn't shake him ff. Neither spoke. They walked as far as Lam Son Square where battered Citroëns and Pugeots competed with the motorbikes and pedicabs in the evening rush hour.

In front of the big hotel, the Continental Palace, that catered to Americans and Europeans he suggested they go in

for a drink. She didn't resist. Her spirit was drained. She wa
exhausted, he realized, and far too vulnerable to deal wit
what he'd said.

The cocktail lounge was dark. Most of the tables wer
taken by reporters, tech-reps, embassy people, French entre
preneurs and well-to-do Vietnamese. As they took places at
small table, Michael realized that Inge Holz, even gaunt an
weary, was more beautiful than any woman there. He felt i
at ease suddenly, as if he had no right to be in such a plac
with her.

They ordered whiskey and waited for it to be served.

Michael said softly, "I was out of line. I shouldn't hav
said that. I know from nothing."

"You know more than I think." She shrugged. "We hav
been . . ." She didn't finish the sentence. What was sh
going to say? Lovers? Discreet? Fools?

"I know how hard it is," he said, "to love someon
impossibly." His thoughts flew to Carolyn.

Her eyes were lit with feeling when she said in a voice h
could barely hear, "It is not impossible."

"Of course it is."

"Then that is because of the war."

"No, the war is what has enabled you to find each other."

After a long moment her eyes went to his and she asked
"Have you loved a woman?"

"Yes," he replied simply.

She looked away from him, tears spilling over her cheeks
She said, "For long I have wanted to talk to someone. I lov
him."

"I know."

"Is that wrong? Is that sinful?"

Michael knew what he'd been trained to answer, wha
Fitzmaurice, Spellman and even O'Shea would have answered
An absolute answer, arrived at absolutely, without hesitation
And he knew what the circumstances of his own decision t
be a priest and his determination to remain one required hin
to answer too. The same thing.

Wrong? Sinful? Those words he applied at last to the war
But the war—ah, there was a moral dilemma, conundrum
tragic problem! Michael knew that the chaplains and bishops

having considered the war from across an infinite stretch of
the ambiguous, had disqualified themselves from passing judgment because military matters were not in the area of their
competence. But was love?

"You love a man," he said. "How can that be anything in
God's eyes but glorious?"

TWENTY-FIVE

"**M**Y darling Carolyn," I said, and at last she looked at me.

"Oh, Durk, I'm dying."

"But not today." I touched her cheek. Even in the fickle light of the baptistry I saw how tan she was, how beautiful. Her face was distorted, though, with feeling. We had been holding each other for a long time. The Vietnamese girl had disappeared from the shadows, and I wondered, Was she there at all? Had I invented her? "Was that your daughter?"

She looked where I was looking, at no one, but she nodded. "Yes, Thuy Thien."

"She is lovely."

"She is heartbroken." Carolyn fell against me once more. "So am I, oh, so am I."

My eye drifted to the coffin, stark and brutal box. Beyond it in the stone wall were bronze plaques, and I realized with a shudder that they marked niches for cineary urns. That was the columbarium, the vault of the dead, and it seemed suddenly so foreign, so unnatural, so Protestant—until the Renewal, Catholics were forbidden cremation—that I wondered again at Michael's being there. But was he really? I looked at the coffin once more. It holds him, I told myself, but didn't believe it. Still, I wanted to get away. Michael Maguire had been more alive than anyone I knew. If he could die, then who or what couldn't? Could the very earth live? Could God? It was a surprise to learn that for all my years, for all my books, for my eternity in the tomb of the monastery, I did not believe in death. I had been assuming like a twelve-year-old that we and the ones we love live forever. I squeezed my eyes against the truth, touched my face to Carolyn's hair. I inhaled her. "Should we go outside," I asked, "where we can talk?"

She pulled back to look at me and I was afraid her steady gaze meant she was offended. Would she drag me to the coffin, lift its lid and make me look at him? No. She nodded.

I led her by the hand, out into the ambulatory and back around the curving, becolumned passageway. And suddenly I was leading her by the hand in a different darkness. Where? What was that sound? A name? A word? A moan? It was waves breaking. It was night. We were walking along the beach at Lake George. I had escaped Saint John the Divine once more in memory. The lake's calm inland surface had been transformed by the wind. It seemed to be a bay of the Atlantic, and in the darkness the water might have stretched for three thousand miles, instead of merely three. The imported sand underfoot was difficult to walk in, made us feel drunk. The house of our friends was behind the trees. We had come out, we'd said, for air. But in fact the endless Scrabble game had bored us.

The wind whipped at our clothes. Carolyn was wearing loose white cotton bell-bottoms and a white Mexican wedding shirt. She was a summer night vision, and what light there was—the moon had set but the stars were brilliant—seemed drawn to her. When we were down the beach, utterly alone, we stopped, wordlessly, as if we'd planned to, and embraced. Her tongue was in my mouth. My hands were on the blades of her back, pressing her against me. Her hands were at my belt. And then in seconds we were naked and on the sand. I was between her thighs, moistening her with my tongue. Then I was on her. She had my prick in her hands and was taking me in. And I was crying out, Oh, God, and trying to raise my head away from her, arching involuntarily, but she was holding me, my face by her face, and as she pumped back at me, swiveling, she breathed in audibly, endlessly. When at last she exhaled, the air was a word, a whisper alive in my inner ear, as if already it had entered my body through my skin.

"Durk!" she said. But it was more than my name. It was a plea, a summons, an expression of pain that I never forgot.

"Durk! Durk!" For once passion seemed to have taken over her. "I do love you!" she said, but what I heard was her emphasis; I *do* love you! As if someone had said she didn't. As if *she* had.

Michael was assigned to duties at Saint Joseph of Arimathea in Alna, a village just north of Newburgh, about a mile west of the Hudson. He was solemnly forbidden to preach or teach anything having to do with Vietnam, but that was no problem in that parish where the pressing issues had been keeping the school open and the people closed. If he participated in antiwar activities in any way, his priestly faculties would be suspended. When this was spelled out to him upon his return that summer from Vietnam, he found it impossible to respond. Something like this had happened to him before when Spellman had coopted him with the Relief Fund job. But this was not sweet persuasion. He was not given a choice this time, and frankly the old pull of priestly obedience seemed less like oppression than rescue. Once more the refuge of certitude and exemption was being offered him, no, forced on him. But now, exhausted and emotionally spent after the events in Vietnam—after seeing the hopelessness of things there—he did not reject that refuge but welcomed it. His one request was to speak in person to Cardinal Spellman. It was refused. Spellman would not see him. The cardinal, the chancellor said, would like never to lay eyes on him again. And he might not have, except for Nicholas Wiley.

But it was a while before Nicholas came back into his life. By then, Michael had grown almost accustomed to the quotidian pastoral life of Saint Joseph's. No big crises, no acts of violence, no napalm; just the early-morning Mass, offered quietly for a few old ladies before dawn; at breakfast he exchanged banalities with his fellow priests and wasn't even tempted to read the papers, as in the evening he wouldn't be tempted to watch the news on television. The world beyond Alna became less and less important as he gave himself to the oddly fulfilling tasks of parish ministry. Instead of the wounded children in primitive hospitals, there were the shy teenagers in his Religion Class. Michael taught them to feel better about themselves. Instead of frantic trekking around Vietnam, there were afternoon games of pick-up at the high school, where boys imitated Michael's slow, loose-wristed jump shot. It wasn't long before Michael was the one they came to with their problems. Instead of terrified refugees, there were addled old people in the local nursing home. Michael talked to them about the Resurrection of the Dead, and if they wanted him to he would, yes, describe heaven to them, golden boulevards, becolumned mansions and all. Instead of demonstrations in the streets of Saigon, there were wakes in the evening at which he lead the rosary or meetings of the Holy Name Society to which each month more and more of the parish men came. But always, rooting him, giving him such solace, such nurture, such pleasure, the priest's version of love-making, were those quiet early Masses, the sharp smell of candles instead of tear gas, the taste of oversweet altar wine instead of fear, and the palpable sense of God's nearness instead of loneliness. His *memento*, still, was for peace, and he always mentioned by name Suu Van Pham and Inge Holz in the prayer for the living, but the war in Vietnam was in another world than his. At Saint Joseph of Arimathea's, in other words, for the better part of a year, Michael Maguire had been condemned to the life of a small town parish priest. The truth was he loved it.

The surprise was, when Wiley showed up, Michael did not feel ashamed.

It was March of 1966. Michael was improvising a system of supports for the star magnolia that he had planted in the churchyard the previous autumn. The tree was one of his first attempts to brighten the place, but the winter had savaged it and it seemed unlikely that spring would revive it. The other priests, the pastor and the first curate, were old men who'd lost their battles years before, and the backwater church of Saint Joseph's, the emblem of their defeat, had taken on their slouch. Michael had planted several trees right away and the beginnings of a rose garden. By Christmas he had organized teenagers to paint the parish hall. This spring he'd already recruited local masons to point the brick facade of the church itself, and he was planning to turn the entire neglected churchyard into a garden. But now he wondered, Was it futile?

"Sad-looking tree," Nicholas Wiley said from behind Michael. "How'd you expect it to survive in this fresh air?"

Michael turned slowly.

The sight of Nicholas Wiley, now wearing a colorful headband and hair to his shoulders and a full beard, threw him. He had never expected to see Wiley again, as if in Alna he'd entered a world to which the likes of this by now full-blown hippie would not be admitted. In a way it was true. Wiley looked like the young people who had staked their claim to the Bancroft Fountain in Central Park. In the city his get-up was as ordinary as the business suits of lawyers, but in the churchyard of a conservative town, it seemed provocative, inflammatory. Michael himself had to stifle an instinctive repugnance at his appearance. But, when he did, when he actually looked at Nicholas Wiley then, he saw that in his own way he looked good. He looked like what he was.

He looked, of course, like Jesus. Remember how for a time America was populated with young Saviors?

Michael dropped his pliers and crossed the lawn, grinning. "You son of a gun," he said.

Nicholas Wiley opened his arms wide. Remember how men began to embrace each other that year?

Michael felt a surge of guilt as they hugged roughly, half-fighting, not about his life at Saint Joseph's but about having left it to Wiley to come to him. When he'd returned to New York he'd written to him, but the short note came back undelivered and Michael hadn't pursued it. Nicholas Wiley was part of what he'd all too willingly left behind. Already Michael's years in Vietnam had receded into the haze of memory. His sharp outrage, his intensely felt compassion for the children, his attachments to the Vietnamese he'd met were like items of contraband he had handed over to stern Customs agents upon his return. He had done it in the name of faithfulness. That irony—that he had broken faith while keeping faith—confused him. Of course he had to shut it out, along with all his feelings and convictions. The conflict implicit in his position was impossible. There could be no such thing as a defiant priest. And so, of course, he'd taken refuge in his belief that the benefit of the doubt, for priests as for married people, had always to go not to intense present feeling but to the solemn promise around which one's life was built.

"You son of a gun," he said again.

"I'd rather you called me a son of a bitch."

Michael pulled back to hold him by the shoulders, expecting to see him grinning. But he wasn't. He'd made the comment earnestly—I'm no son of a weapon—and that was Michael's first warning. "Okay, you're a son of a bitch." Michael tapped his chin. "And it's great to see you."

"It's good to see you too."

"Thanks."

"You're welcome." Now Wiley grinned, but strangely. They separated. Wiley looked around awkwardly. "Nice garden."

Michael looked at the budding trees, the grass with its first splash of green. Mulch still protected the new flower beds and burlap sacks still covered the infant boxwoods. "This is nothing. Come back in a month."

"I don't know if I'll be able to," Wiley said with abrupt solemnity.

"Why not?"

"That's what I came to talk about."

The peace movement with its full-page ads in the *Times*, its teach-ins, marches and draftcard burnings was just picking up steam that spring, and Michael was certain Wiley had come to ask him to join it. He hadn't considered that Wiley might have come to him for help. He chided himself. There was more on this young man's mind than what Michael Maguire did or didn't do to sublimate his guilt and loneliness. He studied him for a moment and read, now that he bothered to try, the signs of his pitched anxiety. Nicholas's beard obscured the facts that he'd lost weight and that his skin had a gray pallor to it. His eyes were unfocused and bloodshot. Where once only his thumbs were gnawed, now all of his fingernails had been chewed to the quick. "Come on inside," he said.

"I'd rather stay out here." Wiley looked nervously toward the grim rectory. "Could we just go for a walk or something?"

"Sure." Michael led the way. Soon they were on an unpaved lane that went up Rattlesnake Mountain, the hill at the base of which the town nestled. Neither spoke until they came to a bright meadow around a house-sized boulder. Michael scurried to the top of it, then reached back to help Nicholas up. When they were sitting, the stone cold beneath them, Michael said, "I come here to think my best thoughts."

"You're going to need them."

"Why?"

"Because I want you to tell me what to do."

"What's up?"

Wiley looked at him strangely. "You know what's up."

"No, I don't."

Nicholas pulled a creased news photo from his canvas bag. He handed it to Michael. It wasn't a picture of a child now, though, but of a Buddhist pagoda in flames. In the foreground, helmeted Vietnamese Rangers were clubbing an aged monk. It was all too familiar. The Buddhist Struggle had resumed as the war had worsened and become Americanized. The cities of South Vietnam were paralyzed daily by thousands of chanting, frenzied demonstrators. There were reports that taxi drivers and shopkeepers were shaving their heads and dressing as monks to replace those who'd been arrested. It was yet to be seen whether Ky and Thieu would be any more effective against them—though they were equally brutal—than Diem had been.

Michael folded the photograph and handed it back to Wiley. "What does it mean to you?" he asked somewhat rigidly. He resolved to keep his own reaction at arm's length until he knew what Wiley wanted.

"Just that we're back where we started three years ago. Catholic government against Buddhist people. Only now the government has three hundred thousand American mercenaries and bombers galore. They're using B-52s now."

Michael hadn't known that. B-52s? Was he so out of touch?

Nicholas shook his head. "The Buddhists don't hope to change their government anymore, you know. They're trying to change us. They know that we're the ones who have to stop the war. We're the ones who pay for it. You and I are the ones who let it happen. And it just keeps getting worse."

Michael said nothing.

Wiley looked sharply at him. "Didn't you learn anything over there?"

Michael felt the blast of the young man's disappointment—it was there after all—and tried to deflect it. "I learned always to put my chopsticks into the hot rice as soon as it was served. It was the only way to sterilize them."

"Is that what you worried about? Germs?"

Michael shook his head, but of course he had worried about germs.

"You were going to save the children! You were going to make the army take care of the wounded!"

"I was naive, Nicholas. I was wrong. You were right. The only thing to be done about the war is to stop it."

"Well, what are you doing here then?"

"I'd convinced myself that you didn't come here to guilt-trip me. You didn't come here to talk about my life; you came to talk about yours. What's going on?"

"I'm pulling out."

"What do you mean?"

"I'm going to serve the people."

"What do you mean, Nicholas? You sound like Chairman Mao." Michael waited for him to answer, but he didn't. The war had obviously possessed him, as surely as some devil, and now Michael could only try to imagine what he was contemplating.

"I have to volunteer," he said at last. "I have to cut my hair and shave and sign up."

What, the army? Did he intend to go in as a medic or something? But the army wouldn't let him within a mile of itself. Was he thinking of going to Asia with a volunteer agency? Michael knew what that impulse was like, and how futile it would be. For Nicholas it would be dangerous. "What do you mean?" he asked again.

"I have been conscripted and I have to go."

"I want to understand what you mean, Nicholas. Help me to understand."

"Is that all you can say?" He clambered to his feet. "What do I mean? What do I mean?" He raised his arms to the sky melodramatically and threw his head back. His hair rained down like an Indian's, like a prophet's. "How the hell do I know what I mean? The fucking war has got to stop! That's what I mean! The American people have got to stop it! The Catholic Church has got to stop it! 'War no more! War never again!' The pope said that! The *pope* said that!'' he began screeching wildly. ''Peace now! Peace now!''

Michael stood quickly. Balance was precarious on the boulder. Before Wiley could fall, Michael grabbed him and held him. The young man deflated and shrunk, falling against Michael who sensed in him an infinite relief. Nicholas began to sob. Michael remembered Inge Holz: Is this wrong? Is it sinful? Am I insane? And he had the same reaction. Was it mere rhetoric, a deflection of his own sense of responsibility for what Wiley had become? Perhaps. But he felt it nevertheless. The madness was not in this boy, but in the war.

Michael knew from his own experience that what Nicholas Wiley needed was some ordinary living, a taste of the pleasures and duties of work and friendship, a spell in the realm of the utterly unnewsworthy where alone he could be safe from the ravaging News. Death held sway over the world, after all; life over only the smallest pieces of it. Over little places like Alna and Saint Joseph's. From what Michael learned on their subsequent walks, Nicholas had become less and less connected in New York. After leaving the *Catholic Worker* he'd attached himself to a settlement house in Harlem for a time, had written for a Quaker magazine, had joined, then quit, the Newman Club at NYU in the Village. He attended demonstrations and had gone to Washington twice, once as part of a group of Quakers who held a vigil outside the Capitol while Congress debated—and passed—a special four-billion-dollar appropriation for the war. It was then he'd begun to fast, and he hadn't eaten right since. Despite all this, his part in the peace movement remained tangential. He'd made no close friends. He was no longer in touch with his family, and along the way he'd stopped seeing his therapist. So Michael offered him a job as his helper in the garden at Saint Joseph's and convinced him to take it. Surely he'd tracked Michael down hoping for such an intervention, even if he couldn't admit that to himself.

Behind the sacristy there was a room with a cot where

Nicholas slept, and he stayed through the spring. At first he was too depressed to express much in the way of gratitude, but that was the last thing Michael required of him. At times he was downright sullen and at other times, often after watching the nightly news in Michael's room, he was hysterical about the killing in Vietnam. But Michael stayed at him. There was no question now of arguing about the peace movement. All Michael wanted to do was help restore the equilibrium Nicholas needed to deal with his experience creatively. Eventually Nicholas began to respond. The rectory housekeeper treated him like the son she wanted, and the hard physical work gave him an appetite for her plain food. He gained weight and a bright sunburn replaced his pallor. Even the pastor softened toward him and said that if he'd shave his beard and cut his hair, he could start taking up the collection at Mass. Nicholas refused, of course, but politely, though to Michael he joked that he was tempted because he could have used the extra income.

One morning, while Michael was taking his vestments off after Mass, Nicholas came into the sacristy from the garden. He wore an expression of pure joy and he said, "Father, you've got to come outside."

Michael followed him.

Nicholas led the way to the star magnolia and with a ringmaster's panache he stepped aside and swept his arm toward the tree's first-ever flower. "I said to the magnolia, 'Sister, speak to me of God,' and the magnolia blossomed." Wiley grinned as he watched Michael approach the branch and put his nose to the flower. "Isn't it great?" Wiley asked. "Isn't it just so great!"

It was the boy who seemed great to Michael; there was such happiness in him. Michael grinned too and said, "And this is just the beginning, Nicholas. You'll have flowers coming up all over the place before you're done."

Wiley nodded. "I think you're right, Michael. I think you're right."

"Hey, guess what?"

"What?"

"You just called me Michael."

"I did?" Wiley leaned toward him, showing his amazement.

"Just now."

"God, I never thought I'd be able to."

Michael felt as though he'd won something, a prize, an important medal. What a strange effect the use of his own name could have on him. "I knew you would, Nicholas."

"Does that mean . . . ?" He hesitated, looked down shyly, blushing.

"It means we're really friends now, Nicholas."

Nicholas looked up at him, tears brimming, relief extravagantly on his face. "Thank you, Michael. Thank you."

Michael shook his head, implying, I should thank you. He struck a pose and recited, "I said to Nicholas Wiley, 'Brother, speak to me of God,' and he called me Michael."

It was absurd, such a small thing, such happiness from it. But they both felt it. They embraced in their rough, athletic way, and they laughed and laughed.

A few days later Michael was going into Manhattan for a clergy meeting and he thought Nicholas might enjoy some time in the city too. But Nicholas didn't show for breakfast. Michael went looking for him. He knocked on the door of the little room behind the sacristy, but there was no answer. He's still asleep, Michael thought, and he opened the door quietly. But Nicholas's bed was neatly made already, army corners and all. He'd gone into Alna probably. Too bad. Michael couldn't wait. He'd have enjoyed the company. He was about to close the door when something caught his eye on Nicholas's table, a copy of the *New York Times*. That was unusual enough, since Nicholas didn't read the paper either, but in that first glance, the front page seemed wrong. Then Michael realized there was a hole in it, something had been clipped, and a clothing ad was showing through from page three. Michael wondered about it, but not for long.

The clergy meeting was at Holy Trinity in Greenwich Village and lasted through lunch. Michael enjoyed the company of priests his own age and was reluctant to return to Alna, but the other priests scattered when the meeting ended. They were big city men and all had their appointments. So Michael decided to take a long walk. It was a beautiful May day. Washington Square was full of painted hippies wading in the fountains, tossing Frisbees, passing marijuana, playing guitars. A pretty girl with hair to her waist was sitting in the grass breast-feeding her baby while her young beau serenaded them on his flute. New York, especially after Alna, seemed charmed, and he wished Nicholas had come with him. For a moment he wondered again where the kid had gone off to so early.

By midafternoon, Michael found himself at Saint Patrick's and he went in to kneel and pray while the tourists gawked and the shoppers, rattling their bags, sat and rested. He loved the place. He couldn't go there without remembering his ordination or reclaiming that sense of hope he'd felt, that sense of God's kindly touch. He knelt for a long time, offering his gratitude, his relief. He was the man, at last, he'd wanted to become.

When he came out into the bright glare he stood at the top step of the cathedral and watched the traffic of Fifth Avenue, the fancy cars and the tricked-out secretaries on their breaks, the most beautiful girls in the world. He thought of Jesus watching the gold-laden caravans from the pinnacle of the Temple. "All this I will give you," the devil had said, "if you will worship me." Michael knew for the first time why Jesus had said no. He didn't need the gold or the cars or the stunning girls. He had everything he wanted.

As he walked down the stairs he saw a group of cops on the corner near a newsstand. One of them looked toward him, and something in the man's eyes drew Michael. There were five of them, and they were craned toward a nearby motorcycle's radio.

As he walked toward them he passed the newsstand, and had to step around a stack of papers, that day's *Times*.

"What's up, fellows?" he asked.

"Hey, Father, you won't believe this one."

"What?" He cocked an ear toward the police radio, but it was all static. He let his eye fall to the newspapers. On the front page was a photograph of a Buddhist monk seated in the lotus position on a Saigon street, and he was aflame.

"Some guy," the policeman said, "over at the U.N. douses himself with gasoline and lights a match. Some peacenik kook."

Michael reeled, exactly as if that cop had jammed his

nightstick into his stomach. As if he'd brought it crashing down onto his skull. No. The cops were so surprised they didn't catch him when he fell.

Nicholas Wiley died that night in the burn unit at Bellevue. Michael was with him. Nicholas never regained consciousness, and when Michael anointed him there was no place he could touch him with the sacred oil that wasn't burned. He bent over him and began to whisper into the charred hole that had been his ear the words of the Act of Contrition. "O my God, I am heartily sorry for having offended Thee . . ." Standard procedure. The idea was that the unconscious person might somehow register what was being said and assent to it.

But Michael was unable to finish the recitation. He began to sob. He wanted to rest his head on Nicholas's chest, even that scorched chest, but he was afraid to touch him for fear of causing pain. The stench of burned flesh was familiar. All too fucking familiar.

Michael began to whisper again when he could, but instead of the Act of Contrition he said simply, over and over, "I'm sorry. I'm sorry. I'm sorry."

Reporters were waiting for him outside the ward. Michael was stunned by their assumption that they had the right to question him.

"Was he your protégé?"

"What?" Michael had trouble focusing on the reporter who'd asked the question. There were a dozen or more, men and women, and some had thrust microphones at him.

"He was your employee?"

"He was my friend," Michael said, and he pushed through them.

"Dorothy Day says he was not a Catholic Worker, the Quakers say he was not a member of any meeting, and the archdiocese says they had no record of him on the Church payroll. Was he connected with your parish or not?"

Michael ignored the question. When a reporter grabbed his arm Michael pushed him roughly aside.

"The cardinal said if he was a Catholic, he's excommunicated."

"What?" Michael stopped and faced the man who'd said that.

"Because it's suicide," the reporter added.

"Suicide?" Michael glared at him.

"He burned himself to death, right?"

"When did the cardinal say that?"

"Shortly after the hospital pronounced the kid dead." The man referred to his notes. "He said, '. . . the Church condemns suicide. Anyone who commits it forfeits the right to a Church burial.' "

"He said that?"

"Well, that's the statement they issued at the chancery. His name was on it."

It was as if a pair of mailed hands reached into Michael's chest and tore his lungs out. He said, "I haven't spoken to the cardinal. I don't expect to. I will speak to Nicholas Wiley's parents, and, if they agree, he will have a Roman Catholic burial at Saint Joseph of Arimathea Church in Alna, New York. We will pray for the repose of his soul."

"You don't condemn suicide?"

A flashbulb went off in Michael's face. He was blind for a moment.

He said, "Nicholas Wiley is a martyr. He is at peace with God. What I condemn is the war in Vietnam, and that is what the cardinal should be condemning too."

The next day Cardinal Spellman summoned Michael to his office.

He had not been in his office since the time nearly three years before when Michael had gone to him upon his first return from Vietnam. Since then, it seemed to Michael, the pin had been removed from the center of the world itself. Everything was out of kilter now. He had only one certainty as he entered the cardinal's residence, that Nicholas Wiley was going to be buried in Church.

The woman at the typewriter in the room off the entrance hall knew who he was this time. His photograph had been in all the New York papers that morning. A tourist's photograph of Nicholas Wiley in flames had been on the front page of every major newspaper in America.

"Father Maguire is here," she said into her phone.

Monsignor Dugan was waiting for him when the elevator doors opened on the second floor. He followed Michael down the hallway to the cardinal's office.

As before, Spellman was sitting at his desk, back to the window, waiting for him when he entered. Spellman did not stand. He needed the desk this time, against this man.

Dugan ushered Michael to the wing chair. Michael took it. Dugan took his place at the large Catalonian table, opened a folder and uncapped his pen.

The cardinal spoke then and his voice was steely. "You have contradicted me publicly on a grave matter of faith and morals. You have disobeyed my explicit order regarding use of the public forum. You are hereby suspended of all priestly faculties. You are not to preach, administer the sacraments, or celebrate the Holy Eucharist."

Michael did not blink. "Your Eminence, I am going to preside at the funeral of Nicholas Wiley at Saint Joseph's. After that I will obey you."

Spellman's face reddened. "You are no longer assigned to Saint Joseph's. You are now assigned to the North American College in Rome where for two years you are to pursue the Licentiate in Sacred Theology. Obviously you did not learn your lessons well enough the first time."

Michael stood. "I respectfully submit, Your Eminence, that there is little point in continuing this. I will leave Saint Joseph's when Nicholas Wiley has been buried there. I will stop preaching and go to Rome when the war in Vietnam is over."

"Consider carefully what you are saying, Father."

"I've considered it for three years, Your Eminence." Michael towered over him. The cardinal seemed small and weary. He had been defeated by the very thing—American Catholic triumph—to which he'd given the best energy of his life. It seemed no surprise at all to discover that this frightened old man could do nothing to punish Michael and nothing to stop him. Nor could Michael want to punish Spellman by denouncing that war as a monument to the man's vanity. He clung to what mattered. "I feel bound in conscience to complete my ministry to Nicholas Wiley. I cannot abandon him, not even to keep my vow to you. I wasn't with him when he needed me most, but I'm with him now."

"But you cannot have a Mass at Saint Joseph's. I will not permit it."

"Then I will do it in Central Park. Is that what you prefer? I have no intention of turning Nicholas Wiley's death into a protest rally." Michael leaned over Spellman's desk, put his hands upon it. He stared at the prelate with cold, threatening eyes and he said, "But if you refuse me access to the small church to which he devoted the last efforts of his life, that's exactly what it will become. And you will have to answer for it, to newspapers, to television, to Rome and to God." Michael straightened abruptly, and his arm shot out, his finger stabbed toward Spellman. "Believe me, Cardinal, you will have to answer."

Spellman could hardly bring himself to speak. He opened his mouth and closed it. He shook his head. Finally he said, "But we are talking about Church law! This is not a matter of my will, Father, or of yours. This is not a matter of individual conscience. You are a priest!" He gestured with both his fists at Michael. "You must condemn the sacrilege of suicide!"

"I will not!" Michael shot back. Now anger choked him too. But he reined it. "Church law on the matter of the burial of the dead—any dead—leaves room for pastoral discretion, Your Eminence. If you don't know that you should. Ask Monsignor Dugan." Michael looked back at the other prelate, who refused to raise his eyes from his notepad. He was a canon lawyer and knew that Michael was right. Michael faced Spellman again. "By your statements you have made the issue that young man's rejection of the war. You have made the issue his standing as a Catholic. You have made the issue your authority. And I am telling you—as I will tell anyone who asks—that in the matter of Nicholas Wiley I refuse to be bound by your authority. The issue is his right to a loving gesture from the Church, and he will have it. Beyond that, I refuse to yield to you in anything related to this evil war."

Cardinal Spellman's lips moved soundlessly around the only words he could think to say: "Get out!"

Michael nodded, a vestige of respect, and left.

Early the next day he prayed the Mass for the Dead, quietly, without music, in the Church of Saint Joseph of Arimathea. In front of him was the pine box containing Nicholas Wiley's remains. Michael had not made the time of the service public, but he'd notified those whom he hoped would come. Very few did. Not Nicholas's parents, not his therapist. No one from the Newman Club at NYU; the chaplain was on retreat. A seminarian and two women from the *Catholic Worker* were there, although not Dorothy Day, who would later bristle when Thomas Merton himself wrote that something was wrong with a movement that led people to kill themselves. Two Quakers with whom Nicholas had worked for a short time were there, and so was the rectory housekeeper.

Michael reminded them, as he threw the first handful of dirt onto Wiley's coffin in the parish cemetery, that Saint Joseph of Arimathea was the stranger who'd taken the body of Jesus from the cross when none of His friends would claim it. He had placed it in his own tomb.

The stone now with which to seal such a hole was in Michael's heart.

TWENTY-SIX

CARDINAL Spellman died in the last month of 1967. In his final Christmas sermon to thousands of American soldiers at Cam Ranh Bay the year before he had christened their efforts as "a war for civilization." He had said that the peace America sought could be had only through "total victory." The troops cheered him, but their applause was far from enough by then. He would return home to a people he had embarrassed, and the Holy Father himself would make clear his displeasure at what was less "faith and morals" than rank jingoism. Even Cardinal Spellman knew that he had outlived values and modes that once he had thought were absolute. His physical death was only the last of many deaths he suffered toward the end, but even so, to others it was a shock. The cardinal? Dead? As if the structures of his Church, his country and his war could not stand without his support, they immediately began to rock like runaway scaffolding in the winds of that typhoon of years, 1968.

First, in January, Tet, that decisive defeat of the Communists in Vietnam that, in the mad logic of that war, assured their victory. Then, little more than a month later, the political defeat of an upstart senator by the president in the New Hampshire primary (the president won 48 percent to Eugene McCarthy's 42 percent) that, in the same logic, sealed the defeat of LBJ and led to his withdrawal from the race. A few weeks later, in the same month, Lieutenant Calley presided over the slaughter of several hundred civilians at My Lai. Some Americans, when they learned of it a year later, would not understand the fuss, and they would be right. Calley was a victim of the army's pretense that what he did was different.

Then on a bright April day a new archbishop of New York and Vicar of the American Military was installed at Saint Patrick's Cathedral, an unoffensive Irishman named Terence Cooke whose first words from the episcopal throne were addressed to Lyndon Johnson, sitting in the front row. He thanked the president for coming and commended him warmly for his valiant search for peace in Vietnam, a search which by then was being conducted by 549,000 U.S. soldiers, none of whom could find it and many of whom, even if they lived, would never have it again. Johnson liked Catholics a lot better now than he had as a boy in Texas, for they were his diehard backers. Demonstrations of the sort paralyzing hundreds of other colleges that spring weren't tolerated on Catholic campuses, and the students weren't inclined to have them anyway. Furthermore, the Catholic bishops issued a rare formal statement about the war. Applying the principles of Vatican II and the classic moral theory of the Scholastic tradition, though not the urgent pronouncements of Pope Paul VI, they said, "It is reasonable to argue that our presence in Vietnam is justified."

No one noticed how cozy Archbishop Cooke and President Johnson were that day, however, because a few hours after the ceremony at Saint Patrick's, James Earl Ray shot and killed the clergyman who had most resolutely condemned the war. In the days and weeks following Dr. King's death, black Americans in a dozen cities set fire to their own neighborhoods. Hardly anyone noticed. But at the end of the month when students took over Columbia before going on vacation, the nation was stunned.

In France, too, the young revolted—one resists saying they were revolting—while in Germany a punk named Andreas Baader committed his first act of arson, and in Northern Ireland Catholics took to the streets for the first time in years, not dreaming how much worse their lives could get. In June, Vietnam became the longest war in U.S. history, and a lunatic Arab saw to it that the war would be as long again still when he murdered the leader of those who opposed it. Robert Kennedy was buried from Saint Patrick's Cathedral, and with him was buried any hope not only for a prompt end to the killing, but for a return to our simple faith in the goodness of our government. Carolyn and I kept the vigil on Fifth Avenue with a million others. On our radios we heard Andy Williams begin the ''Battle Hymn of the Republic.'' A news bulletin reported that the three-month-old siege of Khe Sanh was lifted that day. The marines had held. ''Mine eyes have seen the glory. . .'' What should have felt like victory in that war was always more like defeat. All we could do was hold each other and sing.

In July Catholics who'd thought their Church had changed were jolted by the papal encyclical, *Humanae Vitae*, forbidding all forms of birth control except abstinence and rhythm. Well, it *had* changed because immediately thousands of Catholic priests in Europe and America publicly rejected the pope's authority in the matter. Bishops on the other hand, who had found it possible the year before to ignore Paul's radical criticisms of capitalism, private property and the profit motive in *Progressio Populorum*, now fell in behind His Holiness with a vengeance. When the large majority of seminarians signed a dissenting letter in Boston, Cardinal Cushing fired them without discussion. In Los Angeles Cardinal MacIntyre forced his clergy to take a solemn oath of fealty, and in Washington Cardinal O'Boyle imposed an oath of his own and suspended more than forty of his priests for refusing to take it. Many priests didn't wait to be suspended. In large numbers—tens of thousands eventually—they began to resign their ministry altogether. Meanwhile millions of Catholic lay men and women who had long since decided for themselves in the matter of contraception regarded the squabbling of celibates over other people's sex lives with distaste and a kind of embarrassed pity. So much for the triumph of American Catholicism.

In August the police—Catholics again—rioted in Chicago and the Russians sent tanks into Prague. The first event guaranteed the defeat of the Democratic candidate and the second meant that the Republican candidate—or so he said—could not reveal his secret plan for ending the war. In China the Red Guard had begun their rampage, but we didn't care about China yet.

In October Jacqueline Kennedy married Aristotle Onassis, a divorced man. The Vatican newspaper called her "a public sinner." But now even cardinals began to dissent—authority was in shambles everywhere—when Cushing of Boston countered, "Leave the poor woman alone."

November gave us Nixon.

On December 10 Thomas Merton, with whom we began, having left his Kentucky monastery for the first time in over twenty years, was in Bangkok for a meeting of Zen and Christian monks and masters, an effort toward East-West reconciliation. He was electrocuted while trying to plug in a fan. By now even the most benign American contact with Southeast Asia seemed dangerous, tragic, violent and absurd.

And on Christmas Eve, the last week of the year, the American military elite, our astronauts, preached the homily from the moon. "In the beginning God created the heaven and the earth," one of them read, looking back at us, a blue ball hanging in nothing. "And the earth was without form, and void; and darkness was upon the face of the deep."

Some people were undone by that string of jolts and others were made by it, their energies focused and the essentials of their lives revealed. Michael was one of these, though perhaps he would not have been, frankly, but for me and Carolyn.

After leaving Saint Joseph's, he'd lived with us in Brooklyn. The suspension of his faculties as a priest disoriented him, and he turned to us for the support and friendship he was not getting from his fellow clergy. Oh, there were always a few renegade Jesuits hanging around, junior editors from *America* or young faculty and graduate students whom I'd bring over from Fordham thinking the clerical company would cheer him up. But the radical priests, as Paul Simon called them, were hotshots, hypnotized by their own flamboyance. What seemed to attract them to Michael was his bad standing. The New York press had made much of his conflict with Spellman, and the young antiwar priests and seminarians who sought Michael out seemed to regard such ecclesiastical disapproval as a high achievement. Michael didn't feel that way about it. He was never comfortable with rebels, and he hated it when events made him one.

It was during that time, when he was our guest and before he moved into a small apartment of his own in the East Village, that he and I began to sit up late at night, rediscovering the things that had made us friends. We were both drinking too much, but the booze helped.

During those late-night sessions, Michael talking with an abandon I'd never experienced in him, I first began to perceive the shape of this story. Korea, Lennie Pace, Tim O'Shea, the seminary, the flap with Robert Moses, Vietnam, Spellman, Jack Howe, Nicholas Wiley, Inge Holz and Suu Van Pham. I began to understand what had happened to Michael and why his confrontation with the cardinal, so long postponed, had left him at the mercy of a paralysis of guilt. During that period of his living with us I watched him struggle to fight it off.

One night we were sitting in the living room. Carolyn had gone to bed. Michael and I were sprawled in opposite corners of the same couch because it faced the window that framed the skyline of Manhattan, on which each of us let his eyes play. Surreptitiously I looked at him occasionally. He wore his gauntness more easily by then. His thin, ascetic visage had become the essence of his good looks. I, on the other hand, having quit smoking, had entered a period of overweight. His leanness, like his boldness, represented a kind of rebuke to me. His dark hair was longer than mine, and it made me feel foolish that this priest should have been handsomer, more stylish than I was. I didn't like how he made me feel. Sometimes the silences that fell between us were awkard ones and it had been so repeatedly that night.

"What's wrong, Durk?" he asked at last.

I shook my head. "Nothing's wrong, Michael."

"Have I overstayed my welcome?"

"Hell, no, you kidding?"

"Something's bugging you."

I smiled at him. "There was a time when you'd have let it bug me. You used to believe in holy reticence."

"So anyway . . ."

I worked on my drink for a few minutes and considered whether to say it. Hell, Michael Maguire was a city-wide symbol of integrity. He had his problems with Church authority, and his defiance of it had very nearly derailed him emotionally, but to a lot of the rest of us he'd become the focus of moral opposition to the war. He was already an exemplar. And what did that make me? I was a two-bit professor at a second-rate college, a sometime contributor to small-circulation journals. My professional and even personal concerns, which ordinarily seemed worthy of the best energy of my life, seemed at times like that with Michael, when the silence was on us, utterly trivial. How noble he was! How pure! How unfettered by the banalities of raising a family or earning a living! My job was to correct papers and hire instructors and chair committees and pen scathing insights so that I could pay plumbers and keep my child in barrettes and give my wife the rent money for her studio. Carolyn's work was just being noticed by the midtown galleries. One of my main jobs was to encourage her. I knew what a rare artist she had become. I considered it a privilege to pay her bills. But that was a further clamp on me, wasn't it? And clamps Michael would not have understood. His job, after all, was to speak the truth to power. I forced a smile. "You're a hard act to be in the same ring with, Michael. First a fucking war hero. Now you're threatening to become an antiwar hero. Or is it war antihero?"

"Come off it, Durk. What am I doing? A little draft counseling, what's that?"

"Maybe it's not what you're doing, Michael, but what you *are*. Tell me the truth. You think I'm just a wad of intellectual pretension, don't you?"

"No."

I laughed. "You're just afraid I'll throw you out if you say it."

"I'm not afraid of that. You know how I feel about those diehard resisters, Durk. Come on. They drive me crazy. *They* think you're bourgeois, sure. But I don't. Shit, I'm bourgeois!"

"No, you're not. You're a radical now, Michael, whether you like it or not. And folks like me feel a little uncomfortable around folks like you. A little judged."

"I don't judge you. Who the fuck am I to do that? You know the truth about me."

"What truth?" I stared at him. I was going to make him say it, admit it. Of course I knew.

"That I should have taken on the cardinal seven years ago."

If Carolyn had set herself on fire, I thought, he would have. That I nearly said that revealed to me how drunk I was. I checked myself and forced yet another laugh. "But if you had, then you and Caro would be the couple whom I was visiting. There's the irony, Michael. Is that the regret you feel?"

He shook his head. "What's the point of a regret like that? I'm just saying that I'm not judging anybody. We all have to live with the choices we make, eh?"

"Right. But see, I live with mine, *and* I live with yours. That's all I mean. I build a life that I think is mine, or mine and Carolyn's, or mine and Carolyn's and Molly's, and then, lo and behold, I see that I've built it on a little raft that bobs along in your wake. I'm a raft, Michael, see? And you're a fucking battleship."

He grinned. "But we're in the same bathtub?"

"I guess so."

"I won't be here forever, Durk. I promise."

"That's not what I'm talking about, Michael. If I feel uneasy it has to do with me, not you. I want you here. So does Carolyn. We love you, Michael."

Michael looked away from me, I thought because I'd embarrassed him. But then I realized he was staring at someone. I turned. Carolyn was standing in the doorway, in her bathrobe. Her hair was down to her shoulders. How long had she been there?

"You fellows going for the record?"

"Are we keeping you awake?" Michael asked.

I resented his solicitude. It was easy for him to be gracious because she wasn't his wife. She wasn't the symbol of his domestication. Of course I loved her, and of course I pitied him for not having her, but also—and powerfully at that moment—I hated the feeling of being hemmed in, bound by a hundred responsibilities. Sure, I'd have liked to stop the war. I'd have liked to open myself more fully to the great dramas of the time. But I couldn't and, finally, she was why. I couldn't even shoot the shit with my old buddy. Who the hell was she to sneak up on us? Who the hell was she to criticize our drinking? How I wished, for that moment, to be free of her, of Molly, of my chairmanship, of my house, of my wry, aesthetic, essentially passive sensibility. I wanted to be like Michael: free, pure, simple, direct, alone.

Carolyn shook her head. "Molly was up." She crossed to our couch and sat between us. She rested a hand on each of us.

"The Blessed Trinity," I said, and crossed myself.

Carolyn looked at me with disarming warmth, and I felt guilty for resenting her. "Can I get you a drink?" I asked.

"I'd love some wine."

I stood and started for the kitchen. Michael said, "Bring some bread, would you?"

"Sure."

I didn't think anything of his request. I brought bread and cheese, together with Carolyn's wine. When I'd put the tray on the coffee table Michael said, "Would you guys mind terribly? Praying with me?"

Carolyn and I exchanged a quick glance. The Mass? Bread and wine? Did he mean the Mass?

"Jesus, I'm a little drunk, Michael. So are you."

He sat up and leaned across us, a hand on Carolyn and a hand on me. "You two are so good to me. I love you so much. I never thank you."

"Sure you do," I said, backpedaling. I couldn't handle the confusion of modes. I was a liberal Catholic. My faith was more important to me than ever, and I wasn't cowed by rubrics or regulations. Home liturgies were common among our circle, particularly with Michael as celebrant since he was not allowed to offer Mass publicly, but not in the middle of the night, not as an act of real intimacy, not shorn of everything but a French roll, a glass of muscatel and sentimental blurry-eyed gratitude. Why couldn't he just thank us, kiss us on our cheeks and pass out like other drunks?

But Carolyn said, "That would be nice, Michael."

He took a piece of the bread I'd brought. "Just something simple," he said. He lifted the bread. We all stared at it. After a long silence, a silence that transformed our mood, he spoke softly, naturally, as if to someone who was really there. "Blessed are you, Lord God of the Universe, for through your goodness we have this bread to offer, fruit of the earth and the work of human hands. Let it become for us a spiritual food.'' He paused and looked at each of us. I could feel my reluctance falling away. What was it that drew me in? His intensity, perhaps. His feeling. His, well, holiness. He halved the bread and said, ''He took bread and broke it and gave it to his friends, saying, 'Take this and eat it. This is my body. It will be broken for you.' ''

Then he gave it to us. I ate it and felt as I did a calm come over me. I hadn't known how hungry I was until he fed me.

Carolyn ate and leaned against me. I put my arm around her and felt the relief of one whose only love has returned from a long journey. We watched and listened while Michael blessed the wine. When we drank, the three of us, so quietly, so tenderly, each from the one glass, it was possible to believe that, yes, God was with us.

When Michael first threw himself into work against the war, his purpose was simple and relatively uncontroversial. He was not drawn to street demonstrations or to giving great speeches. He was invited to be on the platform in Washington in October of '67 with Robert Lowell and Norman Mailer, Dr. Spock and William Sloane Coffin, but he refused. He attended the demonstration, but as one of the thousands. Nor was he among those who chose to get arrested at the Pentagon. The self-celebration of the leading resisters made him uneasy. It was to the practical and undramatic activity of draft counseling that he gave almost all of his energy. He spent long hours every day in conversation with young men in a small room in the Protestant chaplain's office at NYU. Ministers, and eventually even priests, from all over the city referred their ''Greetings''-panicked boys to him. In his mind they were a procession of Nicholas Wileys, and if he was compulsively at their service it was only in part to oppose the war. In their trying to decide whether to be objectors or to fake their medicals or to claim to be homosexuals or simply to refuse induction and split, he wanted to give them the support and constructive advice that no one had given Nicholas; that lack, Michael thought, was what had killed him.

He became an expert in the Selective Service laws, which

were toughened several times in that period, and he began to train other draft counselors. As the Justice Department, even under Ramsey Clark, who would come to seem wildly left-wing after John Mitchell, became more aggressive in enforcing draft laws—the army needed more than a million young men in its draft pool now and could not allow the system to break down—Michael became more adept at finding ways to draw out the appeals process and to outflank the VFW fogies who sat on local draftboards. The situation heated up when indictments started coming down not only on the radicals who burned their draftcards and on the ministers, like Coffin, who supported them, but also on kids who, unable to get C.O. status, were laying low, hoping to avoid having to choose between Vietnam and Canada. Pushed by indictments or the threat of them, Canada was it, of course, for thousands, and Michael became part of the network of clergy who helped boys get there. He told me one night that every time he drove back from Montreal he felt he was returning to a damned country that had decided in some perverse, unconscious way to punish itself by banishing the very best of its children.

They were his children, his sons, his Lennies and Nicholases, terrified kids with the balance of their lives in jeopardy. He could not simply watch them, in that primordial image of our generation, falling from the cliff or being pushed from it, from the field of Rye. He had to find a way to catch them. He had to find a way to share their jeopardy and he had to find a way to strike real blows, at last, against the war.

Hence draftboard raids. Hence the destruction of Selective Service files.

It was after midnight, the early hours of December 17, 1968. Merton was dead a week, Bobby Kennedy six months, Spellman a year, JFK and Ngo Dinh Diem five years, and Pope Pius XII ten. Michael and three others, another New York priest and two young Catholic peace workers, were, for their parts, more alive, more alert, more pumped with hunter's nerve than ever. They were inside the federal building in downtown Newark, New Jersey. It had been closed for hours.

The Selective Service office was on the fourth floor, two floors above the office of the U.S. Attorney for Northern

New Jersey. There had been draftboard raids by Catholics in
Baltimore, Catonsville, Milwaukee and the Bronx already,
but this was the first one conducted at night by people who
did not intend to be arrested. It was not their purpose to make
one grand gesture before going to jail. They wanted to do as
much damage to the Selective Service system as they could,
for it had dawned on people by then that it vas the war
machine's one exposed and vulnerable gear. Thousands of
young men in various cities had already been reprieved when
their files were destroyed by having blood or homemade
napalm poured on them, and Michael Maguire and his cocon-
spirators wanted to multiply that number by tens and hundreds.

Michael was the first to leave his hiding place. He had
been huddled since before the building closed in a rarely used
and flimsily locked mop closet in the men's room off the
main post office lobby. Now, following the thin beam of his
flashlight, he crossed that lobby quickly, went into the stairwell and down to the basement snack bar. He rapped on a
storage room door once. The lock was thrown and the door
opened quickly. Father Pete Bryant raised a hand, then
followed. They were both dressed clerically, blacks and collar,
unusual for priests like them by then, but their clothing was
the color of night, and if they were arrested they wanted to be
taken from the start for what they were. They were also
wearing surgical gloves, the clerical dress of burglars.

They went back up the stairs quietly and quickly. On the
second floor were postal offices where clerks worked. Michael knocked once on the ladies' room door. Jerry Dunne
and Joe Reilley had crouched for the hour before the building
closed on the same toilet in a booth they'd marked with an
out-of-order sign. Now they came out promptly, young men
in their mid-twenties. Jerry was a draft counselor whom
Michael knew well, and Joe was his roommate, a math
teacher in a Catholic high school in Queens. Pete Bryant
worked in a parish in Harlem, and he was the one who'd
made the point that by hitting the draftboard in downtown
Newark, it would be young blacks, mainly, whose files the
government would lose. Why should white kids be the only
ones spared a vicious death in Asia?

Another advantage Newark had—the main one—was that

the federal building, like many in the centers of older cities, was not alarmed or guarded at night, and the locks were common ones. Both Bryant and Maguire had learned what they could about picking them and were in fact by then as proficient at it as the average petty burglar. The doors to the offices, also, were paneled in the old-fashioned style, with frosted glass. Jerry Dunne carried tools and suction cups to cut through it if they had to.

They didn't. In minutes they were on the fourth floor and seconds later, having picked a simple tumbler lock—there was a dead-bolt lock that might have stymied them, but the last clerk out had neglected to throw it—they were inside the sprawling, cabinet-lined mammoth room of the Newark Selective Service office. The two younger men had cased the place with visits and they knew what they were after. They led the way to the bank of files where the 1-A forms were stored. Each of the four took a separate cabinet and began to empty its contents into one of the two laundry bags he'd brought; then on to the next cabinet and the next until, within minutes, each man had both his bags stuffed with the papers that identified the thousands of New Jersey boys who were even then in the process of being drafted. Hauling their bags on their shoulders, like Santa's helpers, they left the office. On the glass Michael scrawled with a grease pencil, "Stop the killing! Stop the war!"

The next morning Michael, still dressed as a priest, though now wearing street gloves, went to the *Newark Star-Ledger* and asked the receptionist to take the box he gave her to the city editor. It contained one undamaged Selective Service file from which the draftee's name had been excised, and a plastic bag full of ashes and a letter describing what they'd done. It ended, "If this was Vietnam instead of New Jersey these would be the remains of people instead of paper," and it was signed, "The Catholic Conspiracy to Save Lives."

In the next weeks they took advantage of the Christmas and New Year's lull, which slowed the bureaucracies' ability to respond. Michael, Pete Bryant, Joe Reilley and Jerry Dunne repeated the action in Camden, Albany, Wilmington and Harrisburg. In each case they were able to enter the Selective Service office—in Harrisburg it was only a floor above the

FBI field office—seize the files and get out. Each morning after, Michael presented the ashes of the burned files to a local newspaper or radio or television station. The Catholic Conspiracy to Save Lives was suddenly notorious. In Portland, Oregon, during the night before Richard Nixon's inauguration, another group unknown to Michael raided the Selective Service office in the same way and signed itself, "The West Coast Conspiracy to Save Lives." By the end of January, draftboards in Joliet, Illinois, and San Diego were similarly hit by other groups.

In Washington several things happened. The Selective Service received a special appropriation to begin the immediate microfilm duplication of its records. The General Services Administration issued new guidelines for security in federal buildings and created an emergency fund for twenty-four-hour patrols of buildings housing Selective Service offices. J. Edgar Hoover made the arrest of the draftboard conspirators a top priority for the FBI.

Michael shouldn't have shown himself at the newspapers, perhaps. The FBI had a good description of him and, since his conflict with Spellman and his participation in various demonstrations had been well publicized, he was an obvious suspect. But while his purpose was not to get arrested, neither was it to avoid arrest at all cost or indefinitely. He knew what he was doing. And he knew that if their raids succeeded, the draftboard offices would quickly be made invulnerable anyway to amateurs like him and his friends, both the ones he knew and the ones he didn't.

The FBI, on the other hand, wanted more than Michael. Hoover wanted everyone. Agents were convinced that Michael Maguire was the leader of at least two dozen raiders, and that he had orchestrated the recent burglaries in the Midwest and on the West Coast too. In fact there had already been that many Catholics arrested and freed on bail, and by the end of 1969 forty or fifty more would be. Most of them were priests and nuns, some like Michael in bad standing and some formally defrocked. They participated in draftboard raids not out of subservience to any leader or as part of a centralized organization, but out of subservience to what they'd have described as a vocation to end the war. They were disparate groups, only in the loosest sense conspirators, but they embraced the word *conspiracy* nonetheless. Like true Romans, they loved its Latin etymology, for it means "breathe together." Like true Romans, they liked the draftboard raid for its liturgical simplicity and its moral purity. They were destroying paper to save children.

But governments everywhere fail to understand the spontaneously expressed moral urges of the people. Always governments are fingering agitators and uncovering master plans and tracking down ringleaders. There were a dozen priests like Michael; well known, articulate, charismatic, capable of inspiring boldness in the tame. But the FBI singled him out. Eventually they made him famous. They could simply have arrested him with the evidence they had, and however the trial came out that would almost certainly have ended his aggressive resistance. But, prodded by Hoover and supported fully by the new attorney general, they embarked upon a plan to break the back of what they regarded as the core of the kooky Catholic war resistance.

She came to his office at NYU in early February. Celia Zack, a startlingly pretty Jewish woman in her late twenties. She had lustrous dark hair and eyes dark enough and deep enough to draw anyone in. But her eyes' constant rapid blinking undercut their effect and belied her intelligence, her nerve, and made her seem slightly vacuous. She blinked like that because of her contact lenses.

Michael knew her slightly. She was a board member of RESIST, which had its offices in the same building as his. The antiwar crowd had moved into the religious centers of universities as the alienated kids had moved out. RESIST had sponsored the early draftcard burnings and had more recently focused its efforts on helping draft-dodgers get to Canada. Michael had obtained false papers for a dozen or more of his clients from Celia Zack.

She stood in the doorway of his office.

"Come in," he said.

She shook her head. "Let's go for a walk." She turned the fur collar up on her heavy afghan coat.

When he didn't respond, her eyes went meaningfully to the corners of his ceiling; the room might be bugged.

Michael nodded and got his coat. On their way out he whispered, "You movement heavies flatter yourselves."

It was a brittle day, midmorning, and the only people they passed were walking purposefully, tilted into the cold air.

Celia didn't speak until they'd cut into the park at Washington Square, which was empty even of winos. The fountain in front of the great arch was full of leaves, and on its plaque someone had sprayed, "Ho! Ho! Ho Chi Minh! NLF Is Going To Win!" The trees scratched at the gray sky.

"I know that you're the mystery priest, Michael," Celia Zack said finally.

They kept walking. Michael decided to say nothing.

"Don't you want to know how I know?"

"What's the mystery priest, Celia?"

"Skip it, Michael. Come on. You know what I'm talking about. Newark, Albany, Wilmington, Harrisburg. I suspected you right away. When you weren't around the office I figured there'd be a raid within a few days and there always was."

"Smart. You should be with the FBI."

"I have a proposal to make."

Michael said nothing.

"Well, do you want to hear it or not?"

"Look, Celia, if you have something to say to me, say it." There was something about this woman Michael didn't like. Was it an assumption of superiority? Secular condescension?

"Okay. Let me lay it out for you. I have a friend who works as an office manager at the Selective Service Building on Canal Street. That's the central records depot for the local offices all over the city. It's the largest in the country. It's where the One-A forms are transposed onto IBM, the last step before induction notices are sent out. My friend has helped us a few times by lifting files of particular draft-eligibles and destroying them. It's the best way to beat the system. Without duplicates, it takes them a year to track a kid down again, and then the delay gives him the perfect basis for a complaint in court."

"Why does your friend do that for you?"

"I've been cultivating him for a couple of years."

"What's his name?"

She hesitated, but only for a moment. "Malcolm Dodd. I always thought of him as my trump card, but now he tells me they're going to start microfilming files next week."

"Good things don't last forever."

"And then when I put two and two together about you I realized I'd been thinking much too small. Why not take out all the One-A files for the whole city? We could bring the whole system here to a halt. They'd have to start from scratch."

It was a stunning thought. Michael answered carefully, "How would that work exactly?"

"My friend hands over plans and keys to the offices, codes for the alarm systems, keys and combinations to the cabinets, and the patrol schedule of the night guards. To do the job right would take a lot of people. There are a lot of files."

"And that's why you're talking to me? Because I'm the 'mystery priest'?"

" 'The Catholic Conspiracy to Save Lives,' right?"

"But there are dozens of people in RESIST who'd do it. Why don't you organize them? Imitation, after all, is the sincerest form of flattery."

"I would, but there isn't time. The microfilming will be done in a couple of weeks. An action like this takes discipline obviously, and a group that's been weeded out and tested. A group like yours."

"What do you mean 'cultivating'?" he asked.

"What?"

"You've been 'cultivating' this office manager. How so?"

She shrugged. "I let him fuck me."

Michael looked across the park. No birds, no hippies, no derelicts. "So now we fuck him," he said.

"They probably can't finger him. There are three hundred clerks in that office, and maybe thirty of them could get the keys and plans."

"Filching a file now and then is small potatoes compared to this. Are you sure he'll do it?"

"He loves me."

Michael nodded. "It can make a man pathetic, can't it?"

She looked up sharply. "Yes." She conveyed for an instant only, but effectively, her hatred. And Michael realized what he didn't like about her. He stifled it and said, "I'll have to talk to my people. We'd move on it this weekend."

"How many?"

"Could it handle twenty-five?"

She smiled. Could it ever.

Saturday night, Sunday morning. Two o'clock, then three. Canal Street, a canyon of offices and warehouses and loft-factories, was deserted. A careful observer who knew what to look for could see the figures in the shadows. Michael watched the windows of the old stone building from across the street. In cars and vans up the block and down, people sprawled on seats and floors to be invisible. From a casket warehouse behind him people watched. He could feel their eyes.

He watched. He was waiting for the flashlight beam of the GSA guard to pass by the windows of the stairwell between the third floor and the fourth. It had passed already seven times at intervals of roughly twenty minutes, intervals prescribed in the schedule of rounds he'd memorized. Now when it passed, it was go.

There it was.

He turned his jacket collar up against the cold and stepped into the street. Then he was across and at the door. The key worked. Inside he applied another key to a metal panel and opened it. A maze of wires and toggles, it took a moment to make sense of it. He threw the numbered switches in sequence, then closed the panel. The alarm for floors one through five was deactivated.

Through three sets of locked doors, each key worked. He took the stairs two at a time. On the fifth-floor landing he opened another panel and threw a second set of switches. Now the alarm was off everywhere. He looked at his watch. Four minutes. The guard was in the basement.

On the seventh floor, he entered the main file room. He waited for a moment to let his eyes adjust to that less severe darkness. He had to work without a flashlight there because of the large uncurtained windows, but they admitted sufficient light from the street. Finally he saw the bank of cabinets that he wanted and approached it. He had the small key ready. It took him a second to find the hole, but then he inserted the key. It made a noise. And then he was ripping sheets of paper furiously. The noise of his destruction resounded through the room.

"Freeze!" a man cried.

Lights blinked on.

In quick succession, two burly men hit him, one with his fist just at the kidneys, and another with a vicious chop between his shoulder and his neck. It dropped Michael to his knees, but immediately he was hauled up. His hands were cuffed behind him. And an agent hooked him under the chin and lifted him with the muzzle of a shotgun.

"Where the fuck are the others?" the agent demanded.

Michael said nothing.

Agents crashed into the room behind them. A dozen others already present were poised with their weapons behind desks and cabinets, ready to shoot. There were shotguns everywhere.

"Where the fuck are the others?" A note of hysteria in the man's voice surprised Michael. He himself felt remarkably calm. Everything was going as he expected, although the weapons surprised him. The shotguns. Was he Dillinger? Didn't they know they didn't need weapons?

The agent pressed the gun barrel into Michael's gullet, against his Roman collar. Michael said, "I'm alone."

The agent eased the pressure with the gun. "What?"

"I'm alone," Michael repeated.

A supervisor, one of those who'd been waiting in the casket warehouse, came in. Altogether he had forty-two men in the operation that night, and he didn't like what he saw. He'd pulled people off six squads for this raid, the biggest in New York since the Joe Columbo takedown, and he was going to have to show for it. "Where the fuck are the others?" he bellowed. It was the exact phrase Hoover would use—though without "fuck"—in the morning. "There were going to be twenty-five. Where the fuck are they?" He glared at the agents.

One said, "He was the only one who came in from the street." Another said, "No one came up the back stairs or the freight elevator. No one came in from the alley." The other agents began to holster their guns and to check their watches.

"He says he's alone," one offered.

The supervisor let his eyes fall to the papers that Michael had ripped and strewn. He saw at once that the pages were blank.

The agents had been cued to wait until the perpetrators had actually destroyed documents before arresting them. The charge would be destruction of government property. But what if the fucker had brought his own paper in? What in hell was going on here? If he hadn't actually destroyed draft files, the charge wouldn't even be B&E since he'd come in with keys. All this trouble for illegal entry? Since the federal government did not own the land on which the building sat, it wouldn't even be crime on a government reservation. It would be a local charge, tried in local courts, a step above trespassing! All this trouble for one fucking son of a bitch? For a month's probation? Heads would roll! His head would roll! If the newspapers got it, he'd be sent to Dubuque.

The supervisor yelled, "Out! Everyone out! Check the building again! Every corridor, closet and toilet! Find them if they're here! Goddamnit, find them!"

When the other agents had left, he said to the two who had Michael, "Uncuff him." They did so. "Wait outside." They left too.

Then Michael was alone with the supervisor in the brightly lit cavernous room. They stared at each other for a long time, then the FBI man bent and picked up one of the torn blank pages. At the top were printed the words "The Catholic Relief Service, 350 Fifth Avenue, New York, N.Y." The agent smiled. "Very clever, Father."

"I'm glad you appreciate it."

"I'm the only one who will." The agent gathered the papers, a third of a ream perhaps, and carefully stuffed them inside his coat. Then he fastidiously pulled on his leather gloves. He opened several file cabinet drawers, then withdrew a file folder from one of them. It was about two inches thick. He offered it to Michael. "I think you'll find this material more interesting, Father."

Michael did not answer him, nor did he take it.

The supervisor nodded. "That would have been too easy, wouldn't it? I understand your purposes, Father. Frankly, you're a little naive if you think anyone's going to believe

your version of events here. Now I'll have to ask you to
understand my purposes."

Suddenly his right fist shot into Michael's abdomen. Michael doubled over, clutching himself. Before he could stop
him, the agent had opened Michael's hands and forced the
folder between them. Pages fell to the floor. The FBI man
brought both his fists down on Michael's neck. As Michael
went down, he kicked him in the groin. Michael fell, hands
open, on the scattered Selective Service forms. Fingerprints.
Not many, but enough.

The supervisor picked up a sheaf of papers and carefully
ripped them in two. His hands were perfectly steady. No
hysteria or threat of it in this man. He dropped the pages,
then retrieved another sheaf and ripped those. He let them fall
like leaves. He knocked Michael aside, then picked up the
pages on which his hands had rested. He ripped those and let
them fall. Destruction of government property. Not much,
but enough.

When Michael, gasping and still clutching himself, looked
up, the FBI man said calmly, "Sorry, Father. It's all in the
job."

The next morning the *New York Times* had the story on the
front page of its late edition. "Priest Arrested by FBI in Draft
Office," the headline read. And the subhead: "Priest Charges
Entrapment."

The second paragraph of the story read, "A package delivered to the *New York Times* early this morning contained a
letter describing the one-man draftboard raid and the reasons
for it. The letter was signed, 'Father Michael Maguire,'
although its source has not been verified. The package also
contained a set of wax impressions of keys purported to fit
doors and cabinets in the Canal Street Selective Service Building and which the letter claims were supplied to Father
Maguire by an FBI agent provocateur. The package also
contained a tape recording of a conversation between a woman
identified as Celia Zack, an antiwar activist, and a man
identified as Father Maguire. In the conversation, which was
apparently recorded without the woman's knowledge, she
does raise the subject of the raid on the draftboard that took

place last night. She can be heard describing keys and building diagrams that she says were supplied by a Selective Service employee named Malcolm Dodd and that were apparently being handed over to Father Maguire. The woman also details the patrol schedule of the building guards. If the tape is authentic and if Miss Zack does in fact work for the FBI as the letter asserts, then there may be some basis for Father Maguire's claim. According to *New York Times*'s legal sources entrapment occurs when a criminal act takes place that could not otherwise have taken place without the material assistance of government agents. *New York Times*'s sources maintain that it is illegal for law enforcement officers to actively further the commission of a crime even for the purpose of gaining evidence against a suspect. The FBI had refused comment on Father Maguire's charges as of this writing, although the *New York Times* was able to learn that no one named Malcolm Dodd is employed at the Selective Service office on Canal Street. A spokesman for the U.S. Attorney denied that Miss Zack works for the government and that there was entrapment in this case. The spokesman said, 'The accused can make his case, whatever it is, to the judge and jury.' "

The final paragraph of the news story was a quotation from what it doggedly called "the letter alleged to have been written by Father Maguire." Looking at it now, I find it moving, as I did then, although also somewhat ingenuous. When he wanted to the son of a bitch could croon the *Ave Maria*, warble and all.

"Though as a Catholic priest and the son of a New York City policeman who died in the line of duty I have an inbred respect, even reverence, for the law, I decided to allow myself to be entrapped in this way to expose the illegal and immoral methods used by a desperate government against its own people to keep them from protesting the infinitely more illegal and immoral war it continues to wage against the Vietnamese people. In their name and in God's name and in America's, we say, 'End this evil war before it destroys us all!' "

TWENTY-SEVEN

CAROLYN and I were sitting on a stone bench in the Biblical Garden, a small, tidy plot nestled against the Cathedral Choir and containing with floral fundamentalism only plants mentioned in the Bible: fig trees, mustard plants, lilies, papyrus and the star-of-Bethlehem. Trellised between the buttresses of the cathedral were ten cedars of Lebanon, evergreens that one never sees in the Holy Land now. They were overharvested eons ago, and I was thinking for the first time since leaving Israel of the war in Beirut, the overharvesting of blood.

Another tree caught my eye, a small redbud, the Judas tree. I touched Carolyn's sleeve. "They say that tree descends from the one on which Judas hanged himself. Its flowers are crimson because it blushes with shame."

Carolyn did not speak. I left my hand resting on her sleeve. I remembered sitting self-consciously in a garden like that with Michael at the Cloisters above Inwood. I remembered our laughing hysterically because Jesus cast demons into some poor bastard's swine.

I remembered our sitting on that hill overlooking the river and the bridge.

Carolyn and I had bought our house years later because it overlooked the other river, the other bridge. "Do you remember," I asked quietly, "how we used to have supper on our balcony overlooking the river and the city?"

She nodded. The bright sun and its heat swaddled us.

She took my hand.

"I used to think on those evenings that we would live forever."

"I thought Michael would," she said simply.

Four fruit trees grew in the center of the garden. I could not read the small sign in front of them. Apple trees? Apricot? But of course it was the Tree of the Knowledge of Good and Evil. From one of those Adam plucked fruit and therefore death came into the world.

A large pigeon pecked at gravel near us. What a miserly life! I thought. A few desperate years, odd grains, bread crumbs, the discards of squirrels, then a solitary grotto under shrubs somewhere and a pigeon's heart attack. And is it different for us? The fucking outrage of it! It made me want to kick that bird, kick God.

Michael died of a heart attack. He was just fifty, as I was at that point. He'd been in perfect health, Molly told me, a jogger. He'd quit smoking as a wedding gift to Carolyn.

I knew nothing of the last years of his life, how he earned a living, how he was changed by federal prison, how he was as a father, whether he took up golf, whether he could fix the gutters himself or had, like me, to hire people.

"Where do you live?" I asked.

"In Brooklyn."

"Our house?"

"Yes."

"Good." Could I possibly have meant that? Michael had usurped me utterly. I must have known they were living there. Shouldn't I have been surprised? Had I been a ghost to him around that house? I hoped so suddenly. I hoped I had haunted him. I hoped when the wind blew doors shut in the middle of the night he had thought it was me coming after him. "Did the two of you have supper on the balcony?"

"Not alone, the way you and I did. It's different when the children are older."

"Molly looks wonderful, Carolyn. She fills me with pride."

Carolyn smiled, drew back from her grief.

"And I met your handsome son. You have a Vietnamese daughter. You've been busy." I covered her hand, cupped it between my two. "And you kept painting."

She nodded, but absently. She had no real capacity for talk

about such things, as if her painting, her house, her children even, could have sustained her then. I saw that it would have been wrong for me to steer away from Michael. Memory alone assuages loss, and that was what I was there to help with. It shocked me to realize that I was the one person who could help her navigate that weather. I was there to put heart into that woman. Yet what heart had I? And if I could give her, finally, nothing, wouldn't it be because she had long since taken from me all I had?

We sat in the stillness of the garden. I saw the shadow of the great cathedral creeping toward us, the stillness and the shadow of death.

Finally she said, "Frank, thank you for coming."

"No, Carolyn. I'm the one to thank you. How could I ever have not been here?" I must have shown her more of my feelings than I intended, because all at once she took me in her arms and pressed my face to her breast. *She* consoled *me!*

After a time I pulled away from her. "Carolyn," I said somewhat formally, stifling my emotion, "I want to help you, to be your friend."

"Oh, Frank, I need you! I went to pieces and sent Molly for you, as if you lived in Philadelphia. It was crazy." She shook her head. "What made me wild was when they said we couldn't bury him in sacred ground. It made me crazy when they used that word about him."

"Excommunicated?"

She nodded. "As if he were Hitler or someone. And I didn't know what to do. Someone suggested Saint John's and Dean Evans here has been wonderful . . ." She looked up at the soaring cathedral, the buttresses, the windows, the great bulk of stone. ". . . but it's not . . ." She didn't finish.

"Catholic."

"I didn't think it would bother me, but it does. I can't put his ashes in a wall, a safe-deposit box. I have to commit him to the earth! I have to bury him the way he buried people! This isn't where he belongs, Frank. It's a Protestant church. We can't leave Michael here."

"We could try to think about it in a new way, Caro. So much has changed. Catholics and Episcopalians are so much alike now . . ."

"Oh, but Frank . . ." Her eyes glistened. ". . . none of that matters. This isn't Michael's place."

I'd had the same reaction at first, but I'd put it aside. Now I felt the depth of her pain, her shock. "We're still Catholics, aren't we?" I said it smiling, hoping to bring out the irony—we'd thought ourselves so worldly, but we were just mackerel snappers after all—so we could savor it together.

But her eyes overflowed. I was not prepared for that show of desolation. She had displaced her great distress, loading it on that detail of obsolete ecclesiology. It didn't matter to the dead where they were buried, and did God care if it was Saint John's and not Saint Patrick's? But God was not sitting by me, shattered. What did God know of exile or excommunication or the loss of home?

If it mattered to her, it mattered.

"Molly said you spoke to the chancellor."

"That's when I went to pieces. He was awful to me, cold and legalistic. And when I became so upset no one understood. They said it meant nothing, what bishops think. But I was destroyed, and I knew that no one would understand but you. No one would help me but you." She clutched at me. "Oh, Frank, we have to bury Michael in the Church! We have to!"

"I know it, Caro."

She had my shirt in her fists and was shaking me. "Oh, Frank, I'm the reason he's excommunicated! It's me, Frank! I'm the one they blame! It's me! That's what they think! It's me!"

Of course it was; an undispensed priest marries an ex-nun divorcée, flouting all values, all the holiest traditions. What did she expect? Baby's breath?

She should never have been the one to approach the chancellor. What latitude he might have had—what capacity for compassion—had surely been swamped in his clerical resentment, however clothed it had come in canons.

For myself, I had taken shelter both from that desolation of hers and from my own long-nursed wound in the one unclouded feeling I had. In its womb there was nothing of anger, despair or grief even; not even grief. There was only loving that woman and longing to soothe her.

"Carolyn, I'll talk to him. What time is it? I'll call him now."

She raised her hand, her wrist. The movement drew my
eye along her arm to her bosom. A vision of her nakedness
filled my mind again. It was the image to which instinctively
and, yes, lustfully I returned repeatedly, as to a memory of
the house that gave me shelter from my first storm. I saw her
thighs open, her pelvis tilting at me, her offered cunt.

"It's three-thirty." She fell back against the bench and
laughed crazily. "This is nuts! What's wrong with me? The
service is all set, just four hours from now. The dean of the
cathedral is presiding. It was in the paper. We can't change
it."

"Let me talk to them, Caro. Maybe there's something we
can do." Weren't there dispensations? Rescripts? Absolutions?
Annulments? Weren't there miracles? Was there no way—I
refused to believe it suddenly—for the Roman Catholic Church
to manifest God's mercy toward that man? "I'll call the
chancellor. What's his name?"

It was exactly as if I'd slapped her. "You don't know?"

"No."

"It's Archbishop O'Shea, Frank. Tim O'Shea."

"Michael's friend?"

Tears once more burst out of her.

"Take me to the Catholic chancery."

The taxi driver looked at me dully through the cloudy
plastic shield.

"Behind Saint Patrick's Cathedral," I explained, "on
Madison."

He popped the clutch and punched a button on his meter, a
digital readout. Where was the meter flag? I wanted to ask.
We jolted into traffic.

On the telephone in Dean Evans's office I had learned that
Archbishop O'Shea was there. His secretary wouldn't put me
through unless I stated my business. It had been easy to
picture her, upright in a severe wooden chair in front of an
antique Underwood, the dark reaches of the high-ceilinged
old mansion looming above her. The chancery office of the
archdiocese had been in the south wing of the Villard Mansions since 1948. Fit for a Borgia prince, the building was a
Roman Renaissance palazzo full of Tiffany glass, Saint-Gaudens

sculpture and the murals of John Lafarge. One of the grandest houses in all New York, it had been the vain indulgence not of an Italian aristocrat but of a nineteenth-century railroad baron. It had matched Spellman's position as the drum major of the Church's arrival in America that he should have bought the place and dubbed it the Cardinal Farley Building. It dwarfed his own residence across the avenue, and it seemed almost vengeful when he turned the mansion into the offices of his chancellor. He would not, of course, have grasped the irony that once more Catholics were scooping up the leavings of Protestants. The descendants of Henry Villard and his successor proprietor, Whitelaw Reid, who entertained the Prince of Wales in the house, had long since moved farther north. The fashionable Upper East Side had come into its own. Midtown was fit now only for commerce and for Catholics.

The cab, after cutting through Central Park, went down Fifth Avenue. The traffic was like traffic in Jerusalem, but the people on the sidewalk, their clothing, their lack of it, the shoulders and thighs of women, the glittering store windows in which their bodies were reflected, windows behind which the bodies of mannequins took tribute in glances, plaster nipples stretching plastic blouses, wreaked havoc with my concentration. I wanted to remember everything I could about Timothy O'Shea. I wanted to remember what I'd read in canon law. I was certain the bishop had discretion about who was buried where and how. In death, everyone is excommunicated; therefore no one should be. But I could not think. My mind was taken up utterly by the pretty girls in their summer dresses. Oh early Irwin Shaw!

At Fiftieth Street the driver slowed for a turn. We passed in front of Saint Patrick's, then cut and swerved and were driving along the side of it. An unexpected affection for the spired church surged in me, but I was amazed how small, how ungrand it seemed. Saint John's, even incomplete, was more than twice Saint Patrick's size, and standing as it did on the promontory of Morningside Heights it had a monumentality Saint Patrick's, in the shadow of the skyscrapers of Rockefeller Center, lacked.

New York's nineteenth-century Catholics had been out-

raged when they heard about plans for the heretics' cathedral
in their city. It would be—and was—the largest cathedral in
the world. Ingenuously, in making that claim the Protestants
did not include in the comparison Saint Peter's in Rome,
which, at nearly twice the size again, was the only edifice
bigger. Technically they were right, though, because Saint
Peter's was not a cathedral, but a basilica. Still Catholics in
New York over the years had refused to be cowed by the
relative modesty of their cathedral. It may not have been
designed and furnished by America's great architects and
artists, and it may have been only the size, they would admit,
of Chartres and Notre Dame de Paris, but at least it was
finished. The churches were begun within a decade of each
other. In less than two decades, Saint Patrick's, paid for by
the pennies of millions of immigrants, was completed. Saint
John the Divine, paid for by the sporadic benefactions of the
richest people in America, would probably never be completed.
The house of worship for a dwindling elite, Saint John's,
even at solemn services on Sundays, seemed always nearly
empty. Saint Patrick's, even between Masses on any weekday,
seemed always nearly full. And there was the difference, the
oldest one, the one that mattered. There are fifty million
Catholics in America, two million Episcopalians.

We Catholics have long memories. Take your thumb out of
our ingratiating joviality, of our worldly liberalism, and you
will loose a flood of bitterness. Then watch what we do with
it. In the new age in which neither layman nor priest, progressive nor conservative, chancellor nor cardinal nor pope, even,
wants to be thought unecumenical, small-minded or parochial,
we spare the ancient Protestant enemy and pour the old acid
on ourselves.

Hence my taxi ride. Hence my purpose as the cab swung
north on Madison, cut across the avenue to the far curb and
jolted to a stop in front of the Renaissance palace; I had come
to ask the Roman Catholic archdiocese of New York to lift its
sanction, to ask Holy Mother the Church to have mercy on
her son.

"This place?" the cabbie asked.

"That's right." I was counting bills out for him. The feel
of the money was alien, and not because it was American. I

had not even so much as paid a cab fare in a decade. The bubble of unreality in which I had been living touched ground but did not break.

"This is a hotel, Mac, not the archdiocese."

"What?"

Even in daylight, even in August, the courtyard trees were lined with white Christmas twinkle lights.

"The Helmsley Palace Hotel."

I craned toward the mansion. The windows sparkled. The entranceway glimmered with brass. At a polished revolving door a uniformed man was taking someone's suitcase. And above the three stories of the nineteenth-century masterpiece loomed a huge, gleaming skyscraper.

I paid the cabbie and got out.

At the door the uniformed Hispanic—in earlier days he'd have been Irish—gave me the once-over. What's with the denim shirt and sandals, man? I nodded at him and went in.

The Villard Mansions now served as a showplace narthex—grand staircase, polished pink marble, restored paneling, flashing chandeliers, Oriental runners with brass fasteners—for a piggy-backed run-of-the-mill behemoth hotel. New York's Industrial Brahmins had abandoned their palazzo to upstart Catholic clergy who had bequeathed it now to expense account admen from Dayton and accountants from Houston who wore English suits, knew their *nouvelle cuisine* and preferred a Continental ambience. This was the best Olde World Palace Hotel yet. I made a quick round of the public rooms to convince myself I was not dreaming. Where were the portraits of Farley, Hughes, Hayes and Spellman? In niches where once stood statues of Frances Cabrini, Mother Seton and Isaac Jogues were now flamboyant floral displays. Against the elaborately carved oak wall at the top of the grand staircase where once the huge seal of the archdiocese— the tassled hat, the Greek Cross, the flame, the motto *Fiat Voluntas Tua*—had hung there was now a mammoth portrait of the unsmiling, waistcoated, mustachioed Villard. His successors still displeased him.

In the stunning second-floor library that had served as the office of the chancellor—I had been in it once and remembered the twin fireplaces with Italian marble mantels and the

barrel-vaulted ceiling—afternoon tea was being served on ta-
bes covered with pink damask. A lady touched her napkin to
her mouth and eyed me suspiciously. Would I come over to
her table and sell her a sign-language card? Suddenly I sensed
that she would have bought one. She might have taken me to
her room.

It was the building I remembered, but the gloom was gone,
that cinctured repression, that overhanging threat that swamped
light and life, sucking oxygen from the rooms and spirit from
their occupants. Now, as in all hotels, infidelity was in the
air, the faint smell of sex. Even that matron from Ohio at her
tea knew it, exuded it. She had that Last Chance look in her
eyes and flashed it at me because I was not dressed right,
because I did not belong. She would have been in charge.
She would never have had to see me again. With a shock I
realized she was younger than I was and, yes, I would have
loved to screw her, not in her husband's company's room
upstairs, but in *this* room where once an archbishop of the
Church had sat up to his ass in anathemas. Anathema shit!
Tempus fuck!

I left the room for the corridors and stairs again. The
restoration, the polish, the carpeting and gold leaf had turned
the intimidating shadows of God's offices in New York into
the living illustration of a slick travel brochure. Amenities
and ambience! It was the perfect end for that counterfeit
Roman masterpiece, that New York version of a Hollywood
backlot front. From its beginning that house had offered its
lonely, uprooted American owners the illusion of a past, of a
culture, of a tradition. Ironically, a *Catholic* past, culture and
tradition—as in Michelangelo, as in Dante Alighieri. Its first
owners had stayed most of a century. Its second, the Irish
clergy to whom the Italian Renaissance, however Catholic,
had been as alien, finally, as it had been to the Protestants
who aped it, had stayed a few decades. Now its owners were
guests who stayed the night, had coffee and *brioche* in the
Gold Room and left, pleased with the place and with
themselves.

When a bellboy—no, *concierge!*—saluted me, I wanted to
intone the benediction in plain chant for him. Instead I asked
where to find a phone book and he told me.

I looked up "Chancery," then "Archdiocese" and found nothing. I looked up "Catholic" and found a listing, with multiple departments and centrex dialing, for the New York Catholic Center at 1011 First Avenue, and I understood even before going there what had happened.

It was a new twenty-story rectangular office building with aluminum window frames, beige Levolor blinds and gray facing stone. Unpainted aluminum letters above the entrance identified it straightforwardly: "The New York Catholic Center," and a good thing too, for otherwise I could have taken it for one of the other seven million clone-buildings in this city, the Arco Building, Random House, Lever Brothers. It was the perfect emblem for the new Church. Having rejected as unmodern and antidemocratic the trappings—if not the political structure—of the feudal aristocracy, the archdiocese had embraced the trappings of the American corporation. The clergy who worked in this building did not aspire to be princes but managers. The cardinal was the president and the chairman of the board, and Archbishop O'Shea was "Senior V.P. for Ops," or perhaps "Assistant CEO."

Good, I thought, crossing the street and going in. I slipped by the distracted security guard—not spinster secretary—and into the elevator. The floors were identified by their offices: Catholic Guardian Society, Hospital Apostolate, Insurance Division, Pension Division, Catholic Relief Service, Marriage Tribunal, Communications, Catholic Home Bureau, Catholic New York. At the top, floor twenty, not a palace but the executive suite, the sign said "Chancellor." I wanted to say, No, that's wrong! You can't have it both ways. Thomas More was a chancellor. An absolutist, he drew lines and refused to cross them, but you can't do that. Not in this place, not in this business. You are an American executive, paid to accommodate and compromise. You cannot pronounce anathemas against your middle management. This building professes the new faith, Your Excellency, even if you don't. It is efficient, computerized, unionized, organized, socialized and banalized. In its sterile fluorescent glare we see episcopal arrogance, clerical vengeance and vestigial medieval tyranny—and this is why, finally, one accepts this otherwise tragic transformation as the work of God—for the devils-on-the-loose they are.

The elevator doors opened and, as if by magic I was standing in front of a desk at which a plain young woman sat. She looked up from a ledger with an expression of mild curiosity. On the wall behind her was yet more aluminum, but that was an abstract figure of the Risen Christ, which I recognized only because of the legend below it: "I am the Resurrection and the Life."

The sculpture was an unexpected reminder that that building, like the Villard Mansions before it and like Saint Patrick's and Saint John the Divine, was supposed to be a mere shell, casing, glove of that truth. But what was the Resurrection to me? And what was the Life? They were words from the homily I'd stopped listening to, as easily ignored as the tawdry piece of modern sculpture. I looked away from it, thinking, What complete shit.

"I'd like to see the archbishop, please. My name is Francis Durkin. Tell him I'm an old friend of Michael Maguire's."

The young woman did not see it as her place to screen me. Probably some monsignor in the inner office would do that. She disappeared behind a pair of walnut doors. A moment later she returned, stood at the door and said, to my surprise, "Archbishop O'Shea will see you now."

His office was plushly carpeted, paneled and carefully lit, modern in all respects. A gray hopsack sofa sat adjacent to a polished ebony desk. On a glass and brass coffee table was arranged a selection of the best magazines. The wall behind the desk was entirely glass, and the view of the East River and the Fifty-ninth Street Bridge was stunning.

Archbishop Timothy O'Shea in black shirt and collar, not robes and skull cap, not even suitcoat, was coming toward me with his hand extended. He was in his early seventies. The crown of his hair was white, longish, setting off his bald head. His skin was tanned and he was not fat. He looked like a cabinet secretary. "My goodness," he said with enthusiasm, "Frank Durkin, how are you? Welcome! Welcome!"

It was not what I expected.

We sat on the sofa together. He offered me coffee, tea or sherry, and I took sherry. So did he.

I raised my glass. "Will you drink to Michael?"

"Of course I will."

We did.

"It's why I'm here."

"I heard you were in a monastery in the Holy Land."

"That's true." I indicated my shirt, my baggy trousers and sandals. "This is Benedictine street garb. I came back today for the funeral. I'm here because I can't believe you won't let him be buried in the Church. I've just come from Saint John the Divine. His family is distraught and so am I."

"I understand. It's thoroughly regrettable." He let his gaze drift to the view. After a moment he said wistfully, "I wish it wasn't like this."

My earlier expectation, of an Orson Welles prelate denouncing permissiveness, attacking infidelity and broken vows, had been off the mark. I sensed at once O'Shea's sadness, and it disarmed me.

He said, "It came as a great shock, Michael's death. I'd always hoped to see him again. I missed him."

All at once my heart flowed toward the man. For a moment I laid aside my argument. Perhaps I should have understood what it was from his side. "You were his mentor. Your gift to him in Korea of that little New Testament changed his life."

"Ah!" His eyes widened and he looked at me with such unwalled unhappiness that I realized I had inadvertently touched a nerve. "That New Testament, my God, what a mistake that was."

"What do you mean?"

He shook his head. "How can I tell you without your thinking . . . ?" He put his glass down and pressed the heels of his hands against his eyes. When he uncovered them they were red. "I gave him that New Testament the night before a battle. He'd seen action the day before . . ."

"He blew up that bridge."

"That's right, and I was worried about him."

"That book was just the thing. He said it was what got him through."

"I know, and it made him want to be a priest, and then it made him the best priest any of us knew."

"Well?"

"But when I gave it to him I told him that that particular

copy of the New Testament had been my brother's. I said that my brother had it with him when he was killed at the Battle of the Bulge. That was a lie. It wasn't my brother's at all. I had already given my brother's Bible to another GI, and it moved him so that, well, I used the story with other fellows. I gave away a lot of Bibles and I always said the same thing. You could call it a pastoral technique. I wanted them to treasure the book and I thought it was all right to . . ." He stopped, breathed deeply. "It was an awful thing to do. It didn't matter with the others because I never saw them again, but with Michael, who always treasured that little book, I felt that our friendship was based on a deception of mine, and I was afraid that somehow it would go wrong. And then, of course, it did."

Now when he pressed the heels of his hands against his eyes he seemed like the old man he was, the old fox, the old manipulator. I had to stifle my disgust at his trick, his sodding "technique." I felt sorry for him despite myself.

After a moment he said, "It was the worst thing that ever happened to me, when Michael left the priesthood. He was my son."

"I know that. I know that he considered you his father. But you disavowed him before he left. You broke with each other over the war."

"Yes, but he was right about Vietnam. And now I see that he was right even to break the law, even to go underground the way he did. America needed the moral witness, and so did the Church. If we pulled through that period with our soul intact, perhaps it was due to him and others like him. Michael was a hero to many priests. They were destroyed when he turned his back on them."

"I think he felt they'd already turned their backs on him. You had. And so had the cardinal."

He nodded. "It was a terrible time. Some of us were wrong." He fell silent, then said suddenly, "Now, of course, the leading Catholic pacifists are all bishops. The Catholic Church may end up a Peace Church."

"If it does, Michael will have started it."

"That's true. I'll tell you something. If he was alive today, he'd be a bishop."

"No, he'd be a husband and a father."

O'Shea blushed. "I mean if he was still a priest."

"But in any case, at some point he'd be dead, wouldn't he? And it wouldn't matter what he was. He'd still stand naked and alone before God, in need of mercy."

"That's right."

"Well, why can't he have mercy from the Church?"

Archbishop O'Shea did not answer me, and so I asked it another way. "Can you explain to me why Michael can't have the funeral Mass, the last blessing and burial in sacred ground?"

"You know why." His voice was barely above a whisper.

"No, I don't. I truly don't."

"He's excommunicated."

"By whom?"

"By himself. You know how these things work. He violated his solemn vow, and he did so publicly."

"Your complaint is that he didn't apply for a proper dispensation, or what? From what we hear in the desert, priests rarely obtain papal dispensations anymore, and well-known priests never do."

O'Shea was stiffened now. This was ground on which the moves came naturally. "Excommunication follows *ipso facto* when rejection of authority in a solemn matter is culpable, obstinate and externally manifested."

"All right. Grant that. He broke his vow. He's excommunicated. But he's also dead. Isn't it time to lift the penalty? I know there are rules and canons and proscriptions, but there are also exceptions, and rescripts and absolutions."

He shook his head.

"Why?"

"Because the order of the priesthood is at stake, that's why. Pope John Paul has reestablished discipline on the issue and just in time. Priests everywhere were confused and demoralized. Men like Michael by the thousands had let them down, and Paul VI had no idea how to deal with it. His ambivalence—his desire to be compassionate—only made things worse. This pope is not ambivalent." O'Shea gestured easily and I realized that he had retreated to a rote explanation of the Church's position. Did bishops take seminars in how to pontificate on this shit? "The priesthood is the spine of the Church, and it is forever. It is a radical, absolute vocation, and the Church must proclaim it as such. It is not a mere job or a career, an occupation to pursue for a while or for a phase of one's life. It is a sacred compact with God, a Covenant. 'Thou are a priest forever!' That is what Michael's excommunication means, and if the archdiocese is observing it scrupulously it is doing so not punitively, but, as the Constitution on the Church says, 'for the edification of the flock.' Only by a rigorous, one could even say heartless, observance of this point can this truth be protected and understood."

"But many ex-priests receive the sacraments."

"They did not flout authority. When they die their funerals won't be reported in the *New York Times*."

"So it's a matter of publicity? Forgive me, but I'm trying to understand. It isn't that he flouted authority, because you just said he was right about that."

"About the war. Not about marrying your wife."

His thrust stopped me. I should have known it would come, of course.

He saw his advantage and pressed it. "I'd have expected you of all people to understand our point of view. There are consequences to human acts. Some acts must simply not be condoned in any way."

"That's how I feel about what you are doing. Yes, Michael took my wife. And no, I don't condone it. But he is dead. She's alive. She is the one who is being punished now."

"She is not entirely innocent, it seems to me."

"Who the hell are you to throw that stone?"

"I'm a member of the Church. We loved Michael Maguire and she took him from us."

"You had already failed him! A deception at the heart of your friendship, yes! But not about a little volume of Scripture. The lie that destroyed his priesthood—and my marriage, damn you!—was the one that you priests tell each other, that you are brothers, that you care for one another, that you love each other. You never mistreat each other or exact vengeance upon each other or degrade each other. You only act for the edification of the flock. What shit! You make me sick!"

O'Shea was staring at his hands obsequiously, and his willingness to sit there passively in the blast of my anger only stoked it. "Why am I surprised at your rejection of him now? You treat the dead like you treat the living. No wonder Michael began to wither! No wonder he refused finally to shrivel like the rest of you and become a gutless, conscienceless husk, a walking, Mass-saying, golf-playing, war-blessing carcass! A sacred compact with God? Bullshit! You people are in covenant with privilege. Everything is sacrificed to that, especially members who dare to challenge it. Michael woke up, that was his offense. I saw, when he did, what he was on his way to becoming. He fought it from within, but he was losing and he knew it. I saw his loneliness. It scorched him. It dried the blood in his veins. And do you know what? The Vietnam war saved him." O'Shea looked up at me, a look of confusion on his face. He *was* hearing me. But really, I didn't care. This was my moment to say what had happened and I was at its mercy. "The Vietnam war was probably the best thing that ever happened to Michael. It made him remember that he was a man before he was a priest. It made him remember his first ideals, and it forced him to make his compact with people again. The war destroyed his aloofness and his smugness. It brought him back. All he wanted after that was to be a man and a priest both. But it's impossible. You with your fancy new office and your mild regret at what stiffening the spine of the Church requires—what shit!—are the best evidence of that. He was your son, you said. But when the world fell down around his ears, when he needed support and love and solace and strength for that incredible, heroic resistance of his, could he get it from you? No! Or from the cardinal? No! Or from his fellow priests? No! Or from the Church herself? No! Of course he had to turn to someone else!"

"You were his friend. Why didn't he turn to you?"

The archbishop's second thrust. He had no idea why, but it undid me.

TWENTY-EIGHT

BEGINNING with Michael's trial, this story becomes Carolyn's story and mine too. She and I were stunned by the news of his arrest, and even before we saw him we knew that it would profoundly affect us. In fact it set in motion the events that changed everything.

Carolyn supported him immediately. It took me longer to work through my good-citizen bias, but eventually I too got the point. By the time his trial formally opened in May 1969—it was the month the war peaked; 539,000 GIs were in Vietnam—I had come to see what he'd done as an elegant ethical gesture and I wrote as much for *Commonweal*. My piece on his trial was reprinted in newspapers all over the country. Michael had the article framed, together with an ancient snapshot of the two of us looking like members of the Gashouse Gang.

I was not surprised that so many people were moved by what he'd done. But not everyone was. When he was arrested, the archdiocese issued a statement saying Father Maguire was a previously suspended priest who had acted purely as an individual and in no way as a representative of the Church. The archdiocese would not censure him, but neither would it post his bail.

His bail was set at twenty thousand dollars. Carolyn and I didn't hesitate to post it, though it meant emptying our bank accounts and cashing in our bonds and my life insurance. I had been looking forward to extending an upcoming sabbatical by a year with those savings. I am chagrined to admit it, but I was going to write a novel about growing up in Inwood.

Carolyn and I went to the courthouse together. We delivered the cashier's check to the proper clerk and then went in the company of a federal marshal to the jail. The marshal served the jail-officer with the court order and left. A few minutes later doors clanged and Michael appeared, looking gaunt in his black clothing. Carolyn ran to him and embraced him. Even while he held her Michael stared at me. The desolation in his eyes seemed familiar. When he embraced me in turn, he whispered, "Thanks. It was awful. It was like China."

His terror of confinement had taken him by surprise, and he said that if he'd known what a nightmare recapitulation of his POW experience it would be, he'd never have walked willingly into the FBI ambush. After dinner—we ate in a small Italian restaurant in the Village—Carolyn and I suggested he come home with us. He seemed not to want to. He could go back to his nearby studio apartment. But we insisted. We both insisted. When he agreed, his relief was palpable. He lived with us then again, while preparing for the trial. Our house became the headquarters of his defense committee. Carolyn set aside her painting and arranged for babysitters for Molly in order to work full-time publicizing the trial and raising money to pay the lawyers. I was up to my ears at the university, but I gave every minute I could. I stifled my ambivalence, and found it possible, to my surprise, to see beyond the posturing and self-righteousness of the war resisters. Hell, in my own, didactic way, I became one of them. I wrote against the war every chance I got. Sometimes my desk felt hot beneath my hands. It was a frenzied, anxious, but exhilarating time. Michael had invitations from colleges and church groups all over the country. Even I took to the platform. I was particularly adept, it turned out, at debating the government lackeys who showed up at teach-ins. They were fodder for me. To speak at an antiwar rally, I discovered, was nothing like lecturing in the classroom. About literature I was wry and circuitous, carefully discursive, deliberately understated. I did not display myself in public. But about the war, to my own surprise, I spoke with unrestrained emotion, particularly as we discovered that spring that our new president was not winding down the violence, but intensifying it. I'll always be grateful to Nixon, that worm. Thanks to him even I could feel pristine. It was glorious, how in hating the war and the warmakers, we could love ourselves. Praise the Lord and pass out pompous leaflets! Right on, Mother!

The antiwar movement was a perfect mix of the ridiculous and the profound, of true nobility and blatant solipsism. And its most memorable moments held both elements in tension.

I remember, for example, a rally at Boston University, the self-styled "Berkeley of the East." It was held at the football stadium and students from Boston's half-dozen large colleges had filled the stands to overflowing. It was a balmy spring day, and the kids were tricked out in tie-dyed T-shirts, flowing hair and moccasins. Frisbees sailed to and fro above their heads and, between speakers, a blues band wailed away on amplified harmonicas. Michael and I had driven up from New York and we arrived late. A kid at the gate who didn't recognize Michael said that Dave Dellinger and Tom Hayden had already spoken, but that everybody was waiting to hear Father Maguire. Michael winked at me. The note of deference was a surprise from this kid, at least to me. B.U. wasn't Notre Dame or Fordham. I didn't think a priest, even the celebrity-resister-priest, would make much of a dent there. But that was because I had yet to grasp that draft-age boys particularly regarded Michael as their great defender. And kids who wouldn't have thought of going into a church were as susceptible to the Great American Romance of the Priest as their parents had been. Michael was their Bing Crosby. As we walked into the stands, students began to recognize him. He had taken to wearing a black turtleneck sweater and a black windbreaker, a costume other priests would imitate, and, with his height, his leanness, he was a striking figure. As we walked through the stands toward the platform, students began to applaud. Frisbees stopped flying, though the music continued to blare. The closer we came to the platform the more students recognized him and began applauding. They stood. The ovation crossed the stadium like a wave, following us. By the time we reached the platform the band had stopped playing. The musicians were a scruffy, ill-groomed bunch with the studied look of nihilists, but they were applauding too. Michael looked at me, helpless. Thousands of college kids were cheering him. I clapped my hands theatrically toward him and bowed. As he mounted the stairs to the platform he leaned into me. I could sense that he was moved, but also embarrassed. Who was he? Bob Dylan? This was wacky. "Fuck peace," he whispered.

In May, Michael's case was finally heard. It was a simple procedure, quick and anticlimactic. The judge refused to admit into evidence the tape-recording that had been supplied to the *Times,* and when Michael's lawyer subpoenaed Celia Zack, he learned that she had disappeared. In the end Michael's defense consisted of little more than his own testimony. On the stand he was utterly credible, and it seemed to me the prosecutor's inability to shake his story would be decisive. When he sought repeatedly to refer to the war, the judge interrupted him. The war was not on trial. But when the prosecutor repeated the irrelevant slander that Michael had encouraged Nicholas Wiley to immolate himself, the judge allowed it. In his instruction to the jurors, the judge ordered them to disregard all arguments having to do with entrapment. The government was not on trial either. In fact, Michael had succeeded in making an issue, whether the judge allowed it or not, of abusive patterns the government would repeat against other Catholic resisters, against radicals, against genuine hoodlums and eventually against members of the U.S. House and Senate.

It took the jury less than an hour to bring back its verdict. Michael was guilty of willful and malicious destruction of government property. A week later the incensed Irish Catholic judge handed down a sentence of two to five years in prison.

When that sentence was announced there was a gasp in the courtroom. One of the jurors, present now as a spectator, cried, "No!" And Michael's shoulders sagged. When given a chance to speak, he only shook his head. A moment later, after the judge had left and people had begun to clear the room, Michael turned in his place, looking for us. Carolyn's face was buried in her hands. I knew it was her eyes he wanted. I touched her. She uncovered her face and Michael took refuge in what it showed him.

At a time like that friends stand without defenses in one

another's company. I knew that the level of feeling between Caro and Michael was more intense than ever, but the context for their feelings, their love, had been radically altered. How can I indicate our states of mind, or the common state I presumed we shared? It is important that you understand. We had all been softened by the years. Once, perhaps, even they would have romped into an affair, believing implicitly, as the young do, that there is only one possible form of expression for such feelings. But it was different for them now because their love for each other—I knew this with primordial certainty—existed inside their love for me. It was therefore radically chaste. It was a love I could encourage. Though we were two sides of a love triangle, Michael was not my competitor. It was as likely that Carolyn should have been, in fact. In that courtroom, after his sentencing, the three of us embraced. We stood together for a long time. *That* was the expression we wanted. Carolyn, Michael and I shared a sense of having come home again in one another.

He continued to live with us during the months it took the courts to dispose of his appeal. Though his coming jail term loomed above us, we found it possible to live happily, as one family. Summer came. In August, to escape the rat-race of antiwar work—Michael was more in demand than ever—we rented a cabin at Lake George. At night after Molly was asleep, we would sit on the porch looking up at the stars. Sometimes I read poetry aloud. One verse of Eliot's became a theme of ours, a joke, but more than a joke because it hinted at the mysteries there were and would always be among us.

> *Who is the third who walks always beside you?*
> *When I count there are only you and I together*
> *But when I look ahead up the white road*
> *There is always another one walking beside you*
> *Gliding wrapt in a brown mantle, hooded*
> *I do not know whether a man or a woman*
> *—But who is that on the other side of you?*

During the period leading up to our "vacation," Carolyn had worked herself to a frazzle too. Once she'd laid aside her painting, it was as if all her creativity was channeled into organizing, and she had done it with great success. She shunned the celebrity mode that Michael, like it or not, fell into, and she didn't function as a pinch-hit speaker as I did. Instead she spent long hours arranging events, benefits at art galleries, concerts at which the heroes spoke and cocktail parties at which the rich radicals could make donations to Michael's rich lawyers. At all of these occasions Carolyn would hover at the edge of things, making sure the microphones worked and the bartender had ice and the girl at the table by the door had pens with which the chic supporters could write their checks. And Carolyn always looked lovely. She'd developed a style of dressing that was fittingly unconventional; she was surely no lawyer's wife, no socialite, no BonWit DimWit. But she never embraced the counterculture cult of ugliness—uniform unisexuality; workboots, overalls, fatigue jackets, torn flannel shirts—that held sway in the movement. I remember her in long, high-waisted dresses, sandals, but still with heels, bangles at her wrists, no makeup but her luxuriant blond hair cinctured in bright, trailing silk like Louise Nevelson or Isadora Duncan. You knew she was an artist, just looking at her. It didn't matter that she hadn't painted in months.

Well, it mattered to her. And the fact that she'd fallen into a role, that of an antiwar hostess, that she despised mattered too. Stokely Carmichael had said a woman's place in the movement is on her back. Carolyn's place, she said, with bitterness that shocked me, was at the door, smiling. We were alone in our room one night at Lake George. It was the first time we'd talked to each other about what those months had really felt like. Her alienation, her weariness, were different from mine, and had led her to a vastly different conclusion.

"I've decided to do a raid, Durk."

"What?" I sat forward. I'd been propped against the headboard of our bed. I was wearing pajamas. She wore a T-shirt, no bra, and shorts. A blue engineer's bandanna was tied around her head.

"On the Dow Chemical offices at Rockefeller Center next month. A symbolic burning of napalm against its creators. We're going to burn some files."

"You're not serious."

"I am. There are seven of us. I have to do it, Durk. I haven't done anything."

I stared at her, unbelieving. This was the most insidious thing about the antiwar movement, how it could make such generous, dedicated, zealous workers feel as though they'd done nothing. Shit, she'd done nothing *but,* for months. For the crazies who were always within an inch of taking over, the only contribution to peace that counted was the act of going to jail. It was self-aggrandizement through self-punishment. It was madness. I'd never expected Carolyn to fall for it. I had to control my anger, I had to work at understanding her, at listening. I said quietly, "Why am I only hearing about this now?"

"Well, there wasn't any point to both of us being in on it, was there? We couldn't both do it."

"Because of Molly, you mean."

"That's right."

"Well, I'm glad you thought of her to that extent."

"Don't use Molly against me in this, Durk. Don't be angry at me. I need your support."

I took her hand in mine. "Caro, I think it's brave of you to want to do it. But you can't. You simply can't. They'd use it against Michael."

She shook her head. "He doesn't know about it. We've kept him out of it on purpose. Obviously the court would use any involvement on his part to extend his sentence."

"And when you and who—Jack? Sonny? Kate?—when you get busted in Dow Chemical they're going to think Michael's not involved? He got two to five years, remember? You want to make sure he serves every possible day, is that it?"

"Of course not. But we do want him to know that what he's begun will continue."

"Sweetheart, it can't continue. Not that way. There's only one Michael Maguire. There's only one hero."

She withdrew her hand from mine and looked away. What a disappointment I was to her. It was true. There was only one Michael. I was a disappointment, of course, to myself. But, hell, I was used to that. Nevertheless, I pressed the point, because I was right. "We have to work against the war, Caro, in the ways that *we* can. That means not making Michael's situation worse. And it also means, by the way, staying close to Molly. You'd be in jail a year.''

She looked down at the thin bedspread, smoothed it with her hands. ''But, Durk,'' she said finally, ''I haven't done anything against the war. And I haven't helped Michael.''

''You want to take his place in jail, don't you?''

She looked up and I saw the flicker of her recognition. She nodded slowly and I could read her worry. ''I think I would handle it better than he will.''

I was about to say, ''You would. You're stronger than any of us.'' But before I could I had a recognition of my own. She didn't want to take his place in jail. She just wanted to be with him. The truth stopped me cold. Before I maneuvered past it, Molly cried out sharply from the next room, the panic of a bad dream in her voice. Carolyn went to her at once.

I was alone with unwanted knowledge. Carolyn was far more like Michael than like me. If she'd been a nun still, instead of my wife, she'd have been his virgin princess, his Saint Joan at the head of his army. It did not occur to me to think of her as his Magdalen.

When Carolyn returned she stopped short in the doorway of our room and leaned against the jamb. Wearily she unknotted her bandanna and shook her hair free. Then she looked at me pensively. ''You're right, Durk. I couldn't leave Molly. She's what's kept me from becoming even harder.''

''You're not hard, darling.''

''I hate the war. I hate what it's doing to us. Don't you feel it?''

''Yes. But I didn't know it was the war.''

''What else is it?''

I shrugged. ''Quotidian Distraction, darling.'' I could be so insufferably blasé. I patted the bed, Come sit. She crossed to me. I said, ''Once Michael is gone, you and I can withdraw somewhat from all that antiwar shit.'' She started to protest. I stopped her. ''You know we can. We're both in it because of him. He drafted us, didn't he?'' She nodded. ''You simply *must* start painting again, Caro. You're an artist. That's the longing you feel, the unhappiness. You're not *working*. You must work. Your paintings are the opposite

of war. That's how you resist. That's how you keep faith.
You are an artist, Caro!''

She leaned against me, and I felt the tension drain out of
her. "You mean I can?" she asked. "I really can?"

"What, go back to painting?"

She nodded.

"Darling, you must."

Her arms went around me. "Oh, Durk, you know me,
don't you? You take care of me. No one takes care of me like
you do."

"That's my job, love. I'm your husband."

"You're my best friend."

"Same thing."

"It's why you put up with me."

"I put up with you because I love you, Caro.

"Oh, Durk." She surprised me then by kissing me
passionately. We fell back upon the bed, at the mercy of her
emotions, which I took to be gratitude, relief, and the old
affection.

"I love you," she said. "I've never loved you more." She
clung to me so fiercely I believed her.

Of course I was conscious of Michael's presence in the
room beyond Molly's. I was both grateful to him—he had
drawn from both of us entirely new capacities for feeling—
and sorry for him because he would never experience with
either of us the fullness of intimacy that Carolyn and I, to our
mutual surprise, shared then. I remember restraining myself
at orgasm that night and subsequent ones at Lake George so
that he wouldn't hear, so that he wouldn't feel bereft.

That August Michael and I climbed Black Mountain, one
of the highest peaks in the Adirondacks. Carolyn and Molly
had gone down to Westchester to see her parents. The heat
was ferocious and by the time we arrived at the top of the
mountain we were soaked with perspiration and too weary at
first to bother with the view. In our packs we had liquor. We
sat against the rocks and traded swigs. When I finally looked
out across Lake George the vista—a spine of mountains
running north—made my mind reel. In my dehydrated state,
the gin helped, of course. I felt instantly drunk. I faced away,

but behind us was an even grander view, the Green Mountains of Vermont. I faced west, nestled in the crevice of the rock and tried to focus, for sobriety's sake, on the sun. It had fallen to within two or three hands of the horizon.

We sat in silence for a long time. Maybe we did get drunk. Maybe that was why we said those things.

He began, "All of this I will give you."

"If?" I knew the phrase, the opening of the devil's temptation of Christ. If you will fall down and worship me.

But he said, "I'll just give it to you. There."

"Thanks."

"I would though, Durk. I'd give you the whole goddamn world if I could, for what you've done for me."

"Michael, it's been a privilege. You're a fucking hero. Have a drink."

"Don't say that."

"But it's true."

"I'm not interested in being a hero to you. One time we sat in the Cloisters. Do you remember that?"

"Sure."

"We covered the same ground."

"You were a hero then too."

"Do you remember the Unicorn Tapestry?"

"The Unicorn in Captivity."

"That's right. I pointed out to you that what looked like the blood of the Unicorn was actually the juice of the pomegranate tree dripping down on it. Do you remember?"

"Yes."

"Guess what."

"It was blood after all."

"That's right. And if it wasn't for you I'd have bled to death."

"Get out of here."

"I would have, damnit. I still might." He took my sleeve. "Durk, I've got to tell you, I'm bleeding right now. I'm scared shitless. I think prison is going to do me in."

"Come off it, Michael. You know about fear. It's a reflex It just gets you ready. Fear's your friend."

"No." He draped my neck. He was drunker than I was. "You're my friend."

"We're all your friends, hero!"

"Goddamnit, listen to me! Don't call me that. I'm telling you I'm afraid. I'm afraid because I know the stakes now. I didn't before. When we were kids, you and me, we hadn't a clue how fucking easily things get lost."

"What, like youth?"

"Like faith." He hesitated, took a breath, then declared, "I think I'm losing mine."

Michael was serious. Even in my fog I sensed that he was talking about something important, something more profound than his alienation from Church authority. Michael Maguire was nothing if not a believer. "You mean in God?" I asked carefully.

"I don't trust Him to sustain me. Isn't that the point of faith?"

"I guess." My mind went blank. After all the months of being at the mercy of this man's ordeal, of being, however willingly, at the service of his vaunted integrity, this was impossible to take in. Michael had to believe in God, he was that kind of priest, of man. He had thrown himself over Kierkegaard's edge where there was either grace or nothing. If God did not sustain him—we knew the Church wouldn't—who would or could? Then I panicked; not me, I thought, no way, bud! I can be your friend, but not the Ground of Your Being.

"In China," he said, "the guards told me that World War Three had started, remember that?"

"Yes."

"They told me New York had been hit with the A-bomb and for a time I believed them. I believed that everyone I knew and loved was dead and that half the cities of Europe and America were ash and that a cloud of radiation was hanging over the world. I believed all that, Durk, but I still believed in God. I still believed He loves us and takes care of us. But now . . ." He fell silent.

I became increasingly desperate. He gave me the feeling that somehow I had to rescue him—his faith!—with what I said. I wanted to recite a whole litany of reasons for belief, but I could not think of one. After several swallows of gin I swept my hand toward the horizon grandly. "But look at the

view, Michael. It's the fucking world at our feet. You see
any fucking radiation cloud? Hey, you wanted to give it to
me as a token of your gratitude, right?''

"That's right.''

"Well, that's how God feels. There it is. Mountains,
valleys, rivers, trees, animals, Vermont, New-fucking-York,
Cana-fucking-da, the whole fucking earth!'' I slugged his
shoulder. "And God puts it there for you, hero! Out of
gratitude!''

"You're not listening to me.''

"Because you manifest His conscience for Him, hero.
Nobody does that like you do it. That's why He put you
here.''

"Durk, listen to me, will you? None of that means shit to
me!''

"So you're having a little Dark Night of the Soul, that's
all.''

"No, that isn't all.''

I put my hand on his shoulder. "Look, Michael, if I were
you I'd be sick thinking about what's coming up. But I'm not
you. More to the point, you're not me. You can deal with
it.''

"And you couldn't? Why the hell am I special?''

"I don't know. But you are. That's the fact of it, Michael.
You have a strength the rest of us lack. You're stuck with it.
And that's why more is asked of you.''

"No, more is asked of everybody. If we filled the jails the
war would end.''

"If we filled the jails we'd fill the jails, that's all.''

"Well, that makes me a chump, doesn't it?''

"Why? For manifesting God's conscience on earth? What
better thing for a priest to do? You're a *priest*, Michael!
That's the difference between you and me. It's a big difference.
Priests sustain the rest of us. We draw on you for courage and
for gentleness and for moral example. Maybe we suck life out
of you. That's what we need you for. I see the problem; I see
your problem. Who do priests draw on? Who do priests suck
life out of? Who sustains the sustainer? Well, you have to
answer that one. I can't.''

"In theory, God does.''

"He always has, right?"

"Yes."

"Well?"

"It's different this time."

"Why?"

This was when he could have told me. He was silent for some moments, then took a hit of gin. "I guess because I'm older. I don't know. Maybe I'm afraid of dying. I told you. When we were kids we didn't know how easily things get lost."

I put my arm around his shoulder. "Michael, you won't lose me."

He looked at me sadly. This was the last time we got drunk together. "Just don't call me 'hero,' all right?"

When the appeals process had finally run its futile course, Michael was ordered to begin serving his sentence on the first day of December 1969.

And he might have.

But in late November news stories began appearing about an "alleged massacre" of civilians that was reported to have taken place in a Vietnamese village variously referred to as "Pinkville," "Songmy" and "My Lai." The story came out in disjointed pieces and at first without sensation. Courts-martial of certain junior officers were discreetly under way, and that was what began attracting the attention of reporters. At first the civilian death toll was put at forty-three, then at "somewhat over a hundred." By the end of November more than ten American GIs who admitted participating had given reporters their accounts of the incident.

For most of a day in late March of 1968, dozens of American soldiers, acting under orders of officers, had herded more than five hundred old men, children and women into the village square, into fields and into a large drainage ditch where they fired their automatic weapons on them at close range. This was not the act of frenzied, panic-stricken boys, but of lucid soldiers who had come to regard every Vietnamese person—every "Dink"—of whatever age or position as the enemy. There was one American casualty, a GI who shot himself in the foot rather than obey. The "Combat Action

Report'' about the incident, filed by the lieutenant colonel who supervised from his helicopter, called it an "attack that was well-planned, well-executed and successful."

When *Life* magazine, the last week in November, published nine gruesome photographs, eight in color, showing corpses of babies piled on one another, of toothless old women and Pappa-san men strewn in paddies, of hundreds of villagers stretched along a ditch, the world was stunned. The photographs had been taken secretly and held back until now by a disgusted but frightened army photographer. His pictures and his testimony were the most damning revelations of the whole war.

Only two weeks before, on November 15, a quarter of a million Americans had marched on Washington, the largest demonstration in the capital's history, demanding an immediate end to the war. They had thought that they grasped its horrors in full dimension, but they didn't. Now suddenly the rhetoric of the radicals, crazy youngsters who threw stones at cops and broke windows at peace marches, seemed justified. The first shock of My Lai would lead to others, and it would take months before the full story of that and related atrocities became known. But in those first weeks of the My Lai disclosures Americans grasped viscerally, finally, what the Vietnamese had long known. The war itself was the atrocity.

Still, I was surprised that that was what Michael wanted to talk about. It was snowing lightly, but neither of us paid much attention to the weather. I was aware of Michael's weighty mood and thought he had a right to one, since this was his last day of freedom. We were walking across the plaza at Lincoln Center. It was where we habitually strolled when he came to see me at my office in the new Fordham building on Sixtieth Street. The huge Chagall tapestries dominated the square even from inside the glass facade of the Met. Ahead of us snowflakes dusted Henry Moore's reclining nude, that massive stolid sculpture which I'd come to think of as the steely heart of New York City. It was noontime.

Why the hell was he going on about the war? He was on his way to jail! Wasn't Vietnam someone else's problem now?

"Did you read that about Calley? How he tore that infant

from the Buddhist priest's arms so that he could shoot the priest? And then how he shot the infant? His M-16 must have cut that baby in half.''

Michael's agitation made me impatient, but it alarmed me too. I hadn't felt it at such a pitch since Nicholas Wiley's death. We turned the corner at the far side of the reflecting pool in front of the Vivian Beaumont. In reply I was reduced both by my concern for him and by my despair at the war to saying simply, "It's grotesque."

"No, no, Durk! You miss the point if you think of it as grotesque. Don't you see, it's ordinary! It's commonplace! Calley is what this war has become. The army is full of Calleys now. He's no exception."

"Come on, Michael. Don't go SDS on me."

"Calley does it up close, that's all. But it's the same thing."

"I don't think it's quite—"

"Ask the Vietnamese! It's the same to them!"

"The point is, Calley's being court-martialed, isn't he?"

"Yes, because some kid blew the whistle and forced the issue. So they string up an imbecile lieutenant and a few Pfc's from Tennessee . . .''

"And Captain Medina."

". . . when it's the generals who should be hung, especially Sennett."

"Who's Sennett?"

"Brigadier General David Sennett, the commander of Fort Hamilton in Brooklyn."

"I don't get it."

"He was the Eleventh Infantry Brigade commander in March of sixty-eight. Calley was his boy. My Lai was his operation."

"Look, Michael, if you think the brass will be held accountable for this thing you're wrong. You might as well hope they bring Agnew and Nixon to court for it. Somebody has to be tried for shit like My Lai. Why not the animals who actually did it?"

"Durk, listen to me!" He took me by the arm and pushed me to a low, concrete parapet. We sat. "My Lai gives us a brand-new chance to force the American people to look at

what this war has become, what it's been for years. I'll tell
you who's responsible for My Lai: *we* are! Goddamnit, isn't
that the point, finally? We rejected this war as a people two
years ago, but it's worse than ever! So everyone marches on
Washington. But Nixon ignores it. Thieu uses his army against
his own people. Agnew rants about the kooks. A few of us
timidly break the law and get locked up. And we all throw
our hands in the air and say, 'Well, we tried!' But meanwhile
our boys keep going over there by the thousands after raising
pet rabbits in boot camp so the DI can snap their necks. And
yes, then they're animals! And they *will* do anything! To
anyone! Do you hear me? That's what this war has done! Our
soldiers will do anything to anyone! Do you hear me?''

"Yes. So does half of Manhattan.''

We stared at each other. Steam puffed from his mouth and
nostrils. Finally he said, "West Point is playing basketball
against Saint John's tomorrow night at Madison Square Garden.
The local commander always attends Army games as a kind
of presiding officer. General Sennett's going to be in the front
row at midcourt. There's going to be a demonstration and I
am going to be a part of it.''

"But you can't! You go into custody tomorrow!''

"That's what I wanted to tell you. I'm not turning myself
in. I'm not cooperating with the government anymore, Durk.
Authority has to be legitimate.'' Michael smiled. "Even
Saint Thomas said that. If this government wants me to obey
it, then they can stop the war. If they won't call the real
criminals to account, then we will. If they want me tomorrow,
they can come to Madison Square Garden.''

At first, so domesticated—housebroken—was my mind that
I did not understand what he was saying. Had his lawyer
obtained an extension from the court? Of course not. Even
before I spoke I grasped in its full dimension the enormity,
the audacity, of what he'd said. "You mean you're going
to . . . ?'' I didn't have a word for it.

But he did. "Resist, Durk. I'm going to resist. Not out of
rebelliousness. You know me. I'm no revolutionary. I hate
what I've come to. But I see now what we have to do—
challenge and if we can, destroy America's faith in people
like General Sennett and General Abrams . . .''

"And Nixon?"

"As far as the war goes, yes. GIs have to stop obeying their officers. Teenage boys have to stop obeying their draftboards. And peaceniks have to stop obeying the courts."

"Michael, you've lost me. Honest to God, you've lost me. The last time we talked you told me you'd had it. You were through. You'd done your part."

"I was indulging myself, Durk. I'd become obsessed with my anxiety about prison. What's that next to the sacrifice of the Vietnamese? My Lai reminded me, that's all. At first I thought I was doing this because I *am* afraid of prison, but that's not it. I'll go to jail eventually, but not before I strike a real blow at the war. Americans, if you face them with it, won't tolerate this thing. And that's what I'm going to do, face them with it. Before we're through, Durk, it won't be that kids refuse induction, but that their mothers and fathers won't let the army near their kids."

"Where will you go?"

"To America," he said, utterly without self-consciousness. "If the government wants me they can come out there and catch me, where everyone can see."

The melodrama of his statement, the cartoon-talk about "America" so typical of the time, stands out starkly now as I repeat it, but then it seemed eloquent. His bravado simply took my breath away. My God, I thought, it's the old Michael Maguire, the boy-soldier hero hurtling down a hill against an enemy patrol to save his wounded buddies and their priest, the young idealist handing over the rest of his life in one wrapped package to the Lord, the priest off to Vietnam to rescue children, then defying the cardinal to bury Nicholas Wiley. Yet now Michael seemed readier, as if every previous act of boldness—*'L'audace! Toujours l'audace!'*—was practice for this one.

"And this means," he said, "I'm going to owe you a lot of money. I'll be forfeiting bail. That's your twenty thousand dollars. That's what I'm here to talk about. I'm telling you right now that somehow, someday I'll see that you're repaid."

For a moment I felt sick at the thought of all that money, which was *all* of my money, going up in smoke, the smoke of his sacrifice. I couldn't reply.

He said, "I feel terrible about it," and I saw that he did.

But then it hit me, what was money, even that sum, in such a context? Michael was talking about an ultimate act. He had become, in a way, an ultimate man.

And I? At that moment I was like everyone. I forgot what he'd shown me in secret, the cost of his world-saving, charismatic integrity, the cost in loneliness and self-doubt. I rejoiced instinctively to see him large again, unyielding, the rock of our rejection. My reservations—I thought his decision was quixotic, foolhardy and dangerous—were obliterated by the pride I felt just to be his friend. I thought him right about the war, about America and about My Lai as the turning point we'd been awaiting.

"Forget the money, Michael," I said, "I mean, please. And tell me now exactly what I can do to help."

TWENTY-NINE

And when our work is done
Our course on earth is run
May it be said, "Well done;
Be thou at peace."
E'er may that line of gray
Increase from day to day,
Live, serve and die we pray,
West Point, for thee.

AFTER the robust, throaty rendition of their alma mater, the cadets, a thousand strong and concentrated, a gray mass, in the upper seats, let out one of their startling, sustained roars. The noise, like a balloon expanding in a box, pressed against the walls and girdered ceiling of the Garden. West Point cadets make the best roars in sport because of all that pent-up energy and their acquired knack for unison. Only seminarians could match them in those traits. Seminarians, of course, do not learn to roar since they are not, most of them, being trained for battle.

The roar did not fade until the referee tossed the ball into the air at center court. The Redmen snagged it and immediately moved on Army's basket; three quick passes, a feint, a shot, swish! Saint John's would never lose the lead. By halftime the score was 42–28. Even the automated cadets in the stands had gone slightly limp. The Saint John's fans across the arena looked like long-haired hippies next to the Corps, though in fact they were relatively conservative Catholic kids from Queens and would have looked downright square at Dupont Circle or Haight-Ashbury or, for that matter, in Greenwich Village. But by now even to most of them, the army was the enemy of their generation, and the cadets were traitors to it. They wanted their ballplayers to beat West Point mercilessly.

It was because of the abuse Military Academy teams regularly took at other colleges during the late sixties that the local commanders compulsively attended the games. They always sat, bedecked and accompanied by aides, in a prominent seat. It was like setting up a commandpost on a ridge so that both your enemy and your own forces would behold your nerve and be, in one case, shaken and, in the other, reinforced. At halftime General Sennett stood in his place in the first row at center court and greeted well-wishers, old friends, retired officers and celebrities.

When the priest walked out onto the court with a microphone in his hand, the general assumed, as the guards had, he was some functionary from Saint John's about to begin the halftime program. He looked innocuous in his Clark Kent spectacles, black suit and Roman collar.

"Ladies and gentlemen," he said, "may I have your attention, please." At first the crowd ignored him. Sennett took his seat, however, and the cadets, seeing that, fell silent. Soon the quiet spread across the Garden. The priest was alone in the middle of the court. "Please come forward," he said. Suddenly from seats and aisles in all parts of the arena, men and women filed onto the court. They moved with ceremonial dignity, donning white conical hats as they did so. Sennett was among the first to recognize those as stylized Vietnamese peasant hats, and he was close enough to read what was written on them: "Old Woman," "Infant," "Buddhist Nun," "Village Elder," and so on. The priest, Sennett realized, was staring at him as he said, "Think of these four hundred and twenty-two people as the old men, women and children who lived in a small village in Quang Ngai Province until March 16, 1968. That was the day that you, General Sennett, as the commanding officer of the Eleventh Infantry Brigade, sent Task Force Barker, led by Lieutenant Colonel Frank Barker, including Charlie Company, led by Captain Ernest Medina, including a platoon led by Lieutenant William Calley, against their village, which was called My Lai.'' By this time the several hundred demonstrators had joined the priest on the court. They stood rigidly, like figures in a mime, pointed in every direction, their faces obscured by their conical hats. After a long silence during which there was no sound from anyone in Madison Square Garden, the priest said, slowly and distinctly, the sound system carrying every nuance of his voice, ''General Sennett, we accuse you of and charge you with the murder of these people.''

At that all four hundred and twenty-two demonstrators— the ''infants,'' ''elders'' and ''nuns''—fell to the floor, limp. Like that, snap! They were a mass of corpses! Only the priest remained standing.

After an initial gasp, the crowd was absolutely still, too stunned to react, with the exception of photographers, whose cameras clicked and whirred.

Sennett stared at the priest. His face was a blank mask.

The priest said, ''May God forgive you. We do not.'' And then he took off his glasses, his gesture toward disguise. He walked off the court, stepping around the ''corpses'' as he did so.

The newspapers the next day made much of the fact that at the very moment Michael Maguire was confronting the army general in front of twelve thousand people, the FBI was searching for him in New York rectories. As of noon that day he had become a fugitive priest.

It was a powerful myth for Catholics of the old school. The priest on the run, the outlaw celebrant, the Jesuit with a price on his head. Fugitive priests had founded the Church in the Catacombs while Caesar's legions hunted them. Fugitive priests had kept the last flicker of the true faith alive in Elizabethan England while the queen's men stalked them. They hid in priest-holes, in secret rooms behind fireplaces. They went about disguised as lawyers or teachers, and the people revered them. Their legends grew even while they lived, and when at last they were caught and martyred, the Church remembered them as saints. They were Thomas, James and Peter, Edmund Campion, Robert Southwell and John Fisher. There were fugitive priests in Ireland and then, in our own time, in Europe under the Nazis, in China under Communists, and in Latin America under military regimes. As children my generation of Catholics read comic books about them, and articles in *Our Sunday Visitor*. We celebrated their feast days and prayed to grow up with their courage and their willingness to risk everything for God. We sang how sweet 'twould be if we "like them could die for Thee." Now there was a priest-fugitive in our own country, hounded not by Caesar or the queen, Hitler, Stalin, Mao or some generalissimo, but by that other company of our heroes, the FBI.

Michael taunted them. Within a week of having "gone underground" he began the dramatic series of surprise appearances at rallies and in churches, making speeches, preaching sermons, and giving interviews, stealthily, to reporters. A network of dozens of people from Washington to Boston sprang up to help him, to hide him, to arrange his meetings with students and with antiwar and church groups. Brave strangers drove him from one rendezvous to another.

Carolyn and I were not among that network and neither were his other close friends. For the most part, during his months underground, we did not know where he was. Obviously we were being watched and our phones were surely tapped. Michael was in the hands, mainly, of Jewish professors, ironically, and that was why he succeeded beyond anyone's expectation. The FBI, lumpishly, concentrated on us Catholics.

Still, we heard stories about him. Not many days would pass without some report from that unlikely outlaw subculture about his latest escapade. There we were, sophisticated academics, journalists and professionals all up and down the East Coast, but we were like kids with ears to the radio. *Gangbusters! The FBI in Peace and War! The Shadow!* In the snatches of what we heard we knew that a legend was being made. A legend, unbelievably, for the likes of us.

In Washington in late January there was a meeting of top leaders from around the country of CALC, Clergy and Laity Concerned About Vietnam. About seventy of them, men and women of various denominations, gathered to coordinate plans for the upcoming campaign to lobby congressmen to cut off funds for the war. They were meeting in the basement auditorium of a Baptist church in Northeast Washington, not far, ironically, from Catholic University where Michael had done his training. At the start of their morning session the chairman melodramatically promised the group that before the meeting adjourned that day they would be hearing from, as he put it, "the priest-prophet of the peace movement." No one at that meeting had to have it spelled out that that meant Michael Maguire, and the anticipation that even those hard-boiled activists felt at the prospect of his coming was a distraction of the first order all day.

Sure enough, late in the day, after their workshops and small group meetings, the people reassembled in the auditorium. Word had spread to other local clergy and activists. Even seminarians from Catholic U. showed up, filling the corridors and stairwells outside the basement hall. The uninvited overflow were ushered into the unheated church upstairs, and soon even it was full. There the people stared at an empty sanctuary, the cold air showing the vapor of their breath, and they listened closely to the proceedings downstairs through the squawky sound system. The CALC meeting had turned into an ad-hoc rally. A folksinger led choruses of "Blowin' in the Wind" and "If I Had a Hammer." A black poet in Muslim dress read verses that asked questions of the Vietnamese. (Do you not curse us in your sleeping and your waking?) A gospel choir sang three rousing numbers. A minister from Indian Territory in South Dakota spoke feelingly about the old American custom of genocide. And then silence fell over both groups, down and up, as the CALC chairman took the podium.

No sooner had he introduced Michael than Michael's voice, cutting short the applause, filled the auditorium and the church with heartfelt exhortations addressed expressly to the organizers. "CALC exists to save lives!"

No sooner had his speech begun than half a dozen men, some bearded and wearing fringe-leather jackets and some clean-shaven, dark-suited, looking like clerics, left the pews of the upper church hurriedly. They dashed down the stairs to the auditorium and burst into it, with guns drawn, crying, "Freeze! FBI!" Their FBI colleagues who had infiltrated the auditorium ahead of them looked sheepishly back from their chairs. Those agents hadn't moved because they knew the truth, that Father Maguire's ringing antiwar speech, which had not stopped or slowed or broken cadence despite the interruption, was even then being delivered by a large, reel-to-reel tape machine balanced precariously and quite visibly on the otherwise vacant podium.

Another time Michael appeared at a so-called Celebration of Resistance at the University of Connecticut at Storrs, a typical college town in the farming area north of Hartford. The weekend festival, with music, speeches, "political theater," slide-shows and movies, was held in the huge university fieldhouse. The place was packed for the Saturday night rally because Jane Fonda was appearing. That Father Michael Maguire unexpectedly joined her was like Mick Jagger showing up at a Janis Joplin concert. Fonda embraced the renegade priest chastely when he walked onto the stage. When she turned then and introduced him to the crowd, most of whom had recognized him and were already cheering, the seven widely scattered, overweight and nervous campus policemen got orders from their chief through their walkie-talkies to converge on the platform and arrest him. Students saw the cops moving and spontaneously, good-naturedly, spilled into the aisles, slowing them. Michael spoke only for a moment— "Resistance, yes! Violence, no!"—and then disappeared backstage. He made good his escape inside one of the giant puppet heads of the mime troupe that had preceded Jane Fonda on the evening's program. The papier-mâché head that enabled him to slip by the police was, in fact, a dreary, gray monster, the writhing face of death.

Between these dramatic, much-discussed appearances, Michael shuttled from place to place driven by strangers, people whose names he made a point not to know. In the cities, his movements and contacts were orchestrated by a handful of organizers, four or five at the most, whose identities I never knew. Obviously, given his success, they were people Michael had reason to trust. The longer he was at large—and it had never occurred to them in the beginning that he would elude capture for so many months—the more smoothly the network functioned. He hid out in little attic rooms or apartments over garages. His attitude toward the strangers who harbored him was one of utter trust, a kind of abandon, although he refused to stay with families with young children, who would not understand why their parents and a priest would break the law. He did not go out in daylight even when he was in small towns that seemed far removed from the controversies of the day. Mostly he was sheltered in the nicer suburbs where lived the professors, ministers, rabbis, psychiatrists and social workers his hosts tended to be: Newton outside Boston, Columbia near Baltimore, Summit, New Jersey, Media outside Philadelphia. He avoided New York, where he was so well known, and places like New Haven, Cambridge and Princeton, which the FBI were sure to stake out. Though he was on the platform often with antiwar celebrities, he never hid out with them. And he had nothing whatever to do with the anarchistic underground of the SDS and its spin-off groups of crazies. Instead he lost himself among an anonymous mass of average, essentially moderate people. They were no "underground" at all, but had simply come to hate the war passionately and now welcomed Michael, despite the risks, as a way of turning up the volume on their "no" to it. In the evenings, Michael habitually encouraged his hosts to have friends over so they could talk. Just being exposed to him in such informal settings, knowing that that huge posse of Hoover's agents was outside looking for him, realizing what risks he was taking and most of all experiencing up close his compelling, single-minded but strangely relaxed and self-accepting dedication was enough to change people in fundamental ways. It was commonly said by men and women who met him in such circumstances—I heard this second and third hand often—that for the first time since they'd turned against the war they believed they could make a difference to it, they could help stop it. Michael Maguire, by example, by manner, by what he said and especially by how he lived, was shattering the paralysis of doubt, futility and frustration people felt. When they asked him, as they always did, "But what can *we* do?" he would smile, raise his shoulders and say, "You've already broken the law by being here with me. You are in resistance now. So keep resisting." An act of disobedience had freed him once so that when the opportunity came to strike a real blow against the war he could take it. Now he had become himself the occasion of disobedience for others, and many of those, in fact, found it to be as freeing for action as he had. He left a trail of recruits to the antiwar movement behind him, men and women who would give it their best energy for years.

Ironically, because of him, some of those liberals found themselves reconsidering their attitudes toward that most reactionary of impulses, belief, and that most conservative of institutions, the Church. For whatever else Michael was during that time, he was never more a priest. Perhaps only the unchurched who did not take such things for granted could fully appreciate that the driving force of his resistance was his spirituality. Those who were sensitive to it were moved, and those who weren't still knew that this man had depths they couldn't touch. He was rarely with religious people, and so mostly he prayed by himself. Prayer, the hagiographers would say, became his one steadfast companion.

In the interviews he gave and in his short talks in that variety of settings he hammered away at what My Lai revealed. The story of that massacre and the subsequent army cover-up that was exposed that winter gave him his theme and made his message accessible to a broad public. Not even staunch supporters of the war were unaffected by the news of My Lai. Even military men professed repugnance. Sennett himself was eventually censured, reduced in rank and stripped of his DSM. Horror at the war spread to average people, and Father Michael Maguire gave voice to it. His hit-and-run appearances were widely covered in the media, though not with universal approbation. Editorials blasted him regularly, but the average journalists who wrote the news stories about him hardly disguised how enthralled they were. A surprisingly large segment of viewers and readers followed the dramatic unfolding of his defiance with sympathy. Groups, including apolitical and patriotic ones, began passing resolutions of support for the fugitive priest. Vestries and parish councils began inviting him to their churches to preach. At times organizers of antiwar rallies deliberately began rumors that Michael was coming as a way of drawing television coverage for their demonstrations, and that made it seem as if he was capable of a kind of omnipresence; Father Maguire, more than once, was reported to have been in Washington and Boston on the same night. Hadn't he become like Superman?

Cardinal Cooke steadfastly refused all comment about the notorious priest, although a Vatican spokesman in Rome said the pope was praying for him. Reports from Stockholm had it that he was a candidate for the Nobel Peace Prize (which had yet to be given to Henry Kissinger). It was a period when the sixties ended and the seventies began, and though Michael Maguire's defiance seemed to embody a massive national repudiation of the war, the brutal bombing of the North was resumed in those months and plans were laid for the invasion of Cambodia. We had no idea how utterly immune from influence, moral or political, the warmakers always were.

In January, despite its own condescension toward him, the *New York Times Sunday Magazine* ran a long, dramatic interview with Michael. The reporter described having been searched, blindfolded, and driven in successive cars to a farmhouse well outside of New York City. It was like *Breathless, Bonnie and Clyde* or *Easy Rider,* only this criminal was no psychopath, no weirdo, no loser, but, in the reporter's estimate, an accomplished, intelligent, admirable man. In February his picture appeared on the cover of *Time* and the accompanying article was entitled ''Wanted and Needed.'' If his appeal among Catholics grew out of the myth of the fugitive priest, his appeal to the people as a whole—it seemed eventually that the entire country was rooting for him—grew out of the classic American romance with the decent outlaw—Who was that masked man?—who challenges the crooked sheriff not for his own ends but for the town's.

The door bell rang. Carolyn looked up sharply from her book.

I looked at the clock. It was nearly midnight, a Saturday in February. The house was utterly still. Molly was asleep in her room at last. A school friend was sleeping over and they had drawn out the goodnights endlessly. Carolyn and I had each made trips to silence giggles.

I waited for the bell to ring again. It didn't. Finally I put my own book aside, took my glasses off, and stood. Carolyn stayed where she was.

I opened the door. No one was there. When I stepped out onto the stoop to look down the street I think I half-expected someone to jump on me. No one did. I went back into the house and shut the door. On the floor below the mail slot was a piece of paper the size of a business card. I might have missed seeing it. I picked it up, but was afraid to read it, as if the FBI could see through wood. I went into the living room. The curtains were drawn, as they always were that winter. By Carolyn's lamp I squinted at the piece of paper. "Come to the eleven o'clock at Saint John the Divine," it said, and nothing more. No signature, no peace sign, no Chi-Rho. But the handwriting was as familiar to me as my own. I let Carolyn read it. We did not exchange a word. Then I dropped the note onto the embers in the fireplace and watched it flame.

We left the house the next morning at eight-thirty and spent an hour and a half riding various subway trains, hopping on and off at the last minute the way Cary Grant and Audrey Hepburn would have. We came up at Times Square, caught a taxi to Columbus Circle, walked to the Paulist church, went in one door and out another, and caught another taxi to Saint John's. We arrived feeling exhausted and nervous at ten minutes before eleven.

The organ was playing softly, far from full out, but the tones filled the vast church. On the wooden chairs and needlepointed cushions—not pews with kneelers, the Catholic notes—several dozen people sat and knelt. But in that space dozens counted for nothing. Others arrived as we did, shaking their heavy coats open and walking with a certain timidity into the overwhelming Gothic nave. The mammoth piers, curving stone pillars rising one hundred feet in a single, stark leap, dwarfed everything human. It took an act of intellect to recall that those columns themselves were made by men too; the sacred space itself was human. I watched the other arriving worshipers, hoping they would make the cathedral seem less empty. They were older and well, but not flashily, dressed. The men wore their hair slick and the women wore hats. Except for an occasional young person wearing blue jeans and an angelic expression, the gathering congregation seemed like establishment Episcopalians, as one might have expected. Of course, establishment Episcopalians by then, led by their outspoken Bishop Paul Moore and theologians like

Pike and Stringfellow, were resolutely against the war. Still, that the pulpit of this cathedral might be offered to Michael Maguire, the fugitive priest, amazed me. As I walked well to the front of the center aisle, clutching Carolyn's arm, my anxiety, like the architecture, soared. We took our places. I knelt at once and tried to pray. My mind was whirling along, and in the end, like a schoolboy, I mumbled my Hail Mary and sat.

At the appointed time a blast from the trumpets behind us reverberated the full length of the cathedral. As we rose, I held a hymnal for Carolyn, but neither of us sang. We turned to watch the ranks of choir, clergy and attendants enter. How sparse the congregation seemed! There may have been several hundred, but they seemed a paltry number and the strains of their singing were lost in the vaulted shadows. Still the procession was impressive, with boys carrying medieval banners ahead of the choir. The paired singers passed pompously, and then came the candle-bearers, the crucifer and thurifer whose incense pot spewed forth a pungent, billowing cloud through which strode the subdeacon, deacon and presiding priest. The smoke stung my eyes. There was no sign of Michael.

The last time Carolyn had attended a Solemn High Mass had been at Michael's ordination in Saint Patrick's a decade before. Such liturgy, with chanted prayers, the Gregorian music, the incense, the hierarchy of officiants—as opposed to concelebrants—in old-fashioned fiddleback vestments, was rarely seen in post-Council Catholicism. It seemed strange to think of it as a Protestant service, since it was more familiar to me, and more beautiful, than anything I'd seen in a Catholic church in years.

It was the first Sunday of Lent and there was no *Gloria*. After singing the *Kyrie*, the choir sat and the Scriptures were read by lectors. And then the celebrant, identified by the program as the dean of the cathedral, the Reverend Thomas Reid Evans, mounted the elaborately carved white marble pulpit. Father Evans was a huge man—he had to be in that space—and his head was crowned dramatically with white hair, though he did not impress as old. He wore spectacles, but took them off with a flourish as he began to speak.

"For reasons that will be obvious to you in a moment, it was not possible for me to consult in advance with either the liturgical committee or the standing committee of the board of trustees, and for the sake of limiting possible legal jeopardy, I decided not to consult with the bishop but used my own discretion—my *sole* discretion—as the pastor of this community to invite into our pulpit this morning, on this first Sunday of the Penitential Season, a priest of the Church who has restored to us in all its power the commission priests receive from the Lord Himself to go forth into the world preaching the Gospel of Peace."

Abruptly, with no further comment, he turned and descended the pulpit and resumed his chair in the sanctuary. After a moment a bearded man robed in white and wearing a purple stole walked from behind the carved choir stalls up the length of the Choir. He bowed at the altar as he crossed in front of it, then walked to the pulpit and mounted it.

The beard threw me. He looked like an English actor. But when I heard his voice as he blessed himself and pronounced the sign of the cross, I wanted to cry out with joy for the sight of him. The old son of a bitch! My dearest friend!

Carolyn seized my hand and squeezed it. As we listened to him, I knew that I would never forget what he said.

He recited first this verse from Luke: "And when he drew near and saw the city he wept over it saying, 'Would that even today you knew the things that make for peace.' "

He paused. He seemed to look at each of us in the congregation singly.

"My dear friends," he said softly, "a brief word about the things that make for peace. There are three, Faith, Hope and Love. Faith is the easiest of these because it is an act of God's, not ours. The question is not whether we believe in Him, but whether He believes in us. And we have the absolute promise—the Flesh of His Son—that He does. God is the Faithful One. He is faithful even to us. Therefore we can, as Paul says, move mountains. We can even, perhaps, end wars.

"And Hope. Hope is the ability to see more than is before our eyes. We look at all the damned of this century, a hundred million killed needlessly in war, and know that we have turned the earth itself into the village of My Lai. Yet

instead of seeing mere victims, reasons to hate the living,
Hope sees in that host of war-dead a Communion of Saints
who even now prepare to swoop down on us and seize us and
shake us from our complacency. Live! they say. Stand! they
say. Be what you are, creators of the future with God!
Despair is the conviction that we can do nothing to end the
war. And that is the last sin, the most costly sin. It dooms not
just the one who commits it, but, in this century, the fragile
world itself. In Hope, therefore, we tear that despair from our
bosoms, our stony hearts, and we hurl it at heaven, crying to
all those men, women and children, the victims of our recent
history, 'Come you holy spirits! Renew the face of the earth!'

"And Love. Love, as Dorothy Day insists, is a harsh and
dreadful thing. It is not romance or infatuation or an ocean of
warm feelings. Love is radical communion with all those who
have been forgotten or condemned or brutally massacred.
Love, in our dispensation, is a crucifixion. How can we end
the war? We have been told and told again. Each of us in his
or her own way must take up the Cross and follow. Its road
leads outside the city, away from comfort and security and
the nurture of those who cherish us. The Cross, remember,
puts us in the company of criminals, of fugitives, of those on
whom presidents and generals, tribunes and centurians only
spit. We have never been in better company in our lives.

"Faith, Hope and Love. The things that make for peace.
And the greatest of these, Paul wrote, is Love. It was the
discovery he made while in prison. With chained hands Paul
wrote his messages—his love letters—to those who sustained
him, who held him dear. They feared for him. But he said,
'No! Do not be afraid! Do not lose faith! Do not despair!
Work for peace! We have the promises of Christ! We have
His Word! The presidents and generals, the principalities and
powers pursue me and will imprison me. But they can never
imprison the Word of the Lord!' "

Michael turned in the pulpit toward me, and his eyes found
mine. It was the first indication that he knew I was there. His
sermon until this point had been delivered in a quiet voice,
but his voice rose now as he ringingly repeated the last
sentence. "They can never imprison the Word of the Lord!"
He raised his hand to his mouth. I thought he was going to

bless himself, but instead he touched his finger to his lips, a kiss, and then he threw it to us, to Carolyn and to me. And he turned, went down from the pulpit, and was gone.

There was silence for a moment and then the congregation burst into muted but amazed conversation. "My God," someone behind us said, "that was Father Maguire!" He said it in the awed tone of the cow-town barber: "That was the Lone Ranger!"

Carolyn leaned against me. I felt how drained she was. We clung to each other. I loved her more than ever. Michael—I could admit this at last—was what bound us.

After the Creed Dean Evans knelt and led us in prayer. He prayed for peace, and he prayed for "Our dear brother Michael. Carry him, O Lord, in the palm of Thy hand. Protect him from violent men. And open the ears of all who hear him. And open our hearts, that we too might be instruments of Thy Peace. We pray in the name of Christ."

"Amen," the people answered resoundingly.

By the time the offertory hymn was finished and the wine and bread were prepared, FBI agents had arrived. The congregation had not been unanimously edified after all.

The agents, eight that I counted, walked along the side aisles eyeing us sheepishly. Their hair was close-cropped and they carried their hats in their hands. They were ill at ease and for good reason; they were Catholics. You could feel them itching to genuflect. How strange their business must have seemed to them suddenly. How they'd have preferred to raid a gambling den or a chop-shop. How bizarre that setting must have seemed to them, the Roman liturgy, the Gothic church, the incense, candles, holy water, vestments. Were these Protestants or not? And was their quarry a criminal or a saint? Why weren't such distinctions sharp like they used to be?

I wanted to call out to them, "Sorry, G-Men! You missed him again!

But all at once I felt sorry for them.

At the *Sanctus* we said with one voice, and it seemed to me defiantly, "Blessed is he who comes in the name of the Lord!"

*   *   *

Carolyn and I wanted to meet Dean Evans and thank him, so we went to the coffee hour at the Cathedral House, a Gothic château on the south side of the cathedral compound. The reception was in a splendid room with a gnarled timber ceiling and huge leaded windows and rare carpets on the floor. I was told that originally it was the bishop's house, and when someone faulted it for being too elegant, J. P. Morgan, a trustee, defended it by saying, "Bishops should live like everyone else."

Dean Evans greeted us cordially and introduced us to his handsome, confident wife. To them we were just two of several hundred worshipers. I wanted them to know we had come expressly to hear Michael. I said, "We're friends of Father Maguire. We're Catholics." In another context that would have been a stupid identification, an offensive one, but in that context it was exactly right. The Episcopal dean knew what I was saying. At his ordination Michael had given my faith in God back to me, and now, after a decade in which such distinctions had been blurred, he'd given me back my affiliation. For the first time since my days as a Good Shepherd altar boy, I could take pride in calling myself a Catholic.

"He is the jewel of the Church," the dean said. "I'm glad that you were here."

"Will you be in jeopardy now?" Carolyn asked.

"I hope so."

The dean's wife put her arm through her husband's. "Father Maguire has changed things here," she said.

The dean smiled. "She means he's changed some sheep into lions. It was people like us who began this war. Well, maybe it's time people like us ended it."

Their sense of themselves, so large, though not precisely arrogant—we start, we finish—was what struck me. It wouldn't have occurred to my people to feel responsible for Vietnam, though given its peculiarly Catholic origins, we should have. But in Good Shepherd High School in all its incarnations we learned to feel responsible only for our sex-weakened souls if at all. At Groton, Exeter, Saint Paul's and Choate, which indeed spawned the National Security Clique who ran the war, they were taught to feel responsible for the world. The dean was right. And so was Michael to go after him and his kind. Turn them against the Vietnam war, mobilize *their* anger, unstop *their* impotence and you will have more than torn draft files and burned cards, more than riots in the streets, more than teach-ins and demonstrations. You will have peace.

"Smug, aren't they?" I said to Carolyn as we left. I couldn't quite stifle my inborn Irish resentment.

She shook her head. "I wish Michael got support like that from his own people."

"His own people are chasing him."

We went out into the raw day and were crossing the broad garden, "the Cathedral Close," that was enclosed on one side by the imposing Synod House, yet another Gothic masterpiece, and on the other by the buttressed flank of the cathedral itself. As we walked toward Amsterdam Avenue we had to lean into the wind. It was Lenten weather. I hated it.

At the towering monument in the center of the Close, the platform crowned by the classic spire, Carolyn stopped. "What is that?"

It was the elaborate pulpit, the focus of the outdoor services that had been common before the nave was built, but I teased her. "It's the topmost spire of the Underground Church."

She laughed and opened her arms. I went into them. "Oh, Frank, let's not go home. Let's spend the afternoon together."

"I'd love that. We could ride the ferry like we used to and then get plowed at Desmond's."

"Yes, that's it! Let's!" Her face broke into a smile. "I'd love that. I'll go call Emily and see if she'll stay with Molly through the afternoon."

"I'll wait here," I said. I was glad to have left the Cathedral House crowd behind. I watched Carolyn retrace our steps. She was wearing a dark sheepskin coat and boots. She looked like a Russian princess. I felt a surge of affection for her. How her impulse pleased me!

"Mister Durkin?" A familiar man approached from the direction of the Synod House. He was wearing a dark overcoat and hat and as he drew near I saw him reach into his inside pocket. I knew even before he flashed it at me that he was pulling out his badge. "I'm Special Agent Finnegan, the Federal Bureau of Investigation."

"I remember you. You were at Father Maguire's trial."

"Yes."

"You testified."

"That's right."

"You were the agent in charge."

"I'm not wild about our work right now, Mister Durkin. I gather you're not either."

"That's right."

"Can we talk for a minute?"

"I'm just waiting for my wife."

"She's a pretty lady."

"Thank you."

"Look, Father Maguire is not doing himself any good this way. They're going to throw the book at him, you know."

"Someone has to catch him first, don't they?"

"Oh, we'll catch him."

"People are beginning to wonder, Mister Finnegan. How do you fellows do against Russians or the Mafia if this is how you do against a priest?"

"A priest has certain advantages. Especially if he's right."

"You think he's right?"

"About the war? Yes."

"I find that surprising, frankly."

"We're not numbskulls, you know. Who supports the war at this point? The question is how to end it. I think Father Maguire is keeping it going. Why should the NLF negotiate seriously if they think the U.S. is about to fold?"

"Wait a minute, I thought you said he's right?"

"His ends are right. Not his means."

"A nice Jesuit's distinction. Where'd you go, Fordham?"

"Georgetown."

"You should have heard his sermon. Even the rich old ladies were very moved."

"Where is he now, Mister Durkin?"

"You come right to the point, don't you?"

"You're his oldest friend. Obviously you knew ahead of time he would be here. Or do you always come here on Sundays?"

"Sometimes. It brings back memories of the Tridentine

Mass, you know? They have everything but sixteenth-century underwear.''

"I thought you might see things a little more reasonably than he does. I thought you might help us for his sake."

"Father Maguire's welfare is your main concern, I guess, huh?"

"Obviously not. But I do think the man is hurting himself."

"I'm not interested in discussing this with you further, Mister Finnegan. I simply can't help you." I saw Carolyn coming out of the Cathedral House toward us.

"Do you know where he is?"

"No. Obviously he'd be a fool to let me know. Your boys have me in their sights all the time."

"Except when you shake them in the subway. On that count alone I could take you downtown, you know."

"Feel free."

The agent stared at me. I read his disdain all too easily. What contempt he had for the likes of me! He made me feel guilty, but how could I have explained to him that my true crime till then had been good citizenship?

"I'm going to come back to see you, Mister Durkin. No one will know but you and me." He glanced toward Carolyn and stepped back, blocking her view of himself with a shrub. "And until I do I want to leave you with something to think about." He paused. Was he waiting for me to ask what? I said nothing. He looked toward Carolyn again and withdrew farther. "Your lovely wife," he said, "and your oldest friend, the famous Father Maguire—they've been fucking their heads off together for years."

"Who was that?" she asked.

I was so relieved to turn toward her, to bathe my eyes in the sight of her. The agent's words had jolted me, but not in the crude way he wanted. I saw his ruse for what it was. He was a desperate man, and with reason. Michael had made him the Bureau buffoon. Obviously Finnegan would try anything now.

But without intending to he'd just done me an enormous favor. He'd put my oldest, worst, fear into words and I was

grateful to him because I saw at once, at last, it was impossible.
Impossible.

"A derelict," I said, hugging her. "A bum who wanted a
handout. Churchyards are full of them."

THIRTY

A
RCHBISHOP O'Shea put his sherry glass down with a definitive flourish. In his view our conversation had ended and it remained only for him to shepherd me as gracefully as he could, given the spilled acid between us, toward the door.

But I refused to move. I was staring into the amber liquid of my own glass, and I saw in its swirl the miniature of my face. A pathetic figure, mine. Why did I feel more strongly than ever the need to win him over? Why did I want so desperately to prolong our talk? He was right; it was pointless. His position, the position of the Church, was clear and fixed. And mine? I was a child having crawled back to be domineered again. I wanted the approval of my rigid father, the worship of my unforgiving mother. And it was not for Michael I craved these goodies, or for Carolyn, but for myself.

"Archbishop," I said carefully, "if Michael Maguire cannot be buried in the Church, is there leeway for some other solution? Another gesture?"

"Like what?"

"I thought perhaps you'd want to come to the service. Perhaps you'd offer a prayer."

He shook his head.

Suddenly a vision of what Michael's funeral would look like filled my head: that vast, dark cathedral and, lost in its shadows, the scrawny company of mourners. Who would be there? A few dozen neighbors, the parents of his children's friends, a handful of co-workers. But more evident than who was there would be who was not. Even a hundred in attendance would seem like no one, and the empty chairs of the mammoth church would stand like rebuking ghosts.

As altar boys Michael and I had served at countless funerals at Good Shepherd. We vied for funerals for unworthy reasons—to miss morning classes, to earn the dollar tip, to ride in the priest's limo out to the cemetery in the Bronx—but also because in that parish nothing edified, nothing affirmed, nothing made us cherish who we were more than that large demonstration of loyalty and loss. Perhaps because the Irish are emotionally inhibited, particularly when it comes to the expression of simple affection, they respond to funerals compulsively, as a last, though often first, opportunity to stand with a friend *as* a friend. Funerals in Good Shepherd were jammed, and the numbers—not the liturgy, not the eulogy, not the holy water or the benediction, just the numbers—were what we cared about. And we, imagining our own funerals, knew that one day the aisles would be crowded with our cronies too. *They* would be weeping by the hundreds. *They* would be clutching rosaries. *They* would be passing hats for our wives and children. Their multitude would represent the finest achievement of our lives, that we had accumulated such abundant love. This dream was one of many we had before we realized to our horror and then relief—or was it the other way around?—that Good Shepherd Parish had everything a man could want: comely wives, cozy taverns, rent control, ball fields and cheap transport to the job; everything but oxygen. When we left Inwood our parents were crushed and their friends regarded us as traitors and the guys in the bars swore that we'd be sorry. And now, finally, I was.

I put my glass by his and stood. He stood. When our eyes met I realized I did not remotely understand him. Despite myself I pressed, "There is one other question, Archbishop."

He blinked at me.

"I'm thinking of Korea. You were on a hill waiting for the enemy to come and kill you. Michael stopped them. He saved your life at a huge cost to himself. Did you ever pay him back for that?"

"No. Once I thought he was asking me to, but he never really did."

I shook my head. "Archbishop, he did just now."

For a moment it seemed he was going to respond, but he did not. I imagined him standing in the hatchway of that helicopter firing an officer's sidearm down at the Chinese soldiers, a killer priest. It was impossible to tell now what if anything he felt, and it seemed ludicrous to me that earlier I had found something in this man to pity. But now the secret in this iciness, in this absolute rejection, revealed itself, and at last I understood. "How he must have hurt you."

A moment later I was on the steaming street.

Alone with my panic.

Panic? you ask. Why panic?

Because I had to return then to Saint John the Divine Cathedral, which was empty of people but full of ghosts. Ancient ghosts: Martin Luther, Henry VIII, Edmund Campion, John Fisher and Thomas More. There were the ghosts of Morgans, Potters and Huntingtons who wanted worthy monuments to their own munificence, and there were the ghosts of the Irish coolies on whose backs their colossi rose. There were ghosts with names I knew: Lennie Pace, Mary Ellen Divine, Sister Anne Edward, Dorothy Day, Cardinal Spellman, Tom Dooley, Thomas Merton, two Kennedys and two Ngos. There were the ghosts of Korean refugees and Chinese soldiers, of Inge Holz, Suu Van Pham, of My Lai and of a legion of slaughtered Vietnamese. There were the ghosts of the American dead. There was the ghost of Nicholas Wiley. And in a room behind the great facade, like a room behind the fireplace, a priest-hole, there hovered above his own coffin the ghost of Michael Maguire. Each awaited the tri-une word that I knew had been refused; no "*Requiescat in pace*" here. The Church had spoken. The anathema had been pronounced. The benediction was withheld not from one man or several, but from an age, a generation, a people, an entire world.

It fell to me to be for the dead and for the living a sign of peace, of mercy, of forgiveness, and I knew I could not do it.

By now, of course, you know why. The FBI man came back as he promised he would, and like some Arthurian alchemist, with a mere flick of his finger, he changed the gold of my life to lead.

He turned on the tape-recorder, then left me alone in the

interrogation room. Until then I had thought I was under
arrest. I had thought they'd brought me to their headquarters
to threaten me or bribe me, neither of which would have
worked. They could have tortured me and I would not have
helped them. I would have died first and my last thought
would have been of Michael, my last feelings love for him
and joy that I too, after all, had become a hero, a martyr for
the faith. But, alas, they didn't kill me.

They only made me listen.

I watched the reels spinning and waited for the sound to
crackle on.

A man's voice broke the silence abruptly. "Maguire, tape
forty-seven, Lake George, August nineteenth, nineteen sixty-
nine. Two seventeen P.M."

The silence then was of a different kind. It was the silence
of our summer, of our cabin, of our nights and days, the three
of us together. I remembered climbing Black Mountain with
him. I remembered her clinging to me and saying, "I've
never loved you more."

A door banged open and a woman spoke. Why did it shock
me that it was Carolyn? The door slammed closed and I heard
then the familiar creak of floorboards and the swarming rustle
of bedclothes being torn back.

Michael's first words were, "Oh Christ!"

I listened as to the sounds of a city being razed, the
destruction of all future, all faith, all things, in his phrase,
Luke's phrase, that make for peace.

When Carolyn cried out as she never cried out when I was
in her, it was the Master's "Epheta!" His mud and spittle
were on my eyes. I opened them and I saw their story whole.

Though it spanned twenty-two years, including one of the
most tumultuous decades of the century, and though it swept
across the full range of human experience, from war to
childbirth to death, from virginity to adultery, from celibacy
to parenthood, from sanctity to excommunication, their love
remained until the end what it was in the beginning: the
innocent love between a priest and a nun. Once the epitome
of what is tragic in life, it is the most ludicrous of romances
now and commentators always wink when they speak of it.

Priests and nuns when they fall in love recapitulate the absurd Victorian melodrama of fully grown men and women fumbling through an excess of clothing toward their first nakedness. We are supposed to laugh at them as their habits fall. How superior they make us feel, those of us who succeeded at an early age in purging sex of awe and love of all transcendence. And how smugly do we imagine the desolation of their guilt, those who surrender principle and violate vows and cuckold God Himself. Priests and nuns think love means all things— salvation and damnation both—while for us it is the way, as our music puts it, to make it through the night.

Silence. *This* priest and *this* nun—my dearest, dearest friends. The silence in which they came together deafens me even now. Can the cuckold-husband narrate such a scene? And how could he possibly know of it? Oh, it is so simple; this is the hard-won prize of my work, the very center of the story I have struggled to bring you. I have played it over and over in my imagination, never fussing over diction, over voice, over the length of sentences. It is the curse of sensitivity that we behold more than we want, the blessing that we see the truth. Truth! What is truth? Mere rhetoric? But rhetoric, in Yeats's definition, is will doing the work of the imagination. Alas, I am a man of no will when it comes to this. I am at the mercy of what I have continually imagined. Nay, conjured. Nay, witnessed. Silence. This is what happened. Silence. This.

See him walking across the Brooklyn Bridge on its fabled scaffold high above the black river, a solitary figure in the middle of the night. In daylight and with good binoculars Carolyn could have watched him coming from the balcony not a dozen paces from the bed where she was asleep alone. I was in Cambridge, Massachusetts, delivering a paper on Hopkins at an important Harvard symposium. I'd been honored to be asked and had thought of it as my lucky day. Oh cruel irony. Oh the inscape, the instress, the asshole of Inwood.

It was the night of the day in May 1966 that Nicholas Wiley died.

Michael had left Bellevue, having run the gauntlet of reporters—"You don't condemn suicide?"—from whom he learned of the Church's condemnation of Nicholas. He had found it impossible to return to his parish and had instead walked aimlessly through Manhattan. He went to Chrystie Street, thinking to talk to Dorothy Day—had she renounced Wiley too?—but at the last moment he knew it was impossible to talk to her. From Chrystie Street to the Brooklyn Bridge is no distance, and instinctively he made for it. He could have as easily been coming to me as to her, and there is the irony, the particular pain. What chaos followed from the accident that at the moment of his most brutal desolation, I was away and Carolyn was not.

He rang the bell.

Carolyn stirred, but did not wake up.

He rang again, although he almost decided not to.

Carolyn was frightened by the bell when it finally woke her, and she went immediately into Molly's room. Molly was two and a half years old. She was fast asleep.

When Carolyn saw through the glass that it was Michael, she was afraid at first that he had come with news of me, that I'd been killed in a car wreck. How much simpler for everyone if that had been the case.

"Michael, what's wrong?"

It startled him to see her in her robe and nightgown, her long hair falling over her shoulders, and he realized only then what rudeness it was to present himself at that hour. He didn't answer at first. They stood looking at each other on opposite sides of the threshold.

He shook himself. "I'm sorry, Carolyn. Something awful happened. A young friend of mine burned himself today."

"Oh Michael, I heard about it. He was a friend of yours? Oh God!" She took his hand and pulled him into the house, and in that movement he went into her arms. She held him for some moments, but like a mother would have.

"Come have a drink," she said.

He looked at his watch. "God, Carolyn, I had no idea it was so late. I'm sorry."

"Don't be silly. I'm glad you came."

"I know," he said, following her into the kitchen, "but Durk will kill me."

"He isn't here," she said over her shoulder. "He's in Boston until Friday."

If you imagine Michael shuddering with anticipation at that revelation, you have misunderstood him. He was capable of all the inner urges, of course, but his virility was a function of restraint. He was thirty-four years old and had been faithful to his vow of celibacy, remained in fact a virgin. He had been ambushed on occasion by desire, and masturbation was not unknown to him, but he had not allowed himself in years consciously to fix upon Carolyn's image as the object of his lust, as he would have surely were she not still the owner of his heart.

In the kitchen he sat at the Formica counter while Carolyn brought glasses and the gin. They sipped quietly. Michael told her Nicholas's story. She listened carefully for what it revealed about his own.

Michael was adrift in the aftermath of his futile time in Vietnam. His final surrender to Spellman's tyranny, his upstate banishment to Saint Joseph's and his too-easy embrace of the tranquillity of exile left him profoundly vulnerable to feelings of guilt. The guilt was appropriate because he violated his conscience brutally when he chose to obey the bark of the Church rather than the cry of the Vietnamese. And then he had tried to draw Nicholas Wiley into exile with him, but the young pacifist's conscience was more ruthless. The mistake had been to dam its torrent with the trivialities of life in the country parish. When the dam burst, poor Nicholas was at the mercy of that flood, the rage of it.

"I know it seems silly, Caro, given his age and mine, but I felt like a father to Nicholas. I never felt like a father before."

She touched his arm. "You're a good father, Michael. Only good fathers make good priests."

Michael shook his head slowly. "If I'd been more attentive to him, to what he was feeling . . ."

"Michael, how could you know? He didn't know himself."

"But I did know, Caro." He leaned against her. She caressed him. And they were still.

After a time he said, "It's as if I was forbidden to."

"What?"

He straightened, moved away slightly. She withdrew her

hand and each fussed with the gin. "To pay attention to feelings."

"Well, in a way you are forbidden to do that, aren't you?"

He smiled. She was bitter about her convent experience, and the religious life was a topic they avoided. "I guess I am," he said. "If so . . ." He took a hefty drink. "I'm in the state of disobedience now."

"Because you're feeling . . . ?"

"Like getting drunk."

"Now there's a feeling priests are allowed to have."

He laughed and poured more gin into his glass. "Not 'allowed,' encouraged!" He drank again.

Carolyn watched him. "Which is sad," she said quietly.

"It's the only way, love. As Saint Paul said, it's either that or burn."

"I thought he said, 'Marry or burn.' "

That stopped him. He looked at her abruptly. "That's the issue, isn't it?"

"Is it?"

"I mean that's the point of renouncing feeling. It's the only way to live like this."

"That's the saddest thing I ever heard, Michael."

"But you know it's true."

She wouldn't look at him.

"Don't you?" he pressed.

"Then why live like that?"

"You know why."

"No, I don't, Michael. I honestly don't."

"Well, you did."

Now she faced him squarely, and when their eyes met, he had an impulse to shield his from hers. "Yes, I did," she said. "I knew about the 'Come follow me!' and the 'Not my will but Thine!' and the 'Be ye perfect!' and the *'Fiat Voluntas Tua.'* But I also know about the man who put the Pharisees in their place. And I know who the Pharisees are today. And I know how they maintain their control over good people like you. They make you think that the most precious experience possible to a human being is an evil one. Nicholas Wiley has offered you a chance, Michael, because he's made you *feel* something. Well, don't drown that feeling! And don't talk it away with your Bible quotes!''

''But Carolyn, Nicholas Wiley burned himself to death because of his feelings.''

''Is that what you're afraid of, immolating yourself?''

''No.'' He looked away from her. ''But I am afraid of lunacy.''

Carolyn lifted her gaze to the window. The lights of Manhattan shone in the black, but it was to a reflection in the glass her eyes were drawn. On Michael's face the lines were taut, fierce, unbecoming. She had never seen him in the grip of cowardice before. ''Your refusal is the lunacy,'' she said harshly.

It was the truth between them, the very heart of it. He knew, as I would have, that she meant, beneath the generalities about ''feelings,'' his refusal of her.

He said quietly, ''I wish I could change it.''

''You can,'' she said simply.

Michael waited for her to look at him. ''I'm afraid,'' he said.

''I know.''

Neither breathed. Already they had crossed the threshold; he closed a door behind them by saying, ''Of you.''

Silence, what silence then between them. Michael stared at the counter, Carolyn bowed her head. They could still have drawn back. Each small step required another, bolder one. The wind from the river rattled lightly at the window. The wall clock hummed.

Michael raised his eyes to look at her. The nightgown was closed at her throat. Its white cotton shimmered against the navy blue of her robe, a kimono, full sleeved without lapels. She had belted it tightly. Her waist and bosom were defined, not erotically but with unabashed womanliness. He pictured her as she had been when he first knew her, in the black habit of a Sister of Charity, and then he pictured her stepping from the terrace in Dobbs Ferry, in the near nakedness of an ordinary bathing suit, her long legs, her cropped blond hair, her thighs. Was it possible that first vision of her beauty had occurred only six years before? Those six years, with a marriage, a child, a house, a resolute pursuit of painting, had been for her a long time, but for him they had been an eternity, an infinite stretch in which, while worlds ended outside, nothing happened inside. It had been that long since anyone touched him, since she had.

He reached his hand toward hers where it rested by her glass. Shyly he covered it.

When she looked up at him, tears spilled from her eyes. Her crusty assertiveness had evaporated. When she spoke he could barely hear her. "I have been wanting you to do that."

Michael knew that if he continued touching her all was lost, yet he could not remove his hand. This was what he'd feared—being outdistanced by his racing heart. But Carolyn was ahead of him, she was waiting for him. She at least had been consistent from the start.

He leaned toward her and she brought her face to his. He kissed a tear. He raised his other hand to touch her hair. Suddenly that hand closed on the back of her neck and pressed her face against his. Their kiss was like a blow, stunning them both. Carolyn's lip bled at once, and the taste of her blood made Michael wild. Lunacy, he thought, yes, lunacy! This could make a man set fire to himself. But this had nothing to do with Wiley.

Against the image of a man aflame he buried his face between her shoulder and her neck. "Oh Caro!" Immolation of another kind.

The chair fell out from under him. She took his weight and her hands pulled at him passionately. She brought his face up to kiss him again, pushing her tongue into his mouth, but she began to fall too. They went together to the floor, roughly. Their arms and hands never faltered, hers pulling him on top of her, his pressing through her robe and the thin cloth of her nightgown.

"Stop!" she said. "Stop!" and rolled her face away.

He raised himself on one knee, off her. Oh Christ, what are we doing? This is impossible!

But that was not her meaning.

She stood and took his hand and led him to her bedroom. To our bedroom.

He followed mutely.

She closed the door behind them and by our bed she turned

toward him. She opened her robe and let it fall. "We should be undressed," she said. "We should be naked for each other."

Michael unbuttoned his black shirt. No woman would have done that for him. At his bare chest, hanging from a string around his neck, was a small plain cross of wood, Wiley's cross.

He went to her, understanding that this must happen slowly, deliberately. He would have preferred it that way himself, but preference had nothing to do with it. The storm of his arousal broke. He kissed her, pressed her body against his, and the sensation of her breasts rising beneath the thin cotton against his skin unleashed him. He tore at her nightgown, pulling it down feverishly, even while pushing her away to look, to see those breasts, her waist, the hair of her crotch, to see that she was after all the fulfillment of his lust. She fell back onto the bed, and her legs opened.

He threw off his clothing and was on her, but he was too frantic, too new, too at the mercy of his passion, and he could not find her. All at once he was terrified that he would ejaculate outside her. "Help me!" he said. "Help!"

And didn't that plea of his sum up everything? Why he was afraid; why the suicide of his protégé drove him into her arms, her legs; why this moment had been so long in coming, so terrifying. He was the man who helped others. He had never needed help himself. There was his true virginity.

She knew just what to do and did, guiding his penis successfully, seizing it in the mouth of her womb so that when, seconds later, all that he withheld began to pump violently like Gatling rounds, a new terror took hold of him—many first-time lovers have it—that he would kill her.

When she screamed, how could he have known it was not with pain? In his dream of copulation, brutality was muted but there. But now when she thrashed below him, all was violence. Her arms held him as the walls of her cunt held his prick. Her constrictions came in spasms; she gave what she got. She strangled him.

Then he cried out like a gored beast. They were both killers. Was that the recognition that freed him?

He stopped caring finally what would happen if he fucked her, and simply did.

Remorse, when it came, was gentle. They spoke of me, of course, and would surely have felt horror at their betrayal, but their postcoital happiness reduced it to something like regret. It was as if I was a passenger in a car one of them was driving—it didn't matter which—and then the other's car came out of nowhere. Perhaps it was the highway's fault or the weather's. In the collision I was the only victim. What else could they do but console each other for what they'd done? At least I would never know.

Michael dressed before dawn and at the door he said to her, his finger under her chin, "I love you." Then he left. He went to his rectory in Alna, showered, put on fresh clericals and said the early Mass for the repose of the soul of Nicholas Wiley. Later that morning, in his fateful, final meeting with Francis Cardinal Spellman—"I refuse to yield to you in anything related to this evil war!"—he remembered what, on the scale of moral conduct, was the true blasphemy, not disobedience or adultery, but genocide.

Still he felt an overpowering remorse at having failed Nicholas and at having broken his priestly vows and at having, yes, betrayed me. But the bite of those sorrows was nothing compared to the passion set loose in him at last. There was a woman now, and there was a war, and in relation to each he found the precious treasure that he'd counted lost forever, not the Kingdom of God, but his own manhood. His memory and his manhood had been returned to him by Wiley's soul and Carolyn's body.

I have had twelve years to understand, and I think I do, although I have perhaps accepted less than I have understood.

It was not their purpose to hurt me. On the contrary, they always sought to lull me in the cat's cradle of their lies. And there were times when they even offered me a crack at the truth, but I rigorously avoided that. When Michael spoke to me on Black Mountain of his dread, his discouragement and sense of doom, I chose to hear him always as the hero of resistance, as if the dread was of prison and not of hell, as if what doomed him was his faithfulness and not his betrayal. I was a cooperator in their adultery, and even a beneficiary of it. I'm certain it was true, as Carolyn said, that she loved me more than ever, even while she deceived me. It was Michael who opened her fully, not me. When at last she had him, her joy overflowed. She could not have feigned her happiness, and I, with Molly, saw more of it than anyone.

Surely at some level I knew what had happened. They were secret lovers for three years. I have described already times when the truth—"I *do* love you!"—all but raped me. But I never allowed it entrance to the center of my heart. It was writing in the sand in the wind, and before the last letter was formed the first was always gone. I refused to hold the literal image in my mind; Michael and Carolyn naked with each other? Fucking? Not once in a fit of passion, but every chance they got? Every chance I gave them? Settling into a long, easy liaison that made them not less loving, as the "old morality" swore it would, but more? Carolyn became a great wife and mother, and Michael became a hero-priest because of—who could have explained this?—in a word, sin.

When at last I was made to face what was obvious, I simply could not do so as myself. I became someone else. I became what the FBI man thought I was, and what he wanted.

I watched the tape reels spinning, silent now except for the *flick flick flick* of the tailing brown ribbon. The room, stark white, unornamented, the light glaring fiercely above me, was like the set of a play. One of those modern things, Pinter or Beckett, in which the antagonist representing absolute evil or absolute good—it is never clear and doesn't matter—inflicts his torment from outside the room. He never enters.

But if I was a Pinter character, I would have dismissed what I had just heard with an ironic remark—"Golly, but the good Father paid close attention in Confession all these years!" —and I'd have resumed my life with Carolyn, my friendship with Michael, as if nothing happened. But I'd have become the absolute antagonist outside *their* stark white room.

But I am out of Ibsen, not Pinter. I had no choice but to shake heaven, to bring it down, even if on myself. This was the betrayal I'd foreseen, expected, made possible. Yet it was the one event—even including, say, the arrival on our cities of Russian missiles—for which I was utterly unprepared. There had been no air-raid drills for this.

My reaction watching those reels was no more a matter of choice than it was for the end of the audio tape to go *flick flick flick*. I was possessed by the simplest reflex, the oldest one, an absolute impulse. It taught me the only wisdom I would need in Israel when I got there, the only relevant truth of the Nuclear Age: that when the enemy strikes and we are defeated totally—our cities razed, our future ash—it will not matter that no purpose is served by our destroying in return and with our last effort a Beirut or a Moscow or a My Lai for that matter. Retaliation is the rule of life. That's all.

The door of the interrogation room opened—theater of the absurd now utterly—and the mode of mine walked in.

THIRTY-ONE

MONHEGAN Island is a whale-shaped rock twelve miles off the coast of Maine, only a few miles around and reaching perhaps a hundred and fifty feet above the sea. For three hundred years it has maintained a cruel, stolid indifference to the pounding waves of the Atlantic, to the shrouding weather, to the fierce fishing people who have made it home, to the artists and rare summer tourists who defy the twin hostilities of nature and native, and to the hardy traffic of lobster boats, trawlers and cargo ships for which it remains a fearsome navigational hazard. Nearly a hundred vessels have piled up on its rocks. The story of Monhegan's wild shore is the story of shipwreck.

No savvy fugitive would have gone there, and I could not imagine why Michael would have chosen it. Carolyn and I were clinging to the same stanchion, the upright pipe that supported the flimsy roof of the lobster boat we'd hired to take us out from Boothbay Harbor. It was early in April, much too soon for tourists, and the lobsterman had eyed us warily when we'd approached him. But for fifty dollars he swallowed his qualm. He could be out and back in four hours. It was a Sunday and he couldn't haul traps anyway. What was it to him that the island's one small hotel didn't open up until June? What was it to him that the Monhegan people would shun us? We didn't explain that we had reason to think that a friend of ours was out there already, expecting us.

I pressed the ends of my collar together at my throat. The spray had saturated my citified raincoat, and I dearly wished

for a hat. I was freezing, though the day had begun as balmy
and bright. I tried to focus on the island, which seemed to
undulate mystically ahead of us, though we were the ones
who rose and fell. Our boat was at the mercy of swells and I
considered it a miracle that I had not gotten sick yet. For the
first hour it had frightened me that I could not see the island
through the fog, and all that time the lobsterman's boat had
seemed less seaworthy the farther from land we got. How I
wished for radar. I did not trust his compass or his skill until
suddenly the island appeared ahead of us, like an apparition. I
looked at the man to offer the homage of a nod, but he
ignored me. Carolyn raised her eyebrows with relief. We
were strictly Circle Line sailors. This was fucking awful.

I said, "Why the hell would he come out here?"

"This is why." Carolyn grimaced as the boat dropped.

"But if they came after him, there's no escape. It's a
corner. He's put himself in a corner."

"You just wish he'd stayed in Manhattan, the island with
bridges."

"Damn right I do. Maybe this is the wrong Monhegan
Island. Maybe it's the name of a nice resort in North Carolina."

Carolyn shook her head. The message that fell through our
mail slot, in Michael's writing, had said only, "Monhegan
Island, Palm Sunday morning."

"Besides," she said, sliding her arm through mine, "they'd
never think to look for him out here."

"They have their ways." I pressed her arm between my
elbow and my ribs. The wind feathered the wisps of her hair,
tugging them one after the other out of her scarf. Beads of
water clung to her lashes.

One time we took the boat from Galway to the Aran
Islands. The sea became rough and then rain began to fall.
Neither Caro nor I became sick, but many of our fellow
passengers did, and to escape the cramped, putrid space
below we went up on deck and stood huddled by a lifeboat.
The rain lashed us and the boat bucked like a bronco, but we
loved it. When the tourists came crashing up from below to
be sick, they rushed one after the other for the nearest rail,
but that had them puking into the wind with predictable
results. Perhaps it was cruel of us, but we laughed and

laughed. We were on the largest of the Aran Islands for three days. It never stopped raining, but that did not faze us because we spent the entire time in bed. Our Irish hosts—we stayed in a small, child-ridden B&B—eyed us suspiciously during our rare forays downstairs for meals. That we scandalized them heightened our pleasure. What a surprise to both of us that a gloomy, puritanical outpost of the Kingdom of Repression should have been the scene of our greatest coital excess. Talk about broncos! Carolyn and I rode each other like champions. Because that dreary little world held nothing for us we could focus for a change entirely on each other. In that foreign place we could become the other people we wanted to be. We came together like sex-starved strangers. The weather, having transformed our tourist weekend into a tryst, was a problem in only one regard. Owing to the pervasive dampness, our sperm-soaked sheets never dried out and we were too embarrassed to ask the Missus for fresh ones.

Carolyn leaned toward the lobsterman. "How do local people get out here, if there's no ferry?"

He shrugged. His gaze was fixed on the island. His hands played the wheel, the spokes of which were welded bolts. "Not much call. Local people stay put. Mail boat on Tuesdays. That's it."

"Do they get television out here?"

"Nope. No phones either. Just two-way radio."

Carolyn looked at me and said quietly, "So he can walk around without worrying about being recognized. That might be worth being in a corner."

I asked the lobsterman, "What about newspapers? What about *Time* magazine?"

He shrugged.

"You ask him," I whispered to Carolyn. "He won't answer me."

The boat wallowed as we hit what seemed to be a wake, a wave distinctly larger than what we'd been through. Then the boat's propeller bit again and we steadied. Carolyn hugged me. "I hate this," she said. "I hate it. I wouldn't do it for anyone else."

"Me neither," I said.

Irony does not feature in my recollection of that morning.

Obviously my true feelings toward Michael and toward what I had done, was doing, were coated over by numbing layers. My mind was entirely taken up with the details of our journey, although I do recall thinking that my nausea, once I began to feel it, was fitting. Otherwise it seems to me I was moving through events the way a sleepwalker does, with no sharp sensations of anticipation, fear, bitterness, or guilt.

As we approached the small harbor nestled in the gut between Monhegan and its tiny satellite, Manana, the noise of our boat's engine grew louder, not that our reticent skipper gunned it, but that the sound bounced back at us from the island's looming mass. The irregular, insistent clanging of a floating gong filled the air with tension, then faded as we left it behind. Even before I could distinguish between the gray rock of the shore and the sharp line of scraggly green pine above it, the boat slowed. Inside Manana the water was smooth. When I leaned over the boat's edge I could see the reflection of my own face, which I barely recognized.

I saw no houses until we swung around the tip of a promontory. On the hill above were separate small clusters of rugged-looking cottages. A large white clapboard building with a covered porch and shuttered windows must have been the summer hotel. Poking up from the trees at a higher elevation were a church steeple and the round white tower of the famous lighthouse.

We were cutting through a fleet of moored lobster boats essentially like the one in which we were riding. On their transoms were names like "Lu-Ann," "Beth-Marie" and "Sally-Jo." I nudged Carolyn. "Do you think the women out here have hyphenated names, or do the fishermen credit their wives and girlfriends together?"

Carolyn stared at me as if she hadn't understood. I was thinking that if she had a boat, it would be the "Michael-Frank."

Tied to the pilings at the single thrusting pier was a large oceangoing trawler, the only boat of its size in the harbor. It dwarfed us as we pulled in beside it.

"Goddamn!" the lobsterman said when he saw it. "What's she doing in here?"

There was an emotion in his voice—anger? alarm?—that disturbed me. "What do you mean?"

"These trawlers wreck our traps," he said. "They got no business in this close."

Close? It seemed to me we were halfway to Europe.

"She just better get out of this harbor before the tide goes. Ever seen a whale on the rocks? That's what she'll be."

With effortless skill he slipped in behind the trawler. I reached out to fend us off when we bumped the pier, but the boat slid up to it gently and stopped, just kissing the pilings.

I looked up at the trawler's looming black stern. Rust-stained white letters two feet high arched across it: "Sea Witch. Halifax."

A young man dressed for weather in a yellow slicker and watch cap greeted us from the pier. We clambered out of the boat, which slipped away then as smoothly as it had come in. I turned to thank the lobsterman, but he was intent on the helm and headed out with no farewell. As I watched him leave it was with a pang. Why didn't I just go with him?

The young man led us off the pier and up a dirt road that was lined with open oil drums. An unbearable stench came from them. They were full of rotten fish, lobster bait, and it was then that my nausea got the best of me. I turned away and vomited violently on the side of the road. Carolyn tried to help but I shrugged her off. For perhaps two full minutes, though it seemed like hours, I retched. When the heaves subsided and I recovered some sense of myself, of my situation, I looked around expecting to see unfriendly men laughing at me the way I had laughed on the boat to Aran. But there were only Carolyn and our guide.

I followed them miserably.

I was quite aware that Carolyn could hardly contain her excitement, and only then did the bile coating my mouth seem truly bitter.

The young man led us up the steep hill behind the village, along a rutted dirt path. If there were cars or trucks on Monhegan I didn't see them, and I can't call the trail we followed a road. At the top of the hill was the lighthouse we'd seen from the water, a great phallus fifty feet high. At its base stood a neglected shed. No sooner had we come upon it than our guide turned and left us.

Michael came promptly out of the shed, walking vigorously. He too was dressed like a seaman, and his beard enhanced the ruddy image, but I knew him at once. Despite everything— what I'd learned and what I'd done—my first surge of feeling was of the old affection, the need.

When my father lay dying in a dreary Queens hospital in 1964, Michael never left us. My father had a terrible time. He knew he was dying, and when he was awake he was crazy with fear. His piety had failed him when my mother died several years before, and if it had been up to me to console him, he would have died in the throes of despair. But Michael knew how to help him, with a combination of silence and muted reassurance. Michael talked simply and directly of the Christian faith. He told my father, and me who listened, about the death of Lazarus, about the anguish of Jesus. Another priest had glibly begun describing the Streets of Heaven to my father, who had cursed him in a seizure of panic and railed, "Don't talk to me about heaven! Talk about my dying!" And that's what Michael did. Only when the full terror of that loss—Lazarus', ours—had been plumbed did he broach the subject of resurrection, but by then my father was ready to hear of it.

Eliciting faith from the wary is like getting a wounded bird to walk into your hand, but Michael, a natural priest if I ever knew one, could do it effortlessly. When my father died Michael was holding his hand and they were praying together the Hail Mary. It was the first prayer my father had uttered since my mother's death. He released his grip on life because Michael made him ready to. He believed in God, like me, because Michael did. If he had not been my friend, if he had only been the priest who sent my father on his way, I'd have been in his debt for the rest of my life. But with Michael, as with a brother, it was never a question of owing. At my father's graveside he said to me, "Now we really have to stick together."

I watched Carolyn go into his arms.

They kissed the way I'd seen them kiss dozens of times before, not with great passion certainly—no one's mouth

opened—but with forthright affection. Their bodies were pressed
together, but not sensually. Still I saw their kiss and embrace
differently, and though even then I could not have identified
its signals explicitly I recognized the unmistakable reality of
their intimacy.

I lowered my eyes. Was that an act of deference? Of
bashfulness? Reluctance to intrude upon lovers? Wasn't it my
acknowledgment of their right to be together? From the very
beginning I'd been the outsider in the ill-fated trio. I was the
interloper, the one who'd come between. Perhaps that knowledge was what kept my jealousy at bay. If I trembled it was
with the weak-kneed vertigo of one who'd just puked his guts
out. I was sicker than I'd felt in years. But emotionally I was
in space, floating weightlessly, not like an astronaut, but like
an astronaut's tube of toothpaste.

When Michael turned to me I found it possible to go to him
and embrace him. I did not kiss his cheek.

Hey, I told myself, no big deal. These things happen.
What the hell, he fell in love with the wrong woman, or I
did. It wasn't the end of the world. Just a bit of nastiness
between two mortals. He slugged me; now I was slugging
him. It had been going on since Cain and Abel. No, since
Eve left Adam for the snake. No big deal.

Then why were my legs trembling?

The lighthouse was in the middle of a clearing, but ringing
it were wild, weather-beaten shrubs and vine-tangled trees.
The undergrowth was too thick to see into. Where was the
goddamn FBI? I wanted this shit over with.

Michael took my arm firmly between his two hands. "Durk,
what's wrong?"

When I looked at him, the concern in his eyes, the friendship,
was what set off the charge at last. This fucker! This son of a
bitch! This self-proclaimed saint! How dare he manifest love
to me! Or rather pity! Or was it mere guilt? Out with it, Fuck!
Show me what you really feel, the smug superiority of the
usurper! Oh, you tortured soul! How you condemned yourself
for flourishing a bayonet at those Korean peasants, but what
of the bayonet you plunged in me? My wife's betrayal is
nothing to yours! My first friend, the one who taught me
trust! But what is trust now? Now I feel it, that blade between

my breast and its bone, cutting cleanly, opening a hole in which to bury all past and future, a hole . . .

I caught myself before I cried, *"Et tu!"* No melodrama, no display. I would show the fucker nothing. I covered one of his hands. "I've been sick," I said.

"I think he may be dehydrated," Carolyn explained.

"There's a tap in the cabin. Come in." Michael led me into the shack and Carolyn followed. I put my mouth at the faucet and drank, an act full of history, for as boys we were always finding faucets to drink from. He might have slapped me on the back, "It's my turn, Durk, come on!" But he let me drink my fill. I remembered the Inwood summer ritual of opening the fire hydrants and dancing in the spray. This man was in the middle of every happy memory I had. He'd taken those from me too.

The water tasted of rust, but it soothed me and my stomach felt better at once. When I straightened I was less lightheaded, and I looked around the small shadowy room. Rampant cobwebs held the corners. In the center were two chairs at a plain table, the only furniture, and I took one of them. Carolyn and Michael remained standing, but I didn't care.

"A lighthouse?" I asked. "Won't the coast guard find you?"

Michael shook his head. "They run these things from Portland or someplace now. They're automated. These cabins haven't been lived in for years."

"How long have you been here?" Now when I looked around I noticed that there was no cot, no toilet, no sign of food. A blanket was bunched in a corner.

"Last night. I came out on a boat like yours."

"But you'll be staying here?"

He shook his head. "This was just a rendezvous. I'm pulling out right away."

"What do you mean?" Suddenly I didn't know what to feel or think. Would it be good news or bad if he escaped the FBI? Were they even then watching from hiding places in the woods?

"I'm going away." He looked toward Carolyn. He was explaining himself to her, not me. "That's why I wanted to see you. I'm leaving the country."

"For Halifax?" she asked. She'd been paying attention too.

"Yes."

"Then it's over?" I asked. "Your resistance is over?" Was it possible that the great hero had reached his limit? That the antiwar priest, having spent his passion for peace, would become just another convict on the lam?

No.

He said, "I'm going to Vietnam. This Friday, Good Friday, Suu Van Pham and thirty-two other Vietnamese priests are going to occupy the cathedral in Saigon. They're going to offer it as a sanctuary to anyone who will refuse to fight anymore. I'm going to join them."

"Oh Michael!" Carolyn crossed to him. She did not bother to disguise her impulse now as she embraced him, resting her head on his shoulder. Light glistened off tears in her eyes.

"You'll be a martyr yet," I said with a show of bitterness, despite myself. I was sick of his fucking virtue, his righteousness, his crusade against evil. I was sick of his hypocrisy. Was I the only one who had to suffer it?

But he took me literally. He shook his head. "As usual the risk is mostly someone else's. If I go, though, some American GIs might be moved to join us."

I was impressed despite myself. It was the perfect way to bring his resistance to a close. No mere surrender, but the most dramatic challenge yet to the war and, finally, a fully *Catholic* act of atonement for its Catholic origins. A Good Friday protest against the crucifixion of a people that began with the holy righteousness of Tom Dooley, Ngo Dinh Diem and Cardinal Spellman. Sanctuary in Saigon! Michael Maguire strikes again! His arrest in Saigon and the long transfer back to the States for prison would attract the attention of the world.

Suddenly I felt sorry for Carolyn. No matter what had gone on between them, no matter what understanding they had, he was still putting her second to his sacred vocation. So what that his sacred calling now was to political opposition instead of ecclesial subservience. But clearly Carolyn had accepted second place in his heart. Why shouldn't I have accepted second place in hers?

It was not a question I was interested in answering.

Michael said, "I just wanted to see you both before I went."

He meant me too. "Oh Jesus, Michael . . ." I began, but I had to stop because my voice cracked. Perhaps I was going to tell him what I'd done. Perhaps I was going to accuse him of what he'd done. It doesn't matter, because he interrupted me.

"And I wanted someone in the States to know where I was going in case . . ."

He stopped short of statement because the implication carried. If he was found by the government in Vietnam before the press knew he was there, anything could happen. He could simply disappear forever. He had come a distance from fun and games with the Fordham boys of the FBI.

"You haven't told anyone else?"

"You're the only ones I trust enough."

At last I faced what I was doing. Compared to what rose in my throat then, the vomit had been lemonade. The first full knowledge of the meaning of my act choked me, and I realized that whatever happened to him, I had already destroyed myself. I had committed moral suicide, or in the more familiar phrase, mortal sin. I had made myself over into what he and Carolyn were in relation to me—liars, traitors, egotists. But I lacked utterly the element that mitigated their offense: they at least were driven by love, not hate. And when the coming events laid the truth bare—I saw this clearly for the first time—they would have each other still. I would have not even my own soul. I was disemboweled. Like an Oriental warlord I had, with ceremony but no dispatch, sliced open my own soft middle. It only remained to press against the wound until the flow of blood rescued me from the awareness of what I'd done. Faced with doom like that, there was nothing to do but surrender to it.

But in truth I was not dying. Maybe moral suicide is never fatal. The chasm inside me, having swallowed everything I valued, began to close. Soon all would be smooth again. Air would purify my lungs. The bile would recede. And I could claim like everyone—like Michael, like Carolyn, like the FBI and like the men who ran the war—that life's cruelties force us all too regularly to do what we abhor.

He looked at his watch. "I'm sorry to say it's time to go."

"You have to leave before the tide goes out," I said.

"That's right."

"And from Halifax?"

"To Montreal, then Paris, then Saigon."

"But how? What about visas?"

He smiled. "Vatican diplomat, Durk. I'll be an Irish monsignor with Caritas International as of Wednesday." He laughed raucously. "They still leave the clergy alone, especially if they have a little red at their throats."

"Unless it's lipstick," I said. Carolyn started, but Michael laughed easily.

"Come on," he said. He put his arms out, one to drape each of us. Carolyn and I fell into step with him, and like three chums we strode down the rough trail toward the harbor.

Michael saw it before I did.

He stopped abruptly as we came around the last curve a few dozen yards above the pier.

Sitting in the middle of the harbor, dominating it, was a large white boat, seventy-five feet or longer. On its bow was the red diagonal slash that identified it as a coast guard cutter; on the forward deck was a large weapon, a machine gun or a cannon, at which a man sat. It was aimed at us. A dozen other men in orange life vests stood at various stations on the boat holding rifles.

On the pier were four men dressed like duck hunters. One of them was Finnegan. He was holding his badge aloft. "FBI, Father!" he called. "You're under arrest."

Michael did not move. He did not lessen the pressure of his arm on my shoulder. I stared straight ahead, not breathing, terrified that I would have to look at him.

Someone stirred behind us. Out of the corner of my eye, only a dozen yards away, I saw two more duck hunters by a shack. These had shotguns aimed at us.

"Keep walking!" Finnegan ordered. "We don't want anyone to get hurt."

Michael dropped his arms from me and Carolyn and without a word to either of us stepped away and began to walk to the pier.

Carolyn ran after him, crying his name. She clung to him. Michael tried to pull away from her but couldn't.

I went to them and tried to pull her back. She fought me, but Michael made her release him. When he looked at me I found it possible somehow to meet his gaze. I saw the recognition at the very moment it came to him. "Jesus Christ!" he said, "You!"

Carolyn looked at me. Her realization grew more slowly but with deadlier effect. I watched the flood of horror rising as she stared at me.

Michael turned immediately and walked to Finnegan, who began reading him his rights while the others handcuffed him. I heard one of the agents call him "Father." Later, leaving the cutter in Portland, he would be photographed smiling broadly, like a lottery winner, between two glum agents. He would be flashing the peace sign despite his handcuffs. The fucker was indomitable. The photograph would appear everywhere. I would be certain that he flashed that "V" just for me, to say, "Michael Maguire withstands everything, even you, Durkin!"

Carolyn pulled away from me slowly and backed down to the pier. It was as though she was staring at the Man With No Face. I see that expression of hers vividly, its shock and disbelief. I had done this to Michael, she saw at once, because of what she had done to me. This nightmare began with her, and she knew it. But it ended with me. Shock and disbelief bound us, and also, finally, guilt. Looking at her was like looking in a mirror. Hers was the face, the desolation of that moment and the despair, I had turned on myself ever since. It was what I had fled from and what, even in the desert, in the fourteenth century, I had never escaped.

The agents took her back to the mainland with them. They offered to take me too, but I refused. When the cutter pulled out of Monhegan Harbor, Michael was already below. I never saw him again.

Carolyn was at the railing, staring back at me. I had her full attention at last.

The funeral would begin in less than an hour. Carolyn was napping in the guest room of the dean's house when I returned from the Catholic Center, and so I went to see Molly. While her brother and sister explored the Biblical Garden, my daughter and I sat together in silence on a stone bench. She held my hand. I held hers. That seemed enough. When it came time for me to go to Carolyn, Molly hugged me fiercely, and I knew that I would never be without her again.

I waited for Carolyn in the austere parlor where visitors were received. The maid had the impression I was someone's brother.

The door opened and it was she.

I stood.

There was no sign of sleep in her eyes, but a subtle luster had been restored to them. Her hair was even more tightly pulled back than before. She had changed into a simple black dress, and it enshrined her grief. Her grief had become part of her loveliness. It displayed the fullness of her love and therefore, curiously, made her seem as gifted as bereft.

Without a word she sat on the sofa and I joined her. She looked at me expectantly. I hated that I had failed her. I wanted to report that the cardinal himself was coming. "I'm sorry, Caro. They're adamant."

"Did you see Archbishop O'Shea?"

"Yes. If he wasn't so personally involved . . ."

She looked away. "Well then."

"It doesn't matter," I said without conviction. "The Church is different now. Charismatics, Encounters, Journal Groups, Christian Zen. Michael wouldn't recognize it anyway."

She nodded. "But I can't have him cremated, Frank."

"Caro, even the Catholic Church permits cremation now."

She shook her head. "I can't leave him here. I have to bury him in the ground someplace." She took my hand suddenly. "Will they let him be buried in sacred ground?"

"No, Caro, they won't."

"Oh." She exhaled, dispirited.

Because I thought it would help her to address the detail of where to bury him—isn't concreteness what rescues us?—I pressed it. "Do you go to the country?"

She nodded, then looked at me. "Lake George."

The words pierced me. How I'd cherished our time there. Michael had simply replaced me in my house, in my vacation place, in my daughter's life and in my wife's arms. Did they pretend I never existed? Did they come to think I was simply the part of Michael's personality he outgrew? Had my function only been to save his place until he was ready for it? But my function now, to find him a new place, did not allow such questions. "I recall an old cemetery in Bolton Landing. Do you?"

She nodded. "We went there for stone rubbings." The memory saddened her. The wave of emotion endeared her to me, completed the resurgence of my love.

"Would that be a place?"

For a moment she didn't react. Then she nodded vigorously, decisively. Her teeth cut into her lip.

"It's his remains that will make the ground sacred, Caro."

"I know." Her acknowledgment of my banality made it seem quite true.

Sadness, and with it silence, took over both of us.

I looked at the clock above the mantel. It was nearly six-thirty. I listened to it ticking. Two minutes went by, then five.

Caro whispered my name. I looked at her. She was staring at her hands. "Frank, I wanted you to come because Michael and I both hoped that someday . . ." It frightened me when she stopped. I wanted desperately to talk about it before going into the cathedral, before seeing Michael's face.

"Don't stop, Caro."

"We hoped we could find a way to . . . We . . ." She faced me at last. "Oh, Frank, I'm sorry. I'm so sorry."

It was my impression that tears had come into her eyes, but I was unsure because tears had blinded mine. "You, Caro? You're sorry? But what I did was so much worse."

"Frank, I loved you." She fell against me.

"I know it, Caro. You loved both of us. I understand about that now."

"Will you forgive me?"

"I did that long ago. That's why I came when you asked me to. It's Michael I never finished with. Did he ever indicate how he felt? I mean about what I did?"

She dropped her eyes. "He never spoke of it, Frank."

"Did he speak of me?"

"No."

"Oh, God."

"But that's only because his feelings about you ran so deep. I know that he wanted to be reconciled with you more than anything. He wanted it as much as I did."

"And now he's gone before we . . . Time has healed a lot, but it never healed that."

"But it would have, Frank."

"Do you think?"

"Yes, I'm sure." She stroked me. The gentleness of her touch acknowledged *my* grief, my right to it.

"I feel completely lost, Caro. I've been suspended all this time, floating in space. Now I'll never . . . Michael was like the earth to me. I think I'll never get down to it again."

"But you have to be on earth, Frank, for me. I need you, and so does Molly."

How I wanted to reassure her, to say she had me. But I was telling her the exact truth. The loss of Michael had left me incomplete, like an amputee. Of what use could I be to her or Molly or anyone?

She sat upright, but left her hand on my arm. "It helps just having you here." She was pulling back from the edge. Had she seen over it too? Into that pit, that emptiness? "I appreciate it. I know you've put us first. I appreciate it very much. Now if we can just get through the service."

"As long as we don't have to sing 'A Mighty Fortress Is Our God.' "

We both laughed. In his great hymn, Luther called the pope the Devil.

"You know what?" I said gamely. "We don't need the Catholic Church. We have each other." I punched her shoulder lightly. Even as I said that I knew how untrue it was. The final loss of our Catholicism—for what did the archdiocese's rejection mean if not that?—was as devastating at that moment as the loss of Michael. What was our religion but the cluster of rituals, formulas, beliefs and learned responses by which, *precisely*, we were able to finish the business that every death interrupts? The Church existed to help us say a final word of love or, as in my case, forgiveness. If our religion—our Catholicism—was useless to us then, having become a sign of recalcitrance instead of reconciliation, when would it ever be of use? We were like victims of a shipwreck clinging to each other on an alien shore. Who asked in such a situation whether the compass was at fault or the navigator or the captain? Or was it the fault of the dumb rock we ran upon? All we knew was desolation. We consoled ourselves by insisting that we didn't need the only vessel that could have carried us home.

At that moment, as if to underscore the poignancy of our exile, there was a rap on the door and an oh-so-Anglican clergyman, a canon of the cathedral, opened it.

He was as tall and lean as those upper-class clerics with the best jobs always are. Though he was middle-aged, his face was boyish and his hair was closely cut, giving him the look we once associated with marines, but now with homosexuals. Not that he was one of *those;* his wedding ring flashed. His foppishness was a function of mere breeding, not sexual preference. It was no longer considered bad form to look like what he was. In the sixties men like this let their grooming go and pretended they were the sons of plumbers like the rest of us. But not anymore. In his clerical collar and striped seersucker suit he looked like a chaplain of the British Raj, and I realized it had been glib sophistry to assert that little remained to separate Episcopalians and Roman Catholics. In that "little," revealed in meaningless details like the color of a priest's clothing, were buried millions of colonized and murdered people, many of them Irish and many Catholic. In that "little" were buried my own ancestors and Michael's. In that "little" was lost the distinction between the people who built the Cloisters and the people who clean it. Nothing separated us but history. It was a whole new reason to resent our own Church, that its intransigence abandoned us to the exquisite civility of the rich. For the point was that, at that moment, we would go anywhere and embrace any heritage and accept any offer of hospitality, even the smuggest one, if it included a simple, direct proclamation of the Gospel of Jesus Christ.

"Carolyn?" he began familiarly. Then, seeing me, he put his manicured hand out. "Hello, I'm Martin Putnam, the dean's assistant."

I stood and shook hands with him. I felt oafish in my

monastic mufti. I needed a shave and a shower. "I'm Frank Durkin," I said. The priest stared at me so intently I had to look away. And then my discomfort exploded into humiliation when for the first time it occurred to me that, after all those years, I had a part in Michael's legend too. I was the FBI informant.

Canon Putnam turned back to Carolyn. "I hate to bother you with this, but there are television people outside. I've told them no interviews, of course. But I wanted to know your feelings about letting them film the service."

Carolyn looked at me.

"No," I said without hesitating. "Absolutely not."

Putnam ignored me and continued to stare at Carolyn. "The more dramatic their footage, the more likely they'll use it. What better way to memorialize Michael than to draw attention to the killing in Beirut? Wouldn't he seize the opportunity to denounce . . . ?"

"I beg your pardon, Canon Putnam." I touched his shoulder. "But we don't want camera crews in church." Did I have to explain myself? Did I have to say it's against our religion? The man had the instincts of a publicist. So would you if you had the largest cathedral in the world and no congregation to fill it. No wonder he offered it to aerialists and jazz musicians and renegade Catholics.

Carolyn said, "Television? Why is television here?"

The canon touched her. "Because Michael is still news, my dear. He was a great American when America needed one." How did he manage to make even that tribute seem condescending? I pictured him, years before, as a seminarian who'd gone into the ministry, instead of the family investment firm, to avoid the draft. Nicholas Wiley would have been about his age by now.

He waited for Carolyn to contradict me. When she didn't he said, "All right. But we can't stop them from filming outside." He looked at me. "Just so you'll know."

I nodded at him, but the image of stars arriving at some premiere seemed ludicrous to me. No one would be coming to Michael's funeral. Television was there because Canon Martin Putnam, the Impresario Priest, had called them.

"Dean Evans has mentioned you," he said. "You were a friend of Michael's, weren't you?"

"Yes, I was his friend."

It was easy to read the canon's expression, and he wanted me to: *What friends poor Michael had, you and Archbishop O'Shea.*

Somehow I found it possible to continue looking at him this time. A surge of anger rescued me from my embarrassment. *You Anglicans don't believe in excommunication, do you? And you never betray your best friends either. You have manners.* If he says something ingratiating, I told myself, I will hit him.

When Carolyn took my hand I was surprised. It was a manifestation of her loyalty, and I was grateful for it.

Canon Putnam said to her, "Dean Evans will keep his remarks brief of course. He asked me to tell you that he intends to draw the connection between Michael's ministry and what's happening in Lebanon. Is there any other particular point you want him to make?"

"His remarks?"

"The eulogy."

"Oh."

Why was it a surprise to her? Clearly she had been unable to anticipate in any way the details of the service. Distress distorted her face, but instead of making her seem helpless, it girded her. She was still the strongest woman I had ever known. "Dean Evans has been wonderful to me, but he can't speak for Michael. I'm sorry, but he can't."

"Well, I . . . whatever you . . ."

She turned to me. "Frank, will you?"

THIRTY-TWO

WHEN we were children nuns told us that Pentecost was the birthday of the Church. The silliness of that notion, the banality of it, struck me even as a boy in the overheated classrooms of Good Shepherd School. I am not inclined, like so many, to mock the memory of those earnest women. Such easy targets; my instinct is always to defend them. Nuns made the Church possible, and many of their ludicrous images—the Baby Jesus pretending to a drooling helplessness—made great mysteries available in ways the obtuse categories of theologians—Homoiousian—never could. But the birthday of the Church? I remember squirming at the idea of the Apostles gathering around a cake with one candle. Was I supposed to think of its flame as the fiery manifestation of the Holy Ghost? Was the noise they made with their Gift of Tongues the group's off-key singing of the Happy Birthday song?

Now of course I am an informed Christian and I know what Pentecost really was. I refer to it here not for the sake of some blatant, facile comparison between the lives of Jesus and Michael Maguire, as if finally my point is to make Michael a latter-day Christ, but because at Pentecost was revealed the structure of human hope, which begins, of course, in despair. The followers of Jesus had disgraced themselves. They had all abandoned him, or, as Mark put it, rather more mercilessly, "They all forsook him and fled." They left a stranger, a centurion, one of the crucifiers, to finally and formally acknowledge Jesus: "Truly this man was the Son of God."

Those who claimed to love Jesus simply disappeared. They were terrified that what happened to him was going to happen to them. And so they hid. They dispersed. They went their separate ways. Only one thing could have brought them together again—a miracle. Only a miracle could have changed them from confused, inarticulate, and beleaguered peasants into a company of preachers who would in a generation ignite an empire. Pentecost is the day on which the miracle happened. Not a mountain being moved, not the sun being stopped in the sky, the miracle was a eulogy. A eulogy of Jesus.

The eulogist was no orator, and he was no hero. Of all the disciples he had the least right to stand in the main street of Jerusalem and speak of the Lord because, like Judas, who'd had the decency to kill himself, this man had not merely abandoned Jesus, but had explicitly betrayed him. He was Peter. When he stood up—had Mary asked him to?—and told the simple story of Jesus of Nazareth, everything changed. He told how Jesus went around doing good and how his words and actions fulfilled the promises of Scripture; how he came, like a good Jew, to Jerusalem for Passover, though he knew the leaders of the people plotted against him there; how he was arrested and, though the Romans offered to release him, how the people themselves demanded that he be put to death; how he was crucified among thieves; but also how His Father was faithful to him even in death and so raised him up to glory. In the exposition, the telling of the story itself, those who'd been a part of it were able to grasp its meaning at last, and those who hadn't been a part of it were able nevertheless to see its relevance to their lives.

People from all over the world—Parthians, Medes and Elamites—heard Peter's words as a new language, but one they understood. And in the recitation of facts with which they were familiar but had never seen whole, as forming like every story a coherent structure with a beginning, a middle and an end, the people recognized the narrative that bound them together, that made them a community, that made them what came to be called the Church.

What came to be called the *kerygma*, the Good News, the Gospel, began—and this is the miracle—as the coward's eulogy of the only man he ever loved, the one whom he betrayed.

I was in the huge Gothic cathedral alone, walking the aisles. Michael's funeral was to begin in half an hour. A few people had taken places in pews at great distance from each other. Once more I felt the pang of disappointment for him. In that vast space it would seem that no one came, no one cared. He would have passed from the earth unnoticed, unmourned by all but a meager remnant. If the death of this man was insignificant, whose wasn't?

Yet also, at the same time, the space itself, however it dwarfed us or because it did, was exactly right for that particular liturgy. In the end that structure overpowered its own history, and its associations with class and denomination meant nothing. It was a Gothic cathedral, and to a Catholic its stones were sacred. Its aisles, its nave, its narthex, its crossing, its transept and choir formed the geography of memory. At first I'd felt entrapped by it, but memory is what saves us when we are faced with death. These were the darkened, mysterious aisles along which I'd run with Michael as a boy. Actually I'd run *after* him, for he was the one who led the way in all our explorations, our adventures. He was the one who'd pushed first into tunnels or who leapt into quarries or who sallied forth on the winter's first ice. I, with others, had stood outside those tunnels, back from those cliffs, on those shores, waiting to see if he made it, to see if it was safe. And we'd cried after him, "Go, Michael, go!"

The pointed patterns of color splashing the stone floor from the stained-glass windows signaled the coming of nightfall, for this was evening light, not morning. Yet my memories had not, as I'd feared, condemned me to an end-of-the-day nostalgia. The sun was gone behind the buildings of the city, but its last light and warmth filtered into that immense yet intimate enclosure. The feelings I had for him filled it, and like angels whose wings could be heard fluttering in the reaches, so also did the memories we'd inherited from our people, of *their* adventures. In this place we'd recognized that those adventures going back eons were ours. That communal memory suggested that *we* had hidden from barbarians behind these pillars; *we* had taken the spiraling stone stairways at a clip, yeomen rushing to the battlements; *we* had crept from cavern to cavern, from vigil light to lantern; *we* had attended coronations and installations and heard anathemas pronounced from the great Chair; *we* had been present when saints were named and kings wed and cardinals invested and nonconformists banished; and *we* had lowered our heads and struck our breasts countless times when the anointed one high above us held for all to behold the broken Body of Our Lord. The Gothic cathedral is the Catholic's Holy Land, and even those of us who were raised in pale parish churches carried in our minds, as Jews did Palestine, the image of that homeland. You see, as Catholics we knew that we, like that very place—and isn't this what's gone now?—were made for worship.

I had been grieving for Michael, but for so much more than him. He was the flower of Catholic life, the best we had, the one who went before us and showed that it was safe. Against the numbing sameness of secular culture even as it had encroached upon the Church, he had stood as our champion in exactly the way, as a boy-soldier, he had stood against the enemy for the sake of his friends. He could risk his life because he believed innately that life is made for more than itself. That innate knowledge—what made him a hero—became the conscious religious affirmation—what made him a priest—of his maturity. The world is made for more than itself: that is what Michael meant. That is what the structure of the cathedral meant. No mere achievement or act of heroism could have justified or explained his life, as no organizational function, no bishop's throne, no social or aesthetic purpose could have justified or explained that church. Michael Maguire was the Gothic cathedral of men. He and it were made—I hesitate to introduce the word after all this time in the telling—for God.

If God did not exist, then that building was a cruel, pompous joke on itself. If God did not exist, then Michael Maguire, war hero, resistance leader and priest-against-the-Church was a figure of the absurd. I did not think, in beginning this story, that it would end religiously. I had thought rather that religion was that cluster of false notes we had left behind. I had gone, perversely, to a desert monastery to escape it. And hadn't

Michael abandoned his religion to love a woman and make a family? The Catholic Church, like a good Roman, had fallen on its sword. Hence the unarticulated grief of a generation of sophisticates. We were exactly like the sons and daughters of a suicide, with anger for the past and fear for the future, each so intense we never consciously entertained them. If the Church could not maintain the loyalty of men like Michael, then surely—and wasn't this to be our theme?—God's work on earth had failed.

As it had when His Son was crucified, his disciples having fled. As it had until Peter stood among strangers and told the story.

Is it the core Christian insight that just when we free ourselves from the spell religion casts, we come face to face with God? When we confront failure we succeed? When we die we live? Doesn't the inbuilt tension between forgiveness and sin provide the drama of every human narrative? Aren't the stresses between, in Simone Weil's phrase, gravity and grace what keep the Gothic masterpieces standing?

Michael was dead, but God lived.

Was that enough for me?

Could one believe finally in the Resurrection of the Dead? That is the question this story puts. As it was the question Peter's put. It is the only question left, and has always been.

I was ready now to be with him.

His coffin waited, still, in the baptistry, the priest-hole, and as I crossed in front of the high altar toward that octagonal chamber in which the marble font sat like God's crown, I genuflected, right knee to left heel with an altar boy's precision. The physical gesture reassured me, restored me, reminded me.

On the coldest mornings of winter in Inwood the place we loved to be was in the sanctuary—steaming radiators, undulating linoleum tile, threadbare orientals—of Good Shepherd Church. Each pair of altar boys thought of themselves as halves of one person. Since they, together, held the corners of the priest's chasuble while he genuflected and raised up the Sacred Host, it was natural for altar boys to come to think that together they were worthy of almost anything. But let a

morning come when one of the pair did not appear; the other
was struck with terror at what he had to do alone. What if the
Host fell to the floor? What if the finger-towel got wet? What
if he forgot the secret Latin phrases that the priest's hocus
pocus—"*Hoc est Corpus . . .*"—required?

I always served Mass with Michael because he never failed
to come and he always knew exactly what to say and when to
move the Book. And if the unexpected happened, a tabernacle key missing or a shortage of sacred wafers or a blown-out
paschal candle, I knew that Michael could deal with it. At
those times, I anticipated terrified GIs and Vietnamese priests
and American draft-dodgers, crying after him as he moved
decisively to do whatever had to be done, "Go, Michael!
Go!"

A tower shaped like a lantern and supported by rounded
arches overhung the baptistry. It was nearly dark in there,
shadows dominated, and at first I did not see the coffin. Had
attendants moved it already? But no, for I had just crossed the
intersection of aisles where it would sit during the funeral.
The coffin would be carried into the nave in the opening
procession. As my eyes adjusted I saw the oblong shape
against the arched doorway that led to the columbarium, the
room where ashes were interred in stone, the final prison.
Carolyn was right to want the earth for him, not walls.

Slowly I approached.

I wanted to cast aside our personal history. I wanted to
exchange the end of our friendship for the beginning. Couldn't
we have been two boys lifting up the corners of a golden
chasuble forever? That close to God? That close to one
another? Instead we were two men on a weather-beaten desperate island, separated forever by the woman who united us.
I saw him looking back at me, amazed, through that fog of
pathos which was to blur, then stain, the entire chronicle of
our time. Even the most cherished memories of our innocence
had become polluted by the knowledge of what happened. It
was like wanting to be rid of our *national* history. Oh, if we
could only have been the heroes of the world, vanquishers of
Hitler, defenders of freedom, forever. Oh, if we could only
have had our Kennedy, our Pope John, our Tom Dooley,
Tom Merton, our Cardinal Spellman in his prime, our Martin

Luther King. If we could only have had the Holy Catholic Church we'd first believed in. If we could only have had "America."

Instead we had Vietnam. That evil war forms the center of this narrative, not as the source of all the evil that befell us, but as the great reminder that no nation is holy—not even ours; no Church is sacred—not even this one; any more than a single one of us is free from sin—not even Michael Maguire. The shadow of the Fall has been upon this story from the start, and that, not references to cathedrals, cardinals or the infidelity of priests, is what has made it Catholic. The bronze cock stands on every paragraph, as if it were a barn, a basilica, and like the memory of My Lai, it rattles each time the wind blows. It crows each time we deny who we are. And for every denial there is later put the question, thrice, "Do you love me, friend, more than these others do?" In every paragraph I have tried to answer.

I tell you, Michael, dead as you are, that you and I *ourselves* embodied the age without knowing it. We were the town that had to be destroyed to be saved. We were the immolations and the gunships and the body bags. We were the naked girl running down the road with napalm bubbling her skin. We were the dark-eyed campus beauty at Kent State, screeching above the corpse of her youth. We were the scar on LBJ's belly, and we were the coonskin on the wall. We were what made Cassius Clay change his name. We were the stonewall around Nixon and we were Washington aflame. Instead of in truth or God we believed in our innocence, then in our sorrows, and that is what made us dangerous. You were going to end the war. I was going to create a mansion of literature, love and loyalty.

We had handfuls of each other that we carried like treasures until the day we turned and found that all we carried were stones. What else to do but set them rolling? How did it feel to be all alone? To be on your own? How did it feel? Oh, dear reader, by now dear friend, don't ask me. I could never tell you. Ask Anne Sexton, John Berryman, Delmore Schwartz, Cesare Pavese, Randall Jarrell, Sylvia Plath, Marilyn Monroe, Janis Joplin, Papa Hemingway, William Inge, and why shouldn't our souls be disquieted?

"Go, Michael!" I cried. But also, "Wait for me!" You didn't. You forgot what my life was, and you became hard while I grew soft. You were too far ahead to see it happening when I became totally—overly—dependent on one thing. Not you, God or booze. Just her. She was all I needed and all I had. And no one in the world—not Nixon, Mao or J. Edgar Hoover—could have destroyed our love but you. You took Carolyn from me, you bastard. And I repaid you without a kiss.

And now I was touching the gleaming wood of your coffin, at the end of my recitation.

How could I believe in God, Church or the Resurrection of the Dead when I did not believe you were in that box? You, Michael, in the throes of decay? You, Michael, with a waxen face? A rosary through your fingers? All you ever had were bones and flesh, fleet feet and that fierce conscience of yours. Now they were separated? If flesh was falling from your bones, why did mine adhere? If you were dead, Michael, how could I believe that I was alive? The box alone did not convince me.

And so with a finger under the lip of wood I lifted the cover of your coffin expecting anything—a staring mask, plasticene, lipstick, rouge, a pirate's skull—but you.

Ah. Ah. I had nothing then but silence. Only emptiness. The void. Nothing. And nothing. And nothing.

Later—only moments, but it might have been all of time— Dean Evans interrupted me. He was as imposing as I'd remembered, that great shock of white hair, that physical self-assurance. Also, that quiet earnestness.

"Mister Durkin," he said sadly, "it is nearly time to begin."

"May I have a moment more, please?"

He looked at me, not as if I was ridiculous, which I expected, but as if he'd known I was going to ask. He nodded, and threw a glance at the pallbearers behind him. They withdrew.

"Where's Carolyn?" I asked.

"She's in the pew with her children."

"Is Molly there?"

"Yes."

"Then would you ask Carolyn to come here a moment? Just for a moment?" To help me break the grip of that nothing, which had me, that paralysis.

He nodded and turned.

Then, again after no time or all time, she was standing in the arched entrance of the baptistry.

Her eyes went to the open coffin, and she drew back, shaking her head.

I offered my hand, but said, "Caro, help me make my peace with him. Please help me."

When she looked at me I saw in her eyes finally the glint of understanding. She came and stood by me.

Over his remade, lifeless face.

"Michael, it's me and Caro." I had no idea whether I was speaking this aloud or only in my head. "You died before I said to you that I am sorry, and I so wanted your forgiveness. I wanted to give you mine. Is it too late?"

Carolyn took my hand, pressed it like a dead flower.

He did not speak to me.

I leaned toward him, thinking to kiss those lips. But when he did not breathe on my face I stopped, suspended just above his frozen skin.

Oh, he is dead!

This is death!

There was no kissing now. No forgiving.

Organ music behind me. And a congregation resonant but removed, as if in another sphere, singing, "The strife is o'er, the battle done; Now is the victor's triumph won. O let the song of praise be sung, Alleluia!"

Dean Evans, vested in black cope, motioned at the pallbearers and they came forward.

Carolyn and I stood aside. We should have slipped out then to join the laity, to let the clergy splice their rubrics, but we could not, either of us, leave him.

One of those strangers closed Michael's coffin.

When the pallbearers had it hoisted and began the slow

unsteady procession out into the ambulatory, Dean Evans gestured toward me and Carolyn. "Walk with us," his hand said. Holding each other we fell into step behind the gleaming box.

I was numb. I was as a man upright but asleep. I merely followed, with only one sensation, that of a chill on my face, a frosted patch where I'd expected the warmth of Michael's breath. Outside the baptistry, in the main body of the cathedral, the procession suddenly became elaborate. Ahead of the coffin were dozens of robed choir members, and ahead of them was a huge borne cross, a pair of torches and a white banner emblazoned, "Blessed are the Peacemakers." Interspersed between the choir and the coffin and between the coffin and us were a thurifer carrying a smoking incense vessel and two pairs of surpliced acolytes. And waiting to walk with Dean Evans were vested deacons and more acolytes, candles flickering off every face.

And they were all singing with rolling robust voices, "On the third morn he rose again, Glorious in majesty to reign; O let us swell the joyful strain, Alleluia!"

Slowly we moved. Instead of cutting directly across the near aisle to the sanctuary, however, the procession wound into the north aisle, into the nave, among the pews where the mourners sat.

And it was there that the first jolt hit me, the first surprise, the first miracle. The frontmost dozen rows of chairs—not pews—were full of albed priests, some with stoles crossed on their breasts and gathered in cinctures, some with stoles hanging in stripes from their shoulders. Others wore the vestigial Benedictine cowls, that serve professors now and low church preachers. As the coffin appered, their eyes displayed their loss. They were like firemen, policemen, soldiers gathered by the death of a brother. After the choir passed they began to file out into the aisle ahead of the coffin. As I watched I could feel my concentration slowly coming back, a focus of mind, to grapple with this mystery. Who exactly were they? But at once, recognizing the cut of the albs and stoles, the flash of cassocks and habits under outer vestments, I understood that they were Jesuits, Paulists, Franciscans,

defiant priests of the Roman Catholic archdiocese, as well as
Episcopal vicars and canons, Lutheran pastors and Baptist
ministers. I saw familiar faces, priests from Michael's seminary class—Gene O'Mally—and veterans of antiwar demonstrations. They were clergy of every stripe from New York, but
not only New York. Monsignor Egan, the famous Chicagoan,
was there. Interspersed among the men were women, similarly vested, the new *ordinandi*, the new prophets of several
denominations. There were parish priests and teachers, pastors,
curates and missionaries. There were the famous ones whose
names came back easily as they passed: Harvey Cox, Daniel
Berrigan, William Sloane Coffin, Monsignor Fox, Bishop
Alcott of the Episcopal diocese, John Ferris Smith, Robert
MacAfee Brown, Henri Nouwen, Paul Lannan, and Michael
Hunt. There were more than a hundred, ordained all, brother
and sister priests of the excommunicant.

And with full strong voices they were singing, "O Risen
Lord, all praise to You, Who from our sin have set us free,
That we may live eternally, Alleluia."

The second jolt—miracle—came when our part of the procession resumed, behind the concelebrating clergy, and I saw
at last, moving into the heart of the darkened nave, that the
vast cathedral, the second largest church in the world, was
full.

Full of people. Men, women, children, students, nuns, old,
young, ex-priests, journalists, politicians, peace workers; a
dominance surely of the middle-aged, looking slightly worn,
faded, but above their hymnals, looking also strong, clear-
eyed, resolute. They were Parthians, Medes and Elamites.
They were Jews. There were thousands of them.

And I was stunned. Archbishop Timothy O'Shea was not
there. Terence Cardinal Cooke was not there. Pope John Paul
II was not there. But their people were. People come to bury
Michael Maguire; come to send him on his way.

Who, therefore, were the outcasts? Who the excom-
municants?

"Alleluia, the strife is o'er, the battle done . . ."

The song soared above us.

The procession turned the first corner and then the second.

"Who from our sin have set us free."

And we were striding now down the main aisle, toward the altar and the pulpit. Carolyn had both her hands linked in the crook of my arm and when I looked at her, I saw those eyes, brimming over, fixed upon the coffin.

I saw also, for the first time, what we were doing here, why she had sent for me.

Yes, Michael was dead.

And yes, we were alive. The Church, having died, was reborn. We were the Church, that throng gathered in memory, and also by it. We had been remembering ourselves, becoming part of each other once more. This had been the work of Michael's ghost and the work—Ah, Bright Wings!—of the Holy Ghost. That alleluia there and then outweighed all unfinished business, every anathema and each harbored wound of betrayal. That alleluia outweighed what we had done or not done, what we had lost, had found or had forgot. That alleluia outweighed death.

Yes, we believed in the Holy Catholic Church, the forgiveness of sin, the resurrection of the dead and life everlasting.

Into life everlasting we had gathered to commit our friend. Into life everlasting we wanted to release him.

I had been using memory and remorse to cling to him. He was my saint, my sinner, my hero, my great friend, my last enemy. He was none of these. He was a man. And as a man, not God, he stopped the world for a moment to speak of peace. And if the world had not heard him, we had heard him.

As we approached the altar on which we would break bread, a communion of the living and the dead, of Catholics and Protestants, of Jews and gentiles, of believers and unbelievers, of the reborn and the fallen-away, of Americans and Asians, of the saved and the damned, a communion, in that precious phrase, of saints, I sensed at last—oh gratitude! —the Presence of the One from whom Michael heard the call and toward whom even then Michael, steadfast marcher, was striding. He was striding as always, just ahead of us. And we had come to that act of remembrance and of worship out of the old habit of following him. We yet believed—and this is what our priests must do for us!—because he did.

As my eye fell to the magnificent carved pulpit, the shrine of the eternally unimprisoned Word of God, I knew at last what I would say. That throng needed no sermon, no homily, no eulogy, no explanation or confession, nothing more from me. Michael Maguire's story had been enough. It had brought us here to earth again, and him to the threshold of heaven. It was my place, my privilege just to end it, crying with my fist raised at his remains, "Go, Michael! Go, Michael! Go in peace, dear Michael! Go!"

About the Author

James Carroll was born in Chicago, raised in Washington, D.C., and since 1969 has lived in Boston, where he has written four previously published novels. He and his wife, the author Alexandra Marshall, have two children, Elizabeth and Patrick.